EMPIRE
of the
VAMPIRE

Also by Jay Kristoff

The Nevernight Chronicle
Nevernight
Godsgrave
Darkdawn

LIFEL1K3 Series
Lifel1k3
Dev1at3
Truel1f3

The Illuminae Files Series
Illuminae
Gemina
Obsidio

The Aurora Cycle Series
Aurora Rising
Aurora Burning
Aurora's End

The Lotus Wars Series
Stormdancer
Kinslayer
Endsinger

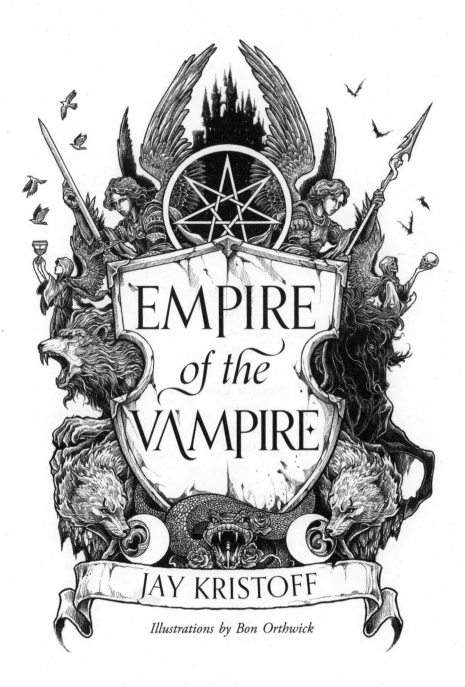

EMPIRE
of the
VAMPIRE

JAY KRISTOFF

Illustrations by Bon Orthwick

HARPER
Voyager

HarperCollins*Publishers*
1 London Bridge Street
London SE1 9GF

www.harpercollins.co.uk

HarperCollins*Publishers*
1st Floor, Watermarque Building, Ringsend Road
Dublin 4, Ireland

First published by Harper*Voyager*
An imprint of HarperCollins*Publishers* 2021
9

Typeset in Adobe Garamond Pro by Palimpsest Book Production Ltd,
Falkirk, Stirlingshire

Printed and Bound in the UK using 100% Renewable Electricity
at CPI Group (UK) Ltd, Croydon CR0 4YY

MIX
Paper from
responsible sources
FSC
www.fsc.org **FSC™ C007454**

This book is produced from independently certified FSC™
paper to ensure responsible forest management.

For more information visit: www.harpercollins.co.uk/green

Take hold of my hand,
For you are no longer alone.
Walk with me in hell.
— Mark Morton

Whitesea

Bag
Tears

BLOOD DYVOK

VELLENE

AVINBOURG

TALHOST

Blind Bay

CHARINFEL

CHARBOURG

SAN MICHON

AVELÉNE

BÁIH SIDE

REDWATCH

TRIÚRBAILE

The Red Strads

SAN GUILLAUME

OSSWAY

DÚN MAERGENN

DÚN CUINN

TOLFIRTH

DHAHAETH

Gulf of Wolves

SUL ILHAM

SUL ADAIR

TUUVE

QADIR

SUDHAEM

LASHAAME

ASHEVE

ALETHE

BLOOD CHASTAIN

Eversea

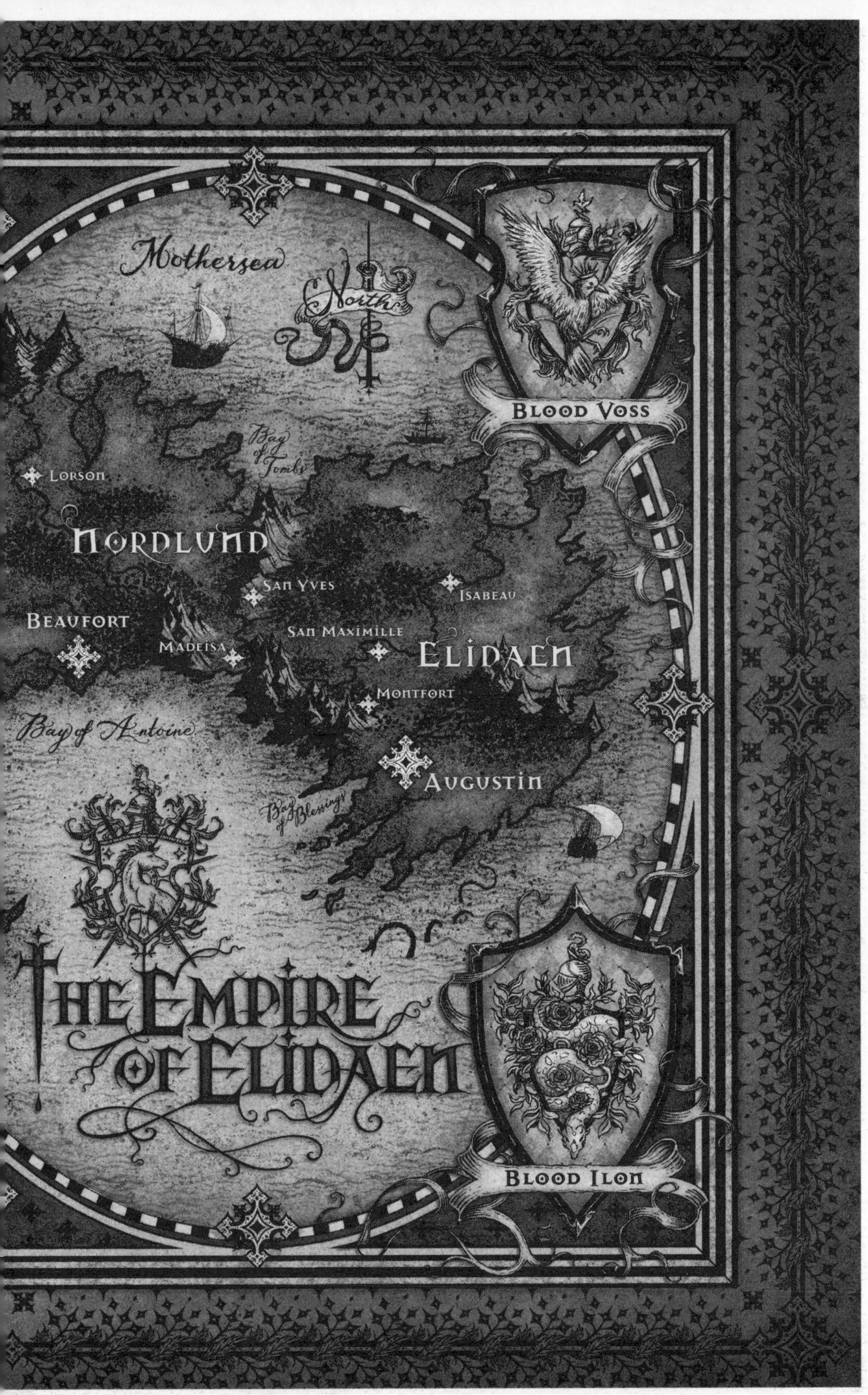

Mothersea

North

Blood Voss

Lorson

NORDLUND

Bay of Tombs

San Yves

Isabeau

Beaufort

Madeisa

San Maximille

Elidaen

Montfort

Bay of Antoine

Augustin

Bay of Blessing

The Empire of Elidaen

Blood Ilon

And in sight of God and his Seven Martyrs,
    I do here vow;
Let the dark know my name and despair.
So long as it burns, I am the flame.
So long as it bleeds, I am the blade.
So long as it sins, I am the saint.
And I am silver.

— The Vow of San Michon

ASK ME NOT *if God exists, but why he's such a prick.*

Even the greatest of fools can't deny the existence of evil. We dwell in its shadow every day. The best of us rise above it, the worst of us swallow it whole, but we all of us wade hip-deep through it, every moment of our lives. Curses and blessings fall on the cruel and just alike. For every prayer heeded, ten thousand go unanswered. And saints suffer alongside the sinners, prey for monsters spat straight from the belly of hell.

But if there is a hell, mustn't there also be a heaven?

And if there is a heaven, then can't we ask it why?

Because if the Almighty is willing to put an end to all this wickedness, but somehow unable to do so, then he's not as almighty as the priests would have you believe. If he's both willing and able to put paid to it all, how can this evil exist in the first place? And if he's neither willing nor able to lay it to rest, then he's no god at all.

The only possibility remaining is that he can *stop it. He simply chooses not to.*

The children snatched from parents' arms. The endless plains of unmarked graves. The deathless Dead who hunt us in the light of a blackened sun.

We are prey now, mon ami.

We are food.

And he never lifted a fucking finger to stop it.

He could have.

He just didn't.

Do you ever wonder what we did, to make him hate us so?

SUNSET

IT WAS THE twenty-seventh year of daysdeath in the realm of the Forever King, and his murderer was waiting to die.

The killer stood watch at a thin window, impatient for his end to arrive. Tattooed hands were clasped at his back, stained with dried blood and ashes pale as starlight. His room stood high in the reaches of a lonely tower, kissed by sleepless mountain winds. The door was iron-clad, heavy, locked like a secret. From his vantage, the killer watched the sun sink towards an unearned rest and wondered how hell might taste.

The cobbles in the courtyard below promised him a short flight into a dreamless dark. But the window was too narrow to squeeze through, and his jailers had left nothing else to see him off to sleep. Just straw to lie on and a bucket to shit in and a view of the frail sunset to serve as torture 'til the real torture arrived. He wore a heavy coat, old boots, leather britches stained by long roads and soot. His pale skin was damp with sweat, but his breath hung chill in the air, and no fire burned in the hearth behind him. The coldbloods wouldn't risk a flame, even in their prison cells.

They'd be coming for him soon.

The château below him was waking now. Monsters rising from beds of cold earth and slipping on the façade that they were something close to human. The air outside was thick with the hymn of bats' wings. Thrall soldiers clad in dark steel patrolled the battlements below, twin wolves and twin moons emblazoned on black cloaks. The killer's lip curled as he watched them; men standing guard where no dog would abase itself.

The sky above was dark as sin.

The horizon, red as his lady's lips the last time he kissed her.

He ran one thumb across his fingers, the letters inked below his knuckles.

'Patience,' he whispered.

'May I come in?'

The killer didn't let himself flinch – he knew the coldblood would've relished that. Instead, he kept staring out the window at the broken knuckles of the mountains beyond, capped by ash-grey snow. He could feel the thing standing behind him now, its gaze roaming the back of his neck. He knew what it wanted, why it was here. Hoping it'd be quick and knowing, deep down, that they'd savour every scream.

He finally turned, feeling fire swell inside him at the sight of it. The anger was an old friend, welcome and warm. Making him forget the ache in his veins, the tug of his scars, the years on his bones. Looking at the monster before him, he felt positively young again. Borne towards forever on the wings of a pure and perfect hate.

'Good evening, Chevalier,' the coldblood said.

It had been only a boy when it died. Fifteen or sixteen, perhaps, still possessed of that slim androgyny found on manhood's cusp. But God only knew how old it was, really. A hint of colour graced its cheeks, large brown eyes framed by thick golden locks, a tiny curl arranged artfully on its brow. Its skin was poreless and alabaster pale, but its lips were obscenely red, the whites of its eyes flushed just the same. Fresh fed.

If the killer didn't know better, he'd have said it looked almost alive.

Its frockcoat was dark velvet, embroidered with golden curlicues. A mantle of raven's feathers was draped over its shoulders, the collar upturned like a row of glossy black blades. The crest of its bloodline was stitched at its breast; twin wolves rampant against the twin moons. Dark britches, a silken cravat and stockings, and polished shoes completed the portrait. A monster, wearing an aristocrat's skin.

It stood in the centre of his cell, though the door was still locked like a secret. A thick book was pressed between its bone-white palms, and its voice was lullaby sweet.

'I am Marquis Jean-François of the Blood Chastain, Historian of Her Grace Margot Chastain, First and Last of Her Name, Undying Empress of Wolves and Men.'

The killer said nothing.

'You are Gabriel de León, Last of the Silversaints.'

Still, the killer named Gabriel made not a sound. The thing's eyes burned like candlelight in the silence; the air felt sticky-black and lush. It seemed for a moment that Gabriel stood at the edge of a cliff, and that only the cold press of those ruby lips to his throat might save him. He felt his skin prickling, an involuntary stirring of his blood as he imagined it. The want of moth for flame, begging to burn.

'May I come in?' the monster repeated.

'You're already in, coldblood,' Gabriel replied.

The thing glanced below Gabriel's belt and gifted him a knowing smile. 'It is always polite to ask, Chevalier.'

It snapped its fingers, and the iron-clad door swung wide. A pretty thrall in a long black dress and corset slipped inside. Her gown was a crushed velvet damask, wasp-waisted, a choker of dark lace about her throat. Her long red hair was bound into braids, looped across her eyes like chains of burnished copper. She was perhaps mid-thirty, old as Gabriel was. Old enough to be the monster's mother, if it had been just an ordinary boy and she just an ordinary woman. But she carried a leather armchair as heavy as she was, eyes downturned as she placed it effortlessly at the coldblood's side.

The monster's gaze didn't stray from Gabriel. Nor his from it.

The woman brought in another armchair and a small oaken table. Placing the chair beside Gabriel, the table between, she stood with hands clasped like a prioress at prayer.

Gabriel could see scars at her throat now; telltale punctures under that choker she wore. He felt contempt, crawling on his skin. She'd carried the chair as if it weighed nothing, but standing now in the coldblood's presence, the woman was almost breathless, her pale bosom heaving above her corset like a maiden on her wedding night.

'Merci,' Jean-François of the Blood Chastain said.

'I am your servant, Master,' the woman murmured.

'Leave us now, love.'

The thrall met the monster's eyes. She ran slow fingertips up the arc of her breast to the milk-white curve of her neck and—

'Soon,' the coldblood said.

The woman's lips parted. Gabriel could see her pulse quickening at the thought.

'Your will be done, Master,' she whispered.

And without even a glance to Gabriel, she curtseyed and slipped from the room, leaving the killer alone with the monster.

'Shall we sit?' it asked.

'I'll die standing, if it's all the same,' Gabriel replied.

'I am not here to kill you, Chevalier.'

'Then what do you want, coldblood?'

The dark whispered. The monster moved without seeming to move at all; one moment standing beside the armchair, the next, seated upon it. Gabriel watched it brush an imaginary speck of dust from its frockcoat's brocade, place its book upon its lap. It was the smallest display of power – a demonstration of potency to warn him against any acts of desperate courage. But Gabriel de León had been killing this thing's kind since he was sixteen years old, and he knew full well when he was outmatched.

He was unarmed. Three nights tired. Starving and surrounded and sweating with withdrawal. He heard Greyhand's voice echoing across the years, the tread of his old master's silver-heeled boots upon the flagstones of San Michon.

Law the First: The dead cannot kill the Dead.

'You must be thirsty.'

The monster produced a crystal flask from within its coat, dim light glittering on the facets. Gabriel narrowed his eyes.

'It is only water, Chevalier. Drink.'

Gabriel knew this game; kindness offered as a prelude to temptation. Still, his tongue felt like sandpaper against his teeth. And though no water could truly quench the thirst inside him, he snatched the flask from the monster's ghost-pale hand, poured a swig into his palm. Crystal clear. Scentless. Not a trace of blood.

He drank, ashamed at his relief, but still shaking out every drop. To the part of him that was human, that water was sweeter than any wine or woman he'd ever tasted.

'Please.' The coldblood's eyes were sharp as broken glass. 'Sit.'

Gabriel remained where he stood.

'*Sit,*' it commanded.

Gabriel felt the monster's will pressed upon him, those dark eyes swelling in his vision until they were all he could see. There was a sweetness to it. The lure of bloom to bumblebee, the taste of bare young petals damp with dew. Again, Gabriel felt his blood stir southwards. But again, he heard Greyhand's voice in his mind.

Law the Second: Dead tongues heeded are Dead tongues tasted.

And so, Gabriel stayed where he stood. Standing tall on colt's legs. The ghost of a smile graced the monster's lips. Tapered fingertips smoothed a golden curl back from those bloody chocolat eyes, drummed on the book in its lap.

'Impressive,' it said.

'Would that I could say the same,' Gabriel replied.

'Have a care, Chevalier. You may hurt my feelings.'

'*The Dead feel as beasts, look as men, die as devils.*'

'Ah.' The coldblood smiled, a hint of razors at the edge. 'Law the Fourth.'

Gabriel tried to hide his surprise, but he still felt his belly roll.

'Oui,' the coldblood nodded. 'I am familiar with the principles of your Order, de León. Those who do not learn from the past suffer the future. And as you might imagine, future nights hold quite an interest for the undying.'

'Give me back my sword, leech. I'll teach you how undying you really are.'

'How quaint.' The monster studied its long fingernails. 'A threat.'

'A vow.'

'*And in sight of God and his Seven Martyrs,*' the monster quoted, '*I do here vow; Let the dark know my name and despair. So long as it burns, I am the flame. So long as it bleeds, I am the blade. So long as it sins, I am the saint. And I am silver.*'

Gabriel felt a wave of soft and poisonous nostalgia. It seemed a lifetime had passed since he'd last heard those words, ringing in the stained-glass light of San Michon. A prayer for vengeance and violence. A promise to a god who'd never truly listened. But to hear them repeated in a place like this, from the lips of one of *them* . . .

'For the love of the Almighty, sit,' the coldblood sighed. 'Before you fall.'

Gabriel could feel the monster's will pressing on him, all light in the room now gathered in its eyes. He could almost hear its whisper, teeth tickling his ear, promising sleep after the longest road, cool water to wash the blood from his hands, and a warm, quiet dark to make him forget the shape of all he'd given and lost.

But he thought of his lady's face. The colour of her lips the last time he kissed her.

And he stood.

'What do you want, coldblood?'

The last breath of sunset had fled the sky, the scent of long-dead leaves kissed Gabriel's tongue. The want had arrived in earnest, and the need was on its way. The thirst traced cold fingers up his spine, spread black wings about his shoulders. How long had it been since he smoked? Two days? Three?

God in heaven, he'd kill his own fucking mother for a taste . . .

'As I told you,' the coldblood replied, 'I am Her Grace's historian. Keeper of her lineage and master of her library. Fabién Voss is dead, thanks to your tender ministrations. Now that the other Courts of the Blood have begun bending the knee, my mistress has turned her mind towards preservation. And so, before the Last Silversaint dies, before all knowledge of your Order is swept into an unmarked grave, my pale Empress Margot has, in her infinite generosity, offered opportunity for you to speak.'

Jean-François smiled with wine-stain lips.

'She wishes to hear your story, Chevalier.'

'Your kind never really hold the knack for jesting, do you?' Gabriel asked. 'You leave it in the dirt the night you die. Along with whatever passed for your fucking soul.'

'Why would I jest, de León?'

'Animals often sport with their food.'

'If my Empress wished sport, they would hear your screams all the way to Alethe.'

'How quaint.' Gabriel studied his broken fingernails. 'A threat.'

The monster inclined its head. 'Touché.'

'Why would I waste my last hours on earth telling a story nobody on earth gives a shit about? I'm no one to you. Nothing.'

'Oh, come.' The thing raised one eyebrow. 'The Black Lion? The man who survived the crimson snows of Augustin? Who burned a thousand kith to ashes and pressed the Mad Blade to the throat of the Forever King himself?' Jean-François tutted like a school madam with an unruly student. 'You were the greatest of your Order. The only one who yet lives. Those oh so broad shoulders are ill-suited for the mantle of modesty, Chevalier.'

Gabriel watched the coldblood stalking between lies and flattery like a wolf on the pin-bright scent of blood. All the while, he pondered the question of what it truly wanted, and why he wasn't already dead. And finally . . .

'This is about the Grail,' Gabriel realized.

The monster's face was so still, it actually seemed carved of marble. But Gabriel supposed he saw a ripple in that dark stare.

'The Grail is destroyed,' it replied. 'What care we for the cup now?'

Gabriel tilted his head and spoke by rote:

> 'From holy cup comes holy light;
> 'The faithful hand sets world aright.
> 'And in the Seven Martyrs' sight,
> 'Mere man shall end this endless night.'

A cold chuckle rang on bare stone walls. 'I am a chronicler, de León. History is of interest to me, not mythology. Save your callow superstitions for the cattle.'

'You're lying, coldblood. *Dead tongues heeded are Dead tongues tasted.* And if you believe for one moment that I'll betray . . .'

His voice faded, then failed entirely. Though the monster never seemed to move at all, it now held one hand outstretched. And there, on the snow-white plane of its upturned palm, lay a glass phial of reddish-brown dust. Like a powder of chocolat and crushed rose petals. The temptation he'd known was coming.

'A gift,' the monster said, removing the stopper.

Gabriel could smell the powdered blood from where he stood. Thick and rich and copper sweet. His skin tingled at the scent. His lips parted in a sigh.

He knew what the monsters wanted. He knew one taste would only make him thirsty for more. Still, he heard himself speak as if from far away. And if all the years and all the blood had not long ago broken his heart, it surely would have broken then.

'I lost my pipe . . . In the Charbourg, I . . .'

The coldblood produced a fine bone pipe from within its frockcoat, placed it and the phial on the small table. And glowering, it gestured to the chair opposite.

'Sit.'

And finally, wretch that he was, Gabriel de León obeyed.

'Help yourself, Chevalier.'

The pipe was in his hand before he knew it, and he poured a helping of the sticky powder into the bowl, trembling so fiercely he almost dropped his prize. The coldblood's eyes were fixed upon Gabriel's hands as he worked; the scars and calluses and beautiful tattoos. A wreath of skulls was inked atop the silversaint's right hand, a weave of roses upon his left. The word P A T I E N C E was etched across his fingers below his knuckles. The ink was dark against his pale skin, edged with a metallic sheen.

The silversaint tossed a lock of long black hair from his eyes as he patted his coat, his leather britches. But of course, they'd taken his flintbox away.

'I need a flame. A lantern.'

'You *need.*'

With agonizing slowness, the coldblood steepled slender fingers at its lips. There was nothing and no one else in all the world then. Just the pair of them, killer and monster, and that lead-laden pipe in Gabriel's shaking hands.

'Let us speak then of need, Silversaint. The whys matter not. The means, neither. My Empress demands the telling of your tale. So, we may sit as gentry while you indulge your sordid little addiction, or we may retire to rooms in the depths of this château where even devils fear to tread. Either way, my Empress Margot shall have her tale. The only question is whether you sigh or scream it.'

It had him. Now that the pipe was in his hand, he'd already fallen.

Homesick for hell, and dreading to return.

'Give me the fucking flame, coldblood.'

Jean-François of the Blood Chastain snapped his fingers again, and the cell door creaked wide. The same thrall woman waited outside, a lantern with a long glass chimney in her hands. She was just a silhouette against the light: black dress, black corset, black choker. She could have been Gabriel's daughter then. His mother, his wife – it made no difference at all. All that mattered was the flame she carried.

Gabriel was tense as two bowstrings, dimly aware of the coldblood's discomfort in the fire's presence, the silk-soft hiss of its breath over sharp teeth. But he cared for nothing now, save that flame and the darkling magik to follow, blood to powder to smoke to bliss.

'Bring it here,' he told the woman. 'Quickly, now.'

She placed the lamp on the table, and for the first time met his eyes. And her pale blue stare spoke to him without her ever speaking a word.

And you think me *slave?*

He didn't care. Not a breath. Expert hands trimming the wick, raising the flame to the perfect height, the oil's scent threading the air. He could feel the heat against the tower's chill, holding the pipe's bowl the perfect distance to render the powder to vapour. His belly thrilled as it began: that sublime alchemy, that dark chymistrie. The powdered blood bubbling now, colour melting to scent, the aroma of hollyroot and copper. And Gabriel pressed his lips to that pipe with more passion than he'd ever kissed a lover and . . . oh sweet God in heaven, breathed it down.

The blinding fire of it, filling his lungs. The roiling heaven of it, flooding his mind. Crystallizing, disintegrating, he drew that bloody vapour into his chest and felt his heart thrashing against his ribs like a bird in a bower of bones, his cock straining against his leather britches, and the face of God Himself just another bowlful away.

He looked up into the thrall's eyes and saw she was an angel given earthly form. He wanted to kiss her, drink her, die inside her, sweeping her into his arms, brushing his lips along her skin as his teeth stirred in his gums, feeling the promise thudding just below the arc of her jaw, the hammerblow beat of her pulse against his tongue, alive, *alive*—

'Chevalier.'

Gabriel opened his eyes.

He was on his knees beside the table, the lamp throwing a shaking shadow beneath him. He'd no inkling how much time had passed. The woman was gone, as if she'd never been.

He could hear the wind outside, one voice and dozens; whispering secrets along the shingles and howling curses in the eaves and shushing his name through the boughs of black and naked trees. He could count every sliver of straw on the floor, feel every hair on his body standing tall, smell old dust and new death, the roads he'd walked on the soles of his boots. Every sense was as sharp as a blade, broken and bloodied in his tattooed hands.

'Who . . .'

Gabriel shook his head, grasping at words like handfuls of syrup. The whites of his eyes had turned red as murder. He looked at the phial, now back in the monster's palm.

'Whose blood . . . is that?'

'My blessed dame,' the monster replied. 'My dark mother and pale mistress, Margot Chastain, First and Last of her Name, Undying Empress of Wolves and Men.'

The coldblood was looking at the lantern's flame with a soft, wistful hatred. A skull-pale moth had surfaced from some dank corner of the cell, flitting now about the light. Porcelain-pale fingers closed over the phial, obscuring it from view.

'But not one more drop of her shall be yours until your tale is mine. So speak it, and as though to a child. Presume the ones who shall read it, aeons from now, know nothing of this place. For these words I commit now to parchment shall last so long as this undying empire does. And this chronicle shall be the only immortality you will ever know.'

From his coat, the coldblood produced a wooden case carved with two wolves, two moons. He drew a long quill from within, black as the row of feathers about his throat, placing a small bottle upon the armrest of his chair. Dipping quill to ink, Jean-François looked up with dark and expectant eyes.

Gabriel drew a deep breath, the taste of red smoke on his lips.

'Begin,' the vampire said.

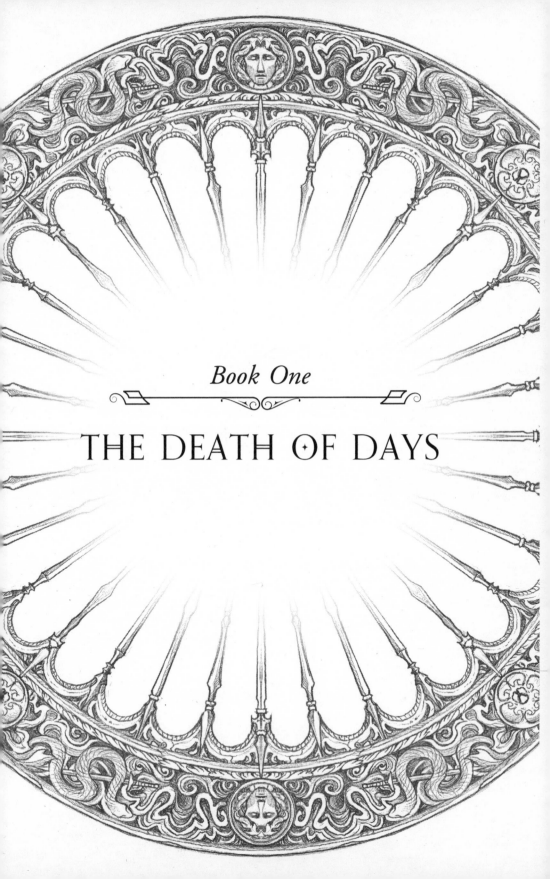

Book One

THE DEATH OF DAYS

And so came, in the year of Empire, 651, a portent most dread. For though the sun still rose and set, it now gave forth its light without illumination, and its glow held no warmth, and no accustomed brightness. And from the time this grim omen took hold the skye, folk were free neither from famine, nor war, nor any other calamity leading unto death.

– LUIS BETTENCOURT
A Complete Historie of Elidaen

OF APPLES AND TREES

'IT ALL STARTED with a rabbit hole,' Gabriel said.

The Last Silversaint stared into that flickering lantern flame as if into faces long dead. A hint of red smoke still bruised the air, and he could hear each thread in the lantern's wick burning to a different tune. The years passed between then and now seemed only minutes to his mind, alight with rushing bloodhymn.

'It strikes me as funny,' he sighed, 'looking back on it all. There's a pile of ash behind me so high it could touch the sky. Cathedrals in flames and cities in ruins and graves overflowing with the pious and wicked, and that's where it truly began.' He shook his head in wonder. 'Just a little hole in the ground.

'People will remember it different, of course. The soothsingers will harp about the Prophecy, and the priests will bleat on about the Almighty's plan. But I never met a minstrel who wasn't a liar, coldblood. Nor a holy man who wasn't a cunt.'

'Ostensibly, *you* are a holy man, Silversaint,' Jean-François said.

Gabriel de León met the monster's gaze, smiling faintly.

'Night was a good two hours off when God decided to piss in my porridge. The locals had torn down the bridge over the Keff, so I'd been forced south to the ford near Dhahaeth. It was rough country, but Justice had—'

'Hold, Chevalier.' Marquis Jean-François of the Blood Chastain raised one hand, placed the quill between the pages. 'This will not do.'

Gabriel blinked. 'No?'

'No,' the vampire replied. 'I told you, this is the tale of who you are. How all this came to pass. Histories do not begin halfway. Histories begin at the beginning.'

'You want to know about the Grail. A rabbit hole is where that tale begins.'

'As I said, I record this story for those who will live long after you are food for worms. Begin gently.' Jean-François waved one slender hand. 'I was born. I grew up . . .'

'I was born in a mud puddle named Lorson. Raised the son of a blacksmith. Eldest of three. I was no one special.'

The vampire looked him over, boots to brow. 'We both know *that* is untrue.'

'The things you *know* about me, coldblood? Well, if you scraped them all together and squeezed them dry, they could almost add up to a fucking thimbleful.'

The thing called Jean-François affected a small yawn. 'Teach me, then. Your parents. Were they pious folk?'

Gabriel opened his mouth for a rebuke. But the words died on his lips as he looked at the book in Jean-François's lap. He realized the coldblood wasn't only writing down his every word, he was also sketching; using that preternatural speed to trace a few lines between every breath. Gabriel saw the lines coalescing into an image now; a man in three-quarter profile. Haunted grey eyes. Broad shoulders and long hair, black as midnight. A chiselled jaw dusted with fine stubble and streaked with dried blood. Two scars were carved beneath his right eye, one long, the other short, almost like falling tears. It was a face Gabriel knew as well as his own.

Because, of course, it *was* his own.

'A fine likeness,' he said.

'Merci,' the monster murmured.

'Do you draw portraits for the other leeches, too? It must be tricky to remember what you look like after a while, if even a mirror won't profane itself with your reflection.'

'You waste your venom on me, Chevalier. If venom this water be.'

Gabriel stared at the vampire, running a fingertip across his lip. In the grip of the bloodhymn – that rushing, pulsing gift from the pipe he'd smoked – every sensation was amplified a thousandfold. The potency of centuries within his veins.

He could feel the strength it gifted him, the courage that walked hand in hand with that strength; a courage that had borne him through the hell of Augustin, through the spires of the Charbourg and the ranks of the Endless Legion. And though he knew that it would fade all too soon, for now, Gabriel de León was utterly fearless.

'I'm going to make you scream, leech. I'm going to bleed you like a hog, stuff the best of you in a pipe for later, and then show you how much your immortality is truly worth.' He stared into the monster's empty eyes. 'Venomous enough?'

A smile curled Jean-François's lips. 'I *had* heard you were a man of ill temper.'

'Interesting. I hadn't heard of you at all.'

The smile slowly melted.

It took a long slice of silence before the monster spoke again.

'Your father. The blacksmith. Was he a pious man?'

'He was a hopeless drunkard with a smile that could charm the unmentionables off a nun, and fists even angels feared.'

'I am put in mind of apples and the distances they fall from their trees.'

'I don't recall asking your opinion of me, coldblood.'

The monster was filling in the shadows around Gabriel's eyes as he talked. 'Tell me of him. This man who raised a legend. What was his name?'

'Raphael.'

'Named for those angels who so feared him, then. Just as you were.'

'And I've no doubt how pissed they are about it.'

'Did the pair of you get along?'

'Do fathers and sons ever get along? It's not until you're a man yourself that you can see the man who raised you for what he was.'

'I wouldn't know.'

'No. You're not a man.'

The dead thing's eyes twinkled as he glanced up. 'Flattery will get you everywhere.'

'Those lily-white hands. Those golden locks.' Gabriel looked the vampire over, eyes narrowed. 'You're Elidaeni born?'

'If you say so,' Jean-François replied.

Gabriel nodded. 'The thing you need to know about ma famille, vampire, before we get down to tacks of brass, is that we were Nordish folk. You're made pretty out east, sure and true. But in the Nordlund? We're made fierce. The winds off the Godsend cut like swords through my homeland. It's untamed country. Violent country. Before the Augustin peace, the Nordlund had been invaded more than any other realm in the history of the empire. Have you heard the legend of Matteo and Elaina?'

'Of course,' Jean-François nodded. 'The Nordling warrior prince who married an Elidaeni queen in the time before empire. 'Tis said Matteo loved his Elaina fierce enough for four ordinary men. And when they died, the

Almighty placed them as stars in the heavens, that they might be together forever.'

'That's one version of the tale,' Gabriel smiled. 'And Matteo loved his Elaina fierce, that much is true. But in Nordlund, we tell a different story. You see, Elaina's beauty was renowned across all five kingdoms, and each of the other four thrones sent a prince to seek her hand. On the first day, the prince from Talhost offered her a herd of magnificent tundra ponies, clever as cats and white as the snows of his homeland. On the second, the prince from Sūdhaem brought Elaina a crown made of shimmering goldglass, mined from the mountains of his birthplace. On the third, the prince from Ossway offered her a ship wrought of priceless trothwood, to bear her across the Eversea. But Prince Matteo was poor. Since the year of his birth, his homeland had been invaded by Talhost, and Sūdhaem, and Ossway too. He had no horses, nor goldglass, nor trothships to give. Instead, he vowed to Elaina he would love her fierce as four ordinary men. And to prove his point, as he stood before her throne and promised her his heart, Matteo laid at Elaina's feet the hearts of her other suitors. Those princes who'd invaded the land of his birth. Four hearts in all.'

The vampire scoffed. 'So you are saying all Nordlings are murderous madmen?'

'I'm saying we're people of passions,' Gabriel replied. 'For good or ill. To know ma famille, to know *me*, you must know that. Our hearts speak louder than our heads.'

'Your father, then?' Jean-François said. 'He too was a man of passions?'

'Oui. But not for good. Not him. He was ill, through and through.'

The silversaint leaned forward, elbows to knees. The cell was silent save for the swift scratchings of the coldblood on its portrait, the myriad whispers of the wind.

'He wasn't tall as I am, but he was built like a brick wall. He'd served as a scout in Philippe IV's army for three years, before the old emperor died. But he got caught in a snowslide on campaign in the Ossway Highlands. His leg broke and never healed right, so he'd turned to blacksmithing. And working in the keep of the local barony, he met my mama. A raven-haired beauty, stately and full of pride. He couldn't help but fall in love with her. No man could. Daughter of the Baron himself. La demoiselle de León.'

'Your mother's name was de León? I was under the impression names are inherited paternally among your kind, Silversaint. Women give up their names when wed.'

'My parents weren't wed when I was seeded.'

The vampire covered his mouth with tapered fingers. '*Scandalous.*'

'My grandfather certainly thought so. He demanded she get rid of me once she started to show, but Mama refused. My grandfather cast her out with all the curses he could conjure. But she was a rock, my mama. She bowed to no one.'

'What was her name?'

'Auriél.'

'Beautiful.'

'Just as she was. And that beauty remained undimmed, even in a mudhole like Lorson. She and Papa moved there with naught but the thread on their backs. She birthed me in the village church because their cottage didn't have its roof yet. A year later, my sister Amélie was born. And then, my baby sister Celene. Mama and Papa were wed by then, and my sisters took his name, "Castia". I asked Papa if I could take it too, but he told me no. That should've been my first clue. That, and the way he treated me.'

Gabriel's fingers traced a thin scar down his chin, his eyes distant.

'Those fists the angels feared?' Jean-François murmured.

Gabriel nodded. 'As I say, he was a man of passions, Raphael Castia. And those passions came to rule him. Mama was a godly woman. She raised us deep in the One Faith, and the blessed love of the Almighty and Mothermaid. But his love was a different one.

'There was a sickness in him. I know that now. He fought in the war only three years, but he carried it the rest of his life. He never met a bottle he wouldn't race towards the bottom of. Nor a pretty girl he'd say no to. And we all preferred his indiscretions, truth told. When he was out whoring, he'd simply disappear for a day or two. But when he was home drinking . . . it was like living with a keg of black ignis. The powder just waiting for a spark.

'He broke an axe handle over my back once, when I didn't chop enough wood. He pounded my ribs to breaking when I forgot the well water. He never touched Mama or Amélie or Celene, not once. But I knew his fists like I knew my name. And I thought it love.

'The day after, the song would be the same. Mama would rage, and Papa would vow by God and all Seven Martyrs he'd change, oh, he'd *change*. He'd swear off the drink, and we'd be happy for a time. He'd take me hunting or fishing, drill me in the swordcraft he'd learned as a scout, the life of the wild. How to make a flame catch on wet wood. The knack of walking across dead leaves with no sound. The crafting of a snare that won't kill what you catch. And more and most, he taught me ice. He taught me snow. How it falls. How it kills. Tapping on that broken leg of his, teaching me the truths of blizzard, of snowblind, of avalanche. Sleeping under the stars in the mountains just like a real father might've done.

'But it would never last forever.

'War doesn't teach you to be a killer," he told me once. "It's just a key that opens our door. There's a beast in all men's blood, Gabriel. You can starve him. Cage him. Curse him. But in the end, you pay the beast his due, or he takes his due from you."

'I remember sitting at table on my eighth saintsday, Mama cleaning the blood off my face. She adored me, my mama, despite all my birth had cost her. I knew it the way I knew the feel of the sun on my skin. And I asked her why Papa hated me, if she could love me so. She met my eyes that day, and sighed all the way from her heart.

'"You look just like him. God help me, you look exactly like him, Gabriel."'

The Last Silversaint stretched his legs out, glanced at the vampire's sketch.

'Funny thing was, my papa was broad and stocky, and I was already tall by then. His skin was tanned, and mine was pale as ghosts. I could see Mama in the curve of my lips and the grey of my eyes. But truth was, Papa and I looked nothing alike.

'She took off her ring – the only treasure she'd brought from her father's home. It was silver, cast with the crest of the House de León; two lions flanking a shield and two crossed swords. And she slipped it onto my finger and squeezed my hand tight.

'"The blood of lions flows in your veins," she told me that day. "And one day as a lion is worth ten thousand as a lamb. Never forget that you are *my* son. But there is a hunger in you. One you must beware, my sweet Gabriel. Lest it devour you whole."'

'She sounds a formidable woman,' Jean-François said.

'She was. She walked the muddy streets of Lorson like a highborn lady through the gold-gilt halls of the Emperor's court. Even though I was bastard born, she told me to wear my noble name like a crown. To spit pure venom at anyone who claimed I'd no right to it. My mama knew herself, and there's a fearsome power in that. Knowing exactly who you are and *exactly* what you're capable of. Most folk would call it arrogance, I suppose. But most folk are fucking fools.'

'Do your priests not preach from their pulpits of the grace that lies in humility?' Jean-François asked. 'Do they not promise the meek shall inherit the earth?'

'I've lived thirty-five years with the name my mother gave me, coldblood, and never once have I seen the meek inherit anything but the table scraps of the strong.'

Gabriel glanced out the window to the mountains beyond. The dark, sinking like a sinner to its knees. The horrors that roamed it unchecked. The tiny sparks of humanity, guttering like candles in a hungry wind, soon to be extinguished forever.

'Besides, who the fuck would want to inherit an earth like this?'

✦ II ✦

THE BEGINNING OF THE END

SILENCE CREPT INTO the room on slippered feet. Gabriel stared, lost in thought and the memory of choirsong and silverbell and black cloth parting to reveal smooth, pale curves, until the soft tapping of quill to page broke his reverie.

'Perhaps we should begin with daysdeath,' the monster said. 'You must have been only a child when the shadow first covered the sun.'

'Oui. Just a boy.'

'Tell me of it.'

Gabriel shrugged. 'It was a day like any other. A few nights prior, I remember being woken by a trembling in the ground. As if the earth were stirring in her sleep. But that day seemed nothing special. I was working the forge with Papa when it began; that shadow rising into the sky like molasses, turning shining blue to sullen grey and the sun as dark as coal. The whole village gathered in the square and watched as the air grew chill and the daylight failed. We feared witchery, of course. Fae magik. Devilry. But like all things, we thought it would pass.

'You can imagine the terror that set in as the weeks and months went by and the darkness wasn't abating. We called it by many names at first: the Blackening, the Veiling, the First Revelation. But the astrologers and philosophers in the court of Emperor Alexandre III named it "Daysdeath", and in the end, so did we. On his pulpit at mass, Père Louis would preach that all we needed was faith in the Almighty to see us through. But it's hard to believe in the Almighty's light when the sun is no brighter than a dying candle, and the spring is as cold as wintersdeep.'

'How old were you?'

'Eight. Almost nine.'

'And when you realized we kith had begun walking during the day?'

'I was thirteen when I laid eyes on my first wretched.'

The historian tilted his head. 'We prefer the term *foulblood*.'

'Apologies, vampire,' the silversaint smiled. 'Have I somehow given impression that I give a solitary speck of shit for what you prefer?'

Jean-François simply stared. Again, Gabriel was struck with the notion that the monster was marble, not flesh. He could feel the black radiance of the vampire's will, the horror of what he was, and the lie of what he appeared – beautiful, young, sensuous – all at war in his head. In some candle-dim corner of his mind, Gabriel was aware just how easily they could hurt him. How swiftly they could dispel his illusions that he was in control here.

But that's the problem with taking away all a man has, isn't it?

When you have nothing, you have nothing to lose.

'You were thirteen,' Jean-François said.

'When I saw my first wretched,' Gabriel nodded. 'It'd been five years since daysdeath. At its brightest, the sun was still only a dark smudge behind the stain on the sky. The snows fell grey instead of white now, and smelled like brimstone. Famine swept the land like a scythe – we lost half our village to hunger or cold in those years. I was still a boy, and I'd already seen more corpses than I could count. Our noons were dim as dusk, and our dusks as dark as midnights, and every meal was mushrooms or fucking potato, and no one, not priests nor philosophers nor madmen scrawling in shit could explain how long it must last. Père Louis preached this was a test of our faith. Fools we were, we believed him.

'And then Amélie and Julieta went missing.'

Gabriel paused a moment, lost to the dark within. Echoes of laughter in his head, a pretty smile and long black hair and eyes just as grey as his own.

'Amélie?' Jean-François asked. 'Julieta?'

'Amélie was my middle sister. My baby sister Celene the youngest, me the eldest. And I loved them both, as dear and close to me as my sweet mama. Ami had long dark hair and pale skin like me, but in temperament, we were as far apart as dawn and dusk. She'd lick her thumb and rub it on the crease between my brows, warn me not to frown so much. Sometimes I'd see her dancing, as if to music only she could hear. She'd tell us stories of an eve, when Celene and I lay down to sleep. Ami liked the frightening ones best. Wicked faelings and dark witchery and doomed princesses.

'Julieta's famille lived next door. Twelve years old she was, same as Amélie. She and my sister teased me fierce when they were together. But one day when we were in the wood picking white buttons alone, I stubbed my toe and took the Almighty's name in vain, and Julieta threatened to tell Père Louis of my blasphemy unless I kissed her.

'I protested, of course. Girls were terrifying to me back then. But Père Louis stood at his pulpit every prièdi and spat of hell and damnation, and a little kiss seemed preferable to the punishment I'd suffer if Julieta told him of my sin.

'She was taller than me. I had to stand on tiptoe to reach. I remember our noses getting entirely in the way, but finally, I pressed my lips to hers, warm as the long-lost sun. Soft and sighing. She smiled at me afterwards. Said I should blaspheme more often. That was my first kiss, coldblood. Stolen beneath dying trees for fear of the Almighty.

'It was late summer when the pair disappeared. Vanished one day while out gathering chanterelles. It wasn't unusual for Amélie to be away longer than she said. Mama would warn her about waltzing through life with her head in the clouds, and my sister would reply, "At least I can feel the sun up there." But when dusk fell, we knew something was wrong.

'I searched with the men of the village. My baby sister Celene came too – she was fierce as lions, even at eleven years old, and nobody dared tell her no. After a week, Papa's voice was broken from shouting. Mama wouldn't eat, couldn't sleep. We never found their bodies. But ten days later, they found us.'

Gabriel traced the curve of his eyelid, feeling the motion of every single lash beneath his fingertip. Chill wind shifted the long hair about his shoulders.

'I was stacking fuel for the forge with Celene when Amélie and Julieta came home. The coldblood that killed them threw their corpses in a bog after it was done, and they were filthy from the water, their dresses sodden with mud. They stood in the street outside our cottage, fingers entwined. Julieta's eyes had gone death-white, and those lips that'd been warm as the sun were black, peeling back from sharp little teeth as she smiled at me.

'Julieta's mother ran out from their house, weeping for joy. She gathered her girl in her arms and praised God and all Seven Martyrs for bringing her home. And Julieta tore out her throat right in front of us. Just . . . fucking peeled it open like ripe fruit. Ami fell on the body too, pawing and hissing with a voice that wasn't hers.' Gabriel swallowed thickly. 'I've never forgot the sounds she made as she began to drink.

'The men of the village toasted my valour for what came next. And I wish I could say it was courage I felt as my sister pushed her face into that flood, painting her cheeks and lips dark red. But I look back now, and I know what truly made me stand my ground as little Celene ran screaming.'

'Love?' the coldblood asked.

The Last Silversaint shook his head, entranced by the lantern flame.

'Hate,' he finally said. 'Hate for what my sister and Julieta had become. For the thing that had done it to them. But more and most, hate for the thought that this moment was how I'd always remember those girls. Not Julieta's stolen kiss beneath those dying trees. Not Amélie telling us stories at night. But *this*. The pair on all fours, lapping blood from the mud like starving dogs. Hate was all I knew at that moment. All its promise and all its power. It took root in me on that chill summer day, and in truth, I don't think it's ever let me go.'

Jean-François turned his eyes to the moth, still beating in vain upon the lantern glass. 'Too much hate will burn a man to cinders, Chevalier.'

'Oui. But at least he'll die warm.'

The Last Silversaint's eyes flickered to his tattooed hands, fingers curling closed.

'I couldn't have hurt my sister. I loved her even then. And so, I picked up the wood axe and I brought it down, right on Julieta's neck. The blow was solid enough. But I was only thirteen, and even a full-grown man will struggle severing a human head, let alone a coldblood's. The thing that had been Julieta fell into the mud, pawing at the axe in its skull. And Amélie lifted her head, bloody drool hanging from her chin. I looked into her eyes, and it was like staring into the face of hell. Not the fire and brimstone Père Louis promised from his pulpit, just . . . emptiness.

'Fucking *nothingness*.

'My sister opened her mouth, and I saw her teeth were long and knife-bright. And the girl who told me stories every night before we slept, who danced to music only she could hear, she stood and she hit me.

'God in heaven, she was *strong*. I felt nothing until I struck the mud. And then she was straddling my chest, and I could smell rot and fresh blood on her breath, and as her fangs brushed my throat, I knew I was about to die. Looking up into those empty eyes, even as I hated and feared it, I wanted it.

'I *welcomed* it.

'But something in me stirred then. Like a bear waking hungry after winter's slumber. And as my sister opened her rotten mouth, I seized hold of her throat. God, she was strong enough to grind bone to powder, but still, I pushed her back. And as she pawed my face with bloody fingertips, I felt a heat flood up my arm, tingling across every inch of skin. Something dark. Something deep. And with a shriek that turned my belly to water, Amélie reared back, clutching the bubbling flesh of her throat.

'Red steam rose off her skin, as if the blood in her veins was boiling. Red tears spilled down her cheeks as she screamed. But by then, Celene's cries had brought the whole village running. Strong hands grabbed Amélie, threw her back as the alderman pressed a torch to her dress, and she went up like a Firstmas bonfire. Julieta was crawling about with my axe still stuck in her curls as they lit her too, and the sound she made as she burned . . . God, it was . . . unholy. And I sat in the mud with Celene crouched beside me, and we watched our sister twirl and spin like a living torch. One last, awful dance. Papa had to hold Mama back from throwing herself onto the blaze. Her screams were louder than Amélie's.

'They checked my throat a dozen times, but I'd not a scratch. Celene squeezed my hand, asked if I was well. Some folk looked at me strangely, wondering how I'd survived. But Père Louis proclaimed it a miracle. Declaring God had spared me for greater things.

'Still, he refused a burial for the girls, the bastard. They'd died unshriven, he said. Their remains were taken to the crossroads and scattered, so they'd never be able to find their way home again. My sister's grave was to stand forever empty on unhallowed ground, her soul damned for all eternity. For all his praise, I fucking *hated* Louis for that.

'I smelled Amélie's ashes on me for days afterwards. I dreamed about her for years. Sometimes Julieta would come with her. The two of them sitting atop me and kissing me all over with black, black lips. But though I'd no idea what had happened to me, or how in God's name I'd survived, I knew one thing for sure and true.'

'That the kith were real,' Jean-François said.

'No. In our hearts, I think we already believed, coldblood. Oh, the powdered lords of Augustin and Coste and Asheve would have thought us backwards. But fireside tales in Lorson were always of vampyr. Of duskdancers and faekin and other witchery. Out in the Nordlund provinces, monsters were as real as God and his angels.

'But the chapel bells had just struck noon when Amélie and Julieta came home. And the day seemed not to bother them at all. We all knew the banes of the Dead. The weapons that kept us safe: fire, silver, but most of all, sunlight.'

Gabriel paused a moment, lost in thought, eyes of clouded grey.

'It was the daysdeath, you see? Even years later, in the monastery at San Michon, no silversaint could explain why it happened. Abbot Khalid said a great star had fallen in the east across the sea, and its fires raised a smoke so thick, it blackened the sun. Master Greyhand told us there'd been another war in heaven, and that God had thrown down the rebellious angels with such rancour the earth had been blasted skywards, and hung now in a curtain between his kingdom and hell. But nobody really knew why that veil had covered the sky. Not then, and perhaps not even now.

'All the folk of my village knew was that our days had become almost dark as night, and the creatures of the night now walked freely in the so-called day. Standing at the crossroads outside Lorson as they scattered my sister's ashes, holding Celene's hand as our mother screamed and fucking screamed, I knew. I think some part of us all knew.'

'Knew what?' Jean-François asked.

'That this was the beginning of the end.'

'Take comfort, Chevalier. All things end.'

Gabriel looked up at that, blood-red eyes glittering.

'Oui, vampire. *All* things.'

✦ III ✦

THE COLOUR OF WANT

'WHAT CAME NEXT?' Jean-François asked.

Gabriel took a deep breath. 'Mama was never the same after my sister died. I never saw my parents kiss after that. It was as if Amélie's ghost had finally killed whatever remained between them. Sorrow turned to blame, and blame to anger. I looked after Celene as best I could, but she was growing up a hellion, always looking for trouble and simply making it if she couldn't find it. Mama was scarred by her grief, hollowed and furious. Papa sought refuge in the bottle, and his fists fell heavier than ever. Split lips and broken fingers.

'There's no misery so deep as one you face by yourself. No nights darker than ones you spend alone. But you can learn to live with any weight. Your scars grow thick enough, they become armour. I could feel something building in me, like a seed waiting in cold earth. I thought this was what it felt like to become a man. In truth, I'd no fucking idea what I was becoming.

'But still, I was growing. I'd sprung up tall, and working the forge had turned me hard as steel. I began noticing the village lasses looking at me that way young girls do, whispering among themselves as I passed by. I didn't know why at the time, but something about me drew them in. I learned how to turn those whispers into smiles, and those smiles into something sweeter still. Instead of having kisses stolen, I found them given to me.

'In my fifteenth winter, I started trysting with a girl named Ilsa, daughter of the alderman, niece of Père Louis himself. Turned out I could be a sneaky little bastard when I chose to be, and I'd steal my way to the alderman's house at night, climb the dying oak outside Ilsa's window. I'd whisper to the glass, and she'd invite me in, sinking into desperate, hungry kisses and those clumsy first fumblings that set a young man's blood afire.

'But my mama didn't approve. We didn't quarrel often, but when it came to Ilsa, God Almighty, we shook the fucking sky. She warned me away from that girl, time and time again. One night we were at table, Papa quietly drowning in his vodka and Celene poking her potato stew while Mama and I raged. Again, she warned of the hunger inside me. To beware, lest it devour me whole.

'But I was tired of my parents' fear that I'd make the same mistakes they had. And furious, out of patience, I pointed at Papa and shouted, "I'm not him! I am *nothing* like him!"

'And Papa looked up at me then, once so handsome, now sodden and soft with drink. "Damn right you're not, you little bastard."

"'Raphael!" Mama shouted. "Do not speak so!"

'He looked at her, and a bitter, secret smile twisted his lips. And it might have ended there if the lion in me hadn't been too enraged to let it lie.

"'I thank God I *am* a bastard. Better no father at all than one so worthless as you."

"'Worthless, am I?" Papa glowered, sliding to his feet. "If only you knew the worth I've shown, boy. Fifteen years, and I've breathed not a word, raising such a sin as you."

"'If I'm a sin, then I'm *yours* to own. And just because you were fool enough to seed a son in the girl you ploughed out of wedlock, doesn't m—"

'I got no further. His fist flew as it had hundreds of nights before. Mama screaming as she'd always done. But that night, Papa's fist never found its mark. Instead, I caught it but a few inches from my face. I was taller than him, but he had arms thick as a baker's wife. He should've been able to swat me like a fly. Instead, I shoved him backwards, his eyes wide with shock. My blood was pounding, and as my papa's skull struck the hearth, that pulse began roaring in the shadows behind my eyes. As he fell, I saw he'd split his scalp upon the mantel. And from the gash spilled a slick of bright and gleaming red.

'*Blood.*

'I'd seen it before, of course. Smeared on my broken fingers and smudged on my swollen face. But I'd never noticed before how vivid the colour, how heady the scent, salt and iron and flower's perfume, entwined now with the song of my thundering heart. My throat was dry, my tongue like old leather, my stomach a yawning, clawing hole as I reached out with one trembling hand towards that spreading stain.

"'Gabe?" Celene whispered.

"'Gabriel!" Mama shouted.

'And like a spell broken at cock's crow, it fell away. That ache. That dust-dry longing. I stood on shaking legs, looking Mama in the eye. I could see secrets there, unspoken. A horror, a weight, growing heavier every year.

'"What's happening to me, Mama?"

'She only shook her head, kneeling beside Papa. "It's inside you, Gabriel. I'd hoped . . . I prayed God it would not be so."

'"*What's* inside me?"

'She said nothing, staring at the shadows on the floor.

'"Mama, tell me! *Help* me!"

'She looked into my eyes. This lioness who raised me, who taught me to wear my name like a crown. I could see it then; the desperation of the mother who'd do anything to protect her cub, realizing she'd only one thing left to do.

'"I cannot, my love. But perhaps I know someone who can."

'I'd no idea what else to ask. Didn't know the answer I needed. Mama would speak no more, and Celene had started crying, and so I saw to my sister as I'd always done. Things were never the same after that night. I tried to talk with Papa, God help me, I even apologized, but he wouldn't even look at me. I watched him pounding his anvil, fist upon his hammer. Great and terrible things, his hands. I could remember them closing around mine when I was a little boy, big and warm, showing me how to set a snare or swing a sword. I remembered them curling into knots and falling like rain. He built things, and he broke things, my papa. And I realized that perhaps one of the things he'd broken had been me.

'My only refuge was the circle of Ilsa's arms. And so, I sought it often as I could, sneaking out at all hours and climbing through her window. Meeting in that place where words have no meaning. We were both raised in the One Faith, and ever the spectre of sin hung over us. But not even God Himself can come between a girl and a boy truly in want of each other. No scripture or king or law on earth has that power.

'One night, we were close. So close we both burned with it. Her night-clothes cast aside and my britches unlaced, my lips almost hurting from the press of her mouth. The feel of her naked body against mine was dizzying, and the want of her was a thirst, welling inside me. I could smell her desire, filling my lungs and making me ache, her long chestnut tresses tangled between my fingers as her tongue flickered against mine.

'"Do you love me?" I whispered.

'"I love you," she answered.

'"Do you want me?" I asked.

'"I want you," she breathed.

'We rolled across her bed, and her breath came quicker, and her eyes saw only me. "But we can't, Gabriel. We can't."

'"This is no sin," I pleaded, kissing her throat. "You have my whole heart."

'"And you mine," she whispered. "But it's my moonstime, Gabriel. My blood is on me. We should wait."

'My belly thrilled at that. And though she spoke again, the only word I heard was *blood*. I realized *that* was the scent, *that* was the want, roaring now inside me.

'I couldn't have told you why. There was no why in my thoughts at the time. But my mouth drifted lower, over the smooth hills and valleys of her body, and I could feel her heart hammering beneath my fingertips as my hands roamed her curves. She shivered as my tongue circled her navel, murmured the softest protest even as she parted her legs and dragged her fingers through my hair. And I sank between her thighs and pressed my mouth against her, feeling her tremble. And a part of me was just a fifteen-year-old boy then, nervous as a spring lamb, begging only to serve and wanting only to please. But the rest of me, the most of me, was filled with a hunger darker than any I'd known.

'Ilsa pressed her fingers to her mouth, clamping her thighs about my head. And as I pressed my tongue inside her, I tasted it, God, I *tasted* it, and it almost drove me mad. Salt and iron. Autumn and rust. Flooding over my tongue and answering every question I'd never known how to ask. Because the answer was the same.

'Always the same.

'Blood.

'*Blood.*

'I felt complete in a way I'd never known possible. I knew a peace I'd never have believed was real. I felt this girl, writhing against the sheets and whispering my name, and though a moment before I'd promised her my whole heart, now she was nothing, *nothing* but the thing she could give me, the treasure locked behind the doors of this silken temple and calling to me without speaking a word. I sensed a stirring in my gums, and running my tongue across my teeth, I felt they'd grown sharp as knives. I could hear the pulse in Ilsa's thighs, pressed tight against my ears, struggling to turn my head as she sighed protest. And then, then God help me, I sank my teeth into her, her back arching, her every muscle taut as she threw back her head and pulled me closer, trying not to scream.

'And I knew the colour of want then. And its colour was red.

'*What am I? What am I doing? What in the name of God is happening to me?* These are the thoughts you might have expected to be rushing through my head. The questions any sane person might have asked himself. But for me, there was nothing. Nothing but my lips against Ilsa's skin and the flood of that punctured vein into my mouth. I drank like parched desert sand, one thousand years wide. I drank as if all the world were ending and only one more mouthful of her could save it, save me, save us all from the grand finale waiting in the darkness. I couldn't stop. I wouldn't.

'"*Stop . . .*"

'Ilsa's whisper broke through the boundless hymn in my head, that choir of our heartbeats entwined. Hers was fading now, weak and frail as a broken bird's and mine thrumming stronger than ever. But still, the part of me who loved this girl realized what the rest of me was doing. And at last, I tore my mouth away with a gasp of ragged horror.

'"Oh, God . . ."

'Blood. On the sheets. On her thighs and in my mouth. And as the spell of my kiss wore off, as the dark desire that had gripped her bled away, Ilsa saw what I'd done. The animal part of her took over, and even as I raised my hands to shush her, she opened her blue-blushed lips and screamed. The scream of a girl who understands the monster isn't under the bed any more. The monster is in it with her.

'I heard running footsteps. A soft curse. Ilsa screamed again, pure horror in her eyes. And that horror had me too, turning my full belly to water. The horror of a boy who's hurt the one he loves, of a boy in bed with a daughter as her father's footsteps come barrelling down the hall, of a boy who has woken from a nightmare to discover the nightmare is him.

'The door burst open. The alderman stood there in his nightshirt, a dagger in one hand. And he cried, "Good God Almighty!" as I dragged myself from the ruined bed, hands and chin drenched red. Ilsa was still screaming, the alderman roared and swung his blade. I gasped as a line of fire sliced down my back, but I was already gone, moving so swift the world was a blur, out through the window and into the dark.

'I landed barefoot in the mud, dragging my britches up as I stumbled, my hands sticky and red. I could hear the village waking, Ilsa's screams ringing across the muddy square, and the tread of watchmen's boots as little lights flared in the dark.

'I was lost and alone and running only God knew where. But I realized with awful wonder that the night was *alive* around me, burning as bright and beautiful as the day once had. My legs were steel, and my heart was thunder, and I felt every inch the lion I was named for. In that moment, I was more alive and afraid than I'd ever been, but my thoughts were clear enough now to question. What was happening to me? What had I done? Had Amélie passed some measure of her curse onto me? Or was I something else entire?

'It started to snow. I heard church bells ringing. And I dashed onwards, towards the only place I thought I might find safety. Where does the cub run, vampire, when the wolves snap at his heels? Who does the soldier cry out for, when he bleeds his last upon the field?'

'Mother,' Jean-François replied.

'Mother,' Gabriel nodded. 'She'd tried to tell me something that night I'd struck Papa low. That night the blood first called to me. And so, I burst through our cottage door and called only for her. She rose from bed, and my little sister stared at me, wide-eyed and fearful at the blood on my hands and face. Papa snarled, "Oh, God, what have you done, boy?" and Celene whispered a soft prayer. But Mama enfolded me in her arms and whispered, "No fear, my love. Everything will be aright."

'Heavy fists pounded on the door. Angry voices. Mama and Papa exchanged a glance, but Papa moved not a muscle. And with lips pressed thin, my lioness wrapped a shawl about her shoulders and took my bloody hand, leading me back out into the cold.

'Half the village awaited us. Some held lanterns, burning brands, or icons of the Redeemer. The alderman was among them, and so was Père Louis, the priest clutching a copy of the Testaments like a sword in his hand. He raised the holy book and pointed at me, his voice hoarse with the same righteous fury with which he'd damned my sister.

'"Abomination!"

'Mama cried protest, but her voice was lost under the clamour. The farrier grabbed my arm. But the blood I'd stolen pounded hot and red in all my hollow places, and I sent him flying as if he were straw. More men came on, and I lashed out, feeling bones break and flesh split in my hands. But they fell on me in a mob, the priest bellowing.

'"Bring him down! In the name of God!"

'"He's one of *them*!" someone cried.

'"Gone like his sister!" another roared.

'Mama began screaming, and Celene was spitting curses, and somewhere in the tumult, I heard my papa roaring too, crying out that I was only a boy, just a boy. I felt the crowd dragging me bloodied and half senseless to my feet, and I thought of Amélie then, dancing and wailing as she burned.

Wondering if the same fate awaited me. I looked into Père Louis's eyes, this bastard who'd denied my sister her burial, hate upon my tongue.

'"Faithless fucking coward," I spat. "I pray you die *screaming*."

'A shot split the air, the crack of a wheellock pistol ringing in my ears. And the mob fell still, all eyes turning to the figures riding slow up the muddy road.

'Two of them on pale steeds, like angels of death from the pages of the Testaments. A thin fellow rode in the lead, gaunt as a scarecrow. He wore a leather greatcoat, black and heavy. His tricorn was pulled low, collar laced about his mouth and nose. All I could see of his features was a strand of dry, straw-coloured hair and his eyes. His irises were the palest kind of green, but the whites were so bloodshot they were all but red. He had a burlap sack over the back of his stout tundra pony. The shape inside was akin to a man. On his shoulder sat a falcon, sleek grey feathers and glittering gold eyes.

'The second rider was younger, broader of shoulder, but again, I could see little of his face. He wore the same gear as the first, a longblade sheathed at his waist. His tricorn was pulled low, and he looked about the mob with an ice-blue gaze.

'The snow was coming heavier, its chill digging into my bare skin. The riders bore small hunter's lanterns on their saddles, and the light glittered on the flakes falling fat and freezing from the sky, the silver sevenstars embroidered at their breasts.

'Papa had fetched his old war sword from the wall, and Mama was breathless, her hair come loose from its braid. Celene stood with her fists bunched in knots, my little hellion stepping in to defend her big brother as those ponies clopped slowly up to our house. We all of us could feel the gravity of that moment. I watched these strange men, and I marked how fine their steeds were, how sharp the cut of their greatcoats, how the thread in those stars at their breasts wasn't thread at all, but actual, *real* silver. And the one in the lead slipped his wheellock inside his coat and called out over the song of my pulse.

'"I am Frère Greyhand, Silversaint of San Michon."

'He pointed at me.

'"And I am here for the boy."'

✦ IV ✦
LAMB TO SLAUGHTER

'THE WIND HOWLED like a hungry wolf, the snow clinging to my bloody skin. I looked to Père Louis and saw his brow darken. "Monsieur, this boy is a practitioner of witchery and foul blood rites. He is evil. He is *damned*!"

'An angry murmur rippled among the assembly. But this man called Greyhand simply reached into his greatcoat and took out a vellum scroll. It was adorned with the imperial seal; a unicorn and five crossed swords in a hardened blob of apple-red wax.

'"By word of Alexandre III, Emperor of Elidaen and Protector of God's Holy Church, whom no man under heaven may gainsay, I am empowered to recruit any and every citizen of my choosing unto our righteous cause. And I choose him."

'"Recruit?" the alderman blustered. "This *monstrosity*? Into what?"

'The man drew his longblade from its sheath, and I caught my breath. Bleeding and battered as I was, I was still a blacksmith's boy, and that sword was enough to dream wet about. The steel was run through with threads of silver, like bright whorls in darker wood. The pommel was a star – seven-pointed for the Seven Martyrs, surrounded by the circle of the Redeemer's wheel. In the dim lanternlight, it seemed almost to glow.

'"We are the Ordo Argent," Greyhand replied. "The Silver Order of San Michon. And monstrosities are *exactly* the recruits we need, monsieur. For the enemies we fight are more monstrous still, and if we fail, so too shall God's mighty church, and his kingdom on earth, and all the world of men."

'"Who is this enemy?" Père Louis demanded.

'Greyhand looked at the priest, lanternlight shining in blood-red eyes. The falcon on his shoulder took wing as the frère turned to the sack on the back of his steed, loosed the chains about it, and slung it into the mud. It grunted as it struck the earth, and as I thought, the shape inside was that of a man. But the thing that dragged its way free of the burlap was nothing close.

'It was clad in rags, deathly gaunt. Flesh stretched over its bones like a skeleton dipped in skin. It had death-white eyes, wasted lips drawn back from its teeth, but those teeth were long and sharp as a wolf's. It reared up out of the mud, and a sound like boiling fat bubbled from its throat. All the villagers about me cried out in terror.

'Suddenly, I was thirteen years old again, standing in the muddy street the day Amélie and Julieta came home. And I was terrified, to be sure. But along with that fear came the memory of my sister. I felt that old, familiar hate, scorching in my chest and tightening my jaw. There's strength to be found in hatred. There's a courage forged only in rage. And instead of crying out or stumbling back as the men about me did, I stood with feet apart. And I drew a breath. And I raised my fucking fists.'

'Impressive,' Jean-François murmured.

'I didn't do it to impress,' Gabriel growled. 'Knowing what I know now, I wish to God I *had* run. I wish I'd pissed my pants and wailed for my mama.'

Gabriel dragged a hand back through his hair and sighed.

'Call it what you will. Instinct. Stupidity. It's just the way we're birthed. There's no changing it, any more than you can change the will of the wind or the colour of God's eyes. Of course, that thing lurching towards me gave no shits about my raised fists. But a silver chain binding it to Greyhand's saddle drew it up short, its hands flailing at my face. The frère slipped from his mount, and at the sound of his boots striking mud, that gaunt and starving monster turned, and I swear by all Seven Martyrs, I heard it whimper. Greyhand raised his arm, sword gleaming in the dark. And he struck, God above, so quick I could barely see it.

'The silvered pommel crashed into the monster's jaw. I saw a spray of dark blood and teeth. Greyhand was terrifying with that blade, and I flinched as he struck the monster again, again, until it collapsed in a moaning, battered heap. As Greyhand pushed the thing's face into the mud with his boot and looked to Père Louis, I saw the same hatred in him that boiled in my own heart. "Who is our enemy, good Father?"

'He gazed about the terrified villagers, red eyes finally settling on me. "'The Dead.'"

There in his chill cell, Gabriel de León paused, running a hand across his stubbled chin. He could hear those words so clearly, Greyhand might well have been imprisoned with him. He was almost tempted to check for the old bastard over his shoulder.

'Such melodrama,' Jean-François of the Blood Chastain yawned.

Gabriel shrugged. 'Greyhand had a flair for it. But as he looked me over with those bright and bloody eyes, I could feel him taking my measure. He reached up with one gloved hand, unlaced his collar so I might see him. Death-pale skin. A face carved from cruelty. He looked as if he'd leave bruises in the sheets where he slept.

'"You've seen one of these before," he said, nodding to the monster.

'I had to search long and hard for the words. "My . . . my sister."

'He glanced at my mama and back to me. "Your name is Gabriel de León."

'"Oui, Frère."

'He smiled like my name struck him funny. "You belong to us now, Little Lion."

'I turned to Mama then. And when I saw the resignation on her face, I understood at last. These men were here at her behest. This Greyhand was the help I'd asked her for – the help she herself couldn't give. There were tears in her eyes. The agony of a lioness who'd do anything to protect her cub, knowing there was nothing now left to do.

'"No!" Celene spat. "You will *not* take my brother!"

'"Celene, hush now," Mama whispered.

'"They will not take him!" she cried. "Get behind me, Gabe!"

'I stepped between the frère and my baby sister as she raised her fists, hugging her tight as she glowered at the riders behind me. I knew she'd have scratched Greyhand's eyes out of his skull if given half a chance. But meeting the fellow's cold stare, I could see the truth of it.

'"These are men of God, sister," I told her. "This is his will."

'"You can't go!" Celene snapped. "It isn't fair!"

'"Perhaps not. But who am I to gainsay the Almighty?"

'I was terrified, I'll not lie. I'd no wish to leave ma famille, or my little world. But the villagers were still gathered about us, looking at me with fearful, furious eyes. My teeth were dull as they'd once been, but the red rush of Ilsa's blood yet lingered in my mouth. And it seemed for a moment that everything stood poised on the edge of a knife. You feel those moments in your soul. These men were offering me salvation. A path to a life I never imagined. And still, I knew there'd come a terrible cost for it. And Mama knew it too.

'But what choice did I have? I couldn't stay, not after what I'd done. I didn't know what I was becoming, I didn't have any answers, but perhaps these men did. And as I'd asked my sister, who was I to challenge the will of heaven? To defy he who made me? And so, drawing a deep breath, I reached out and took what Greyhand offered.'

Gabriel looked skywards and sighed.

'And that was it. Lamb to slaughter.'

'They took you then and there?' Jean-François asked.

'They gave me a moment with ma famille. Papa had little to say, but I saw the sword in his hand, and I knew that when my life was on the line, he'd done what little he could to save it. I was afeared at what might happen to Celene without me to look after her, but there was naught I could do. Still, I warned Papa. I *fucking* warned him.

'"Mind your daughter. She's the only child you have left."

'Mama wept as I kissed her goodbye, and I was weeping too, holding Celene in my arms. Mama told me to beware the beast. The beast and all his hungers. All my world was coming to pieces, but what could I do? I was being swept up in a river, yet even then, I was old enough to know; there's a difference between those who swim with the flood and those who drown fighting it. And its name is Wisdom.

'"Don't go, Gabe," Celene pleaded. "Don't leave me alone."

'"I'll return," I promised, kissing her brow. "Look after Mama for me, Hellion."

'The young fellow who rode behind Greyhand prised Celene off me, offering no words of comfort as he pushed me up onto the back of his pony. Then he wrapped that whimpering monster back up in silver chains and burlap, slung it over Greyhand's mount. The frère looked about the gathering with pale, bloody eyes.

'"We captured this monster three days' west of here. And there shall be more of them before there are less. Dark days come, and nights yet darker. Set candles at your windows. Invite no stranger into your homes. Ever keep the fires burning in your hearths and the love of God burning in your hearts. We *will* triumph. For we are silver."

'"We are silver," the young fellow echoed.

'Little Celene was weeping, and I held out my hand in farewell. I called to Mama that I loved her, but she was just staring at the sky, tears freezing on her cheeks. As we rode out of Lorson, I can't remember ever feeling so lost, and I watched ma famille through the falling snow until they grew too distant to see, and the gloom swallowed them whole.'

'A fifteen-year-old boy,' Jean-François sighed, stroking the feathers at his throat.

'Oui,' Gabriel nodded.

'And you name *us* monsters.'

Gabriel's eyes found the vampire's, and his voice became steel.

'Oui.'

✦ V ✦

FIRE IN THE NIGHT

JEAN-FRANÇOIS SMILED FAINTLY. 'So, from Lorson to San Michon?'

Gabriel nodded. 'It took us a few weeks, riding along the Hollyroad. The weather was freezing, and the coat they'd given me did nothing to keep the chill from my belly. I was still reeling with it all. The memory of what I'd done to Ilsa. The dark heaven of her blood in my mouth. The sight of that monster that Greyhand had dragged from his sack, still slung behind him on his saddle. I knew not what to make of any of this.'

'Did Frère Greyhand tell you what was in store?'

'He told me one-fifth of three-eighths of fuck all. And at first, I was afraid to ask. There was such a fire in Greyhand, it seemed he might scorch you if you stood too close. He was all skin and bone, sharp cheeks and chin, hair like dirty straw. He chewed his food like he hated it, spent almost every moment of rest at prayer, pausing occasionally to whip his back with his belt. When I tried to speak to him, he'd just glare 'til I fell silent.

'The only affection he showed was to that falcon he rode with. He called it Archer, and he doted on that fucking bird like a father on a son. But the strangest part of him was revealed the first morning he washed in front of me.

'As he removed his tunic to bathe in our bucket, I saw Greyhand was *covered* in tattoos. I'd seen inkwork before – fae spirals on Ossway folk and the like – but the frère's tattoos were something new.'

Gabriel ran his fingers over the inkwork atop his own hands.

'The ink was like this. Dark, but metallic. Silver in the pigment. Greyhand had a portrait of the Mothermaid covering his entire back. A spiral of saints-rose and swords and angels ran down his arms, and he wore seven wolves for the Seven Martyrs across his chest. The young apprentice who rode with him had less inkwork, but he still wore a beautiful weave of roses and serpents on his chest. Naél, the Angel of Bliss, covered his left forearm, Sarai, the Angel of Plagues, filled his bicep, her beautiful moth wings spread wide. And both of them had the sevenstar inked in their left hands.'

Gabriel turned his hand over, showed the vampire his palm. There, among the calluses and scars, sat a seven-pointed star inside a perfect circle.

'I am curious,' Jean-François mused, 'why your Order profaned your bodies so.'

'Silversaints called it the aegis. There's no sense wearing armour when fighting monsters that can crush platemail with their fists. Armour makes a man slow. Noisy. But if your faith in the Almighty was strong enough, the aegis made you *untouchable*. No matter what monster of the night you stalk – duskdancer, faekin, coldblood – none can abide the touch of silver. And God hates your kind in particular, vampire. You fear even the *sight* of holy icons. You cower before the sevenstar. The wheel. The Mothermaid and Martyrs.'

The vampire gestured to Gabriel's palm. 'Then why do I not cower, de León?'

'Because God hates me more than he hates you.'

Jean-François smiled. 'I presume you have more?'

'Much more.'

'. . . May I see?'

Gabriel met the thing's eyes. Silence passed between them, three breaths deep. The vampire ran his tongue over his lips, bright red, wet.

The silversaint shrugged. 'As you like it.'

Gabriel stood, the chair creaking beneath him as he rose. Reaching up slow, he sloughed off his greatcoat, unlaced his tunic and dragged it over his head, leaving his torso bare. A small sigh, gentle as a whisper, slipped over the vampire's lips.

The silversaint was sinew and muscle, lanternlight shadows etched deep on the furrows and troughs of his body. A bevy of scars decorated his skin – from bladework and claws and Redeemer knew what else. But moreover, Gabriel de León was covered in inkwork, neck to navel to knuckles. The artistry would've been breathtaking if the historian had breath to take. Eloise, the Angel of Retribution, ran down the silversaint's right arm, sword and shield ready. Chiara, the blind Angel of Mercy, and Eirene, the Angel of Hope, were on his left. A roaring lion covered his chest, sevenstars in its eyes, and a circle of swords stretched across the taut muscles of his belly. Doves and sunbeams, the Redeemer and Mothermaid – all decorated his arms and body. A dark current ran thick in the air.

'Beautiful,' Jean-François whispered.

'My artist was one of a kind,' Gabriel replied.

The silversaint dragged his tunic back on and sat once more.

'Merci, de León.' Jean-François continued to sketch him, apparently from memory. 'You were speaking of Greyhand. What he told you before you arrived.'

'As I said, as little as he could at first. And so, I was left to wonder in silence. How badly had I hurt Ilsa? How was it I'd grown strong enough to throw grown men about like toys? I'd thought the alderman's dagger had sliced me to the bone, but now, the wound seemed not so bad. How in the Almighty's name was *any* of this possible? I had answers for none of it.' Gabriel shrugged again. 'But finally, it all came to a head. Our motley little band was bedding down one eve in the Nordlund wilds, in the shadow of dying pines just off the Hollyroad. We'd been travelling nine days.

'The young rider who accompanied Greyhand was an initiate of the Order named Aaron de Coste. An apprentice, if you like. He was a princely looking lad; thick blonde hair and bright blue eyes and a face girls swooned for. He was older than me. Eighteen, I guessed. "Coste" was the name of a barony in western Nordlund, and I supposed he might be related to them somehow, but he told me nothing of himself. The only time he ever spoke to me at all was to order me about. He referred to Greyhand as "Master", but he called me "Peasant", spitting the word as if it tasted like shit.

'Whenever we were forced to stop in the open, Greyhand would hang that corpse he'd captured from a nearby tree branch. I'd no idea why he didn't just kill the thing at the time. De Coste would order me to gather wood, then light a fire as high and hot as he could. The apprentice or his master would sleep while the other kept watch, often smoking a pipeful of an odd, blood-red powder as they stood vigil. When they smoked, I saw that their eyes would change hue, the whites flooding so bloodshot they turned red. I asked de Coste for a taste one night, and the boy just scoffed.

'"Soon enough, Peasant."

'Anyway, de Coste was sharpening his sword that eve. Beautiful weapon, it was. Silver and steel, with the Death Angel Mahné at wing on the cross-guard. Archer sat on a branch above, bright falcon's eyes shining in the dark. Greyhand's captive corpse had been dangling inside its burlap bag for hours, unmoving. But one of the logs in the fire burst with a crack, and de Coste slipped, sliced his finger nice and deep. And all of a sudden, that thing on the branch above started moaning and bucking like a landed fish.

'Greyhand was at prayer, as usual, his back red raw from self-flagellation. He opened his eyes and snarled, "Shut up, leech." But the corpse only thrashed the more.

'"Feeeee," it begged. "Feeeeemmmeee."

'I looked at the blood dripping from de Coste's finger, my stomach curdling even as the scent of it sent a small thrill along my skin. And Greyhand spat the darkest curse I'd heard in my young life, climbed off his knees, and drew his beautiful silvered sword.

'Then he stomped around the fire, tugged the burlap loose, and laid a beating on that thing like I'd never witnessed in all my years. It screamed as he struck it with the pommel, the silver hissing where it touched its wasted skin. Greyhand kept swinging, and the monster's cries turned to whimpers, and still he beat it, bones crunching, flesh pulping, until, as God is my witness, the thing started blubbing like a child.

'"*Stop!*" I cried.

'Greyhand turned on me, eyes like fire. Fucking brave or fucking stupid, you can decide, but monster or no, this seemed a kind of torture to me. And I looked to that awful thing sobbing on its branch and declared, "It's had enough, Frère, for pity's sake."'

Gabriel sighed, elbows on his knees.

'God Almighty. I thought I'd seen rage in my papa before. But I'd seen nothing so terrifying as the look that crossed Greyhand's face then.

'"*Pity?*" he spat.

'He stalked towards me, and I recognized the look in his eyes – the same that Papa wore when he was about to raise his fists. I tried to push Greyhand off, but God, he was strong, hauling me to my feet and backhanding me across the face. My lip split, black stars bursting behind my eyes. I felt Greyhand dragging me towards that thing hanging from its tree, holding me out by the scruff. And like a flame doused by water, the weeping died and the corpse came alive again. Madness burned in its eyes. Hunger like I'd never seen. I roared in horror, but Greyhand edged me closer as the monster clawed towards my bleeding lip.

'"You *pity* this abomination?"

'"Please, Frère! *Stop* it!"

'Greyhand slapped me again, harder than my papa ever had, sending me sprawling. I looked up from the frozen mud to de Coste for aid, but the apprentice didn't move a muscle. Greyhand towered over me, flame and fury in his eyes.

'"Rid your heart of pity, boy. Light a fire in your chest and burn it out at the root! Our enemy knows not love, nor remorse, nor bonds of fellowship! They know only *hunger*!" He pointed to that thing, still keening for my blood. "Were this abomination permitted to, it would rip you privates to chin and glut itself like a hog at trough. And tomorrow night, perhaps the next, you might rise, just as soulless as the thing that slew you! Seeking only to slake your thirst on the heartsblood of *fools* who speak the name of pity!"

'His shout rang over the crackling fire, the hammer of my pulse. Looking into that living corpse's eyes as it pawed towards my bloody mouth, I felt myself filled with that same loathing, that same hatred as the day my sister came home.

'"What are they?" I heard myself whisper.

'Greyhand's gaze burned like the bonfire. "We call them the wretched, Little Lion."

'"But what *are* they?"

'He stared at me, and much as I wished to, I refused to look away. A quiet stole over him then. Regret softened the cruel lines of his face. He offered his hand, and knowing no better, I took it. And Greyhand brought me over to the fire's edge and sat me down, staring into the crackling blaze while de Coste watched on in silence.

'"What do you know of coldbloods, boy?" Greyhand finally asked.

'"They feast on living blood. They're ageless. Soulless."

'"Oui. And how is one made?"

'"All those slain by them become them."

'Greyhand looked at me then. "Thank God and Redeemer that's not true, boy. Were it so, we'd already be lost."

'Silence fell, broken only by the crackle of the fire. I could feel a weight in the air. A rush of adrenaline. These were the first real answers Greyhand had offered in nine days, and now that he was speaking, I didn't want him to stop. "Please, Frère. What *are* they?"

'Greyhand ran his hand over his pointed chin, stared deep into the flames. I put his age at only thirty, but from the lines of care about his eyes and mouth, he seemed a much older man. I still feared him – feared his fists as I'd feared my papa's – but I wondered what it was that had made him so. If once, he'd been a boy just like me.

'"Listen close now," he said. "And listen well. Coldbloods do give their curse to those they slay. But *not* always. They cannot choose who their affliction is passed on to. And there seems no rhyme or reason as to which of their victims will turn and which will simply stay dead. It could be the victim rises only a few heartbeats after death. But more often, days or even weeks pass. And in the meantime, their corpse will go the way of all flesh. When it rises, a coldblood's victim will be locked forever in the state in which it turned. Beautiful and whole. Or otherwise." He glanced to the hanging monster. "Times past, if a victim turned many days after dying, the sun would quickly end them. The brain rots with the body, you see. And knowing no better, mindless coldbloods would simply perish with their first dawn. But now . . ."

"'Daysdeath,'" I whispered.

"'Oui. The sun no longer harms them. So they live on. Wandering. And killing. And in the seven years since the daystar failed us, multiplying."

"'How many are there?'" I murmured, licking at my split lip.

"'In the west of Talhost, past the Godsend Mountains? Thousands."

"'Seven Martyrs . . .'"

"'It's worse than you know, Little Lion. The oldest and most dangerous, the beautiful ones who call themselves highbloods? It used to be they lived in secret. But four months ago, a highblood lord led an *army* of wretched against the walls of Vellene. He stalked the streets like the angel of death, pale and fey and impervious to any blade. He slew His Imperial Majesty's own cousin, and claimed the keep for his own. He encroaches farther through Talhost even now, and with every massacre his dark brood commits, more Dead join their number. A few rise as highbloods, forever young and deathless. Yet more become wretched, hideous and rotten. But *all* those slain are bound to his will. Rumour has it he is the most ancient coldblood that walks this earth. His name is Fabién Voss. But he has declared himself the Forever King."

'My stomach turned at the thought. I tried to picture entire *legions* of coldbloods, laying siege to human cities. Creatures old as centuries stalking the day with earthly feet.

"'And how . . .'"

'I shook my head, my throat dry. I remembered the honey of Ilsa's blood cascading over my tongue. The bliss as my teeth slipped through the smooth skin of her thigh. My canines were no longer sharp like they'd been, but still, I could feel them, and that thirst, lying in wait beneath my surface. Wondering if, *when,* it might rise again.

"'How do I fit into all this?'"

'Greyhand looked at me sidelong. A log cracked in the fire, a shower of sparks spilling into the dark. "What do you know of your father, Little Lion?"

"'He was a soldier. A scout in the armies of Phili—"

"'Not the man who raised you, boy. Your *father.*'

'And I understood then. Realization like an avalanche. I knew why my papa's fists had fallen only on me, not my sisters. What he meant when he said he'd raised a sin beneath his roof. My lips felt numb and swollen. The words too big to speak.

"'My father . . .'

"'Was a vampire.'

'It was Aaron de Coste who'd spoken, staring at me now across the flames.

"'No," I breathed. "No . . . *no*, my mama would never . . .'

"'She'd hoped you were not his. They both did." Greyhand patted my knee, and something close to pity softened his gaze. "Fault her not, Little Lion. To eyes that cannot truly see, highbloods are beautiful. Powerful. Their minds can bend even the strongest will, and their mouths drip sweetest honey."

'I thought of Ilsa, helpless with passion as I drank her almost to death. I looked at that corpse hanging from the tree branch, and then down at my hands in absolute disgust.

"'I'm . . . like *them*?"

"'No, Peasant," de Coste said. "You're like *us*."

"'You are a halfbreed, boy," the frère said. "What we call a paleblood."

'I looked between the pair, saw that their skin was white as ghosts, just like mine.

"'The change comes upon us near manhood," Greyhand said. "And worsens yet with time. We inherit some of our fathers' gifts. Strength. Speed. Other boons, depending on the bloodline they belonged to. But also, we inherit their thirst. The bloodlust that drives them to murder, and us to madness. We are products of *sin*, boy. Make no mistake, we are the accursed of God. And the only way we might recover his eternal grace and win a place in heaven for our damned souls is to fight and die for his Holy Church."

"'This . . . Silver Order you spoke of?"

"'The Ordo Argent," Greyhand nodded. "We are the silver flame burning between humanity and the darkness. We hunt and kill those monsters that would devour the world of men. Faekin and fallen. Duskdancers and sorcerers. Risen and wretched. And oui, even highbloods. Once, vampires lived in the shadows. But now, the highbloods do not fear the sun. And the Forever King's dark legion grows nightly. So we, the sons of their sin, must pay the burden of the cost. We shall stand, or all shall fall."

"'So we . . . we're supposed to fight this Forever King and his army?"

"'Armies fight armies. But Empress Isabella has convinced Emperor

Alexandre he has need of a razor as well as a hammer. The Ordo Argent is that razor. We are a brotherhood with a hallowed tradition, but never before have we operated with royal patronage. The Emperor's generals will lay their sieges and muster their lines. But *we* will strike the serpent's head. We will slay the shepherds, and watch their sheep scatter."

"'Assassins,'" I murmured.

"'No, boy. *Hunters*. Hunters with a divine mandate. Hunters of the most dangerous game." Greyhand looked back to the flames, the fire returning to his eyes. "We are hope for the hopeless. The fire in the night. We will walk the dark as they do, and they shall know our names and despair. For so long as they burn, we shall be flame. So long as they bleed, we shall be blades. So long as they sin, we shall be saints."

'Greyhand and de Coste both spoke then, their voices as one.

"'*And we are silver.*"

'Frère Greyhand gazed into my wondering eyes. I felt his stare like a fist about my heart. Then he stood, returning to his prayers, as quiet as if he'd never spoken.

'But he *had* spoken. And his words now filled my mind. I was afraid like I'd never been. Horrified at the truth of what I was. I'd just learned that my whole fucking life had been a lie. My father was not my father. Instead, I was the child of a monstrous sin, now growing like a cancer inside me. And yet, Aaron and Greyhand were sons of that same darkness, and they stood tall in defence of the Emperor, the Church, the Almighty Himself.

'Brothers of the Silver Order of San Michon.

'My mother had always spoken of the lion in my blood. But for the first time in my life, I could feel it waking. My sister had *died* at the hands of these coldbloods. And though I couldn't save her then, I *could* avenge her now, and perhaps, redeem my damned soul besides. Though I was born of darkest sin, this seemed a salvation. And looking into those flames, I vowed that if I were to join these men, I'd be the best of them. The fiercest. The most faithful. That I'd not falter, not fail, not rest until every one of those monsters was sent back screaming to the hell that birthed them, and there, give my sister my love.'

Gabriel sighed and shook his head.

'I had no fucking idea what I was in for.'

✦ VI ✦

A MONASTERY IN THE SKY

'WE ARRIVED AT San Michon on the last findi of the month, wreathed in snow-grey fog. Frère Greyhand led the way, Aaron de Coste came next, me on the saddle behind him. As I rode into the monastery's shadow, I didn't quite know what to feel. Fear of the sin inside me. Sorrow at all I'd left behind in Lorson. But in truth, what I felt most as I looked to the bluffs above was awe. Simple, jaw-dropping awe.

'San Michon seemed born from a faerie tale. It was built in a valley along the Mère River, nestled among rocky black crags. Seven massive pillars of lichen-covered stone rose up like spears from the valley floor, as if left there by giants in the Age of Legends. The river flowed between the granite pillars it had carved, like a serpent of dark sapphire. And on those mighty pedestals, the monastery of San Michon awaited me.

'At a nod from Greyhand, Aaron unslung a silver-trimmed horn and blew a long note through the valley. Bells answered above, butterflies dancing in my gut as we rode down mushroom-covered shale towards the central pillar. Its base was hollowed, the entrance sealed by iron gates wrought with the sevenstar. I caught a whiff of horse within, realizing the silversaints had built their stables inside.

'Next to the gates, a broad wooden platform was being lowered on heavy iron chains. After handing over our horses to two young grooms, Master Greyhand slung his captured wretched over his shoulder, then strode to the elevator with Aaron and me on his heels. The platform swayed ominously as we rose a hundred, then two hundred feet off the valley floor. This high, I could see the Godsend Mountains to the northwest – that great spine of snowcapped granite splitting Nordlund from Talhost.

'Archer circled us as we ascended, and I found myself hanging onto the rails with a white-knuckle grip. I'd never climbed anything so high. Instead of looking down, I turned my eyes up, to a place I thought could exist only in a children's tale. A monastery in the *sky*.

'"Scared of heights, Peasant?" Aaron sneered.

'I glanced at the blonde lad, my grip tightening. "Leave off, de Coste."

'"You cling to that railing like to your mother's tits."

'"I'm actually picturing *your* mama's tits. Though I'm told you favour your sister's?"

'Greyhand growled at us both to simmer down. De Coste kept his tongue behind his teeth, glaring at me the rest of the ride. But I couldn't really bring myself to care. After three weeks of being treated like something Aaron had found smeared on his boot, I was finding this highborn prick's company about as pleasant as a case of crotch lice.

'Our platform creaked to a halt. To our left, a toothy fellow in black leathers manned the winch house. His hair was long and greasy, and I noted no silver on his hands.

'"Fairdawn, Keeper Logan," Greyhand nodded.

'The thin man bowed, spoke in a heavy Ossway brogue. "Godmorrow, good Frère."

'Gazing down, I guessed we were near five hundred feet off the grey valley floor. Master Greyhand simply glowered at me until I prised my fingers from the railing.

'"No fear, Little Lion."

'"Not if I don't look down," I said, trying to conjure a grin.

'"Look forward instead, boy."

'I dragged the windswept hair from my eyes and sighed. "Now *there's* a sight . . ."

'Before us loomed a cathedral – the first I'd ever seen in my life. Our tiny chapel in Lorson had seemed a palace to my young eyes, but this – *this* was a true house of God. A great circular fist of black granite with spires that bled the sky. In its courtyard stood a fountain of pale stone set with a ring of angels. Chiara, the blind Angel of Mercy. Raphael, Angel of Wisdom. Sanael, the Angel of Blood, and his twin, my namesake, Gabriel, Angel of Fire. The Cathedral's stonework was crumbling, some of the windows boarded over, but still, I'd never seen *anything* so grand. Workmen crawled over it like ticks on a fallen log, and gargoyles grinned atop the eaves. Huge double doors were set in its east and west faces, and in the stone above the dawn-doors was a magnificent window of stained glass.

'It was fashioned like a sevenstar, each point depicting the tale of one of the Seven Martyrs: San Antoine parting the Eversea, San Cleyland guarding the gates to hell, San Guillaume burning the faithless on their pyres. And, of course, San Michon and her silver chalice, all flaxen hair and fierce eyes, staring into my very soul.

'A man awaited us atop the eastern stairs, dressed in the greatcoat of a silversaint. He was Sūdhaemi born; his skin dark as polished mahogany, his eyes a pale green rimmed with kohl. He was older than Greyhand, black hair knotted in long, winding braids. A vicious horizontal scar cut deep through both cheeks, twisting his mouth into a permanent, humourless smirk, and there were beautiful silver tattoos atop his hands. He was broad-shouldered like my papa, but he radiated a gravitas that my papa and his fists never did.

'*This*, I thought to myself, *is a leader of men*.

'Greyhand bowed low before him, as did de Coste.

'"Welcome home, Brothers. We've missed you at mass." The mighty man turned to me, his voice deep as cello song. "And welcome to you also, young paleblood. My name is Khalid, High Abbot of the Ordo Argent. I know you have travelled long to be here. And this life may not be what you imagined for yourself. But it *is* your life now. You have been both blessed and accursed, called by Almighty God to this holy task. You must not shirk. You *cannot* fall. For if you do, so shall all we know and love."

'I bowed to him. I didn't know what else to do. "Abbot."

'"Until you take your vows as a full-blooded frère of the Order, you will look to your master for guidance. Initiates are not permitted to leave Barracks after evebells, nor may they visit the Great Library's forbidden section. Duskmass will be held tonight, and you'll have your maiden taste of silver. On the morrow, your training begins." Khalid glanced towards Greyhand. "If I might have a word, good Frère?"

'"By the Blood, Abbot. De Coste, show our Little Lion the grounds."

'"By the Blood, Master." Aaron glanced at me and growled, "Follow."

'Leaving Greyhand and Khalid to confer, de Coste led me across one of the broad stone walkways. I realized all seven pillars must have been naturally connected once, but the hands of time had brought most of those bridges low, replaced now with long spans of rope and wood. Instead of looking to the dizzying fall, I gazed to the skyline, at the beautiful, ancient buildings around us and the men crawling the walls.

'"What are all the cranes for? The workmen?"

'"You will refer to me by the title of Initiate, Peasant," de Coste replied, not even looking at me. "When Frère Greyhand is absent, I am senior member of this company."

'I bit my tongue. I was well and truly sick of Aaron's shit. But he *did* outrank me.

'"In answer to your question, the Silver Order has only recently gained patronage of Emperor Alexandre. This monastery stood for centuries before that, and for long years, these buildings were let run to rot. Not always have we enjoyed the favour we hold now."

'I chewed on that for a moment, gazing with a peasant boy's eyes at the buildings about us. They were dark stone, grim and stately in design, arrayed on towering spires above the Mère Valley like the crowns of ancient kings. I wasn't certain what I'd been expecting to find here among this hallowed order of monster slayers, but even rundown and crumbling, San Michon was the most wondrous place I'd ever been in my life.

'Aaron motioned to the building behind us. "The Cathedral is the heart of San Michon. The brethren meet for mass twice daily, dusk and dawn. If you miss mass, you'll find yourself missing testicles shortly after."

'De Coste waved northwest, at a many-windowed structure in modest repair.

'"The Barracks, where we lay our heads. The refectory is on its lower level, as are the privies and washhouse. Silversaints spend much of their lives on the Hunt, so I'd usually advise you to take advantage of the baths while you may. But I doubt a lowborn maggot like you would know a lump of soap if it hit you in the teeth."

'I rolled my eyes as de Coste nodded to the southmost structure – a circular building with blood-red banners embroidered with the sevenstar fluttering on the walls.

'"The Gauntlet. While staying in San Michon, you'll spend much of your time training there. In the star, you'll be taught bladework. Unarmed combat. Marksmanship. The Gauntlet is the furnace where silversaints are forged."

'My jaw clenched at that, and thinking of my sister, I nodded.

'"I'm ready."

'Aaron scoffed. "If you last more than two weeks in there, I'll send a personal missive to the Grand Pontifex, proclaiming it a miracle." De Coste nodded to another building, round and roofless. "To the north is the Breadbasket. The kingdom of good Frère Alber. There, we keep our food stores and henhouses, the glasshome where we grow our herbs. To the north-east is the Priory, where the Sisterhood sleep."

'". . . Sisterhood?"

'Aaron sighed as if I were somehow supposed to know all this already. "The Silver Sorority of San Michon. Before our Order found patronage in good Empress Isabella, it was their work keeping this entire monastery afloat."

'I saw small figures in long black habits walking out from that grand and gothic building. Their cloth fluttered in the mountain wind, lace veils whipping about their faces.

"'Are they palebloods like us?" I asked.

"'There *are* no female palebloods. The Almighty saw fit to spare his daughters our curse. These Sisters are godly women, devout in the One Faith and brides of the Almighty."

"'I'd not expected to find nuns among an order of warrior brothers."

"'Mmm." De Coste eyed me sidelong. "And you've spent a great deal of time among warrior brothers, Little Kitten?"

'I blinked at that. "I—"

"'The Great Library." De Coste nodded to the sixth pillar, the beautiful hall of stained-glass windows and tall gables atop it. "One of the finest collections of lore and learning in the empire. There is a forbidden section within, and if Archivist Adamo catches you even *looking* at it, he'll skin your hide and use it for book binding. I'd normally recommend you investigate the general shelves in your free time, but I doubt you can actually read."

"'I can read fine," I scowled. "My mama taught me."

"'Then I'll be sure to send you a letter when I start giving a damn." Aaron waved back at the Library. "Books are kept on the lower level, and the Silver Sisters work in the bindery above. Along with the Brothers of the Hearth, they create the most beautiful tomes in the empire." He raised his hand to interrupt my question. "There are two castes within the Ordo Argent. The Brothers of the Hunt are palebloods like me and Greyhand, men who get their hands dirty stalking horrors in the dark. The Brothers of the Hearth are simple men of faith who keep the Library, craft our weaponry and . . . other tools. Speaking of . . ."

'De Coste pointed at a sprawling building ahead. It had few windows, but many chimneys. They all spat black smoke, save one, which trailed a thin finger of red fumes.

"'The Armoury." Aaron squared his shoulders and smoothed back his thick blonde hair. "Follow. You'll want to see this."

"'Wait," I said. "What is that?"

'I pointed to a stone span jutting out from the Cathedral's pillar. It seemed a bridge, save that it led nowhere at all, ending in a balcony without a railing and a plunge down into the river Mère. A large chariot wheel sat at the edge, locked in a stone frame – the same kind of wheel the Redeemer had been flayed upon, and that now graced the necks of every priest and holy sister in the realm.

'"That," Aaron said, "is Heaven's Bridge."

'"What's it for?"

'The young lordling clenched his jaw. "You'll find out soon enough."

'De Coste turned on silver heels and marched to the Armoury. Pushing open great double doors wrought with the sevenstar, he led me into the vast entrance hall. And there, I breathed a sigh of wonder.

'The space was lit by myriad glass spheres suspended from the ceiling. I knew not how, but each glowed like a burning candle. It was as if the long-lost stars of my youth had come back to the sky, bathing the hall in honeyed light. And looking about, I saw that warm glow playing on a multitude of weapons, lined up in vast racks along the walls.

'I could see swords like the ones Greyhand and de Coste carried, the steel run through with traceries of silver. Longblades, bastard swords, axes, and warhammers. But there were stranger weapons too – the kind I'd only heard whisper of. Wheellock pistols and rifles and pepperboxes, wrought of beautiful metal and engraved with scripture.

'I AM THE SWORD THAT LAYS THE SINNER LOW. I AM THE HAND THAT LIFTS THE FAITHFUL HIGH. AND I AM THE SCALE THAT WEIGHS BOTH IN THE ENDING. SO SAY'TH THE LORD.

'If I was in love with the monastery before that moment, now I was utterly smitten. I'd been raised the son of both a blacksmith and a soldier, remember. I'd been drilled hard in use of a blade, but I also knew the art of making weapons this beautiful. The smiths who worked this armoury were geniuses . . .

'"Wait here," de Coste ordered. "Touch *nothing*."

'The lad stepped through another set of doors, and I caught the familiar song of hammer and anvil beyond. I saw figures in leather aprons, muscular arms glinting in forgefire. I ached with homesickness at the sight. I missed my sister Celene, Mama, oui, even my papa. I supposed I needed to stop calling him such in my head, but Seven Martyrs, that was easier said than done. I'd lived my whole life thinking of Raphael Castia as my father. Never once guessing I was the son of a *real* monster.

'As the heavy doors swung shut behind Aaron, I stepped closer to the longblades, marvelling at their beauty. Each pommel was decorated with a sevenstar, the crossguards all some variation of the Redeemer hanged upon his wheel, or angels at wing. But the silver patterns in each blade were like whorls in lengths of fine timber; each subtly different from the next. I reached for the closest sword, and brushing the back of my hand against the edge, I was rewarded with a sliver of pain and a thin line of red across my skin.

'*Razor sharp*.

'"You have fine taste," came a deep voice behind me.

'I turned, startled to find a young Sūdhaemi man watching me. He'd entered the hall through a second doors, lithe as a cat and quiet as a mouse. He was in his early twenties, ebon-skinned like all his folk. He wore no tattoos on his flesh, but the scorched hairs on his forearms and the leather apron he wore told me this young man was a smith, through and through. He was tall, crushingly handsome, hair worn in short, knotted braids. Striding across the hall, he took the sword from my hand.

'"Who told you how to test a blade like that?" he asked, nodding to my cut.

'"A swordsman's strength rests in his arm. But his finesse lies in his fingers. You don't risk them on the blade's edge. My papa told me that." I caught myself then, clenching my teeth. "Well . . . the man I thought was my papa, anyway . . ."

'He nodded, soft understanding in his eyes. "What's your name, boy?"

'"Gabriel de León, my lord."

'The young man laughed then, so deep and loud I felt it in my own chest. "I'm no lord. Although I am his devoted servant. Baptiste Sa-Ismael, Brother of the Hearth and Blackthumb of the Silver Order, at your service."

'"Blackthumb?"

'Baptiste grinned. "It's Forgemaster Argyle's expression. They say a man with a love for growing things has a green thumb. So we with a love for the anvil and the fire and the rule of steel . . .?" The smith shrugged. Cutting the air with the longsword, he smiled at it fondly. "You've a keen eye. This is one of my favourites."

'"You forged all these?"

'"Only some. My brother smiths crafted the rest. Every blade in this hall was made for recruits like you. A tiny piece of the maker's heart left in every blade. And once forged and cooled and kissed farewell, the silversteel waits here for the hand of its master."

'"Silversteel," I repeated, enjoying the word on my tongue. "How is it made?"

'Baptiste's grin widened. "We all of us have secrets within these walls, Gabriel de León. And *that* secret belongs to the Brothers of the Hearth."

'"*I* have no secrets."

'"Then you're not trying hard enough," he chuckled.

'At first, I suspected he might've been mocking me, but there was a warmth in the blackthumb's eyes I took an instant liking to. Folding his arms, he looked me over, toe to crown. "De León, eh? Strange . . ."

'Turning to the weapons behind us, Baptiste walked down the row. Almost reverently, he took a blade from the wall. And returning to me, he placed it in my hands.

"'I forged this beauty only last month. I knew not for who. Until now."

'I looked at him in utter disbelief. ". . . Truly?"

'In my shaking hands was the most beautiful sword I'd ever seen in my life. Eloise, the Angel of Retribution, was wrought on the hilt, her wings flowing about her like silver ribbons. Bright whorls of silver rippled along the blade's darker steel, and I could see beautiful script from the Testaments engraved down the length.

'KNOW MY NAME, YE SINNERS, AND TREMBLE. FOR I AM COME AMONG THEE AS A LION AMONG LAMBS.

'I met Baptiste's dark eyes and saw him smile. "I think perhaps I dreamed of you, Gabriel de León. I think perhaps your coming was ordained."

"'My God," I said, all awonder. "Does . . . does it have a name?"

"'Swords are only tools. Even those wrought of silversteel. And a man who names his weapon is a man who dreams others will one day know *his* name too."

'Baptiste glanced about us, his eyes twinkling as he leaned close to whisper.

"'I call mine Sunlight."

'I shook my head, unsure what to say. No blacksmith's boy under heaven had ever dreamed of owning a sword as peerless as this. "I've . . . I've no way to thank you."

'Baptiste's mood grew sombre. His eyes were far away then, as if lost in distant shadow. "Kill something monstrous with it," he said.

"'*There* you are . . ." came a voice.

'I turned and found Aaron de Coste at the door he'd left by. The dark mood that had fallen on Smith Baptiste vanished as if it had never been, and he strode across the room, arms open. "Still alive, you bastard!"

'Aaron grinned as he was caught up in the older boy's bear hug. It was the first genuine smile I think I'd ever seen on his face. "Good to see you, brother."

"'Of course it is! It's me!" Baptiste released Aaron from his embrace, nose wrinkling. "Sweet Mothermaid, you stink of horse though. Time for a bath, methinks."

'"Such is my intent. Once this filthy peasant is situated. You," Aaron growled. "Little Kitten. Come grab your damned gear."

'De Coste carried black leathers, a heavy greatcoat, stout boots with silvered heels like his. Without ceremony, he dumped the lot onto the floor. But I'd no interest in new boots or britches. Instead, I hefted my magnificent new sword, testing the balance.

'The silversteel gleamed in the dim light; the angel on the crossguard seemed to smile at me. The uncertainty I'd felt as I stepped into the monastery faded just a breath, the thought of home made me ache just a little less. I knew I had much to learn; that in a place like this, I had to walk before I ran. But truth was, despite the sin I was born of, the monster that lived inside me, I still felt God was with me. This sword was proof of that. It was as if the smiths of San Michon knew I was coming. As if I were *fated* to be there. I looked down at the beautiful scripture on my new blade, mouthing the words to myself.

'I AM COME AMONG THEE AS A LION AMONG LAMBS.

'"Lionclaw," I whispered.

'"Lionclaw," Baptiste repeated, stroking his chin. "I *like* it."

'The smithy handed me a belt, a scabbard, a sharp silversteel dagger to match the blade he'd gifted me – the Angel of Retribution spreading her beautiful wings along the crossguard. And looking at the sword in my hand, I vowed I'd be worthy of it. That I *would* slay something monstrous with it. That I'd not just walk. Not just run.

'No, in this place, I'd fucking fly.'

✦ VII ✦

SHAPED LIKE HEARTBREAK

'IT WAS LATE afternoon of that first day when I met her.

'I'd washed the filth of the road away in the bathhouse, changed into my new gear. Black leather britches and tunic, heavy boots, knee-high and silver-heeled. The soles were embossed with the sevenstar, and I realized I'd leave the mark of the Martyrs wherever I walked. In casting off my old clothes, in some way I was casting off what I'd been. I'd no idea what I might become yet. But as I returned to Barracks, I found Abbot Khalid waiting, a smile in his eyes to match the one that haunted his cut-throat's face.

'"Come with me, Little Lion. I've a gift for you."

'I followed the abbot to the gatehouse, marvelling at the sheer size of the man. He was a mountain walking, long knotted braids trailing down his back like untamed serpents. The elevator swayed in the chill wind as we descended, and I watched him sidelong, eyes drifting to the horizontal scars bisecting his cheeks.

'"You're wondering how I got them," he said, eyes on the cold valley below.

'"Apologies, Abbot," I said, lowering my gaze. "But Frère Greyhand . . . he said we palebloods heal as no ordinary men do. The night he took me from my village, I was cut so deep the knife struck bone. But now, there's barely even a mark."

'"You shall heal all the faster as you grow, and your blood thickens. Though we do share some of the weaknesses of our accursed fathers – silver will cut us deeply, for example, and fire will leave its mark. But you are wondering what scarred me so?"

'I nodded mutely, meeting his green, kohled stare.

'"The dark is full of horrors, de León. And though coldbloods concern us most these nights, brothers of the Silver Order have hunted all manner of evil, and been hunted in kind." He traced his scars. "These were gifted to me by the claws of a duskdancer. A monster, accursed, who could take the form of beast and man. I sent her to the hell she deserved." His scarred smile widened a fraction. "But she refused to leave without a goodbye kiss."

'We touched down, and with a soft chuckle, Khalid patted my shoulder and led me onwards, a hundred questions brawling behind my teeth.

'The stable was carved within the heart of the Cathedral's pillar, supported by columns of dark rock. It stank inside, as stables do: horse and straw and shite. But ever since the night I'd drunk Ilsa's blood, I could swear my senses had grown sharper, and beneath the everyday stink, I caught a whiff of death. Decay.

'Two boys were saddling a shaggy chestnut mare near the entrance – dark-skinned Sūdhaemi lads like Khalid. The first was around my age, the other, perhaps a year younger. They were fit, dressed in homespun with dark curls cropped close to their scalps. By the shared hazel of their eyes and the cut of their chins, I guessed they were famille.

'"Fairdawning, Kaspar. Kaveh." The abbot nodded to the older lad, then the younger beside him. "This is Gabriel de León, a new recruit to the Order."

'"Fairdawning, Gabriel," Kaspar said, grasping my hand.

'"Godmorrow, Kaspar." I nodded, looked to his brother. "Kaveh?"

'"Apologies," Kaspar said. "My brother was born tongueless. He does not speak."

'The younger lad stared at me as if in challenge, and I could guess why. In superstitious parts of the empire, such affliction might have been taken as the taint of witchery, the babe burned, his mother beside him. But my mama had taught me such thinking was folly, born only of fear. That the Almighty loved *all* his children, and that I should strive to do the same. And so, I offered my hand.

'"Well, I'm not that interesting to talk to anyway. Fairdawning, Kaveh."

'The lad's scowl softened as I spoke, and as our palms met, his lips curled in a smile. Abbot Khalid grunted approval, called out across the stables in his warm baritone.

'"And a fairdawn to you also, Prioress Charlotte. Sisternovices."

'Following the abbot's eyeline, I saw a half-dozen figures around a stack of feedbags – Sisters from the Priory above, I realized. They were all clad in dove-white novice robes and coifs, save a severe-looking woman in a black habit, who stood where the others sat. She was older, so thin she was almost gaunt. Four long scars cut down and across her face – as if she'd been attacked by some wild animal.

'"Godmorrow, Abbot." The woman glanced at her charges. "Give blessing, girls."

'"Godmorrow, Abbot Khalid," the sisters sang, all in unison.

'"This is Gabriel de León," Khalid said. "A new son of the Ordo Argent."

'I kept my head bowed out of respect, but looked the sisters over through my lashes. All were young. Sitting on the bags with blocks of paper on their laps, charcoal sticks in hand. They'd been drawing the horses, I realized. I noted a novice among them so slight she seemed almost a child, with big green eyes and freckled skin. And seated at their forefront, like an angel fallen to earth, was one of the most beautiful girls I'd ever seen.'

Jean-François rolled his eyes and leaned back in his chair.

Gabriel looked up and scowled. 'Problem?'

'I said nothing, Silversaint.'

'I heard a distinct groan just now, coldblood.'

'The wind, I assure you.'

'Fuck off,' Gabriel growled. 'She *was* beautiful. Oh, perhaps not the kind you'd find hanging in a portrait gallery or gracing some rich bastard's arm. She wasn't a beauty you wrapped in silk or hid inside a golden bower. But I can still recall the sight of her that afternoon. All the years between then and now, and it seems only yesterday.'

Gabriel fell so still he seemed a mirror to the vampire opposite. Even the monster seemed aware of the weight in the air, sitting patiently until the silversaint spoke again.

'She was older than me. Seventeen, at a guess. A beauty spot was placed as if by the Mothermaid herself, just to the right of her lips. One eyebrow was arched higher than the other, giving her a constant air of mild disdain. Her skin was milk; her cheek, the curve of a broken heart. There was no perfection to her. But her asymmetry commanded . . . fascination. She had the face of a half-heard whisper, of a secret unshared. She sat with a block of parchment in her lap, partway through a beautiful drawing of a big black gelding.

'Abbot Khalid looked at her work. It was hard to tell with his scars, but I realized he was genuinely smiling. "You've a keen eye and a keener hand, Sisternovice."

'The girl lowered her eyes. "You honour me, Abbot."

'"'Tis the Almighty that guides our hands," Prioress Charlotte said, with a disapproving glance at the young sister. "We are merely his vessels."

'The girl looked up to her prioress and nodded. "Véris."

'I knew I shouldn't gawp. On the road to San Michon, Greyhand had told me silversaints swore vows of celibacy, for fear we might perpetuate the evil of our birth and make more paleblood abominations like ourselves. After what I'd done to Ilsa, I confess that the thought sat well enough with me. I could still see the terror in her eyes if I tried, and the horror that I'd hurt her haunted me still. I'd no desire to touch another girl as long as I lived, and these weren't just girls, either – these were novices of the Silver Sorority. Soon to be married to God Himself.

'But still, something about this girl drew me in. As I watched, her eyes flickered up and met mine. I didn't look away. But surprisingly, neither did she.

'"Well, Godmorrow, godly daughters." Khalid bowed. "Mothermaid bless."

'"Fairdawning, Abbot." The prioress snapped her fingers. "Back to work, girls."

'I broke my stare, and the abbot clapped my shoulder, led me to the stable's heart. And all thoughts of raven-haired sisternovices fled my head at what I found there.

'A throng of horses waited in a wide pen. They were tundra ponies from Talhost – that hardy breed known as sosyas. Smaller than their Elidaeni cousins, sosyas have shaggy coats and stomachs of iron, ideally suited to the years of privation that followed daysdeath. Those bastards will chew on *anything*. I once knew a man who swore blind his sosya ate his fucking dog. These beasts seemed of the finest stock. But as I stood admiring them, again I caught that whiff of decay. And looking up, I finally discovered its source.

'"Mother and Maid . . ."

'Two wretched coldbloods were hanged from the ceiling. An older male, thin and rotten, and a boy, no older than I. Their skin was pallid, their clothes were rags, and their eyes burned with hunger and malevolence as they glared down at me.

'"Have no fear, de León," Khalid said. "Bound in silver, they're helpless as babes."

'Looking close, I saw that the vampires were strung up by silver chains, swaying like ghastly chandeliers. The grooms and sisters and even the animals themselves seemed entirely unconcerned. And at last, I realized why these coldbloods were here.

'"You keep them for the horses . . ."

'"Just so," the abbot nodded. "God's creatures cannot abide the presence of monsters of the night. But these steeds are meant to bear us into battle against the dark. So, we expose them early and often, that they become accustomed to the evil of the deathless." Khalid gave one of his scar-face smiles. "You've a sharp mind, Little Lion."

'I nodded, seeing the wisdom in it. The abbot handed me a few sugar cubes – a luxury since the crops had all failed, but one that San Michon could apparently still afford with the Empress's patronage. "Take your pick, son."

'"God's truth?"

'Khalid nodded. "A gift, for your trials to come. And mind you choose well, lad. This horse will bear you into battle against all the horrors that call the dark home."

'"But then . . . how should I decide?"

'"Trust your heart. You'll know the one."

'Ma famille hadn't owned so much as a sheep when I was a lad. It was only the nobleborn who could dream of keeping beasts as fine as these. Marvelling at the fortune that saw me gifted my own sword and steed on the same day, I stepped into the pen. And there in the throng, I found him. His stare was deep as midnight; his shaggy coat, darkest ebony. His mane was tied in thick plaits, his tail the same, switching from side to side as I approached. I realized he was the same gelding that the talented sisternovice had been drawing, and glancing in her direction, I found her dark eyes upon me again. She seemed to bristle as I closed in on the horse. But still, I did.

'"Hello, boy," I murmured.

'He took the sugar cube I offered. Nickering, he nuzzled my face in search of more, and I stroked the shaggy satin of his cheek, laughing for joy.'

Gabriel shook his head.

'Cynics say there's no such thing as love at first sight. But I loved that fucking horse the moment I met him. And feeding him another cube, I knew I'd made a friend for life.

'"What's your name?" I asked, bewildered at his beauty.

'"His name is Justice."

'Turning, I saw the sisternovice had spoken, furious now. But before I could ask what I'd done to earn her ire, the prioress's voice cut the air. "Sisternovice Astrid, be silent!"

'"I will *not*." Her drawings spilled as the girl stood, and I saw every sketch was of this same horse. "Why should this *peasant* have Justice's keeping? I—"

'The girl's words were cut off by the prioress's slap.–

'"How *dare* you take tone with me," Charlotte glowered. "A sister of the Silver Priory owns no goods. She covets no earthly possession. And she obeys her betters."

'"I am *not* a sister of the Silver Priory," the girl spat, defiant.

'I winced as the prioress brought the girl to her knees with another slap, her scarred face twisting as she snarled, "Continue with this insolence, and you never will be!"

'"Good! I never wanted to *be* here!"

'"That much is plain! But there are two places in this world for a bastard daughter, Astrid Rennier! Before God's altar on her knees, or in a brothel on her back!"

'An awful still settled over the stables. Astrid stared up at the prioress, furious. I looked to Khalid, but one glance told me he wouldn't intercede. So, fool that I was . . .

'"I beg pardon," I said. "If the horse belongs to the good demoiselle—"

'"She is no demoiselle," the prioress spat. "She is a sisternovice of the Silver Priory. She owns nothing, save the cloth on her back. She deserves nothing, save the punishment she is due. And unless you wish to share it, *you* would do well to mind your tongue."

'"Stand down, de León," Khalid commanded.

'I looked to the abbot, uncertain. The prioress reached into her sleeve and drew out a leather thong tipped with a short spur of iron.

'"Beg God's forgiveness," she commanded the girl.

'The novice only glared. "I beg for nothi—"

'Her words became a strangled cry as the thong landed across her back.

'"Beg it, whorechild!"

'The girl lifted her head and spat in fury. "*Fuck* you."

'A gasp rang out among the novices. I was astonished at the hate in the girl's eyes, bewildered at her stubbornness. But more and most, sickened at the violence being done to her. I knew what it was to suffer a beating like that. I knew the courage it took to bear it without a sound. The strap fell six more times, and still, the girl refused to yield. So finally, fearing she wouldn't beg until it killed her, I begged instead.

'"Prioress, stop, please! If punishment must be meted—"

'Strong fingers took hold of my arm, so hard I winced. Turning, I found Abbot Khalid behind me. "This is not your place to speak, Initiate."

'"Abbot, this is cruelty beyond—"

'His grip tightened, so hard I could feel my bones groaning. "Not. Your. Place."

'I felt a cur. My mouth gone sour and my belly turned cold. But with that crushing hold on my arm, and only a boy after all, I dared not speak again. Charlotte kept striking, the scars on her face turning a livid red with her rage. My stomach churned as those awful cracks rang in the stillness. And finally, like anyone would have, the girl broke.

"'Godsakes, *stop*!"

"'Do you beg the Almighty's forgiveness, Astrid Rennier?"

'*Crack*.

"'*Oui!*'

'*Crack*.

"'Beg, then!"

"'I'm sorry!" she screamed. "I beg God forgive me!"

'The prioress finally eased back, her voice like ice. "*Get* up."

'I looked on helpless as the weeping girl took a moment to gather her strength. And then she struggled upright, arms wrapped about her. I glanced among the sisternovices and saw fear of the prioress in their eyes. Fear of God above all. There was only one who seemed truly concerned – the tiny girl with green eyes and freckles, who looked at Astrid with the same pity I felt in my own heart. But Prioress Charlotte clearly felt none.

"'You will learn your place, whorechild. Do you hear me?"

"'O-oui, Prioress," the girl whispered.

"'That goes for *all* of you!" Charlotte rounded on her charges, fervour flashing in her eyes. "You are promised to God now. You will serve him and His Church as faithful wives should. Or you will answer to me, and hell itself!"

'The woman glowered at me as if inviting reply. But though the words roiled behind my teeth, Abbot Khalid still held my arm. And so, I stayed mute.

"'My apologies for the unseemly display, Abbot," Charlotte said, lips thin.

"'Unnecessary, Prioress," Khalid replied. "*The sheep that stray are prey for wolves.*"

"'Just so." The thin woman nodded curtly at the Testaments quote, turned to her novices. "Come along then, girls. We shall spend the day in silent contemplation. Sisternovice Chloe, assist Sisternovice Astrid."

'The small freckled girl nodded, helped her fellow novice collect her things. Astrid's hands were shaking. She met my eyes briefly – a clouded, fleeting glance stained with tears. It was only when they were out of sight that Khalid released his grip on my arm.

"'A strong will shall serve you well on the Hunt, young brother," he said softly. "And a good heart shall prove a shield against the perils of the dark. But if ever you question my orders again, I will drag you to the wheel and flay the skin right off your back. You are a servant of God. But you are *my* soldier now. Do you understand?"

'I looked into Khalid's eyes to see if he was angry, but his voice was matter-of-fact, his stare steady. The Abbot of the Ordo Argent didn't rage. Didn't raise his voice. It was at that moment I learned a true leader didn't need to.

"'Oui, Abbot," I bowed.

'Khalid nodded, as if the matter were already forgotten. Looking to the gate the sisters had left by, he murmured, "Prioress Charlotte is a godly woman, devoted to the Almighty and Mothermaid. And if she is of a temper this day, you must forgive her. Mass this eve will be painful for you, young-blood. But for most of us, it will be agony."

"'Why? What happens at mass this evening?"

"'Someone dies, de León."

'Khalid heaved a sigh, and stared out into the cold.

"'A good man dies.'"

✦ VIII ✦

THE RED RITE

'AS THE FEEBLE sun set, I was ushered to the Cathedral by the song of mighty bells.

'Figures were answering the call from around the monastery, and I was struck by how few there were. Half a dozen silversaints, perhaps a dozen apprentices, workmen and servants and sisters of the Silver Sorority. But ascending the Cathedral's steps with Aaron de Coste beside me, I still had goosebumps on my skin. No matter how old or empty it appeared, I could sense the sanctity in this place. And stepping inside, I found my breath stolen from my lungs.

'The Cathedral was carved of dark granite, circular like the sigil of God's Holy Church. As was tradition, two pairs of great graven doors were set in its walls – one in the east, for the dawn and living, and one in the west, for dusk and the dead. Graven pillars rose up to the dome, taller than the grandest trees, and the space was softly lit by the same glass globes that hung from the Armoury ceiling. Many of the windows were under repair, but those uncovered were breathtaking. Dark light struggled through the great sevenstar window in the façade, casting dim rainbows on the floor. Wooden pews were arranged in concentric circles around a stone altar at the building's heart, and above it hung a great marble statue of the Redeemer upon his wheel. His hands were bound, back flayed open, throat cut ear to ear.

'Upon that altar sat a brazier, and a glass bowl filled with bubbling silver liquid. Before it sat a single silver chalice.

'I'd no ken what the brazier was for, but every God-fearing soul knew the Grail. Like every other church in Elidaen, this was only an imitation, of course. But while that chalice was present in the room, so too was the Redeemer's spirit. And I swear, I could *feel* it.

'Despite the Cathedral's size, there were only four dozen at mass. Baptiste Sa-Ismael sat close by, along with three others who were certainly fellow blackthumbs. My master, Frère Greyhand, knelt in the front row among a handful of men in silversaint garb. They were dour-faced and black-clad, and each seemed a living legend to me. But I noticed many were mutilated somehow; wrists absent hands and faces missing eyes. At the end of their row sat a silversaint with lank greying hair. I saw he was rocking softly, back and forth. His stare was deeply bloodshot, his face carved with lines of pain.

'The air was filled with ghostly music, angelic and beautiful. I saw sisters of the Silver Sorority in a loft above, clothed in black, singing all in unison. Their voices made my skin tingle, the beauty of their song filled my chest with ancient fire.

'From a spiral stair below the floor, Abbot Khalid ascended to the altar. He was clad in black robes, the scars in his cheeks twisting his lips into that odd forever smile. As he lifted his hands, I saw silvered ink on the dark skin of his forearms – Sanael, the Angel of Blood, a weave of swords and doves, the Mothermaid holding the infant Redeemer.

'"*I am the word and the way, sayeth the Lord,*" Khalid intoned. "*By my blood, the sinner shall find salvation, and the penitent, the keys to my kingdom eternal.*"

'All in the Cathedral answered "Véris" – the customary reply of congregation at mass. It was an old Elidaeni word, meaning *A truth beyond truth*.

'"We welcome a new brother into this, your house, oh Lord." Khalid looked right at me. "His birth, an abomination. His life, a transgression. His soul, bound for perdition. But we beseech you, give him strength that he might overcome the misdeed of his making, and stand tall against this endless night."

'"Véris," the brothers replied.

'The altar bell rang. I could feel the very breath of God upon my neck.

'"Gabriel de León," Khalid commanded. "Approach."

'I looked to Master Greyhand, and he nodded once. Making the sign of the wheel, I found myself standing before that brazier and the bowl of silver liquid atop it.

'Six figures ascended the stair, bathed in the soft, warm light from those globes above. Prioress Charlotte stood at their fore, followed by three women in black habits, silver-trimmed. Their heads were veiled in lace, faces powdered white, crimson sevenstars painted over their eyes. But the two figures following wore novice white, their faces uncovered and unadorned.

'As they took up places at the altar opposite me, I recognized both from the stables that afternoon. The first was the tiny lass with the green eyes and freckles – Chloe, I remembered she'd been called. The second was the beautiful raven-haired girl who'd been beaten by the prioress for her disobedience. Her dark eyes once more meeting mine.

'Astrid Rennier.

'I watched Sisternovice Chloe unroll a leather satchel embossed with the sevenstar. A host of needles was arrayed within, long and gleaming in the honeyed light.

'"As he gave to the Redeemer upon the wheel," Khalid said, "we pray God gives you strength to endure the suffering of nights to come. For now, we grant you a taste."

'I looked to the abbot, wondering what he meant.

'"Place your left hand upon the altar," he commanded.

'I did as I was bid, placing my hand on the wood. It was only when Sisternovice Chloe gently turned my palm upwards that I understood what was happening. She wiped a cool cloth over my skin, and I smelled strong, sharp spirits. Astrid Rennier dipped a needle into the metallic liquid bubbling atop the burner. And looking into my eyes, she spoke, echoed by the other sisters around her.

'"'This is the hand,
'"'That wields the flame,
'"'That lights the way,
'"'And turns the dark,
'"'To silver."

'Astrid stabbed the needle into my palm. The sensation was sharp and bright, but brief, and I flinched only a little. Looking down, I saw a tiny spot of blood and silver etched into my flesh. Prioress Charlotte leaned close to inspect the needle stroke, gave a curt nod. I drew breath, swallowed hard. Thinking the sting hadn't been all that bad.

'Astrid stabbed my palm again. And again. By the twentieth prick of the needle, discomfort had become pain. And by the hundredth, pain had become agony.'

Gabriel shook his head, staring at the star tattooed on his left palm.

'It's a strange thing, being marked so. The hurt becomes delirium. The brief relief between each needle stroke seems both heaven and hell. My stepfather beat me like a dog on his bad days. But I'd never felt anything like the pain I knew at Astrid's touch. It was . . . incandescent. Like I stood outside my body, watching through a fever dream.

'I didn't know how I'd manage it. And still, I knew this was a testing – the first of many. If I couldn't endure a needle, how was I to face the monsters of the dark? How was I to avenge my sister, defend God's mighty Church, if I couldn't win through this?

'I tried to concentrate on the choirsong, but heard it only as a dirge. I closed my eyes, but felt only dread at not knowing when the next stroke might fall. And so, I looked to the Redeemer above.

'They'd flayed him alive, the Testaments said. Priests of the Old Gods, refusing to accept the One Faith – they hung him from a chariot wheel and scourged him with thorns, burned him with fire, then cut his throat and cast him into the waters. He could have called on his Almighty Father to save him. Instead, he accepted his fate, knowing it would be the catalyst that united this Church and spread his word to every corner of this empire.

'*By this blood, shall they have life eternal.*

'And now, that empire stood imperilled. That Church under siege by the deathless Dead. So, I looked up into his eyes, and I prayed.

'*Give me strength, brother. And I will give you everything.*

'I couldn't tell you how long it took. By the end, my palm was a bleeding, fucking mess. But Astrid finally leaned back, and Chloe poured burning spirits onto my skin. And through the boiling haze, I saw it, etched in my palm; the mark of the Martyrs, in silver ink.

'A perfect sevenstar.

'"Frère Greyhand," said Khalid. "Approach."

'Master Greyhand made the sign of the wheel and stepped forward.

'"Do you vow before Almighty God to lead this unworthy boy in the tenets of the Ordo Argent? Do you vow before San Michon to be the hand that guides, the shield that protects, until his damned soul stands strong enough to protect this realm himself?"

'"By the Blood of the Redeemer," Greyhand answered. "I vow it."

'Khalid turned to me. "Do you vow before Almighty God to commit yourself to the tenets of our Order? To overcome the vile sin of your nature and live a life in service to God's Holy Church? Do you vow before San Michon to obey your master, to heed his voice, to be guided by his hand until you stand sainted yourself?"

'I thought of the day my sister came home. Knowing that among this brotherhood, within this holy order, I'd find the strength to stop such horror from ever happening again.

"'By the Blood, I vow it.'

"'Gabriel de León, I name you initiate of the Silver Order of San Michon. May the Almighty Father give you courage. May the blessed Mothermaid give you wisdom. May the One True Redeemer give you strength. Véris.'

'I met the abbot's eyes, and my whole body tingled with pride as his lips twisted a little further in his cut-throat smile. Greyhand gave a small nod – the first sign of approval he'd bestowed since saving me in Lorson. My head felt light, the pain now a benediction. But through that haze, I felt more at peace than I'd ever been.

'Greyhand returned to his place, and I walked beside him. A bell rang, signalling the congregation should rise. The sisters and novices around the altar bowed their heads. Khalid turned his eyes to the stained-glass window of the Martyrs.

"'From brightest joy to deepest sorrow. We beg you bear witness, blessed Michon. We pray you, Almighty God, to open the gates of your eternal kingdom.' His eyes fell on the greying silversaint at the end of our row. "Frère Yannick. Step forth.'

'The choir had fallen silent. I watched the man clench his jaw, lift his gaze to heaven. Frère Yannick's face was gaunt, sleepless lines carved around bloodshot eyes. Beside him, a younger, sandy-haired lad squeezed his hand, pale with grief – another apprentice, I realized. And drawing a deep breath, Yannick stepped forward before Abbot Khalid.

"'Are you ready, Brother?' Khalid asked.

"'I am ready,' the man replied, his voice like cracked glass.

"'And are you certain, Brother?'

'The silversaint looked at the sevenstar in the palm of his left hand. "Better to die a man than live a monster.'

"'To heaven, then,' Khalid said softly.

'Yannick nodded. "To heaven.'

'The choir took up their song again, and I recognized the hymn sung at funeral masses; the grim and beautiful "Memoria Di." Khalid walked up the Cathedral's western aisle. Frère Yannick drifted behind like a man sleepwalking. One by one, the rest of the congregation followed, out through the doors for the dead to the courtyard beyond. I dared not speak and break the awful sanctity I could feel in this moment. But Master Greyhand knew the questions in my head.

"'This is the Red Rite, Little Lion,' he whispered. "This is the fate that awaits us all.'

'We formed up in the courtyard, watching Abbot Khalid and Frère

Yannick marching onto the stone span I'd seen earlier – the one de Coste had named "Heaven's Bridge". I saw the wheel on the balcony's edge, looking out over the drop into the river far below. And a part of me knew then, what was coming.

'"We are the children of a terrible sin," Greyhand murmured to me. "And eventually, that sin corrupts us all. The thirst of our fathers lives inside us, Little Lion. There are ways we can quell it for a time, that we might earn our place in the Almighty's kingdom. But eventually, God punishes us for the sacrilege of our making. As palebloods grow older, we grow stronger. But so does the immortal beast that rages within our mortal shell. The terrible thirst that demands to be slaked upon the blood of innocents."

'"Yannick . . . he killed someone?" I whispered. "He drank . . ."

'"No. But the thirst has become too much for him to bear. He feels it, spreading like a poison. He hears it when he closes his eyes at night." My master shook his head, voice hushed. "We call it the *sangirè*, Little Lion. The *red thirst*. A whisper at first, dulcet and sweet. But it grows to an endless scream. And unless you silence it, you *will* succumb to it, becoming naught but a ravenous beast. Worse than the lowest wretched."

'Greyhand nodded to Frère Yannick, his voice thick with sorrow and pride.

'"Better to end this life than lose your immortal soul. In the finale, that is the choice before every paleblood alive. Live as a monster, or die as a man."

'I could still hear the choir in the Cathedral. I watched Frère Yannick slip his greatcoat off, remove his tunic. His body was covered in beautiful silver ink: icons of the Martyrs and Mothermaid, the Angels of Death and Pain and Hope. That ink told the story of a life spent in service to God. Outside, he seemed hale and strong, but one look in his eyes told me all was not so within. And I remembered my night with Ilsa, then. The chorus of her veins flooding into my mouth. The beat of my raging heart growing stronger as hers weakened with every swallow. The thirst that had driven me to such depths.

'What would it become as I grew older?

'What would *I* become?

'"We beg you bear witness, Almighty Father," Abbot Khalid called. "As your begotten son suffered for our sins, so too shall our brother suffer for his."

'"Véris," came the reply around me.

'Yannick turned to face us, placed his hands upon the wheel. My mouth ran sour as I saw Prioress Charlotte approach with a leather whip adorned with silver spurs. But the prioress only pressed the whip to Frère Yannick's shoulders – seven ritual touches for the seven nights the Redeemer suffered. A candle was kissed to the brother's skin, to mimic the flames that burned God's begotten son. And then, Abbot Khalid lowered his head, drawing a silvered knife. The choir was near the end of their hymn.

'"Blessed Mothermaid . . ." I breathed.

'"From suffering comes salvation," Khalid intoned. "In service to God, we find the path to his throne. In blood and silver this 'saint has lived, and so now dies."

'"Into your arms, Lord!" Yannick cried. "I commend my unworthy soul!"

'I flinched as the blade flashed in the abbot's hands, slicing the frère from ear to ear. A great rush of blood spilled from the wound, and Yannick closed his sleep-starved eyes. The final notes of the Memoria Di rang out over the congregation. I couldn't find air to breathe. And with a gentle shove, like a father guiding his son to sleep, Khalid sent Yannick tumbling off the balcony, down towards the waters five hundred feet below.

'About me, the gathering made the sign of the wheel. Cold horror had settled in my belly. Among the novices, I saw Sisternovice Astrid, watching me again with those dark eyes. Abbot Khalid looked about as the bells tolled. And he nodded, as if content.

'"Véris," he said.

'"Véris," the others echoed.

'I looked down to the new tattoo in my palm. Throbbing with pain. Burning like fire.

'"Véris," I whispered.'

✦ IX ✦
SWEETEST AND DARKEST

'THERE WAS NO sleep for me that night. I bedded down in the Barracks, listening to the old oaken rafters creak overhead. True silversaints had individual cells on the floors above, but we initiates slept in a communal room. There were more cots than needed – enough for fifty at least. But as we returned from mass, only a dozen or so came with me.

'I lay down, my head reeling. In the space of a day, I'd been gifted the finest possessions I'd ever owned, been inducted into a holy order, promised my life to God. But I'd also seen a member of that same order ritually murdered before he succumbed to the madness within him, and learned that eventually, the same fate awaited me.

'Not if. *When.*

'"The first day is one of the strangest."

'I looked to the initiate in the cot beside mine. He was the boy who'd squeezed Frère Yannick's hand before he approached the altar – the dead brother's apprentice. He was a big lad, sandy-haired, and his formal accent told me he was Elidaeni born. His blue eyes glittered as he glanced at me sidelong. I could see them bloodshot from tears.

'"Quite a day," I agreed.

'"I wish I could promise it gets easier. But I've no liar's tongue."

'"I'll not fault you for it," I nodded. "My name is Gabriel de León."

'"Theo Petit," the boy said, shaking my hand.

'"My condolences for your master. I'll pray for his soul."

'His eyes flashed then, voice growing hard. "Save it for yourself, boy. Pray you live long enough to face the same choice as he. And show the same courage in the making of it."

'Theo blew out the lamp, plunging the room into darkness. I lay there in the gloom, staring up into the black. Tossing and turning until de Coste eventually growled from the bed opposite mine.

"'Go to sleep, Peasant. You'll have need of it amorrow.'

'I'd no idea how true Aaron's words would prove. Next morn, I was roused by the Cathedral bells, and felt I'd hardly slept at all. I was half-eager, half-terrified, wondering what was to come. The tattoo on my hand was aching, bloody, and after a sombre dawnmass, Frère Greyhand gifted me a jar of sweet-smelling salve.

"'Angelgrace,' he explained. 'The silver in your ink means it will heal slower than a regular wound. The 'grace will help until your blood does its work. Now, follow me. And leave that sword here. It's not your todger, you can take your hand off it occasionally.'

'I did as my master bid, following him into the morning air. I remember it was so cold that day, my bollocks felt like they'd crawled up inside my body. The dim morning light across the monastery was frail, beautiful, and making our way along the rope bridge towards the Gauntlet's silhouette, I could feel butterflies warring in my belly. Archer cut through the chill air around us, calling to Greyhand as he soared overhead.

"'Master . . . where do we go?' I asked.

"'Your first trial.'

"'And what should I expect from this trial?'

"'What you should always expect from this life, Little Lion. Blood.' Greyhand looked to the river winding through the pillars below and sighed. A fey mood was on him, but whether it was thoughts of the Red Rite last night or other troubles, I knew not. 'A part of me envies you this day, boy. The first taste is ever the sweetest. And the darkest.'

'I'd no idea what he meant, but Greyhand seemed in no mood for questions. As we strode through the great double doors of the Gauntlet, I saw that San Michon's proving ground was fashioned like a vast arena; circular, open to the sky. Its flagstones were granite, but a great sevenstar was wrought in pale limestone on its surface. Training mannequins and strange apparatus skirted the edge, and banners with unfamiliar crests adorned the walls.

'In the centre of the star, a group awaited, their dim shadows reaching out towards me. The foremost was Abbot Khalid, standing with arms folded, his greatcoat billowing in the wind. A beautiful silversteel sword was slung at his back – double-handed and deadly, taller than I was. The big man nodded as we approached, and Greyhand and I bowed low.

"'Fairdawning, Initiate de León. Frère Greyhand.'

'"Godmorrow, Abbot," we replied.

'Khalid motioned to the people about him. "These are the luminaries of the Silver Order, de León. Come to bear witness to your Trial of the Blood. Good Prioress Charlotte, head of the Silver Sorority and Mistress of the Aegis, you already know."

'I bowed to the dour woman, eyes downturned. She was clad head to foot in her black sister's habit, and her skin looked waxen in the thin dawn light, those four scars cutting angry pink lines across her face. I idly wondered how she'd earned them as she gave me a thin, bloodless smile. "Fairdawning, Initiate. Mothermaid bless."

'Khalid nodded to an elderly man in a black robe beside him. "This is Archivist Adamo, master of the Great Library and keeper of the history of the Ordo Argent."

'The fellow blinked at me, looking slightly befuddled behind his thick spectacles. His skin was wrinkled like waterlogged paper, his hair, white as the snows of my youth. His back was bent with age, and I could see no silver ink atop his liver-spotted hands.

'"Argyle á Sadhbh," Khalid said, motioning to a towering fellow among the group. "Seraph to the Brothers of the Hearth and Forgemaster of San Michon."

'The huge man met my eyes, nodding greeting. He was Ossway born for sure – flaming red stubble covered his scalp, and his jaw was heavy as a granite brick. But his left eye was milky white, the left side of his face was marred by a deep burn, and strangest of all, his left hand was metal, not flesh – some clever simulacrum forged of iron, strapped to his forearm with a leather bracer. His biceps were thick as a man's thighs, his fair skin pocked by spark scars from his forge. He was a smith, through and through.

'"Initiate," he grunted. "May God grant ye strength this day."

'"This is Sœur Aoife," Khalid said. "Adept of the Silver Sorority."

'The abbot motioned to a young sister beside Charlotte, watching me with curious blue eyes. She was slender, pretty, a hint of auburn curls at the edge of her coif. She held a thin box of polished oak, and her fingernails were chewed to the roots.

'"Godmorrow, Initiate." She bowed. "Mothermaid bless you."

'"The good sister will be assisting in today's trial. And as for your trial master," here Khalid shared his cut-throat's smile with Greyhand, "I shall allow him to introduce himself."

'I glanced to the brother in question, standing beside the abbot like a sharp black shadow. His dark grey moustache was so long it could've been tied in a bow atop his shaved skull, and his eyes looked like piss holes in his head. He seemed older than Khalid and Greyhand – past forty, I guessed. He was slight of build, his greatcoat collar laced high and tight about his throat. Save for a long cane of polished ashwood, he was unarmed.

'"My name is Talon de Montfort, Seraph of the Hunt," the thin man declared in a sharp Elidaeni accent. "You will learn to hate me worse than the whore who spat you from her belly, and the devil who squirted you into it."

'I glanced at my master, then at Khalid, taken aback. This Talon was Seraph of the Hunt, the second-highest 'saint in the Order. But still, no bastard alive speaks that way about my mama. "My mother was n—"

'*Swakk!* came the sound of Talon's cane across my legs.

'"Ow!"

'"During this trial, you will speak when spoken to. Am I understood?"

'"O-oui," I managed, massaging my whipped thigh.

'*Swakk!*

'"Oui what, you pig-buggering little shitwizard?"

'"O-oui, Seraph Talon," I gasped.

'"Splendid." The thin man glanced to Greyhand, the other luminaries. "You may take your places in the rings, godly Brothers and Sisters. The weather is chill, but this shall not take overlong. By hour's end, the Trial shall be concluded or the funeral underway."

'I blanched a little at that. But my master only patted my shoulder.

'"No fear. Heed the hymn, Little Lion."

'Greyhand turned, and with Abbot Khalid and the prioress beside him, he marched up to the bleachers. Argyle assisted Archivist Adamo, the old man taking the smith's iron hand and shuffling slowly from the star. Cold winds whispered between Talon and me, tossing my hair into my eyes. Sister Aoife stood beside the seraph, that wooden box in her hands. The thin man looked at me like an owl summing up a particularly juicy mouse, and I watched that switch in his hand as if it were a viper set to strike.

'"What do you know of the coldblood who sired you, boy?" Talon asked.

'The question caught me off-guard, mostly because I had no good answer. I thought of my mother then, a pang of resentment in my chest. All those years she spent warning me of the hungers within, and never once did she warn me of what I truly was. I supposed she was ashamed by the sin of it all. But she could have told me *something* . . .

'"Nothing, Seraph."

'*Swakk!*

'"Ow!"

'"Speak up, you ill-bred twatwaffler!"

'I glanced to the stony faces in the gallery, spoke louder. "Nothing, Seraph!"

'He nodded. "Now, I need ask this question like the world needed your mother to shit you into it, but are you at all versed in the divine mysteries of chymistrie?"

'My heart quickened at that. Chymistrie was a dark craft, spoken of in hushed tones about my village. My mama once told me it was something between alchemy, witchery, and lunacy. But to be on the safe side, I shook my head.

'Talon sighed. "Then let me enlighten your so-called mind, you spunk-brained fuckweasel. The foes you will face on the Hunt are the deadliest creatures under God's own heaven. Coldbloods. Faekin. Restless. Duskdancers. Fallen. But the Almighty has not left you bereft of tools in the endless night. And we shall teach you how to craft them *all*. Black ignis powder that explodes with all heaven's fury at a single spark. Silver caustic to burn the flesh of your foes like acid. Kingshield. Angelgrace. Ghostbreath. Griefthorn . . ." From within his greatcoat, Talon produced a phial of dark scarlet dust. "And last, his greatest gift of all."

'My mouth ran dry. It was the same powder I'd seen Greyhand and de Coste smoke along the Hollyroad, their eyes flooding blood-red as they breathed it down.

'"What *is* that, Seraph?"

'"This, you lackwitted piss-puddle, is sanctus. A chymical distillation of the essence in our enemies' veins. Through it, we alleviate the dark thirst inherited from the monsters who sired us. *And* unlock the gifts God granted us to help send them back to hell."

'"You mean that's . . ."

'He nodded. "Vampire blood."

'"Fuck *me*," I breathed.

'"The Testaments name sodomy a deadly sin, so I'd rather not." Talon offered a brief smile. "But you're very pretty, de León, and I appreciate the offer."

'I chuckled, thinking he was making a jest.

'*Swakk!*

'"Ow!"

'"Sanctus is the holy sacrament of San Michon. A paleblood's greatest weapon against the endless night, and our damned natures. Today, you begin to wield it, and your gifts. And our first step, my cherry pauperstain, is to determine which of the four bloodlines your father's deathless cock belonged to. But before we begin . . ." He twirled his cane between his fingertips and scowled. "You must give me permission to do so."

'I swallowed, massaging my leg. "Permission, Seraph?"

"'It is forbidden for palebloods to use their gifts upon each other without consent, under punishment of the lash. We are brothers-in-arms, in purpose and in blood, and we must trust one another above all else, de León. So. Do you consent?"

'I looked to Sister Aoife, uncertain. "What happens if I don't?"

'Swakk!

"'Ow!"

"'Do. You. Consent?"

"'I consent!"

'Talon nodded, narrowed his gaze. I felt the strangest sensation then. Like fingertips brushing soft along my scalp. Like a whisper slipping through my eyes. I winced as if looking into the sun, my head swimming. "What . . . w-what are you doing?"

"'All vampires have common abilities, which palebloods inherit. But each bloodline also has unique talents." Talon pointed to one of the un-familiar crests on the wall – a white raven wearing a golden crown. "The *Ironhearts*. The kith of Blood Voss. They have flesh akin to steel. It can turn aside silver. The eldest among them can even withstand the fury of the flame. But far more sobering is their ability to read the minds of weaker men."

'I realized *that* was the sensation I felt – the seraph was *in my fucking head*. I could feel him now, like a shadow inside my skull. But just as swift as it began, the feeling ended.

"'You must learn to better guard your thoughts, my dribble-chinned gibbercuck," Talon warned. "Or Voss's kin will pluck them right out of your shit-witted head."

'I blinked hard, realizing Talon's father must have been one of these Ironhearts, and that his son had claimed their gifts as his own. I wondered again about my own father, then. Who was he? What boons had his accursed blood bestowed upon me? I was unnerved Talon could simply force his way into my mind if he chose, but at the same time, a part of me felt a thrill that such a gift might also be mine.

'The seraph pointed to another banner, embroidered with two black wolves and two ornate red circles – the twin moons, Lánis and Lánae.

'"Blood Chastain. The *Shepherds*. These coldbloods exert their will over denizens of the animal world. See through their eyes. Control them like puppets. The eldest can even assume the forms of the darker creatures of earth and sky. Bats. Cats. Wolves. Trust no beast when you hunt a Chastain, boy. For the eyes of the night are theirs to command."

'The seraph nodded to a third banner; a heart-shaped shield set with a beautiful weave of roses and snakes. "Blood Ilon. The *Whispers*. A line more dangerous than a sackful of syphilitic serpents. All vampires can bend the weak-hearted to their will. But the Ilon can manipulate all manner of emotion. Heighten rage. Provoke fear. Inflame passion. And the hunter who cannot trust his own heart can trust nothing."

'Talon whipped his switch at the final banner; a blue field adorned with a white bear and a broken shield. "Blood Dyvok. The *Untamed*. Possessed of a strength even the other foul bastards of the night would shit their unholy pantaloons over. These creatures can tear apart full-grown men with their bare hands. Their ancients can smash down castle walls with their fists, and make the earth quake beneath their boots. Even other coldbloods look like helpless children beside them."

'My mind was swimming as Talon turned to the young woman next to him.

'"Good Sœur?"

'Aoife opened her oaken box, producing an ornate silver pipe. It was fashioned in the guise of Naél, the Angel of Bliss, her hands cupped to form a bowl. As I watched, Talon poured a tiny measure of sanctus into the angel's palms.

'"Now, the monster who bellied up your mother belonged to one of these four lines. And you will possess his bloodgift, albeit in a lesser form. Do you recall the first time you exhibited some strange ability? Did you show an affinity for animals as a boy? The knack of constantly getting your way? Perhaps you knew what others would say before they spoke?"

'I chewed my lip. "My sister Amélie. She was murdered by a coldblood and returned to our village as one of the wretched. I fought her off with my bare hands."

'"Mmmn." The thin man nodded. "Dyvok, perhaps. The same accursed blood as flows within our abbot. Very well. We shall begin there."

'I looked to the bleachers, where Khalid met my eyes and nodded. The thought I might be the same bloodline as a man so mighty set the butterflies loose in my belly once more.

'Talon beat his cane upon the ground three times. I heard the oiled grinding of stone upon stone, and saw the centre of the sevenstar opening wide.

'Rising up on a plinth of dark granite was the very same wretched that Greyhand had hauled to the monastery from Lorson. Its flesh was a wasteland, blotched and grey; its mouth, a pit of razors. A silver chain bound it to the floor, metal sizzling where it touched that rotten skin. Looking into the wretched's empty eyes, I found myself back in my village, the day my sister came home.

'Other segments of the sevenstar opened, and on the rising plinths, I saw a pack of rough-bred mongrels – half wolf, half dog – held fast by steel chains. They were going berserk, snarling at the wretched in the centre of the star. But the monster stared only at me, eyes filled with an endless, ageless hunger.

'Talon lifted the long-stemmed silver pipe towards my lips.

'"Breathe deep," he advised. "As San Michon caught the Redeemer's blood upon the wheel, and turned the sin of his murder to God's own holy cause, so too do we remake our own sin. From the greatest horrors are the greatest heroes forged."

'I glanced to my master, then to Sister Aoife, still uncertain. Her brilliant blue eyes met mine, and beneath her veil, I saw the sister's lips moving. Mouthing the very same words Greyhand had spoken to me:

'*Heed the hymn.*

'My heart was beating quick. Fear in my belly. But if this was a testing, I was determined not to fail it before the eyes of every luminary in the Order. Seraph Talon placed the pipe on my lips, striking his flintbox and bidding me breathe, *breathe.*'

Jean-François was sketching in his book, his voice a low murmur.

'The first taste is ever the sweetest. And the darkest.'

'So Greyhand promised,' Gabriel nodded. 'If only I knew then what I know now. I would have run until I reached my mama's arms, slamming the door on the dark and the monsters who haunted it and these men who walked it with silver heels. Because it wasn't a hero Talon forged that day as I breathed that beautiful poison into my lungs. It was a *chain*. And one I shall never break.

'I saw it begin in that angel's silvered hands. A thin wisp of scarlet, dancing on my tongue. I felt it crash upon me, heavy as lead and light as feathers, all of me aflame. And inside it, I heard the first notes of a symphony, bright as heaven and red as blood.

'*Heed the hymn, Little Lion.*

'"Oh, *God*," I gasped. "Oh, sweet and blessed Redeemer . . ."

'I know not how long I lost myself. Fighting to ride that bloody wave, to bring my scattered senses to bear, awash in boiling crimson. I only remember the sound that finally dragged me up and out of it. Beneath that blood-red symphony, another noise was building, sharp enough to shake me, loud enough to wake me. Metal on stone.

'I opened my eyes and saw it. My heart dropping and thudding in my chest.

'The wretched was charging right at me.'

BLOOD OF THE FRAIL

'SERAPH TALON AND Sister Aoife were nowhere to be seen. I was alone. Unarmed. Minutes were hours, moments were minutes, the monster running at me with fingers curled like claws. The mongrels were barking, driven mad in the coldblood's presence. My heart was racing. And in the palm of my left hand, a fire was burning, silver bright.

'I'd been raised deep in the One Faith. I'd gone to chapel every prièdi as a boy, still said my prayers before I slept every night. I loved God. Feared God. Worshipped God. But for the first time in my life, I could actually *feel* God. His love. His power, made manifest in me. And I moved then, as if my shoulders were crowned with angel's wings. The wretched's mouth was agape, tongue swollen between its fangs. But I twisted aside from its grasping hands, and the monster stumbled past, ploughing into the wall.

'I snatched up the silver chain still wrapped about the wretched's neck, cracking it like a whip. The creature turned, and I felt its unholy strength as dead hands closed about my throat. But I found myself just as strong – as strong as I'd been the day Amélie came home. I rolled my arm, once, twice, wrapping that silver chain around my fist. And drawing back, I smashed it right into that monster's black fucking maw.

'Bone shattered. Teeth splintered. I struck again, dimly aware of the dull, wet crunch of silver into rancid flesh. My old friend hatred crouched upon my shoulder, my mind alight with the sight of my sister dancing to music only she could hear, the hymn I could now hear also – red, red, red. And when I was done, the monster's head was a dark splatter upon the wall behind it, a ragged pulp lolling at the end of a broken neck.

'*Heed the hymn, Little Lion.*

'I let the body drop. A red wash flooded my eyes, all the angels singing in time. My right hand was a bleeding mess, knuckles ripped back to bare bone. I was so fucking high I could have stood on tiptoe and kissed the lips of the Mothermaid herself. But Talon called from the gathering in the bleachers, "I fear not. Next!"

'I heard running feet, claws on cold stone. And turning, I saw that pack of starving mongrels charging across the circle. I gripped the chain in my bloody hand, uncertain what to do with myself. There were a dozen of the bastards bearing down on me like arrows, eyes wild, teeth bared. In a growing panic, I swung the chain about me to fend them off. The dogs slowed, snarling and barking, forming a tight circle around me as I backed up to the wall. I'd no ken why they were attacking me. I'd no wish to hurt them, but I'd no wish to be dinner either, my mind racing with the bloodhymn as that length of bloody chain *whooshed* around my head.

"'Tell them to stand down!" Greyhand called. "Command them!"

"'Sod off!" I bellowed at the beasts. "Away with you, bastards!"

"'Not with your voice, you cack-brained yak-fiddler!" Talon spat. "With your mind!"

'I hadn't the first clue how to do what the seraph wanted, but still, I tried. Swinging my chain to keep the mongrels at bay, I fixed my stare on the biggest – a snaggle-toothed brute with mottled fur and flashing eyes. I bared my teeth and roared at him in my head, feeling an utter fool all the while. And as I focused my attentions on the big fucker, one of the little shits took his chance, darting under my chain and leaping at my chest.

'With a curse, I battered him aside. But something heavy struck me from the flank, and I felt fangs sinking into my forearm. I screamed as my flesh ripped, punching and flailing at the dog who had me. Another struck my legs and bore me down, I felt teeth rip into my shoulder, hot blood spilling down my back. I lashed out again, bodies flying, but there were so many of them, I didn't know which way to turn. My arms were up around my face, and I was roaring as they tore me up, wondering what drove them to such madness. They seemed possessed, almost as if their wills were not their own.'

'Ah,' Jean-François said. 'I see.'

'Oui,' Gabriel replied. 'And as swift as they'd come on, the jaws around my limbs unlocked. I rolled to my feet, covered in blood, snatching up my chain again. But the mongrels were backing away, licking bloody jowls, their eyes now fixed on Frère Greyhand. My master waved one hand, and the half-wolves returned to their places in the sevenstar, like trained Nordish sheepdogs at their shepherd's call.

'As the others looked on, Seraph Talon stepped back into the circle. His boots rang on stone as he walked towards me, Sister Aoife beside him. I could barely stand, hot blood running down my shredded arms and legs. The bloodhymn was a dirge in my ears, the sanctus still rushing in my veins along with my rage at what they'd done.

'"Well, you're definitely not Chastain. No affinity for beasts in you, sure and true." Talon took hold of one of my tattered hands. "Nor a Voss, either, by the look. Your lily flesh ripped easy as paper, didn't it, boy?"

'"Get your fucking hands off me!"

'Talon called to Khalid. "I believe he's upset, good Abbot!"

'"They could have *killed* me!"

'Talon scoffed. "You're a paleblood, boy. You don't die that easily. In a few hours, you'll have not a mark on you." The seraph smoothed his impressive moustache, spun his accursed cane between his fingers. "Our gifts manifest in times of duress. This trial is designed to inflict that. So cease your whining, you buck-toothed little gongfarmer."

'"You did this on purpose?" I looked to the eyes above. "Are you *mad*?"

'"Are *you*, whoreson?" Talon smiled.

'I gritted my teeth. Feeling my fingers curling into a fist.

'"I wouldn't do that if I were you, my little bumblefuck," Talon warned. "Striking a Seraph of the Silver Order unprovoked would see you whipped like an inquisitor on the feastday of the Angel of Bliss." He brushed his long dark moustache, a small smile creeping onto his face. "But perhaps . . . if I were to strike you first . . ."

'". . . What?"

'"If I strike you first, you can strike me back. Blood for blood, eh, Abbot?"

'Up in the bleachers, Khalid nodded. "Blood for blood."

'"So make me do it, you worthless gobblecock," Talon spat. "Take the anger. Take the fury. Take the indignation that sets that pretty lip all aquiver, and force it onto me. If I hit you first, you can hit me back. So make me angry, boy. Make me *furious*."

'"I . . ."

'*Swakk!*

'"Do it! Make me feel it!"

'"I don't . . ."

'*Swakk!*

'"Seven Martyrs, fucking *stop* it!"

'"Give it to me!" Talon slammed me back into the wall, frightening strong. His face was inches from mine, and I could see his eyes were run through, red with blood as he hissed with bared fangs. "Embrace what is within you! The *curse* within your blood!"

'I clenched my jaw, temples pounding. Sister Aoife made no move to help me. The Order's elders looked on, cold and pitiless. But I knew this was still a testing, and I wanted desperately to carve myself a place here, to learn the truth of the gifts my father had passed down to me. So, I tried to do as Talon bid. I embraced my fury, that Nordling fire within my blood, so real I could feel its heat beneath my skin. And I imagined the seraph burning with it instead, flames flooding out from me and setting him ablaze. Bloody fists clenched, chest heaving as I gathered up all my anger and all my pain and pushed it onto him.

'Talon's eyes widened. He drew one short and shallow breath.

'"No," he finally sighed. "Nothing at all."

'Talon released my tunic. Piss-hole eyes twinkling, the Seraph of the Hunt turned away, stroking his moustache as he glanced to the luminaries above. Seraph Argyle was scowling, his iron hand cupped to Khalid's ear as he whispered. Greyhand's face was a mask. Archivist Adamo seemed to have fallen asleep on Charlotte's shoulder. I hovered, uncertain, the pain of my wounds a dim fire under the sanctus rush. Blood dripped down my fingers, puddled inside my boots. Sister Aoife looked at me with concern, but still, she took no steps to help me. The seraph scuffed his heels as he turned a slow circle, lips pursed.

'"We haven't seen one of you in a while. How very depressing."

'". . . What do you mean?"

'"I mean you're not particularly strong." Talon motioned to the crushed wretched. "Strong as an ordinary paleblood, of course, but certainly not one descended from the Blood Dyvok. You have no affinity for beasts, no resilience to wounds of the flesh, so that strikes Chastain and Voss off the list. But it seems you've as much talent for emotional manipulation as a cuntful of cold water, so you can't be Ilon, either."

'"So . . . what am I?"

'Talon looked me over with sour expression. "You're a frailblood."

'I looked to my master. "A what?"

'"The child of a vampire too young and weak to have passed on his legacy," Talon replied. "You have no bloodline. No bloodgifts, other than those we all of us share."

'The pain of my wounds was forgotten. I could feel my belly sinking without quite knowing why. "A-are you certain? Perhaps you've not tested me ri—"

'"I have been Seraph of the Hunt for a decade, boy. I have conducted this Trial enough to know a frailblood when I see one." Talon's lip curled. "And I see one in you."

'Sweeping his moustache, the seraph stalked away across the sevenstar. Sister Aoife at last reached out towards me, patted my bloody shoulder as she murmured, "You shall still do God's work here, Initiate. Keep the Mothermaid's love in your heart and the Almighty's teachings in your head, and all shall be well."

'I looked to Greyhand and Abbot Khalid, my gut sinking. And as I stood there in the rush of the bloodhymn, my torn limbs shaking, sweat-damp hair hanging over my eyes, I heard Talon's parting blow like a punch to my belly.

'"Disappointing."'

✦ XI ✦
HOW STORIES WORK

'*DISAPPOINTING.*

'That was the word hanging over my head later that night. If Master Greyhand was discouraged at the news about his new apprentice, he hid it well – remaining stoic as ever as he walked me back to Barracks. But still, Forgemaster Argyle's dark scowl, Prioress Charlotte's pursed lips, Seraph Talon's words – none of them would leave me. And as I sat on my bed cleaning the blood out of my new boots, I could still hear his voice ringing in my ears.

'*Disappointing.*

'"Should've knocked his fucking block off anyway," I growled.

'"Well, look what the maggots left behind," came a voice.

'I glanced up and found Aaron de Coste staring at me from the Barracks door. He stood with another initiate – a tall, dark-haired lad named de Séverin, who carried himself in the same silver-spoon-up-his-arse manner as de Coste. From the shit-eating grin on Aaron's face, word of my Trial had already circulated among the other initiates.

'"I knew you were lowborn, Kitten," he sneered. "But not so low as that."

'"Eat shit, de Coste. I've not the patience for this now, I warn you."

'"I suppose it makes sense," the lordling mused to de Séverin. "Vampire peasants bedding human peasants. All part of the gutter's rich tapestry?"

'His crony chuckled as the fire inside me flared.

'"My mother was no peasant. She was of the house of de León."

'"Oh, madame of the manor, I'm sure. That squalid little hole we dragged you out of was her summer home, then?" Aaron frowned, as if in thought. "Summer hovel, perhaps?"

'De Coste was older than I. Three years, give or take, and he had a few inches on me back then. I wasn't certain I could take him, but I swore to God if he made one more crack about my mama, I'd fucking try.

'"So I've not got a bloodline," I snapped. "I'm still paleblood. I can still fight."

'De Coste chuckled. "I'm certain the Forever King is trembling in his boots."

'"He fucking should be," I spat, returning to cleaning mine.

'The lordling wandered to his cot, picked up a copy of the Testaments by his bedside. But he still stared at me. "That's how you see yourself, is it? Plucky little Gabriel de León, charging up to Fabién Voss's throne of corpses with his new silver sword and saving the realm single-handed?" Aaron chuckled. "You really have no bloody idea what's happening here, do you?"

'"I know all I need to. I know I was fated to be here. And I know this Order is the one true hope against the Forever King."

'"We're the true hope against *nothing*, Kitten."

'I scowled. "What do you mean by that?"

'"I *mean* that my brother Jean-Luc is a chevalier in the imperial army at Augustin. The Golden Host. The forces being mustered in the capital will *annihilate* the Forever King before his shambling mongrels ever reach the Nordlund. Oh, our cause might be righteous. But the sad truth is, nobody at court believes the silversaints will make a difference." Aaron waved to the Barracks about us with lip curled. "The only reason this monastery is being financed at *all* is because Empress Isabella is enamoured of mysticism, and Emperor Alexandre enjoys getting his cock sucked by his new bride."

'"That's horseshit, de Coste," I said.

'"And what would you know about it, frailblood?" de Séverin sighed.

'"I know God meant for me to be here. My sister *died* at the hands of these monsters. And if I can do something to stop them, I will."

'"Good for you," Aaron said. "But in the end, for all your faith and fury, you'll be nothing but piss in the wind. I mean, look at you. Ma famille can trace our lineage back to Maximille the Martyr. My mother is baronne of the richest province in Nordlund and—"

'"And yet she wasn't above bedding a vampire."

'De Coste fell silent as Theo Petit stepped through the doorway. The big lad was dressed in his leathers, but his tunic was unlaced, and I could see a hint of metallic ink beneath. A beautiful angel was tattooed from knuckles to elbow on his left forearm, and what looked to be a snarling bear was scribed on his chest. He had a plate of chicken legs in hand, and he flopped into bed, chewing noisily.

'"That's the funny thing about highborn women," Theo mused. "They're the same height as any other when they're down on all fours."

'"Blood from the gutter and a mouth from the sewer," de Séverin sneered. "If it isn't Theo Petit. The answer to the question no one was asking."

'"We're all the Dead's bastards here, Aaron. We're all shit on the bottom of the Emperor's boots. We're *all* damned." Theo stuffed a chicken leg into his face and spoke to de Coste with his mouth full. "So give the tortured nobleson sermon a rest, eh?"

'Aaron only scowled. "Just because you lost your master to the sangirè doesn't give you leave to forget your manners, Petit. *I* am the senior initiate of this company."

'Theo stopped chewing a moment, eyes flashing.

'"You make mention of my master again, we might have to test that theory, Aaron."

'De Coste looked the big lad up and down, but didn't seem keen to press. Instead, he lay back on his pillow, muttering beneath his breath. "Softcock . . ."

'Theo scoffed, put his boots up on the bed. "Your sister sings a different tune."

'I chuckled softly, marking the ledger in my head.

'"What the hell are you laughing at, Kitten?" Aaron snarled.

'I shot a poisoned glance at de Coste, but the matter seemed settled for now. I met Theo's eyes, nodding silent thanks, but the big boy simply shrugged in return – I guessed the quarrel was less about Theo defending me, and more about his dislike of de Coste. And so, silent and bruised and still friendless, I returned to cleaning my boots, trying not to think too much about my failure in the Gauntlet. I had no line and no gifts to call my own, save that which we all shared. I'd learned nothing of my father. But despite all Aaron said, despite the Trial, I still felt I was fated to be there. God *did* want me in San Michon. Frailblood or no.'

Gabriel paused a moment, lacing his fingers as he stared down at his hands.

'But you want to know the awful thing, coldblood?'

'Tell me the awful thing, Silversaint,' Jean-François replied.

'I lay in bed later that night, my wounds nothing but a memory, and I thought on what de Coste had told me about his brother in the army. About the restoration of this monastery being only an empress's whim. And my first thought wasn't for the people who might be spared if the Forever King was crushed by the Golden Host. It wasn't of the soldiers who might die defeating him, or the horror that this conflict had come at all. My first thought was to pray that the war wouldn't be over by the time I got there.'

Gabriel sighed, and met the historian's eyes.

'Can you believe that? I was actually afraid I was going to *miss out.*'

'Is such not the desire of all young men with swords? Win glory, or glorious death?'

'Glory,' Gabriel scoffed. 'Tell me something, vampire. If death is so glorious, how is it meted so cheaply and so often by the most worthless of men?'

The Last Silversaint shook his head.

'I'd no idea what was coming. No clue what they were going to make of me. But I *did* know this was my life now. And so, I vowed again to make the best of it. Whatever Aaron said, I felt in my bones that San Michon would be the salvation of the empire. I truly believed that I'd been chosen, that all this – my sister's murder, what I'd done to Ilsa, the cursed and bastard blood in my veins – all of it was part of God's plan. And if I trusted in him, if I said my prayers and praised his name and followed his word, all would be well.'

Gabriel scoffed, staring down at the sevenstar on his palm.

'What a fucking fool I was.'

'Take heart, de León.' The coldblood's voice was soft as the scratching of his pen. 'You were not alone in your hopes. But none can best a foe that cannot die.'

'The snows at Augustin weren't soaked red with mortal blood alone. You died in droves that night, coldblood.'

A slender shrug. 'Our dead *stay* dead, Silversaint. Yours rise against you.'

'And you believe that a *good* thing? Tell me, do you never wonder where all this ends? After the monsters you've birthed drain these lands dry of every man, woman, and child, *all* of you will starve. Wretched and highblood alike.'

'Hence the need for a firm rule.' Pale fingers brushed the embroidered wolves on the vampire's frockcoat. 'An Empress with the foresight to build, rather than destroy. Fabién Voss was wise to harness the foulbloods as a weapon. But their time is at an end.'

'The wretched outnumber you fifty to one. There are four major kith bloodlines, and all have corpse armies in thrall. You think those vipers are going to give up their legions without a struggle?'

'They may struggle all they wish. They shall fail.'

Gabriel looked to the monster then, cold calculation in his eyes. The bloodhymn still thrummed in his veins, sharpening his mind as well as his senses. The coldblood's face was stone, his eyes, liquid darkness. But even the barest rock can tell a story to those with the teaching to see it. Despite it all – the carnage, the betrayal, the failure – Gabriel de León was a hunter who knew his quarry. And in a blinking, he saw the answer, as clear and crisp as if the monster had written the words in that damnable book.

'*That's* why you seek the Grail,' he breathed. 'You think the cup can bring you victory against the other bloodlines.'

'Children's stories hold no interest for my Empress, Silversaint. But *your* story does.' The monster tapped the book in his lap. 'So return to it, if you'd be so kind. You were a fifteen-year-old boy. The halfbreed bastard of a vampire father, dragged from provincial squalor to the impregnable walls of San Michon. You grew to be a paragon of the Order, just as you vowed. They sang songs about you, de León. The Black Lion. Wielder of the Ashdrinker. Slayer of the Forever King. How does one rise from beginnings so low to become legend?' The monster's lip curled. 'And then, fall so very far?'

Gabriel looked to the lantern flame, his mouth pressed thin. The bloodsmoke roiled inside him, sharpening not only his mind, but his memory. He ran one thumb across his tattooed fingers, the word P A T I E N C E etched below his knuckles.

The years at his back seemed mere moments, and those moments were clear as crystal. He could smell silverbell on the air, see candleflame reflected in his mind's eye. He could feel smooth hips swaying beneath his hands. Eyes dark with want, lips red as cherries open against his, fingernails clawing his naked back. He heard a whisper then, hot and desperate, and he echoed it without thinking, the words slipping over his lips in a sigh.

'*We cannot do this.*'

Jean-François's head tilted. 'No?'

Gabriel blinked, found himself back in that cold tower with that dead thing. He could taste ashes. Hear the screams of monsters that had denied death for centuries, delivered at last by his hand. And he met the coldblood's gaze, his voice tinged with shadow and flame.

'No,' he said.

'De León—'

'*No.* I've no more wish to speak of San Michon just now, if it please you.'

'It does *not* please me.' A thin frown marred Jean-François's flawless brow. 'I wish to hear of your years in the paleblood monastery. Your apprenticeship. Your ascendance.'

'And you'll hear about all of it in time,' Gabriel growled. 'We have all night, you and I. And all the nights we'll need thereafter, I'd wager. But if you seek knowledge of the Grail, then we should return to the day I found it.'

'That is *not* the way stories work, Silversaint.'

'This is *my* story, coldblood. And if I have the right of it, these will be the last words I'll ever speak upon this earth. So if this is to be my last confession, and you my priest, trust that I know how best to impart the tally of my own fucking sins. By the time the telling is done, we'll have returned to Lorson. The Charbourg. The red snows of Augustin. And oui, even San Michon. But for now, I'll speak of the Grail. How it came to me. How I lost it. And all between. Believe me when I say your Empress will have her answers by the end.'

Jean-François of the Blood Chastain was displeased, a hint of fangs in his silent snarl. But in the end, the monster ran his tapered fingertips over the feathers at his throat and acquiesced with a tilt of his chin.

'Very well, de León. Have it your way.'

'I always did, coldblood. That was half the fucking problem.'

The Last Silversaint leaned back in his chair, steepled his fingers at his chin.

'So,' he sighed. 'It all began with a rabbit hole.'

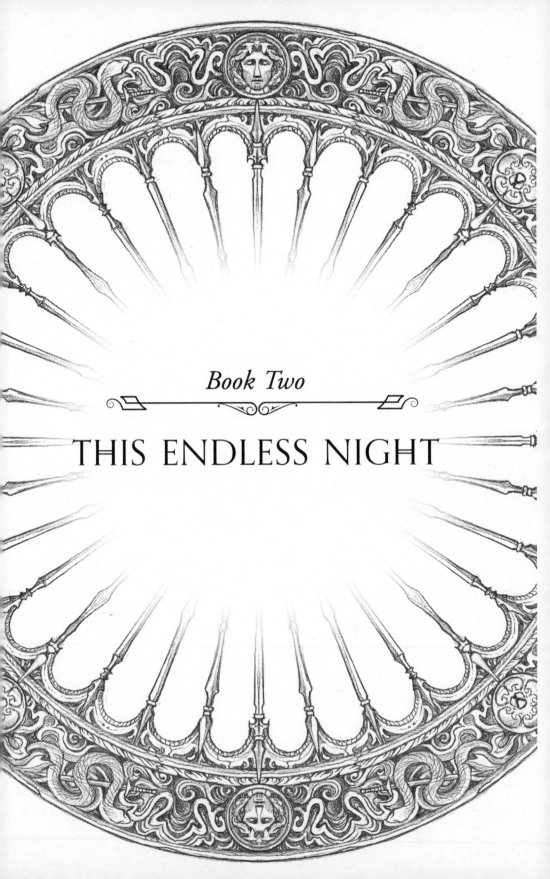

Book Two

THIS ENDLESS NIGHT

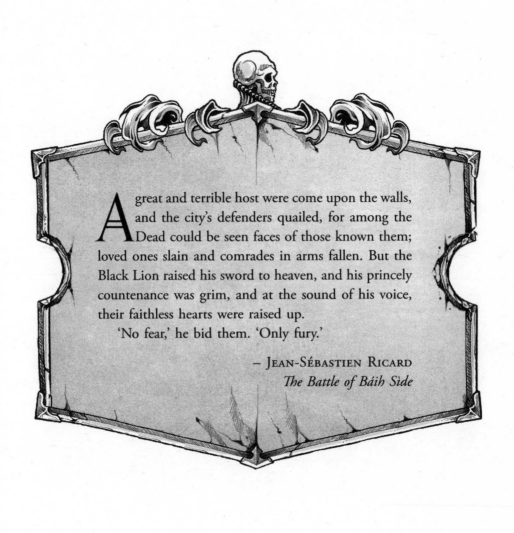

A great and terrible host were come upon the walls, and the city's defenders quailed, for among the Dead could be seen faces of those known them; loved ones slain and comrades in arms fallen. But the Black Lion raised his sword to heaven, and his princely countenance was grim, and at the sound of his voice, their faithless hearts were raised up.

'No fear,' he bid them. 'Only fury.'

— JEAN-SÉBASTIEN RICARD
The Battle of Báih Side

✦ I ✦

INJUSTICE

'NIGHT WAS A good two hours off when it happened,' Gabriel said. 'I was riding north through ruined farmlands, soaked with grey drizzle. The first bitter bite of winter was in the wind, and the land about me had a haunted air. Dead trees were hung with ropes of pale fungus, the road naught but miles of empty black slurry. The villages I passed through were ghost town – buildings empty and cemeteries full. I hadn't seen a living person in days. It'd been more than a decade since I travelled through the realm of Emperor Alexandre, Third of His Name. And all seemed worse than when I'd abandoned it.'

'How long ago was this, exactly?' Jean-François asked.

'Three years back. I was thirty-two years old.'

'Where had you been?'

'South.' Gabriel shrugged. 'Down in Sūdhaem.'

'And why did you leave your beloved Nordlund?'

'Patience, coldblood.'

The vampire pursed his lips, but made no reply.

'I wore my old greatcoat to keep off the rain. Faded bloodstains. Black leather. Tricorn pulled low, collar laced high, like my old master taught me. It'd been years since I'd put that kit on, but it still fitted like a glove. My sword hung in a beaten scabbard at my waist, my head bowed against the weather as we rode through the miserable so-called day.

'Justice hated the rain. Always had. But he rode hard as he always did, on into the cold and empty quiet. A beauty he was: black and brave and solid as a castle wall. For a gelding, that horse had more balls than most stallions I'd ever met.'

Jean-François glanced upwards. 'You still had the same horse?'

Gabriel nodded. 'He was a little creakier than he used to be. Just as I was. But it was as Abbot Khalid had told me – Justice was my truest friend. He'd saved my life more times than I could count by then. We'd ridden all the way through hell together, and he'd brought me all the way home. I loved him like a brother.'

'And you kept the name that foul-mouthed sisternovice gave him? Astrid Rennier?'

'Oui.'

'Why? Was the girl of some significance to you?'

Gabriel turned his eyes to the lantern, the flame dancing in his pupils. 'Patience, coldblood.'

Quiet hung in the cell, the only sound the whisper of nib on parchment. It was a long while before the silversaint continued.

'I'd been riding months without much rest. I'd planned to be over the Volta before wintersdeep struck, but the roads were harder going than I expected, and the map I carried well out of date. The locals had ripped down the tollway at Hafti and destroyed the bridge over the Keff, for starters. There were no ferrymen plying trade that I could find, no living soul for fucking miles. So, I'd been forced to double back and head upstream.'

'Why?' Jean-François asked.

Gabriel blinked. 'Why did I double back?'

'Why did the locals destroy the bridge over the river Keff?'

'As I said, this was just three years ago. It'd been twenty-four years since daysdeath. The lords of the Blood had turned the realm into a slaughter-house by then. Nordlund was a wasteland. Save for a few coastal duns, the Ossway had fallen. The Forever King's armies were drawing ever closer to Augustin, and masterless wretched crawled northern Sūdhaem like lice on a dockside jezebel. The locals had smashed the bridge to cut off their advance.'

The vampire tapped his quill, brow creased. 'I told you, de León. Speak as if to a child. For what reason did the locals tear down the bridge?'

The silversaint stared hard, his jaw clenched. Then he spoke, not only as if to a child, but as if to one who'd been dropped repeatedly and enthusiastically on the head by its mother.

'Vampires can't cross running water. Except at bridges, or buried in cold earth. The most powerful among them might manage it with a supreme act of will. But to the newborn Dead, a fast-flowing river may as well be a wall of flame.'

'Merci. Please, continue.'

'You sure? No other fuckmumblery to which you already know the answer?'

The vampire smiled. 'Patience, Chevalier.'

Gabriel breathed deep and marched on. 'So. I hadn't smoked since morning, and my thirst was quietly creeping up on me. I knew I'd not make it much farther that day. But consulting my old map, I saw that the town of Dhahaeth lay not an hour's ride north. Presuming the place was still standing, the promise of a fire and something hot in my belly was enough to keep the shakes at bay. So, hoping to make up lost time, I cut off road, through a rolling carpet of whitecaps and into a forest of living fungus and long-dead trees.

'I was barely ten minutes into the woods before the first wretched found me.

'A woman. Perhaps thirty when she was murdered. She was silent as ghosts, but Justice caught wind of her, ears pressed against his skull. A second later I saw her, moving like a hunter, right at me. Her hair was a wild blonde tangle, and she came at me wolf-quick, thin and naked, skin hanging in damp folds around a gaping wound at her neck.

'She was running *quick*. Far quicker than a mortal man. I'd no fear of a single wretched, but these bastards are like minstrels – where there's one, there's always others, and the more that find you, the more aggravating they get. So I gave Justice a nudge and we were running, off through the ship-wrecked trees.

'I loosened my sword in its sheath as I saw another wretched off to my right. A little Sūdhaemi boy, dashing through the tall spires of tubers and toadstools. I spied another ahead, then. And another. All quiet as corpses. All running swift. None of them moved quick as Justice, mind you. But I could tell they were a pack. Each at least a decade old.'

Jean-François raised one eyebrow, tapped his quill. 'As if to a child, de León.'

Gabriel sighed.

'Newborn wretched are dangerous, don't mistake me. But on a scale of one to ten, with one being your average Ossway pub brawl, and ten being the most fearsome nightmare hell's belly can spit, they rate about a four. Not even the eldest among them is a match for a highblood. But older wretched can't be underestimated. Your kind grow more powerful the longer your blood has to thicken. These ones were dangerous, and they were many. But Justice charged on through the deadwood, weaving through the mush-room thickets at full gallop. His hooves were thunder and his heart was dauntless, and we soon left those bloodless bastards in our wake.

'We burst from the woods a while later, damp with sweat, out into the rain. A chill grey valley lay below us, thick with fog. A little way northeast, I could see a dark ribbon of road in the gloom. A few miles beyond lay the river ford, and safety.

'I patted Justice as he galloped down into the valley, murmured into his ear.

'"My brother. My best boy."

'And then his hoof found the rabbit hole. His foreleg sank into the earth, the joint snapped with an awful *craaack*, his screams filling my ears as we fell. I smashed into the ground, felt something break, gasping with agony as I rolled to rest against a rotten stump. My sword had slipped from its scabbard and was lying in the muck. My skull was ringing, fire raging down my arm. I knew in a heartbeat I'd snapped it – that familiar broken-glass grind under my skin. Not so bad it wouldn't be healed by morning. But the same couldn't be said for poor Justice.'

Gabriel sighed, long and deep.

'I rose up from my boy's wreck, hands and chin blacked with mud. Looking at the shank of bone torn through his fetlock as he tried to rise, brave to the last.

'"Oh no," I breathed. "No, *no*."

'Justice screamed again, wild with agony. I turned my face to the heavens above, a familiar rage swelling in my chest. I looked down at my friend, my arm bleeding, throat tightening, heart breaking. He'd been with me since that first day in San Michon. Through blood and war, fire and fury. Seventeen years. He was all I had left. And now . . . this?

'"God fucking hates me," I whispered.

'*And why think ye that might be, m-might be?*

'The voice came as it always did. Silver-soft ripples inside my head. I ignored it best I could, watching as my brother tried to stand on his broken leg. His fetlock bent wrong, and down he went again, big brown eyes rolling in his skull. His agony was my agony.

'*Know ye what must be d-done, Gabriel,* came the silvered voice again.

'I looked to the longblade at my feet, naked and spattered with mud. The double-handed haft was bound in black leather, its silvered hilt crafted like a beautiful woman, her arms spread to form the crossguard. The blade was curved and elegant, shaped in an archaic Talhostic style, but still possessed of a deadly grace. Forged from the dark belly of a fallen star in an age whose name was legend. But it was broken. Lifetimes ago, it seemed now.

'Six inches snapped from the tip.

'"Shut up," I told it.

'*They shall smmmell him. Tear him to p-pieces, aye, sticky red, red sticky, as he screams and screams and screeeeams. This be sugarsweet mercy.*

'"Why do you always tell me what I already know?"

'*Why do ye always n-n-need me to?*

'I looked my horse in his eyes, the pain of my broken arm forgotten. Of all those I'd called friend over the years, Justice was the only one who remained. And through his pain and fear, in the darkest of all his hours, he looked to me. His Gabriel. The one who'd met him as a boy in the stables at San Michon, who'd ridden him from that place into exile when not a single one of his so-called brothers had come to say farewell. He trusted me. Despite his hurt, he knew I'd somehow make it all right.

'And I put my sword right through his heart.

'It wasn't the swiftest end I could've gifted him. I had a shot loaded in my wheellock. But nightfall was only two hours away, and the town of Dhahaeth was at least four on foot. The wretched were apparently thick as flies on shite around these parts now, and a man unhorsed is just a meal uneaten.

'Always better to be a bastard than a fool.

'But still, I sat with Justice as he died. His head sinking heavy into my lap as he bled his last out into the mud. The sky was dark with shadow, my tears hot in the freezing rain. My broken longblade was stabbed into the muck, bright with my friend's blood. I stared up to the heavens above, the God I knew was watching.

'"Fuck you," I told him.

'*G-gabriel,* the blade whispered in my head.

'"And fuck you too," I hissed.

'*Gabriel,* she repeated, more urgent.

'"*What?*" I glared at the sword, my voice choked. "Can you not give me one breath to mourn him, you unholy bitch?"

'The blade spoke again, chilling my blood.

'*Gabriel, th-they are coming.*'

✦ II ✦

THE THREE WAYS

'THE BOY RAN first. The little one. No more than six when he Became. He moved swift as a deer, down the valley right towards me. The others followed: the blonde woman, a haggard man, another man shorter and broader. At least two dozen in the pack now.

'With a gasp, I was on my feet, broken arm swinging useless at my side. The pain returned as I tore my saddlebags loose with my good hand, sheathing my broken blade. I bid my poor brother farewell, and then I was running, down the valley towards that ribbon of distant road. The ford was at least three miles past it. There was little chance I could outpace a pack of wretched for that long. But I knew they'd stop for Justice – his blood was pooled in the mud, ripe in the air. Mongrels like these wouldn't be able to resist.

'I could feel the shakes, the thirst making my heart stutter, my belly ache. Stumbling, almost slipping in the mud, I snatched a glass phial from my bandolier. Just a pinch of powder remained in the bottom, the colour of rose petals and chocolat, the promise of it making my hand shake all the worse. But reaching into my greatcoat, my heart sank into my boots as I realized my flintbox was gone.

'"Fuck my face . . ." I whispered.

'I groped around my belt, my coat, but I already knew the tale; I must have lost it when Justice threw me. And now I had no way to even the odds stacked against me.

'And so I ran on, slinging my broken arm up inside my bandolier and wincing in agony. It would heal with time, but the wretched would give me none. My only hope now was the river, and that was slim hope at best. If they caught me, I'd be dead as Justice.'

Jean-François looked up from his tome. 'You feared them that much?'

'The graveyards of the world are full of fools who thought of fear as anything but a friend.'

'Perhaps your legend has swelled in the telling, de León.'

'Legends always do. And ever in the wrong direction.'

The vampire brushed his golden curls aside, dark eyes roaming Gabriel's broad shoulders. 'It is said you were the most fearsome swordsman who ever lived.'

'I wouldn't go that far.' The silversaint shrugged. 'But let's put it this way; you'd not want to flip me the Fathers if I had something sharp nearby.'

The vampire blinked. 'Flip you the Fathers?'

Gabriel raised his right hand, fingers extended, then cupped his forearm with his left. 'Old Nordish insult. It implies your mama had so many men in her bed that your paternity is impossible to determine. And insulting my mama is a good way to get your face stabbed.'

'Then why flee? A paragon of the Silver Order? Wielder of the Ashdrinker himself? Running like a whipped pup from a pack of foulbloods?'

'Law the Third, vampire.'

Jean-François tilted his head. '*The Dead run quick.*'

Gabriel nodded. 'There were two dozen of the bastards. My swordarm was broken in at least two places. And like I said, I had no way to smoke.'

Jean-François glanced to the bone pipe on the table before them.

'So reliant upon sanctus, were you?'

'I wasn't reliant on sanctus, I was *addicted* to it. And oui, I had other tricks among my gear, but my arm was twice-fucked, and it was too much to risk fighting that many. I'd little hope of outpacing them either, truth told, but I've always been too stubborn to just lie down and die. And so, I tried to boot it. Rain in my eyes. Heart in my throat. Thinking of all I'd meant to do returning here and wondering if I'd ever get to do any of it. I glanced back and saw the wretched were finishing with Justice's body. They rose from the mud and came on, lips red, teeth bright.

'I reached the road, staggering in the mud as thunder rolled above. I was almost done by then. The wretched close to my heels. Drawing my sword in desperation.

'*If thou art b-brutally murdered here*, she whispered, *and I end my days hanging on the hip of a m-mindless shamble-bag of m-maggots, I shall be* terribly *upset with ye.*

'"The hell do you want from me?" I hissed.

'*Run, Little Lion*, she replied. *RUN.*

'I did as the blade told me. One last burst of speed. And as lightning arced across the skies, I squinted through the drizzle and saw it before me. A miracle. A carriage, drawn by a miserable grey draught horse, sitting in the middle of the road.'

'Divine intervention?' Jean-François murmured.

'Or the devil loves his own. The carriage was surrounded by a dozen soldiers. Feed was scarce those nights, and keeping a horse had never been a poor man's game. But each of these men also had a mount – good stout sosyas, standing downcast in the rain while their riders argued, shin-deep in the muck. I saw their problem in a heartbeat – the weather had turned the road into a quagmire, and their carriage was sunk to its axles.

'The soldiers were well geared and well fed. Clad in crimson tabards and iron plate caked with filth, they tried to drag the carriage free. And standing at their head, whipping that poor dray as if the mud were the horse's fault, were two tall, pale women. They were near-identical – twins maybe. Their hair was long, black, cut in pointed fringes, and they wore tricorns with short, triangular veils over their eyes. They were clad in leather, and their tabards were also blood-red, marked with the flower and flail of Naél, the Angel of Bliss. I realized these were no ordinary soldiers, then.

'This was an inquisitor cohort.

'The men heard me coming, but didn't seem too ruffled. And then they spied the pack of corpses on my tail, and all of them looked fit to shit. "Martyrs save us," breathed one, and "Fuck me," gasped another, and the inquisitors' jaws near dropped off their heads.

'*Gabriel, 'ware!*

'The whisper rang in my mind, silver behind my eyes. I turned with a cry as the first wretched caught me. It was close enough that I could smell its carrion breath, see the shape of the little boy it'd been. Rot had set in hard before it turned, but it moved quick as flies, dead doll's eyes glinting like broken glass.

'My sword cut the air, an offhand swing that was far from poetic. The blade met the monster's thigh and just kept going, sending the thing's leg sailing free in a gout of rotten blood. It fell without a sound, but the others came on, too swift to fight and far too many to best. The sosyas screamed in terror at the sight of the Dead, bolting in all directions, hooves thundering. The soldiers shouted after them in rage, in fear.'

Gabriel steepled his fingers at his chin. Pausing for thought.

'Now, there's three ways a person can react when they look their death in the eye, coldblood. Folk talk about fight or flight, but in truth, it's fight, flight, or *freeze*. Those soldiers saw the two dozen corpses charging them down, and each chose a different path. Some raised their blades. Some messed their britches. And those inquisitor twins glanced to each other, drew long, wicked knives from their belts, and sliced through the harnesses binding the horse to their carriage.

'"Run!" one cried, scrambling onto the terrified beast's back.

'The other leapt up behind her, gave the dray a savage kick. "Fly, you whore!"

'*Gabriel, ye mu—*

'I sheathed my sword, silencing her voice in my head. And I reached to my belt, left hand shaking as I drew my wheellock. The pistol was silvered, a sevenstar embossed in the mahogany grip. The shot I could've given Justice was still loaded in the barrel. And glad I'd saved it, I gave it to the inquisitors instead.

'The shot rang out, the silver slug ripped through one woman's back in a spray of blood. She toppled from the dray with a cry, the horse rearing up and throwing her sister into the muck. Breathless, I bolted past the baffled soldiers and leapt onto the dray's back.

'"Wait!" the first woman cried.

'"B-bastard!" the other coughed, bloodied in the mud.

'But I'd no time for any of them. Clutching the dray's mane with my one good hand, I raised my heels for a kick. But she needed no encouragement, screaming in terror as the wretched came on. The horse dug her hooves into the mire and bolted, and in a spray of black mud, we rode away towards the river without a backwards glance.'

Gabriel fell silent.

A quiet rang in that cold cell, long as years.

'You left them all there,' Jean-François finally said.

'Oui.'

'You left them all to die.'

'Oui.'

Jean-François raised an eyebrow. 'The legends never called you coward, de León.'

Gabriel leaned into the light. 'Look into my eyes, coldblood. Do I strike you as the kind of man who's afraid to die?'

'You strike me as the kind who would welcome it,' the vampire admitted. 'But the silversaints were meant to be exemplars of the One Faith. Slayers of monsters most foul and warriors of God most high. And you were the best of them. You weep like a child over a dead horse, but shoot an innocent woman in the back and leave God-fearing men to be slaughtered by foul-bloods.' The historian frowned. 'What kind of hero are you?'

Gabriel laughed, shaking his head.

'Who the *fuck* told you I was a hero?'

✦ III ✦

SMALL BLESSINGS

'WE FORDED THE Keff a while later. The river rose up to my horse's shoulders, but she was a strong one, and I suspect, glad to be rid of the inquisitors and their whips. I didn't know her name, and I supposed I'd not be keeping her long. So I just called her "Jez" as we rode on through the dark.'

Jean-François blinked. 'Jez?'

'Short for "Jezebel". Since I'd only know her for a night and all.'

'Ah. Prostitute humour.'

'Don't fall down laughing, coldblood.'

'I shall do my very best, Silversaint.'

'My arm was slowly healing,' Gabriel continued. 'But I knew I'd need a dose of sanctus to really see it right. And without my flintbox, I'd no sensible way to light a pipe, let alone a lantern, so we ran blind to Dhahaeth, hoping against hope that the town was still standing. Whatever light the sun gave was long gone by the time I saw them in the distance, but my heart still surged at the sight: fires, burning like beacons in a black sea.

'Jez was just as uneasy as I in the dark, and she rode harder towards the light. From what little I'd heard of Dhahaeth, it was a one-chapel milltown on the banks of the Keff. But the place I drew up outside was like to a small fortress.

'They couldn't afford much stonework, but a heavy wooden palisade had been erected on the outskirts, twelve feet high, running all the way down to the riverbank. A deep trench skirted the palisade, filled with wooden spikes, and bonfires blazed atop it despite the rain. I could see corpses blackened by fire in the ditch as we halted outside the gate, and figures on a highwalk behind the palisade's spikes.

'"Hold," a voice with a thick Sūdhaemi accent cried. "Who goes?"

'"A thirsty man with no time for bullshit," I called back.

'"There's a dozen crossbows pointed at your chest right now, fuckarse. I'd be speaking more polite if I were you."

'"Fuckarse, that's a clever one," I nodded. "I'll remember it next time I'm climbing aboard your wife."

'I heard a soft guffaw from one of the other figures, and the voice spoke again. "Good luck on the road, stranger. You'll 'ave need of it."

'I sighed softly, pulled off my glove with my teeth, and held my left hand aloft. The sevenstar inked in my palm glinted dully in the firelight. And I heard a whisper then, running through the figures like red fever.

'"Silversaint."

'"*Silversaint!*"

'"Open the bloody gate!" someone cried.

'I heard the heavy clunk of wood, and the palisade doors yawned wide. I gave Jez a nudge, my eyes narrowed against the torchlight. A cadre of guards waited in a muddy bailey beyond, nervous as spring lambs. I could tell at a glance they were pressganged militia – most had seen too few winters, the others, far too many. They wore old, boiled leather and carried crossbows, burning torches, ashwood spears – all pointed in my vicinity.

'I climbed off Jezebel, gave her a grateful pat. Then I turned to the stone font to the right of the gate. It was crafted in the likeness of Sanael, Angel of Blood, his outstretched hands holding a bowl of clear water. The militiamen tensed, weapons ready. And looking them in the eye, I dipped my fingers inside and wiggled.'

Jean-François blinked in silent question.

'Holy water,' Gabriel explained.

'Quaint,' the vampire replied. 'But tell me, why insult the gatekeeper? When you could simply have proffered your palm and entered without fuss?'

'I'd just murdered my best friend. Almost lost my life to a pack of mongrel corpses. My arm was throbbing like a virgin's pecker on his first trip into the woods, I was tired and hungry and fiending for a smoke, and I'm something of a bastard on the best of days. And that day was hardly my best.'

Jean-François's gaze roamed Gabriel, toe to crown. 'Nor this one, I fear?'

Gabriel tapped an empty leather pouch at his belt. 'Behold the purse in which I keep my fucks for what you think of me.'

The vampire tilted his head and waited.

'The militiamen stepped aside,' Gabriel continued. 'Most had never seen a silversaint, I'd guess, but the wars had been raging for years by then, and all had heard tales of the Ordo Argent. I could see wonder in the youngers, quiet respect among the older men. I knew what they saw when they looked at me. A bastard halfbreed. A Godsent lunatic. The silver flame burning between what was left of civilization, and the dark set to swallow it whole.

"'I don't 'ave a wife," one said to me.

'I blinked at him. A buck-toothed young Sūdhaemi scrap he was: dark skin, tight cropped hair, barely old enough for fuzz on his taddysack.

"'You said you'd be climbing onto my wife later," he said, defiant. "I don't 'ave one."

"'Count yourself blessed, boy. Now, which way to the fucking pub?'"

✦ IV ✦

ON THE PERILS OF
MATRIMONY

'THE PLACARD ABOVE the taverne's door read THE PERFECT HUSBAND. The faded lettering was accompanied by a picture of a freshly dug grave. I hadn't yet set foot in the place, and I was already fond of it.

'The town had seen better nights, but twenty-four years after daysdeath, there were few places in the empire that wasn't true of. Truth told, it was lucky to have survived at all. Dhahaeth's streets were freezing mud, her buildings leaning on each other like drunkards at last call. Ancient cloves of garlic or braids of virgins' hair were nailed to every door, churlsilver or salt scattered at every window – for all the good it would do. The whole place stank of shite and mushrooms, the streets crawled with rats, and the folk I passed took one look at me and hurried on through the freezing rain, making the sign of the wheel.

'The town got enough traffic to still have a stable, though. The groom caught the ha-royale I flipped him, pocketing the coin as I dismounted. "Give her your best fare and a good rubdown," I told him, patting Jez's neck. "This dame's well and truly earned it."

'The lad stared at the sevenstar on my palm, awed. "Yer a silversaint. Do you—"

'"Just mind the fucking horse, boy."

'My hands were shaking as I handed over the reins, and the ache in my broken arm and empty belly made it easy to ignore his wounded look. Without another word, I stomped across the mud, under a wreath of withered silverbell, and pushed my way through the doors of the Perfect Husband.

'Despite the grim signage, the pub was comfortable as an old rocking chair. The walls were plastered with playbills from one of the bigger cities up in Elidaen – Isabeau, or maybe even Augustin. Bordello shows mostly, and burlesque. The framed watercolours about the commonroom were of scantily clad femmes in lace and corsetry, and a full-length portrait above the bar was of a beautiful green-eyed lass with deep-brown skin, wearing naught but a feather boa. The commonroom was softly lit, jammed full of patrons, and I could see why. Every taverne I've ever visited has the impression of its owner soaked into the walls. And this one's was as warm and fond as an old lover's arms.

'Conversation stilled as I entered. All eyes turned to me as I unbuckled my swordbelt, sloughed off my greatcoat with a wince. I was soaked underneath, deathly cold, leathers and tunic clinging to my skin. I'd have boxed my own grandmama in the baps for a hot bath, but I needed food first. And a smoke, Almighty God, a fucking smoke.

'I hung up my coat and tricorn, stomped across the commonroom. The table closest to the fire was occupied by three youngbloods in militia kit. In front of them sat a few empty plates, and more important, a candle burning in a dusty wine bottle.

'". . . Do you wish to join us, adii?" one asked.

'"No. And I'm not your friend."

'Uncomfortable silence hung in the room. I simply stood and stared. And finally getting the hint, the lads excused themselves and vacated the table.'

Jean-François chuckled, pen scratching. 'You *were* quite the bastard, de León.'

'Now you're catching on, coldblood.'

Gabriel scratched at his stubble, dragged a hand through his hair as he continued.

'Tugging off my boots, I put them near the fire. I was reaching for my pipe when a taverne lass materialized beside me.

'"Your pleasure, adii?" she asked in a gentle Sūdhaemi accent.

'Glancing up, I saw dark tresses. Green eyes. I blinked at the portrait over the bar.

'"My mama," she explained, with the wounded air of someone who had to do it often. She nodded to a woman behind the counter, generously proportioned and twenty years older, but definitely the painting's subject. I idly wondered if she'd kept the boa.

'"Food," I told the girl, fumbling with my pipe. "And a room for the night."

'"As you like it. Drink?"

'"Whiskey?" I asked, hopefully.

'She scoffed, rolling her eyes. "Does this look a laerd's keep to you?"

'Now, a tiny part of me had to admire this maid giving me cheek while those militia boys had folded like a bad hand of cards. But most of me was just getting shittier by the breath. "It looks far from a laerd's keep indeed. And you, far from a lady. So keep the lip on your face, mademoiselle, and just tell me what you have."

'Her voice grew colder then. "We have what everyone has, adii."

'"Fucking vodka."

'"Aye."

'I scowled. "A bottle, then. The decent stuff. No pigswill."

'She dropped into the laziest sort of curtsey, turned away. I should've known better than to ask. Grain liquor was as hard to find as an honest man in a confessional by then. Since daysdeath, farmers had been reduced to growing crops that could sprout in what little light the bastard sun still gave us. Cabbage. Mushrooms. And of course, the dreaded potato.'

The Last Silversaint sighed.

'I fucking *hate* potatoes.'

'Why?'

'Eat the same thing every day of your life, coldblood, see how bored you get.'

Jean-François studied his long fingernails. 'A finer argument against the sacrament of matrimony I have never heard, Silversaint.'

'I nodded thanks as the lass delivered my liquor. The patrons returned to their small talk, pretending not to watch me. The taverne was crowded, and among the Sūdhaemi locals, I noted other folk with pale skin, grubby kilts, and a desperate look – refugees from the Ossway, fleeing the northern wars mostlike. But the distraction of my arrival seemed over at least. And so, I reached to a glass phial in my bandolier.

'I didn't usually take to the smoke in company, but the need was weighing on me, heavy as lead. I measured a healthy dose, then took the wine bottle with its blood-red candle and held my pipe near the flame.

'There's an art to smoking sanctus. Hold the flame too close, the blood will burn. Hold it too far, it'll melt too slow, liquefying rather than vapourizing. But get it right . . .' Gabriel shook his head, grey eyes twinkling. 'God Almighty, get it right, and it's magik. A bright red bliss, filling every inch of your sky. I leaned into the pipe's stem, conscious of the stares aimed my way, but caring not a drop. It was the poorest kind of blood I was smoking. Thin as dishwater. But still, as soon as it hit my tongue, I was home.'

'What is it like?' Jean-François asked. 'San Michon's beloved sacrament?'

'Words can't describe it. You might as well try to explain a rainbow to a blind man. Imagine the moment, that first second you slip between a lover's thighs. After an hour or more of worship at the altar, when everything else has run its course and there's naught but want for you in her eyes and finally she whispers that magik word . . . *please*.' The silversaint shook his head, glancing at the pipe on the table between them. 'Take that heaven and multiply it a hundredfold. You might be close.'

'You speak of sanctus as we kith speak of blood.'

'The former was a sacrament for the Silver Order. The latter, mortal sin.'

'Do you not find it hypocritical that your Order of monster hunters was just as reliant upon blood as the so-called monsters you hunted?'

Gabriel leaned forward, elbows to knees. The long sleeves of his tunic slipped up over his wrists, exposing the ornate tattoos on his forearms. Mahné, the Angel of Death. Eirene, Angel of Hope. The artistry was beautiful, ink glinting silver in the lantern's light.

'We were our father's sons, coldblood. We inherited their strength. Their speed. We shrugged off wounds that would put ordinary men in their graves. But you know the horror of the thirst we were cursed with. Sanctus was a way for us to sate it without succumbing to it, or to the madness we'd fall into by denying it completely. We needed *something*.'

'Need,' Jean-François said. 'That was your Order's weakness, Silversaint.'

'Everyone has an empty place inside,' Gabriel sighed. 'You can try to fill it with whatever you like. Wine. Women. Work. In the end, a hole is still a hole.'

'And sooner or later, you all crawl back into your favourite one,' the vampire said.

'Charming,' Gabriel murmured.

Jean-François bowed.

'As that smoke reached my lungs,' Gabriel continued, 'the room came into sharpest focus. I could feel the patrons' eyes on me. Hear their every whispered word. Flames singing in the hearth and rain drumming on the roof. The weariness slipped off my bones like a rain-soaked greatcoat. My arm stopped aching. All of me – taste, touch, smell, sight – *alive*.

'And then, like always, it started. The sharpening of my mind along with my senses. The weight of the day hit me like a hammer. I could see my poor Justice again, hear his screams in my head. The faces of those soldiers I'd left for dead, the inquisitor I'd shot. The ruins in my wake, and the shadow following. Fear. Pain. All of it amplified. Crystallized.

'And so, I reached for the vodka. My beast had been fed, and I wanted to be numb. I drank a quarter of the bottle in a single draught. Another a few minutes later. I slumped beside the fire, closing my eyes as the liquor fought the bloodhymn, black drowning the red, welcoming the onset of sweet, silent grey.

'I drank to forget.

'I drank to feel, see, hear nothing.

'And then, I heard someone speak my name.

'"Gabriel?"

'It was a voice I hadn't heard in years. A voice that put me in mind of younger days. Glory days. Days when my name was a hymn, when I could do nothing close to wrong, when the Dead spoke of me with fear, and the commonfolk with awe.

'"Gabe?" the voice asked again.

'They called me the Black Lion back then. The men I led. The leeches we slew. Mothers named their children for me. The Empress herself knighted me with her own blade. For a few years there, I honestly thought we were winning.

'"Seven Martyrs, it *is* you . . ."

'I opened my eyes then, and knew I was dreaming. A woman stood before me, tiny and sodden, big green eyes brimming with question.

'Her shape was blurred by the drink, but still, I'd have known her anywhere. And I wondered why my mind had conjured *her*, of all people. Of all the faces I might have seen when I closed my eyes at night, I'd have picked hers for last.

'But then she stepped to my side and threw her arms around me. And I could smell leather and parchment, horse on her skin and old blood in her hair. And as she whispered "God be praised" and crushed me to her breast, the part of my brain least numbed by the drink finally realized this was no dream.

'"Chloe?"'

✦ V ✦

DIVINE PROVIDENCE

'THE LAST I'D seen her, Chloe Sauvage was wearing the vestments of the Silver Sorority; a starched coif and a black habit embroidered with silver scripture. She'd been weeping then. She was clad as a warrior now; a dark, padded surcoat over a shirt of mail, leather britches and heavy boots – all soaked from the rain. A wheellock rifle hung on her shoulder, a longblade was slung at her belt with a silver-trimmed horn beside it. A silver sevenstar dangled about her neck.

'She was still weeping, though. I have that effect on my friends.

'"Oh, sweet and blessed Mothermaid, I thought I'd never see you again!"

'"Chloe," I murmured, my face still buried in her chest.

'"In my heart I hoped. But the day you left—"

'"Ch-chloe," I wheezed, struggling to breathe.

'"Oh, sweet Redeemer, I'm sorry, Gabe."

'She released her grip on my head, finally letting me inhale. I blinked hard, black spots clearing in my eyes as she patted my shoulder. "Are you well?"

'"Still alive . . ."

'She squeezed my hand, smiling wide. "And I thank the Almighty for it."

'I smiled thin, looked her over with a careful eye. She'd always been small, had Chloe Sauvage. Freckled skin and wide green eyes and a stubborn mass of brown curls. Her accent was pure Elidaeni, prim and nobleborn. If there was a woman under heaven more at home in a nunnery, I'd yet to meet one. But she seemed harder than she'd been back in San Michon. Nothing like the girl who'd stood at the altar the night I'd been branded with my sevenstar. Chloe was road-worn now.

She wore no holy vestments, but the sevenstar still hung about her throat, etched on the pommel of that longblade at her waist. The sword was too big for her by far.

'*Silversteel*, I realized.

'She glanced across the commonroom, and I saw four figures had come in behind her. An elderly priest stood at their fore, grey hair shorn to stubble, his beard long and pointed. Like most of the folk around us, he was Sūdhaemi born, dark eyes and deep brown skin, wrinkled with age. But he had a bookish look to him – supple hands and spectacles perched on a pointed nose. I summed him up in a blink: soft as baby shite.

'A tall young woman stood beside him. Strawberry-blonde hair was shaved on one side of her skull, knotted into slayerbraids on the other, and two red stripes were interwoven on her face, running down her brow and right cheek. *Naéth*, I realized; the warrior tattoos of the Ossway Highlanders. She wore a collar of tooled leather, a heavy wolfskin cloak on her broad shoulders, and more blades than a fucking butcher. An antlered helm was slung under her arm, and a battleaxe and shield at her back. I didn't recognize the clan colours on her kilt at first. But she could crush a man's throat between those thighs of hers, and no mistake.

'A young fellow stood behind her, and I picked him for a soothsinger at a glance. He was perhaps nineteen, lock-up-your-daughters handsome – big blue eyes and a square jaw dusted with stubble. A six-string lute of fine bloodwood was slung on his back, he wore a silvered necklet with six musical notes hanging on it, and his bycocket cap was tilted in a fashion that could safely be described as "rakish".

'*Wanker*, I thought.'

'And last among the group, stood a boy. Fourteen maybe. Thin and gangly, not yet grown into his bones. He was pale, pretty, maybe of Nordlund blood. But his hair was white – and I don't mean blonde now, I mean white as a dove's feathers. He wore it messy, draped over his eyes in a tumble so thick I wondered how he could see at all.

'One glance at his wardrobe, you'd be forgiven for thinking him a prince-ling. He had a beauty spot on his cheek, and he wore a nobleman's frockcoat, midnight-blue with silver curlicue, ruffled sleeves. But his leather britches were patched at the knees, and his boots were falling to pieces. He was gutterborn for sure, pretending to be something finer.

'The boy saw Chloe standing with me, made to walk across the common-room to us. But the woman held up her hand, almost too quick.

'"No. Stay with the others, Dior."

'The lad glanced to my half-empty bottle, then fixed me with suspicious eyes. I met his gaze, and he squared his scrawny shoulders in his stolen coat and stared in silent challenge. But our contest was put to rest by the landlady's shriek.

'"Mother and blessed Maid!"

'The commonroom filled with gasps as a final newcomer slunk over the threshold, dripping rain onto the boards as it shook itself, nose to tail. It was a cat. Well, a fucking *lion*, if I'm honest – one of the mountain breeds that used to haunt the Ossway Highlands before all the big predators died off for want of game. Its fur was russet red, its eyes speckled gold, a scar cutting down its brow and cheek. It looked a beast that'd gobble newborns for breakfast, then wash them down with a healthy serving of toddler.

'Men about the commonroom reached for their weapons. But the Ossway lass with the slayerbraids only scoffed. "Take yer wobbling baps in hand, ye damn blouses. Phoebe here'd nae hurt a mouse."

'The publican pointed a shaking finger. "That is a *mountain lion*!"

'"Aye. But she's tame as a hoose cat."

'As if to prove the point, the beast sat on the doorstep and began cleaning its paws. I saw it had a leather collar, tooled with the same design the lass wore. But still, the publican remained on the safe side of unimpressed. "Well . . . it cannot come in here!"

'"Tch." The Ossian lass rolled her eyes. "G'wan, then. Oot to the stables, Phoebe."

'The big cat licked her nose and huffed.

'"Don't sass me, ye cheeky bitch! Ye know the rules. Oot!"

'With a soft growl, the lioness hung her head and slunk back out into the rain. The Ossian lass settled into the booth with no more fuss, the priest and dandyboy slipping in beside her. The wanker called for drinks. As a semblance of calm returned to the commonroom, I turned my eyes back to Chloe, one brow raised.

'"Friends of yours?"

'She nodded, pulling up a chair. "Of a sort."

'I smirked, the vodka bringing a warm glow to my cheeks. "A nun, a priest, and a lioness walk into a bar . . ."

'Chloe smiled briefly, but her tone was grim. "How've you been, Gabe?"

'"All sunshine and flowers, me."

'"Last I heard you were living in Ossway?"

'I shook my head. "South. Past Alethe."

'Chloe whistled softly. "What are you doing all the way back up here?"

"'I know a leech who needs killing."

"'Eleven years, and you haven't changed a bit." Chloe brushed back her impossible curls and grinned. I saw the thought form in her eyes. The inevitable question.

"'. . . Is Azzie with you?"

"'No," I replied.

'Chloe craned her neck and searched the booths, as if expecting to see her face.

"'Astrid's at home, Chloe."

"'Oh." She nodded, settling in her chair. "Of course. Where else would she be?"

"'Oui. Where else."

High in the reaches of that lovelorn tower, Gabriel de León leaned forward, rubbing his stubble, and he sighed from his very heart. The historian looked on in silence. The wind whispered about them as Gabriel hung his head, long locks of ink-black hair tumbling about his scarred face. Sniffing thickly. Spitting once.

'Astrid Rennier,' Jean-François finally said. 'The sisternovice who named your horse. Tattooed your palm. You still knew her then? After all those years?'

Gabriel glanced at his chronicler. His jailer. He realized Jean-François was illustrating another page – an image of Dior. Frockcoat, vest, fine features and pale eyes.

'You have the gift,' he commented, grudging.

'Merci,' the vampire murmured, continuing to draw.

'Can you see him in my eyes? Or in my head?'

'I am of the Blood Chastain,' Jean-François replied, not looking up. 'Our dominion is over the beasts of earth and sky. Not the mind. You know this, Silversaint.'

'I know it's not for nothing that Margot names herself Empress of Wolves and Men. But the blood is fickle. Ancien coldbloods can display . . . other gifts.'

'I believe you are attempting to unlock my secrets, de León. But I am master of keys here, not you. It had been seventeen years since you entered San Michon. More than a decade since you'd roamed the roads of the empire. Who was Astrid Rennier to you now?'

Silence rang out in reply, the scratching of the vampire's pen and the song of the mountain wind the only sounds. And when Gabriel finally answered, he ignored the question, marching on with his tale instead.

"'So this leech you're hunting," Chloe said. "Where is it?"

"'Elidaen. Somewhere near Augustin."

'"You're heading north, then." She raised her eyes heavenwards. "Thank God."

'I took a swig from my vodka, wincing at the burn. "Thank him for what?"

'Little Chloe nodded to her comrades gathered in their booth. The priest had his head bowed in prayer. The ashen-haired boy was smoking what looked to be a traproot cigarelle, staring at me like something he'd found on the bottom of his boot.

'"We're travelling that way too," Chloe said. "We can share the road."

'"Ohhhh," I breathed, taking another drink. "Won't that be lovely?"

'Chloe frowned, uncertain at my tone. "There's safety in numbers. Ossway is rough country, believe me. And some of the feet following us don't belong to mortal men."

'"Only some?"

'Chloe fell silent as the taverne lass returned, plonking my room key down in front of me, along with a bowl of steaming mushroom ragout and a slab of potato bread. Eyeing the spudloaf with contempt, I began shovelling down the rest.

'"Anything else, adii?" the lass asked.

'I took another swig to wash down my ambitious mouthful. "More vodka."

'The lass eyed me with clear scepticism. "Are you certain?"

'"*Terribly* certain, mademoiselle."

'The girl glanced at Chloe and then shrugged, spinning on her heel. I smiled as I felt the room spin in her wake, pushed my bottle across to Chloe. "Drink?"

'The sister was looking at me strangely. Pretty green eyes roaming my face, the sword on the table in front of me, the needle holes in the breast of my greatcoat where a sevenstar had once been stitched. She sat silently as I finished my meal. I even stuffed the potato bread down in the end. And finally, she spoke.

'"Are you well, Gabriel?"

'"I'm fucking marvellous, Sœur Sauvage." I thumped the empty vodka bottle down. "But forget me. Last I saw, you were holed up in the San Michon Library, eleven years and a thousand miles ago. The hell are you doing down here in Sūdhaem?"

'Chloe glanced around the taverne, wary of the few curious eyes still on us. She pulled her chair closer, speaking in conspiratorial tones. "God's work."

'I looked at the gear she was wearing, the companions she travelled with. "I wasn't aware Sisters of the Sorority were permitted to leave San Michon unaccompanied by silversaints? Let alone dressed like a common sellsword?"

"'It's . . . complicated." Chloe lowered her voice to a whisper. "I'll not speak of it here. But things changed a great deal around the monastery after you and Astrid—"

'She caught herself, looking up into my scowl.

"'Go on," I told her. "After we what?"

'Chloe combed one mousy curl off her freckled cheek. She spoke slow, choosing her words with utmost care. "You and Azzie didn't deserve what they did to you. I was sick with it every day afterwards, and I'm sorry that—"

"'So sorry you didn't even come to tell us goodbye?"

"'You know I wanted to. Don't be a bastard, Gabriel."

"'In life, always do what you love."

'Chloe frowned then. "You're drunk."

"'You're perceptive."

'The lass returned with my second bottle, and I gave her a dramatic bow, apparently charming enough for her to muster a smile in return. My arm didn't hurt at all any more.

"'Merci, chérie," I sighed, breaking the wax. "Your blood's worth smoking."

"'Perhaps I should leave you to it." Chloe eyed me up and down as I took a fresh swallow. "We can talk more in the morn when you've a clear head."

"'. . . Talk about what?"

"'About the road we're to share. When you wish t—"

"'I don't think we'll be sharing roads anytime soon, mon amie."

"'You said you were travelling north?"

"'Oui." I toasted her with my new bottle. "But I plan to float, not walk."

'Chloe's frown deepened. "Gabe, this is no jest. The roads through Sūdhaem and Ossway are thick with the Dead. I've need of a sword like yours."

"'Have you now?"

'The sister turned her stare to the blade on the table before us, speckled with mud and blood. "It's not through chance alone that I find the Ashdrinker again tonight. Nor blind luck to be reunited with her master after all these years." She looked up at me, fire in her eyes. "This is Almighty God's will. And blessed are we who share in his divine providence."

"'Well, huzzah *and* hurrah," I nodded, swallowing another burning mouthful.

'Chloe glanced around the room again. Leaning forward, she lowered her voice, barely audible above the taverne's hubbub. "Gabe, I've done it. I've *found* it."

'"Congratulations, Sœur." There were three Chloe's in front of me now, and I directed my query at the middle one. "But . . . what's *it*?"

'"The answer." She reached out her little hand and grasped my own. "The weapon we need to win this war, and finally put an end to this endless night."

'"A weapon?"

'She nodded. "One no coldblood under heaven can withstand."

'I felt my brow furrow. "Is it a blade?"

'"No."

'"Some work of chymistrie, then?"

'Chloe squeezed my hand again, her voice brimming with fervour. "It's the Grail, Gabriel. I'm talking about the bloody *Grail*."

'I looked Chloe Sauvage in her big, pretty eyes.

'I leaned slowly back in my chair.

'And then, I fell off it laughing.'

✦ VI ✦

PROMISES, PROMISES

'THE GRAIL OF San Michon,' Jean-François murmured.

'Oui,' Gabriel replied.

'The cup that caught the blood of your Redeemer as he died.'

'So the Testaments say.'

'Pretend you are more of an expert on scripture than I, Silversaint. Explain.'

Gabriel shrugged. 'Well, after his acolytes betrayed him, the Almighty's one begotten son was captured by priests of the Old Gods. At the end of seven nights of torture, the priests strung him up on a chariot wheel. They flayed his skin away to appease Brother Wind, burned the flesh beneath to please Father Flame, cut his throat to feed Mother Earth. And at the end, they tossed his body into the Eternal Waters. But his last faithful follower, the hunter Michon, was so aggrieved at seeing her master's blood lost in the dust, that she caught it up in a silver chalice. That cup became the first relic of the One Faith. And Michon, the first Martyr.' Gabriel sniffed. 'Bugger of a job, really.'

'Children's tales,' the vampire mused.

The Last Silversaint leaned back, laced his fingers behind his head. 'As you like it.'

'This Sauvage woman must have been a simpleton.'

'She was one of the shrewdest bitches I ever met, truth told.'

'And yet she put stock in peasant superstition?'

'Twenty-seven years ago, leeches were considered peasant superstition by most. And your Empress Undying must put stock in it too. Else, I'd already be dead.'

Jean-François looked Gabriel over with glittering eyes.

'The night is young, Chevalier.'

'Promises, promises.'

'You first scoffed at the tale, same as I.'

'That I did.'

The vampire brushed the edges of his quill with one sharp fingernail. 'How did Sister Chloe react, then, when you laughed in her face?'

'Well, she wasn't turning cartwheels. But I was too shitfaced to care by then. Chloe looked down on me with something between pity and anger as I rolled on the floorboards of the Perfect Husband, laughing as if she were jester to Emperor Alexandre himself.

'The old Sūdhaemi priest made his way over, hands tucked in his sleeves. His skin was wrinkled as a walnut's, dusk dark. He wore the sigil of the Redeemer's wheel about his neck; a perfect circle forged of pure silver. Worth a fortune those nights.

'"Is everything well, Sister Chloe?" he asked, looking at me with bemusement.

'"Oh, it's more than well, Father," I chuckled, wiping away the tears. "Our Chloe here has found the answer, don't you know?"

'"Mind your tongue, Gabriel," she murmured.

'"She's found the end to the endless fucking night, no less!"

'"Shut your *mouth*!" she commanded, kicking my shin.

'The chatter around the commonroom had stopped, and every patron in the pub was busy with the spectacle of me making a complete twat of myself. The serving lass looked mournfully at the mess I'd made. The lad Dior was staring at me with pure contempt through his cigarelle smoke, though the young soothsinger raised his cup and grinned.

'It was at that moment the taverne door opened, admitting a blast of freezing sleet and a doughy, middle-aged Elidaeni man. His face was flushed, his powdered wig askew. Sausage fingers were adorned with silver rings, and he clutched a crook staff. His red robes were embroidered with scripture, and the sigil of the wheel hung about his neck. He was surrounded by militiamen from the gate.

'Glaring about, the man's gaze settled on the publican.

'"Mme Petra," he said. "Are visits to your establishment from honoured gentry so frequent no one thinks to fetch me when a *silversaint* arrives in it?"

'"We were afeared of disturbing you at prayer, Bishop Du Lac," the woman replied, eyes downturned. "Apologies."

'I looked this priest over. Noted the way the mood had fallen in the commonroom at his entrance. Even though he was Elidaeni born, he clearly had the run of the town. In the nights of famine and suffering after daysdeath, there wasn't a single game in the empire that prospered like the Holy Church. When hell had opened its gates, it was only natural commonfolk turned to the priesthood for guidance. But I've met believers in my time, coldblood. And I've met politicians. And I'd have bet my troth ring that this bastard was the latter. Too well fed, too well dressed, and too fucking sure of his welcome in the world. So, I tossed the hair from my eyes. Raised one unsteady finger at his robe.

'"I just *love* your dress."

'"You'd do well to mind your tongue, monsieur," the man warned, "lest I have you whipped through the streets like a disobedient hound."

'"Well that's not very polite."

'He looked me over – sprawled on the boards with vodka in hand, unshaven jaw, bare, dirty feet. "And you hardly look a man deserving of politeness."

'Leaning on his silvered crook, the man puffed up like a peacock.

'"I am Alfonse Du Lac, Bishop of Dhahaeth. I am informed a member of the Ordo Argent is come among us." He looked about each patron in turn. "Pray, where is the good frère? I desire a word or three, none of which can wait."

'The serving lass nodded to me. "That's him, Your Grace."

'The bishop's mouth fell open. "It . . . is?"

'The man glanced at Chloe beside me, who simply shrugged. My stomach burbled a sternly worded complaint as I swayed to my feet. The suspicion I shouldn't have downed an entire bottle of peasant-still vodka was slowly rising, along with the threat of second dinner.

'To his credit, the bishop recovered quick, crossing the commonroom and shaking my hand so vigorously his wig began slipping. "It is my honour, Holy Brother."

'"As you like it," I growled, dragging my hand free.

'Du Lac straightened his wig, altogether flustered. "Your pardon, I beg you. Had I known you were en route, I would have met you at the gate. Long months have I beseeched High Pontifex Gascoigne to send us aid against the marauding Dead. I thought perhaps His Holiness might send a few troops. If I had known he would send a bona fide *silversaint*—"

'My stomach burbled ominously. I held it still with one hand as the rest of me swayed with the building around us. "Should've never eaten that spudloaf . . ."

'Chloe held my arm to steady me. "Gabe, you should sit down."

"'Frère, please," the bishop begged. "I'd speak with you alone, if I may."

'I squinted at the powdered curls atop the man's head. "I think your cat's dead."

"'Gabriel, you should drink some water," Chloe warned.

"'Pardon me." The bishop glared at Chloe, cheeks flushing. "I am conducting official parish business here. Who exactly are you, madame?"

"'Well, first and foremost, I'm not a dame. I'm a demoiselle."

"'Forgive me. I presumed you'd be wed. A woman of your age—"

"'I *beg* your pardon?"

"'He doesn't look too well," one of the militiamen said, eyes on me.

"'He doesn't feel too fucking well either," I confessed.

"'You just drank an entire bottle of vodka, Gabriel," Chloe scowled.

"'Who are you, my mama?"

"'I wish to God I were. I'd have taught you not to make an arse of yourself in public."

"'In life, always do what you love."

'The rest of Chloe's comrades had joined the growing commotion on the commonroom floor. The Ossian lass with the slayerbraids was standing beside Chloe, one hand close to her many blades. The dandyboy stood behind her, that mop of ash-white hair hanging over his eyes. I had the almost irresistible urge to brush it the fuck out of his face.

'The handsome one was at the bar, chatting up the serving lass.

"'Good Frère," the bishop said to me. "We should dine in my home. How long will you be staying with us? Have you missive from Pontifex Gascoigne?"

"'Why would I have a letter from that tubby shitstain?"

'Chloe elbowed my ribs to shush me. "Bishop Du Lac, apologies, but the good brother is not in Dhahaeth on His Holiness's business. He's leaving with us in the morning."

'The dandyboy piped up. "No, he's not."

"'Dior." Chloe turned to the lad. "Please let me handle this."

"'He's not coming with us."

"'Do you even know who he is?"

"'I don't *care* who he is."

"'Dior, this is Sir Gabriel de León."

'A gasp washed over the commonroom. I felt a tremor roll among the militiamen, the bishop looking at me with renewed wonder as he made the sign of the wheel.

"'The Black *Lion* . . ."

'"This man has killed more coldbloods than the sun itself," Chloe explained. "He's a sword of the empire. Knighted by Empress Isabella's own hand. He's a *hero*."

'The boy dragged on his cigarelle, looked me up and down. "Hero, my shapely arse."

'"Dior—"

'"He's not travelling with us."

'"Damn right I'm not," I growled.

'"See? He doesn't even want to come."

'"Damn right I don't."

'"And what need have we for a drunken pig anyway?"

'"Damn ri—wait, what the fuck did you say?"

'"You're a drunken pig." The boy puffed up in his fancy coat and blew smoke in my face. "And we've as much need of you as a bull has of tits."

'"Fuck you, you little shitgrubber," I growled.

'"Ah. A rapier wit to boot."

'"Speaking of boots, perhaps you fancy one of mine up that so-called shapely arse?"

'"You're not wearing any, monsieur."

'The Sūdhaemi priest chuckled into his beard. "Touché."

'"Who the fuck asked you, god-botherer?"

'"Enough!" The bishop stomped his polished heel. "Everyone not directly involved in town business will vacate this establishment, immediately! Alif, clear this room at once!"

'The man beside the bishop nodded, and the soldiery set about rousting the clientele. The townsfolk grumbled, but the militiamen cared little. And then one of the soldiers reached towards that smart-mouthed dandyboy, and sudden hell broke loose.

'The Ossian lass seized the soldier's wrist. Twisting him about smoothly, and with a swift kick to his arse, she sent the man staggering into his fellows. "Dinnae *touch* him."

'Predictably, the militiamen reached for their cudgels. But quick as snakes, the clanswoman slung that battleaxe off her back, beautiful and gleaming. Monsieur Ladykiller over by the bar was suddenly standing atop it, a crossbow slung off his back. And Chloe drew that silversteel longblade faster than I'd ever seen a nun move.

'"No closer," she warned, blowing a rogue curl out of her eyes.

'"I am bishop of this parish, and my word is law!" Du Lac bellowed. "Lay down your blades, or by Almighty God, there will be blood!"

'Patrons ducked beneath tables as the soldiers drew their steel. The familiar threat of violence hung in the air, hammering in my veins with the bloodhymn, the vodka's fire, the adrenaline in my still-grumbling belly. This whole scene was headed south of heaven quicker than a back-alley wristjob.

'So, with a sigh, I picked up my fallen sword and drew it.

'The blade's song rang in the air. Everyone in the room fell still, eyes on the weapon in my hand. Unreadable glyfs were etched down its length, the dark starsteel glinting like oil on water. Its edge was curved, its point jagged, half a foot missing from the tip. The beautiful woman on the hilt held her arms wide, silvered, ever smiling.

'"The Ashdrinker . . ." the rake breathed.

'*They know us, Gabriel,* came her voice in my head. *The b-blade that cleft the dark in twain. The man the undying feared. They r-remember us . . . e'en after all these years.*

'I turned a slow circle among the mob, making certain everyone was still.

'*Ye hast the look of hammered shite, by the by.*

'"Shut up," I whispered.

'The bishop's face was shining with sweat. "I said nothing, Chevalier."

'"Keep it up, then." I glanced at Chloe, then back to the militiamen's blades. "Mayhaps you and your friends have outstayed your welcome, Sœur Sauvage."

'"Mayhaps." She nodded, backing towards the door. "Where's your horse?"

'I scoffed. "I'm not going with you."

'"But, Gabriel . . ."

'"Ah, splendid." The bishop smiled, mopping his lip with a kerchief. "This rabble are of no consequence. I bid you come to my home, Chevalier, we have mu—"

'"I'm not going with you either, god-botherer."

'"But . . ." Du Lac glanced among his men. "Where, then, will you go?"

'"I'm going to fucking bed."

'The room broke into sudden babble.

'"But, Chevalier, the Dead grow in numbers every d—"

'"Our meeting isn't just by chance, Gabriel, this is God's w—"

'*Damn ye, Gabriel, listen to h—*

'"Shut *up*!" I roared, squeezing the sword's grip.

'Silence rang in the commonroom, and blessedly, inside my head.

'"I already lost one old friend today, Your Grace," I warned the bishop. "And I'm apparently taking it rather badly. So I'd advise you and your men to let this one go in peace." I glanced into sad, pretty eyes. "But that's as far as I stretch for you, Chloe."

"'Gabe—"

"'Chevalier—"

"'Let him go."

'The voice was clear, crystal, bringing a strange stillness to the room. All eyes turned to Dior, standing behind the ring of his comrades. The boy crushed out his cigarelle underheel, tossed his head, ashen hair flipping from his eyes, and for the first time, I saw they were a pale and piercing blue.

"'Dior . . ." Chloe began.

"'Can't you see?" the boy scoffed. "He doesn't give a damn about you. He doesn't care about this town or its problems. He's no hero. He's just a drunk. And a dead man walking."

'A silver whisper echoed in my head.

'*From the mouth of b-b-babes—*

'But I silenced the voice, slamming Ashdrinker back into her sheath. A little unsteady, I wobbled towards the hearth to retrieve my boots. Straightening with a wince, I peered around the room, settling on the blurry triplets of the publican behind the bar.

"'I'll take breakfast at noon, if you please, madame."

'Chloe looked at me with wounded eyes. The bishop and his men with simple bewilderment. But without a backwards glance to anyone, I staggered upstairs to bed.'

✦ VII ✦

STARS IN A YESTERDAY SKY

'I WOKE WHEN dark ran deepest, and hope seemed farthest from the sky.

'I opened my eyes in the velvet black. I could still taste vodka on my tongue, a hint of candlesmoke, the scent of leather and dust hanging in the gloom like an old promise. My arm didn't hurt any more. I wondered where I was, what had woken me. And there it came again – the sound that always did, that set my heart beating swift against my ribs and dragged me up through the tattered wall of sleep.

'Scratching at the window.

'I sat up, bedclothes tangled about my legs, squinting towards the sill. And though my room sat on the taverne's upper floor, still, I saw her outside, waiting for me. Floating, as if submerged beneath black water, arms open wide as she trailed her fingernails across the glass. Pale as moonlight. Cold as death. No breath on the window as she brought her heartbreak-shaped face closer and whispered.

'"My lion."

'She wore nothing save the wind. Her hair was silken tar, flowing about her body like ribbons on a moonless tide. Her skin was pale as the stars in a yesterday sky, her beauty born of spiders' songs and the dreams of hungry wolves. My heart hurt to see her – that fearful kind of hurt you couldn't hope to bear, save for the emptiness it would leave if you put it behind you. And she looked at me, out beyond the window glass, and her eyes were black gravity.

'"Let me in, Gabriel," she breathed.

'She ran those pale hands up her body, lingering over the bare curves I knew as well as my own name. Bloodless lips parted as she whispered again.

'"*Let me in.*"

'I stepped to the window and opened the latch, invited her into my waiting arms. Her skin was cold as shallow graves, and her hand was hard as tombstones as she wove it up through my hair. But her lips were pillow-soft as she dragged me down, my eyes fluttering closed at the sound of her sigh, and I could feel my tears running down my cheeks, staining our kiss with salt and sorrow.

'Her hands were on my body and her mouth urgent against mine, and I tasted fallen leaves and the ruin of empires on her tongue. I felt her teeth then, sharp and white at my lip; an ecstatic stab of pain and a rush of bloodwarm copper, and her whole body shivered as she leaned harder into my embrace. She pushed me backwards towards the bed, and her teeth grazed my throat as she stripped away the cloth and leather between us, leaving me more naked with every kiss.

'And then she was atop me, bare and pressed against me, all shadow and milk-white, growling in the hungry hollow of her breast. Her kisses descended, and she hissed in pleasurepain at the sizzling touch of silver ink to her mouth. But there were no tattoos below my belt, no aegis to bar the way to her prize, and there at last she sank, sighing as she reached into my britches and set me free, aching and hot in the cool of her hand. I gasped as she gently stroked me, blew breathless breath upon me, as she wet red lips with the tip of her tongue and then ran it up my length, leaving me shaking, aching.

'"I miss you," she sighed.

'Her lips brushed against my crown as she spoke, curling into a dark smile, teasing tongue and gentle touch setting every inch of me aflame.

'"I love you . . ."

'And she parted those ruby lips and swallowed me whole, and my back arched and the timbers creaked as I gripped the bed and held on for dear life. I was powerless then. Adrift in the motion of her hand, her lips, her tongue, a rhythm as old as time and deep as graves and warm as blood. She dragged me ever higher into a starless, burning heaven, and all I knew was the feel of her, the sound of her, the hungry moans and silken flickers pulling me ever closer to my brink.

'And at last, as I fell, somewhere between the sighs and blinding light and the flood of my little death into her waiting mouth, I felt it; the stab of twin razors, a slice of agony amid the bliss, a rush of red before the rush of my ending.

'And she drank.

'Long after I was finished, still she drank.'

✦ VIII ✦

AT THE GATES

'I WOKE TO find a legion of tiny devils throwing a revel inside my skull.

'Most were taking turns kicking at my brain with rusty hobnail boots, though one had apparently crawled into my mouth, vomited, and died. I risked opening my eyes, rewarded with a shear of light so blinding, I thought for a moment daysdeath had finally ended, and the sun had returned to full and blessed glory in the skies.

'"Fuck my *face*," I groaned.

'My arm had healed as if the break had never been. I reached up to my neck, down into my britches, felt no trace of wounds. The thirst crouched on my shoulder like an unwelcome friend, magpie and mockingbird. I pushed away the memory of pale curves and lips red as blood as what sounded like an enraged stallion kicked at my door.

'"Chevalier de León?"

'The hinges screamed as the serving lass poked her head into the room. I was lying on my bed shirtless, britches unlaced and dragged dangerously low. The window was unlatched. After a shy glance at my tattooed skin, the lass turned her gaze downwards. "Pardon, Chevalier. But the bishop sends for you."

'"What t-time is it?"

'"Past noon."

'I squinted at the pitcher in her hand. "Is that m-more vodka?"

'"Water," she replied, handing it over. "I thought you'd have need."

'"Merci, mademoiselle."

'I took a long, slow gulp, then upended the rest onto my face. The strangled daylight streamed through the open window like a white-hot lance.

My insides began making noises like they'd prefer to be outside, and could find their own way if I refused to show them.

'"Chevalier," the girl said, voice unsteady. "The Dead are at the gates."

'I hauled myself upright with a groan, dragging the sodden hair from my face. "No fear, mademoiselle. You've men aplenty and strong walls besides. A few wretched won't—"

'"These are no wretched."

'I glanced up at that. My sluggish pulse tripping quicker. "No?"

'The girl shook her head, eyes wide. "The bishop bids you come with all speed."

'"All right, all right . . . Where are my britches?"

'"You are wearing them, Chevalier."

'". . . Seven Martyrs, I can't feel my legs."

'I pushed my knuckles into my eyes. My skull was pounding like I'd been thrice fucked in it. The lass stepped up as I tried to stand, and with her help, I wobbled upright, holding my brow and hissing with pain.

'"Should I fetch more water?"

'"What's your name, mademoiselle?"

'"Nahia."

'And with a sigh, I shook my head. "Just find my pipe, Nahia."

'Ten minutes later, I trudged through the mud towards Dhahaeth's southern gate, freezing sleet about my shoulders, rats about my heels. Nahia followed, wringing her hands. I'd shrugged on my greatcoat, mercifully dry, and hauled on my boots, sadly still damp. But pulling on my kit, I couldn't help being reminded of younger days. Glory days. And with Ashdrinker at my waist, I hoped I looked a fucksight more imposing than I felt.

'The bishop waited at the gate. In the water-thin light, the militia lads looked even less impressive than they had last night. Word of my name had no doubt worked its way among their number. Talk of last night's drunken fuckarsery in the pub obviously had too.

'"Thank the Almighty," the bishop began. "Chevalier, doom has come t—"

'"Take your jewels in hand, Your Grace."

'A cry came from beyond the palisade, a voice that made the men about me quaver. "Bring him out! Eternity we might have, but we'll waste it not on lowing cattle!"

'I set boots to stairs, old nails creaking, climbing until I stood on the rough, splintering timber of the highwalk. I hugged the shadows like old friends, hidden behind the palisade's highest spikes, the bishop following on my heels with clear reluctance. A dozen men stood up here, clad in worn leather armour and rusty tinpot helms. The skinny prick who'd given me lip last night stood among them, along with a man I presumed was their leader. He was a bulky fellow with a busted face and walnut skin, a whalebone pipe at his lips. Callused hands. Scarred chin. The only real soldier among them.

'"Capitaine," I nodded.

'"Chevalier," he grunted, looking beyond the walls. "Fine day to meet your maker."

'The man's voice was steady, his jaw set. But every one of his fellows seemed ready to fill their britches. And peering between the timbers, I saw the source of all their fear.

'A coach sat in the middle of the road. It was finely wrought; glossy black paint and gold trim, two lanterns casting a moon-pale light through the sleet. But instead of horses, the coach was drawn by a dozen wretched. Each had been a teenage girl before she was murdered. Ragged and rotten, they stared up at the men on the walls with nothing but hunger in their dead eyes. And sitting in the driver's seat was something hungrier still.

'It wore the shape of a young lass, too. But unlike the coldbloods hauling the coach, this one was a perfect beauty. She wore a leather corset, a half-skirt, high boots. Her lips were painted glossy dark, deep blue eyes ringed with kohl and framed by long black hair. Her skin was white as death, her chin smudged with faint stains of murder.

'"Dyvok, I'd wager," the capitaine grunted.

'"No," I replied, looking the coldblood over. "She's a Voss."

'"Ancien?" the bishop asked, trembling.

'I shook my head. "Just a fledgling, by the look."'

The historian suddenly tapped his quill on the tome in his lap.

'Really?' Gabriel sighed. 'Again?'

'As to a child, de León,' the vampire said. 'How could you tell this one's bloodline just by looking at her?'

'Because I wasn't fresh fallen from the last rains? You Chastains seldom travel by carriage. The Dyvoks were still busy razing the Ossway, and the Ilons were far too subtle to make an appearance this gaudy. But the Forever King's get had grown arrogant after their famille's successes in the Nordlund. *All Shall Kneel* was the creed of the Blood Voss, and Fabién's children saw themselves as vampiric royalty, destined to rule the endless night from atop thrones built of the old empire's bones. Rolling up to a peasant mudhole in a fancy carriage drawn by a dozen corpses was *exactly* a Voss's style.'

Jean-François nodded. 'And the term you used? *Fledgling?*'

'You *know* what a fucking fledgling is.'

'Nevertheless, I would like you to explain it.'

'Well, I'd like a glass of fine single malt and a courtesan with thousand-royale tits to read me a bedtime story, but we don't always get what we want.'

The vampire glowered. 'Margot Chastain, First and Last of her Name, Undying Empress of Wolves and Men, does.'

Gabriel bit back an insult, drew a calming breath.

'There are three stages to a coldblood's existence. Three ages to your so-called life. The new Dead are called fledglings. Young, comparatively weak, still shedding the remnants of their humanity and finding their way in the dark. After a century or so of murder, a fledgling can be thought of as mediae; a vampire in full possession of its gifts, *extremely* dangerous, and devoid of anything approaching human morality. The last, and most deadly, are the ancien. The elders.'

'And you can tell the difference at a glance?'

'Fledglings, sometimes.' The silversaint shrugged. 'Even though they don't breathe any more, they'll do things like gasp in surprise. Blink out of habit. A few even delude themselves that they can see mortals as anything other than meals. But everything erodes. *Everything* ends. And by the time you're mediae, you're something else entirely.'

'Something more,' Jean-François nodded.

'And much, much less,' Gabriel replied.

The vampire ran his fingers along the feathered tips of his lapels, lantern-light glinting in dark eyes. 'How old do you think I am, Chevalier?'

'Old enough to have nothing left inside you,' Gabriel replied.

And, unwilling to play the game, the silversaint returned to his tale.

'I looked down on the coldblood from atop the palisade, weighing her up. She climbed off the driver's seat, heels sinking into half-frozen mud. Stalking past those hollow, wretched girls hauling the coach, she approached Dhahaeth's walls through the freezing sleet, altogether unconcerned about the arrows aimed at her chest.

'I guessed she'd been no more than thirteen when she was killed, her body trapped a year or two shy of adulthood's shore. Her smile was razor-blade sharp as she looked among the militiamen above. The fear of her washed the walls like pale fog.

'"You are all going to die," she declared.

'One of the younger men lost his nerve at that. Loosing his crossbow with a sudden *twang*. The boy's aim was true, but the arrow simply *thumped* against the coldblood's chest as if she were made of ironwood. Eyes fixed on the lad who'd shot her, the vampire reached up and plucked the bolt free of her breast. Black lips parted, she licked the tip with a long, clever tongue.

'"You first, boy," she promised.

'"Loose!" the capitaine cried.

'Crossbows sang, a dozen other quarrels sent speeding after the first. But the coldblood simply stood her ground. The arrows hit her in a dozen places but, again, did almost nothing. One struck her full in the face, leaving naught but a scratch in her porcelain cheek. And when the rain was done, she looked mournfully down at the holes in her outfit, plucking another arrow loose and tossing it to the mud.

'"I was *fond* of this dress . . ."

'"Oui," I murmured. "She's Voss for certain."

'"Pitch shot!" the capitaine called. "At the ready!"

'The militiamen reloaded. But the tips of these new quarrels were bound in homespun, dipped in tar. The archers of Dhahaeth gathered about their burning barrels, ready to set their shots aflame.

'The coldblood paused at that. She might've made a show of standing in the rain, but if there's one thing all Dead fear, it's fire. A small tremor of courage ran along the wall at her hesitation.

'And then the carriage door cracked open.

'A figure stepped out onto the mud, closing the door with a gentle hand. Through the sleet, I could see he was dressed as gentry – a dark frockcoat, silken undershirt, a beautiful sabre at his belt. A long duellist's cloak of thick wolf fur hung from one shoulder, lined with red satin. Dark hair was slicked back from his pale brow in a sharp widow's peak. He was beautiful as a bedful of fallen angels. But his hems were spattered red, and his eyes were like black knife holes in his skull. He joined his companion and took her little hand in his, and a thrill of perfect rage ran through me, toe to crown.

'"*That's* an ancien," I breathed.

'". . . You know him?" the capitaine asked.

'I nodded, not believing my fortune. "That's the Beast of Vellene."

'A murmur rippled along the walls. Bishop Du Lac turned pale as babies' bones.

'"My name is Danton Voss," the male declared. "Child of Fabién and Prince of Forever."

'The coldblood plucked the ruffled edges of his sleeves, smoothed a stray lock of dark hair from his brow. The wretched girls pulling the carriage remained stone-still, deathly silent. I knew they were all the Beast's offspring now – held motionless by their maker's immortal will. The little female was also his get most like, but she'd Become before she had a chance to rot. The monster's gaze settled on Du Lac, lip curling at the sight of the wheel dangling from the bishop's neck on its thin silver chain.

'"Bring him to me, Your Grace. Lest I come in there and fetch him."

'I could feel the power in that voice. Cold as tombs and centuries deep. The other militiamen aimed uneasy glances my way. I'd seen the corpses impaled around the fortifications – these men had fought the Dead before today. But it was plain not a one of them had faced foes like these, and plainer still that none were in the mood to die for me.

'"Do you think he means it?" the bishop asked.

'"I think he does," I replied.

'The capitaine glanced around at the boys and greybeards he led, every one of them aquiver. Chewing his whalebone pipe, he blew a plume of grey smoke into the air.

'"Then I think we're fucked."'

✦ IX ✦

THE BEAST OF VELLENE

'I LOOKED DOWN at the coldbloods, wondering if today might actually be my last, or the day it all began. I checked the bandolier across my chest, my phials of black ignis and silver caustic and holy water. Then I nodded to the smoke drifting from the burly man's lips.

'"Can I borrow your flintbox, Capitaine?"

'I struck the flame to my pipe as I descended the stairs, dragging dead-red smoke into my lungs. The bloodhymn was rushing by the time my boots touched mud, the thirst in me forgotten, my hangover nothing but a smoke-dream, the war-drum beat of my pulse, primal and screaming and wanting and needing, focused only on that thing waiting outside. I slipped my pipe away, laced my collar about my face and nodded to the gateman.

'The timbers groaned, the wooden palisade opening wide. I stepped beyond the shelter of Dhahaeth's walls, a bitter wind blowing my greatcoat about me, head lowered as the gate creaked shut behind.

'The Beast of Vellene looked at me through the falling sleet, black eyes narrowed as I tipped my tricorn.

'"Fairdawning, Danton," I called. "Does your papa know you're here?"

'The Dead lass stepped closer, black gaze roaming my boots, my greatcoat, up to my blood-red eyes. "Step aside, mortal."

'"Aside? You're the one who demanded I come out, leech."

'She sneered. "We come here not for you?"

'I blinked at that. Thoughts racing with the sanctus in my lungs. I'd supposed they were hunting me; that the Forever King had perhaps gathered some second thoughts, sent his son to finish the job he'd begun. But a glance into those flint-black eyes told me Danton hadn't even recognized me yet.

'I was a dead man, after all.

'My mind returned to the taverne last night. The words Chloe had spoken: *Some of the feet following us don't belong to mortal men.* And I recalled the good sister's comrades, their fervor and flashing blades, the way they'd stepped in to protect . . .

'"The boy," I realized. "Dior."

'"Bring him to us," the fledgling commanded, empty eyes on mine.

'"I'd tell you to say please, little one. But he's not even here."

'"Will you lie as sweet, I wonder, with your bleeding tongue in my palm?"

'"I'd certainly talk a fucksight less than you do, chérie."

'The fledgling glowered, black lips pressed thin. But Danton peered at me more carefully, then to the town behind. His long-dead eyes roamed the spiked palisade, the militia atop it. All was silent save for the moaning wind, and he, as still as stone.

'The Beast of Vellene they called him – the Forever King's youngest son. He'd earned the name seventeen years back, when his father's army crushed its first capital west of the Godsend. When Vellene's gates came down, the Endless Legion slaughtered every man and woman therein. But Danton had a taste for young maidens. Infamous for it, he was. Rumour had it, he'd murdered every girl in the city under the age of sixteen with his own hands.

'I glanced to the coach behind Danton now. Saw those wretched lasses, completely in thrall of the one who'd massacred them. And Danton turned his black gaze to me, and spoke the way hammers fall.

'"*Tell us where the boy went.*"

'I felt his mind pushing into mine. His will pressing against my own, all the power in his long and darkling years tingling on my skin and in my soul. The desire to obey, to *please,* was as undeniable as time itself. I wanted to relent. Abase myself before him. But my hate for this thing, for his famille and what they'd taken from me, for what he was and pretended to be, sang even louder. I blinked hard. And I shook my head.

'"You didn't honestly expect that to work on a silversaint, did you?"

'Danton brimmed with contempt as his eyes flickered over me. I mustn't have looked much – haggard and muddy, eyes pouched in shadows.

'"A black coat and a lungful of cur's blood does not a silversaint make," he said.

'I drew the blade at my belt, the silver music of its voice in my head.

'*I was . . . having the strangest d-dream . . .*

'"Time to wake up, Ash. We've work to do."

'*Oh? . . . Oh, ohhhh yesss yesyes . . .*

'The wretched pulling the coach stirred. Their mouths slack, their fangs sharp. Danton's pale lip curled. And with a blink, he released them from his hold.

'They dropped the crossguards and came on in a rolling flood, vicious and soulless and quick. There were almost as many as the day before, when I lost poor Justice and ran for my miserable life. But today, I wasn't just a man unhorsed and a meal uneaten. Today, the sanctus was pounding in my veins and my swordarm was iron. And as Ashdrinker began humming an old broken nursery rhyme inside my head, I was running at them, their empty eyes filling with surprise as my blade began to dance.

'It's a strange thing, to fight in the grip of the bloodhymn. Each moment feels a decade long, and yet, the whole world moves in a blood-red blur. I cut through those dozen coldbloods like a straight razor through silk, and in her wake, the air was filled with the ashes my blade was named for. Sweet release was the only gift I could give those poor girls, and so I did, to every one. And when I was done, I stood there in the muddy road, my coat, my skin, my blade, all slicked with gore and streaked with grey, and for a terrible moment, I wondered how on earth I could've left all this behind.

'"Almighty God," I heard someone whisper on the walls above.

'"Magnificent . . ." the capitaine murmured.

'My senses were as sharp as the sword in my hand, my pulse athunder. I flicked a sluice of blood off Ashdrinker's blade and into the cold mud at my boots. And brushing a speck of soot off my lapel, I looked the Beast of Vellene in the eye.

'"What do you want with the boy, Danton?"

'The vampire gave no reply, his gaze flickering briefly to the carnage at my feet, the bloody sword in my hand. I searched those dark eyes, looking for a scrap, a crumb.

'"I heard some nonsense about the Redeemer's cup?"

'The female sneered. "You know nothing, mortal."

'"I know you made a mistake, leech, coming here with the sun still up."

'I saw *that* blow land at least. A tiny flicker of it in Danton's dusk-dark eyes as he threw a glance to the watercolour sky above. The Beast of Vellene was a child of the most powerful vampire under heaven. He'd obviously ridden up to these walls thinking he'd roll right through them and the peasants atop them. But instead, he'd found me.

'The fledgling's eyes narrowed, fangs glinting. "Who are you?"

'"You mustn't be much, chérie," I sniffed, "if you don't even know who I am."

'*Show them, G-gabriel,* came a silver whisper.

'I reached up, unlacing my collar so they could look upon my face. The female didn't blink, but Danton surely did, recognition splintering the black ice of his eyes. He glanced again at the broken blade in my hand. The place on my coat where the sevenstar had once been stitched. The tip of his tongue pressed to the edge of one sharp canine.

'"De León. Ye live."

'"Sadly."

'"*How?*" he hissed.

'"God didn't want me. And the devil was afraid to open the door." I took one step forward, eyes narrowing. "You look frightened too, Danton."

'"I fear no man," he sneered. "I am a Prince of Forever."

'I laughed at that. High as heaven was wide. "There's no one more afraid to die than those who believe they're undying. Your big sister taught me that."

'Fury flashed in his eyes. "Ye meddle in affairs ye cannot possibly comprehend."

'I shrugged. "Other people's business was always my favourite kind."

'They moved then. A stuttering flash of black cloth and marble skin. My wheellock was in my hand in a blink, tracking the female as she charged. She was swift, no doubt. But a pistol shot moves faster than a fledgling, hits ten times harder than any arrow. And with a fresh dose of sanctus in my veins, I wasn't one to miss at that range.

'The silvershot struck her in the face, right in the tiny crack at her cheek where the arrow had already hit, sending her reeling backwards with a bubbling shriek.

'Danton moved faster, and I was on my back foot in an instant. He came on like a cannon blast – older, stronger, just a blur of dead eyes and flashing teeth. His sabre glinted like lightning in his hand. His strikes were a hurricane. A slash from his blade almost took the jaw off my face, blood running red and hot down my neck. His boot landed in my belly, and I felt my insides rupture as I flew thirty yards back into the freezing mud.

'All coldbloods are tough as nails. Like palebloods, they ignore wounds that would orphan most men's children. But the flesh of the Voss bloodline can turn silver aside. Their eldest can even resist the kiss of flame. For all my taunts, this bastard was deadly, and I knew if I slipped just once, he'd slice my arse up like fresh spudloaf.

'I rolled back to my feet, wove aside from his blows, the bloodhymn ringing in my veins. Like I said, the batch I'd smoked wasn't top-shelf. But just because you coldbloods can prance about in the day now, doesn't mean you still aren't ten times more fearsome in the dead of night. Feeble as it was, the dark sunlight made Danton weaker than if it had been pitch black. And in the end, that was the edge I grabbed hold of.

'I reached to my bandolier, flinging a glass phial at the vampire's face. It exploded with a flash, a cloud of black ignis and silver caustic bursting in the air. The silverbomb was barely enough to singe him, but some of the dust *did* reach his eyes, and Danton reeled backwards, flailing. And hard as I could, I brought my blade down.

'Ashdrinker sheared the air, still humming off-key in my head as she took Danton's swordarm off at the elbow. His flesh was iron, but in daylight, the blade was its match, all my hate and rage behind the blow. Danton's severed hand exploded into ashes, years of denied decay turning in a heartbeat. He snarled, claws hissing past my chin as I smashed a phial of holy water into his face. His snarl became a scream, eyes wide with agony and running red with blood.

'"Ye *dare* . . ."

'I reached for his throat then, desperate to clutch him. One handful would be all I needed. But my fingers caught only air. The Beast of Vellene stood forty feet away now, back in the tumbling sleet, clutching his severed arm. The stump was smoking, his sabre lying in the mud. I reached inside my greatcoat, unslung my silvered chain and flail. Gasping and bleeding. Broken ribs stabbing with every breath.

'"Not staying for the funeral?" I wheezed.

'I took another step forward, but the vampire flashed twenty feet back in the blink of an eye. The Beast of Vellene had weighed the scales, and though he'd kicked the shite out of me, he still plainly found the balance wanting. The sun was up. The foe he faced was one he wasn't prepared for. You don't live for centuries by being impatient.

'Unlike me, Danton had time.

'I heard a cry behind me then, turning to see the fledgling dragging herself up from the bloody muck. A ragged black hole had been blasted through her face, her one good eye fixed on her maker. "Master?"

'I marched back across the mud to where she was trying to rise. She shrieked, voice ragged with agony and fear, eye still on her dark father.

'"*Master!*"

'The fledgling turned to run, but my silver flail tangled up her legs, bringing her back down to the mud. As she tried to drag herself away with her hands, I drove Ashdrinker down through her back, pinning her to the freezing earth. She twisted to bite me, but my boot forced her face into the muck, and reaching to my swordbelt, I drew a sharp knife made of pure silversteel, the Angel of Retribution soaring on the hilt.

'"No, w-what are you doing, what are y—"

'The monster screamed as I drove the blade into her back, began sawing at the ribs just below her left shoulderblade. Fledgling she might've been, but she was still a Voss, and it was more than thirsty work, the thing bucking beneath me, thrashing and wailing.

'"Danton, *help me!*"

'*Not a girl, Gabriel. Not a human. Just a m-m-mmmmmonsterliketherest-ofthem.*

'My teeth were gritted, face spattered with ashes and rotten blood – no peerless swordsman, just a butcher now. And as I worked, silvered blade slicing through bone as hard as iron, I felt that old familiar thrill, that dark joy rising as I looked into this thing's eyes and saw realization dawn – that after all the murder, all the nights of blood and beauty and bliss, here was where it all came to an end.

'*No fear.*

'"Please," the monster begged as I drew out an empty phial. "P-please . . ."

'*Only f-fury.*

'I forced my fingers between the fledgling's ribs. Her plea became a scream as my fist closed about her heart and tore it from its moorings. The organ began rotting as soon as it was free; stolen years rushing back with a vengeance. But I held it in my fist, squeezing a rush of luscious, dark blood into my phial before all turned to ashes. The vampire's spine arched as the thief of time took hold, stealing back what was his. And in a moment, it was over – little more than a husk remaining inside that pretty dress it had been so fond of.

'I breathed deep. Grey and red. I looked down on the monster, the wreckage, the little girl at my feet. And then, up into the eyes of the one who'd murdered her.

'"Did you tell her you loved her, Danton? Did you promise her forever?"

'The Beast of Vellene stared at me across the bloody ground. Holding his ruined arm, looking on the ruin I'd made of his children, eyes like burning coals in his skull.

'"Thou shalt suffer for this, Silversaint. And it shall be *legendary*."

'And with little more than a whisper, he vanished into the fog.'

RED SNOW

'*THEY CAME DURING the d-day, Gabriel.*

'"I know," I said, marching back towards the Dhahaeth gate.

'*E'en in a mud puddle like this, a Prince of Forever putting himself arisk under the n-noonday sun . . . desperate must he b-be to find this boy afore something else does. We must track them down. We m-mmmust know the truth of it, t-truth of it.*

'"I always find it so pleasing," I said, looking down at the blade, "when you insist on telling me shit I already know."

'*Ye should have listened to Chloe, Gabriel. Both then and now, n-now and then. Think of all we m-may have been spared, if thou hadst b—*

'"Shut up, Ash," I warned.

'*The fault is mine as m-mmmmuch as—*

'I slammed Ashdrinker back into my scabbard, silencing her voice as the gate opened wide. The militiamen waited beyond, the taverne lass, other townsfolk, all watching me with horror and awe. Du Lac came down from the battlements, and I glanced at the wheel around his neck, up into his eyes.

'"Merci for the assistance, Your Grace."

'Du Lac had the decency to look ashamed. "You seemed to have matters in hand . . ."

'"Which way did they ride?"

'". . . Whom do you mean?"

'"From the taverne last night, you powdered prig," I snarled. "The short woman with the big hair. The priest. The boy. Did they head north like they said?"

'"I *beg* your pardon, but—"

'"Oui, Chevalier," the taverne lass said. "They rode out north."

'"Merci, Mlle Nahia," I nodded, striding past. "I say again, your blood's worth smoking." Glancing to the highwalk, I called to the militiamen. "I'll be keeping your flintbox if all's well with that, Capitaine."

'The grizzled man nodded. "With my blessing, Chevalier. God go with you."

'"I'd rather he minded his own fucking business, if it's all the same."

'I made my way to the stables, haggled for a saddle, provisions and harness to replace the ones I'd lost when poor Justice died. I probably left town a few royales lighter than I should've, but I was too fretful to harp on it.

'Broken and befuddled though she was, Ashdrinker had spoke true. Vampires were creatures who lived forever if they played their cards right. Ancien were seldom stupid and *never* reckless. I could scarce believe a creature as old as Danton had put himself at such risk. And if that boy Dior was so important that a son of the Forever King hunted him . . .

'I saddled up Jezebel and rode hard through Dhahaeth's north gate. Chloe and her band had a good head start, and I'd have to ride swift to catch them. The gash Danton had given my face was slowly closing, but my broken ribs still ached with every breath. The dark sun threw a feeble light on the road ahead, autumn noon as bleak as winter sunset.

'I knew this used to be wheat country decades back – that these lands would once have swayed with stalks of gleaming gold. Now, the few farms that had managed to stay afloat grew the only things they could: potatoes and other roots, and great, rolling fields of mushrooms. Fungus sprouted *everywhere*. Luminous maryswort crusted the fence lines and rocks. Pale tendrils of asphyxia wrapped themselves around the long-dead trees, and thick growths of massive toadstools encroached into the muddy road.

'Rot. Swelling. Spreading.

'As we rode north, the sanctus began wearing off, my hangover catching up with the comedown and the pain of my beating kicking in. The farmlands receded, and Jez and I reached open road. The Ūmdir River was a silver serpent in the distance, and I could see thick deadwood through the gloom to the east, a hill crowned with a ruined watchtower. We passed a sign hammered into a lifeless elm, overrun with fungus.

'DEAD AHEAD.

'Ashdrinker was a heavy comfort on my hip. The thought of the blood I'd milked from that fledgling's heart was a greater comfort still. The thirst was already creeping back on me with red and slippered feet. Night drifted closer, I heard the rush of the Ūmdir ahead. And squinting through the darkness, I felt my heart sink.

'"Face*fuckery* . . ."'

'Allow me to guess,' Jean-François ventured. 'The folk of Dhahaeth had destroyed the bridge.'

'Oui,' Gabriel scowled. 'That prick of a bishop could have warned me at least. As I reached the riverbank, I saw only mooring stones and a few broken archways midstream. I'd come across no wretched on the road, so cutting off the crossings was obviously helping to keep the Dead out of the province. But the river was too fast and deep for Jez to cross.

'And to top it all off, it started snowing.

'I pulled my tricorn lower, gave Jez a mournful pat. "Sorry, girl. Should've warned you that the Almighty enjoys shitting in my brisket at every opportunity."

'The mare nickered in response.

'There was no sign of Chloe and her band. I checked my map for the closest crossing and rode on, following a dirt track up into a deadwood hill as dark deepened. Picturing the holy sister's face from the night before. Her whisper as she squeezed my hand.

'*It's the Grail, Gabriel. I'm talking about the bloody* Grail.

'I'd been a prick to her, and I knew it. Justice's death had been weighing heavy, and I'd been tired and drunk. But that wasn't the whole truth of it. Truth was, the sight of my old friend had dredged up a flood of memories I'd thought long buried. And now the past was rising again, just like the Dead.

'*What the hell did Danton want that boy for?*

'The blackened sun had slunk below the horizon, and the snow was falling heavy as I rode into the long-dead woods. I managed to get my lantern lit, hung it from Jez's saddle. But I knew we were one stumble away from a repeat of yesterday's funeral.

'"Might be time to call it a night, girl."

'A sound pierced the storm then. Blinking snow from my eyes, I tilted my head. A shot from a wheellock, I swore it. Another sound followed – a long note, high and muffled, the kind that had once borne me on silver wings into the jaws of hell. And I remembered Chloe in the pub last night. A rifle at her shoulder. And a silver-trimmed horn at her belt.

'"Shit," I hissed.

'I slapped Jez's rump, and we were charging up the jagged hillside. The dray wasn't spry, but she had grit, galloping headlong into the dark. I heard the horn again, adrenaline souring my tongue, a rush of memories from nights in San Michon – the vow on my lips, my brothers around me, love my shield and faith my sword.

'*And in sight of God and his Seven Martyrs, I do here vow; Let the dark know my name and despair. So long as it burns, I am the flame. So long as it bleeds, I am the blade. So long as it sins, I am the saint.*

'*And I am silver.*

'I heard a distant cry, saw the ruined watchtower rising before me. Dark shapes were moving towards it through the deadwood, lifeless eyes and sharp fangs. The horn blew again, a silver-sharp note rising above the thudding footfalls of the Dead. Because the Dead were here, and running quick – at least a dozen wretched drawn towards the figures I now saw through the falling snow.

'I drew Ashdrinker in one hand, my other fist wrapped in Jez's reins.

'*Where are w-we, Gabriel?*

'"We're in shit, Ash," I hissed.

'*Ohhh. Just another day, another d-day, then?*

'I could see Chloe standing at the base of the ruined tower, sword in hand, hacking at an oncoming wretched like a lumberjack at a tree. She fought with all hell's fury, but she was a nun, after all, and that sword was far too big for her. The soothsinger stood beside her, stubble crusted with snow, a burning brand in one hand, a steel longblade in the other. Behind them, pressed against the tower's broken walls, stood the boy Dior. He had a silvered dagger in his fist, an unlit cigarelle hanging from his lips, cold rage in his eyes.

'"Get back, you unholy bastards!" the soothsinger yelled.

'"Chloe!" I bellowed.

'I'd no idea where the Ossian lass or her lioness were, nor the old priest. But these three were in the deepest kind of shite. The soothsinger was quick with that torch of his, catching a wretched across the skull and setting its head ablaze with a cry of triumph. Chloe lashed out with her longblade at anything that strayed too close, and the silversteel ripped through Dead flesh like rotten straw. But the wretched were too many.

'Jez was brave or stupid, or just moving too fast to slow down. We ploughed into one wretched, knocked it flying. But as the other Dead turned on us and bared their rancid fangs, the mare lost her nerve, rearing up so hard she almost threw me.

'Ashdrinker at least seemed to have her head in the game now.

'*She be not a warhorse, shitwit, what in name of* Gods *do ye play at?*

'I kicked loose from my stirrups just as another wretched came at me out of the dark. The thirst was back on me, the lanternlight wild and strobing. This was a bad wager and I knew it, but I'd little choice now save roll hard or die.

'"Gabe, look out!" Chloe roared.

'*Behind!* Ashdrinker warned.

'I spun in time to fend off clawing hands, the coldblood flailing as I split its chest apart. Even with odds like these, I wasn't without a trick or three. I snapped the seal on a glass phial and tossed it. Two wretched toppled in a blast of silver caustic, their skin blackened, eyes bubbling as the silverbomb ripped the air.

'These were only fledgling Dead, but enough ants can slay a lion. Ashdrinker whispered warning as another wretched lunged through the dark – an old man with gore-matted hair. He should've died in his bed, this fellow, surrounded by loved ones. Instead, he ended beneath some broken tower south of the Ūmdir, his head sailing free as my sword flashed in the dark. I tossed a phial of holy water, heard another peal from Chloe's horn as glass shattered and Dead flesh sizzled.

'A wild-eyed man with bloody hands made it past the soothsinger's torch and struck Chloe from the side. She cried out, silversteel blade sailing from her hand, screaming as the thing plunged its fangs into her arm.

'"Chloe!" Dior cried.

'"Sister!" the 'singer roared.

'The man lunged to save her, only to have another wretched strike him from behind. Dior picked up the fallen torch, stabbed at the flailing cold-blood. A soulless screech of pain rang through the woods as the monster went up in flames, arms pinwheeling as it fell, and as I watched in aston-ishment, the boy spun the torch between his fingers and lit his fucking cigarelle. I hurled my last phial of holy water, emptied my wheellock into another wretched's face. But that many foes, my thirst burning brighter, I was beginning to suspect we might be proper fucked.

'And then, I heard a whisper. Saw a flash of midnight-blue, a ribbon of red. One wretched collapsed headless, another fell back convulsing, crimson steam rising from its eyes. A figure moved among the monsters now, sharp as the north wind, quick as the lightning in an Eversea storm. Long black hair and a red sword, cutting through those wretched like a dose of bad medicine.

'*Stand n-not amazed, Gabriel, fight!*

'I set about it, hacking at the coldbloods as this newcomer flickered among the dead trees, scattering the wretched like flower petals about its feet. And as we dispatched the last of the monsters together, I knew what kind of monster it was.

'The highblood stood now among the scattered corpses. Not sweating. Not breathing. She was dressed in a long red frockcoat and black leathers, a silken shirt parted from her bare and bone-white chest, throat wrapped in a red silk scarf. She had the body of a maid, though I knew she was nothing close. The sword in her hand was as tall and graceful as she was, gleaming red and dripping onto the bloodied snow at her feet. Her hair was the blue-black of midnight, running down to her waist, parted like curtains from a dead thing's eyes. But her face was covered in a pale porcelain mask, painted like a madame at winter court – black lips and dark kohled eyes.

'I glanced over my shoulder to a gasping, bleeding Chloe. "She with you?"

'"God Almighty, no," she replied, retrieving her fallen blade.

'The newcomer offered one slender hand to Dior. Her voice was soft as pipe smoke, but she spoke with a strange, hissing lisp. "Come with usss, child. Or die."

'*'Ware this one, Gabriel. She f-feels . . . wrong.*

'Ashdrinker's whisper rang in my mind as I stepped between the vampire and the others. For the first time, the highblood turned eyes towards me. Her irises were bleached like old linen. The air around us was freezing, my breath spilling over my lips in pale clouds.

'"Stay back," I warned.

'"*Ssstep assside,*" she commanded, soft and venomous.

'But even as her will came down on my shoulders like lead, I stood my ground. "I've hunted your kind since I was a boy, leech. You're going to have to try harder than that."

'Her eyes roamed my body then, lingering on the broken blade in my hands. "We heard you were dead, Silversssaint."

'"Who's *we*, you unholy bitch?"

'The highblood scoffed softly, as if I'd said something amusing. She turned dead eyes back to Dior, sharp fingernails glinting as she beckoned. "*Come with uss, ch—*"

'A fierce light stabbed through the trees. Ghostly and bright. Looking over my shoulder, I saw the old priest stumbling towards us, the wheel he'd worn around his neck now in his fist. He held the holy symbol aloft, spitting scripture like a sailor spat curses.

'"*I am come among thee as a lion among lambs!*"

'Light was spilling from his wheel as if from a mirrored lantern. The highblood flinched as it struck her, death-pale eyes narrowed against the flare. I was awed for a moment, remembering the nights when my faith shone as bright as this priest's did, when the sight of the ink on my skin was enough to burn the Dead blind. And as the old man ran towards us, a roar rang through the woods. I saw that red lioness from the taverne barrel out of the darkness, scarred face twisted as she bared her fangs. The Ossian slayer ran through the snow behind, antlered helm on her head, that beautiful battleaxe in her fists.

'At the sight of the she-lion, the priest's burning light, the highblood hissed. Her pale gaze was still fixed on Dior, but fear of that holy man was overcoming her will, the chill in the air fading as the priest finally crashed into the clearing, wheel held high.

'"I banish you!" the old man bellowed. "In the Almighty's name, *away!*"

'"Wretched priessst," the thing spat, hand up against the light. "You d—"

'"And I say to you, my children, I am the light and the truth!" The old man stepped forward with the wheel in his wrinkled fist. "You have *no* power here!"

'Another hiss spilled from behind that cold, painted mask. The lioness roared again, charging closer, and the coldblood's body seemed to tremble at its edges. And as the beast leapt towards her, claws outstretched, the vampire swept her coat about her and dissipated into a storm of tiny wings – a thousand blood-red moths spilling into the darkness and vanishing up into the falling snows.

'I swallowed hard, the taste of dust and bones in my mouth.

'It was over.

'I looked around the gathering. Chloe clutched her arm where the wretched had bitten her, face twisted with pain. The soothsinger knelt beside her, pale with worry. The slayer stared at me, her axe glinting in the fading light of the old priest's wheel.

'But I had eyes only for the boy. He was crouched in the muck, his burning brand still held in one white-knuckled fist, a smoking cigarelle hanging from his lips.

'*Lackwitted strumpet-stain, ye almost s-saw us killed. What in Gods' names w—*

'I slipped Ashdrinker into her scabbard to quiet her. Looked the lad up and down. There seemed nothing particularly odd about him. But still, and despite what my blade might have said, I was no one's fool.

'"So what's your fucking story?"'

✦ XI ✦

OUT OF THE STORM

"'SAY NOTHIN', DIOR," the clanswoman warned.

"'I'd no plans to, Saoirse," the boy replied, scowling at me.

"'Sister, are you aright?" The young soothsinger knelt at Chloe's side. "Is it deep?"

"'It's fine, Bellamy," she replied, lifting her blood-soaked sleeve. "A scratch."

'One glance told me the wound was anything but. Chloe's bicep was bleeding from a vicious bite, skin already bruising from that monster's unholy strength.

"'Wretched mouths are rife with rot," I said. "That'll fester if we don't treat it. I've some kingshield and gut in my saddlebags. Strong spirits too."

'Dior dragged on his smoke. "We'd hate to part you from your revels, hero."

"'It's medicinal alcohol, boy. You'd have to be thick as pigshit to drink it."

"'You just leave the door wide open, don't you?"

"'Look, who the fuck *are* you?"

"'Perhaps introductions can wait?" Chloe winced, waving at the storm and carnage about us. "Stench of dismembered corpses notwithstanding, it's getting worse out here."

"'A brave woman enjoys the wild's kiss on her skin, Sister," the slayer said.

"'And a wise man knows to come in from the rain," the priest smiled.

'The soothsinger nodded to the ruined tower. "Let's shelter inside."

'The company gathered their possessions, the rake helping Chloe stand while I went to fetch Jezebel. I found the mare a few hundred yards away, standing in the lee of a naked elm. I gave her a soft pat and a thorough looking over, but luckily she seemed none the worse for wear. And taking her reins, I led her back to the tower.

'I got a better look at the ruin as I approached – three storeys high, dark stone, crowned with broken battlements. The walls were crawling with old lichen and new fungus, the mortar crumbling to dust. It'd stood for centuries, mostlike – built by Sūdhaemis back when Elidaen was still five feuding kingdoms, and San Michon began her crusade to bring the One Faith to every corner of the land.

'The company was gathered within, sheltered from the rain as best they could. The slayer glowered in the shadows, twin interwoven lines inked down her brow and right cheek, clawing the braided hair from her face as that she-lion curled about her feet. Dior was brushing the snow from his fine stolen coat. The priest and rake gathered around Chloe, cleaning her bloodied arm. I shooed the pair away, knelt beside my old friend, placing a small bottle of pure spirits and a phial of pale yellow powder on the stone.

'"This'll burn like a strumpet's nethers when the fleet is in town," I warned. "But it's a fucksight better than gangrene."

'"Merci, mon ami," Chloe nodded.

'I set about the wound, my hands quick and sure, washing and sterilizing as Chloe hissed in soft agony. "Right, so who *are* you lot? Aside from a lodestone for the Dead?"

'"F-friends," Chloe winced.

'"Chosen," the slayer replied.

'"Believers," the priest murmured.

'"Oh, Seven Martyrs save me," I sighed.

'"My name is Bellamy Bouchette," the young rake declared with a small bow. "Soothsinger, adventurer, lover of women, and songsmith to emperors." He flipped damp brown curls from sparkling blue eyes. "A pleasure to make your acquaintance, Silversaint. I've heard your exploits sung all the way from Asheve to the shores of the Mothersea. I fear your legend does your reality . . . no justice at all."

'*Oui,* I thought to myself. *Definitely a wanker.*

'"This is good Père Rafa Sa-Araki," Bellamy said, nodding to the Sūdhaemi priest. "Scholar, astrologer, and devout member of the Order of San Guillaume. Never was there a man under heaven more in need of having his lute professionally strummed, but he's a splendid fellow beneath the repression, really."

'The old priest spoke with a voice that would've sounded like music on any pulpit in the land. "My thanks for your aid, Chevalier. Seven Martyrs bless you."

"'Our resident butcher, baker, and candlestick maker," Bellamy said, waving to the Ossian lass. "Mlle Saoirse á Rígan. She's terrible at baking and candles, by the by, but her skill at butchery more than makes up for it. Her four-legged companion there is Phoebe. I'd advise against trying to pat the little scamp if you're at all fond of your fingers."

'The lass just stared at me, hands on her axe, while the lioness licked her chops.

"'Our good Sœur Sauvage, you already know," Bellamy continued. "Which leaves the youngest of our band." The soothsinger waved to the ashen-haired boy. "Gabriel de León, may I present Dior Lachance, Prince of Thieves, Lord of Liars, and incorrigible little bastard."

"'You forgot whoreson," the boy muttered around his smoke.

"'Dior, a gentleman never refers to a lady plying honest trade as a whore."

"'My mother was no lady. And you're no gentleman, Bellamy."

"'You wound me, monsieur," the fellow grinned, tipping his idiotic hat.

'I finished cleaning Chloe's wound, a steel needle between my teeth as I fetched my spool of gut. "So now I've your names. But I still don't know who the fuck you are." I cast my eyes over the group, settling at last on the boy. "You in particular."

"'I'm no one special."

"'Is that so?" I looked to Chloe, hoping to slice through the bullshit. "Someone came to Dhahaeth looking for Monsieur Nobody Special after you left. And they'd have run through that town like a dose of the scratch if I hadn't been there to stop them."

"'I told ye." Saoirse glanced around the group. "Phoebe could smell them miles away. We've had coldbloods on our trail since Lashaame."

"'This wasn't just a coldblood," I replied. "This was Danton Voss."

"'. . . Who?"

"'Sweet Mothermaid, you lackwits have no fucking idea what you're doing, do you?"

"'Mind yer tongue, Silversaint," the lass spat.

"'Danton Voss is the youngest heir of Fabién. A direct descendant of the most powerful vampire that walks this earth. If the Forever King wants someone found, Danton is the child he sends, and he's not failed his father yet." I glowered at Chloe as I began stitching her bleeding arm. "You want to tell me what you did to make the Forever King set his most faithful bloodhound on your tail?"

"'Seven Martyrs.'" Chloe made the sign of the wheel. "The Beast of Vellene."

"'I saw him off,'" I said, still scarcely believing it. "But only because he came to those walls during the day and found me instead of you. Why would a creature as old as Danton risk himself like that, Chloe? Is it this Grail nonsense you were spitting last night?"

'The group looked at Chloe, aghast.

"'Ye *told* him?'" Saoirse hissed.

"'Not everything.'" Chloe glanced about the company, wincing as I stitched. "But Gabe was the man who put me on this path to begin with. *Years* ago. And God brought him to us for a reason. He's the greatest swordsman of the Silver Order who ever lived."

"'Fat lot of good swordsmen o' the Silver Order have done ye so far, Sister.'"

"'We *need* him, Saoirse.'"

"'Why?'"

"'Because the Beast will be back. And next time, he'll come at *night*.'"

"'What does Voss want with this boy?'" I demanded. "It's sure as shit got naught to do with children's tales."

"'The Grail is no children's tale, Silversaint,'" Père Rafa said, cleaning the muck from his spectacles. "*From holy cup comes holy light; the faithful hand sets world aright. And in the Seven Martyrs' sight, mere man shall end this endless night.*"

'I glanced at Chloe. "We're spouting shitty poetry now?"

''Tis no mere poem,' the priest said.

"'It's a prophecy, Gabe,'" Chloe said. "The Forever King. The Endless Legion. Daysdeath. The Grail can put an end to *all* of it."

"'This isn't one of your library books, Chloe. I thought you'd have outgrown that shite by now. One of you mad fucks best start talking straight-wise.'"

"'The cup of the Redeemer's blood *can* end this darkness,'" the priest insisted.

"'Bull*shit*,'" I spat. "The cup has been lost for centuries! And even if you had it, there's ten thousand Dead amassing north of Augustin. Nordlund's gone. North of the Dílaenn, the bloodlords have torn the empire to ribbons! How is a fucking cup supposed to fix that?"

"'Because it holds the Redeemer's blood. God's own son, who died upon the whe—'"

"'Spare me, god-botherer.'"

"'Gabriel, ask yourself this," Chloe said. "If the Grail is such nonsense, if the prophecy such rot, why has the Forever King got his son chasing us?"

"'I don't fucking know! What's the Grail to do with *any* of you?"

"'He knows where it is."

'I looked to the slayer, who was watching me like a hawk watches a hare. Her strawberry-blonde braids hung about her eyes as she stared me down, her gaze finally flickering to Dior as the snow danced in the air outside.

"'The bairn," she said. "He knows where it is."

'I looked at the lad. Dior cast an accusing glare at the slayer, then at Chloe.

"'*You* know where the Grail is?" I demanded.

'The boy shrugged, blowing a plume of thin grey smoke from his lips.

"'The silver chalice of San Michon," I scoffed. "The cup the Crusaders carried before them as they fought the Wars of the Faith, and forged the five kingdoms into one empire."

'The boy crushed his traproot cigarelle underheel. "So the Testaments say."

"'He's full of shit," I spat, glowering at Chloe.

"'No, Gabe." Chloe winced as I wrapped her wound. "He knows where the Grail is. And the Forever King *knows* he knows. Why else would the Beast of Vellene be hunting us?"

'I stared at the boy, thoughts at war in my head. This seemed the darkest shade of lunacy. The kind of rot that pulpit-riders feed children when they're scared of the night. There was no magik spell, no holy prophecy that would bring an end to this darkness. This was our here and our now and our forever.

'But apparently Fabién Voss believed. And if the Forever King was desperate enough to send his own children to hunt this boy . . .

'Chloe stood with a grimace, flexing her bandaged arm, whispering thanks. And taking my hand gently, she drew me away so the others might not hear.

"'This is a fool's errand, Chloe Sauvage."

"'Then call me a fool, Gabriel de León."

"'I'll call you that and more. Where do you plan to lead this pageant of fuckarsery?"

"'San Michon."

"'San Michon? Have you taken leave of your senses? You're taking these fucking children into the Nordlund? You're *never* going to reach the monastery before wintersdeep sets in. Danton is going to find you, and when he does—"

"'I need you, Gabriel. I told you, it's not by accident we met again. For us to find each other after all these years, in the midst of all this dark . . . you *have* to see the hand of the Almighty at work here, you—"

"'Fucksakes, give it a rest, Chloe. You've been bleating the same tune since Astrid dragged you into that Library seventeen years ago."

'Her scowl darkened. "I wish to God she was here, then. Azzie could always make your pigheaded, dim-witted, prettyboy arse see sense."

'I chuckled at the insults, despite myself. Scratching ruefully at my chin. "Making her husband see sense is the lot of every bride, it seems."

'Chloe's eyes widened. "You're . . . *married?*"

'I lifted my hand to show the silver troth ring on my finger. "Eleven years."

"'Oh, Gabriel," she whispered. ". . . Children?"

'I nodded, eyes shining. "A daughter."

"'Sweet Redeemer." Chloe's blood-slicked hands slipped into my own. "Oh, merciful God in heaven, I'm so happy for you both, Gabe."

'I could see pure joy in her smile then. The kind of joy only the truest of friends feel, to learn their friends have found joy also. Her eyes brimmed with tears. And I remembered what a good heart she had, Chloe Sauvage. Better than mine ever was.

'And then her smile slowly died. Her shoulders slumped, and she looked over her little band, bloodied and alone in the dark. I could see the road ahead in her eyes. The war-torn wastes of the Ossway. The barren hell of Nordlund beyond. The growing sea of darkness in which humanity's light guttered like a candle, soon to be extinguished entirely.

'Chloe hung her head. "I can't ask you to risk all that."

'She released her grip, my tattooed hands falling away from her own.

"'Tell Azzie hello for me. Tell her . . . tell her I'm happy for her." Chloe sniffed and swallowed thickly, damp curls tumbling about freckled cheeks. "Adieu, mon ami."

'And she turned to walk away.

"'. . . Chloe."

'She looked back at me, eyebrow raised. I opened my mouth to speak, not knowing yet what I'd say. And it seemed for a moment that everything stood poised on the edge of a knife. Those moments happen only once or twice in a lifetime. I could see two paths, either side of the blade. One where I helped this old friend of mine. And one where I left her to die.

"'. . . I can ride with you awhile. See you to the Volta, at least."

"'I can't ask you to do that, Gabe."

"'You didn't ask. Which is why I'm offering." I glanced around the ragged company, eyes settling on Dior. "Who am I to stand in the way of divine providence?"

"'But Astrid . . . Your daughter . . ."

"'They'll understand. I'll be back with them soon enough."

'I saw my words sink in, Chloe's chest caving, all the weight she'd been carrying lifted from her shoulders. A sob slipped over her lips, smothered at once by a fierce grin. She threw her arms around my shoulders, so short she had to take a running leap. I tried not to laugh as she squeezed me tight, smooshed her lips to my cheek.

"'You're a good man, Gabriel de León."

"'I'm a bastard, is what I am. Now stop kissing me. You're a nun for fucksakes."

'Chloe released her embrace. But still, she gave my hand one last squeeze, and all the light and life was shining once more in her eyes, just like when we were young. She looked up at the ceiling of that broken tower, tears spilling down her cheeks. And she put her hand to the sevenstar around her throat and whispered, "Almighty God be praised."

'I could see her joy, the relief of faith rewarded, and that faith itself, undimmed by toil or time. And for the briefest moment, I envied her more than anyone I'd ever met.

"'What's her name?"

"'Eh?"

"'Your daughter," Chloe urged. "What's her name?"

'I breathed deep, running my thumb over my knuckles.

"'Patience.'"

✦ XII ✦

TWO GLASSES

'NO,' THE VAMPIRE said.

Gabriel glanced up. 'No?'

'No, de León, this will not do.'

'Will it not?' Gabriel replied, eyebrow rising.

'It will *not*.' Jean-François waved his quill as if vexed. 'When last you mentioned her, this Rennier girl was but a novice sister in the monastery that trained you, and now I learn she became your *wife*? The mother of your child? It is my Empress's will to know the whole of your tale.'

Gabriel reached into his battered britches, fished about under the monster's stare. Finally, he retrieved a tarnished royale from his pocket. 'Here.'

'What is that for?' Jean-François demanded.

'I want you to take this coin to market, and buy me a fuck to give.'

'This is *not* the way stories are told, Silversaint.'

'I know. But I'm hoping the suspense will kill you.'

'You will take us back. Back to the walls of San Michon.'

'Will I?'

The coldblood held up the phial of sanctus between forefinger and thumb. 'You *will*.'

Gabriel stared for a long and silent moment. His jaw twitched, and he gripped the armrests of his chair so hard the wood creaked. It seemed for a second he might rise, might lash out, might let loose the terrible hatred that roiled deep and dark behind his eyes. But Marquis Jean-François of the Blood Chastain was unperturbed.

Gabriel stared hard into the vampire's eyes. Gaze drifting to the phial between those tapered fingertips. The bloodhymn was still sharp in him, but that didn't mean his thirst was sated. One pipe wasn't enough.

It had never been enough, had it?

Truth was, he didn't know if he was ready to go back. Unwilling to dredge up the ghosts of the past. They were hungry too. Locked inside in his head, the door rusted shut from long disuse. If he were to prise it open . . .

'If I'm going back to San Michon,' he finally declared, 'I'll need a drink.'

Jean-François snapped his fingers. The door opened at once, that thrall woman waiting on the threshold. Her gaze was downturned, thin red braids draped across her eyes.

'Your will, Master?'

'Wine,' the vampire commanded. 'The Monét, I think. Bring two glasses.'

The woman met the Dead boy's eyes, a sudden flush rising in her cheeks. She dropped into a low curtsey, long black skirts whispering as she hurried away. Gabriel listened to her retreating down a stone stairwell, glanced towards the now-unlocked door. Faint sounds of life drifted up from the château beneath – tromping feet, a snatch of laughter, a thin, warbling scream. Gabriel counted ten steps from his chair to the door. A bead of sweat trickled between his shoulderblades.

He saw Jean-François was illustrating the company of the Grail, now. Père Rafa in his robes, the wheel about his neck, the priest's warnings echoing in Gabriel's head. He saw Saoirse with her slayerbraids and hunter's stare, the she-lion Phoebe beside her like a red shadow. Bellamy with his rake's cap and easy smile, and at the front, little Chloe Sauvage, with her silversteel sword and freckled cheeks and all the hope in the world shining in her liar's eyes.

The vampire glanced up. 'Ah, splendid . . .'

The thrall stood at the doorway, holding a golden platter. Two crystal goblets sat upon it, alongside a bottle of fine Monét from the Elidaeni vineyards. A vintage like that was rare as silver these nights. An emperor's fortune in dusty green glass.

The thrall placed the two goblets on the table, poured a generous helping into Gabriel's. The wine was red as heartsblood, its perfume a dizzying change from mouldy straw and rusted iron. The second glass stood empty.

Wordlessly, Jean-François held out his hand. The silversaint watched, mouth running dry as the woman sank to her knees beside the monster's chair. Her cheeks were flushed, bosom heaving as she placed her hand in his. Again, Gabriel was struck by the notion that she looked old enough to be the vampire's mother, and his stomach might have soured at the lie of it all were it not for the thought and thrill of what was to come.

The vampire looked to Gabriel as he raised the woman's wrist to his lips.

'Pardon,' he whispered.

The monster bit down. The woman moaned softly as ivory daggers slid through her pale skin and into the supple flesh beyond. For a moment, it seemed all she could do just to breathe, fallen into the spell of those eyes, those lips, those teeth.

The Kiss, they called it – these monsters who wore the skins of men. A pleasure darker than any sin of the flesh, more honeyed than any drug. Gabriel could see the woman was lost now, adrift on a blood-red sea. And awful as it was, a part of him remembered that desire, pounding hot at his temples, down between his legs. He could feel his teeth growing sharp, a needle-bright stab of pain as he pressed his tongue against one canine.

Under her lace choker, he spied the old bite scars at the woman's neck. His blood stirring as he wondered where else she might hide the marks of their hungers. The woman's head sank back, long tresses flowing down her bare shoulders as she pressed her free hand to her breast, lashes fluttering. Jean-François's eyes were still fixed on Gabriel, narrowing slightly as a tight gasp of pleasure escaped his lips.

But then the monster broke his unholy kiss, a thin, ruby string of blood stretching and snapping as he pulled the woman's hand away. Eyes still locked with the silversaint's, the vampire held the thrall's open wrist above the empty glass and the blood spilled, thick, warm, crimson into the crystal. The scent of it filled the room, making Gabriel's breath come quicker, his mouth now dry as tombs. Wanting. *Needing*.

The vampire sliced the tip of his own thumb on his fangs, pressed it to the woman's lips. Her eyes flashed open and she gasped, suckling like a starving babe, one hand pressed between her legs as she drank. When the goblet was full, *drip, drip, drip*, the vampire lifted the woman's wounded wrist. And like a forgetful host, he offered it to Gabriel.

'We could share her? If it please you?'

The woman's eyes flickered to his, chest heaving and fingers strumming as she drank. And Gabriel remembered then – the taste of it, the warmth of it, a dark and perfect joy no smoke could ever match. The thirst reared up inside him, a thrill pulsing from his aching crotch all the way to his tingling fingertips.

And it was all he could do then to hiss through clenched and knife-sharp teeth.

'No. Merci.'

Jean-François smiled, licked the woman's bleeding wrist with a bright red tongue. Easing his thumb from her mouth, the monster spoke, thick and heavy as iron.

'Leave us now, love.'

'. . . Your will, Master,' she whispered, breathless.

The woman rose on trembling legs, steadying herself against the monster's chair. With the wound at her wrist already closing, she sank into a shaking curtsey, and with a final wanton glance to Gabriel, slipped from the room.

The door locked softly behind her.

Jean-François lifted the blood-filled glass. Gabriel watched, fascinated, as the vampire held it against the lanternlight, twisting it this way and that. So red it was almost black. The monster's lips curled in a smile, eyes still on the silversaint's.

'Santé,' Jean-François said, wishing him health.

'Morté,' Gabriel replied, toasting his death.

The pair drank, the vampire taking one slow mouthful, Gabriel downing his entire glass in a single draught. Jean-François sighed, sucking the plump swell of his lower lip and biting gently. Gabriel reached for the bottle and refilled his glass.

'So,' Jean-François murmured, smoothing his waistcoat. 'You were a fifteen-year-old boy, de León. A frailblooded Nordling brat, dragged from the squalid mud of Lorson to the impregnable walls of San Michon. They made a lion of you. They made a legend. A foe even the Forever King learned to fear. How?'

Gabriel lifted the goblet to his lips, downed it with a long gulp. A trickle of wine spilled down his chin, and as he wiped it away, he looked at the wreath of skulls tattooed atop his right hand. Those eight letters etched across his fingers.

PATIENCE

'They didn't make a lion of me, coldblood,' he answered. 'Like my mama said, the lion was always in my blood.'

He closed his hand slowly, and sighed.

'They just helped me turn it loose.'

Book Three

BLOOD AND SILVER

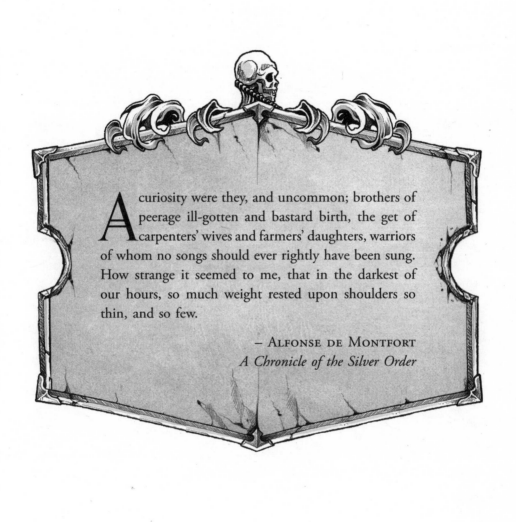

A curiosity were they, and uncommon; brothers of peerage ill-gotten and bastard birth, the get of carpenters' wives and farmers' daughters, warriors of whom no songs should ever rightly have been sung. How strange it seemed to me, that in the darkest of our hours, so much weight rested upon shoulders so thin, and so few.

– Alfonse de Montfort
A Chronicle of the Silver Order

✦ I ✦

AUSPICIOUS BEGINNINGS

'HALF A YEAR had passed since I was sworn as an initiate of the Silver Order, and every day of it, Frère Greyhand had worked me to the fucking bone.

'As Aaron de Coste had promised, the Gauntlet was the fire in which I was to be forged, or melted to slag. The dance was different every day, and for months on end, I was put to the test by my master, or by ingenious devices built by the Brothers of the Hearth.

'There was the "Thorned Men" – a knot of ever-moving training dummies that could strike you back when you hit them. "The Thresher" was a rotating series of oaken poles, thirty feet off the stone – one slip during a spar meant you'd be nursing broken bones for the rest of the day. The shifting obstacle course called "the Scar", the speed run named "the Scythe" – all designed to make us harder. Faster. Stronger.

'The sanctus they gave me to smoke every evemass was awaking the beast inside me: the strength, the reflexes, the sharpening of my paleblood senses. I felt like a blade that had been kept in a cold cellar, finally unsheathed in the sun. And yet, I knew I wasn't as sharp as the other boys around me, and never would be.

'Frère Greyhand made no mention of my frailblood heritage after the Trial of the Blood, but the taunting from Aaron and his cronies was reminder enough. Initiates at San Michon came and went, stopping days or weeks, then returning to the Hunt with their masters. Many were nobleborn, which made a kind of sense – highbloods usually liked to feed among high society. But in the end, what that meant for me was a constant stream of stuck-up tossers who looked down on me for my birth *and* my blood. Arseholes, all. I swear, there were more pricks in those Barracks than at a hedgehog's bachelor feast.

'When he could, Aaron kept company with a boy called de Séverin – son of an Elidaeni baronne. De Séverin had dark eyes and pouting lips; his face reminded me of a dead fish's, truth told. Aaron's other crony was a handsome nobleson, brown of hair and blue of eye. There was a cruelty to his stare – I reckoned the servants in his father's house would've trod carefully around the heir apparent. His name was Mid Philippe.'

Jean-François blinked. '*Mid* Philippe?'

'Emperor Alexandre's father, Philippe IV, sat upon the Fivefold Throne for twenty years. Some parents name their brats for the famed, in the hope that fame rubs off. There were *three* Philippes among the initiates. We nick-named the smallest Lil, the tallest Big, and the one between, Mid.'

'Ingenious, de León.'

'There are worse nicknames teenage boys can conjure, believe me. And I heard every one. Of the two dozen initiates I met over those six months, there were only a couple who didn't treat me like outright shite. Theo Petit, the big sandy-haired lad who'd defended me from Aaron when I first arrived at San Michon, and a wiry Ossian boy named Fincher. Finch had a face like a dropped pie and mismatched eyes, one green and one blue. Didn't bother me much, but it made the other lads nervous.'

'Why?' Jean-François asked.

'Superstition. Some folk believe a blemish like that marks you as faekin. That someone back in your famille line was fucking with the wealdfolk. But I liked Fincher. He was of Voss blood, hard as nails. And he slept with a carving fork under his pillow. Even took it in the bath. Mad as a bucket of wet cats, he was.'

'Why a carving fork?'

'I asked the same. "Gift from me grammy afore she died," he told me, twirling it between his fingers. "Real silver, boyo."'

'But even Finch and Theo weren't really my *friends*. They just didn't outright fuck with me. Every other initiate in the monastery took the same road as de Coste. "Peasant". "Boylover". "Little Kitten". These were the names they called me, Aaron worst of the lot. Porridge in my boots. Shit in my bed. All my life I'd been no one special, and even there, among these chosen of God, it seemed I'd been relegated to the bottom of the pile for what I was. The name itself spoke of weakness.'

'*Frailblood.*'

Jean-François nodded. 'Hardly an auspicious beginning, de León.'

'It was nothing to write home about, to be sure. So, even though I wondered about my true father, who he was and how he'd known my mama,

I didn't write home at all. My baby sister Celene sent me a letter every other month, keeping me informed of all that went on at home in Lorson. My little hellion sounded like she was getting up to no good, but I wasn't in a position to change any of it. I had my own shite to deal with. So, I ignored her.'

Gabriel shook his head.

'Shames me to think about it now. But I was young. Young and foolish.'

'Can it really be true, though? The Black Lion, hero of Augustin, wielder of the Mad Blade and slayer of the Forever King himself . . . a water-blooded wretch?'

'Some people are born lucky, coldblood. And some people make their own.'

'Surely there was somewhere in San Michon you exceeded expectations?'

'Not at first. I was good with a sword. But only because Papa had drilled me hard as a lad. I liked being in the Gauntlet. I *loved* learning the hymn of blades Greyhand showed us. Steel never judged me, see. Steel was mother. Steel was father. Steel was friend. But I never walked into anything and found I was simply *good* at it. The only way I shone at anything in my life was being too much of a stubborn bastard to quit.'

'You *are* quite the bastard, de León, I shall grant you that.'

'I don't like to lose, coldblood.'

'The sin of pride serves you well, then.'

'See, I never understood that. Why pride is looked on as an evil. You work hard at something you're not born good at? Damn right you should be fucking proud. There's nothing comes of quitting besides the knowledge you didn't finish.'

Gabriel shook his head.

'It's only in faerie tales that everything works out for the best with a magik spell or a prince's kiss. It's only in storybooks some little bastard picks up a sword and wields it like he was born to it. The rest of us? We have to work our *arses* off. And we might not ever taste triumph, but at least we dared to fail. We stand apart from those cowards whispering on the sidelines about how the strong did stumble, while never daring to set foot in the ring themselves. Victors are just folk who were never satisfied being vanquished. The only thing worse than finishing last is not beginning at all. And *fuck* finishing last.'

The vampire glanced to the night just outside the window, the empire rising beyond. 'I'd have thought your kind accustomed to it by now, de León.'

'Touché.'

'Merci.'

'Smartarse.'

'So after six months, you were not yet a full-fledged 'saint of the Order?'

'Not even close. I needed to complete two more trials before I'd even finish the bare bones of my aegis.' Gabriel ran his fingertips up his left arm, over the silver tattoos. 'This arm got inked after the Trial of the Hunt – presuming you survived. Your other arm would be filled after you'd killed your first horror with your own sword. The Trial of the Blade.'

'What then, had you earned in the Trial of the Blood?'

Gabriel pulled down the neck of his tunic, showing a hint of the roaring lion on his chest.

'That looks like it was painful,' the vampire mused.

'Didn't tickle. But as usual, I'd no idea what I was in for the day I got it.' Gabriel shook his head, smiling faintly. 'I was so excited the night before, I couldn't sleep. The inkwork on Greyhand and Abbot Khalid and the other silversaints had always held a fascination for me. But this was to be the first part of my aegis. The first true sign I actually *belonged* there.

'As I marched into the great Cathedral of San Michon on findi morn, I saw four figures awaiting me at the altar, bathed in soft light and choirsong. Even beneath her veil, I recognized the scarred, dour face of Charlotte, Prioress of the Silver Sorority. She and the sister beside her wore black habits, faces daubed white, red sevenstars painted over their eyes. But the other two figures wore the dove-white robes of novices. The first was short, green-eyed and freckled, a rogue curl of mouse brown escaped from the edge of her coif.'

'Your Chloe Sauvage, I presume?' Jean-François asked.

Gabriel nodded.

'And looking at the girl beside her, I saw dark smoky lashes, a raised eyebrow, a beauty spot beside quirked lips. I realized this was the sisternovice I'd met in the stables the day I chose my horse. The same who'd inked my palm at my first mass.'

'Astrid Rennier,' the vampire said.

'"Remove your tunic and lay upon the altar, Initiate," Prioress Charlotte commanded.

'I did as I was told. Sisternovice Chloe bound me down with leather straps, shiny steel buckles, and I winced at the chill of the spirits she poured on my skin. These four were holy women of the Silver Priory, brides or betrothed of God Himself, and I dared not even glance at them. Instead,

I looked to the statue of the Redeemer above. But still, I could feel Sisternovice Astrid beside me, smell the rosewater in her hair, hear the soft whisper of her breath as she ran a straight razor over the muscles of my chest.

'There was something impossibly intimate about it. Even with other eyes upon us. Her touch was gentle as feathers, the press of her fingertips to my skin had goosebumps crawling over every inch of me. My heart was all a-gallop. And despite my best efforts, I found my blood rushing to a place I'd absolutely *no* desire for it to be.'

Gabriel chuckled to himself.

'You ever get an erection in front of a pack of nuns, coldblood?'

'Not that I can recall, no.' Jean-François frowned slightly. 'Although admittedly, I've never found myself in need of one where nuns are concerned.'

'Well, it's not ideal. To their credit, if any of the sisters noticed, they were too polite to call attentions. I thought perhaps the thrill of the sister-novice's touch would fade once Prioress Charlotte began stabbing those needles into my skin. But as I saw Astrid take up a long silver lance, I realized she herself was to do my inking.

'"Blessed Michon," she prayed, "First of the Martyrs, heed this prayer in blood and silver. We anoint this flesh in your name, and offer this boy in your service. May all heaven's host bear witness, and all hell's legion tremble. Sweet Mothermaid, give me patience. Great Redeemer, give me strength. Almighty Father, give me sight."

'"Véris," the other sisters replied.'

Gabriel shook his head, sighing soft.

'The room was filled with choirsong, yet all was silence. We were surrounded by sisters of the Priory, and somehow, completely alone. There was only pain between me and that girl then. Pain and promise. Her breath was cool on my bare and bleeding skin. Her hands warm as firelight as she hurt me, again and again.

'I'd thought my sevenstar was painful, but it was a honeyed bliss compared to this. Thirteen hours I lay on that altar, bathed in candlelight and pain from the hands of that strange and beautiful girl. It was agony. It was euphoria. And somewhere in the middle of it, both became interlinked. I couldn't bear another moment. I never wanted it to end. I wanted her to stop, and I wanted her to keep hurting me, some dam of pressure breaking loose inside. Pain had been punishment when I was a boy. But now it had become reward. Bliss in torment. Salvation in suffering.

'I didn't realize I was crying until it ended. And Sisternovice Chloe poured

a measure of what felt like freezing fire over my bleeding skin, and Astrid
Rennier spoke like an angel into my ear.

'"This is the hand,
'"That wields the flame,
'"That lights the way,
'"And turns the dark,
'"To silver."'

The Last Silversaint shrugged. 'And then it was done.'

Jean-François continued writing in his tome, though his eyes flickered
to Gabriel's small and secret smile. 'The design is of some importance?'

Gabriel blinked hard, as if coming back to himself. And slowly, he nodded.

'The chestpiece of the aegis signifies a silversaint's bloodline. De Coste
had that wreath of roses and snakes, which along with his ability to crawl
right on my tits marked him as the Blood of Ilon. Theo and Abbot Khalid
both wore the broken shield and roaring bear of the Dyvok. The wolves on
Greyhand's chest were for the Blood of Chastain, which explained his affinity
with Archer. I'd often thought that falcon could understand when he spoke
to it. Turns out, I wasn't wrong.'

'And that is why you wear the lion,' the historian smiled. 'Your dear
mama.'

'I'd no vampire bloodline to call my own. I knew nothing of my father,
nor what my mama had been to him. His lover? His victim? His slave? But
whatever uncertainty I had about the vampire who'd sired me, I knew at
least I was hers. So I clung to that truth she'd given me as a boy. *One day
as a lion is worth ten thousand as a lamb*. I wore that ink like armour. I
worked harder than I'd ever worked in my fucking life, no matter what shit
the other boys threw. Not just in the Gauntlet, either. We were expected to
master all manner of knowledge – the geography of the empire, catechisms
of the One Faith, and tactics of great battles. The banes of the horrors we
hunted, the preparation of chymical weapons – black ignis, silver caustic,
hellspark, and sanctus most important of all.

'I'd never been much for schooling. Seraph Talon gave us lessons in the
Great Library or Armoury, aided as ever by his dutiful assistant, Aoife. The
good sister was a patient tutor, and no slouch when it came to the arte of
chymistrie. But Talon was a bastard, plain and simple. That damned ashwood
switch of his tasted my palms more times than I can remember. My every
mistake was met with a bloody thrashing and a creative curse about the shite

in my veins or my mother's virtue. But his punishments only spurred me on.

'I cut gashes into my heel to remember the ounces of brimstone in a one-pound silverbomb. Each morning, I'd prick the measure of shadeberry for a jigger of angelgrace or the amount of yellowwater in a charge of black ignis into my fingertips with my sword. Every day for four weeks, I plucked hairs to etch the number of hollyroot drops in a dose of sanctus into my mind. Anything, *everything* I could do to remember.'

'You plucked hairs from your head to remember a recipe?'

'Not my head.'

The historian glanced down at the silversaint's crotch, one eyebrow raised. Gabriel nodded. 'Every day for four weeks.'

'How many hollyroot drops are in a dose of sanctus?'

'Sixteen,' Gabriel answered immediately.

'Good God Almighty, de León.'

'I told you, coldblood. Some people are born lucky. And some people make their own. I'd had nothing ever handed to me, save this curse in my veins. But this was my life now. And if I were to spend it among these hunters in the dark, then I'd damned well be the best of them, or die trying. And my opportunity for the latter finally arrived, after half a year of blood and sweat and silvered ink.

'A frail summer had been and gone at San Michon, and winter's chill was in the air. I was training at the Thorned Men, nursing a split lip and cracked cheekbone. Master Greyhand was atop the Thresher, wailing away on Aaron. It was around noonbells when the Gauntlet doors opened wide and Abbot Khalid strode into the training ground.

'I was in awe of Khalid. Greyhand was a swordsman both sharp and swift, but the abbot was a force of nature. The Blood Dyvok flowed in his veins as in Theo's, and I'd seen him at training, wielding twin two-handed swords, one in each grip. All palebloods were strong, but Khalid was fucking terrifying.

'He strode into the sevenstar circle, and Greyhand and Aaron leapt down from the Thresher. All three of us bowed in respect as Khalid's kohled green eyes met our master's.

'"The town of Skyefall has been struck by malady. A wasting sickness none can explain. Mayhaps witchery. A fae curse, or cultists of the fallen. For my part, I smell a coldblood's work. But regardless, our Emperor Alexandre demands answers. Go with God and Martyrs to seek the truth of it."

'Greyhand made the sign of the wheel. "By the Blood."

'Khalid nodded, then glanced to me. "Do us proud, Little Lion."

'Archer wheeled through the sky above, his shrill call piercing the air. My heart swelled in my chest. After six months of tireless work, I'd finally been deemed worthy to leave San Michon. De Coste's proud jaw was set. As Khalid spun on his heel, Master Greyhand turned to us. And though his features were stone as always, I thought I caught a hint of a smile in his voice.

"'At last, lads," he said. "We Hunt."'

II

THE FIVE LAWS

'GREYHAND'S BLADE SCYTHED towards my throat, glinting red in the firelight. With a gasp, I turned it aside, feeling the strength of his blow jar my arm as he sent me tumbling.

'"Initiate de Coste," he said. "When stalking vampires, what is Law the First?"

'Aaron stepped aside from Greyhand's strike, countered with a stab of his own. Our master met de Coste's thrust, locking the lad up and waiting for his answer.

'We'd been travelling two weeks through Nordlund, and the mining town of Skyefall was but a day's ride away. We'd camped in the foothills below it, just south of the Velde River. And as was our nightly ritual, before we ate, we earned our fucking dinner.

'"Law the First," Aaron panted. "*The dead cannot kill the Dead.*"

'"Good. What does it mean?"

'"We can't kill coldbloods if we're killed ourselves, Master."

'Greyhand's boot collided with the boy's chest, sent him flying back into the corpse of a nearby fir. De Coste struck the trunk hard enough to crack the roots, and the whole tree tilted like a two-pint drunkard. Twirling his blade, Greyhand spoke as if out for a stroll on prièdi.

'"Indeed. Of all the prey that silversaints stalk, coldbloods are perhaps the most dangerous. You must be cunning and cautious in pursuit of the Dead. They surely didn't survive for centuries by being less so. Mistake not stupidity for courage. Do not be fear's slave, but its friend. Look. Think. Then act."

'"Don't be a dumb fuck," I murmured.

'Greyhand parried Aaron's charge, smashed his blade aside, and punched

him full in the face, sending the lordling onto his backside. Turning, he
stalked across the frozen ground back towards me. "Since you're feeling
talkative, de León, recite Law the Second."

'I ducked below the sweep of his blade, skipped backwards towards the
fire. "*Dead tongues heeded are Dead tongues tasted*, Master."

"'And what does that mean?"

"'Listen to nothing they say."

'Greyhand feinted, and like a fool, I took the bait. Swift as a serpent, he
struck at my swordarm, opening up my bicep to the bone. I cried out, felt
my legs swept out from under me, crashing onto the muddy ground.

"'Very good, Little Lion," Greyhand said. "All highbloods can bend the
minds of men. Their gaze can mesmerize, their words are iron-clad commands
to the weak-willed. Especially the Blood Ilon. But moreover, their currency
is deceit. Coldbloods are foxes and serpents all. Listen not to a *word* these
bastards hiss, lest you find yourself their meal."

'I rose from the ground and Greyhand met my strike, pale green eyes
flashing. We exchanged a flurry of blows, firelight dancing on steel. Fast as
a hummingfly's wings, Greyhand buried his pommel into my stomach so
hard I almost puked. And with a savage uppercut from his hilt, I was sent
flying in a spray of blood and spit.

"'Now, young Lord de Coste. Law the Third?"

'Aaron dodged Greyhand's strike, parried another. "*The Dead run quick,*
Master."

"'I know you can speak by rote, boy. What do you *think*?"

'Aaron struck back, opening up a thin line of red along Greyhand's chest.
"Our enemy runs quick." The lordling twirled his blade in triumph. "Quicker
than *we* do."

"'Excellent." Greyhand ran his fingers through his blood and smiled.
"Mark this one well, Initiates. Your enemy is stronger than you are. Faster.
More resilient. A single wretched is a match for a dozen men. An ancien
highblood can break your bones with a touch, and move fast as winter wind.
You have weapons and training to even the scale. But underestimate this foe,
and you *die*."

'Again, Greyhand lunged, but this time, twice as fast and sure. Aaron
moved too slow, and with expression unchanged, Greyhand thrust his sword
through the lordling's belly and right out through his back. Aaron gasped
as Greyhand *twisted* the blade loose and dropped him groaning to the floor.

"'Law the Fourth," Greyhand said, turning to me. "*The Dead feel as beasts,
look as men, die as devils*. What does it mean?"

'I raised my sword in my off-hand, heart hammering. "They're . . . complicated."

'Greyhand came at me like a thunderbolt. I recognized his patterns from the Gauntlet, countering with my own. I came close to spitting the bastard, too. But then he smashed my blade aside and drove his sword through me so hard I was pinned to the tree behind me. Moaning in agony, I clutched the five feet of steel now skewered through my chest as Greyhand wandered back to the fire to check on dinner.

'"Complicated, oui," he mused, stirring the steaming pot. "But in many ways, coldbloods are at root, the same. Oh, they may act as men. But you need only starve one for a night or two to discover what lies under the silken finery and cherry lips. A mortal man will fight with all he has to protect his famille. But I swear by Almighty God and all the host of heaven, you've not seen true fury until you've witnessed the jealous rage with which these devils fight to preserve their own lives."

'Aaron had picked himself up, bloody drool leaking from his mouth. His face was paler than usual, blonde hair plastered to red cheeks. But Greyhand held up a hand.

'"Nono, it's almost ready. Help de León."

'De Coste gave a weary nod. Thrusting his training blade into the muddy ground, he trudged around the fire to assist me. I had both bloodied hands wrapped around Greyhand's sword, trying to drag it free from the tree he'd spitted me upon.

'"You forgot Law the F-fifth, Master," I groaned.

'Greyhand took a sip from his iron ladle, smacked his lips. "Needs salt."

'Aaron took hold of the sword embedded in my chest, giving me a sadistic smile. *"Even the Dead have laws."*

'"*Even the Dead have laws,*" Greyhand nodded, sprinkling the pot with a fingerful of seasoning. "This is the simplest, Initiates, and most comforting. For even though these monsters are spat straight from hell's maw, they are still governed by *rules*. They can cross no rivers save at bridges, nor enter a dwelling without invitation. They cannot set foot upon sanctified ground, nor bear the sight of sacred icons wielded by a person of pure faith. They have *weaknesses*, is the point. Weaknesses you will learn to exploit."

'I tried not to cry out as de Coste wrenched the blade loose. Falling to my knees, I pressed hard to staunch the blood, the chest wound bubbling as I breathed.

'"De León, being headstrong isn't a boon in combat, it just means you're easy to fake," Greyhand declared. "This is swordplay, not loveplay. Don't go where your partner leads you, go where you need to be."

"'Oui, Master,'" I groaned, dragging my knuckles across my bloody chin.

"'De Coste, your feint announces its approach from two provinces over, and you're too cocky by half. Don't start celebrating 'til your quarry is in the damned ground.'"

"'Understood, Master,'" the lordling said, spitting more red.

"'Good. Now come eat while it's hot.'"

Jean-François was staring at Gabriel, his expression somewhere between amusement and disbelief. '*This* was how your master trained you in blade-work?'

Gabriel shrugged. 'It wasn't like he was doing any permanent damage. We were palebloods, and our sparring blades were ordinary steel. The flesh wounds would be gone in an hour. Even the worst of it would heal by dawn. But the *pain*, that was real. You want to teach someone a lesson about keeping their guard high, stab them in the baps a few times, they'll get the message.

'Bruised and bloodied, we settled down around the fire. Greyhand said the Godthanks as always, and I served the meal while Archer watched from the branches above. Dinner was mushroom ragout, one of our master's favourites. He wasn't the finest cook in the empire, but all I could taste was my own blood anyway.

'The brief summer was done, and winter's bite was in the wind. I could barely recall the springs of my youth, all the world cloaked in flowers. I remembered my sister Amélie weaving wreaths for Mama's hair when we were children. Celene and I running in green fields. But snow fell six months of the year now, and all the land seemed soaked in gloom and the smell of brimstone. Miserable leaves clung to the branches of failing trees, slowly being overgrown with a new luminous fungus called maryswort. The chill cut to the bone. The river's song was distant, muffled, and a thought struck me as we ate, brought on by Greyhand's talk of Law the Fifth.

"'Master? What happens when the rivers freeze?"

'De Coste scoffed, holding his wounded belly. "Aside from the obvious?"

"'Must you be a sour-tongued prick all your life? I'm talking about the armies of the Forever King. If coldbloods can't cross running water, but rivers freeze . . ."

"'You've the truth of it, Little Lion," Greyhand said. "Wintersdeep is not our friend. In summer, the Emperor's generals can guard bridges against the Forever King's host. Stop him crossing, or at least force a battle of their choosing. But when the freeze sets in again . . ."

'"Voss can cross wherever he likes," I murmured.

'"So we fear," Greyhand nodded, stirring his bowl.

'"How long until he marches?"

'"We know not. Scouting in those freezing wilds is difficult, but we've had no word out of Talhost in months. The region is surely a wasteland by now. The Forever King likely waits in Vellene upon his corpse throne for the freeze to begin, yet it's only a matter of time before he pushes east to feed his legion. But still, we have advantage." Greyhand nodded to the snowcapped peaks above. "There are only two places he can strike, after all."

'I looked to the dark silhouettes of the mountain range around us, listening to the wind howl among its reaches. In times past, that great spine of granite marked the edge of Nordish civilization, and the beginning of the untamed lands of Talhost to the west. Hence its name: the Godsend. Each mountain in the range was named for an angel of the heavenly host. The peak above us was Eirene, Angel of Hope. The range stretched the entire northwest edge of the Nordlund, and there were only two natural gateways into the east. Two choke points guarded by two of the mightiest fortresses in the realm.

'"Avinbourg in the north," de Coste murmured. "Or Charinfel in the south."

'Greyhand nodded. "Those two cityforts have guarded the Nordlund's flank since the Wars of the Faith. And Voss must take one of them if he wishes to take the empire. We know not which he'll strike, but one thing is certain. When the rivers freeze, his hammer falls."

'Greyhand looked to the darkened skies, his mood growing fey.

'"Is it true what you told me, Master?" I asked. "About the attack on Vellene?"

'"'Tis true," Greyhand nodded, his voice grim. "Voss took the city and slaughtered all within the walls. It's said one of his heirs, the beast Danton, murdered every virgin maid in Vellene with his own hand. The dark twins Alba and Alene set the grand cathedral ablaze with a thousand or more people inside, murdering anyone who fled the flames. And Fabién's youngest daughter, Laure, gathered all the newborn babes in Vellene, filled the fountain in the market square with their blood, and *bathed* in it."

'My stomach did a slow, sickening turn inside me.

'"Laure Voss," Aaron murmured. "The Wraith in Red."

'"An abomination made flesh," Greyhand spat. "But it's not for their brutality that the Forever King's brood should be feared. Nor the legend that Fabién himself cannot be slain by any warrior of woman born. No, the true reason to fear Voss is his ambition. In nights before daysdeath, to beget a wretched was considered an embarrassment among kith society. But it was Voss who first thought to forge the wretched's growing numbers into an army. It was Voss who foresaw a way vampires might conquer this empire."

'Greyhand set aside his bowl, stared up into black skies.

'"But that's not the darkest part of it, lads. Kith are hateful and solitary creatures. Territorial. Vindictive. But the Voss are *famille*. Fabién has seven highblood descendants that we know of. And though creatures so soulless as they are incapable of true love, it *can* be said of all the world, Voss's children hate each other the least. Their unholy father calls them the Princes of Forever. Abbot Khalid says they are the deadliest creatures that walk on God's own earth. But no matter the name by which you call them, strike at one, you strike at seven. And their unholy father besides."

'Greyhand looked among us again, his voice as cold as stone.

'"So *we* will have to kill them all."'

III

HUNTERS AND PREY

'THE TOWN OF Skyefall crouched on a hillside of black stone, wreathed in grey mist. As wealthy as a priest after the collection plate has been passed around, and as strange as the idea that the creator of heaven and earth needs the money in the first place. For a boy who'd grown up in a mud puddle like Lorson, it seemed the grandest metropolis. But riding into its shadow on that cold winter day, I'd no notion of the horrors we'd find there.

'Skyefall's fortune had been made in silver. Only eleven months had passed since the Forever King decimated Vellene, and back in those days, it still wasn't well known just how important that noble metal would be in future nights. Rumour had begun spreading, of course, dribbled from the lips of drunken prophets or screamed by wandering lunatics. But the gentry of Skyefall paid little heed to hearsay about Dead armies massing to the west, or coldbloods stalking freely along the hamlet roads.

'They were rich. God had clearly blessed them. And that was enough.

'Skyefall's streets were cobbled, her cathedral marbled and gilt. The architecture was baroque and gothic – all grand spires and stairways leading who knew where. But as our company plodded through her gates, I felt a shadow on that town. She was built on a granite slope, winding roads and grey buildings looming on all sides. Fog hung heavy in her streets, and her walls were decorated with reliefs of flowers that hadn't grown since the sunlight failed. In the town square stood a crow-pecked gibbet with a rotting skeleton inside – WITCH, the sign assured us. Streetwalkers with scabbed knees stood at lonely alley mouths, and miners with filthied faces staggered through the streets, sullen and drunk.

'The air hung chill. Damp. And far too quiet.

'I knew not what, but something in this place felt *wrong*.

'Justice was ever a rock beneath me, his head held high as he steamed and stomped. But as we rode up Skyefall's twisting streets, the roads grew too narrow and the stairs too treacherous. Eventually, we were forced to leave our mounts behind at a communal stable and continue on foot through the haze, up towards the noble quarter above the town.

'Greyhand marched in front, de Coste came next, and me last of all, my silver heels ringing on the stones. Local folk watched as we passed by their doors and windows, some with awe, some with fear. And yet . . .

'"They all stare at us, Master," I murmured.

'"Such is the curse in our veins," Greyhand replied. "And it shall only deepen as you grow older. Folk are drawn to the dark within us, Little Lion, just as they are drawn to the coldbloods who made us." He looked at me sidelong. "Surely you noticed it, even as a boy?"

'I thought of the girls in my village then. Their eyes following as I passed by. Their kisses given so freely. But had they been given to me? Or this thing inside me?

'"Oui," I muttered. "Perhaps."

'"As we grow older, so too do we sink deeper into our curse and the power it gifts us." Greyhand nodded to the townsfolk. "Yet always, regular folk will smell something of the predator beneath your skin, de León. Some shall hate you for it. Others adore you. None will ignore you. A wolf cannot long hide among sheep. But Almighty God knows who we *truly* are. And our service to His Holy Church shall be rewarded in the kingdom of heaven."

'I took comfort in that. Buoyed by the notion that, though I was accursed, though I still didn't truly understand what I was or was becoming, all this was the will of the Almighty above. And through him, I would find salvation.

'"Véris," Aaron and I replied, making the sign of the wheel.

'Our master strode over a long, cobbled bridge and onto an avenue of fine estates. Lanterns on wrought iron posts lit up the fog about us. The houses we passed seemed like strangers' faces, their windows, sightless eyes.

'"When we arrive, say nothing," Greyhand warned. "If there is a coldblood at work in this place, some of these townsfolk may be thralls. Mortal servants of the enemy."

'I blinked at that. "You mean people willingly serve these devils?"

'"Cows," Aaron growled. "Cows praying for the night they might become butchers."

'"But why would folk submit to such devilry?" I wondered. "Coldbloods can't choose who they turn. It's not as if immortality can be offered as a reward."

'Greyhand scowled. "It might surprise you, de León, what some folk would risk for even a *chance* to live forever. Coldbloods truck in temptation. Their power is in darkness. Their power is in fear. But most of all, their power is in desire. Drinking the blood of ancien can slow mortal ageing, and undo wounds that would send any man to his grave. But moreover, the act itself is addictive. Drink from the same vampire on three separate nights, and you will be enthralled. Helpless to resist its commands. In every sense, a slave." He patted the pipe in his pocket. "Hence we smoke a distillation of it, rather than drink it."

'We came to a halt outside the walls of a grand estate. Archer circled in sullen skies above, keeping a watchful eye on his master. The frère pulled down his high collar and breathed deep. "This town reeks of sin."

'I watched my master from the corner of my eye. Though Greyhand was dour and cruel, still I'd grown to admire him over the last seven months. He beat his back bloody at prayer every night. He read to us from the Testaments for an hour every morn. His devotion was a beacon, his faith a bright comfort. And though I was frailblood, he didn't judge me for it. He was as like to a father as I'd ever known, and I wanted to make him proud.

'De Coste rang an iron bell at the gate. *Him*, I admired far less. I had to admit he worked hard – even with his talk of San Michon not making a difference, Aaron still seemed to *believe* in what we were doing. And yet, he treated me like common shite. In seven months, he'd not called me by my name once.

'Hard worker or no, I hated his fucking guts.

'From the look, the house before us was the grandest in Skyefall. The grounds might once have been bright with greenery, but now, only fungus grew at the feet of withered fruit trees. A magnificent mansion loomed in the estate's heart, all graven pillars and shuttered windows. Fog hung heavy on the grounds.

'A short fellow in a fine coat and powdered wig strode through the mist towards us, lantern in hand. He stopped behind the gate, looked us over.

'"This is the house of Alane de Blanchet, Alderman of Skyefall?" Greyhand asked.

'"I am his humble servant. Who might you be, monsieur?"

'Greyhand took out his vellum scroll. The servant's eyes widened as he saw that blob of blood-red wax, embossed with a unicorn and five crossed swords: the seal of Alexandre III, Benefactor of the Order of San Michon, Emperor of the Realm and Chosen of God Himself.

'"My name is Frère Greyhand. And I will speak to your master."

'Five minutes later, we stood in a grand parlour, holding glasses of choc-olat liqueur. The walls were decorated with fine art, and an ornate suit of plate armour stood guard over a grand shelf of books. De Coste looked perfectly at ease. Unimpressed, even. But I'd never seen wealth like this in my life. This man's ashtrays could have fed ma famille for a year.

'Greyhand had unlaced his collar, removed his travel-worn tricorn. As ever, I was struck by how cold our master's features were. I fancied if I touched his face, he'd feel not like flesh, but stone. Still, I watched him like a hawk, soaking in all he did and said. *This* was the Hunt, I realized. And more than anything, I wanted to be a hunter.

'"Initiate de Coste," he murmured. "When the master of the house arrives, I want you ready to use the gifts of your blood. If tempers flare, keep them dampened. If good cheer is required, provide it."

'"By the Blood, Master."

'"Initiate de León . . ." Greyhand glanced at me then. My heart sinking as I realized a frailblood had nothing special to offer here. "Don't touch anything."

'The parlour door opened, and a portly man entered with sparse ceremony. He was in his early forties, well fed and well heeled, an ornate green alder-man's sash across his chest. But despite the noble fashion of the time, he wore no wig. His hair was dishevelled, tied back in a thin, greying tail. He had the eyes of a man who had forgotten what sleep tastes like, his shoulders bent by some hidden weight.

'Behind him came another gent, a little younger. He wore black vestments and a stiff red collar, signifying the cut throat of the Redeemer. Thick dark hair was cut in a short bowl, and the sigil of the wheel hung about his neck. Skyefall's parish priest, I guessed.

'Our master removed his gloves, offered his hand. "M. de Blanchet, I am Frère Greyhand, brother of the Silver Order of San Michon."

'As the alderman took his grip, Greyhand pressed his tattooed palm atop the man's hand. *Touching him with the silver*, I realized. *Testing him for corruption.*

'"The pleasure is mine, Frère," the alderman said, his voice thin as paper.

'"These are my apprentices," Greyhand nodded. "De Coste and de León. We are here by imperial command to investigate rumour of a malady among the godly people of Skyefall."

'"Thank the Mothermaid," the priest breathed.

'"It is true, then? This town is afflicted?"

"'This town is *accursed*, Frère," the alderman spat. "A curse that has already plucked the brightest flowers from our garden. And now, threatens all we have left in this world."

The priest placed a comforting hand on the alderman's shoulder. "M. de Blanchet's wife, Claudette, is taken ill with the sickness. And his son . . ."

'De Blanchet broke, as if his face were splitting at the seams. "My dear Claude . . ."

"'Have strength, M. de Blanchet," the priest counselled.

"'Have I not shown the strength of titans, Lafitte?" he snapped, pushing the priest's hand away. "The strength a father must conjure to put his only son in the ground?"

'De Blanchet slumped on a velvet longue, head low. Greyhand turned on the young priest, cold green eyes flickering to the silver wheel about his neck. "Your name is Lafitte?"

"'Oui, Frère. By grace of God and High Pontifex Benét, I am priest of Skyefall."

"'How long has your parish suffered this malady, Father?"

"'Young Claude passed just before the feast of San Guillaume. Almost two months ago." Lafitte made the sign of the wheel. "Precious child. He was only ten years old."

"'He was first to die?"

"'But not the last. At least a dozen of the town's finest have fallen since. And I hear rumour from the poorer quarter. A wasting sickness sweeping the riverside." The young priest pressed his lips thin. "I hear other whispers also. Of folk gone missing in the night. Of witchery and shadows. I fear this town *is* accursed, good Frère."

"'And now Mme de Blanchet is afflicted?"

"'As if heaven has not tested me enough," the alderman whispered.

"'Take us to her," Greyhand ordered.

'De Blanchet and Père Lafitte led us up a winding stairwell in the estate's heart, and though I tried to pay heed only to Greyhand, the opulence of that place struck me hard. Famine had cut the Nordlund to ribbons in the years after daysdeath. Whole communities had been destroyed, cities flooded with farmers and vintners and the like – folks whose livelihoods had wilted and rotted when the sun failed. It was only Empress Isabella's request for her husband to open the imperial granaries that had saved the people in those years before we found our new normal. Through it all, this man had lived like a lord, surrounded by objets d'art and polished mahogany and grand rows of unread books.

'But for all his wealth, it hadn't been enough to save his son.

'We arrived at double doors, and de Blanchet hesitated. "My wife is not . . . properly attired for company."

'"We are servants of God, M. de Blanchet," Aaron replied. "*Have no fear.*"

'I heard the inflection in de Coste's voice, saw a predator's gleam in his pale blue eyes – the gift of the Blood Ilon. The Ilon were known as *the Whispers* among kith society, and their ability to influence the emotions of others was unparalleled. Aaron had inherited the same from his vampire father, and as he spoke, de Blanchet's face slackened. With a murmur of assent, the alderman pushed through the doorway, and with a nod to de Coste, Greyhand followed, with me on his heels.

'A roaring fireplace cast a ruddy glow in the room. Glass doors opened onto a stone balcony, but the curtains were almost closed. Marble mantelpiece. Gold trim. I smelled sweat, sickness and dried herbs. And resting on a mountain of pillows in a magnificent four-poster bed, was a woman who looked on the verge of death.

'Her skin was waxed paper, thin breast rising and falling swift as a wounded bird's. Though the boudoir was uncomfortably warm, her nightshift was laced to her chin, blankets piled atop her. She shivered in her sleep.

'Greyhand crossed the room, pressed the sevenstar upon his palm to her sallow brow. The woman moaned loudly, but her eyes remained closed.

'"How long has she been such?"

'"Seven nights," de Blanchet replied. "I have tried every tincture. Every cure. And yet, each day my Claudette worsens, as did our Claude. I fear my wife soon shall follow our son to the grave." The alderman looked skywards, his shaking hands in fists. "What sin is mine that you would pass this measure unto me?"

'Greyhand lit a posy of dried silverbell and placed it on the mantelpiece, murmuring a prayer and watching it burn. Reaching into his bandolier, he dashed handfuls of metallic powder on the floor around the bed, studying the patterns.

'"What is that, Frère?" the priest asked.

'"Metal shavings. Faekin leave footprints no cold iron will touch. Tell me, M. de Blanchet, have you noticed the shade of your fires tilting towards blue near midnight? Milk souring in the morn perhaps, or cocks crowing as the sun sets?"

'". . . No, Frère."

'"An abundance of lowborn beasts about the manor? Black cats, rats, or suchlike?"

'"Nothing of the sort."

'Greyhand pursed his lips. I knew he was eliminating possibilities – witchery or the fae or servants of the fallen. "You will forgive me, monsieur. But I must examine your wife. I fear this may be uncomfortable to watch. I understand if you wish to wait outside."

'"I will do no such thing," the alderman replied, standing taller.

'"As you like it. But I warn you not to interfere with my examination."

'Aaron sidled up to the alderman, spoke comforting words. Again, I saw that predatory gleam in his eyes, and de Blanchet's resolve melting. Not for the first time, I found myself envious of my fellow palebloods. The power their fathers had given them. Control over beasts. Mastery of men's minds. And there I stood, with little to do save stare.

'Greyhand turned to Madame de Blanchet and opened the neck of her nightshift. The alderman tensed, Père Lafitte frowned, but neither spoke protest as Greyhand prodded the woman's throat. Finding nothing amiss, he inspected her wrists, muttering softly.

'I stood by one of the balcony doors, and as much as I wished to study Greyhand, it seemed improper to gawp at a sleeping woman in her nightwear. I cast my eyes to the floor. And there, between my boots, I spied a tiny, dark spot on the wood.

'"Master Greyhand . . ."

'He turned from the bed, saw me pointing.

'"Blood."

'Greyhand nodded, slipped his gloves back on. And with no further ceremony, he took hold of the woman's nightshift, and tore it open.

'Father Lafitte cried protest, and the alderman stepped forward. "Now see h—"

'"I am here by order of Emperor Alexandre himself," Greyhand snapped. "If the nature of your wife's affliction is such as I fear, it may be that I can save her life. But not without risk to her modesty. So decide now, monsieur, which you hold more dear!"

'De Coste patted the alderman's arm. "*All is well, monsieur.*" And bristling with rage, de Blanchet stood down. It was a testament to Aaron's craft that the man hadn't already rebelled – if someone had stripped my wife half-naked in front of me, I'd be breaking their fucking skull open.

'"Initiate de León, bring that light closer."

'I did as Greyhand commanded, holding a lantern above Madame de Blanchet. Parting the ruined nightshift, he began inspecting the woman's sallow, naked body. But as soon as he placed one gloved hand on her breast, the alderman finally broke.

'"This is an outrage!"

'Aaron seized de Blanchet's arm. "*Calm yourself, monsieur.*"

'Père Lafitte stepped forward, "Please, Frère, I must insist—"

'I turned to the priest, warned him to be still. The alderman shouted for his servants, and the room descended into chaos before Greyhand's bellow split the air.

'"HOLD!"

'Our master looked to de Blanchet, his voice dark with loathing.

'"Come see, monsieur."

'De Coste released his grip, and straightening his coat with an indignant huff, de Blanchet stalked to his wife's bedside. Greyhand pointed as I held the lantern high. And there, in the dark flesh of Madame de Blanchet's right nipple, we saw small, twinned scabs.

'"There are more between her legs," Greyhand said. "Hard to spot. But fresh."

'"Plague sores?" the priest whispered.

'"Bite marks."

'"What in the name of Almighty God . . ." the alderman breathed.

'"Did any visitors come to Skyefall around the time your son fell ill?"

'The alderman's eyes were fixed on those tiny wounds in his wife's flesh, sheer horror on his face. Greyhand snapped his fingers for attention.

'"Monsieur? Were there visitors?"

'"This . . . th-this is a mining town, Frère. We have visitors constantly . . ."

'"Anyone strange that young Claude might have come into contact with? Wanderers, or travelling performers? The kind of folk who come and go with ease?"

'"Certainly not. I'd never allow my son to mix with suchlike. I . . . I believe he spent time with the Luncóit boy while his mother conducted her affairs on the outskirts. He was a little older than Claude, but a fine lad of good breeding."

'"The Luncóit boy," Greyhand repeated.

'"Adrien," the alderman nodded. "His mother was come to Skyefall to survey a claim farther down the Godsend. She is from an old prospecting famille in Elidaen. She spent most of her time surveying the land around the town, and thus, Adrien kept Claude's company while his mother worked. Marianne, her name. A fascinating woman."

'The young priest folded his arms, his face darkening.

"'You did not find her so fascinating, Father?" Greyhand asked.

"'I . . . I am being uncharitable," Lafitte said. "I admit I never met her."

"'Not even at holy services?"

"'She worked, even on prièdi," he said, obviously displeased. "Though she had time aplenty for soirees and suchlike, she never attended mass."

'Greyhand looked de Blanchet square in the eye.

"'Where did you bury your son, monsieur?"'

+ IV +

HOUSE OF THE DEAD

'"DE COSTE, DE LEÓN, we three will check the tombe de famille,"
Greyhand said. "If the boy has Become, he is only a fledgling. But he may
not be alone by now, and even young, he is still deadly. Keep your heads,
and remember the Five Laws."

'We'd returned to the stables to fetch our horses, and my heart was
pounding like I'd just been at spar. The de Blanchet tomb stood in the heart
of the Skyefall necropolis, and with a few hours until sunset, Greyhand had
decided to investigate. We'd no true idea if little Claude was responsible for
the dark predations upon his mother, or the other deaths around town. But
removing him from the list of suspects was the next sensible step.

'Greyhand took a spiked flail with a long silver chain from his saddlebags.
"If pressed, keep your swords sheathed. If he's Become, I want this boy
caught, not killed."

'"To what end, Master?" de Coste asked.

'"Perhaps it's naught." Greyhand glanced to the dark sun, now sinking
towards the mountains. "But the name *Luncóit* means *raven child* in old
Elidaeni."

'"The sigil of the Blood Voss is a white raven," I murmured.

'"As I say, perhaps nothing. But perhaps this Marianne has a dark sense
of humour."

'Greyhand took a phial from his bandolier, coating his hands and face
and rubbing down his leathers with the chymical concoction inside. As he
passed it to de Coste, I saw the glass was marked with a wailing spirit.

'*Ghostbreath*, I noted. *To mask our living scent from the Dead.*

'I busied myself with my gear – black ignis and phials of holy water. I
checked that my wheellock was loaded, then took the chymicals de Coste

passed me. Aaron slung a length of silver chain about his chest along with his bandolier. He seemed to stand a touch taller, wrapped in his black leathers with a gleaming sevenstar at his breast. If I didn't know better, I'd have said the spoiled little prick almost looked like a vampire killer.

'"Let's away." Greyhand mounted his horse. "Sunset waits for no saint."

'Skyefall was a town of tiers and levels, with richer folk living up the hillside and the poorer down the slopes. The necropolis lay in the lower end, close to the towering cathedral. We cantered through grey fog, past scowling townsfolk and a few trundling wagons. As we crossed one of the old stone bridges, I imagined the rivers to the north, the coming wintersdeep, the armies of the Forever King. Wondering what role San Michon was to play in stopping him, and if I'd be a part of it.

'The cathedral was a circular spire of marble on the edge of a shallow cliff. The doors were bronze, crafted with eerie reliefs of angels battling the fallen. Great bells rang in the belfry, Archer calling out in answer as we followed a winding road to the cliff base, and at last, found the entry to Skyefall's houses of the dead.

'As was custom, two archways led into the necropolis – one facing west for the dead, the other, which would usually face east, for the living. Large reliefs were carved into the stone – human skeletons with angels' wings, and the Mothermaid holding the infant Redeemer. Wrought above the entrance were words from the Book of Laments.

'I AM THE DOOR ALL SHALL OPEN. THE PROMISE NONE SHALL BREAK.

'I tried to keep my nerves steady as we dismounted. Greyhand closed his eyes, one hand outstretched towards the necropolis. I wondered at his game, but in a few minutes, my answer appeared in the form of several mangy rats. They emerged from the shadowed stairwells leading to the crypts, snuffling and blinking in the fading daylight.

'"Fairdawn, little lords."

'My master knelt on the cold stone and offered the vermin morsels from one of his pockets. Again, I felt that stab of envy, watching him commune with those beasts. The Blood Chastain was a curse, but still, it must have been a kind of wondrous to speak to animals of earth and sky. I patted Justice, giving him a swift hug and wondering what it would be like to know something of his mind. Something of where I'd come from.

'"What tidings, little lords?" Greyhand asked. "What troubles?"

'The boldest rat, a fat fellow with a missing ear, chittered angrily. Greyhand nodded in sympathy, like an old friend griping over a mug of mulled wine.

'"A sad tale. We shall mend it presently."

'Our master stood, and the rats scampered back into the gloom. "They speak of *darkthings* in the crypts. *Wrongthings*." Greyhand shook his head. "Even the lowest of God's creatures recognize the evil of the Dead. But it seems there are more than one."

'"How many?" I asked.

'"They're rats, boy, not bookkeepers. They only know *one* and *more than one*."

'Greyhand nodded to himself, now certain: Coldbloods were at the heart of the disease afflicting this town. I felt a warm thrill in my belly as my master drew a phial of sanctus from his bandolier, tipped a dose into his pipe. In San Michon, on the road, we took the sacrament at dusk, a routine part of our daily prayers. But we were given only the smallest taste to keep our thirst quelled.

'Greyhand was measuring a heavy dose. Obviously expecting trouble.

'He lit his flintbox, offered the pipe to de Coste. I watched the lordling breathe in, his every muscle stretching taut. Exhaling a cloud of scarlet, I saw that Aaron's teeth had grown long and sharp, his eyes flooding blood-red. It was my turn next, and the dose hit me like a warhammer to my chest, setting all my blood afire. Greyhand took the unholy sacrament last, finishing the pipe and breathing it down, his whole body trembling. When he opened his eyes, they were the colour of murder.

'He took two flasks of hellspark from our saddlebags, upending them over the stairs into the necropolis. When he was done, both stairwells were soaked with the oily red liquid and reeked of sulphur so thick my eyes watered.

'"De Coste, you guard the duskdoors. De León, the dawn. If you hear the sound of my horn, the kith have evaded me. Light the hellspark to cut off their escape."

'"By the Blood, Master," we both answered.

'"God walks with us this day, boys. Stand your ground and fear no darkness."

'Greyhand stripped off his greatcoat and tunic, leaving his tattooed torso and arms bare. He was pure muscle, wiry and iron-hard, his aegis etched in beautiful lines of silver. Slinging on his bandolier and flail, he tipped his tricorn, then stepped into the gloom.'

Jean-François tapped his quill on the page, bringing Gabriel's tale to a halt.

'. . . Honestly?' the silversaint glowered. 'You're interrupting me *now*?'

'A brief clarification. But an important one.' The historian raised one tapered brow. 'Are you truly saying warriors of the Ordo Argent stripped half-naked to fight?'

Gabriel nodded. 'Being silverclad, we called it. Modesty is of little use to a corpse. And armour is of even less use when your opponent can crush steel with its fists.'

'But what about thralls? Surely they used blades and other weapons mundane?'

'We weren't worried about lackeys, coldblood. We were worried about their masters. The people who die in battle? They mostly die once the battle is done. It's not the swordblow or arrow that kills you. It's the bleeding you do afterwards. We were palebloods. We *healed*. So while an angry, well-trained thrall with a nice sharp broadsword was a threat, it paled in comparison to the threat of having your heart shown to you by the unholy bastard who just ripped it out of your chest with its bare fucking hands.

'It's not as if the aegis made us impervious either. But it served as a conduit by which God's power could be felt on the battlefield. The light of the aegis burns the eyes of the unholy. Its touch scorches their flesh. It's like an armour of blinding faith, making us harder to focus on, punishing to hit. It was an edge, and against faekin, duskdancers, coldbloods, we needed every one we could get.' Gabriel leaned back in his chair. 'Now, can I get on with my story? Or would you like to fucking tell it?'

Jean-François waved his quill. 'As you like it.'

'Right. So Greyhand descended into the necropolis. De Coste and I exchanged a red glance, but there was little for us to say. Aaron remained at the duskdoors while I trudged downhill to cover the other entrance. And there, I settled to wait.

'Paleblood senses are sharp at the best of times, but with a dose of sanctus in us, the whole world comes alive. I could hear the town above: wagons on the cobbles and the choir practising in the cathedral and the calls of a hungry babe. I watched Archer circling endlessly in the grim skies overhead. The hellspark on the stairs was pungent, but I couldn't smell myself under the ghostbreath. Lionclaw hung heavy in the scabbard at my hip. I read the inscription above the necropolis door, over and over. Words from the Book of the Redeemer.

'KNOW ONLY JOY IN THY HEART, BLESSED CHILD. FOR ON THIS DAY, LIFE IS THINE.

'Ten minutes passed without a sound. Then twenty. I stepped farther into the entrance, head tilted, but all I could hear was a faint drip somewhere within.

'"He's been gone an age," I called.

'De Coste looked up from the small, tight circle he'd been pacing. "Breathe easy, Peasant. Greyhand is a cautious hunter. The dead can't kill the Dead."

'I nodded, but my unease was growing. I felt useless standing there on guard. I was a ball of nerves and restless energy, a long-tailed cat in a room full of rocking chairs, that infamous Nordlund fire hot in my veins. And then came a faint sound up the crypt stairs.

'"Did you hear that?"

'". . . Hear what?"

'I stepped back beneath the arch, squinting down the stairs. "A cry?"

'"It was the wind. Unknot your gizzards, you quivering peon."

'"I heard a cry just now. What if Greyhand is in need?"

'"Greyhand was stalking the dark before your worthless father slipped his dead cock into your peasant mother. Now shut up, frailblood. Hold your ground."

'I clenched my teeth, straining to hear. I *swore* I'd caught wind of something in the depths. Definitely a cry, faint, but . . . perhaps pained? My pulse was thumping in my ears, the bloodhymn raging in my head. If Greyhand had fallen foul of the things within these tombs, and we just stood here doing nothing . . .

'And then I heard it for certain. A distant call. A man in pain.

'"Did you hear *that*?"

'De Coste's eyes were narrowed. "I think . . ."

'"Greyhand's in trouble," I said, unslinging my flail. "We have to help him, de Coste."

'"No, what we have to do is exactly what he *told* us to do. Hold your damned ground, Peasant. In Greyhand's absence, I am senior member of this company."

'"Hell with that," I said, checking my wheellock again. "You want to wait up here with your thumb in your cackhole? God bless you. But I'll not stand idle."

'"De León, wait! Greyhand told us to *stay here*!"

'I felt the press of his will on mine then, the Blood of Ilon at work in my mind. But the hymn sang louder, the sanctus and my own pigheadedness drowning out Aaron's command. And with flail in fist, heart in throat, I strode into the house of Skyefall's dead.'

Jean-François sighed. 'Foolish.'

'Oui. But remember, I'd not even turned sixteen. I'd worked my arse to the bone in the monastery. But the displays of de Coste's and Greyhand's gifts had me of a mood. No matter how much I pretended it didn't bother me, being a frailblood made me feel less than my fellows. I was desperate to prove my worth, and *this* could be my chance.

'I wasn't a complete shitwit – I lit the hellspark as I departed. It ignited with a dull roar, and I flinched back from the raging heat. I heard de Coste yell again, but paid no heed. And with shoulders squared, I bounded into the tombs in search of my master.

'A long corridor stretched into darkness, but my paleblood eyes saw clear as day. The walls were lined with stone doors, carved with names of the corpses beyond. Poorer folk had no tombs at all, bones piled atop one another in dusty niches. The slabs under my feet were also graves, and it struck me as eerie to be walking on dead bodies. But I was no coward to be frightened by old bones or the thought of death. The only thing that scared me back then was the thought of dying without ever having done something worthwhile.

'I found myself at a crossroads leading deeper into the necropolis. Rats scurried past my heels, the scent of old death filled the air. I listened but heard nothing, cursing beneath my breath. Perhaps it was my imagination, but the stone halls below this town seemed *far* older than the town itself.

'"Master Greyhand?" I called.

'No reply, save the whispering wind. And so, praying to God, I strode on through a warren of twists and turns, past piles of nameless skulls. Statues of beautiful angels loomed at each corner, guarding those who slept eternal in the tombs beyond.

'And then, in the dark ahead, I heard a cry.

'With a gasp, I was off, boots pounding the grave slabs, fist curled around my flail. I could see dim light ahead now, a silver-cold glow on the walls. I heard another shout of pain, a loud voice I finally recognized as my master's.

'"Come on, you accursed dogs!"

'"Greyhand!" I roared.

'I rounded the corner, skidding to a halt at the sight before my wondering eyes. A large crypt lay before me, ringed by a dozen sarcophagi. The floor was slabbed by gravestones, and a statue of Mahné, Angel of Death, loomed over the scene with his great sickles in hand. Beneath him stood Greyhand, his flail singing as it cut the air, locked in combat with two fleeting shadows.

'Goosebumps prickled on my skin – not at the freezing cold, but at the sight of the tattoos on my master's flesh. The Mothermaid and Redeemer, the angels of the host, the seven wolves, throat to wrist to waist. That holy magik,

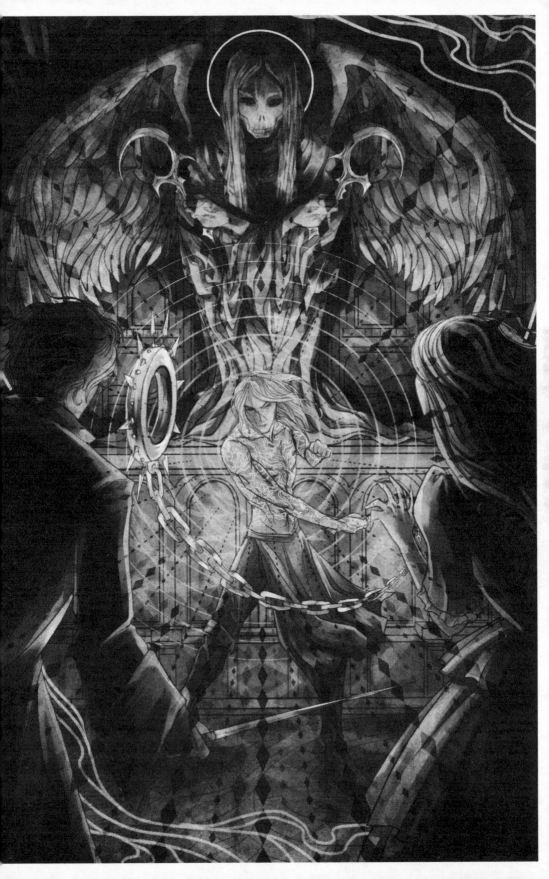

wrought by the hands of Silver Sisters. The armour of the silversaint. The aegis.

'And it was *glowing*.

'Greyhand was a white star burning in the dark, a circle of illumination spanning fifteen feet about him. I felt my left hand growing hot, as if too close to flame, and taking off my glove, I saw the sevenstar on my palm burning with that same terrible light.

'Two coldbloods wove through the dark, wearing the clothes they were buried in. A brunette woman in an elegant black dress, and a tall gent in a long frockcoat armed with a fine swordcane. Each was a pale beauty, skin like ivory, eyes like jet, and my belly rolled at the sight of them. I'd seen wretched before, oui – those monstrosities born of rot and the coldblood curse. But these two were locked forever in a dark perfection. The first highblooded vampires I'd ever laid eyes on.

'The man's speed was unholy, his eyes black lanterns. He stood before the woman as if to protect her, all his dark strength brought to bear. But Great Redeemer, Greyhand was magnificent. I thought I'd felt the presence of God as I faced the Trial of Blood, but now I felt it true, bathing me in the light of heaven's shoreline.

'"Leave us alone!" the woman pleaded.

'"Stay away from her!" the man shouted. "Stay away, or by God, I'll *kill* you!"

'"God?" Greyhand spat. "You profane his name with your black tongue, leech."

'Greyhand flung a silverbomb, and I flinched as it exploded in a ball of flame and white light. The coldbloods scattered and Greyhand lashed out with his flail, wrapping it around the man's legs. Bound in silver, his limbs became as useless as lead, and he collapsed to the stone. The woman cried out, "Eduard!" and flashed into the light, Greyhand's sword crashing down on her outstretched arm. She screamed, clutching the shattered bone as she drew back her hand, and I knew it true, then – these vampires were the Blood of Voss. Any other fledgling would have been holding nothing but a smoking stump after a blow like that.

'"Master!" I shouted.

'"De León? I told you to stand your—"

'A third fledgling came out of the dark behind Greyhand – a street waif in rags, rotten fingers curled into claws. My master gasped as the girl flung herself upon his back, but the silver on his skin scorched the leech like flame, and she tumbled back, mouth wide in agony.

'Greyhand turned towards the wretched child, burning with blessed light. He flung a phial of holy water, the glass shattering against the little girl's skin. She shrieked, stumbling farther backwards as my master drove his blade through her chest.

'"*Lisette!*" the woman screamed.

'The fallen man had unwrapped Greyhand's flail from his legs, his hands now blackened and smoking. He turned to the woman in desperation. "Vivienne, run!"

'"No, Eduard, we—"

'"RUN!"

'The coldblood turned to me, dead eyes glinting as he came on like a pistol shot. But I raised my left hand, rewarded with a hiss of agony as the light from my sevenstar pierced those cold, dead eyes. Months of training kicked in, and I drew a silverbomb from my bandolier, hurled it into the monster's chest. A silver flash and a black scream split the air.

'Greyhand tore his sword from the waif's chest and with four mighty blows, hacked her head clean off her shoulders. But untended, the woman took her chance. She had no form, no training, but still, she struck with terrifying force, smashing me into one of the sarcophagi and shattering it like glass. I felt something inside me snap, collapsing in a tumble of broken stone and old bones. And with none left in her way, she dashed down the corridor I'd entered by, just a flash of silk and dark hair.

'"Seven Martyrs, *stop her!*"

'Greyhand drew his wheellock pistol and took a knee. Aiming carefully, he struck the spring and fired a burst of silvershot at the fleeing coldblood. He hit her leg but missed the bone, and she staggered on. Clutching my ribs, I fired off a crooked shot as Greyhand blew a long note on his horn. But even if he wanted to seal off the entrance, Aaron couldn't now – I'd already lit the hellspark to cover my back. I just prayed God it was still burning.

'My master turned, the fallen male crawling backwards as the frère came on. The vampire's pale flesh was blacked from my silverbomb, his funeral finery a smoking mess.

'"No," he pleaded. "No, God, we did not ask—"

'Greyhand struck at the thing's throat. Though the force would have been enough to cleave steel, the vampire's skin didn't split, cracking like stone under a hammer instead. Another phial of holy water smashed against his face, and the coldblood howled as Greyhand struck again, finally opening up his neck. A part of me felt a whisper of pity for this thing, wed to the same thirst as murdered him. But I could see bloodstains on his cuffs, his scorched lapel – this monster hadn't been idle in the nights since he Became.

'*The Dead feel as beasts, look as men, die as devils.*

'With one final effort, the vampire threw itself at my master. Heedless. Hateful. Greyhand stepped aside, spun and followed through, and with one final, terrible blow, the vampire's head was loosed from his neck, the body collapsing in ruin.

'My master dashed off in pursuit of the woman as I hauled myself out of the smashed sarcophagus. Limping and bloodied, I couldn't keep up the chase, but I knew where it led. Reaching the exit, I saw the stairs were black and smoking, but the fire had died. And cursing myself for a fucking fool, I dragged my sorry arse into the dark daylight.

'Greyhand was on his knees beside de Coste. My fellow initiate was sprawled on the cobbles, lips split, nose broken, thick blonde hair soaked with blood. He threw a look of pure murder at me as I climbed the stairs. Master Greyhand rose to his feet, and I saw his fangs had grown long with his rage. "You simple-minded, bullheaded *lackwit.*"

'He flashed towards me, hand to my throat, slamming me back into the cliff face.

'"I told you to stand your ground!"

'"I th-thought I heard—"

'"You *thought*? You thought you'd be a damned hero is what you thought! Your disobedience has cost us our quarry, and mayhaps another innocent life! *Think* on that!"

'"I'm s-sorry, Master! P-please . . ."

'He choked me a moment longer, then let me slither down the wall. De Coste rose to his feet, nose dripping blood. He shot me another glare of hatred.

'"Did you find the de Blanchet boy, Master?"

'Greyhand took a moment to find his calm, spitting on the cobbles.

'"No. His tomb was empty. But he definitely stalks these streets. Along with the unholy daughter this *fool* allowed to escape." Greyhand rubbed his pointed chin, scowling. "There was a dusting of grit in the boy's tomb, a smell like blasting powder. He may be alternating between nests. De Coste, you and I will search the mines before the sun fails."

'". . . What about me, Master?"

'Greyhand turned on me, glowering. "Until you learn to act like a hunter, I'll treat you like a damned hound. You will return to the alderman's estate and stand guard by Mme de Blanchet's bed until we return."

'He placed his bloody silversteel sword on my shoulder, gentle as first rains.

'"And if *ever* I give an order to you that is not followed direct again, I vow by Almighty God and all Seven Martyrs, I will *end* you, boy. I will put you in your grave before I allow your impatience and glory-seeking to put an innocent in theirs."

'I hung my head, tongue thick with shame. "Understood, Master."

'Greyhand lowered his sword, offered me his hand.

'"Now get up. You have bodies to burn."'

✦ V ✦

A BEAUTIFUL VIEW

'"TEA, INITIATE?"

'Père Lafitte's voice broke me from my reverie, and I glanced up from the fireplace. The sight of a little girl's burning corpse was etched in my head. The stink was on my clothes, the horror fresh, and all had put me in mind of my sister again. Amélie's death felt a lifetime ago now, and I'd thought the boy who'd watched her burn was just a ghost. And yet, I'd proved myself a boy again that day. Headstrong and foolish.

'"No," I replied. "Merci, Father."

'De Blanchet's manservant nodded, placed the tray he carried on the mantel, and left the room. The pot was silver, the cups of finest porcelain. The tea's scent was sweet, sharp, only half remembered from around my mama's table in my childhood.

'The sun had fallen outside, and my comrades still hadn't returned. Wounded as she was, I knew the highblood who'd escaped us would be more dangerous in the dead of night. My fellows at deeper risk. For the hundredth time, I cursed my own stupidity.

'"What troubles, my son?" Lafitte asked, sitting opposite me.

'My seat was near Madame de Blanchet's bed, Lionclaw within easy reach. The longue was red leather and plush velvet, large enough to lose myself in. I turned my eyes to the dame ensconced in her mountain of pillows. Her breath was shallow and rapid, her skin pale as paper. The alderman was at work in his study down the hall.

'"Nothing worthy of note, Father," I sighed.

'"You look exhausted."

'I shook my head, knowing the bloodshot red of my eyes was only a residue from the sacrament. "I'll not sleep this night."

"'I have heard only rumour of your holy order," Lafitte remarked. "My papa met one of your number once. He said the man slew a witch who plagued his village as a boy. Tracked her down and nailed her soul into her body with a length of cold iron before setting her alight. I'd thought it stuff and nonsense, truth told."

"'I've met no witches, Father. But I *have* seen evil. And it walks now among us, doubt it not." I swallowed. "There will be dark nights ahead."

"'The folk you found in the catacombs. They were . . . changed?"

'I nodded. "I've fought the Dead before, but . . . not like that. The woman seemed . . . afraid. The man told her to run. It was like they remembered what they'd been."

"'I knew them both," Lafitte said, dabbing his sweating lip with his kerchief. "Parishioners of mine. Eduard Farrow and Vivienne La Cour." His fingertips hovered over the silver wheel about his neck. "They were to be married in spring."

"'And the little girl? Her name was Lisette."

'Lafitte shrugged. "There are many strays in a town this size, Initiate de León. Many who come and go, and more yet who would not be missed. A tragedy."

"'It's God's will," I declared. "All on earth below and heaven above is the work of his hand."

"'Véris," the priest smiled. "But come, if we are to stand vigil 'til dawn, you should drink something. A tea this fine is a rarity these nights. It would be sin to waste it."

'I took the cup Lafitte offered, staring into the flames. I remembered my mama, brewing tea in her big black kettle in the years before daysdeath. My sisters and I sitting at table, Amélie scoffing while Celene and I squabbled over a game of knucklebones. I missed my baby sister, felt guilty about not answering her letters. I wondered if I should write to my mother and ask her the truth about my father. A part of me didn't want to know. The rest of me desperately needed to.

"'Santé, Initiate," Lafitte said, raising his cup.

"'Santé, mon Père," I replied.

'I swallowed the draught with a wince. Bitter and too hot. Lafitte put his cup aside, watching me. He was quite handsome, truth told – Nordish stock, dark of hair and eye. A rich man's son most like, to have been posted by the Pontifex to a town this wealthy at his age.

"'How long have you served the Ordo Argent, Initiate de León?"

'I glanced to Madame de Blanchet as she moaned in her sleep. "Seven months."

"'Are there many brethren of your holy order?'"

"'A few dozen,' I replied, rising from my chair. "Though it's hard to tell sometimes. The Hunt keeps us often from home. It's rare that we're all at San Michon at once.'"

"'Why so few of you? If dark nights come as you say, could you not recruit more?'"

'I checked Madame de Blanchet's temperature, and she groaned as my sevenstar touched her skin. "The birth of a paleblood is no common thing, Father. We are like the coldbloods we hunt. Our making is happenstance. A curse, and one not to be encouraged.'"

'He frowned. "Coldbloods are made by other coldbloods, are they not?'"

"'Oui. But not all the folklore is true. Their affliction is capricious, Father. Only passing to their victims by chance. Some stay dead. Others rise as mindless monsters.'"

"'Chance, you say?' Lafitte frowned. "Curious.'"

'I rubbed my sweating brow, sloughed off my greatcoat. "That's the shame of all this. The vampire who started this mess may not have even known Claude de Blanchet turned.'"

"'Mme Luncóit did not strike me as a careless woman.'"

'I blinked. "I thought you said you didn't know Mme Luncóit?'"

"'Only by reputation. The folk she dealt with in Skyefall regarded her highly. Even the alderman seemed under her spell.'"

"'What other folk did she deal with?' I asked, wiping sweat from my lip.

'But Lafitte made no reply. His head was tilted as if he were listening, his tea untouched. My head was throbbing. My eyes stinging and blurred.

"'Seven Martyrs, it's sweltering in here . . .'"

'The priest smiled at me. "Open the window. It's a beautiful view.'"

'I nodded, trudging over to the glass bay doors. Eyes still stinging, I took hold of the drapes, dragged them apart. And there, gleaming moon-pale in the dark outside, was the face of little Claude de Blanchet.

"'Sweet Redeemer!'"

'Ten years old. Coal-black hair and grave-white skin. He was dressed in noble's finery, black velvet and gold buttons, a silken cravat at his throat. But his eyes were the darkest part of him, heavy-lidded and gleaming like wet jewels. And he fixed them on the priest, and pressed his hand to the glass.

"'Beautiful, isn't he?'"

'I turned and saw Father Lafitte, now holding my sheathed sword. The priest's eyes were filled with a thrall's rapture, gazing at that pale shadow beyond the glass.

'"Let me in," it whispered.

'"Lafitte, *no!*" I shouted.

'"Come in, Master," the priest breathed.

'The doors slammed apart, the glass cracking in the frame. I barely had time to turn before Claude de Blanchet was on me, slamming me back into the wall. The plaster split, the ribs I'd cracked earlier in the day bursting into new flame. I saw Lafitte walking to the balcony, but I was too busy fighting the boy off to do anything but roar protest as he tossed my sword out the window. As if roused by the thing's unholy presence, Madame de Blanchet was now sitting up in bed. She'd loosed her nightshift, arms outstretched.

'"My boy," she breathed, tears in her eyes. "My sweet baby boy."

'That sweet baby boy slammed me back into the wall, his fingernails iron-hard and sharp. The whole room was blurring, a bitter tang on my tongue, and I understood at last that Lafitte had slipped some toxin into the tea, dimming the bloodhymn in my head. As the vampire fixed me in his black gaze, I realized I was in the deepest shite of my life.

'"*Kneel,*" Claude commanded.

'The word hit me like a pistol shot, wrapped in satin. The desire to please this thing was as real as the air I breathed. I knew if I simply relented, everything would be all right. Everything would be *wonderful.* But in some dim corner of my mind, I could feel Greyhand's blade skewering me against that tree, the fire of his words burning away the dark.

'*Listen not to a* word *these bastards hiss, lest you find yourself their meal.*

'I reached for the teapot on the mantel. Bright and gleaming silver. I felt my fury rising, my canines growing sharp. And as the vampire spoke again, "*Kneel!*" my fingers found purchase, and spitting, "Fuck you!" I smashed the pot right into his ruby lips.

'Claude wailed in pain, staggering. The pot crumpled like paper, but it gave me a moment to breathe as the bedroom door burst open. The alderman stood on the threshold, pale with shock. He took in the chaos – wife screaming, Father Lafitte drawing a knife from his sleeve as I smashed the monster in the face again. But de Blanchet's eyes were fixed on the thing I brawled with, the dark remnant of the boy he'd buried months ago.

'"My son?"

'I lunged for my bandolier of holy water and silverbombs, but the priest leapt upon my shoulders, stabbing me with his little blade again and again. Lafitte's strength was impressive, his knife puncturing my chest a dozen times. But I was no fucking thrall like him. I was a paleblood, an initiate of the Ordo Argent, trained at the feet of a master of the Hunt. Smashing his jaw with my elbow, I heard bone splinter, a scream from the treacherous prick's broken mouth. I speared myself backwards, felt Lafitte's ribs crumble as we collided with the wall hard enough to shatter the bricks.

'But by then, little Claude was upright again, delivering a blow to my bollocks so thunderous, it actually made me vomit. I doubled up in agony, and he slung me down into the floorboards. Sitting on my chest, the vampire lunged towards my throat.

'A burning piece of timber crashed over the boy's head, splintering in a shower of sparks. Claude screamed in agony, his hair smouldering. Rising off me, he turned to his father, standing at the fireplace with a shattered log in hand.

'"Papa," the vampire hissed.

'"No son of mine," de Blanchet whispered, tears in his eyes.

'He struck the boy again, the thing shrieking as the fire blacked its skin. A scream rang out in the room then, and Madame de Blanchet snatched up Lafitte's fallen dagger, launched herself at her husband's back. The blade punched through the alderman's flesh, the man gasping as he and his wife collapsed onto the blood-slicked floor.

'"Claudette! S-stop . . ."

'Vomit in my mouth, blood streaming down my chest, I lunged for my bandolier again. I heard hissing breath, felt strong hands sling me across the room, demolishing Madame de Blanchet's magnificent bed. I raised my left hand as Claude landed atop me, the unholy little fuck shrieking as the silver in my palm flared bright. But still he struck me like a hammer, driving the breath from my punctured lungs. With one clawed hand, he grabbed my arm, forcing the light of my tattoo from his eyes. With his other, he reached for my throat. And desperate, gasping and bleeding, I seized hold of his wrist.

'My strength versus his. His will against mine. He loomed above me, cherubic face scorched and spattered red. I remembered those two highbloods in the crypts, the semblance of their old lives still clinging to their corpses. But this fucking monster atop me, glutted on months of murder, this, *this* was what they really were.

'"*Hushhhhhh now* . . ."

'I was thirteen years old again. Lying in the mud the day Amélie came home. And there, just as before, with death breathing cold upon my throat, I felt heat flood up my arm. Something stirred once more inside me, tenebrous and old. And with a shriek of agony, Claude de Blanchet reared back, clutching the hand that clutched his.

'His flesh was blackening in my grip, as though it burned without flame. The boything tried to pull away, and beneath my clenched fingers, I saw his porcelain skin bubbling and splitting, red vapour rising from the cracks as if the very blood boiled in his dead veins. His voice was a child's again, bloody tears in black eyes.

'"Let *go!*" he squealed. "Mama, *make him stop!*"

'His hand was a charred ruin now, scalding blood spilling down my forearm like hot wax. Still, I held on, horrified, amazed. I heard boots up the stairs. Greyhand's shout. Little Claude gasped as my master's flail wrapped about his throat and chest. And bound at last by silver, the little bastard tumbled to the floor. Madame de Blanchet flew off her husband and towards me, but de Coste wrestled her to the ground.

'"I'll kill you! You hurt my baby, bastard, I'LL KILL YOU!"

'The woman was drenched in blood, her husband dead by her own hand, and she had no thought but for the leech laying helpless beside me. Claude de Blanchet stared up at me, soulless eyes brimming with malice. I pictured the bite wounds upon his mother's breast and between her legs, trying not to imagine the shape of his nightly visitations. And I wondered if I'd ever walked so close to hell as this.

'Greyhand placed his hands under my arms, eased me to my feet. My legs were shaking so badly I could barely stand, head spinning from Lafitte's poison. My master surveyed the carnage: the crushed priest, the moaning highblood, the murdered alderman and his screaming wife. I was drenched in sticky red, stab wounds in my chest, ribs broken. My hair hung about my eyes in a matted, bloody curtain, mind racing with the thought that I'd somehow boiled that vampire's blood just by *touching* him.

'"What did I do?" I whispered, looking at the boy's black flesh. "How did I do it?"

'"I've no idea."

'Greyhand patted my shoulder, gave me a grudging nod.

'"But fine work, Little Lion."'

✦ VI ✦

THE SCARLET FOUNDRY

'WE ARRIVED BACK at San Michon two weeks later, those mighty stone pillars rising from the sunset mists before us. In truth, I knew not how to feel. I'd both failed and flown on my first Hunt. My impatience had bested me, put innocent lives at risk. I'd killed a man with my own hands, and it's no small thing to be the one who takes a life from this earth. You make the world less by it, and if you're careless, make yourself less besides.

'But instead of regret, I felt only vindication. That I'd defended God's faithful from the evil that beset them. That I'd done *right*. And more and most, I'd defeated a highblood single-handed. I admit I was feeling more than a touch full of myself on that – sitting tall in Justice's saddle with a smile that never quite left my lips.

'Claude de Blanchet and Vivienne La Cour were both trussed up in silver chains on Greyhand's horse. The boy's arm had yet to fully heal from the wounds I'd inflicted on him, and Greyhand had to silence his wails with a gag. But the questions of exactly what I'd done, and more important, *how* I'd done it, were still unanswered.

'Despite my insubordination, Greyhand paid me a grudging respect – I could tell he was impressed at the prowess I'd shown in taking the boy down. But de Coste's eyes were full of loathing when he looked at me. My disobedience had seen him get his skull broken by a fledgling, and I'd gone on to thrash its maker unarmed and alone. Aaron had been overshadowed, and I knew he'd have a bone to pick once out of Greyhand's sight.

'We pulled our horses to a halt outside the stable gates, and I walked inside to fetch the grooms as Aaron and Greyhand unloaded our captive coldbloods. I called out to Kaspar, my eyes adjusting to the dim light of the chymical globes. And in the shadows, I saw two figures, starting as if surprised. The first was Kaveh, Kaspar's mute brother. And the second, her face paling a little at the sight of me, was Seraph Talon's assistant, Sister Aoife.

"'Fairdawning, Initiate," she stammered, bowing low.

"'Godmorrow, good Sister." I nodded slowly. "Kaveh."

'The lad lowered his eyes, mute as always.

"'You are returned from the Hunt?" Aoife asked. "I am told all went well? Archer arrived last week with news of the cargo you carry."

'I looked Aoife over, head tilted. It was uncommon strange to find a sister of the Silver Sorority unchaperoned in the company of a stableboy. Kaveh was still refusing to meet my eyes. But in the end, I supposed it no concern of mine.

"'Oui," I nodded to the sister. "Two highblood fledglings, both of the Blood Voss."

"'Wonderful," Aoife smiled, straightening her habit. "I shall accompany you."

'The good sister followed me outside, and Kaveh hurried to bring our horses in from the cold. Aaron and Greyhand bowed in greeting to Aoife, and together we ascended San Michon's dizzying heights, with me hauling the de Blanchet boy and Aaron carrying La Cour. I watched the sister sidelong as the platform rose, but Aoife's face was stone. Archer wheeled above us, singing to the wind in joy at his master's return. Greyhand lifted his arm, and as the falcon alighted at his wrist, his lips twisted the closest to a smile they ever got.

'I thought we might report to Abbot Khalid or fill our bellies, but Aoife led us straight to the Armoury. As ever, the windows were lit by forgefire, the chimneys belched black smoke – all save one, spitting that thin wisp of scarlet. Awaiting us on the steps was Seraph Talon himself, his greatcoat's collar laced painfully tight, his ashwood switch in hand.

"'Fairdawn, Frère Greyhand," Talon said in his cool highborn tone. "De Coste."

"'Godmorrow, Seraph," they answered.

'The Seraph of the Hunt looked directly at me, stroking his long, dark moustache like a six-year-old strokes a favoured kitten. "Fairdawn, my little shitblood."

"'Godmorrow, Seraph," I sighed.

'Talon gave a small toss of his head, and we four followed him into the Armoury. The warmth of the forges was a blessed change from the road, the chymical globes glittering like stars in the gables overhead. The walls were lined with silversteel, and there among the racks, I saw Baptiste Sa-Ismael, the young blackthumb who'd forged my sword. His dark skin was damp with sweat, muscles glinting as he wheeled a barrow of raw coke for the forges. He stopped when he saw us, wiped his brow.

'"Fairdawn, Seraph," he said in his warm baritone. "Sister Aoife."

'Talon nodded, and Aoife bowed. "Godmorrow, Sa-Ismael."

'The smithy gifted the rest of us an impeccable grin. "And a fairdawn to you all, Brothers. Returned in triumph, I see?" He looked to the sword at my waist. "How did Lionclaw fare on her maiden voyage, de León? Slay me something monstrous?"

'"She was piffed out a window by a bent priest, Brother. So, I fear not."

'Baptiste glanced towards Aoife and grinned. "Well, it sounds like you gave her an adventure, at least. Ladies do enjoy that sort of thing." He slapped my shoulder with one warm hand. "Have no fear, Little Lion. God will grant your chance to do his will."

'Bloody hell, I liked Baptiste. And I wasn't alone. De Coste lost all trace of his usual arrogance when in the blackthumb's company. Even Greyhand looked close to dropping his customary scowl around the young smith. Baptiste had a smile that felt made just for you, a rich laugh, a good soul. But he glanced to Talon as the seraph cleared his throat.

'"I see you've business to attend, Brothers. I'll not keep you from God's holy work. We can share your tales in the refectory tonight over a glass."

'"Or a bottle," Aaron countered.

'The smithy laughed, dark eyes flashing. "By the Blood. Tonight, mes amis."

'We nodded farewells, and followed Seraph Talon and Sister Aoife to an area of the Armoury I'd not visited before. Massive silver-clad doors barred the way, opened with a silver key around Talon's throat, and beyond, a large room of dark stone awaited us. The taste of old blood laced the air. Tall ceilings lit with chymical globes arched overhead, the walls covered with anatomical illustrations of coldbloods, faekin, and other monstrosities. But the room was dominated by a large apparatus, the likes of which I'd never imagined.

'It seemed a kind of forge, dreamed in an unquiet mind. A serpentine nest of pipes surrounded a row of large stone slabs. Channels were carved into the stones in the shape of the sevenstar, and on half a dozen, I could see the emaciated forms of vampires, bound in silver. Many were wretched, but at least one was highblooded – a pretty monsieur with long hair of Ossway red. Their flesh was lifeless grey, withered like old fruit. Silver tubes had been stabbed into their chests, and I could hear the *drip, drip, drip* of blood into glass jars.

'I glanced to Aoife beside me and whispered, "What is this place, Sister?"

'"The Scarlet Foundry," she explained. "The hearts of coldbloods do not really beat, you see. And without a pulse to drive it, their blood goes only where they will it. The Foundry is the most efficient means of harvesting their essence, and thus, producing the greatest quantity of sanctus."

'Looking around the room with jaw slacked, I could feel a strange current crawling on my skin. This device seemed born half of science, half of sorcerie.

'"De Coste," Greyhand said. "De León. Make our guests comfortable."

'Aaron and I obeyed, placing our captured coldbloods on the slabs. Both were gagged and blindfolded, but a low moan of agony slipped over Vivienne La Cour's lips as Aoife fixed silver manacles about her wrists and ankles. As her flesh began sizzling, I had to remind myself again that these things weren't anything other than leeches wearing human skin.

'"From the punishment they withstood, they're definitely Voss," Greyhand said.

'Talon nodded to the boy. "This was first of the brood?"

'"Oui," Greyhand nodded. "Frightening little bastard for a fledgling."

'"Poor soul," Aoife sighed softly. "He's barely more than a babe."

'"Never to become a man," Greyhand scowled.

'"We will examine him thoroughly," Talon said, with rather more relish than was comfortable. "Flame shall reveal whatever his blood does not before he leaves us for hell."

'Aoife made the sign of the wheel. The seraph glanced down at the boything's forearm, still scorched from my touch. I saw him exchange a glance with our master.

'"You two." Greyhand turned to Aaron and me. "Go get yourselves bathed and fed. We may be ahunt again sooner than you think. De León, I'll be arranging extra duties for you until we depart San Michon again."

'". . . Duties, Master?"

'"Starting amorrow, you'll report to the stables before each dawnmass and muck out those pens until they're spotless. I'll inform Kaspar and Kaveh tonight. I'm sure our young grooms will enjoy the extra hour sleep your labours will avail them."

'I blinked in disbelief as Aaron stifled a triumphant smile.

'"I'm to shovel dung every morn? I took down this thing *single-handed*."

'"Disobedience has its price. You think I'm being unfair?"

'I bristled with the indignity of it, but gave a stiff bow. "No, Master."

"'Good. Off with the pair of you. I'll follow presently."

"'By the Blood, Frère." De Coste bowed. "Seraph. Sister."

'Aoife smiled farewell. Talon nodded vaguely, still peering at little Claude's arm as Aaron and I marched out into the freezing eve. Standing on the Armoury steps, I gritted my teeth, trying to hold my temper. I'd disobeyed Greyhand, no doubt. And despite capturing the de Blanchet boy, I knew I deserved punishment. But this?

'De Coste dragged his hand through his grubby mop of blonde and smiled. "Up to your shins in shit every morn, eh, Peasant? It'll be just like home."

"'Speaking of home, how's your mama? Tell her I miss her, will you?"

'De Coste turned to face me. As he stepped close, I noticed that even though he was older, I was almost as tall as him now. Able to meet his pale blue stare.

"'*Close your eyes*," he said.

'Aaron's words slipped into my ears like the cleverest knife. Not the velvet gunshot of that darkling boy's command in Skyefall. Something subtler, and more frightening. It was forbidden for palebloods to use their gifts on each other, and part of me raged that he'd dare to do so. But for the rest of me, it seemed the most reasonable thing in the world. *Aaron is your friend*, came a whisper within. *You trust him. You like him.*

'And so, I closed my eyes.

'His punch took me right in the belly, and all the breath left my lungs. I sank to my knees on the Armoury steps, holding my aching gut.

"'You h-hit l-like a lord," I managed.

"'I don't like you, you ill-bred little bastard."

"'You m-mean this isn't a . . . m-marriage proposal . . .?"

'Aaron loomed over me, sharp teeth at the corners of his mouth. "You made a fool of me in front of Greyhand. I owe you fucking *blood* for that. Our master might be content to have you swing a shovel for a while, but I surely won't be. Now that he's not around to watch your back every minute, you'd best sleep lightly, frailblood."

'Aaron spat onto the steps beside me, stalked off to the Barracks. He'd broken the laws of San Michon using his bloodgifts on me, and I was half-tempted to throw a parting jab about his cowardice. But truth told, I was just glad he'd left me the fuck alone. I'd caught that glance Greyhand and Talon had exchanged, and I wondered if the seraph knew something of the wound I'd inflicted on the de Blanchet boy.

'With Aaron's eyes off me, I aimed now to find out. So, I simply flipped the Fathers at his back, and holding my bruised belly, stole back inside the Armoury.

'My heart was racing, but all those nights I'd spent stealing out to Ilsa's bedroom came back to me in a flood. I could still be a stealthy bastard when I chose, even without warm lips waiting for me at the end. I crept through the weapon racks, low honeyed lights shining above. And soon enough, I was crouched back outside the Foundry doors.

'Peering inside, I saw Greyhand and Talon beside little Claude's body. Sister Aoife was on the other side of the room now, busy at the Foundry's workings.

'". . . large infestation considering the time this maggot spawn had to hunt," the seraph was saying. "It only turned two months ago, you say?"

'"Almost three," Greyhand nodded. "But, oui. The blood runs thick in this one."

'"Interesting that the leech who made it abandoned it?"

'"She may not have known the boy Became. Apparently, she departed in haste."

'"Mmm." The boything shrieked behind its gag as Talon slid one of those silver-tipped tubes into its skin. "And this burn on its arm? Archer's message said it was of import."

'Greyhand glanced to Aoife, lowering his voice to a conspiratorial whisper. "The boy did that with his bare hands."

'"De Coste?"

'"De León."

'Talon scoffed. "That water-blooded little cockgobbler?"

'"Those wounds were inflicted two weeks ago," Greyhand said. "They should have healed at next dawn, and yet they linger. When I burst into the room, I could still see the blood *boiling* under this leech's skin where de León touched it."

'". . . Boiling? You're certain?"

'"I saw it. I *smelled* it. You know what this is, Talon."

'"I know nothing of the sort."

'"Damn you, open your eyes, man. This is *sanguimancy*."

'Crouched at the doorway, I felt my whole body tense. I'd no understanding of the word's meaning, but the way Greyhand whispered it sent a chill through my aching belly. I could hear wonder in my master's voice now. Wonder, and fear.

'"Impossible," Talon hissed. "That line is extinguished. Centuries past."

'"Centuries are nothing to these creatures. What if the stories are wrong,

Talon? Or lies?" Greyhand glanced to Aoife, lowering his voice further. "De León failed every testing in the Trial of the Blood, but we never tested him for this. What if the leech who seeded his mo—"

"'Then we should take him to Heaven's Bridge right now,' Talon growled. "Cut his throat and give him to the waters."

'Again, I felt a surge of butterflies. I'd been taught there were only four kith houses. Voss. Chastain. Ilon. Dyvok. Had I heard aright?

'*Were they talking about a fifth bloodline?*

'*And was I . . . one of them?*

'I pressed back against the doors. I wasn't sure if my chest had fallen into my gut, or my gut had leapt into my chest. My master had lied to me when he said he'd no idea what I'd done to the de Blanchet boy. And Talon was talking about *ending* me. I wondered if I should run for it. Just head back to the stables, saddle up Justice and bolt.

"'We should do nothing rash until we've spoken to Khalid,' Greyhand whispered. "I am the boy's master. He's impatient. Arrogant. Far too keen for glory. But he's one of the finest swords I've trained, and he took down this highblood alone, drugged to the eyeballs on rêvre. If what I suspect of his line is true . . . he could be the greatest of us, Talon."

"'Or the most terrible."

"'Is that not for God to decide?"

"'God helps those who help themselves, old friend.' Talon leaned on the slab and sighed. "You *are* the boy's master, and I'll not gainsay you. But if Khalid bids we end him . . .'

'Greyhand nodded, grim. "So be it. We shall speak to the abbot after duskmass."

'The taste of iron and adrenaline was heavy on my tongue. I slipped away before Greyhand could spot me, stealing back across the Armoury. Out the doors, dashing across the rope bridge to Barracks, my head swimming with all I'd heard.

'A hidden gift named sanguimancy.

'A fifth bloodline of the kith.

'What did it all mean? Why did Greyhand speak of them with fear? And could I really be born of this mysterious line, and not the frailblood Talon had marked me for?'

Jean-François dipped his quill in the ink jar, chocolat eyes on his tome. 'Could you not simply ask Abbot Khalid?'

'Fuck no,' Gabriel scowled. 'All I'd heard, I'd eavesdropped. Greyhand had *lied* to me in Skyefall. God Almighty, Talon was willing to take me to the Bridge over this. Besides, it wasn't in my nature to go bleating to adults when the road got rocky. You grow up with a stepfather like mine, you learn to solve your own fucking problems.'

Gabriel's thumb traced the small, raised ridges of the sevenstar in his palm.

'So solving my own problems was exactly what I set out to do.'

✦ VII ✦

A LIBRARY OF GHOSTS

'THAT EVE, I did something I never imagined myself doing when I first entered San Michon.'

'And that was?' Jean-François asked.

'I broke the rules.'

The vampire's eyes widened in alarm. '*Scandalous.*'

'Mock if you will.'

'Merci, I believe I shall.'

'Fuck you,' Gabriel scowled. 'You've no ken what it was like, you blood-less prick. All my life, I was raised in the One Faith. Deception sat as well on me as a rope around my neck. San Michon was a *holy* place, and in the last seven months, the commandments of the Order had become as the laws of the Almighty to me. In breaking them, I felt I was going against God Himself, and being paleblood, I knew my soul was already at eternal peril. But there was nothing for it. And it wasn't the blood of lambs that flowed in my veins.'

Gabriel sighed, gulping a mouthful of wine.

'I never used to drink anything but water at meals, for fear of what the liquor had done to my stepfather. But Aaron had shared a bottle with Baptiste as promised, and as I bedded down that night, he was already drooling into his sheets. His crony de Séverin lay on his back, breathing softly, returned from a recent Hunt near Avaléne. Theo Petit was snoring loud enough to shake the floor. But I was wide awake, and taut with fear.

'I lay there with Lionclaw hidden under my blankets, one hand wrapped around its hilt. Heart hammering. Mouth dry. Waiting to hear Talon and Greyhand open the door, set to drag me to Heaven's Bridge. I knew I couldn't take them, yet I vowed to fight with all I fucking had if they came for me.

But hours slipped by, and I heard no heavy footfalls, no death march to the foot of my bed. And finally, I realized Abbot Khalid must have deemed that I be allowed to live. That whatever the truth of my bloodline, it wasn't yet worth killing me for.

'I let myself breathe a sigh of relief. My belly slowly unknotting itself. But despite my reprieve, I knew no peace. Greyhand had deceived me. Talon loathed me. My life might still be at risk, I wanted the truth of all this, and there was only one place I could think to find it.'

Jean-François raised an eyebrow in mute question.

'The Great Library. The forbidden section. There must have been a reason that we initiates weren't allowed to visit it. If any word about this fifth bloodline could be found in San Michon, I supposed it awaited me there.

'The Barracks were locked after nightfall, but I'd already pondered a way out of the doghouse. I rose shaking from my bed, and on whispering feet, found my way to the privy.

'Waste disposal in San Michon was a simple affair – the Barracks was built with one wall jutting out over the vast stone pillar it rested upon. A bench ran along that wall, a dozen holes cut into it, with the waters of the Mère River waiting five hundred feet below.'

'Sounds charming,' Jean-François murmured.

'Better than chucking it out the window.' Gabriel shrugged. 'I lifted the privy cover, looking down to the silver ribbon of the Mère and wondering if I was insane to be doing this. I was already on thin ice after Skyefall. If I were caught sneaking out after evebells, Talon might convince Greyhand to take me to Heaven's Bridge and be done. But this wasn't just idle curiosity now. My life might be at risk. I knew no other way to learn the truth of what I was. And after drubbing that vampire barehanded, I was still feeling a touch invincible. So, taking a deep breath, I slipped down through the privy spout.'

Gabriel paused, staring at the coldblood.

'. . . Well?'

'Well, what?'

'This is the part you make some quip about human waste and my relationship to it.'

'Please, de León, I stopped being a twelve-year-old decades ago.'

'No jabs about how I was throwing my apprenticeship down the sewer or suchlike?'

'If I *were* to quip, I'd be far more amusing than that.'

Gabriel scoffed. 'The wind was knives, snatching at my hair and turning my fingernails blue. I swung down onto the scaffold into a crouch, hands out for balance. An ordinary man would've broken his legs in that drop, but though I wasn't yet a man, I was nothing close to ordinary either. Slipping along the timbers, then scaling the rock wall barehanded, I found myself perched on a thin ledge skirting the building. Refusing to look down, I shuffled until at last, a touch light-headed, I reached the Barracks courtyard.'

'There were no guards? No nightwatch?'

'I could see a chymical lantern near the Ossuary, held by a dark figure that I guessed was Gatekeep Logan. But other than that, not another living soul. I made the sign of the wheel as I passed under the Cathedral's eaves, begging God to forgive my disobedience. As I stole over the next bridge, I wondered if he'd just pluck it loose and send me plunging to my death. But soon enough, I found myself before the entrance to the Great Library.

'The doors were sealed, of course. Huge copper-clad slabs they were, fashioned in baroque legends of the Martyrs – Cleyland with his key to hell and Michon with her silver chalice. I wondered if I'd have to force them to get inside. But strangely, as I pressed one hand upon them, I found the doors already unlocked. And with held breath and thumping chest, I crept into the vast hollow of San Michon's Library.

'The room was one vast chamber, lined floor to ceiling with books. Brass fixtures gleamed in the dim light, and the ceiling above was frescoed with angels of the host. Ladders on runners stretched to the loftiest stacks. Peering about the gloom with paleblood eyes, I saw the familiar sight of leather-bound volumes, dusty scrolls, beautiful tomes. Awash with dull rainbows of moonslight, spilling through windows of stained glass.

'Most curious of all, the floor was painted as a great map, outlining the empire and the five kingdoms it had been forged from. To the northwest, the frozen reaches of Talhost, now lost to the Forever King. To the east, the seat of Emperor Alexandre, great Elidaen. Nordlund ever in between, and Ossway and Südhaem to the south, the mighty spine of the Godsend Mountains running down Nordlund's west flank. It was ever the strangest feeling, walking through the Great Library. The knowledge of the entire empire was gathered on the shelves around you, and the empire itself laid out beneath your feet.

'I stole through long shadows, past countless books with countless stories to tell, until I reached the heavy wrought iron gates sealing off the forbidden section. Through the thick bars, I could see a long room, a maze of overflowing shelves. Strangely, I could smell candlesmoke. And ever so faint on the air, the soft perfume of . . .

'"Blood," I whispered.

'My hackles were up now. My mouth watering. I'd been given the sacrament at duskmass as always, but the beast within was never truly sated, and I could feel it stirring. I remembered Frère Yannick having his throat slit in the Red Rite the first night I arrived in the monastery. That fate awaited every paleblood alive.

'Me sooner than others, if Talon got his way.

'I set my mind back to task, and took hold of the gates into the forbidden section. I thought perhaps to prise the bars wider with my dark strength and slip inside, but as I flexed, they parted like the waters of the Eversea before San Antoine's prayers.

'*Already unlocked* . . .

'The hinges made not a whisper as I stole inside. The scent of blood grew stronger as I navigated a warren of dusty shelves, loaded with books and scrolls and the strangest curios. The skulls of men with the teeth of beasts. Sevenstars made of human bones. Metal puzzle boxes carved with arcane glyfs. I saw a skeletal creature pickled in a glass jar, and I *swore* it blinked at me as I passed by. The tomes were all shapes and sizes, but each was bound in pale leather, bleached with time. They were like the corpses of books rather than books themselves. It felt as if I stalked through a library of ghosts.

'I could see faint light ahead. My unease growing along with the bloodscent. And rounding a shelf of bleached and silent secrets, I found the strangest sight I'd yet seen in the Library.

'"God Almighty . . ." I whispered.

'A table of stout oak, piled with books and surrounded by leather chairs, lit by a single candle. A girl in the pale vestments of a sisternovice was slumped flat upon the table, long dark hair over her face, blood puddled thick around her cheek.

'Sweet Mothermaid, it smelled like heaven's perfume . . .

'It looked like someone had struck the girl while she sat there reading, cracking her skull. I crept forward, heart thumping. And as I reached out to move her hair in search of a wound, the girl opened her eyes, looked right at me, and fucking screamed.

'I yelped and leapt backwards. She reared up from the table, face slick with blood, lifting the candlestick to brain me. And looking about with wide, dark eyes, she pressed one pale hand to her heart and whispered in a crisp, highborn accent.

'"Oh, you *cunting* bastard . . ."

'". . . I beg your pardon?"

'The girl dragged a shaking hand through her long dark hair and sighed. "Beg all you wish, boy. You almost gave me a fucking heart seizure."

'". . . You're the sisternovice who inked my aegis," I realized. "The one I saw getting whipped in the stables."

'"And you're the peasant who took my horse."

'"I'm no peasant," I scowled. "I'm an initiate of the Silver Order."

'"Those are hardly mutually exclusive properties."

'"Are you aright?"

'She shrugged. "Just resting my eyes, if that's any of your concern."

'"Facedown in a pool of blood?"

'The sisternovice blinked then, realizing her face was sticky red, yet more blood pooled on the table in front of her. "Oh, *fuck* it all," she snarled, reaching into her vestments for a bloodstained kerchief. "Apologies. It looks rather more dramatic than it is."

'I stared at the blood on her lips, pulse drumming in my temples. This was the first time I'd been alone with a girl since I'd almost killed Ilsa. Remembering the sensation of that warm red rushing into my mouth as she writhed and sighed . . .

'"I thought your skull was broken," I managed.

'"It's my nose," she replied, swabbing her face. "It bleeds a great deal lately. I suspect it's something to do with the altitude in this godforsaken pigsty."

'My mind was awash. I wondered what in the Sevens' names this girl was doing there. Alone, after dark, against the rules. But more, and despite the blood – or likely *because* of it – I couldn't help noticing how beautiful she was. Skin like milk. Beauty spot beside the gentle bow of her bloody lips. She had the eyes of a dark angel.' Gabriel smiled. 'And the mouth of a she-devil on the rag.

'"I've seen you about," she declared with a toss of her hair. "And though I've stabbed you repeatedly, we've not been formally introduced. My name is Astrid Rennier."

'"Gabriel de León," I replied, still more than a little flustered.

'"Oui. De León." Dark eyes roamed me, toe to crown. "You don't look much of a lion. Then again, you *are* out of bed after evebells. Which means you've more courage than the rest of these boorish little boys."

'Ever so slowly, she extended her hand.

'"I think we shall get along famously."

'I blinked at her hand as if it were a serpent coiled to strike. This girl had seen me half-naked, after all, touched me in places few others had. The scent of her blood was stirring that memory now, and my own blood besides. But she was a novice of the Silver Sorority, soon to be wedded to God. I was an initiate of the Silver Order, servant of that same Heavenly Father. I shouldn't even have been *talking* to her, let alone . . .

'"Courtly manners dictate a gentleman kiss a lady's hand when he meets her," Astrid said helpfully, wriggling her fingers.

'"Suppose I don't want to kiss it."

'"Then I suppose you're the ill-mannered peasant I first took you for."

'She gifted me an ingénue's smile, but I saw the trap she'd laid: Obey her command or be rude. Problem was, I wanted to do neither. Holy vows and godly laws aside, this girl reminded me of Aaron de Coste and the other initiates who made my life such a misery, with their lordly accents and upturned noses. Beautiful as she was, *incredible* as she smelled, Astrid Rennier struck me as something of a bitch.

'Still, she'd done an artful job with the ink on my chest. And Mama had raised me to always treat girls the way I'd want them to treat me. *There are three ways men view the women of the world, Gabriel. Enemies to be overcome. Prizes to be won. Or as people. My advice is choose the latter, my love. Lest they begin considering you the former.*

'And so, I took Astrid Rennier's hand.

'Her skin was wondrous warm after the chill outside. I could smell the scent on her hair – rosewater and silverbell mixed with the dizzying perfume of her blood. I suppressed a shiver at the memory of her touch upon my bare chest, the pain of her needles in my skin. And supposing a chaste kiss couldn't anger God too much, I brushed my lips across her knuckles, trying to sound courtly.

'"Enchanted, mademoiselle."

'"Not yet," she promised.

'"What are you doing in here?"

'"I could ask the same of you, good Frère."

'"I'm not a brother of the Order yet. My proper title is Initiate."

'"Oh, is that what we're being now?" She raised one dark eyebrow. "Proper?"

'I peered at the books Astrid was reading. Most were written in languages I'd no ken of, but the ones I could comprehend seemed a strange mix. The pages were covered in mad scrawls, filled with strange geometrical shapes and arcane symbols. I ran my finger along one of the pale spines, murmuring aloud.

'"*A Full and Complete Accounte of that Peril Which Godly Men Did Name the Aavsenct Heresy, Told in Seven Partes, This Being Parte the Thirde.*"

"'Not a very creative title, is it?"

"'*Of Astrological Portents and Prognostications Dire – A Complete Historie.*"

"'Look, do you fucking mind?" Astrid said, covering the books protectively.

"'What are you reading about in here? And why at night?"

"'What business is that of yours?"

"'None at all. Which I suppose is my favourite kind."

'She smiled a little at that. "Still. Why would I share mine with you?"

"'We're both breaking the rules here." I shrugged. "Honour among thieves?"

"'I'm no thief, Gabriel de León. But if you *must* know, I am reading at night because Archivist Adamo won't permit sisternovices into the forbidden section during the day. Even if I *were* a full-fledged sister, I'm still possessed of a pair of breasts, which disqualifies you from all sorts of things around here. And I am wading through this collection of horseshit, pig spunk, and lunatic nonsense in an attempt to get to the bottom of daysdeath." She blew a dark lock of hair out of her eyes. "Satisfactory?"

"'Daysdeath," I whispered, suddenly intrigued. "Have you found anything?"

'She pointed at a few books, one at a time. "Horseshit. Pig spunk. Lunatic nonsense. Honestly, I think the only reason half this collection is forbidden is out of the profound embarrassment someone was fucking stupid enough to collect it in the first place."

'Sitting beside her, I looked at the books with renewed interest. "Why are you searching for the secret to daysdeath?"

"'Well, as long as I'm stuck in this arsehole, why wouldn't I be? The empire shall soon be under siege by an ever-expanding mob of bloodthirsty corpses. It's all well and good for *you*. You get to gallivant about the countryside in fabulous leather coats, turning coldbloods to ashes and peasant girls to puddles. But nobody in authority seems particularly concerned about what caused the phenomenon that led to this fucking calamity to begin with. They're just . . ." – the sisternovice flailed her hand – "*reacting* to it."

"'I've sometimes thought the same myself," I confessed.

"'Well, then, it seems the Almighty gifted you a functional brain. Huzzah and hurrah. They seem in rather short supply around this fucking place."

'I just stared. She was a curious one, this girl. One second turning on her charm easy as breathing. The next, spitting venom like a greensnake.

"'Apologies," she sighed, dabbing again at her nose. "I'm a dragon on her moonstime when I'm fiending. We should remedy that."

'She rose from her chair, walked to one of the shelves and fished about behind a stack of books. From some secret hiding place, she drew a long-stemmed pipe, and to my astonishment, I saw it was solid gold. I watched her take out a peck of powdered traproot and a larger pinch of a sticky green substance from a small golden case.

'"What's that?" I asked.

'"Rêvre," she replied.

'". . . Sisternovices are allowed to smoke dreamweed?"

'"Of course. I just sneak out for a pipeful in the freezing dead of night for the jollies."

'I rolled my eyes. "Touché, I suppose. Where'd you get it?"

'She shrugged. "Keeper Logan and Kaveh both owe me favours."

'"Kaveh?" I asked. "Kaspar's little brother?"

'Astrid nodded. "He goes on the supply runs to Beaufort with the good Keeper, and I've still some friends down there who keep him well-paid and me well-supplied."

'Truth told, and to my shame, I admit I'd mistaken Kaveh as something of a simpleton. But between his odd meeting with Sister Aoife, and now this revelation, it seemed there was more to the mute young groom than first met my eye.

'Astrid frowned, tongue protruding between her lips as she blended the rêvre and traproot. Packing her pipe, she slipped it between her lips, and leaning into the candle, she drew down a deep draught. Her long, smoky lashes fluttered against her cheeks, and she rocked back, holding her breath.

'Traproot was common enough – it had been a favourite among Sūdhaemi sailors for centuries, and served in pipes across the empire now that the tobacco plant had become too hard to grow. But dreamweed was a hard narcotic, favoured of soothsingers, authors, and other worthless tossers. It was near impossible to cultivate since daysdeath, and cost a small fortune; this girl obviously had wealth. And staring at the golden case, I was astonished to notice its embossed design: a unicorn rampant against five crossed swords.

'"Where did you get that?" I breathed.

'Astrid held up a finger, still holding her lungful. My mind was racing through the ways she might have acquired such a prize. Larceny seemed most obvious for a dreamfiend, but I forced myself to truly study this girl. Looking past the beauty, the blood, and thinking like the hunter they were training me to be.

'From the softness of her hand, she'd not done much hard work in her life. She carried herself like Aaron de Coste, not some gutter-running drug addict – that same accent and arrogance, softened by her looks and charm. And the seal on that case . . .

'Astrid moved to the window, breathed a soft grey sigh into the night outside. "Martyrs and Mothermaid, *that* is better."

'I pointed to the case again. "That's the crest of Alexandre III. Emperor of all Elidaen."

'"So?" Astrid asked, her voice now lazy and soft.

'"So either you're a common thief or some kind of princess."

'Astrid lifted her pipe. "I told you already. I am no thief, Gabriel de León."

'I scoffed. "Princess, then?"

'She drew deep on the smoke and said nothing for a long time, simply holding her breath. But finally, she exhaled a sweet narcotic cloud into the dark beyond the glass. And she spoke then, the warm blur in her bloodshot eyes belied by the steel in her voice.

'"I'm no princess. I'm a fucking queen."'

✦ VIII ✦

DEALING WITH THE DEVIL

'"THAT SEEMS UNLIKELY," I replied, trying my best to look unimpressed. "There's but one female sovereign of this realm, and her name is Isabella the First."

'"Devils fuck that syphilitic whore," Astrid growled.

'Again, that shook me. The Emperor was chosen by divine right, his union blessed by God Himself. To speak so of the Empress was not only treasonous, but blasphemous. And this sisternovice seemed to give not a beggar's cuss about either.

'As if remembering herself, Astrid offered me the pipe.

'"Merci, no."

'"I thought you palebloods enjoyed your smoke?"

'"Sanctus is a holy sacrament," I scowled. "Not an indulgence of base vice."

'"Whatever scratches your itch, Initiate." Astrid took another drag, exhaling out the window. "My mother is Antoinette Rennier, former courtesan in the court of Emperor Philippe IV, and favoured mistress of his son Prince Alexandre."

'"You mean *Emperor* Alexandre."

'"Well, he wasn't emperor when mother started bedding him."

'"You're . . . daughter of the ruler of all Elidaen," I breathed, my eyes awonder. "Benefactor of the Order of San Michon, Protector of the Realm and Chosen of God Himself."

'"You make my father sound *far* more impressive than he is, trust me."

'I could scarce believe what I was hearing. But I could feel the weight in her words. Astrid Rennier had the air of nobility, oui. But more, behind the smoke-blur in her eyes, I could sense an indignity and rage that left me little doubt she spoke truth.

"'You're actually . . . *royalty* . . .'"

"'A bastard is what I actually am.'"

"'. . . I never really thought of girls being bastards.'"

"'That's because girls can't inherit property. But I *am* indeed a royal bastard.' Astrid tucked a lock of raven black behind her ear. 'Sometimes a royal bitch besides.'"

"'Well, I wasn't going to be the one to suggest it . . .'"

"'Ah, he shows some teeth at last. Perhaps there *is* a lion in him, after all.'"

"'What are you doing in San Michon?'"

"'Being kept out of sight and mind,' she replied, toying with the stem of her pipe. 'I was raised at court, you see. My mother kept in customary fashion of a prince's mistress. But once the prince became emperor and got himself an empress, his new bride took exception to our presence. And so, we suffered the fate of all unwanted noblewomen in this empire. Whisked off to the silence and security of a nunnery.' Astrid's lips twisted in a bitter smile. 'Better than a brothel, I suppose.'"

"'. . . Your mother is here, too?'"

"'No. Bitch-Empress Isabella thought it unwise to keep us together. Mother's in Redwatch. The Priory of San Cleyland. I haven't seen her in a year.'"

"'I'm sorry. That seems . . .'"

"'Unjust,' Astrid murmured. '*Unjust* is what it is.'"

"'. . . That's why you named him so,' I realized.

'She looked at me then, her bloodshot eyes puzzled.

"'The gelding. You named him Justice.'"

"'Ah.' She nodded, her mood growing fey again. 'One more thing they took from me. They're very good at that in this place. Taking, I mean.' She folded her arms, lips thin. 'What did you name him instead? Some clichéd nonsense like Shadow or Sooty?'"

"'He kept the name you gave him. Justice suits him well.'"

'I watched the beauty spot beside her lip as she smiled sadly. "Merci."

"'I'm sorry. That they took him from you.'"

"'Hearts only bruise. They never break.' Astrid shrugged, as if to banish the shadow on her shoulders. 'But I appreciate you stood up for me against the prioress that day, Gabriel de León. Peasant-born or no, that took a noble soul.'"

'I felt aflame with her flattery. Altogether confounded in her presence. She was older. Obviously deeper in the ways of the world. The ink on my very skin had been carved by her hand. Truth told, though I was taller, stronger, hardened by years of labour and months of bladework, I felt a blundering child around this girl.

"'How did you get in here?" she asked. "Did you steal a key?"

"'I'm no thief either, Sisternovice."

"'Then how were you planning to make your way about? That surly old bastard Adamo usually has everything locked up of an eve."

"'I thought I'd bend the bars. But to be honest, I hadn't really planned that far ahead. I'm not even sure how I'm going to sneak back into Barracks."

"'Presumably the same way you got out?"

"'No way to do that without wings. I crawled out through the privies."

"'That sounds like a shit plan, Initiate.'"

Jean-François paused his writing, chuckling faintly. 'You see, *that* was amusing, de León.'

'Fuck off, vampire.'

The historian gave a small bow and continued scribbling.

'I hung my head, realizing the sisternovice was right. Greyhand had warned me about my impetuousness in Skyefall, yet apparently, I hadn't learned my lesson.

"'It *was* a touch foolish, I suppose," I admitted.

"'Welllll, let's just call it reckless," Astrid declared. "Recklessness is a far more admirable quality in a member of the Ordo Argent than foolishness, wouldn't you say?"

'Looking into her smile, I found myself smiling back.

"'Enchanted *now*, aren't you?" she asked.

'Astrid offered the pipe again.

"'Not much left."

"'Merci, no. I didn't come here to smoke."

"'Then why *are* you here, Initiate de León?"

'I studied this sisternovice, trying to ignore the shiver-sweet fragrance of her blood between us. The fact that she was in the forbidden section – and speaking with such disdain for the powers that be – told me she probably wouldn't go shouting about it if I told her the truth. I didn't know if I should trust her. But God knew I trusted no one else.

'And besides, she was right. Forget enchanted. By then, I was damn-near enthralled.

"'Have you ever heard the word *sanguimancy*?"

"'No. It sounds some measure of blood witchery?"

"'I don't know what it is. But apparently, it's a gift that's been passed to me."

'"But . . . you're frailblood, aren't you?"

'I chewed my lip, remembering the tingle of her fingertips across my skin as she inked the lion on my chest. I reached down to my right hand, toying with the ring my mama had given me as a boy. Wondering why she hadn't just given me the truth instead. "Seraph Talon *told* me I was frailblood. But Greyhand suspects I'm descended from another kith bloodline altogether. A fearsome one, and ancient, thought extinguished centuries ago."

'Astrid leaned forward, intrigued. "Your father . . . ?"

'"I never met him. But I came here tonight in the hope I'd discover something of all this in these archives. I can't ask Greyhand. He already lied to me about it. He and Talon were talking about *killing* me for it. But I need to learn about this sanguimancy if I'm to master it, and understand the truth of what I am. The last seven months I've wandered about here thinking I was the lowest of the low. And now I discover I've some gift that might make me the greatest silversaint ever known?"

'One eyebrow rose. "And is that what you want? To be great? To be known?"

'"My sister was murdered by a coldblood," I said, tone growing fierce. "She was twelve years old. And instead of being left to rest in her grave, Amélie rose again, nothing but a monster herself. If by being here, I can save one child, spare one mother the hell of what mine suffered, I'll do whatever I can to do it well. And damn right I want to be fucking great. Don't you? Don't you want your life to count for something? To *matter?*"

'"More than anything." Her eyes were brief fire as she looked to the window. She whispered then, and her words sounded more like a prayer. "I'd tear the wings off an angel to fly this cage. I'd claw down the sky to carve my name into this earth."

'I nodded. "One day as a lion is worth ten thousand as a lamb."

'The sisternovice tilted her head, looked me over.

'"Interesting," she murmured.

'"What is?"

'"*You* are."

'I turned my eyes to the rows of countless tomes on the shelves about us. All those silent secrets. Astrid drummed her fingers on the book beside her.

'"Ask nicely," she said.

'". . . What?"

'"There are far too many books in here for you to search alone. Even if you'd a thousand nights and could read all the languages they're written in.

And any day, you're like to be sent off on another Hunt. So you're thinking to yourself, *If she's already looking for word about daysdeath, she might keep one eye open for mention of this gift of mine?*"

"'. . . You'd do that? Why?'"

"'Perhaps I appreciate that you stepped to my defence in the stable that day. Perhaps your tale of your sister touched my black and withered little heart. Perhaps I just like those pretty grey eyes of yours.'"

"'Or perhaps you like the idea of me owing you favours? Like Kaveh and Keeper Logan and God knows who else?'"

'Her lips curled into what was perhaps the first true smile she'd gifted me all night. "You know, privy-diving aside, you're actually quite clever for a peasant boy.'"

'I rolled my eyes again. "Why do I feel like I'm striking a bargain with the devil?"

"'Oh, I'm twice as crafty as the devil, Gabriel de León. But we'll not be striking anything lest you ask me nicely.'"

"'What does that even mean?'"

"'Say please, of course.'"

'I looked at her there in the gloom, again struck with the feeling that Astrid Rennier was toying with me. Back in Lorson, a lingering look was all it took to win favour from most of the lasses in my village. But here in Astrid's presence, I felt a particularly plump mouse bargaining with an especially hungry cat.

'But she spoke truth. This archive was too vast for me to search alone. And so, I got down on one knee. And I took her hand. And again, I brushed my lips against her knuckles.

"'Please, Majesty.'"

"'Majesty?'" she scoffed.

'I shrugged. "You're a fucking queen, remember?"

'She looked me in the eyes, her own glittering as she smiled.

"'Oui. We *shall* get along famously.'"

Gabriel fell silent, refilling his drink. Lost in remembrance of an angel's eyes, a devil's smile. Despite the wine, the memory was sharp as broken glass. He feared he'd cut himself if he lingered in it too long. And yet he remained, holding tight as he could.

'De León?' Jean-François finally asked.

'We stayed up for hours,' he said, pale grey eyes coming back to focus. 'Reading in silence. It's strange how much you can learn about a person by just sitting together and shutting your fucking mouth. Astrid Rennier read swiftly, and in at least a dozen tongues. She sat straight-backed like a lady of breeding, swore like a taverneful of Ossian sailors, and chewed her fingernails like a girl with far too many secrets.

'As she warned, most of the forbidden section read like the rantings of moonstouched fanatics. But I knew this search might take months. And so, undeterred, perhaps an hour from dawn, Astrid Rennier and I said our farewells.

'"Godmorrow, Initiate."

'"Will you be back again this eve, Sisternovice?"

'Astrid smiled. "*That* enchanted, are we?"

'"I've a will to get to the bottom of this swift as I may."

'She inclined her head. "I sneak out most nights for a smoke. If you think I'm bitchly now, you should see me after a few days without a pipe. I arrive around midnight. If you've a notion to meet again, might I suggest you climb through the roof on your return to Barracks? The tiles are old in this place. They come away easily."

'"Merci, Majesty." I bowed. "God go with you."

'She curtseyed like a lady at court. "And you, Initiate."

'With nothing else to say, we stole out the front door, which Astrid locked firmly behind us. I'd no ken where she'd got her keys, but I suspected she'd lie if I asked. The wind was freezing after the Library's shelter, cutting through my coat like knives as we parted.

'Mornbells rang in the Cathedral belfry, rousing cooks to the kitchens, brothers to the Breadbasket. I'd lingered longer than intended – I was supposed to report to the stables for my first date with a barrow and fucking shovel. I could see Logan by the sky platform, silhouetted by his chymical lantern. Cutting across the monastery, I approached as if from Barracks, hands in my leathers. The thin gatekeeper grunted greeting in his Ossway brogue.

'"Fairdawn, young cub."

'"Godmorrow, good Keeper. I'm to report below to—"

'"Aye, aye, Greyhand tol' me all aboot it. Yer first 'unt sounded a dark one, laddie. Dead chil'ren and all. Bad business." The keeper spat on the winch and unlocked it, squinting at my swordarm. "Decided what ye'll 'ave inked yet?"

'I shrugged, climbing aboard the sky platform. Skin tingling as I wondered if Astrid would again do the inkwork. "Almost."

'"Well, my congratulations, young'un. Not all survive the Trial of the 'unt. An' you pay nae mind to what those other lads say behind yer back neither. Yer blood might be thin as watered Sūdhaemi cat's piss, and yer stock might be sheep-rutting Nordish trash, but yer doin' God's work. When ye die, I'll say a prayer o'er yer stone, sure and true."

"'. . . Merci, good Keeper."

"'Too right, laddie."

'Logan gave a toothy grin and lowered me down. The valley was still shrouded in gloom and freezing mist, the platform alighting with a heavy *thump*. Kaspar and Kaveh would usually be at work already, but Greyhand had informed the grooms of my punishment as promised. A shovel and barrow sat in the snow before the stable gates, a note pinned to the unlit lantern within.

'GATE UNLOCKED. DOWN AFTER MORNMEAL. MERCI! — K & K

'Cursing beneath my breath, I hung the lantern from the barrow, and wheeled through the creaking gates. I spared a hello for Justice, giving him a long hug and one of the sugar cubes he loved so much.

'And spitting on my hands, I started shovelling shite.'

BLOOD ON THE STAR

'SUCH WAS TO be my life for the next two weeks. Horseshit in the morning, training during the day, and after a few hours of stolen sleep, dusty tomes and the company of Sisternovice Astrid Rennier. Truthfully, I could conjure worse ways to spend my evenings.

'The days were another matter.

'Even though we were only newly returned to San Michon, Greyhand gave Aaron and me no reprieve. Instead, he'd set us straight to work in the Gauntlet, working us until we were dripping, despite the chill. Though I knew Greyhand might have ended me if Khalid had ordered it, the fact that I'd not been taken to the Bridge told me his wisdom had won out over Talon's fears about my lineage. Cruel and hard as Greyhand could be, he'd spoken my praises to the seraph in the Foundry. Some part of me yet wanted to please him. The rest of me just feared him. In truth, I knew not where I stood with my master now.

'A few other initiates were returned from the Hunt, and the Gauntlet was almost crowded. We were training one day; de Coste and his fish-faced crony de Séverin working on the Scythe, me pounding away at the Thorned Men with young Fincher beside me. Our form was being studied by the watchful eyes of Greyhand and Fincher's master – a hulking brother with a booming voice named Frère Alonso.

'Alonso was broad, dark-haired, Nordish born. A long, jagged scar was torn down the left side of his face, giving him a frightening, feral mien. He'd cast off his greatcoat, revealing heavily scarred arms covered in beautiful portraits of the Mothermaid, Raissa, the Angel of Justice, and my namesake, Gabriel, Angel of Fire. He watched Finch and me like a hawk, sipping occasionally from a silver flask.

'"You're dragging that foot again, de León," Greyhand warned.

'"Oui, Master," I said, shifting my stance.

'"And tie those pretty locks back properly, or I'll shear you like a sheep."

'"Your boy moves well, Greyhand," Alonso muttered. "For a frailblood."

'I felt my hackles rise at that, pausing in my bladework to bow. "Merci, Frère. The highblood I kicked the shite out of in Skyefall single-handed certainly thought so."

'"Enough of that, de León," Greyhand growled. "Pride is a sin."

'But big Alonso only chuckled as he took another swig. "You've spirit too, lad. Nordish fire. Think you've enough to best young Fincher here?"

'I looked to my fellow initiate as Finch paused his practice, staring at me with his mismatched eyes. He was swift and sharp, but shorter than me. He had no reach. And the Voss blood in his veins wouldn't make a difference to his bladework.

'"Enough to best Fincher," I declared. "And every initiate in this Gauntlet besides."'

Jean-François raised an eyebrow. '*Really*, de León?'

'What can I tell you?' The silversaint shrugged. 'I was still feeling a little full of myself after taking down the de Blanchet boy. But more important, I'd worked my arse off in that circle, and I was sick of being treated like shite for the blood in my veins. Especially if I wasn't a frailblood at all.

'Greyhand glowered at my boasts, but Alonso roared with laughter. ·

'"The balls on this little bastard! Come on then, Finch! In the circle. You lads!" Alonso bellowed to de Coste and de Séverin, holding up a shining coin from his pocket. "We'll have ourselves a tourney, eh? A gold royale for the victor, I say!"

'Greyhand frowned darker, but if my mouth was big enough to bury me in shite, he wasn't the kind to dig me out of it. De Coste and de Séverin made their way across the circle, standing at the edge of the pale sevenstar. Fincher squared up against me, lips pinched thin. Glancing to his master, he spat on the cold stone.

'"I'ma have to kick yer arse now, Lil Kitty. Nae offence, like."

'The boy moved quick as flies, darting forward and slashing at my throat. But swift as spiders, I blocked his strike, skipped sideways, and struck his sword from his hand.

'Stepping back, I let him retrieve his blade.

'"None taken."

'Fincher scowled, slicing his sword through the air. He came on again, more cautious this time, weaving a blinding strike pattern, head, chest, head, belly. But I knew this song. I'd sung it so often by then, it was burned into my bones. Steel was mother. Steel was father. Steel was friend. And I struck the sword from Fincher's hand again, and with a savage jab from my elbow, split his lip all the way to his chin, dropped him to the circle floor. Standing over him, I levelled my blade at his throat, heart thrilling at the sight of his blood.

'"Yield, Brother."

'Fincher wiped at his split lip. "Best two ae three?"

'"Kittens can't count that high," I smiled.

'Finch glanced to his master, then grumbled. "Yield, then."

'I offered my hand, helped him up off the ground. Finch winced and rubbed his jaw, but to his credit, he didn't seem too dark on it. Frère Alonso smacked broad hands together and grinned. "Fine strike, de León. Fincher, it seems we've work to do."

'"Aye, Master," the lad muttered, eyes downturned.

'"De Séverin, you're next," Alonso crowed, eyes on the bigger lad. "Let's test this frailblood's measure against a Dyvok, eh?"

'De Séverin glanced to Greyhand as if to seek permission, but again, my master made no move to stop any of this. My mouth, he figured. My trouble. And so, the big nobleson hefted his training blades, smirked to de Coste, and strode onto the star.

'De Séverin's tunic was unlaced, and I could see a roaring bear etched across his chest – the sigil of the Blood Dyvok. All palebloods were preternaturally strong, but the Dyvok lads were fucking terrifying. Most wielded two-handed blades with only one, and there was an unspoken rule that they train with wooden swords in the Gauntlet, lest they cut their sparring partners in half.

'De Séverin lifted blades big as small trees, one in each hand.

'"Au revoir, frailblood."

'The blades boomed as they cut the air, scything just shy of my head. I skipped backwards, eyes wide as de Séverin came on like thunder, no room for quarter. We danced for a time, him swinging with measured fury, me staying out of his range. De Séverin's blades were six feet in length, his strength fearsome, though truth told, he was mostly brawn, little finesse. But more, and truer still, there's just no one with more to prove than the boy at the bottom of the pile. You feed a man your table scraps, he grows hungry *long* before he grows thin. And hunger can turn pups into wolves, and kittens into fucking lions.

'I sideslipped a strike from de Séverin's true hand, turned aside a blow from his off and stepped inside his reach. This close, those big swords were too unwieldy, unholy strength or no, and he was too slow to stop me from bringing my pommel up into his jaw, sending him flying backwards in an arc of saliva and brilliant blood. De Séverin struck the stones hard, spitting curses. And standing over him, I lowered my blade to his throat.

'"I yield," the boy growled, fangs glinting.

'Alonso raised a bushy eyebrow at Greyhand. "Scrappy little bastard, this one."

'"For a frailblood," I said, chest heaving.

'Alonso smiled crooked at that, scar twisting his face. "De Coste. You're next."

'"I think we've seen enough," Greyhand said.

'"Ah, come now, Brother," Alonso grinned. "A splash of claret is good for the—"

'"I said enough," Greyhand repeated, meeting Alonso's eyes. Though he was smaller, slighter, my master's tone brooked no dissent. "These are my apprentices both, Brother. I'll not have them blooding each other for no good reason."

'I had to respect that – the fact Greyhand was ever looking out for us, despite his mask of cold cruelty. But there was still ill feeling between de Coste and me, so thick we could have cut it with our training blades. His beating and threats still burned in my memory. And I could see he was still salty about being overshadowed in Skyefall.

'"Master," he said. "I'll happily teach this—"

'"I said no, Initiate. And I'll not say it again."

'I stared into Aaron's eyes, my lip curling. "Angel Fortuna smiles on you, dog."

'". . . What did you call me, Peasant?"

'"You threw me a dog punch the other day, and you know it. Come at me straightwise, I'd knock your fucking teeth out of your skull. You're a *coward*, de Coste."

'And that was all it took. Aaron came at me, hammer-hard and serpent-swift. His handsome face was twisted with rage, and he swung at my throat as if he genuinely wanted to kill me. I knocked aside his blow, but he crashed into me, and like a pair of five-year-olds, we fell to brawling. Aaron grabbed my tunic, buried his elbow in my throat. I mashed my knuckles into his mouth, smiling as I felt his lips split against his fangs.

'"Enough!" Greyhand grabbed our necks and dragged us apart. De Coste and I scrabbled for a moment more, until Greyhand dropped me on my arse and shoved Aaron backwards with a snarl. "You are not mongrels in a robber's yard!"

"'He fucking started it!"

"'And I'll finish it too, you frailblood bastard! I'll fucking *kill* you!"

"'*Enough!*" Greyhand bellowed.

'The rage in our master's voice brought us to heel. Aaron and I stared at each other across the circle while Alonso, Finch, and de Séverin looked on in silence.

"'Remember yourselves, and where you are!" Greyhand demanded. "You are initiates of the Ordo Argent! *Both* of you! Brothers in blood and silver. Your lives might be in each other's hands one night. Never forget, the Dead care not for our creed or kin. To them, we all taste the same! Now make your pax!"

'Aaron and I glowered, eyes burning with hatred.

"'Make. Your. Pax."

'We hung still a moment longer. But grudgingly, de Coste and I finally shook hands, murmuring a wish for peace that neither one of us shared.

'I knew this feud wasn't done. Not by a damn sight.

'As punishment, Greyhand worked us harder that day than I could ever recall. Long after Fincher and Alonso left, even after de Séverin took his leave, still our master drilled us – as if he could *sweat* the enmity from our bodies. Reprieve arrived only when bells rang for duskmass, and when services finished, Greyhand took us *back* to the Gauntlet for more. By the time I crashed into bed, I was almost comatose, falling into the kind of sleep that only corpses enjoy.

'So it was I awoke in the dark, hours later, gripped with sudden dread.

'I was late for my rendezvous with Astrid.'

✦ X ✦

AN ERRANT SPECK OF FLOTSAM

'IT WAS BLOODY freezing as I stole out of bed. The night after we first met, I'd followed the sisternovice's instructions and found myself a way out through the old tiles of the Barracks roof. Since then, I'd been sneaking out to meet her every night. Now I moved swift as I could, cutting across the monastery and dodging Keeper Logan, but it was close to second bell by the time I stole through the Library's front door.

'The gates to the forbidden section were unlocked as always. But sneaking through the warren of forgotten lore, I found Astrid's table empty. Looking around the long rows of books and curios, I could smell candlesmoke and the scent of silverbell and rosewater, but I couldn't see a soul. It seemed the sisternovice had tired of waiting.

'"Shit," I sighed.

'"Indeed," came a voice behind.

'"Sweet *fucking* Redeemer," I gasped, spinning in fright.

'"Flattering. But I prefer when you call me Majesty."

'Astrid stood there between the shelves, dark eyes sparkling, skin pale as starlight. It seemed for a moment she was a piece of the night itself come alive. I smiled at the simple sight of her, but that smile died quickly as I spied a figure in the shadows beside her. As it stepped into the candlelight, I saw wildly curled mousy brown hair, pretty green eyes and freckled skin. A girl Astrid's age, but almost a foot shorter.

'". . . I know you," I frowned.

'"Gabriel de León," Astrid said. "May I present Sisternovice Chloe Sauvage."

'"Fairdawn, Initiate," Chloe murmured. "A pleasure to see you again."

'I looked to Astrid in question. As far as I was aware, we were meeting as we'd done the last fortnight – to search for mention of the fifth line, discover the truth of daysdeath.

"'Chloe is a friend, Gabriel," Astrid said. "The dearest I have within these walls."

"'I've no doubt. But what's she to do with me?"

"'You owe me favour, do you not?"

'I groaned inwardly. "Oui."

"'I owe Chloe more than one. Services rendered and suchlike." Astrid waved a hand vaguely. "It's all a rich tapestry. Point is, you shall repay your boon to me by repaying her."

"'And how should I do that?"

"'Sisternovice Sauvage wishes to learn the art of the blade."

"'Learn *what*?"

"'The art. Of the blade. All that cutting and thrusting and whatnot." Astrid looked down to my hands, up to my eyes. "I have it on good authority you thrashed two initiates in the star today without so much as a scratch. And while I understand this is no Gauntlet, Chloe would like some pointers. Journeyman to novice, as it were."

"'But . . . she's a girl."

'Astrid looked at the little lass beside her, leaning in close to squint at Chloe's chest.

"'My God. You're right."

"'I told you this was a foolish idea," Chloe hissed. "They don't teach girls here."

"'Patience, ma chérie," Astrid murmured. "Our good initiate will eventually figure out that your breasts, whilst *magnificent*, aren't any real impediment to combat prowess."

'Chloe's cheeks burned a furious red. "They actually do get in th—"

"'Hush now, love," Astrid said, patting Chloe's hand. "Here it comes."

"'You told the sisternovice what we're looking for in here?" I asked.

"'Have no fear, Initiate. Chloe can keep a secret."

"'I can't sneak out as easily as Azzie," Chloe declared. "My room is right next to the prioress. But one night a week, she keeps a vigil in the Priory chapel, and I can steal away."

"'. . . And you're willing to help?"

"'I'm not at all convinced the answers to daysdeath lie in this library. It's through prayer and piety we shall regain the Lord's love. Through *his* words," Chloe gestured to the shelves about us, "not these. But all this talk about a fifth bloodline is intriguing."

"'It's as Mama always said, ma chérie," Astrid smiled. "When in a storm, the wise woman prays to God. But she also rows for shore." The sisternovice glanced to me. "Chloe can read Old Talhostic. And Ancient Ossian. Which I cannot. So, for two hours a week, you will teach her the art of steel. And for the rest of the night, she will help us search. Agreed?"

'I was uneasy at this. I didn't know Chloe Sauvage as far as I could spit her. But Astrid trusted her, and I *did* owe her a debt. I wasn't a treacherous dog like de Coste. I dealt my cards straight and paid what I owed.

"'We don't have swords," I finally declared.

"'See?" Astrid smiled to Chloe. "A man of his word." Reaching into her cloak, the sisternovice produced two wooden training blades.

"'Where did you get those?" I asked.

'She waved vaguely. "All a rich tapestry."

'I glanced about the room; the countless tomes, the illegible spines, the tangle of words that might contain the secret of what I was. I knew I'd struggle to read a quarter of it, and that the secrets of an ancient line would likely be written in an ancient tongue. So finally, I took the practice swords from Astrid's hands with a scowl.

"'Seems I've little choice."

"'I did warn you. I'm twice as crafty as the devil. So, you two had best get on with it. Cut. Thrust. Have at thee, villain. All that wonderful, sweaty nonsense."

"'. . . You don't want to learn too?"

"'Sweet Redeemer, no. I shall stay well out of the way and make appreciative noises while you try to bash each other's skulls in. Leave war to the fucking warriors."

'I moved the table and chairs, clearing us a space. Astrid retired to the windowsill, producing a stick of charcoal and a small sketchbook from her robes while I turned my gaze to Chloe. The lass was rolling up her sleeves, a blush on her freckled cheeks. She wore novice robes same as Astrid, but she was obviously ill at ease about being out of bed in the presence of a *boy*. She struck me as a quiet girl. Studious. Steady. And above all, devout.

"'Why do you want to learn the sword, Sisternovice?"

"'Not knowing how to use one is a good way to get killed by one, Initiate."

"'Good answer. Have you ever wielded a blade before?"

"'I've studied it . . . in books. And I know I'm small. But I learn quickly."

'I sighed. This maid was green as grass. But Astrid was right – the fact that Chloe was a girl was no reason she couldn't swing a sword. Unarmed,

a lass that small would get murdered in a fight, sure and true. But by their very nature, weapons are force multipliers. *Equalizers.* And so, I put the point of my sword under Chloe's chin, and lifted her head.

"'You *are* small. But skill with a weapon counts for far more than power. So. First lesson, Sisternovice. Always look your enemy in the eye."

'Chloe met my stare. I saw a faint twinkle in her own. She clenched her jaw, lifted the practice sword. "Always look your enemy in the eye."

'We trained. Just basics. Shifting around the room while Astrid sketched by the tall stained-glass windows. By the end of our two hours, Chloe was dripping with sweat, and I was dry as dust. But the tiny girl's eyes were alight, her smile bright as forgefire.

"'He's a very good teacher," Chloe whispered as Astrid rejoined us on the floor.

"'I saw." Astrid kissed her sweaty cheek. "But you were also *brilliant.* A blade to match the Angel Eloise herself. Do you not think so, Initiate?"

"'She was . . . excellent for a beginner."

'Astrid glowered at me sidelong. "Such praise could make angels weep."

"'It's all right, Azzie," Chloe smiled. "The Lord decrees we walk before we run."

"'And I'm sure you'll be running circles about the good initiate soon, ma chérie."

'I saw Chloe blush at Astrid's praise, just as I had when we first met. Sisternovice Rennier's charm could turn glaciers to puddles, sure and true. But still . . .

"'Shall we get to it? We've only a few hours to dawn, Sisternovices."

"'Oui," Astrid nodded. "This gibberish won't read itself, I fear."

'I moved the table back into place, hefting it effortlessly. Running her eyes along the shelves, Chloe took down an ancient brass-bound tome, its spine carved in a language so alien it almost made my eyes ache. I sat at table, with Sisternovice Sauvage to my left. Placing her sketchbook in front of her, Astrid curled up in the leather chair to my right, a dusty scroll in her lap, candlelight on her skin.

'Glancing at her sketches, I saw she'd been drawing Chloe as we practised. Astonished at how she could conjure such life from simple lines on a page.

"'Beautiful work, Sisternovice," I murmured.

'Astrid shrugged, chewing a well-worn fingernail. "I was trained by the masters of the Golden Halls as a girl. I used to be quite good. Rubbish now, though."

'Chloe scowled. "The Prioress would never have apprenticed you if *that* were true."

'"It's not like she has a choice," Astrid scoffed. "Charlotte's eyes are failing. The old bitch needs to train replacements in inking the aegis while she may."

'"Astrid!" Chloe gasped, making the sign of the wheel.

'"What? She *is* an old bitch. Trust me. Takes a young bitch to spot one." Astrid gazed at her sketchbook, a faraway look in her dark eyes. Her face was a beautiful mask – the kind a mistress's daughter would have learned to wear early in the Golden Halls. "When Mama insisted I be schooled in the arts, I'm not sure she imagined I'd be carving silver into halfbreed vampire boys' skins, before sending them off to die in the dark."

'"Well, they made a fine choice in you," I murmured, brushing fingertips over the lion beneath my tunic. "You've a keen eye and a keener hand, as Khalid said."

'Astrid glanced at my chest. "You were my first, actually. I hope I didn't hurt you."

'"Not too grim," I lied.

'She smiled at that, the beauty spot beside her mouth black as sin.

'"A little pain never hurt anybody, eh?"

'Chloe looked back and forth between Astrid and me, lips pressed thin. And my belly thrilled then, goosebumps tingling as a thin line of blood spilled from Astrid's nose. The scent of it stabbed the air, the flood of rust and copper rushing through my skull, into my chest, and then, lower still. As always, I'd taken the sacrament at duskmass to quiet my thirst. But I found myself averting my eyes, reaching into my leathers.

'"Nose," I said, holding out my kerchief.

'"Oh, fuck it *all*," Astrid hissed. Tilting her head back, she spoke, voice smothered by the kerchief. "Merci. It'll stop in a minute."

'I swallowed hard, pushing the thirst down, past my groin and into my boots where it belonged. Looking anywhere but at Astrid until she'd cleaned up that slick of brilliant, luscious *red*. I could feel Chloe's stare, my teeth growing sharp, and for a moment, I felt horribly ashamed of what I was. The sin of my birth. My hunger. My nature. It was all well and good to be part of the silver flame burning between humanity and the darkness. But I could never allow myself to forget that darkness lived also in *me*.

'The three of us settled in the candlelight, and once the press of my thirst abated, I was struck with how pleasant it was simply to be still for a time. The last seven months, my life had been sweating, praying, hunting, bleeding. I never thought I'd find such peace in simple *reading*. The words were a kind of magik, taking me by the hand and sweeping me into lands unseen, times unremembered, thoughts unimagined. Through all my years in San Michon, all the blood and sweat and darkling roads I walked, I learned one of my greatest lessons sitting in that Library with those girls in the still of the night.

'A life without books is a life not lived.

'Still, I found myself stealing glances at Astrid when I could, the scent of her blood tingling on my skin. She read swift as a storm, chewing through whole tomes while I managed chapters. I realized for all her cursing and brashness, Astrid was just as fierce a scholar as I was a swordsman. A girl who wielded books like blades.

'She rose after an hour, fetching her golden pipe. Wordlessly, she mixed a blend of rêvre and traproot, tongue poked between her lips. I watched her breathe down that sweet smoke, and she seemed a statue in the dim light, carved by the hand of God.

'The God she'd soon be married to . . .

'"My head hurts," Chloe murmured, rubbing her temples.

'"Oui." I nodded, cracking my neck. "I've paleblood eyes, and still they're aching in this candlelight. Almighty only knows how you're both managing."

'Astrid sighed grey out the window. "All this *would* be easier if we were allowed access to this drivel during daylight. Such as daylight is. But we're both girls, and you're an initiate, and none of those circumstances looks set to change anytime soon. So, I'm afraid we're at the mercy of Archivist Adamo and his idiotic rules."

'Chloe nodded and sighed. "What a world this would be, were it not held wholly and solely in the grip of stubborn old men."

'Astrid scoffed. "Oui."

'"I venture it's less to do with the fact they're men," I said. "More that they're old."

'Astrid's dark eyes flickered to mine. "You'd venture that, would you?"

'"Oh dear . . ." Chloe murmured.

'I shrugged. "Prioress Charlotte seems just as bad as Archivist Adamo."

'"A fine riposte," Astrid ceded. "But Prioress Charlotte is a product of Church indoctrination. And the Church is held wholly and solely in the grip of stubborn old men."

'". . . You're going to make a very strange nun, Astrid Rennier."

'"Honestly, look around you. You haven't noticed there's not a single woman in a position of real power in this monastery?"

'"I had," I admitted. "But what about San Michon? *She* was a woman."

"'Don't get me started on the pantheon. There's Seven Holy Martyrs, Gabriel de León. And *one* dame among them. We're half the fucking population, you know.'

"'Well, what of the Mothermaid? She's a woman. Second only to God Himself.'

"'Oh, oui, the holy virgin.' Astrid rolled her eyes. "Let me tell you, if the Almighty offered me the platter of shit that constitutes divine motherhood and yet denied me the pleasure of a good roll in the hay beforehand, I'd have told him to go fuck himself.'

"'Astrid!' Chloe gasped, making the sign of the wheel. 'Blasphemy!'

"'Oh, he knows I don't mean it,' she scoffed, glancing up. 'He knows *everything*.'

'I was taken aback also, and not simply at the sisternovice's sacrilege. To hear her talk so reminded me just how vast the gulf between us was. Astrid was half royalty. I was half monster. She was a child of the Golden Court. I was a brat from the provinces. But more, and most, Astrid Rennier was a courtesan's daughter. She'd likely seen and done things I could scarce imagine. Wonderful things. Wicked things. I lowered my gaze then. Chewed my lip. Astrid looked at me through coal-dark lashes.

"'How old are you?'

"'. . . My saintsday is in five days,' I realized. 'I'll be sixteen.'

"'Almost a man.' She tilted her head. 'And still I make him blush.'

"'That mouth of yours could make a *sailor* blush, Astrid Rennier.'

"'Good God Almighty . . .' Chloe breathed.

'I glanced up at the awe and fear in the sisternovice's voice, followed her eyeline to the windows. Light flared in the dark outside, and for a terrible moment, I feared some discovery. But Astrid pushed the glass open, breathing a wondering sigh.

'Chloe and I clustered behind. And looking into the dark above, I beheld a sight I couldn't recall seeing since I was a child. A sight none of us understood at the time. A sight that was to change my life, and the shape of this entire empire.

'A falling star.

'Its light was dim, and yet it must have burned with impossible fury to be seen through the daysdeath pall at all. I followed its path across the shadowed heavens, felt my skin prickling. Looking to Astrid beside me, I saw her smile, that falling radiance reflected in the bloodshot dark of her eyes, tracing a pale luminance down her cheek.

"'*Beautiful*,' we both whispered.

'She glanced to me, and I turned away, looking up to the dark above. Was this an omen? A portent of evil or harbinger of chaos? I didn't know whether to pray or panic. Still, in the end, I was a peasant boy. Folklore about my village held that shooting stars were the spirits of new saints, ready to begin a life here on the earth. And so, I did what any lad from the Nordlund provinces would've done.'

Jean-François smiled, writing in his tome. 'You made a wish.'

'That I did.'

'How quaint. What did you wish for?'

Gabriel stared for a long moment at the wine in the bottom of his goblet. Watching the way the light played in the red, the sound of broken glass and breaking hearts echoing in his head. He drained the last of it, poured another.

'Doesn't matter. Didn't come true.'

'But the appearance of that star changed your life?'

Gabriel nodded. 'We'd not learn 'til years later what it actually meant. But the sight alone was enough to push the pebbles that would become the avalanche. Chloe's jaw hung open as she looked up to that falling light in wonder, and from there, into my eyes.

'"Auspicious," she murmured. "Most auspicious indeed."

'"What do you mean?"

'She looked around the forbidden section, the dust-dry tomes and words forgot. "I mean it's not by chance the three of us met among these shelves tonight. That much is plain for any with eyes to see."

'". . . Chloe?" Astrid asked.

'The little sisternovice looked back to that burning star above. "The divine light of the Almighty shines upon us. I admit I doubted, but I was right to trust you, Azzie. God Himself has marked this moment." She glanced between us, a fervent smile on her lips. "I think he intends great things for us, mes amis. I think this meeting was *ordained*."'

In the reaches of that lonely tower, Jean-François of the Blood Chastain stifled a yawn. 'She sounds positively unbalanced.'

'As I said, Chloe Sauvage was one of the shrewdest bitches I ever met.'

'An errant speck of flotsam plummets through the firmament, and she feels the breath of God upon her neck? The girl was clearly deranged, de León.'

'No.' The Last Silversaint shook his head. 'To a simpleton's mind, she might've appeared such. To someone not raised in a place like San Michon, surrounded every day by trappings of the holy and words of the Almighty. But Chloe Sauvage was no lunatic. She was something twice as dangerous. Something I was too back then. But will never be again.'

'And what is that, Silversaint?'

Gabriel met the vampire's eyes, a bitter smile on his lips.

'A *believer*.'

✦ XI ✦

SILVER HEELS

'THE STAR WAS still lancing through the dark as I slipped from the Library, and in my heart, I felt a strange sense of hope. I wasn't certain if I believed in this portent as deeply as Chloe, or if we were God-fated to meet as she said. But I admit the sisternovice's fervour was contagious. I was only a peasant boy, like I said. But more, perhaps for the first time since I'd come to San Michon, I felt I'd found people I truly belonged with.

'Not brothers. But friends.

'Snow was falling from the burning heavens as I stole across the monastery. I could see lights in the windows about me, folk silhouetted against the glass as they peered skywards. It was still an hour until I'd start my stablework, and I wanted nothing more than to get back to bed. But as I drew near Barracks, I froze, as still as the angelic statues in the Cathedral cloister.

'In the gloom ahead, I'd seen another figure.

'A lad in a black cloak was sneaking from the Armoury doors. As I ducked out of sight near the Gauntlet, he looked to the marvel above, and I recognized him by its holy light.

'Aaron de Coste.

'Initiates weren't allowed out after evebells, and though I was guilty of the exact same crime, my hackles were up as I watched Aaron pull his hood low and sneak back to Barracks. Our brawl in the Gauntlet was fresh in my mind. His warning that I should watch my back ringing in my skull. Why was this insufferable prick faffing about in the Armoury?

'I checked the Armoury doors and found them locked. Listening within, I heard no sound, pondering now what to do. If de Coste was only just sneaking back to bed, he'd never miss me doing the same, and he'd squeal about it for certain. And so, I decided to seek shelter elsewhere while I waited out the hour.

'The Cathedral.

'I crept through the double doors in the east wall – the doors for the living and the dawn, taking shelter in an alcove by the votive candles. I always felt at peace within the Cathedral, breathing deep of the still and whispering a prayer to the Almighty. I looked to the great sevenstar window above, the Martyrs etched in stained glass. My eyes fell on Michon; armour-clad, the Grail held high in her hand as she led her army of the faithful. My mind was still on that falling star. And then, I heard it. Soft in the dark. A sound that told me I wasn't alone.

'The sound of weeping.

'I squinted in the gloom, illuminated by the harbinger's pale light. And down by the altar, I saw a figure knelt in the front row. Though I couldn't see her face, my paleblood senses recognized her auburn curls, the tune of her voice.

'It was Sister Aoife. Seraph Talon's aide.

'Her head was bowed, sobs echoing on dark stone. I knew not what made the young sister weep, and she sounded heartsick with it. But though she'd been ever kind to me, to ask her troubles was to reveal the fact I was out of Barracks. So instead, I held still and listened to her cry. Only once in that whole hour's weeping did she speak; a plaintive prayer to a statue near the altar. Her arms wrapped tight around herself as she whispered, "Oh blessed Mothermaid, show me truth. Be this curse or blessing you've gifted me?"

'I sat still in the dark, silent as graves. Finally, the belfry rang to rouse the cooks to the kitchen. Sister Aoife smoothed her curls and tried to find some measure of calm. Before she could spot me, I slipped out the doors and into the night outside. Skirting the fountain of angels, I stole away from the Cathedral, finding Keeper Logan by the sky platform.

'The thin man's eyes were fixed on the faint light still above. "D'ye see it, boi?"

'"Oui." Once more, I looked to that harbinger tumbling from heaven. "I see it."

'"D'ye fancy it bodes for good or ill?"

'I thought of Sister Aoife weeping in the Cathedral, Chloe's proclamation that all this was ordained, the light of that falling star playing on the curve of Astrid's cheek.

'"*All on earth below and hea'en above is the work of my hand,*" I said.

'"*An' all the work o' my hand is in accord with my plan.*" Logan made the sign of the wheel as he finished the Testaments quote. "Well said, laddie."

'"I have my moments."

'The keeper looked at me from the corner of his eye, smiling fondly. "You know, you're not half the snivelling backwater scab the other lads make ye oot to be, de León. I quite like ye, in fact. For a Nordish-born prettyboy sheepfucker, like."

'". . . Merci, good Keeper."

'Logan winked. "Too right, laddie."

'Just like every morn before, the stables were dark, my faithful shovel and barrow awaiting me at the gates. The horses were skittish, which I put down to the star tumbling from above. I left my barrow and lantern near the first pen, and wandering down the row, I arrived at my Justice, the horse snuffing and stomping at the sight of me. I gifted him a sugar cube and a hug, pressing my smooth cheek to his shaggy one.

'"Fairdawn, boy."

'Justice nickered and sniffled at my tunic, and I laughed and gave him another hidden cube. Wheeling my barrow into the main pen, I cast a wary glance at the two wretched suspended from the ceiling, wrapped in their silver chains. The pair were kept here to get the steeds used to the presence of the Dead, but that didn't mean the horses *liked* them, and in truth, working underneath them the last fortnight had my hackles up too. Both were male, one a portly older corpse, the other a thin scrap, maybe seventeen when he was murdered. Their hungry eyes were fixed upon my throat as I hauled off my tunic, hefted my shovel, and got to it. Each pen was rife with shite, and I had to work swift – my punishment would only worsen if I missed dawnmass.

'I was seven barrows into it when the vampire hit me.

'This story would have been a far shorter one had I not been given warning. But as the shadow flew at my back through the stable gates, Justice shied and shuddered enough for me to turn my head. And so, as the monster crashed into my back and bore me down to the ground, her fangs tore a gouge through my shoulder instead of my throat. Roaring and lashing out with my fists, I realized who'd struck me.

'Vivienne La Cour.

'The vampire bit deeper, teeth sinking into my flesh. I bellowed again, slamming my elbow back into her head as we rolled in the dirt. She was in a frenzy, claws locked about my neck. I tried to throw her off, but mighty God, she was strong, pushing my face into the muck as she gulped another mouthful of my blood. The rapture of the Kiss rushed through me then, my skin thrilling, veins singing, and I realized how easy it would be to close my eyes and let it take me, drown me, swallow me whole.

'It was a tempting thought. To die in bliss instead of pain.

'*Could I?* I wondered.

'*Would I?*

'I heard a wet thud, the crack of splitting bone. La Cour shrieked as she was flung backwards, rolling to rest against one of the stable's pillars. Opening my eyes, I saw Justice above me, nostrils flared, eyes wild – he'd smashed clean through his pen to save me, delivered a pummelling kick to the vampire's ribs. The awful bliss of her kiss faded, and I realized how close I'd come to death. And as I staggered to my feet, blood streaming down my chest, I found that red heaven replaced with my oldest, dearest friend.

'Hatred.

'Vivienne rose to face me, still dressed in her funeral finery. Her skin was grey, sunken and drained by that dreadful machine in the Foundry. Her wrists and lips were blackened by the silver that had kept her bound, dark eyes fixed on me, bloody tears spilling down her cheeks.

'"You killed them," she whispered. "You killed Eduard and Lisette."

'About us, the horses whinnied their distress, but Justice stood like a rock at my back. I'd no weapon save my shovel and the silver on my skin, but I'd taken down a highblood barehanded before. Again, I felt that burning in my palm and chest; the holy fire of God alight in the ink of my aegis. I raised my hand, sevenstar flaring bright, the vampire hissing a black curse as she turned her head.

'"Get back, leech," I spat.

'"Leech?" she whispered, fangs glittering. "You holy men. You children of God. You bind us in silver and suck us dry and dare name *me* parasite!"

'She circled the edge of my light, eyes cold and black with malice.

'"How did you escape the Foundry?" I demanded, edging towards my wheelbarrow.

'La Cour's blackened lips curled in a smile then. "Mayhaps your holy kin do not love you so dear as they should, boy."

'I spat in the straw. "Dead tongues heeded are Dead tongues tasted."

'"Come taste it, then!"

'She lashed out with her charred fist, and too late, I saw she'd manoeuvred closer to the chain holding those other wretched suspended above the pens. With a crack, the bracket snapped, and unmoored, the chain slithered free. The two wretched plummeted from the ceiling into the main pen, crashing in the midst of the now-shaken horses.

'And just like that, it was three on one.

'Vivienne flew at me out of the dark, burned hands twisted into claws. Still, her eyes were near blinded by my sevenstar, the lion upon my chest, and I stepped aside, bringing my shovel down across her skull. The haft snapped, the blade buckled like paper, but it was enough to stagger her, bloodied and gasping.

'An unholy howl tore through the stables. The older wretched was loose from its chains, charging me. I raised my left palm, silver flaring bright as the monster brought its hands up to shield its face. And swinging overhand, I buried what was left of the shovel's handle into its eye socket, the broken spar bursting out the back of the coldblood's skull.

'The second wretched was still trying to drag its way loose from the silver that bound it, and I leapt the pen's fence and dashed past the now-rattled horses towards it. But Vivienne La Cour struck me out of the darkness again, slamming me into another pillar. She was strong as death, eyes closed against the light of my aegis as her mouth sank towards my throat. I pressed my palm to her cheek, rewarded with her unearthly shriek of pain. She reeled backwards and I kicked her hard, sending her crashing through the fence.

'Free of his chains, the younger wretched came on now, mad with bloodlust. But he'd likely been a peasant boy when he died, and I'd trained at the feet of one of the finest swords of the Silver Order. I seized his arm, slinging him into the pillar beside me. His shoulder popped as I twisted, forcing him down into the straw. I hadn't brought Lionclaw along to muck out the stables, but I realized I still carried silver wherever I went. And lifting my foot, I stomped up and down on the wretched's head with my silvered heels until its skull burst like ripe fruit, rotten brains splashing the straw.

'I was hit from behind, the other wretched smashing me face-first into the pillar, the shovel spar still rammed through its skull. My nose broke, my cheek split, and I roared as it bit into my neck. I might have ended then and there, but again, Justice came to my aid, and with a savage kick, the wretched was sent flying with a staved-in chest.

'As my horse began stomping on the roaring monster, Vivienne struck like a serpent, hands knotted in my hair as she dragged my head back towards her fangs once more. Desperate, I tore myself away with all my strength, howling in pain as I left a thick chunk of ripped and bloody scalp dangling in the vampire's fist. Rolling across the straw to my barrow, I snatched up the lantern and hurled it into La Cour's chest. Glass burst. Oil sprayed. And the black scream that tore up out of her throat seemed born in the belly of hell.

'Daylight. Silver. Fire. These were the banes of the deathless. La Cour tore out of the stables, a living torch lighting the dim dawn. The horses broke then, Justice with them, fleeing the flames that had sprung up in her wake. Crushing the other wretched's skull under my heel, I followed La Cour out into the snow. The stink of burning meat and hair filled my lungs. Flesh scorched down to the bone, Vivienne wailed one last time – a cry more of sorrow than pain. And then she sank to her knees, skin popping like tinder as she collapsed, and the death she'd cheated came to claim her at last.

'The stables were burning, other horses thrashing in their pens as the blaze grew fierce. And though my shoulder and throat gushed blood, my head had been peeled like fruit, I dashed back in to save them. I heaped the barrow with snow, flinging it onto the rising flames. Another barrow followed. And another. Smoke choking my lungs. Heat scalding my skin. But though wounded, I was still a paleblood, and by the time a baffled Kaspar and Kaveh arrived to begin their day's labours, I was sitting amid the stink of burned flesh and straw and shite, my chest and shoulder and hair soaked red, the fire defeated, and all three vampires in fucking ashes.

'"In the name of Almighty God . . ." Kaspar breathed.

'Kaveh boggled, mute and wide-eyed as his brother knelt beside me.

'"What happened, Little Lion?"

'I nodded to La Cour's ashes, still smoking in the new snow.

'"Tried to kill me," I slurred around my broken jaw.

'The Sūdhaemi lads put the puzzle together in their heads, staring in wonder. Between the two of them, they hefted me to the sky platform. Dark hands soaked with blood, Kaspar pressed my tunic to the wounds those dead fangs had ripped as Kaveh went to round up the horses. Kaspar's eyes lingered on the black stain of La Cour's remains below as we rose up out of the snow.

'"A miracle you bested them barehanded, mon ami," the lad said.

'"God be praised," I murmured.

'Kaspar made the sign of the wheel as I sank to my backside on the platform. Unable to feel the chill, let alone the bleeding tears in my flesh, the ache of my broken bones. Instead, I was reliving the words Vivienne La Cour had spat before she died.

'*Mayhaps your holy kin do not love you so dear as they should.*

'And though I knew the currency of the Dead was deceit, though I knew

I could trust not a single word that unholy bitch had hissed, I couldn't help wonder how the fuck she'd got loose from the Foundry.

'I remembered that figure I'd seen sneaking from the Armoury doors.

'Shrouded in black. Creeping like a thief.

'*Aaron de fucking Coste.*

'And I murmured again. Softer this time.

'"Tried to kill me . . ."'

✦ XII ✦

A LETTER FROM HOME

'THE INFIRMARY OF San Michon smelled of herbs, incense, and above all, old blood.

'It sat on the ground floor of the Priory building, with the sisterhood quartered above it. The entrance hall was a grand, open space, deep-red light spilling through tall arched windows, chymical globes glittering along the ceiling. Tapestries hung on the walls – grand portraits of the Mothermaid and infant Redeemer, angels of the host. But the cell I was recuperating in was more austere: white walls, soft cot, clean sheets. Above my bed was a beautiful stained-glass window depicting Eloise, the Angel of Retribution, face in hands, weeping her tears of blood.

'The Infirmary was the domain of a sister named Esmeé, and it was into her tender care I'd been placed by Kaspar. Esmeé was a huge woman, with great ham hocks for hands. She seemed as out of place in a priory as a regular nun would be in an actual brothel.'

Gabriel waved one hand vaguely.

'Specialist services notwithstanding, of course.'

'More prostitute humour,' Jean-François sighed. 'How very droll.'

'Fuck off,' Gabriel suggested cheerily, raising his glass of Monét.

'I think you've had rather enough wine, Silversaint.'

'I think you're the last bastard in the world to lecture a man about his drinking habits, vampire.' Gabriel leaned back, taking another long mouthful. 'It'd been hours since the stable attack, and my bones were mending. But the wounds torn by those dead fangs would take time to scar over, even for a paleblood. And so, I was in the Priory's care.

'"You can certainly take a beating, Little Lion. I'll give you that."

'I looked up at the voice and saw Greyhand at my doorway, watching with keen eyes.

'"If I didn't know better, I'd say you were the Blood of Voss," he declared.

'It took me a few moments to realize my master was trying to jest. And though this was the first time I could ever recall him doing so, I was in no mood for merriment.

'"How's the throat?" he asked.

'"I'll live," I murmured, jaw still aching.

'"Three on one," he nodded, drumming his sword hilt. "Impressive, boy."

'"I am what my master made me."

'"God be praised. Else we might be filling two graves this day."

'I blinked. Tilting my head, I realized I could hear faint weeping out in the Priory proper. A soft multitude in tears. "La Cour . . . she killed someone during her escape?"

'Greyhand nodded. "A sister of the Priory. Young Kaveh found her body when he was fetching the horses. Drained dry and thrown from the monastery's heights."

'Dread froze my belly.

'*Chloe and Astrid had been out of the Priory last night . . .*

'"Which sister, Master?"

'"Aoife." Greyhand made the sign of the wheel. "Poor lass."

'I felt a guilty relief flooding through me, a soft sadness at Aoife's death. She'd been a faithful daughter of God, and she'd always offered kindness to me. She'd been on holy ground when I saw her last night, but I supposed La Cour must have caught her as she left the Cathedral, then made her way to the stables to strike at me. I wondered if I'd said something to Aoife, comforted her in her grief, perhaps I could have saved her?

'But why had she been in the Cathedral in the first place? And weeping, no less?

'My eyes narrowed as I looked to Greyhand.

'*Too many mysteries here by half.*

'"How did La Cour escape, Master?"

'Greyhand sighed. "Drained by the Foundry and charred by the silver, her hands were thin enough to slip her bonds. Talon is wracked with guilt over it, poor bastard. Aoife has been his aide for years. She was as close to a daughter as he will ever know. But he vows by the Almighty and all Seven Martyrs it will never happen again."

'". . . Has it happened before?"

'"Not that I recall, no."

'I kept my face still, but inside, my belly was churning. I couldn't be sure, but I'd have bet my bollocks Aaron de Coste had freed that bitch with the intent she'd do me over. He knew damn well I'd be down in the stables alone. He'd already proven himself a dog, using his bloodgifts on me, *and* he'd sworn to kill me in the Gauntlet. This was the perfect way to have his hands stay lily white and keep himself senior member of our company.

'But was Aaron dark enough to actually want me dead? Over wounded pride?

'And had his vendetta got an innocent sister murdered?

'Greyhand was my teacher. My protector. I wanted to trust this man. But he'd already lied to me once. And I was still in the shite for my disobedience. Sharing my suspicions with him would be less than worthless, especially without proof.

'My master mistook my silence for sadness. He patted my shoulder, awkward, like a father who never had any want to be one. "No sin is grief. But Sister Aoife is with the Martyrs now. And you did well, Little Lion. Fighting off two wretched and a highblood alone was no mean feat. And barehanded, no less?"

'I shrugged. "Justice did his share."

'He studied me carefully. "No strangeness, then? As in Skyefall?"

'I remembered little Claude's blood boiling at my touch. Talon's words: *We should take him to Heaven's Bridge right now. Cut his throat and give him to the waters.*

'*If Khalid had've given the order, would Greyhand really have ended me?*

'"No, Master," I said.

'He grunted, as if he almost believed me. "Well, best heal up quick and be ready to ride, boy. Sunset waits for no saint."

'Butterflies took wing in my belly. "We're to Hunt again?"

'Greyhand nodded. "Talon finished testing the de Blanchet boy. As I suspected, his blood was frightening thick for a fledgling. Kith grow stronger as they age, but some measure of potency is always passed from maker to made. Talon has declared that the creature who turned little Claude was most definitely ancien."

'"An *elder* Voss?" I whispered.

'"Oui," Greyhand nodded. "Abbot Khalid has commanded we track her down. And with prey this dangerous, we do not Hunt alone. Talon himself rides with us."

'I groaned inwardly at the thought of that surly prick plodding behind me through the provinces. "But Talon is seraph. Is he not too important to risk?"

'"An ancien is lethal quarry. And the seraph is the eldest of the Blood Voss in San Michon. He will be schooling you and de Coste in defending yourselves against our prey."

'I nodded, grudging. "When do we leave?"

'"Amorrow. So you'd best drink some mortar and harden up, Little Lion. Butchering fledglings is one thing. But this prey will test your mettle, sure and true." He reached into his greatcoat, his face soft as it ever got. "Something to read while you recover."

'Greyhand passed me a letter sealed with simple candle wax. All pain from my injury vanished as I realized who it was from. My master nodded and left me to it, and I broke the seal with shaking hands, scanning the beautiful flowing script.

'My dearest Brother,

'I pray God and Martyrs this letter finds you well. Know that I am quite furious with you, this being my fifth missive and you not having written *once* in the months you've been away. But in a moment of weakness, I found myself missing you again, and Mama said I should write to let you know. So here it is.

'I am very well, but still wishing you were here. Life in Lorson is dreadfully dull without your shameful behaviour to divert attentions from my own misconduct. In a desperate attempt to prove to Papa I am the God-fearing daughter he tried to raise, I am serving in the chapel as a candlemaid these days. You will be pleased to learn Père Louis is just as insufferable as ever – the alderman's daughter is to be married in spring, and he has insisted we practise *every week* until the blessed day. I am putting serious consideration into poisoning his sacramental wine. Do you have any advice on the herbs to use?

'In other news, I am being pursued in matters amorous by the mason's boy, Philippe. His enthusiasm is laudable, but I have decided to never wed. Instead, I think I shall become an adventuress, wandering the lands in search of fame and fortune and a conquest more inter-esting than a tradesman's son. Perhaps I shall drop in on your little monastery sometime and box you about your ears for not having the common decency to answer your beloved sister's letters.

'Mama misses you too, most dearly. She says she hopes you are eating well and not getting up to foolishness. I asked if she had anything else to say, but she is crying now, so make of that what you will.

'I trust you are enjoying yourself, traipsing about the countryside chasing bugaboos. Please do me the distinct favour of not getting yourself killed. I'd never hear the end of it.

'And for Godsakes, write your bloody mother.

'Your loving sister,

'Celene

"'My little hellion . . ." I whispered.

'My eyes were burning as I crushed my baby sister's letter to my chest. I hadn't realized how much I'd been missing her, and ma famille back in Lorson. I pictured Celene writing at the kitchen table, Mama working at the stove, and for a moment, their absence was so keen, I feared I'd cut myself on it. The news that my old flame was betrothed was also a rock in my belly. A part of me knew Ilsa must hate me after what I did to her, and anyway, silversaints could take no wives. Still, I felt a soft sadness that my old world seemed to be coming along just fine without me.

"'Fairdawn, good Initiate," came a voice.

'I looked up from Celene's letter and saw her framed in the doorway. The dim daysdeath light seemed a halo about her head, and her coal-black eyes were as unreadable as ever. But looking into her face, I felt the sorrow on my heart lift.

"'My name is Sisternovice Astrid. Let's get you fed and watered, shall we?"

'She bustled into the room with a tray of soup, sat by the bed. "Open wide!"

"'I—"

'My protest was silenced as she shoved a loaded spoon into my gob. She waited 'til I chewed, then shovelled in more. She was acting out of character, and I wondered if she might be upset about Aoife's death, until I saw Sister Esmeé trundle past outside, weeping loudly. Once the big woman was out of earshot, Astrid whispered, furious.

"'I know I said recklessness is a more admirable quality than foolishness. But fighting three coldbloods armed only with a fucking shovel might be taking things a touch far?"

"'Good to see you too, Majesty."

"'Oh, pack that schoolboy smile a lunch and send it walking," she scowled, stuffing another spoonful into my mouth. "It holds no weight with me, Gabriel de León."

"'You work in the Infirmary?'"

'Astrid scoffed. "Bedpans and these hands? I think not."

"'Then why are you here?'"

"'The sister who assists Esmeé was close to Aoife. Béatrice is out of sorts after the . . . incident." Astrid shrugged. "I volunteered to take her duties today.'"

"'Let me guess. For a favour?'"

"'I certainly didn't do it out of the generosity of my black and shrivelled heart.'"

'Something in Astrid's voice told me she might be lying about that, but I didn't press. "All well and good, but you haven't answered my question. Why are you *here*?"

'The sisternovice pursed her lips, set the meal aside.

"'I am displeased. You've broken your word to me, Initiate.'"

"'I would nev—'"

"'It's not entirely your fault," she said, raising a hand against my protest. "But I hear you'll be unable to train Chloe in her bladework next week, given you'll be off murdering an ancien of the Blood Voss with a garden spade or suchlike.'"

"'I . . . fear it will be a touch more difficult than that.'"

"'As you like it." She smoothed back a lock of long, dark hair. "But I wished to ensure our arrangement is still in place. I will continue the search for secrets of your heritage in the Library while you are gone. And you will continue to train good Chloe upon your return.'"

'I looked into her eyes. And though her stare was as unfathomable as ever, I couldn't help but note the weight she'd placed on that final word. I realized Astrid was afeared for me. After Aoife's murder, the attack in the stables, perhaps it had been brought home to her just how dangerous the waters I swam in truly were. And I wondered, then, if Astrid Rennier might be saying something without actually speaking it.

"'I'll return," I nodded. "I'm a man of my word, Majesty.'"

"'Not quite a man yet." She mustered a small smile. "Sixteen next week, is it not?'"

'Astrid handed me a sheaf of rough paper, and unfolding it, I felt my heart skip three beats. It was a page from her sketchblock, but it might well have been a mirror. Her artistry was flawless as always, but instead of Justice or Chloe, this time Astrid had drawn me.

'Staring down at that boy's face, I could see how much he'd changed since he arrived in San Michon. Long, dark hair. Sharp jaw. Grey eyes. Beside me, she'd drawn a lion, fierce and proud, eyes the same shape as my own. It was as if Astrid had seen beneath the lad I was, and conjured the lines of the man I'd become. Meeting her stare, I found myself smiling again. This girl was a sisternovice of the Silver Order. She owned nothing save the cloth on her back. And still, she'd found a way to give gift to me.

'"Happy saintsday, Initiate."

'". . . Merci for your gift, Sisternovice."

'She blinked. "You seem . . . unimpressed?"

'I looked at Celene's letter on the sheet beside me. "It's a wondrous gift, no doubt. I'm just wondering if I'm brave enough to beg another."

'"Have you heard the phrase 'pushing one's luck'?"

'"I've had word from my baby sister. She's been writing me for months, and I haven't really known what to say. But her letter has put me in mind of my mama. I'm wondering if I shouldn't write to her about my father. My *true* father, I mean." I shook my head. "But truth told, I'm not certain I want anyone else in San Michon reading her reply. Many folk in this monastery owe you favour. Do you think you might get word passed to her in secret?"

'Astrid's dark eyes softened as she looked at Celene's message.

'"Of course. A letter unanswered is like a kiss ignored. And your mama misses you, no doubt." She produced her sketchblock from within her dove-white habit, tore off a page, and handed me a stick of charcoal. "Hide your letter under your pillow before you leave. I shall see your mama gets it while you're traipsing across the countryside butchering leeches and making all the peasant girls swoon."

'"Merci, Majesty," I smiled. "I owe you. Truly."

'"And I'll not forget it. Have a care, Initiate." She looked to the dim daylight beyond the stained glass. "Soon you'll be indebted enough that you'll be forced to help me escape this ghastly place. And by a kinder road than poor Aoife travelled."

'"Is it so bad?" I asked gently. "To be here?"

'"Bad?" she chuckled, suddenly cruel and cold. "I have nothing. I own nothing. The blood of emperors flows in these veins, and yet, I'm a boat in a storm with no rudder, blown wheresoever the winds choose. There is no hell so cruel as powerlessness."

'My heart sank a little at that. San Michon was my home now, but to Astrid, it was naught but a cage. I'd only known this strange, infuriating girl a few weeks, but still, I wondered what this place would be without her. I watched as she gathered the tray, stalking away across the cold stone. As she reached the door, she turned one final time.

'"A weak and foolish girl would wish you fortune on your Hunt, Gabriel de León. A weak and foolish girl would pray God bring you blessings and guard you from all harm."

'"But you're not a weak and foolish girl."

'"No. I'm a fucking queen."

'And with that, she was gone.'

✦ XIII ✦
EVERY SHADE OF BLOODY

'I STARED AT the place where Astrid had stood for a long moment, noting how the room seemed smaller now she'd left it. And then, with a sigh, I took up the charcoal and began to write. A scrap of parchment was no place to say all I needed to, but I did the best I could. Enough time had passed since we said goodbye. Enough nights filled only with questions.

'Dearest Mama,

'Please forgive me for not writing sooner. I received all Celene's letters, and pray God this one finds you in the best of health. We did not part on sweetest terms, but know that I am well, and thinking of you and the hellion. I miss you both very much.

'The sin of my birth has been explained by the brothers of San Michon, and I do my best to struggle with it each day. I understand why you did not reveal the truth to me sooner, but now I need know all you may tell me. What was my father's name? How did you meet? Does this monster still live, and if so, where may he be found?

'My very life may depend upon this, Mama. If you have any regard for me, I pray you tell me all I need know. Please give all my love to Celene, save that which you would keep for yourself. You both have as much as I can give.

'Your loving son
'Gabriel

'P.S. Tell the hellion I shall write to her soon. For now, I have bugaboos to chase.

'I folded the letter tight and hid it beneath my pillow as Astrid bid. I'd no idea how long Mama might take to reply, but I wasn't left to wonder.

'By the morrow, I was given the nod from Sister Esmeé. And after a dawnmass shrouded in mourning song for poor Sister Aoife, I was down in the stables again, saddling up Justice. Kaspar and Kaveh were there to assist, both lads looking stricken at Aoife's murder. I watched Kaveh in particular, pondering that strange meeting I'd interrupted between him and the dead sister. I wondered what it might have meant, but it wasn't like I could ask him – even if the lad weren't mute, he'd likely just lie.

'The stink of char and burned hair still hung in the air from my battle against the coldbloods. Master Greyhand and Aaron were there with me, as was the dour bastard set to accompany us. The ashwood switch that had wrought such a bloody toll on my knuckles those many months was nowhere to be seen – Seraph Talon was kitted like a brother of the Hunt. He wore a long greatcoat and a bandolier loaded with silverbombs, his breast adorned with a silver sevenstar. The idea that Abbot Khalid was sending a seraph along with us brought home just how dangerous our quarry was going to be.

'Talon's face was grim, his cheeks pinched with sorrow. I could've been mistaken, but I fancied I even saw tears in his eyes. "Merci, boy. For avenging poor Aoife. Fine work."

'I bowed. "For a frailblood."

'"Three coldbloods, unarmed and single-handed?" Aaron looked at me sidelong. "You'll have to tell me how you survived that one, Little Kitten."

'I smiled at de Coste, wondering. "Cats have nine lives, Aaron. Lions too."

'"And you shall have need of all of them," Greyhand growled, hefting his saddle. "And the grace of Almighty God, to see us through this Hunt unscathed."

'I nodded as de Coste fixed me with his cool blue stare. His voice was soft, but he spoke clear in the quiet. "I thank Almighty God you fought them off, de León."

'"I thank him too," I replied. "And you for your concern, Brother."

'Aaron went back to packing his gear. Greyhand grunted softly, content there seemed some measure of pax between us. But saddling up Justice, I knew there was nothing of the sort. I'd no real proof, yet I was damn-near sure de Coste had set the La Cour woman free from the Foundry. Why else would he have been fucking about in the Armoury?

'This slick prick had set a highblood on me over the sake of stung pride, and his vengeance had cost poor Aoife her life. It wasn't lost on me how easily it might've been Astrid or Chloe who got caught by that monster instead. And now, I was headed out on the most dangerous Hunt I'd ever faced, with de Coste watching my back.

'Still, I had no choice. An ancien of the Blood Voss was stalking the Nordlund. It made little sense an Ironheart so powerful was east of Talhost, if the Forever King was amassing all his strength in Vellene. And so, with Seraph Talon leading us through the tumbling snows, we set out on the trail back towards the Godsend Mountains.

'None of us understood the horror we'd find at the end of that road. Nor that this would be the last Hunt Greyhand, Aaron, and I would take together. But undaunted, eager even, I placed my fate once more in the hands of God, and set out after our prey.'

In a quiet prison cell high in the midst of a solemn keep, the Last Silversaint reached to refill his glass. Finding only a few drops of Monét left, he spat a soft curse. He was too much a drinker for a single bottle to dull him much, and the sanctus they'd given him was beginning to wear off. Gabriel could feel it now, tickling in the depths of his belly, scratching on the backs of his eyes. His dearest enemy. His hated friend.

'Thirsty?' Jean-François asked, sketching in his damnable book.

'You know I am.'

'More wine?' Chocolat eyes drifted up to meet Gabriel's. 'Or something stronger?'

'Just get me a fucking drink, you unholy cunt.'

Gabriel pressed his shaking hands together as the vampire snapped his fingers. The iron-clad door opened, that thrall woman ever lurking on the threshold. The bite at her wrist was only two faint scratches now, the blood she'd supped from her master's veins healing the wound almost as if it had never been. But Gabriel could still smell the perfume of her blood, turning his head so he didn't have to meet her eyes.

He felt he'd been in this room all his life.

'More wine, my love,' Jean-François said. 'And a fresh glass for our guest.'

The woman curtseyed. 'I am your servant, Master.'

Gabriel's foot tapped a rapid, broken beat upon the floor. His stomach was slowly twisting into an ice-hard knot. That ghost-pale moth had returned, beating in vain upon the lantern's glass chimney once more. Leaning forward, tracing those teardrop scars down his right cheek with one fingertip, Gabriel peered at the tome in Jean-François's lap. The vampire was finishing a picture of Astrid as she'd been that night in the Library: framed by burning candles and windows of stained glass. Forever young. Forever beautiful. The likeness was so near, it made his chest hurt.

'So,' the vampire murmured. 'An elder of the Ironhearts, roaming the Nordlund.'

'Oui,' Gabriel replied.

'Rather clumsy for an ancien? To have left a trail for you to follow?'

Gabriel shrugged. 'Even elders need tó feed. And for all their power, the Voss had no way to travel the empire other than means mundane. If the Forever King had a way to speak to beasts of the sky direct, this whole tale might've been a different one. But you Chastains were still cowering in the shadows back then.'

'Do not mistake patience for cowardice, de León.'

'A song sung by every bottom feeder I've ever met.'

The vampire raised one blonde eyebrow. ''Tis not a Forever King who shall rule this empire in the end, halfbreed. 'Tis an Empress of Wolves and Men. And you are hardly one to make mock of carrion eaters, given the bloodline you are descended from.'

'I was wondering when you'd circle back to that.'

Rubbing his stubbled chin, Gabriel met the monster's eyes.

'Forty,' he mused. 'Perhaps fifty.'

Jean-François blinked. 'I beg your pardon?'

'You asked what I thought your age was earlier.' Gabriel shrugged. 'Now we've spent a little time together, I can hazard a guess. You carry yourself like ancien, Historian, but you're no elder. In fact, I'd put you not much older than I.'

'Indeed? And what makes you say so, de León?'

'You're not frightened enough.' Gabriel tilted his head. 'Tell me, when your dark mother and pale mistress, Margot Chastain, First and Last of Her Name, set you this task, did you think she was locking me in here with you, or you in here with me?'

'I have nothing to fear from you, de León,' the vampire sneered. 'You are a drunken wretch, descended from a house of dogs, who allowed the last hope for his species to slip through his fingers and shatter like glass upon the stone.'

'The Grail.' Gabriel nodded. 'I was wondering when you'd circle back to that too.'

'I circle nowhere, Silversaint.'

'If only you knew how true that is, you fucking parasite.'

The door opened, and the thrall stood at the threshold, golden tray poised upon one hand. She sensed the tension in the room, eyes upon the historian.

'Is all well, Master?'

The vampire brushed one golden curl from his eyes. 'Quite well, Meline. Though it seems our guest's temper frays when his tongue is parched. See to it, merci.'

The woman drifted into the room, placed a fresh glass of wine on the table, the bottle beside it. Gabriel kept his eyes forward, locked on the illustration in the vampire's book. The memories of Astrid were fresh now. The wound reopened. The longer he told their story, the sooner he must come to the end of it, and he knew he'd not drunk anywhere near enough for that. And so, he turned his stare to the monster opposite. This horror in silken brocade and sable feathers and gleaming pearl.

'I can talk more about the Company of the Grail,' he offered. 'Chloe. Dior. Father Rafa and the others. If you like.'

'I do *not* like,' the vampire protested, perhaps a touch too strongly. 'You cannot bounce around the telling of this tale like a rabbit in heat, Silversaint.'

'I think you'll find I can do whatever the fuck I please, vampire. At least until your Empress has what she wants.' He studied his black and broken fingernails, the dried blood and ashes and silvered ink upon his hands. 'And what she wants is the story of the Grail. What became of it. How I lost it. So what say you we drop the pretence for a spell? At least until I'm drunk enough to return to San Michon.'

The vampire kept his face unchanging. But Gabriel knew well enough to recognize the spark glittering in those chocolat eyes. He could feel it, floating like smoke between them. Smell it, entwined with the wine and blood.

Want.

'As you like it,' Jean-François said, keeping his voice flat.

'Are you certain? As you said, you've no use for children's tales.'

'I am commanded by my pale mistress to record *all* of your story, de León. Personally, I care not either way.'

'Dead tongues heeded are Dead tongues tasted.'

'Is that what you want, Silversaint?' the vampire asked, dark eyes searching pale grey. 'A taste of me? I had heard you'd developed an appetite for us.'

Gabriel picked up his fresh glass of wine, took a long swallow.

'You're not my type, Chastain.'

Jean-François smiled at the stink of the lie, dipping his quill. 'So. Chloe Sauvage and her tattered company. A girl you knew as a sisternovice in San Michon. A girl who'd claimed your first meeting was ordained by the Heavenly

Father himself. Discovering you in Sūdhaem seventeen years later must have done little to dissuade her insane notions.'

'Far from it. Chloe was a believer, like I said.'

'You had evaded Danton, the Beast of Vellene and youngest son of the Forever King, who seemed intent upon the boy Dior. You had rescued Chloe's company from a band of wretched, seen off yet another mysterious highblood who also harried young Dior's footsteps. And this boychild claimed to know the location of the Grail. The lost chalice of San Michon, that caught the blood of the Redeemer as he died upon his wheel.'

'It's almost as if you've been paying attention.'

'But why agree to accompany Chloe to the River Volta?' Jean-François nodded to the P A T I E N C E inked across the silversaint's fingers. 'Your wife and daughter awaited you at home. And you clearly didn't believe this Dior knew the chalice's location.'

'No. I had the boy picked for a fucking liar, and Chloe for a fucking fool. But Danton Voss clearly thought Dior was worth chasing, even if I didn't. I had business with the famille of the Forever King. Unfinished, and every shade of bloody. Liars and fools they might've been, but Chloe's company could serve me in one respect at least.'

'. . . Bait,' Jean-François realized.

'Oui.'

The vampire looked Gabriel over, lips pursed.

'What happened to the boy to whom deception sat like a rope around his neck? Who held life so dear he'd charge into a burning stable to save a handful of horses? Who would do *anything* to save one child, spare one mother the hell that his own mother had suffered?' Jean-François glanced at the sevenstar on Gabriel's hand. 'The boy whose faith in the Almighty shone bright as silver, and lit the dark like holy flame?'

'The same thing that happens to all boys, coldblood.'

The silversaint shrugged and finished his glass.

'He grew up.'

Book Four

LIGHT OF A BLACK SUN

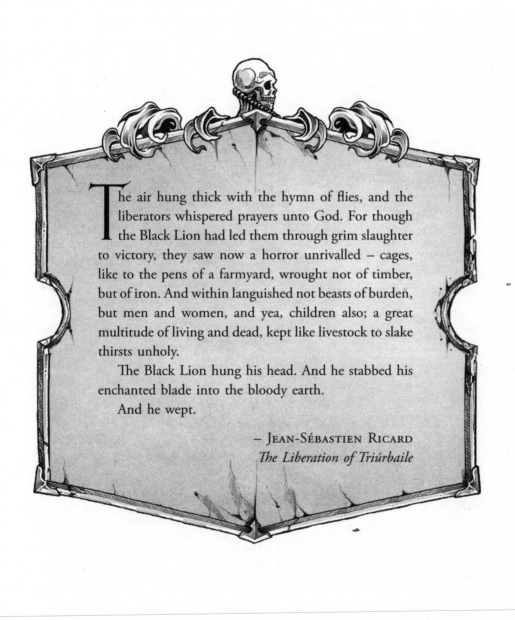

The air hung thick with the hymn of flies, and the liberators whispered prayers unto God. For though the Black Lion had led them through grim slaughter to victory, they saw now a horror unrivalled – cages, like to the pens of a farmyard, wrought not of timber, but of iron. And within languished not beasts of burden, but men and women, and yea, children also; a great multitude of living and dead, kept like livestock to slake thirsts unholy.

The Black Lion hung his head. And he stabbed his enchanted blade into the bloody earth.

And he wept.

— Jean-Sébastien Ricard
The Liberation of Triúrbaile

✦ I ✦

DEEP AND DEEPER

'WE'D RIDDEN THROUGH the night, as if hell itself followed on our tails. The first winter snows were falling, the bloodstains from our battle at the watchtower still caked upon my hands. But it wasn't 'til the sun dragged its sorry arse into the sky that I felt somewhere near safe. Daylight was no bane to the Dead any more, but Danton Voss wasn't fool enough to strike at anything less than full strength again.

'Next time, he'd come in the night.

'We travelled into a long stretch of dead oaks choked with fungal snarls. The north wind whispered cold secrets, biting at ears and blue fingertips. I rode on the flank, studying this strange company sidelong and wondering just how deep the shite little Chloe Sauvage had dragged me into truly was.

'It'd been over a decade since I'd seen her, but I was still surprised at how much she'd changed. Chloe had always been a bookish sort, prim and painfully devout. But her freckles had faded, and her eyes were older – a woman now, where once had stood a girl. She was dressed more like a soldier than a nun; a dark surcoat over a chainmail shirt, a silversteel sword at her side and a wheellock rifle on her back, that infuriating mass of mousy brown curls bound into a long tail. But as we rode through the ghostwood, still she rubbed the silver sevenstar about her neck endlessly, lips moving in silent prayer.

'Dior rode behind Chloe, the boy's arms encircling the holy sister's waist as he chattered almost incessantly. He was an odd one – a manor lord's frockcoat and a beggar king's britches, that tumble of ash-white hair hanging in bright blue eyes. He carried a silvered dagger in his coat, and a heavy chip on his shoulder. I'd have put him at maybe fourteen, but there was an edge to him, glass-sharp and gutterborn. He looked at me like he'd slit my throat for half a brass royale.

'Saoirse travelled on foot, with Phoebe loping along at her side. Of all the company, the slayer impressed me most – she stole through the deadwoods like a wraith, and moved with a grace that told me those blades she carried weren't for the jollies. Under her wolfskin cloak, she wore beautifully tooled leathers and chainmail, a kilt of black and three shades green. Two interwoven stripes were inked down the right side of her face, bloody scarlet. That big red mountain lion she ran with made most of the horses nervous, and the pair spent the day scouting tirelessly, returning only now and then for a check-see.

'Last came Père Rafa and Bellamy Bouchette, the priest and soothsinger riding side by side. Rafa's robes were the pale, homespun cloth you'd find on the backs of most monastery men. His skin was dark and worn like old leather, thick square spectacles perched precariously at the end of a long, thin nose. He looked skinny enough to snap with my smallest finger, but I still recalled our battle by the watchtower – that wheel around his neck burning like a bonfire as he saw that strange masked highblood off our backs.

'Bellamy wore a fine dark-grey doublet, mail, a cloak of what might've been greyfox. A silvered chain with six musical notes was strung about his neck. His longblade hung at his side, his grey felt cap tipped so rakishly it's a wonder it didn't fall off his head. His jaw was like to a shovel blade, and I wasn't sure how he managed it, but his stubble was still a perfect three days' length. He rode beside the priest, and though I put him at maybe twenty, he played with his fine bloodwood lute like a thirteen-year-old boy with his cock.'

'Artfully?' Jean-François asked.

'Constantly. I fucking *hate* soothsingers. Almost as much as spuds.'

'Why?'

'Poets are wankers,' Gabriel sighed. 'And minstrels are just poets who're allowed to strum themselves in public. It's a self-important prat who believes his thoughts are worth putting to parchment, let alone writing a fucking ballad about.'

'But *music*, de León . . .' The vampire leaned forward, animated for perhaps the first time since their conversation began. 'Music is a truth beyond telling. A bridge between strangest souls. Two men who speak not a word of each other's tongues may yet feel their hearts soar likewise at the same refrain. Gift a man the most important of lessons, he may forget it amorrow.

Gift him a beautiful song, and he shall hum it 'til the day the crows make a castle of his bones.'

'Very pretty, vampire. But truth is a sharper knife. Truth is, most men write songs so they can hear themselves sing. And the rest sing not for the song, but for the applause at the end. You know what most men don't do enough of?'

'Tell me, Silversaint.'

'They don't shut the fuck up. They don't just sit and listen. It's in *silence* we know ourselves, vampire. It's in stillness we hear the questions that truly matter, scratching like baby birds on the eggshells of our eyes. *Who am I? What do I want? What have I become?* Truth is, the questions you hear in the quiet are always the most terrifying, because most people never take the time to listen to the answers. They dance. And they sing. And they fight. And they fuck. And they drown, filling their gullets with piss and their lungs with smoke and their heads with shit so they never have to learn the truth of who the fuck they are. Put a man in a room for a hundred years with a thousand books, and he'll know a million truths. Put him in a room for a year with silence, and he'll know *himself*.'

The vampire watched the silversaint drain his wine to the dregs, then refill his glass all the way to the trembling brim.

'Do you know what irony is, de León?'

'They make swords out of it, don't they? Mix it with coally and hit it with a hammery?'

'Halfway through his second bottle, sweating for another pipeful, and he chastises others for their vices.' Jean-François tutted. 'The only thing worse than a fool is a fool who thinks himself wise.'

'I've spent my time in that silent room, vampire. I *know* what I am.'

The silversaint raised his goblet and smiled.

'I just don't like it very much.

'We finally crossed the Ūmdir at a shallow ford, the waters rushing up along the flanks of our horses. Dior seemed to get his back up as the river got deep, and I wondered if the boy was afraid of getting that fine stolen coat of his soaked. It stopped his chatter for a while at least. Jezebel didn't seem to mind the wet, though, and I gifted my big dray a fond scratch behind her ears. Despite her change in circumstances, the horse seemed glad to know me – I supposed I was a kinder master than that pair of inquisitors I'd pinched her from. I just wished I had some sugar to gift her.

'As we clopped up the freezing bank, I unfurled my beaten map, pulled out my spyglass, and took one last look at the lands behind. In our wake lay the Sūdhaem; warmer climes and little patches of civilization still free of coldblood hungers. But ahead, between us and the Volta, the war-torn wastes of Ossway awaited. The river was at least a month's ride, presuming no one harried our steps. But truth told, I was hoping someone would.

'"Why did Voss set the Beast of Vellene on your trail?" I called.

'The question had been chewing at me all night and day, and now that we were across the water and safe-ish, it needed asking. I still felt too far in the dark about Chloe and her little band – where they'd come from, how all this started. If they were to be my bait for Danton, I wanted to know exactly what I was putting on my hook.

'"How does the Forever King know about this Grail bullshit at all?"

'I looked over my shoulder to Chloe, Dior sitting behind her. We were riding a thin strip of mud that could barely qualify as road. The dead trees were thick with shadow and frozen blooms of fungus, crusted with grey snow. But Chloe's eyes were closed, and heavenward. Lost in prayer mostlike.

'"Chloe?"

'"I fear the fault is mine, Silversaint," old Rafa sighed.

'"Well, best start talking straightwise, priest. We've one of the most dangerous leeches in the empire hunting us, and I'd have the why of it. As soon as Danton gathers strength enough, he'll be at us like a shoreleave swab to the nearest doxyhouse."

'The wanker paused his strumming. "He means to say 'enthusiastically', Père."

'"Merci, Bellamy, I understood the implication." The old man turned dark eyes to me. "And I fear this Prince of Forever will not be the only shadow at our backs, Silversaint."

'"I've no patience for riddles, old man. Best start at the beginning."

'Rafa breathed deep. "I have served God since I was a young man. As a b—"

'"Hold, hold." I held up one hand. "When I said *the beginning*, I didn't mean I wanted your fucking life story. Get to the part that matters, priest."

'That earned some sideways looks from the company; Chloe opening her eyes and raising one brow, Dior scowling, the wanker chuckling over his lute. And oui, I was acting bitchly. But it'd been over twenty-four hours since I'd smoked that pipeful upon Dhahaeth's walls, and the thirst had me by the bollocks. The blood I'd squeezed out of that fledgling's heart was still stowed inside my greatcoat, and I could practically taste it already. But we'd had no time to scratch ourselves, let alone to cook a hit of sanctus, so I'd been rationing what little I had left, smoking just enough to keep the edge off.

'Mostly, anyways.

"'Well, quite.' Rafa cleared his throat. "But to my point, I have served the Order of San Guillaume for forty-one years. I am a linguist and astrologer. A student of the universal spheres." He lifted his arms skywards like a conductor afore a symphony. "And when the shadow fell across our sun, I devoted my life to uncovering how it might be undone."

"'What Père Rafa is too modest to say," Chloe interrupted, "is that he's one of the most pre-eminent scholars on daysdeath in the empire."

'The old man smiled with small, worn teeth. "You flatter me, good Sister."

'Chloe bowed. "Flattery well earned, good Father."

"'Oui, oui, I'll tickle his taint later," I growled. "But San Guillaume is a distillery, not a library. Used to be the finest barley fields in the Ossway on those hills. Even nowadays they make a vodka that'll peel the paint off walls."

"''Tis true my brotherhood made coin from the fruits of the bottle," Rafa nodded. "But that coin has always been spent in acquisition and preservation of knowledge. San Guillaume boasts one of the finest libraries in the empire, Silversaint."

"'I've been searching for daysdeath lore in the San Michon Library the last seventeen years, Gabe," Chloe said. "But ten years back, I heard tell from Frère Fincher that a monk in San Guillaume was also a keen scholar on the topic. I sent a missive, and Rafa answered."

"'Thus began a long correspondence.' The old man smiled, fond as a father. "And the finest of friendships, with one of the keenest minds I've encountered in all m—"

"'Fuck me," I sighed. "She's already married, priest. And to God no less."

"'Are you *trying* to be a bleeding arsehole, hero?" Dior scowled. "Or are you just naturally gifted?"

"'Shut your noise hole, boy. The adults are talking."

'Chloe squeezed the lad's hand. "Dior . . . please . . ."

'The boy fell silent, staring bright blue daggers at my neck.

"'Over the next decade," Rafa continued, "Sister Chloe and I traded information. Following a fragile thread through *thousands* of texts. With the good sister's advice, I searched the Library with fresh eyes. And within the pages of a timeworn tome, I unearthed a message. Written in a manner that I believe *you* are familiar with, Silversaint."

'I met Chloe's eyes, nodding slow. "What kind of message?"

"'A poem. Penned in Old Talhostic. *From holy cup comes holy light; the faithful hand sets world aright. And in the Seven Martyrs' sight, Mere man shall end this endless night.*"

"'It's a prophecy, Gabe." Chloe's eyes blazed with a familiar fervour. "A prophecy about the Grail, and ending daysdeath once and for all."

'I scoffed. "And the abbot let you leave San Michon on the back of *that*? Alone?"

"'I finally convinced him there might be merit in all this a little over a year ago. The war had grown so deep by then, he could spare few 'saints for so thin a gambit. But he *did* send two brothers with me on the road. Frère Theo Petit and his apprentice, Julién."

"'I remember Theo," I smiled. "A good man. A better blade. How is the old dog?"

'Chloe lowered her eyes. Old Père Rafa made the sign of the wheel.

"'We were ambushed one night," he said. "Crossing the Ossway, shortly after I'd been collected from San Guillaume. A war party of the Blood Dyvok. Brother Theo and Julién . . ."

'I glanced to the silversteel sword Chloe wore, realizing who it had belonged to.

"'Shit . . ."

'Rafa nodded. "We travelled on undaunted, more than a year now. But we needed more help. Young Bellamy joined us in Sul Ilham half a year back—"

'I glanced at the wanker as he struck a note on his lute for dramatic effect.

"'Young Saoirse has travelled with us perhaps three months," Rafa continued. "And M. Lachance here is the newest addition to our little band."

"'Right, so madman's poetry and little Lord Shitinhisbritches aside, how did the Forever King get word of any of this?"

"'As I say, I fear the blame is mine," the priest said, scratching his pointed grey beard. "Once Chloe and I assembled a compelling case, I informed the head of my order, and Abbot Liam sent word of my discovery to Pontifex Gascoigne in the capital. We fear someone among the Pontifex's inner circle may be . . . compromised."

'I sucked my lip, scowling, my mind running over the tale. "Well, it still all sounds like horseshit to me. But if the Forever King has set the Beast of Vellene on you . . ."

"'Why do they call him the Beast of Vellene?"

'It was Dior who'd spoken, the rest of the group falling silent. I looked the boy over, the swagger, the scowl. He had one of those traproot cigarelles dangling from his lips, unlit. As I met her eyes, Chloe shook her head in warning. But I figured the little prick could do with some waking up about the shite we were all in.

'"Vellene was the first city that fell to the Forever King," I said. "Seventeen years ago. After the gates came down, Voss had every man and woman within slaughtered to bolster the numbers of his legion. His daughter Laure murdered every babe in the city, and made a bath of their blood. But Voss's baby boy Danton has a fondness for untouched girls. Rumour has it, he herded every maid he could find into Vellene's dungeons. Locked them up. Kept them fed. And every night, he'd release ten of them from the city gates."

'Dior frowned. "What for?"

'"For sport. He'd promise they'd be spared if they eluded him 'til dawn. And then, one by one, he'd hunt them down. Tracking them across the frozen wastes, slaughtering them like hogs before setting off after the next. He hunted and killed every girl in the city that way. Took him *months*. And the last of them, a hollow and broken shell by then, he let live, releasing her only so she might babble tales of the slaughter."

'"Great fucking Redeemer . . ." the soothsinger whispered.

'"Blasphemy, Bellamy," Chloe murmured.

'"That's who we have hunting us, boy," I said. "*That's* the kind of blood-hound we . . ."

'My voice drifted off as I heard the faint thunder of hooves. My pulse quickened, and I wondered if by speaking of the Beast, I'd somehow conjured him. But all thoughts of Danton evaporated as I lifted my spyglass and spotted a dozen riders rushing up the muddy track behind us. Most were men, soldiers, clad in crimson tabards. But the pair in front were women, long black hair cut in sharp fringes over veiled eyes. My belly sank into my boots as I recognized them. Tight leathers. Dark mail. So identical they couldn't be anything other than twins. They wore black gauntlets on their right hands, blood-red tabards marked with the flower and flail of Naél, the Angel of Bliss.

'*That inquisitor cohort* . . .

'"Fuck," I sighed.

'"Fuuuck," Dior said.

'". . . Fuuuck?" I asked.

'"*Fuuuuuuuuck*," he nodded.

'A horn blast rang over a distant shout. "Halt! In the name of the Inquisition!"

'"Mothermaid curse them," Chloe hissed.

'Bellamy slapped his horse and roared, "Hoof it!"

'And we were off, pounding down the muddy trail with the cohort at our backs. We ran hard, but old Rafa wasn't a rider's arsehole, and our mounts were in need of a breather after a hard night's slog. Glancing behind, I saw the cohort were gaining. And if you're going to have to fight, coldblood, don't waste the best of yourself fleeing.

'I took hold of Ashdrinker's hilt, drew her into the dull daylight.

'*Be that not the n-nun ye shot, y-ye shot?*

'"That's her."

'*She looks upset. You should s-send her flowers. Girls like f-flowers, Gabriel.*

'"Stow that lute, Bouchette!" I roared. "There's heads need kicking!"

'"Nae!" came a cry.

'I caught a flash of movement, saw Saoirse barrelling through the trees swift as a deer, strawberry-blonde braids streaming behind her. Phoebe came running on the slayer's tail, the lioness just a russet blur. With a skill I'd rare seen like of, the clanswoman leapt aboard Rafa's galloping horse, shoving the priest back and grabbing his reins.

'"Nae place to fight that many! Follow!"

'Saoirse steered the horse into the deadwood around us. Chloe and Dior followed, Bellamy tipping me a wink as he galloped past, lute still in hand. I slowed long enough to crack off the shot in my wheellock, and then I was away, riding hard on the soothsinger's arse as we crashed through rotten scrub and towering spires of 'shrooms and 'stools.

'The light plunged dimmer as we rode, branches stretched overhead like a tangle of beggar's hands. I heard pursuit behind, another shout: "Halt in the name of the Inquisition!" but when the fuck has that worked, honestly? I knew not where she was headed, but the slayer's woodslore was tip of the top, and she led us along a switching path through frozen bramble and branch before charging us down into a narrow gully.

'The earth had split wide and deep, the roots of old trees and tendrils of fresh asphyxia forming a matted roof over our heads. Her lioness was nowhere to be seen, but Saoirse held up a hand for a halt, finger to her lips. Chloe's head was bowed in prayer, old Rafa rubbing his wheel between forefinger and thumb. I heard another peal from that horn, the dim thunder of approaching hooves.

'"Talya!" a woman cried. "Can you see them?"

'"Valya! This way!"

'*I like her voice. She sounds pretty, is she p-pretty?*

'I scowled at the sword in my hand, the silvered dame on the hilt.

'*I be not in the mood to slay nuns this d-day, Gabriel. I have done that enough f—*

'"Shut up," I growled.

'Rafa glanced over his shoulder. "I said nothing, Silversaint."

'"Hssst!" Saoirse hissed.

'The hoofbeats grew louder, and I heard the ragged breath of horse and man as the riders closed in. If those god-bothering pricks had caught us in that gully, it'd have been red slaughter. But my heart eased as they crashed past, all thunder and fury, a few dozen yards southwards. Chloe made the sign of the wheel, Dior sitting behind her with dagger in fist, cheeks pinched pink with chill, that unlit cigarelle still dangling from his lips. The boy met my eyes through his mop of white hair, and I saw he was more furious than afraid.

'Whatever else he might have been, it seemed Dior Lachance was no coward.

'The hoofbeats faded. I flinched in my saddle as a shadow fell over me, but looking up, I saw only Phoebe, standing on the gully's lip above. The mountain lion stared with glittering golden eyes, the scar cutting through her brow and cheek seeming to curl her jowls into a smile as she growled.

'"We're clear," Saoirse whispered. "Let's be oot an' off."

'Wordlessly, we obeyed, nudging our horses from the gully. Turning north, we trotted through falling snows, Phoebe loping along at the back of the line and watching Jezebel and me with hungry eyes. I heard the Inquisitors heading away from us, but I knew it'd be only a matter of time before they realized they'd been duped.

'"You knew them."

'Glancing up, I saw Dior watching me from the back of Chloe's horse.

'"Those bitches. You *knew* them."

'"We've met. Briefly."

'Bellamy glanced at me sidelong, Père Rafa fixed me with a curious stare. Even Chloe threw me an eyeful on the wrong side of suspicious. "Met how?"

'"I shot one in the back and stole their horse."

'Dior scoffed. Chloe's jaw dropped. "Gabriel de León, you *shot* a *nun*?"

'"Not to kill. Well . . . not technically." I scratched my chin, a little chagrined. "I'm impressed those wretched didn't murder them, though."

'Chloe simply boggled as I shrugged.

'"Long story."'

Up in their lonely tower, Jean-François cleared his throat, tapped his quill upon the page impatiently. 'As if to a—'

'The Inquisition is a sorority of the One Faith,' Gabriel sighed. 'Charged with rooting out heresy in the Church. Unlike most holy orders, the sisterhood don't swear to God or Mothermaid or Martyrs, but to Naél, the Angel of Bliss. Which makes about as much sense as I do after my fourth bottle of wine.'

'Meaning what, exactly?' the vampire asked.

'Meaning they're a pack of fucking sadists. They believe bliss can be appreciated only in the absence of pain, and the only prayer they partake in is torture.' Gabriel lifted his glass to his lips. 'Gossip bridles. Heretic forks. Breast rippers. Those twisted bitches invented them all. When old Cardinal Brodeur was accused of heresy back in sixty-four, he was given to the gentle keeping of the High Inquisitrix in Augustin's Tower of Tears. Word is they flayed his skin off, then packed him in salt overnight to stave away the sepsis. Poor bastard confessed after a day. They kept him alive seven more. In the end, they cut off his wedding tackle, fed it to him, then let him bleed out of his misery.'

Jean-François raised an eyebrow. 'Is that true?'

'Fucked if I know,' Gabriel shrugged. 'Never let the truth get in the way of a good yarn. Point is, they make terrible dinner guests. Unless you enjoy conversations about not being hugged enough as a child and the best way to kick puppies off bridges without getting blood on your boots.

'And fair enough, I'd shot one in the back. And those bitches were fond of grudges. They say the best revenge is living well, but there's still a lot to be said for dancing beneath the blood moons in a cloak made of your enemy's skin. But noting the nervous glances my new comrades were sharing, I guessed that cohort hadn't been headed to Dhahaeth to sample the vodka when I stumbled across their bogged wagon and stole Jezebel.

'We already had the son of Fabién Voss on our tails. But it seemed Chloe's little band had earned the attentions of the Inquisition too.

'The shite I was wading in had just got about three feet deeper.'

✦ II ✦

GODTHANKS

'WE BEDDED DOWN near sunset in a wooded gully, a chill mist strung through the air. A huntsman's hovel had stood there long ago, but it was only a few broken walls and a firepit now. The trees were long dead, groaning under the weight of fungal flowers, every shade of pale. But at least we were out of the damned wind.

'I'd been awake thirty hours straight by that point, and Mothermaid only knows how long it'd been since I smoked. My eyes were sandstone in their sockets, my skin ready to fling itself off my bones. As the others flopped down in the shelter of ruined walls and sad, mouldy trees, I started snapping off the lowest branches. Chloe watched, huddled beside Dior in the warmth of a thick dark fur. "What are you doing, Gabe?"

'"Practising my penmanship."

'"Is it wise to light a fire, Silversaint?" Père Rafa asked. "What if—"

'"Those inquisitors need sleep too, priest. And if the Beast of Vellene finds us, oui, we want a fire. Hot as the belly of hell." I snapped off another branch. "But our dark prince will hold off a while. He needs to find a bridge across the Ūmdir, for starters. And it'll take a week or so for his arm to grow back, depending how much he feeds."

'Bellamy shook his head in wonder. "You cut the arm off an ancien Voss?"

'"The sun was up. I was lucky. Next time, don't count on either."

'"Nae fear, Father." Saoirse eased herself down between the roots of a rotten oak and nodded at Rafa. "After we rest a spell, Phoebe and I'll keep watch."

'"We'll *all* take turns at watch. You. Boy," I growled at Dior. "Don't slack arse-ways when there's work needs doing. Get that smoke out of your mouth and find something to burn."

'Dior scowled, but after a nod from Chloe, he unwrapped himself from the shelter of the sister's furs. Tucking his cigarelle behind his ear, he turned up his fancy collar against the cold and trudged over to the Ossian lass. "Can I borrow your axe, Saoirse?"

'The girl parted her braids from her face and blinked. "Afor?"

'"Our hero wants firewood."

'"Ye want to use Kindness to hack at trees? I should take ye o'er my knee."

'Dior lifted the edge of his coat, wiggled his narrow arse.

'"Tease," Saoirse laughed. "G'wan, off with ye."

'"No need to chop anything, boy," I said. "Just grab kindling. Dry as you can find."

'The lad's smile turned sour, but he obeyed, scouting about the ruins for tinder. Chloe watched him like an eagle to her chick. "Don't wander too far, Dior."

'I roamed the trees, studying the slayer from the corner of my eye. Saoirse's kit was impressive: heavy boots and britches tooled in a beautiful pattern of clawed hands, same as her shield. But the axe in her lap was the true work of art – double-bladed, engraved with a stunning pattern of everknots. Unless I was mistaken, its haft was pure trothwood. "*Kindness*, eh?"

'She watched me with cool eyes, scratching her she-lion's ears. "So I can—"

'"Kill people with it. Very clever. You know, someone once told me a man who names his blade is a man who dreams others will know *his* name one day."

'"Good thing I'm no' a man, Silversaint." Saoirse sniffed, green eyes falling on the broken blade at my hip. "Is that why ye named it Ashdrinker?"

'"I didn't give this sword a name, girl. She came with one."

'"An' so did I. So I'll thank ye to use it an' leave that 'girl' shite right out."

'"*Ashdrinker*." Bellamy cooed the name as he wandered over from the horses. "I never thought I'd live to see her in the flesh. They still sing songs about you and that sword in Augustin, Chevalier. The Black Lion and his bloody blade." He tipped his cap back, flashed me a smile most would have described as dashing. "Good God, the stories I've heard . . ."

'"An' what have ye heard?" Saoirse asked.

'"My heart sings to hear you ask!" Bellamy sank by the firepit and took his lute off his back. "But there's no story sweeter than a song, Mlle Saoirse. So, behold! I heard this one in Ossway, in the court of Laerd Lady á Maergenn. They call it, *The Battle of Báih Sì*—"

'"No, you fucking don't," I spat. "You want to make yourself of use, balladboy, gather more wood. Or I'll put that lute to proper service and burn it."

'Young Bellamy flashed me a grin, unflappable. "After dinner, then?"

'Père Rafa was well provisioned, and he set a pot boiling, mixing a soup that would've smelled delicious if I didn't have another hunger in mind. I fetched my small chymist's foundry from my saddlebags, set the cast-iron contraption near the fire to heat. Rafa and Bellamy watched in fascination as I filled the outer sphere with salted water. And with shaking hands, I reached into my greatcoat, withdrawing a glass phial brimming with bright and beautiful red.

'"What's that?" Dior asked, staring across the flames.

'"All that remains of Danton Voss's daughter," I replied.

'I poured the blood into the foundry's inner chamber, tweaked the pressure valve. It'd take hours for it to desiccate enough to blend with the other components in my bags, so I took out my pipe and tipped a peck of my dwindling sanctus into the bowl. Just enough to kill the thirst while the good batch cooked.

'"That's blood," the boy realized. "You use blood like *them*."

'I struck my flintbox, pipe to my lips. "I'm *nothing* like them, boy."

'"The silversaints are good men, Dior," Chloe said, wrapping the lad tighter in her furs. "They may be born of vampire fathers, but they fight on the side of the light. Sanctus is a holy sacrament, keeping their unholy thirst at bay. Gabriel is a faithful warrior of God."

'I dragged the smoke into my lungs, and I saw the boy's eyes widen as my own flushed crimson. The blood was pauper's quality, but still, I felt that need drift off my bones, all the night growing bright and beautiful, sharp as pins and soft as petals and deep as dreaming.

'Père Rafa made the sign of the wheel. Saoirse watched with curious eyes. Bellamy's gaze was on Ashdrinker as he strummed a few chords, and I sighed red, red smoke.

'"How long have those inquisitors been hunting you, Chloe?"

'The sister met my eyes. Dragging a curl from her cheek, she glanced around the fire. I felt the secrets under their skins then. It'd been a long time since I'd seen her, but there was history between us, so it stung a little to realize Chloe didn't trust me as she once had. "Almost two months. Since Lashaame."

'"And what happened in Lashaame?"

'"Ye've no need for the knowing o' that, Silversaint," Saoirse scowled, her big lioness purring like thunder as the girl scratched under her leather collar.

'"Do I look a fucking mushroom to you? *You're* the people who asked *me* to this dance, so if you plan to keep me in the dark and feed me shite all day—"

'"I dinnae ask ye the colour o' sky, Silversaint. Yer here at the sister's request, nae mine. And if ye've a will to plod along with us to the Volta and chock that sword at the bastards tryin' to gaff us, so be it. But ye know as much as ye need to fer that."

'Bellamy gave an uncomfortable cough. I glared at Chloe, but she remained mute. She was saved from a bollocking by the intercession of Père Rafa, who tapped his steaming cook pot and smiled. "Soup's ready."

'The priest served his fare in wooden bowls, and after a day without a morsel, I had to admit it smelled good enough to marry. I put my back against one of the broken walls, all set to tuck in when Rafa cleared his throat and held up the wheel strung about his throat.

'All about the fire bowed their heads, eyes closed for the Godthanks.

'"Heavenly Father," Rafa said. "We thank you for this bounty, gifted by your hand most divine. We thank you for this fellowship, assembled by your will most holy. We welcome our new friend, Gabriel de León, and we ask you gift the chev—"

'"Oi!"

'Rafa flinched as a chunk of broken brick crashed into the fire, sparks scattering skywards. He looked to me, silent and shocked as I raised another chunk in warning.

'"Don't you pray for me, old man. Don't you dare."

'Silence rang around the flames. Rafa glanced to Chloe, watching with worried eyes.

'"Forgive me, Chevalier. I sought only to seek the Almighty's bless—"

'"You want to waste your breath, have at it. Just leave me out of it."

'"*No breath is wasted that sings the praise of Almighty God. And no—*"

'"*—no call unheeded that by faithful hearts is sung to heaven.* I know the Testaments, priest. Sell that horseshit to the rubes on prièdi."

'Rafa glanced to the sevenstar on my palm. "Are the sons of San Michon not faithful servants of the Lord most high?"

'"Servant?" I scowled, blood-red. "Do I look a man on his fucking knees to you?"

'The crackle of flames filled the cold quiet between Rafa and me. I gobbled down my soup, tossed the empty bowl at the old man's feet, and rose to mine.

'"You want to spit in the dirt and call it an ocean, so be it. You want to sing songs to the deaf, I'll find not a care to give. Just keep my name out of your fucking mouth when you do it. You hear me, god-botherer?"

"'I hear you, Chevalier. And the Almighty hears you too.'"

"'I've no doubt he does, old man. I just doubt he gives a shit.'"

'I struck my flintbox again, breathed down the last of my dose. Reaching into my saddlebags, I fetched one of the vodka bottles I'd brought from Dhahaeth.

"'Get some sleep. I'll take first watch.'"

'Hand on Ashdrinker's hilt, I trudged out into the dark. I could feel their stares between my shoulderblades, but paid them no mind. The night was alive and singing, bloodhymn rushing in my veins. And by the firelight at my back, I heard Dior mutter to Chloe, soft enough no ordinary man would've heard.

"'Faithful warrior of God, my arse . . .'"

MONSTERS WHO WEAR THE SKINS OF MEN

'IT WAS SOMEWHERE near dawn when I awoke.

'The bloodhymn was soft in my veins, stale vodka on my tongue. My slumber had been haunted by dreams that made me wish I'd just stayed awake. I needed sleep, though, curling beneath my furs and trying to burrow back into it. But looking across the embers, I saw Dior's bedroll was empty.

'Muscles aching, I stood in the bitter chill. The dark before dawn was the kind that seemed made of glass; still and black and sharp. The snow had ceased. Rafa, Chloe, and Bellamy were curled close to the smouldering coals, the horses huddled together for warmth, Jezebel right in the middle. Saoirse had volunteered for dawnwatch, but I could see no sign of her. And kicking Dior's furs with one silver-heeled boot – oui, they were empty.

'I checked my foundry by the firepit, saw the fledgling's blood had reduced down to a thick dark scab. Nudging the contraption away from the heat, I went for a look-see.

'Saoirse's scent was easy to follow, iron and leather through the mournful trees. I wound my way up the gully, eyes bright in the dark. And perhaps a hundred yards from the camp, I found her, leaning against the corpse of an old oak.

'Dior in her arms.

'Their lips were pressed together in a tender kiss. She was taller than him, arms about his shoulders, the boy's around her waist. Saoirse's fingertips traced Dior's jaw, threading up through his pale curls. The boy pulled her in gently, their kiss deepening. Dior's hands roamed lower, and Saoirse laughed as he reached the edges of her kilt.

'"Slow down, flower," she whispered. "Nae rush."

'His eyes shone as he smiled at her. "You're beautif—"

'"Not interrupting I hope?"

'The pair hissed and broke apart, and Saoirse's axe was off her back in a blinking. Her eyes narrowed with soft rage as she straightened her kilt, lips bruised pink from the press of Dior's mouth. Behind her, the boy looked aghast, hastily fixing his buttons.

'"You're supposed to be on watch," I said, staring at Saoirse.

'She wiped her chin and scowled. "Ye seem to be watchin' enough for both o' us."

'"Get a good look?" Dior demanded.

'"If the things hunting us strike us unseen in the night, *you're* going to get a good look, boy. At your fucking insides."

'Saoirse shook her head, tucking a knotted braid behind her ear. "There's nae a mouse within a mile of us hasn't already been marked, Silversaint."

'"I waltzed right up behind you, and you'd no ken I was here."

'"P'raps not. But *she* did."

'I smelled her before I heard her – a hint of feline musk and a low growl at my back. Turning to the dead trees behind, I saw golden eyes, slitted and glittering. As Phoebe prowled out from the darkness, I had to admire the beast – paleblood senses or no, I'd no idea the lioness had been stalking me.

'"She'd have carved your pretty backside up like saintsday cake if she fancied you a threat." Saoirse smiled. "Phoebe sees what I don't, Silversaint. Nae fear with us awatch."

'Dior had finished buttoning his coat, hissing through clenched teeth. "So perhaps you'd best mind your fucking business in future?"

'Cheeks still burning with embarrassment, the lad shot me a look to kill by and stomped back towards camp. I watched him stumbling over uneven ground in the gloom, cursing up a storm. Stone-faced, I turned back to Saoirse's cold, green gaze.

'"He's a little young, isn't he?"

'The lass leaned on Kindness and tossed her braids off her shoulder. Mute and fierce as the lioness now circling through the rot-roots to my left.

'"There's not many lads his age with sense enough to rebuff a tumble from a pretty girl. But I'd have thought you'd know better than to offer one. What are you, twenty? And him *maybe* fourteen?"

'"I'm nineteen."

'"Oh, well, pardon me all to hell."

'"Yer nae his da. Yer nae his friend. Why do ye give a shit, Silversaint?"

'I chewed on that a minute. Saoirse hadn't been shirking her watch as

I'd suspected. That lioness of hers moved softer than I did and probably saw just as well in the dark. So finally, I shrugged. "You know, you're right, Mlle Saoirse. I *don't* give a shit."

'And turning on my heel, I made to leave.

'"Why are ye here?" she demanded.

'I turned back to face her. Studying her like hunter to prey. She was tall, broad-shouldered, hard-muscled – she'd likely trained with that axe and shield all her life. Her wolfskin cloak and mail were adorned with trinkets of red moons in crescent, her braids threaded with gold rings. Her leathers were embossed with patterns of entwined claws, the collar about her throat woven of everknots – the same design that graced the neck of her lioness. All that to say, she came from wealth. And perhaps, a little bit of witchery.

'"Just helping an old friend," I replied.

'"Bollocks," Saoirse sneered. "Ye were quick enough to turn that old friend aside in Dhahaeth. More concerned with helping yerself to the bottom of a bottle, way I remember it. And yer surely nae stickin' around out of religious sentiment."

'"Same could be said of you."

'"Oh, aye?"

'I pointed to the patterns of black and green on her kilt. "Took me a while to remember the weave. It's similar enough to á Rígan. But I met one of your lot at the attack on Báih Sìde. You lied to Chloe and the others. You're not Clan Rígan. You're Clan Dúnnsair."

'Phoebe growled at me, low and deep.

'I bared my fangs at the she-lion and growled right back.

'"So what?" Saoirse yawned.

'"So while you might mime along while old Rafa mumbles the Godthanks, we both know you've as much of the One Faith in your whole body as I've in my little toe."

'"I've faith aplenty, Silversaint. Just nae fer Almightys and Martyrs and suchlike."

'I nodded, looking at the two stripes of ink woven down her brow, eye, cheek. "Keeping it all for the Mothermoons, eh?"

'"I keep it for them who deserve it."

'"But that boy is supposed to know the wheres of San Michon's Grail. The chalice that caught the blood of the holy Redeemer himself. Which begs the question: why the fuck is a godless pagan risking her life to find a cup she wouldn't even believe existed?"

'"Risking my life?" Saoirse bared her teeth in a bright, feral smile. "I risk

naught, Silversaint. It's not my fate to die today. Nor tomorrow, neither."
She tapped the tattoo on her face. "Nae man can kill me. And nae devil
would dare try."

'"No jest now. Why are you travelling with Dior?"

'"He's a fine kisser."

'"Depends how raw you like your meat, I suppose."

'"Nice and bloody like you, eh, halfbreed?" Saoirse's eyes drifted to the
pipe in my coat. "You know, me grammy warned me about folk like you."

'"Folk like me?"

'"Monsters. Monsters who wear the skins of men."

'Saoirse stepped closer, just a few inches away now, six foot if she was
an inch. I could hear the lioness circling at my back, feel the heat of her
breath.

'"You've nae need to know my reasons for being here, Silversaint. We
reach the Volta, and ye'll be back home to yer pretty wife and pretty daughter
and a nice deep bottle, no a care in the world. 'Til then, keep yer eyes to
yerself and yer opinions likesame, and we'll get along smashing well. Fair
enou'?"

'The slayer didn't wait for a reply, tossing her braids and stalking past
me. The lioness lingered a moment before slinking into the shadows after
her mistress.

'Following along behind, I sighed.

'"Fair enough."'

✦ IV ✦

ONE CAPITAINE, ONE COURSE

"'WITH ALL DUE respect, good Father, you've your head square up your backside."

"'With all respect due *you,* good Sister, a man my age simply isn't that flexible."

'I returned to the gully and found Chloe and Rafa debating around the burning fire. Chloe was finger-combing her hair, head circled with a halo of impossible curls. Saoirse was still out somewhere in the woods, Bellamy strumming his lute – quickly stowed as he heard me stomping back towards camp. Dior was sulking in his furs, dragging on a cigarelle and looking at me with the *exact* measure of fury you'd expect a fourteen-year-old boy to have for the man who'd just scuppered his chances of getting his taddies tickled.

"'San Michon is our path, Rafa," Chloe was saying. "Our answers are there."

"'Of that I've no doubt," the priest replied, stirring a steaming pot. "But San Michon is over a thousand miles away. San Guillaume is far closer."

"'San Guillaume is a distillery, Rafa," Chloe sighed. "San Michon is a fortress. When the Forever King swept through the Nordlund, he took one look at those spires and decided it was easier simply to go around them. It's *there* the end to daysdeath awaits us."

"'If we're to trek a thousand miles, we'll need to resupply. We cannot eat snow, Chloe."

"'The good father raises an excellent point, Sister," Bellamy said.

"'But we'll need to trek weeks out of our way just to *get* there," Chloe said.

"'The good sister raises an excellent point, Father," Bellamy nodded.

"'Is that fucking potato?" I scowled, peering at Rafa's soup.

'"Oui, Chevalier," Rafa nodded. "My speciality."

'"Of *course* it is."

'"What do you think, Gabe?" Chloe asked.

'I looked between the pair as I served myself a steaming bowlful. In truth, I didn't care where they headed – the boy would serve as bait for Danton just as well on either path. "I think the best way to steer your ship onto the rocks is to have two capitaines at the wheel. So one of you should take the helm. And the other should shut their noisemaker."

'Chloe squared her jaw, stared Rafa down. "San Michon, then."

'The old man pushed his spectacles up his nose, scratched the grey stubble on his scalp. "As you like it, good Sister."

'"Accord!" Bellamy cried. "Huzzah!"

'"Shut the fuck up, Bouchette," I growled.

'We took to our horses, Saoirse leading us through the gloom. Snow began falling again, and we trekked through the wood for two days before spilling onto a muddy northbound road winding into the Ossway. I could see what would've been rolling green hills, now run to muck and mushrooms. Another deadwood awaited like a stain on the horizon. We passed a crow-pecked gibbet at a crossroads, creaking in the bitter wind. The word WITCH was carved into the rusting metal. Rafa and Chloe made the sign of the wheel as we passed, Dior staring with his jaw clenched tight.

'The remains inside the cage belonged to an old woman.

'It's a better storyteller than me who can make miles of silent drudgery sound interesting, coldblood. Saoirse and Phoebe scouted ahead. The rest of us rode hunched in our saddles. Rafa squinted at his battered copy of the Testaments, rubbing his silver wheel between forefinger and thumb. I pored over my beaten map, Bellamy played with his wooden cock while Dior chattered away to the soothsinger about any and all. The weather was purest misery. But I'd crushed up that fledgling's blood before we'd left the hunter's hovel, and my bandolier was loaded with a dozen doses of high-grade sanctus, which made me as happy as a pig in shite.

'We met the refugees five days in.

'A thin handful at first – a farmer and his famille, shuffling towards us. But through the falling snow, I spied a multitude behind. Hundreds of them. They dragged hand-drawn carts, the burdens of abandoned lives, small children on their backs. I even spied a world-weary donkey among them, sad and starved. They passed us without a word – even when Père Rafa called out, they simply trudged on like ghosts. Feet scraping through dirty snow.

'"Great fucking Redeemer . . ." Dior whispered.

'"Blasphemy, Dior," Chloe murmured.

'"Where are they all coming from?"

'"Ossway folk," I replied, nodding to the kilts among them. "There's a hamlet long west of here named Valestunn. A bigger village northeast called Winfael—"

'"Gabriel de León?"

'I blinked to hear my name, looking for the voice that spoke it. There among the line of refugees, I saw a mud-spattered man, thirty and some, with a young fair-haired lass on his shoulders. He was tall, grizzled, bright blue eyes shining in a mask of dirt.

'"Martyrs and Mothermaid, it *is* ye!"

'I frowned, trying to recall the man's face as he limped across the road, hand outstretched. Tipping my tricorn back from my brow, I slipped down into the snow, grasped his forearm. There was barely any meat on it, but his grip was iron.

'"Ye'd nae remember me," he said. "But we fought together at Triúrbaile. I was a hammerman in Lady á Cuinn's company the day ye liberated th—"

'"Lachlunn," I said, snapping my fingers. "Lachlunn á Cuinn."

'". . . Tha's right!" He blinked in surprise, looked up to the girl on his shoulders. "D'ye see that, poppet? The Black Lion hisself remembered your old da!"

'"Good to see you again, mon ami," I smiled. "How fare?"

'"Ah." The man sighed. "Tried to make an honest living after the troubles, with my drumstick fucked, like." Here he tapped his leg with a walking stick. "Mushroom farmer, aye? But the Dyvoks took Dún Cuinn last winter, and once the castle fell, just got too dangerous. We're headed over the Ūmdir into Sūdhaem before wintersdeep hits."

'I nodded grim, but spared a smile for the little girl. "And who's this wee slayer?"

'"Aisling." He tickled the girl's cheek. "Say hello, flower."

'The girl ducked her chin so her hair tumbled about her face.

'"Ah, apologies, Lion. She's shy, like."

'"Fairdawn, Mlle Aisling." I took her hand, kissing her dimpled knuckles. "This ugly old troll steal you from the fae? Or do you just take after your pretty mama?"

'The girl looked to the ground, and the man's smile fell away like a broken mask. And I knew the tale in a heartbeat then, without their needing to speak it. I'd heard it a thousand times across a thousand miles and a thousand lives already.

"'Condolences, á Cuinn," I murmured. "For your loss."

'The man sniffed and spat, rubbing at grubby lashes. He peered about the company, Rafa and Chloe making the sign of the wheel, Dior watching with cold blue eyes.

"'I heard tell ye were dead, Lion."

"'They tried."

"'Where ye headed?"

"'The River Volta."

"'North?" The man raised an eyebrow. "There's nae much north o' here but ruins and wretched, Silversaint. An' west is worse. We're come from Valestunn, and there's nae hope there. The wretched are thick as flies on shite since the dún fell."

"'These wretched. Is there a bloodlord leading them?"

"'Nae. The local ones are just dregs. The Dyvok lords are looking westwards now, pushing to Dún Maergenn. But ye know how it is. Bastards roam in packs with or without something pulling their strings. Dozens of 'em up here. And everyone they kill is just as like to rise rotten as stay dead. Best to head south afore the freeze. We hear it's better there."

"'A little," I nodded. "Don't stray too far towards sunset, though. The Chastains have everything west of Sul Adair now."

"'Sweet Mothermaid," he whispered.

"'Dark days," I nodded. "And nights darker."

"'Still. With the Black Lion ahorse once more, ye'll set it to rights." He slapped my shoulder, brightening. "Still remember that day in Triúrbaile, ye know. Greatest o' my life. Like the hand of God Almighty, ye were. Barechested and bloodied, like the legends of old. The whole *battlefield* bathed silver. Never seen the fuckin' like." He shook his head, eyes shining. "I named my youngest for ye after that. Gabrael."

"'You honour me, mon ami." I smiled, hand to heart. "And where is this young lio . . ."

'My voice failed as the man hung his head, his daughter peering at me with tear-stung eyes. I knew that tale as well. And with held breath and shaking hand, I patted his shoulder, knowing it made no fucking difference at all.

"'Safe travels, á Cuinn."

"'God go w'ye, Silversaint."

'We watched the folk stumble by, their lives on their backs, headed towards a flame that would sputter out all too soon. I looked to Dior, my lip curled, filled with contempt that this little bastard would plant a hope where none could bloom. There was no magik silvershot, no divine prophecy, no holy fucking chalice that would end this darkness. This was our here and our now and our forever. And if it weren't for the fact he was my bait for Danton, I'd have kicked the little cunt's teeth out his arsehole then and there.

"'Still want to head north, mon amie?" I asked Chloe.

"'One capitaine, Gabe," she replied, meeting my eyes. "One course."

'I nodded, looking to the deepening gloom ahead.

"'As you like it.'"

✦ V ✦

A HARD THING TO COME BY

'THE STORM HIT us like a hammer from hell two days later. The wind screamed in from the north, the snow fell like knives, and the tiniest part of me hoped Lachlunn and Aisling á Cuinn had found someplace warm to lay their heads. The rest of me, the *most* of me, was just busy trying not to freeze to death.'

Gabriel reached forward to top up his wineglass, glancing at Jean-François.

'Can you remember what it's like to be cold, coldblood?'

The vampire paused, a small frown marring his porcelain brow. 'I take it this is another attempt at homespun comedy, Silversaint. Perhaps you should cleave to jests about prostitutes. At least there, you appear on familiar ground.'

'I mean *really* cold,' Gabriel said. 'Not the cold of the grave. The cold that puts you *in* one. When your hands ache so bad you can't make a fist. When your troth ring feels like ice on your finger, and it hurts to even breathe. *That* kind of cold.'

The historian tilted his head, pale fingertips brushing the Chastain emblem at his breast as he spoke the creed of his line: 'The wolf frets not for the ills of the worm.'

Gabriel took a long swallow of wine. 'You don't miss it?'

'Miss what? The futility of building a life that must one day crumble to dust?'

'The softness of a pillow after a hard day's work? The smile in your daughter's eyes as you step through the door? The joy of a lover in your arms?'

'A lover who must grow old and wither, while I remain unchanged?' Jean-François smiled, cold and thin. 'Unless I kill them, of course. Praying

God and Angel Fortuna that my love rises whole and beautiful, rather than some rotten abomination? Or simply remains dead by my hand?' The vampire shook his head. 'Romance is a mortal's folly, Silversaint.'

'Sounds like someone's talking from experience.'

'The ache of an empty belly. Or a full bladder. Or a cold fireplace.' The historian waved one hand, a golden curl tumbling across his eyes. 'Flesh, Silversaint. All the concerns of weak flesh. There is no mortal pain that can touch me. No sin of the skin that can compare to the blood of some ripe young thing, spilled velvet and lush upon my tongue. The callow thief of time shall never lay claim to my beauty. And when the temple of your body rots for the maggots, de León, when your ribs are their rafters and your belly their ballroom, I shall remain, *exactly* as I am now. Perpetual. Eternal. And you ask if I *miss* it?'

Gabriel smiled, lifted his wineglass. 'Trust me, vampire. Nothing lasts forever.'

'My patience, certainly.' Jean-François tapped his quill. 'The storm.'

'The storm.' Gabriel sighed, stretched out in his leather chair. 'Cold as a loveless bed, it was. The winters had been worsening, year by year, no time to thaw between. But I'd spent too long down in Sūdhaem, where spring still lightly lingered. Hunched in my saddle, hands in my armpits, I wasn't the cosiest of cats. So it was I breathed a white sigh of relief when Chloe called over the howling wind, "Gabe, we can't stay out in this!"

'"I know!" I nodded across bleak hills. "I think Winfael is only a few miles nor'east of here! We can cut across country, be there in a few hours!"

'"Do you know the way?" Bellamy shouted.

'"*We* know the way!"

'Saoirse materialized out of the blinding snows, wolfskin wrapped about her face. Phoebe prowled beside her, the she-lion's brow and whiskers white with frost.

'"Lead on, fair mademoiselle!" Bellamy shouted. "Whither thou go, I follow th—"

'"Shut the fuck up, Bouchette!"

'We reached the town hours later, Saoirse leading us like an arrow into a snowstruck valley. A great loch filled its belly, grey as the skies above. On its shores rested a fishing hamlet, a spiked palisade encircling it like a mother's arms. But peering through my spyglass, I could see the defences had been smashed in places, several buildings levelled by fire. The town had clearly been attacked – and I'd bet my wedding singer I could guess by what.

'"Anything moving?" Bellamy shouted.

'I shook my head, tongue pressed to sharpening teeth.

'"We can't stay out here!" Dior cried. "Rafa's freezing!"

'The old priest was curled in his saddle, beard and spectacles encrusted with frost. "I shall adm-m-mit I lost all feeling b-b-below my waist several m-miles ago."

'I nodded. "Come on!"

'We worked our way down in the gale, finally reaching the palisade. The defences were solid – heavy lumber reinforced with iron brackets. The gates were still sealed, but the palisade itself had been smashed by colossal impacts, beams snapped at the root like driest kindling. Phoebe loped through the ragged gap first, and I rode after the lioness, drawing Ashdrinker as I peered at the shattered timbers.

'*A vulgar display of p-power,* came her voice. *Dyvok, most like, most like.*

'I nodded. "Strong enough to be mediae at least."

'*The damage be n-not recent. Doubtful I think it, that highbloods linger here.*

'"Oui. But other maggots might've crawled into the grave they left behind."

'*We sh-should make haste to Triúrbaile, Gabriel. The attack is set for findi morn.*

'I looked to the beautiful silvered dame upon the hilt, my voice soft with pity. "Ash . . . the attack on Triúrbaile happened thirteen years ago . . ."

'"Who the fuck are you talking to?" Dior demanded.

'"The Ashdrinker!" Bellamy shouted over the wind, nodding to my sword. "The blade of the Black Lion is enchanted, Dior! Magiks from the Age of Legends! The Ashdrinker *speaks* to the mind of her wielder. Some tales have it that the blade steals the souls of all she slays, and sings with their voices as she kills. Others say she knows the truth of how every man under heaven shall die, and she speaks those secrets to the man who masters her!"

'I looked to the sword in my hand, eyebrow raised.

'*I am fond of thy new j-j-jester. He is most amusing, m-most amusing.*

'"Come on!" I pointed to a belfry above the rooftops. "We can shelter in the church!"

'We trudged between tight-packed buildings, down a snow-clad boulevard. The storm was pummelling, but the houses were silent and still. Winfael seemed more a memory of a town than a town itself, doors a-hang like broken jaws, old bloodstains on dusty glass.

'Truth told, it reminded me a little of my Lorson . . .

'"So much for tha' idea, Silversaint," Saoirse growled.

'Looking ahead, I saw the cathedral in the town square – hollowed by flame, broken rafters scraping the sky like an empty ribcage. The belfry tower still stood, but the clapper had long since rusted and fallen free, leaving the bell to swing in the bitter wind.

'Voiceless.

'Pointless.

'Rafa was almost dead ahorse, Chloe and Dior both shivering uncontrollably. There was no respite on holy ground here, but there was shelter at least, just across the square.

'"Let's go to the pub!"

'It was a two-storey affair, its sign bearing a bearded man with a leather apron swimming in a tankard of ale. THE HAMMERED SMITH was printed in faded letters beneath. The windows were barricaded, door locked tight, but a swift kicking would see it open . . .

'"Hold!" Dior shouted. "You smash the door off the hinges, what shelter will it be?"

'I lowered my boot as the boy bustled past. "You've got a key, smartarse?"

'"To every lock in the empire, dumbarse."

'Dior fetched a flat leather case tucked into his boot. Within, I saw iron picks, a torsion hook, a small hammer and wedge, all well-kept and oiled.

'"Thieves' picks," I growled. "Why am I not surprised?"

'"Not just a fuckugly face, I s'pose?" the boy muttered.

'I glanced to Chloe, and the sister simply flashed me a wry smile. And though it was freezing, his fingers trembling, the boy had that lock open quicker than a pisshead's purse when the pub bells ring. With a triumphant grin, Dior pushed the door wide, dropping into a flashy bow as Saoirse gave a small round of applause. And stepping inside, he jumped three feet backwards with a frightened yelp. "Shit!"

'Grabbing his fancy coat, I hauled the lad from the doorway and stepped inside, Ashdrinker raised. I looked about the commonroom, fangs bared: musty, cold, empty.

'"What?" I demanded. "What did you see?"

'The boy pointed. "Rats."

'Sure enough, the floor was crawling with them, thin and black and sleek, peering at me with eyes like jet. But they scattered as I stepped inside, swarming through splits in the floorboards, up into the mouldy walls. I glowered at the boy over my shoulder.

'"I fucking hate rats, aright?" he pouted.

'Shaking my head, I led the company inside while Bellamy took the horses to the stable. Dust coated the furniture, old wine bottles lay on tables or scattered on the floor. The walls were spackled with dark mould, and all smelled of rot and ratshit. But we were out of the wind at least, and with any luck, I'd find something to drink.

'"I'll look upstairs," I said. "Saoirse, stay here with the others."

'"A please'd be welcome."

'I tilted my head at her. "What did you say?"

'The young slayer rested her axe on her shoulder. "I'm nae some hammerman ye fought wi' in days of glory. Nor some lackey to be ordered aboot. A please'd be welcome."

'"We're half-near frozen to death. In the corpse of a town that's obviously been gutted by coldbloods. And you want to pull out our cocks and measure them now?"

'"Ye've been swingin' yer tadpole aboot every chance ye get already, man. Why should now be any different?"

'I walked across the creaking floorboards until we were chest to chest.

'"Pretty please. With fucking sugar on it. Stay here with the others."

'Saoirse scowled. I turned on my silver heel and stomped upstairs, paying a visit with my boots, door to door. Ashdrinker was singing an old nursery rhyme in my head, and I did my best to ignore her as I went from room to room. The bedchambers were small, dusty, all empty save for a handful of rats who looked slightly outraged at my presence. But it seemed we had somewhere to sleep at least – presuming we were allowed to.

'Bellamy came in from outside, slamming the door against the weather just as I returned to the commonroom, sheathing Ash to quiet her disjointed song in my head. The others were in the kitchen – rusty knives on the walls, pots of old cast iron. But there wasn't a trace of food. Nor liquor, more's the pity.

'"Clear upstairs." I glanced to Dior, shuddering. "Save for all the *rats*."

'"Gabe, stop it," Chloe murmured.

'"Huge bastards, they are." I measured a yard with my hands. "Well fed too, by the look. I swear God, one of them was wearing a waistcoat of human skin."

'The boy flipped me the Fathers. "Suck my cock, hero."

'"We can wait here until the weather breaks," Chloe declared. "Warm up. Sleep."

'Rafa was slumped by the hearth, shivering head to toe. The sister knelt beside him, arm around the poor old bastard for warmth. Bellamy scruffed the snow from his still-perfect three-day stubble, stomped his feet to get the feeling back. "I'll get a fire going."

'I nodded, looking to Saoirse. "Where's that cat of yours?"

'"Phoebe wanders. She'll be back when she gets bored."

'"Right. I might go for a look-see myself. Rest of you stay here, stay warm. Pretty please." I glanced to Chloe. "Trouble finds you while I'm gone, belt that horn of yours, Sœur Sauvage."

'Chloe spared me a small, grateful smile. "Walk careful, mon ami."

'"I'll be back. Quick as a bishop up an altar boy."

'Rafa blinked, shivering. "I think p-perhaps your experience with b-bishops differs from mine, Silversaint."

'I stepped out into the sleet, shoulders hunched as I made a slow circuit of Winfael. I trudged through tight-packed streets, checking houses and cellars, then down to the edge of the freezing loch. A tangle of old nets. Boats abandoned. Water cold as a bog hag's tit. The houses were stripped, whether by folk who lived here or scavengers after, I'd no ken. But save for the vermin, there wasn't a soul alive in this whole forsaken place.

'No Dead either, at least.

'I circled back to the main square, silver-heeled boots crunching in new snow. The ghosts in the houses whispered old secrets to the storm. Through the flurry ahead, I caught a hint of blue and silver, disappearing through the doors of the burned church.

'*Dior.*

'It was freezing, and I was itching for a smoke, but I trusted that fancy little shit as far as I could piss into this wind. And so, I stomped across the square and through the buck-toothed dawndoors of the Winfael Cathedral.

'It was a modest affair – circular, limestone blacked by flame. Its roof had collapsed, snow drifting into its hollow belly. The windows were old stained glass, mostly shattered on the floor. But in the nor'most wall, the glass was intact – a scene depicting Michon leading her army during the Wars of the Faith. The first Martyr was tall, flaxen-haired, fierce as a hundred angels. Dior stood before the window with a puzzled look on his face.

'"The fuck are you doing?"

'The boy startled as I spoke, spinning on his heel. His silver dagger was out of his coat in a blinking. I had to admit it – the little prick's hands were as quick as his tongue.

'"I thought I told you to mind your business, hero."

'"And who said that you get to tell me anything at all, boy?"

'"Your mama," he scowled. "After I rumped her on your papa's sheets."

'I chuckled at that, tipped my tricorn. "You've got balls, Lachance. I'll give you that. But my boots are bigger. What are you doing in here?"

'He gestured to the broken pews around the altar. "Bellamy needs fire-wood."

'"Mmf." I nodded. "Fine idea. Worthless made worthwhile."

'"You honestly can't imagine the relief I feel at meeting your approval, hero."

'Dior stalked among the pews, gathering up the crushed timber. I reached into my greatcoat for my pipe, packed a neat hit of sanctus into the bowl. I'd been working my way through the new batch I'd cooked nice and slow, and that fledgling's blood was rich as fine wine. I probably didn't need another smoke yet. But Need and Want are two different masters entire.

'That sharp snap of iron on flint. That sorcerie of heat and vapour slipping like the sweetest blade into my chest, face upturned, snowflakes pressing gentle kisses upon my fluttering lashes, as close to heaven as I'd ever get.

'"Any opportunity to feed that need, eh?"

'Dior's voice brought me back to earth. I exhaled a crimson lungful and looked him over with eyes the same shade. Elidaeni haute couture on his back. Cheap Sūdhaemi leather on his feet. Nordlund blood in his veins. Button missing from his right sleeve. Left-handed. Gutter thin. Black beauty spot on his right cheek. Fingers stained grey from his traproot cigarelles. And for the first time, I saw he had scars across his palms – knife wounds carved in his skin, long and deep. Only a couple of months old, by the look.

'"And what would you know about it, boy?"

'"I know you suck on that pipe like you were getting paid for it." Dior lifted his foot and snapped a shattered pew in half. "I know you got a shadow on you, hero."

'"You know shit, Lachance. Keep talking it, see what happens."

'The boy sneered and nodded to himself. "And there it is."

'"There's what?"

'"The first resort of every man like you I ever met."

'"Don't make the mistake of thinking you know me, boy."

'He shook his head, glanced to my pipe. "I've known people like you all my life. No matter if it's the bottle or the needle or the smoke, the same's true for every one of you. Once that hook's in your skin, it just drags out the worst in you."

'"You've never seen the worst in me."

'"I've seen enough. You treat the people around you like shit."

'"I treat the people around me like they deserve. It's just most people deserve to be treated like shit." I fixed him in a bloody stare, watching his eyes. "Liars, especially."

'The boy matched my gaze, unafraid. "Everybody lies."

"'That they do. But you're not half as good at it as you think, boy. With your big cock swagger and your beggar's boots and your fancy coat."

"'Not just fancy, hero." The boy brushed his midnight-blue lapel. "This coat's *magik*."

"'Magik." I scoffed. "Bullshit. Just like the rest of you."

"'As you like it."

'I lifted my pipe, staring at the stained-glass likeness of the first Martyr.

"'The Grail of San Michon, eh? You want to tell me how a gutterborn thief from the arse end of Sūdhaem learns the whereabouts of the most priceless relic of the Holy Church?"

"'No," Dior replied. "No, I don't."

'I stepped closer, watching his pupils dilate, listening to his heart beating a touch quicker. "Danton Voss. Sisters of the Inquisition. Dúnnsair slayers. Soothsingers and holy men. You've got a strange crop tangled up in this bullshit of yours, Lachance. And normally, I'd be struggling to find a reason to care. But the Silver Sister in that taverne back there who believes in you *so* hard? She's a friend of mine. And they're thin enough on the ground these nights for me to feel overprotective about the few I have left."

'Dior clenched his jaw. "Sister Chloe saved my life. I'd never do *anything* to hurt her."

"'Except drag her through hell for the sake of a cup that doesn't exist?"

'His eyes twinkled then. "But there's the joke, hero. It *does* exist."

"'Is that right?" I smiled, stepping closer. "Why don't you tell me where it is, then?"

"'And why would I do that?"

"'Because if anything happens to my friend because of your bullshit . . ." I put my hand on his shoulder, teeth sharp against my tongue, ". . . it won't go well for you."

"'There it is again," he whispered. "The first resort of every bad man I ever met."

"'The world needs bad men, boy. We keep the monsters from the door."

"'But that's the problem, hero. Bad men never realize when the monster is *them*."

"'Gabe? Dior?"

'I turned, found Chloe at the broken doors, wind howling at her back. Her cloak was up over her curls, scarf about her face. But her big green eyes were fixed on me.

"'Are you two well?'"

"'Just chatting.' I gave Dior's shoulder a squeeze. Hurting just enough to let him know it could hurt far worse. "Man to man.""

"'. . . Dior?'"

'The boy shrugged my hand off, and spitting on the ground at my feet, he hefted his armful of broken lumber and stalked out the doors. Chloe watched him go with a mother's eyes, and I wondered what in God's name made her cleave to this lad so hard.

'Mayhaps because she'd never have a son herself?

'*Could it be that simple?*

"'Phoebe just returned," Chloe murmured. "Saoirse says we may have problems.""

"'Well, there's a pleasant change.'"

'I crunched across the broken pews towards the doors, but Chloe grabbed my arm as I tried to pass. I looked down: barely five feet of her, nunnery-raised, small and slight. But I felt the strength in her grip. Saw the fire in her eyes. "Can I trust you, Gabe?""

"'Why wouldn't you be able to trust me, Chlo?'"

"'You seem . . . different. What you said to Rafa the other day. About God—'"

"'I said I'd see you to the Volta, and I will. I'm not the one you should be fretting on.'"

"'Dior's not what you think, Gabriel.'"

"'A grifter? A thief? He's all that and more. I can smell it in his sweat. Hear it in his heartbeat. He's a fucking *liar*, Chlo. And I'm wondering if all those years you spent buried in those books have turned you so blind you can't see the horizon. If you want to believe in this holy cup nonsense so badly, you'll swallow anything anyone hands you.'"

"'Trust me," she whispered."

"'Why? What makes you so fucking certain?'"

'She pressed her lips thin. "You remember when you used to train me in the Library? *Always look your enemy in the eye? Never draw your sword unless you mean to use it?*"

"'I remember.'"

"'I took those lessons to heart." She pulled off her glove, and I saw her palm was callused, fingers rough where once they'd only been papercut. "I'm not that little girl any more, Gabe. I *know* what I'm doing. And if I can't tell you all, then I beg you forgive me. But God above, truth told, it's best you *don't* know all." She squeezed my hand in her tiny fist. "I need your blade, mon ami. I need your strength. But most of all, I need your faith."

'I reached down, slowly pulled my hand out of hers.

'"Faith's a hard thing to come by these nights, Sister."

'And head bowed, I walked out into the cold.'

✦ VI ✦

THE PLAN

'"WRETCHED," SAOIRSE REPORTED. "A pack o' them. Headed this way."

'We were gathered in the commonroom of the Hammered Smith, the dark sun slinking towards the horizon as if it'd earned a rest. Bellamy had got a fire roaring, and I had my gloves off, warming my hands in the twice-blessed heat. Saoirse crouched beside Phoebe, scratching the big cat under her collar. The lioness yawned, steam rising off her russet fur as she stretched out beside me, close to the flames.

'Old Rafa's voice was muffled inside the blankets he'd stolen from upstairs.

'"How many?"

'"A dozen, mebbe," Saoirse replied. "Phoebe spied them a few miles east. Moving slow in the storm, like. But they'll move quicker when the sun goes all the way down."

'"They may pass us by," I said. "We've no reason to think they know we're here."

'Chloe met my eyes. "They know, Gabe. They're coming for us."

'". . . How can you be certain?"

'Saoirse hefted her axe and shield. "They're comin', Silversaint."

'I sighed, dragged my hand through my hair. A dozen wretched were nothing to scoff at, but at least we had warning they were on the way. So I reached out to give Phoebe a grateful pat. "Merci, mademois – fuck!"

'The lioness snarled and bared her fangs, and I snatched my hand back before she took it off at the wrist. Saoirse looked down at my tattooed fingers and grinned.

'"Might want to be keepin' yer hands to yerself. Like most lasses, Phoebe's not wild about touchin' without permission."

'The she-lion licked her scarred chops, growled deep enough for me to feel it in my chest.

'"So noted." I slipped my gloves back on and stood. "Right, well. If we're certain these unholy bastards are on the way, we'd best get our garters up and our pants back on."

'"You mean to fight them?" Rafa asked.

'"We sure as hell can't run in this storm. Once we repair the palisade, we have a fortified position. And we've a lake behind us."

'Bellamy frowned. "Old ballads speak ill of armies that fought with water to their backs, Chevalier. If memory serves, you yourself won the Battle of Tarren Moor by—"

'"What do you get when you add a priest to water, Bouchette?"

'"In this weather?" Dior frowned at the shivering Rafa. "Pneumonia?"

'I picked up a dusty wine bottle and twisted the old candle stump from its neck. "Watch and learn, you little shitweasel."

'We set about it, and though Saoirse still rankled a little at being told what to do, Chloe's faith in me was enough to carry her over the line. I drew a map of the town in charcoal on the Hammered Smith's floorboards and set each member of the company a task. Thinking swift. Talking swifter. It'd been more than a decade since I led the defence of anything more than a moment of peace and quiet on the privy, but the mantle slipped over my shoulders like a well-worn coat.

'Bellamy and I set about repairing the defences, tearing timbers from abandoned houses and piling them in the palisade breaches. I took another hit from my pipe, blood-red and brimming, and the young soothsinger stood wide-eyed as I rammed broken timbers into the frozen earth by hand, smashing them deeper with a sledgehammer scrounged from the stables.

'After an hour or so, Dior came crunching through the howling snow, pushing a barrow piled with wine bottles full of cloudy loch water. Climbing the stairs, the boy began stacking them on the highwalks beside the breaches.

'Bellamy tipped his cap and grinned. "All's well, M. Lachance?"

'The boy shrugged, called over the roaring wind. "Saoirse found an old barrel of tallow in the pub cellar, and Sister Chloe is fashioning some fire arrows with it. Père Rafa's spitting blessings fast as he can." Dior hefted one of the bottles in hand, glanced at me. "I have to admit, I'm two-thirds of one-eighth impressed, hero."

'I slammed another timber downwards, teeth gritted as it crunched into the ground. "You honestly can't imagine the relief I feel at meeting your approval, boy."

"'If you're impressed now, Dior, wait 'til tonight. You're like to see a sight unrivalled." Bellamy pulled his cloak tighter, grinning. "To witness the Black Lion himself in battle . . . the Ashdrinker unleashed. God Almighty, that'll be worth a song and no mistake."

'I slammed another timber home. Dior climbed down from the palisade, gazing at Ashdrinker. I worked easier with the blade off my hip, and so I'd set her against the barricade. The boy's eyes roamed the beaten scabbard, the silvered maid on the crossguard.

"'Does it really . . . speak to you?"

"'More's the pity," I grunted, slamming another beam down.

"'Where'd it come from?"

"'Ah, there's the rub, Dior," Bellamy replied. "No one knows. A mentor of mine, the famed soothsinger Dannael á Riagán, sings that the Black Lion took the blade from the halls of a sleepless barrowking, deep in the weald of Nordlund. But the historian Saan Sa-Asad tells that the chevalier won Ashdrinker in a riddle contest with a nameless elder horror, deep in the bowels of the Godsend Everdark. I even heard one tale that the Lion took Ashdrinker from the trove of the dread faequeen, Ainerión. Her kiss spells death for any mortal man, Dior, and yet the Lion loved Ainerión so long and so sweetly, he was able to steal the enchanted blade from her bedside after she collapsed in exhaustion. But as far as I know, the chevalier has never once confirmed *any* of these tales."

'Bellamy looked to me hopefully, one eyebrow cocked.

"'Shut the fuck up, Bouchette."

"'How'd it break?" Dior asked, eyes still on the sword.

"'Eh?" Bellamy blinked.

"'The end," the boy said. "The pointy bit, whatever you call it."

"'The tip?"

"'Oui. I saw it when we came through the walls. It's been broken off."

'Bellamy tilted his rake's hat back and rubbed his chin. "I confess I didn't notice. No tale ever mentioned the blade being broken at all. But . . . to the bold, the bouquet." The youngster walked towards Ashdrinker, hand outstretched. "Mayhaps we can ask her?"

"'Oi!" I snapped. "Touch that sword and you'll be playing your lute with your fucking toes, Soothsinger."

"'I jest, mon ami." Bellamy tipped me a wink and a roguish smile. "A fellow who lays a familiar hand on another man's blade might as well be laying hand on his bride. And I never touch brides without *express* invitation."

"'You're a bastard, Bel," Dior grinned. "A scoundrel, a bounder, and a cad."

'"I'm a *romantic*, M. Lachance. Stick with me long enough, I'll teach you how."

'"Meantime, how about the pair of you get the fuck back to work?" I growled.

'The soothsinger pulled his cloak tighter and scratched his dark curls. Dior scoffed and trudged off into the snow. We piled the breaches as high and thick as we could, leaving only the main gate unlocked for Saoirse to return by. Stacking the boulevard and narrow streets with broken furniture and timbers, we created an inner ring to fall back to if things went tits up. It was bitter cold, and by the time we were done, night had fallen like an anvil. But still, I was satisfied. Between our walls and weapons, we could see off a dozen wretched. With the storm raging on, Bellamy and I trudged back to the Hammered Smith.

'The company were within, Rafa bent over a pot steaming in the hearth.

'"Is that fucking potato again?"

'"I have turnip, if you prefer," the old priest smiled.

'"Where's Saoirse?" Chloe asked.

'"Still scouting with Phoebe," Bellamy replied. "They'll return anon."

'I grabbed a bowlful of accursed spuds, scoffed them quick enough not to touch the sides. Walking a slow circle, I scuffed the charcoal map I'd drawn on the boards with my bootheels. For a moment, I was reminded of San Michon's Library; that great, grand map of the empire across its floor.

'"Through blood and fire, now dance with me."

'I glanced up as Chloe murmured, saw her eyes fixed on mine. I knew she was living the same moment I was. How long ago it all seemed then. And how far away.

'"Right." I tapped the map with one toe. "I'll man the gates, with little Lord Talkstoomuch on the highwalk. Chloe, you and Saoirse take the east breach, Rafa and Bellamy the west. If you hit trouble, sing out. I'll be there. If we're overrun, fall back to the inner circle, then the cathedral. Holy ground will keep them at bay as a last resort."

'"Why not retreat to the cathedral now?" Rafa asked.

'"And then what? Hole up inside until we starve to death? These things can wait forever if they've a want to. But don't concern yourself, priest. These rotten bastards will come at us mindless and frontways without a bloodlord leading them."

'Dior was finishing off his second helping, talking with ballooning cheeks. "You asked the soldier we met about that. What's a bloodlord?"

'"Highbloods can control the lower caste of vampires, Dior," Chloe replied.

"The deeper their blood, the more wretched they can keep under sway. With an intelligence directing them, wretched are far more dangerous. But this rabble seem to have none."

'Rafa nodded, signing the wheel. "Thank the Almighty for his mercy."

'The boy swallowed his ambitious mouthful, staring at me. "And what did that soldier mean? When he said you bathed the battlefield silver?"

"'Ah, the *aegis*," Bellamy smiled. "The holy magik for which the silversaints are named and famed, Dior. See that ink on the Black Lion's hands? In truth, it covers most of his body. And in battle, it serves as a conduit for his faith in our Lord above."

'The boy's eyebrows disappeared into his hair. "You mean . . . you fight . . . naked?"

"'Not entirely," Chloe smiled. "Being silverclad, the Order names it."

'Bellamy nodded, eyes alight. "When the chevalier fights tonight, you'll see the aegis aglow, like a *thousand* torches. At the siege at Tuuve, it's said the Black Lion burned so—"

"'Shut the fuck up, Bouchette," I growled. "The holy water we've stocked in those wine bottles will scorch them better than acid. Likely not enough to kill them, but it'll soften them up some. If they make it through the palisade, fire burns these leeches better than a gigolo with the clap. So if you're not wielding silver, a torch is your best weapon."

'Rafa's fingers brushed his wheel, eyes on the sevenstar around Chloe's neck. "I can think of another weapon, Silversaint. Faith is more than a match for any flame."

"'Mayhaps you could pray for an angel or two, then? See if any show up?"

'The old man smiled at me, dark eyes twinkling over his spectacles. "I think God has already sent us angels enough, mon ami. But I shall pray he watch over us this night nevertheless."

"'And what's the point of that, priest?

'Rafa blinked. "What is the point of—"

"'Praying. Oui."

'The old man looked at me as if I'd asked the point of breathing. "I . . ."

"'Two soldiers stand on a field of battle," I told him. "Both are convinced God is on their side. Both pray to their Lord and Redeemer to smite their enemy low, and to the Mothermaid to protect them from all harm. But somebody's going to lose. *Somebody's* wasting their fucking time. Maybe, just maybe . . . it's both of them?"

'The priest frowned. "God cannot be said to be on the side of the Dead."

"'You're missing the point, old man. *All on earth below and hea'en above is the work of my hand . . .*"

"'. . . *And all the work of my hand is in accord with my plan.*"

"'You think those refugees we met on the road didn't pray with everything they had to not lose their homes? You think Lachlunn á Cuinn didn't pray for his wife and son to stay alive? See, that divine plan shite is what the pulpit-hucksters feed you when things start to go wrong. After they've passed around the collection plate, of course. When your crops fail or your cancer spreads or whatever else you've begged him for doesn't come to pass. That's the solace they'll offer. *It's God's will,* they'll tell you. *Part of the divine plan.*

"'What they don't point out is, if he *has* a plan? There's no sense praying for anything. If *His will be done* is the golden rule, then God's going to do what he wants, regardless of how hard you beg him. And imagine, just for a second, the sense of entitlement it takes to ask him for anything in the first place. The fucking ego you'd need to think that this is somehow all for you. What if you ask for something that's not his will? You want him to alter the course of the divine plan? For *you*? See, that's the grift of it all. That's the *genius.* You get what you pray for? Huzzah, God fucking loves you. But your prayers go unanswered?" I snapped my fingers. "Just wasn't part of the plan."

'I tipped a dose of sanctus into my pipe under Chloe's worried gaze.

"'I've stood in the houses of the holy, priest. I've read his scripture cover to cover, I've sung praises to his name, and I tell you now and tell you true: one hand holding a sword is worth ten thousand clasped in prayer."

"'*There be no tree with branches that reach to heaven,*" Rafa quoted, "*that hath not roots that stretch to hell. And we h—*"

"'Chloe!"

'The priest fell silent as the slayer burst through the door, eyes wide.

"'Saoirse?" Chloe rose to her feet. "What is it?"

"'Phoebe's back." The girl clawed the snow from her braids, stomping her feet. "The wretched are ten minutes oot. But there's nae a dozen."

'Dior stood, his face pale. ". . . There's more?"

'The slayer hefted her axe, nodded grim. "Fifty. At least."

"'Fifty wretched . . ." Chloe breathed. "Against seven of us."

'Bellamy looked around the room, eyes wide. "My God."

'I struck my flintbox and chuckled, meeting the priest's eyes.

"'Sure you don't want to pray for those angels, old man?'"

✦ VII ✦

THE BATTLE OF WINFAEL

'THE MOST UNSETTLING thing is the quiet.

'Coldbloods don't need to breathe. Which means they don't speak without conscious thought. And if the vampire you're facing has a brain that rotted to mush before it Became, it isn't capable of much thought beyond "hungry" and "food". There's degrees to it, of course. A coldblood who lay bloating in a ditch for a day or two might remember enough of itself to vocalize. But a monster who rotted in a shallow grave for a week or more won't be anything but instinct. So while some wretched might gabble half-words at you, or scream when you hurt them, most are too far gone even to remember how to inhale.

'So when they come, they come in total silence.

'That's what they did, there at Winfael. A bloody-eyed horde, charging through the snows at our thin walls, making no fucking sound at all. But that instinct still resides. That bestial drive at the heart of us all – mate, kill, feed, repeat. And while the mindless ones just crashed against the closest breach and started to tear through, the less rotten ones, the *smarter* ones, they split up, circling the palisade looking for weak spots. Other ways in to the luscious bags of blood they could smell just beyond the walls.

'"There's too many!" Dior shouted.

'"Just keep that holy water coming!" I roared.

'The boy hurled another wine bottle, and I heard shattering glass and the sizzle of fatty bacon on a skillet in the mob below. We stood on the highwalk above the gates where the wretched were thickest, the boy throwing bottles, me cutting down any bastard who tried to climb. Saoirse was on the eastern walk, loosing burning arrows into the horrors, Chloe flinging bottles alongside her. Bellamy and Rafa stood atop the west walk, the soothsinger shooting his crossbow, the priest hurling holy water and prayers.

'Wretched burn like tinder on a hot summer's day, and the flaming shots were doing goodly work. Problem was, there were far more vampires than we had arrows. The holy water burned dead flesh like hellspark, but even the weakest fledgling would only get softened up by a bottle anywhere but the head. And we were running out of bottles too. It was only a matter of time before—

'"*Gabriel!*"

'Chloe's cry rang across town, bright with fear, followed by the note of a silver horn.

'"Fuck my *face*," I spat. Twisting the fuse on one of my few remaining silverbombs, I hurled it into the wretched below. They were tight-packed, and the explosion flared like a tiny sun. Limbs flew and bellies burst, silver caustic stinging in my paleblood eyes.

'"Can you hold them?"

'"I'll try!" Dior flung another bottle. "Go help her!"

'I leapt twenty feet into the snow, charging towards Chloe's voice. Saoirse and she were atop the highwalk, and I saw a handful of wretched had scaled the walls, flanked them either side. Chloe fought fierce, silversteel in one hand, sevenstar in the other. The sigil burned like white flame, illuminating the tempest around her and the wretched in front of her. At Chloe's back, Saoirse had abandoned her bow, hewing away with shield and axe. She was a vicious bitch, and though Kindness wasn't silvered, that axe still somehow cleaved dead flesh like a hot blade in snow. But in defending the highwalk, they'd ignored the breach, and the wretched had broken in, spilling in a silent flood through the palisade.

'I charged into them, bloodhymn bright and burning, Ashdrinker like a bloody feather in my hand. The blade sang no songs, stole no souls, instead mumbling what sounded like a recipe for mushroom soup, but she sheared through Dead flesh like paper. I saw a flash of russet red, Phoebe blurring out of the darkness, roaring as she crashed atop the corpse of some ill-fated farmer's lad and ripped his head from his shoulders. A coldblood fell from above – enough left inside it to make it wail as Saoirse took its legs off at the knees and sent it tumbling from the highwalk.

'"Where's Dior?" Chloe cried.

'"Still at the gates!"

'"You left him *alone*?"

'*Four tablespoons of butter* . . . Ashdrinker whispered.

'I cut another wretch into the snow, fangs bared in a snarl. "He's fine! You need t—"

'"*Silversaint!*" came a distant cry. "*De León!*"

"'Bellamy?" Saoirse cried.

"'I'll go fetch them! Fall back to the inner circle!" I shouted. "Pretty please!"

'*One tablespoon of oil* . . .

"'Get Dior!" Chloe cried. "Gabriel, he's all that matters!"

"'Just go, damn you! I'll get them all!"

"'Phoebe, go wi'!" Saoirse split a wretched's head in half, spun on her heel and chopped another one's guts clean through. "Go!"

'I dashed off through the dark, wiping blood from my eyes. The lioness dashed ahead, razor-quick. Crossing the thoroughfare and leaping our barricade, I glanced towards the gates, saw Dior hurling bottles and shouting triumphant curses. "Suck my *cock*, you fuc—"

"'Lachance, fall back!"

"'But they're not through yet!"

'*Two onions, finely d-diced* . . .

"'Give it a rest, Ash! And get your scrawny arse back behind the barricade before I feed you to the Dead, boy!"

'Heart pounding, I dashed through a twisted alleyway towards the westward breach. Ahead, I saw a ghostly glow, ripe with sounds of murder and the stink of burning flesh. And rounding the corner, I skidded to a halt, hand up to shield my eyes.

'Père Rafa stood like a beacon in the dark, silver wheel in one skinny fist. Long shadows were etched in grey snow, the sigil casting a blinding beam of light into the dark before him. Bellamy stood beside the priest, bleeding from a vicious gash above his eye, longblade in one hand, a flaming torch in the other.

"'The Lord is my shield, unbreakable!" Rafa cried. "He is the fire that burns away all darkness!"

'*Impressive,* Ashdrinker whispered.

"'Nobody asked you," I replied, lopping another wretched head into the snow.

'*I remember n-nights when ye shone just as—*

"'Shut up, Ash," I hissed.

'The blade spoke truth – old Rafa *was* impressive. Wherever his light struck the wretched, they fell back as if touched by fiercest flame. Problem was, the light shone only where the priest pointed it. Bellamy was doing his best to keep the bastards off the old man's back, swinging that torch like a club. But the pair were encircled now.

'I dashed into the freezing dark, hacking through the coldbloods and roaring over the storm. "Bouchette! Rafa! This way!"

'The pair broke through the gap I'd carved, dashed into the alleyway at my back. I followed, hand up against Rafa's light as the priest covered our retreat. The wretched scattered, some seeking other paths, others scrambling on our tails. Bellamy helped Rafa over our barricade, the old man gasping and holding his chest. I cut down the wretched on our backs – a maid with cherry curls, a soldier with scarred arms, an elderly man, naked and sagging – no thought for what they'd been but only what they'd become, and my old friend hatred burning bright for the one that had let it all come to this.

"'Gabriel!" Chloe cried. "Why aren't you silverclad?"

'I ignored Chloe's cry, hacking at the bastards in the barricade. Their numbers were thinning, but not yet enough. Fearless, mindless, they crashed against the timbers, clawing and climbing. Dior came running from the gates with a mangled mob on his tail, leaping the barricade like a dancer and rolling to his feet.

"'Dior, get back to the cathedral!"

"'I'll not leave you, Sister Chloe!"

"'Dior, Godsakes, do as I *say*!"

'The boy ignored her, stabbing at a coldblood's eyes with his silver dagger. Chloe and Saoirse stood back to back, the sister keeping the wretched off the slayer's arse as Saoirse sowed mayhem. Phoebe struck beyond our blockade, ripping the Dead to ribbons before slinking back into the dark. The wretched's numbers were thinning, bodies fallen around my feet. If I squinted hard, I could see light at tunnel's end.

'But then, as always, came the dark.

'A pack of the cleverest Dead had stolen over the rooftops, dropping into our midst. Dior cried warning, lashing out with his silver knife. But the boy squealed as the monsters leapt upon him, and at his screams, Rafa and Chloe turned their holy light towards him.

'The wretched atop Dior flinched backwards, scrabbling, scrambling, but both priest and sister had left their backs unattended. Phoebe and Saoirse held off the flood, but armed only with his torch, Bellamy couldn't manage. The wretched ripped over the barrier, the soothsinger crying out as Dead weight bore him down, Dead teeth tore his skin. Like dominoes falling, the collapse began, the corpse of a spry teenage boy leaping onto Rafa's back with a blacktooth grin. The priest roared, old knees and old hands failing him, his wheel glinting silver as it flew from his fingers.

'Rafa screamed "God help me!" as the deadboy ripped out a bloody mouthful from his neck. The wretched flinched back, gurgling as Ashdrinker sent its head spinning into the dark. Bellamy was flailing, blood on his hands and face as he punched and kicked at the corpses piling atop him. I carved through them, Chloe beside me, silversteel sword flashing as she screamed from the Book of Vows.

'*"Turn ye now, oh faithless kings of men! And look upon thy queen!"*

'It was foolish. Necks ripped like that, arteries opened like love letters, Rafa and Bellamy were already dead. And in helping them, we'd left Dior – the boy now crying out as a quick-fingered, blood-slicked horror bore him back down into the snow. Another piled atop him as he stabbed and stabbed, and his squeal ripped the night as his arm was wrenched backwards, the wretched lunging like raptors and biting deep into his skin.

'*"Dior!"*

'I heard a sound then. Like not to a sound, but a *movement*, as if the earth shook once and then all upon it, human and beast and them between, held their breath. And those wretched atop the boy reeled back as if struck by the fist of God, and bloody eyes wide, I saw it begin – a glow, burning white-hot in those greedy throats. It spread like flame to tinder in dim-remembered summers, and in a heartbeat, each wretched screamed as if it remembered what it was to hurt, and burst into a pillar of white-hot flame.

'The fire seethed, burning them to bones and ash, and above the sound of bursting bellies and crackling bones I heard Ashdrinker's silvered cry inside my head:

'*Fight, ye pretty fool!*

'I did as I was bid, hacking at the remaining Dead. Some had sense enough to flee, others stood dumbstruck in the glow of that flame, brought low by me or Phoebe or Saoirse. And in a few heartbeats, the tide had turned, our foes scattered into the storm or spattered red in the soaking snows at our feet.

'"Dior!" Chloe skidded to her knees at the boy's side. "Oh God, are you aright?"

'Face splashed with blood, I thrust Ashdrinker into the snow. Dragging the coldblood corpses off the fallen priest, I sank to my knees beside him. Saoirse did likewise with Bellamy, the soothsinger gasping as blood frothed from his torn throat. He was barely more than a boy, the poor fool. Rafa was facedown in a widening puddle, and I rolled the old bastard onto his back, pressed my hand to his sundered throat. The once-gushing river was now only a trickle.

'Soon to be nothing at all.

'His dark eyes were fixed on mine, the perfume of his blood rising over the sanctus rush, and despite the horror of it, setting a dark, delicious hunger in my belly. I cursed then – what I was and what I'd become and what he, in his omniscience, had made me. And looking into the priest's fading eyes, I shook my head and sighed.

'"Where's your God now, old man?"

'"Get the *fuck* out of my way!"

'Dior slammed into me, gasping and furious, blood-soaked hair in his eyes.

'"The bloody hell are you doi—"

'"Gabriel, stand aside!" Chloe cried, pulling me back.

'I shrugged off her bloody hand and glowered at the sister, her surcoat and blade spattered with gore. But she had eyes only for the boy. I saw Dior press his hands to the rends in the priest's throat, his eyes wide and wet with tears.

'"Seven Martyrs, he's finished, boy. Let the man die in p—"

'"Shut the fuck up!"

'Dior's arm was still bleeding, his neck too, and the boy smeared the blood from his own wounds onto his palm. And as I watched, he pressed that crimson hand to the gaping hole in Rafa's throat, and my heart fell still. Because I swear by God and Mothermaid and Redeemer too, at his bloody touch, that wound stitched itself closed.

'"Chloe . . ." I whispered.

'Dior scrambled across the snow, Saoirse removing her grip from Bellamy's throat. The soothsinger's lips were pink with froth as the boy slicked his palm with his own blood again and pressed it to those awful wounds. And just as with the priest, I stood amazed as the gashes knitted closed before my eyes, not a scar nor scratch in their wake.

'"Bellamy?" Dior whispered, desperate. "Can you hear me?"

'The young soothsinger still seemed weak, skin sheened with sweat. But his breath came easy and his eyes shone, and he pressed a bloody hand to Dior's.

'"M-merci, M-monsieur Lachance."

'"Great fucking Redeemer . . ." I breathed.

'I looked to Rafa, sitting up in the snow. The old man was shaking, robes drenched red. But still, he was hale and breathing, where a heartbeat ago he'd been almost a corpse.

'"Y-you asked me . . . where my God was, Chevalier de León."

'The priest looked to Dior and managed a bruise-blue smile.

'"And *there* he is."'

✦ VIII ✦

FROM HOLY CUP

'"WHAT IN THE name of the Father, Mothermaid and all Seven Martyrs is going on?"

'I stood in the Hammered Smith, hands crusted with ashes and blood. Bellamy and Rafa were slumped by the fire. Chloe stood beside Dior, Saoirse nearby, cleaning the gore off Kindness. Phoebe had followed the wretched, whether to take them down one by one or ensure they retreated, I hadn't a clue. But I'd no care for a few ragtag corpses.

'My eyes were fixed on Chloe, Ashdrinker in my hand. My old friend was avoiding my eyes, tending the wounds at Dior's throat and arm. The little bastard's cravat and shirt were soaked with blood, but the boy was staring me down, defiant as ever.

'"Well?" I demanded. "Spit it out, Chloe. What did I just see?"

'*Know ye, what we have w-witnessed, Gabriel.*

'I glared at the blade in my hand, sharp teeth gritted.

'*Faithless may ye be, but yet ye have eyes to see, to see. A mirac—*

'I slammed the sword home and silenced her voice, glowering at Chloe. She tutted and fussed about Dior like a mother hen, wrapping his wounds in swaddling until at last the boy winced and waved her off. "I'm fine, Sister Chloe. God's truth."

'Chloe sat back, bloody hands to hips, a bone-deep fear in her eyes. "Blessed Mothermaid, that was too close, Dior. I *told* you to run to the cathedral."

'"And I told *you*," the boy said. "I'll not leave my friends to fight my battles for me."

'"You can't risk yourself like that! You're too *important*!"

'"Why?" I demanded.

'Chloe finally met my eyes. Secrets locked behind her lips.

"'Goddamn you, Chloe Sauvage, speak! *You're* the one who dragged me into this cavalcade of arsefuckery, and the enigmatic silence is wearing thin. You want my help, you'd best start singing, else I'll leave the lot of you to the fucking Dead!"

'The holy sister slumped cross-legged upon the floor, glanced around the room. Saoirse shook her head, scowling black. Bellamy licked bloodstained lips and nodded once. Rafa remained silent, staring at Dior.

'The boy was looking at me, wincing as he slipped his arms back into his pretty coat. As he glanced to the blade at my side, I could see a grudging respect in his eyes – the knowledge they'd all likely be dead if not for me. But still, his gaze slipped to the pipe in my coat, the scarlet wash glazing my eyes, and I saw that same contempt I'd seen in the church.

'*Bad men never realize when the monster is* them.

'Dior glanced to the holy sister, and finally, reluctantly, he nodded.

"'. . . Do you remember the night you first trained me in the Library, Gabe?"

'I looked to Chloe, and back across that ocean of time. It stood so deep and far, I almost couldn't see the shoreline. The current was black and perilous, threatening to drag me into the depths as I pictured the two of us sparring in the stained-glass light, Astrid sketching by the window. Such a simple moment, so unsullied by blood and death and futility that it made my chest hurt.

'*Godsakes, we were only children . . .*

"'I remember."

"'We trained. Then we read. Then we talked. You, me, and Azzie."

"'*What a world this would be,*" I smiled, "*were it not held wholly and solely in the grip of stubborn old men.*"

'She smiled too, and I could see the girl she'd been in her eyes. "And then?"

"'. . . The star," I finally realized. "That falling star."

'She nodded, eyes shining. "I told you at the time it was auspicious. I said God intended great things for us. And I was right. But far grander than the three of us meeting, that falling star marked another triumph. One it took me almost sixteen years to find the truth of. A *miracle*, Gabriel."

'Chloe looked to the boy standing bloodied and bruised by the fireside.

"'And there he is."

"'What the fuck are you *talking* about, Chloe?"

"'How well do you know your Testaments, Chevalier?" Bellamy asked.

'I glanced to the soothsinger, huddled by the fire. "A damn sight better than you, I'll wager."

"'And what do you know of the Aavsenct Heresy?" Rafa asked.

'I frowned, scratching at the drying blood on my chin. "I think . . . I remember a book about it, perhaps? In the forbidden section of San Michon?"

"'There's a tale to be told here, Silversaint." Rafa nodded to the 'singer. "I think we should leave it to our expert to do so."

'I glanced at Bellamy. "You're not going to fucking sing it, are you?"

'The wearied man perked up. "Would you like me to?"

'Scowling at Chloe, I rummaged in my saddlebags by the door. Grabbing one of my vodka bottles, I pulled a chair to the fire. "Talk."

'Undeterred, the soothsinger brushed back his perfect curls. He looked about the room, drawing a deep breath. And he launched into his tale then, with all the flourish of a young buck who'd carved a hundred bedpost notches with his silver tongue.

"'Perhaps a thousand years ago, somewhere in Nordlund, a boy was born. His name is lost to time, but he'd come to be known as the Redeemer. As he grew to manhood, he became an itinerant priest, preaching that there was only one God. Not only did he proclaim the Old Gods a lie, the Redeemer claimed to be the *son* of this true God. He performed miracles. Raised the dead. And in time, an *army*. Marching west, he spread his 'One Faith' at the point of a sword. The conflict was bloody, and decades long."

"'Fucksakes, Bouchette, you're not telling m—"

"'Hush, Gabriel," Chloe growled. "*Listen.*"

'Bellamy leaned into his tale. "The Redeemer was betrayed by his disciples, and murdered on the wheel by priests of the Old Gods. But his last loyal follower, the hunter Michon, caught his lifeblood in a silver chalice as he died. Michon took up the war in her Redeemer's name, until she herself was martyred in battle. But the *ideals* of the One Faith endured. And centuries later, the warlord Maximille de Augustin and his famille finally united five kingdoms into one empire, under the One True Faith."

'I sighed, necking the bottle. This was nothing I didn't already know.

"'Pay attention, Gabe," Chloe insisted. "What you're about to hear could get you and everyone you love flayed to death on the wheel. This is the darkest heresy in the empire."

'I swallowed deep and sighed. "Out with it, then."

'Père Rafa bent forward, liver-spotted fingers steepled at his lips. He glanced to Dior, and I could see the fear in him – as if even *speaking* these words were a sin.

'"Chloe and I pieced this tale together over many years, Silversaint. Fragments of knowledge. Merest scraps of truth, mixed among miles of madmen's scrawl and lies. To this day, we know not the half of it. But one thing is certain, and two for sure. Michon was not only the Redeemer's disciple."

'The old man sighed as if from his bones.

'"She was his lover."

'If the priest expected that shot to strike home, it fell well short of the mark. "God's begotten son enjoyed a tumble like the rest of us." I shrugged. "So what?"

'"So the Testaments were first written in Old Talhostic, Silversaint. And in Old Talhostic, the words for *lifeblood* and *essence* are almost the same: *Aavsunc. Aavsenct.*"

'"Michon didn't capture the Redeemer's lifeblood in some cup, Gabe." Chloe pressed one hand to her belly. "She captured his *essence* in her own. And nine months after his death, she gave birth to his child. A daughter. Named Esan."

'My eyes narrowed at that. "That's Old Talhostic too. For *Faith* . . ."

'Chloe nodded and murmured. "Esan*i.*"

'"Faith*less* . . ." I whispered, looking at the vein in my wrist. "What the *fuck* . . ."

'"A direct descendant of God's son," Rafa murmured. "But within a year, her mother was dead. And fearing persecution, Esan's guardians moved her to Talhost. Eventually, she had children of her own. The Redeemer's descendants often exhibited signs of divinity in their blood, but kept their origins secret. They built a dynasty, and eventually, began an uprising against the Emperor himself. Claiming a divine right to sit upon the Fivefold Throne."

'"The Aavsenct Heresy . . ." I murmured.

'"So it was named by the Pontifex of the One Faith," Chloe said. "The idea of the Redeemer taking a mortal lover was declared a sacrilege, and the descendants of Esan, blasphemers. And in the following purge, their line was all but wiped out – ironically by the Church their progenitor Michon had helped forge."

'"All records were expunged from Church archives," Rafa said. "Only scraps remain. Esan's bloodline diminished to almost nothing, and lost all knowledge of itself. The blood thinned. The line was almost broken."

'"Almost."

'Chloe looked to Dior, the boy silhouetted against the flames.

'"But that falling star we saw? That star marked the moment of Dior's birth. Rafa and I have searched for more than a *year*. Following tales of magik, witchcraft, sorcerie. We'd almost given up hope when we heard of a boy whose blood worked miracles. Even brought people back from the edge of death."

"'Great fucking Redeemer,' I breathed.

"'Blasphemy,' she smiled weakly.

"'You're telling me this skinny little fuckstain . . .'

"'. . . is the last-known scion of Esan's line. Dior doesn't know where the Grail is, Gabriel. He *is* the Grail. The cup of the Redeemer's blood."

"'*From holy cup comes holy light,*' Rafa said.

"'*The faithful hand sets world aright,*' Bellamy murmured.

"'*And in the Seven Martyrs' sight,*' Chloe whispered.

'Dior met my eyes and shrugged. "*Mere man shall end this endless night.*"

'The crackling flames were the only sound to fill that silence. I looked around the room, pulse hammering in my temples. This sounded like the darkest shade of madness. The chill in the air seeped into my chest, and I stood, sudden enough that Saoirse lifted her axe, jaw clenched. Chloe stared at me with eyes wide; Rafa's hand was inside his sleeve. But I only paced the room, dragging one hand back through my hair before stopping to stare at the boy – that pale streak of seagull shit in his stolen coat and busted boots. He looked nothing like the salvation of the world. But I'd *seen it* with my own fucking eyes. Those monsters bursting into flames as his blood touched their lips. Those red hands dragging Rafa and Bellamy back from the edge of death. Drinking the blood of an ancien kith might heal a wound as deep as those two had suffered, but Dior was a living, breathing boy.

'*How could this be?* I wondered.

'*Could this be?*

'I walked slowly towards Dior, and the boy simply watched. I stopped a few inches away, and he looked up at me, unflinching. I could feel Saoirse at my back, Bellamy's fingers now slipping to his blade. But I only reached down beside me and the boy, snatched up my vodka. Gulping a mouthful, three, four, I felt my eyes watering at the burn. And tossing the empty into the fireplace, I said the cleverest thing I could think of at the time.

"'Well, *fuck* my face . . .'"

✦ IX ✦
TWO WORDS

'"GABRIEL."

'My eyes flashed open, pupils dilating in the dark. A bird with broken wings beat swift inside my belly. For one blessed moment, I thought I was in our bed back home. The peaceful rhythm of my daughter's breath drifting down the hall, the bare branches of the sycamore outside our room scraping against the window. All was peace, and all was well, and I held tight, closing my eyes against the truth.

'But then I smelled rot in the walls, vague hints of fresh blood and stale mould and rat. The soft sounds down the hall belonged to Dior, the boy now moaning in his sleep. And the silk-soft scratching at the window belonged to . . .

'"Gabriel."

'I sat up in bed and saw her, suspended and breathless in the night beyond the window. Her hair was blackest velvet, her cheek, the curve of a broken heart. Her skin was pale and bare as the barrow-bleached bones of long-forgotten queens. In her eyes, I saw the answer to every question, every wanting, every fear I'd never known the naming of, and she pressed herself to the glass, hands and lips and breasts, all smooth curves and shadows full of promise, whispering soft as the sleep she'd stolen me from.

'"Let me in."

'I rose from my furs, bare feet on hard boards, bare chest in chill air. The silver troth ring on my finger felt heavy as lead. She tracked my movement like a wolf ahunt, and she swayed, drifting away into the snow-kissed dark and then surging back, pressing harder now against the window. Black fingernails whispered up over her hips, sinking like claws into the soft swell of her shoulders, dragged deep down her arms and then, red and dripping, scribbling, scratching, on the glass once more. Eyes on mine, she bit down, a dark pearl of promise welling on her lip.

'"Let me in, my lion."

'All that stood between us now were two words. Strange how so much power, so much peril and promise, resides in so tiny a thing. Two little words can carry weight enough to see empires rise and kingdoms fall. Two little words can begin the end of everything. How many hearts have been made complete by words so small as *I do*? How many more have been shattered with a breath as tiny as *It's over*? Little sounds that reshape or unmake your entire world, like great spells of old to redraw the very lines by which you see yourself and all else about you. Two little words.

'"*Forgive me.*"

'"*Do it.*"

'"*I can't.*"

'"*You* must."

'I could already feel her lips, warm as old autumn, the taste of burning leaves on her tongue. I could imagine pale hands slipping into my britches, pale legs wrapped tight around my waist, my teeth grazing her lip and her blood singing between us, filling the empty inside. She pressed against the window as I drew closer, hunger and sheerest wanting, and she smiled, all the colours of despair. With shaking hands, I unlocked the window and pulled the sill up slow. And with a voice that sounded not quite like my own, I spoke two words.

'Two little words.

'"Come in."'

✦ X ✦

NO FLOWER BLOOMS

'THE STORM BROKE four days later, and all the land was empty grey.

'The weight of it still hung on me, heavy as the broken sword at my side. Every time I looked to Chloe and Dior, the strangeness struck me harder. Over the course of my life, I'd seen my share of impossible. Castle walls crumbling under blows from long-dead fists. Monsters who danced in the skins of beasts and wore the faces of men. Legions of the Dead and the eyes of a king eternal, boring black and bottomless into my own.

'"*I have forever, boy.*"

'Truth told, I'd never tasted impossible like this. I'd only agreed to accompany Chloe for a chance to strike at Danton. But I couldn't forget what I'd seen.

'And so, the morn we prepared to leave Winfael, I'd gone searching. I found the boy in the ruined cathedral again, staring up at that window of San Michon like it held an answer to some unspoken question. The floor was thick with new-fallen snow, my breath hanging chill. I could smell his wounds – old, scabbing, a bandage at his throat where he'd been bitten. As miraculous as his blood was, the boy didn't seem able to heal himself.

'As I walked inside, Dior glanced over his shoulder and sighed. "What do you want?"

'"Chloe's fretting on you. You shouldn't wander alone."

'"I need your advice like I need a donkey dancing on my dick, hero."

'"You know, that chip on your shoulder must get awful heavy some days. And most folk would spare a merci for the man who saved their lives, Lachance."

'"If you just came here to give me shit—"

'"I came to give you this."

'The boy looked to my outstretched hand. In my palm was an old sanctus phial, the sacrament long since smoked, the glass now filled to the stopper with ripe, fresh blood.

'"I don't smoke that shite, what am—"

'"It's not vampire blood. It's *mine*." I gritted my teeth, scowling. "I have . . . gifts, boy. Gifts that most palebloods don't. I don't know the working of many of them, but I know if you carry this with you, I can sense you. Follow you. Find you anywhere in the empire."

'"And why would I want you to do that?"

'"If what Chloe said was true—"

'"If?" He folded his arms, scoffing. "You know, when Sister Chloe and Father Rafa found me, I admit it took a while to believe what they said. You grow up like I did, it's best to assume everyone you meet is a fucking cunt. That way, when they turn out to be just regular cunts, you'll be nicely surprised. But you? You grew *up* with all this. Martyrs and Mothermaids and Redeemers. And there's still not a drop of belief in you for any of it." He looked from the phial in my hand, up into the grey of my eyes. "I don't want your blood, hero. I don't want you following me. I want you to sod off back home to your wife and your sprat and your bottle and your smoke, and leave me right the fuck alone."

'He spat once on the floor. And shouldering past, he strode out the door.

'So we set out, the seven of us, into falling snows. We left Winfael behind, trekking northeast, Dior scowling up a storm behind Chloe on her horse. And though I couldn't conjure much affection for the little bastard, I still had to face it. I still had to wonder. Could it be true? A descendant of the son of God?

'An end to daysdeath, here in the palm of my silvered hand?

'Chloe believed. Rafa and the others. The Inquisition, sweet fucking Mothermaid, even Danton Voss believed, which of course meant his father did too. I finally understood a fraction of what was at stake here. The boy wasn't just bait on my hook any more. This was bigger than me. Bigger than all of it.

'I could feel dark currents about us, deeper than I could see the bottom of. And I thought again of that mysterious highblood who'd accosted us at the watchtower outside Dhahaeth. Midnight-blue hair and bloody blade, dead eyes narrowed as she held out her hand to the boy. "*Come with usss, child. Or die.*"

'*Too many mysteries here by half . . .*

'"That coldblood bitch with the mask and fancy red coat," I called. "The one Rafa saw off with his wheel. Have any of you seen her before?"

'The group shook their heads, silence all around.

'"Why do you ask, Silversaint?" Rafa replied.

'I looked to the falling snow behind. "Danton will have found a way across the river by now. We lost days to that storm. And we still have the Inquisition to worry about. I'm wondering where that other highblood stands. No friend of our Forever Prince, I wager."

'Bellamy tilted his head. "The enemy of my enemy—"

'"Is just another enemy, Bouchette. I'm only pondering which will pay a visit first."

'"Well, *I* still believe we should pay visit to San Guillaume," Rafa said. "The abbot may have got word from Pontifex Gascoigne by now. For all we know, there is an army of God-fearing soldiers in his Holiness's colours, waiting to escort us to San Michon."

'"For all we know, the Pontifex will declare our tale a heresy," Bellamy said.

'"The Church has been ruled by fear and misplaced fervour in past nights, 'tis true." Rafa nodded. "But Pontifex Gascoigne is a *good* man. He near emptied the Church's coffers feeding the dispossessed who flooded to Augustin after daysdeath fell. He is a true and holy servant of God."

'"Trust me, Father," I scoffed. "He's like every politician I've known, holy skirts or no."

'The priest ignored me, looking to Chloe. "We should head to San Guillaume, Sister."

'"One capitaine," Chloe replied. "One course."

'Rafa pursed his lips, but held his objection along with his tongue.

'"What's in San Michon that you're so keen to get back to, Chlo?" I asked.

'"There's no safer place for Dior in all the empire. And it's not just the silversaints. San Michon also has its Library. The forbidden section, the secrets inside. Words are our greatest weapons in this war, Gabe. It's not just the tale of Esan. The Prophecy speaks of a way daysdeath can be ended, and I believe I found that too." She looked to the boy behind her, and her eyes shone as if she looked upon the Redeemer reborn.

'Adoration.

'*Belief.*

'"Dior is going to save us *all.*"

'The boy smiled, but I saw uncertainty in his eyes. For all the holy sister's fervour, the shit he'd given me, I could tell Dior himself still wondered at all this. I knew what it was to be a lad that age. To have a weight on your shoulders you'd no wanting of. Truth told, he handled it better than most. But he met my gaze, and I saw his own harden.

'"The fuck are you gawping at, hero?"

'I shook my head and sighed.

'*Still an obnoxious little prick, though . . .*

'We headed north, days on end through the rising chill. This stretch of Ossway seemed utterly abandoned, its folks likely fled south after Dún Cuinn fell. We passed ruined farmsteads, roadside tavernes, ghost towns – all empty, save for the rats. Those bastards swarmed thick, grown fat and fierce on the dead and all they'd left behind. I knew why this place had been left to rot. With no Laerd Lady to protect them, there'd be little sense staying here to be preyed upon. One more slice of the empire gone. One more jewel snatched from old Alexandre's hollow crown.'

The Last Silversaint tilted his head 'til his neck popped, drained the last from his wineglass. Jean-François looked up from his tome.

'Laerd Lady?' the vampire asked.

Gabriel nodded, refilling his glass. 'Ossway was a matriarchal nation. Before it got fucked seventeen times sideways by the Blood Dyvok, anyways. The whole region had been part of the Elidaeni Empire for centuries, of course. Alexandre III ostensibly ruled it all. But the individual fiefs were ruled by femmes. Clan council run by venerable dames. Husbands from outside the clan took the matriarch's name when wed.'

'Sounds positively enlightened,' the vampire murmured.

'Depends who you ask. The practice was steeped in worship of the Old Gods. A feminine aspect of the Wild, the Hunt, the Moons, called *Fiáin*. But the Holy Church beat the paganism out of the Ossians over time. A few traditions survived. Women fought in wars beside their men. Women had the rule of the hearth. But instead of Fiáin, local worship shifted to the Mothermaid after the Wars of the Faith. There were more churches and abbeys devoted to her in the Ossway than anywhere else in the empire.'

Gabriel leaned back, sipped at his wine.

'It was only in the most remote corners where the ancient ways truly lived on. *Old* World religion. Worship of Fiáin. Wild Hunts. Fae witchery. All rare enough to be considered folklore by most. But the silversaints knew better. Even before daysdeath, there were places in Ossway where a man wouldn't dare be caught alone after dark. A few clans up in the Highlands who still took that shit *seriously*.'

'Such as the Dúnnsair?' Jean-François asked.

Gabriel nodded. 'Such as the Dúnnsair.'

'Your good friend Saoirse was one of these . . . fae witches, then?'

'Well . . .' Gabriel shrugged. 'There's magik, and then there's *magik*. But there wasn't an ounce of silver in that axe of hers, and Kindness still went through coldbloods like Philippe the First through his mistresses. And young Saoirse didn't tattoo her face just for the aesthetics. There's power in ink, coldblood. And not just the silvered kind.

'We bedded on high ground when we could. The weather was worsening by the day, but if we were elevated, at least we might spot them coming. Only Phoebe and I could see for shit in the dark, and it'd have been ludicrous to light torches. And so we camped at night, and slept barely a wink. We could risk no flame to cook by, either, so meals were even more of a misery march. And worst of all? The fear that was really chilling my piss?'

'That Danton must surely be tracking you?' Jean-François asked. 'That you knew nothing of that masked highblood, yet she seemed to know you exact? That the Inquisition was surely still stalking you, and yet you'd seen no sign of them since the Ūmdir?'

'No.' The silversaint scoffed. 'My vodka was running low.

'I was sat in the bare branches of an ancient oak, bottle propped beside me, cursing beneath my breath. The tree was one of a dozen in a tall copse atop a rugged hill. The wind blew so fierce and constant from the north that the trees had grown in crooked, the branches swept sideways like windswept hair, wrapped with ropes of asphyxia.

'"I hate this fucking place," I growled. "Nothing grows, save in the wrong direction."

'"What *is* that, Silversaint?"

'Bellamy lay on the branch above, nodding to the parchment in my hand. I was shading in the lands of the Cuinn with charcoal, fingertips smudged black. "Old map of mine. Just keeping track of the knucklebones Alexandre has lost in this game."

'"Do you know where we are?" Chloe called from the tree next door.

'I shrugged, tracing a dark line on the parchment. "Must be close to the Dílaenn by now. Things might get easier once we cross, but I'm not sure where we can do that. There used to be a bridge up past Haemun's Hill, but I've no clue if it's still standing."

'"We can ask Saoirse when she returns," Chloe said.

'Bellamy shivered, curling over in his furs. "I must confess, mes amis, when I set out from the capital two years back, I'd no notion I'd end up in a place such as here. Not that the company isn't of finest quality," he added hastily, "but on nights like this, I miss Augustin. Her little cafés and broad boulevards, doe-eyed lovers wandering her canals arm in arm." He shifted on his branch, sending a smattering of snow onto my head, and he sighed all the way from his soul. "My heart aches to see her again. My Augustin, and her empress divine."

'I scowled upwards, brushing the snow from my hair. "*You* know Isabella?"

"'Know her?" The soothsinger smiled, those pretty blue eyes staring out into the dark. "I can say I serve her, as loyally as any knight or maid-at-arms. I can say I have written songs for her, as beautiful as could make angels weep. But know her?" He shook his head. "What man can truly say that of Isabella, Silversaint?"

'I looked at Bellamy with his silly hat and his perfect stubble and his dreamer's eyes, and it struck me how young he was then. How young *all* of them were.

"'Leastways you've been to the capital," Dior muttered, blowing on his hands and shoving them in his armpits. "I've never even *seen* it."

'The soothsinger brightened then, handsome as a pocketful of princes.

"'We shall see it together, mon ami." His voice grew deep and dramatic, hand sweeping the sky. "When all this is done, I shall take you there myself. Good Sœur Sauvage and Père Sa-Araki can visit the Cathédrale d'Lumière, there to pray in the honey-warm glow of the light eternal. Mlle Saoirse can bathe in the perfumed fountain beneath the Pont de Fleur – heaven knows she needs it." He winked at the boy, eyes shining. "And you, me, and Chevalier de León shall take in a show on the Rue des Méchants."

"'You shall *not*," Père Rafa scowled.

"'Why?" the boy asked. "What happens on the Rue des Méchants?"

"'Sex," I replied, taking a long swallow of my vodka.

'Chloe scowled, made the sign of the wheel. Bellamy tutted and tipped his ridiculous cap. "That is not *all* that happens there, Silversaint . . ."

"'Well, no, not all," I admitted. "There's a great deal of gambling. A goodly dose of dreamweed dealers and poppydens and burlesque. But there's also a tremendous amount of sex. In fact, I bet you'd not be able to fling a royale on the Rue des Méchants without hitting someone either openly offering, desperately looking for, or enthusiastically engaged in s—"

"'Godsakes, Gabriel, we *understand*."

'A hot blush was pinking Chloe's cheeks, and I threw her a teasing wink. "Do you really? I didn't think the books in the forbidden section were *that* risqué, Sister."

'Chloe aimed a furious scowl my way, signed the wheel. I chuckled, leaning back in my branch and wondering if I should have another smoke now, or stretch it out an hour more. Dior watched the flush die in the Silver Sister's cheeks, pouting in thought.

'"Did you always want to be a nun, Sister Chloe?"

'My old friend glanced up to the boy, breathed deep. "Since I was a little girl."

'"Did you . . ." The lad cleared his throat, uncertain. "I mean to say, have you ever . . ."

'"Careful, boy," I growled. "You're sailing awfully close to the shores of a little island most call None of Your Fucking Business."

'"There are many kinds of love, Dior," Chloe said. "If you are asking what I think you are asking, I gave up the love of men for the love of God most high."

'"Do you . . . miss it?"

'"A woman who has never seen the night cannot miss the moons."

'"Aright, then, do you not . . . wonder?"

'Chloe glanced sidelong to me, both of us aware of how thin the ice she now trod upon was. But still, I felt a flicker of cool anger as she spoke. "Desire is no sin, save when we indulge it. But I'm sure Père Rafa would agree God's love sustains beyond all earthly appetite."

'"True." The old man shrugged. "Still, I miss it."

'Four heads swivelled to the priest. Four sets of eyebrows shot to the sky.

'"I miss it like . . ." The priest waved a vague hand, pushed his spectacles up his thin nose and glanced to the soothsinger. "Help an old man out, Bellamy?"

'"Like . . . the desert misses the rain?"

'Rafa winced. "A touch clichéd."

'"Like the dawn misses the dusk?" Bellamy sat up straighter and snapped his fingers. "No . . . like a large-breasted woman misses lying on her stom—"

'"Shut the fuck up, Bouchette."

'Dior was looking at the priest with a wicked grin. "Père Rafa . . . you've . . ."

'"I was not always a servant of the cloth, Dior." The old man smiled fondly. "I was once a young man like you. I even came close to marrying once."

'"What was her name, Father?" Bellamy asked.

'"Ailsa." The priest looked to the dark above, sighing her name like sugared smoke. "A huntress who sold vellum to San Guillaume. I was an acolyte when we met, my vows still unsworn. We fell in love, so deep and sudden I was tempted to leave behind all I'd studied for. But Ailsa could see my suffering, torn between love of her and love of God. She told me no flower blooms that grows in two beds, and still, I could not decide. So one day, she kissed me farewell, set out ahunt, and never returned to San Guillaume. I searched for her. Months and miles. But I never saw my sweet Ailsa again."

'Bellamy sniffled, reaching for his lute. "No flower blooms that grows in two be—"

"'Don't you fucking dare, Bouchette . . ."

"'That's sad," Dior murmured, looking at the priest. "I'm sorry, Rafa."

'The old man smiled. "It was God's will. If I had married Ailsa, I would never have been contacted by Sister Chloe, never have found *you*, Dior. And the good Sister is correct. God's love sustains me where no mortal love could ever have endured." He clutched the wheel about his neck in one wrinkled, liver-spotted hand. "This weak flesh melts all too soon, my child. But the love of the Lord is evergreen. And it shall see me to his kingdom eternal."

"'Seems a little sadistic, though, doesn't it?"

'Rafa spared me an indulgent glance. "What does, Chevalier?"

"'Giving you desires, then denying you the sating of them? Look, but don't touch? Taste, but don't swallow? Why make you want what you can't have?"

"'To test our faith, of course. To judge if we are worthy of the kingdom of heaven."

"'But he's all-seeing, isn't he? All-knowing? God *knows* whether you're going to pass his test before he ever gives it to you. And if you succumb to your desire? He condemns you to burn. He sets you up to fail, then has the balls to question his own handiwork."

"'It is not for mortals to know the mind of God, Silversaint."

"'The wise man knows you don't blame the blade, priest. You blame the blacksmith."

"'A parent's kindness is oft-times cruel. You have a daughter, do you not? I would wager the crown jewels to a ha-royale you love her more than anything under heaven."

"'Of course I do."

"'Did you ever deny your Patience that which she wanted as child? The sweets she cried for before supper? A smack to her knuckles before she burned herself on the flame? The pain you inflicted came from a place of purest adoration, though she may not have understood it at the time. But you hurt her for her own good."

"'My stepfather beat the shit out of me as a child, priest. And all it ever taught me was how to hate him." I fixed Rafa with a glower. "It's the lowest kind of man who raises a fist to his child and calls it love. And it's the worst kind of tyrant who demands you adore him above all others." I shook my head, looking the old man up and down. "That wheel hanging around your neck won't keep you warm in the dark, priest. It won't ever love you back. And silver it might be, but one night, you're going to learn just how little it's actually worth."

'Dior looked at me then, blue eyes drifting to the silver on my skin. It seemed as if the lad were about to speak, when . . .

"'*Chloe!*'

'I glanced up at the distant shout, eyes narrowed in the dark. I could see Phoebe loping across the snowy hillside, the lioness just a shadow on the grey. And behind her . . .

"'Saoirse?" Dior called, sitting up on his branch.

'The slayer was waving as she dashed towards us, and I tucked away my map and bottle, dropped down from my branch, and ran out to meet her. As she reached my side, Saoirse bent double, chest heaving like a bellows. The slayer looked as if she'd sprinted all the way from Alethe.

"'Troubles?"

'The girl nodded, gasping to find her breath. "Yer b-bonny . . . prince . . ."

'My belly filled with tiny cold butterflies. "Danton."

"'He rides," Saoirse gasped. "But a handful o' miles south. A dozen men and horses."

"'Horses?" Bellamy demanded. "I thought beasts of earth and sky feared the Dead?"

"'The blood," I told him. "Drink three times over three nights and you'll be a slave to your master's will. No matter how much you fear him. Danton could have thralled a hundred men and horse by now."

"'Nae that many." Saoirse straightened, met Chloe's eyes. "But plenty."

"'Gabe?" Chloe asked. "Do we fight?"

'I looked to my old friend, standing wide-eyed in the snow with her ragged company: Slayer and Soothsinger and Priest and Pet. In truth, I gave not a speck of shit for any of them save her. But last of all, shielded behind Chloe like she might protect him from all the hurts of the world, stood the Boy.

'My Bait.

'He'd brought Danton to me. Just as I'd hoped. And with a mere dozen men at his side, I put my odds about even I could get my hand around that bastard's throat. I owed his famille blood. And the longer we ran, the longer Danton would have to build a force I couldn't hope to face. Stray wretched, sellswords, other highbloods seeking the Forever King's favour. Better to strike now, with some fodder to throw, with a bandolier full of silverbombs and the faith of two true believers to blind him. I could protect Chloe. What matter if the others fell? What were these people to me?

'Nothing.

'*Nothing and no one.*

'But the Boy. The Bait. The Blood. Washing across those open necks and sealing them closed. Burning in the gullets of those wretched and setting them aflame. I'd known the truth for years. There was no magik silvershot, no divine prophecy, no holy fucking chalice that would bring an end to this darkness.

'This was our here and our now and our forever.

'*Wasn't it?*

'Looking skywards, I found myself trying to remember what it had been like to actually see stars overhead. I could recall them dimly from my youth – cradled like diamonds in the midnight arms of heaven. All was blackness now, only the crescents of dim red moons to light my way. But for the first time in as long as I could remember, I wondered.

'"Gabe?" Chloe asked, desperate now. "Do we *fight?*"

'"No," I sighed. "We flee."'

✦ XI ✦

A BLACK CROWN

'"RIDE FOR THE river!"

'Wind whipping our skin. Sleet slashing our eyes. Jezebel was an engine of muscle and bone beneath me, the company at my back. I took the lead, riding as hard as the others could follow. The light from my hunter's lantern bounced and strobed, throwing mad shadows ahead. I could hear Chloe and Dior behind, Saoirse and Rafa coming next, Bellamy in the rear. Chill snatching the breath from our lungs, we rode. We rode as if all our lives hung in the balance. As if the devil himself rode behind us. Because of course, he did.

'And he was gaining.

'Grace three times the tongue of man or woman with the blood of the kith, and they will be a slave. But not some callow serf, with broken back and battered heart. Some measure of unholy strength will be gifted, master to thrall, making them more than a match for any man. Horses and hounds aren't so different to humans, save the former tend to die with dignity and the latter with blubbery. I knew not where Danton had found his mounts or his men, but it mattered little in the end. He had both in abundance – a burly dozen, their thralled sosyas running harder and faster than ours could hope to match. And behind, with all the insufferable arrogance of a bastard who believes in his bones that he was born to rule, came the youngest son of the Forever King.

'The Beast of Vellene.

'He'd returned to Dhahaeth after I'd left, and he'd fetched his fucking coach. But rather than the corpses of murdered girls, it was now drawn by four swift sosyas, the horses' eyes flushed crimson, their mouths frothing blood. I hoped the folk of Dhahaeth had given Danton what he wanted without resistance – that he'd been so keen to avenge himself on me, he hadn't stopped to wreak vengeance upon them.

'I hoped. But I doubted it.

'Riding off road was too deep a risk in the dark – one rabbit hole or cruel branch under Chloe's horse and all would be undone. And so we hammered down a muddy road, dying trees at our flanks. I glanced to the Silver Sister, the boy behind, the pair riding fierce as they dared. The fate of the world just a few feet away.

'"Why run, de León?" came a call from behind. "When I can follow forever?"

'The bastard spoke true and I knew it – at this pace our horses would break within a few miles, and on foot, we could never outrun a highblood. I'd no clue how far the river could be, and if Haemun's Bridge was still standing . . .

'Chloe cried out, hand to brow. Her horse thundered on, but Dior had to lunge for the reins, clutching the small woman in his arms.

'"Sister Chloe!"

'"He . . ." Chloe gasped, wincing. "He's in . . . m-my head . . ."

'I turned in my saddle and saw him. Like a shadow at morning striding behind you. His eyes were red and full as children's graves, sharp teeth and a butcher's smile. He leaned out the carriage window, hair swept back from his widow's peak. On the driver's perch sat a girl with dark skin and pretty green eyes. Faint red stain at her chin. I recognized the serving lass from the Perfect Husband. Refusing to remember her name.

'"Guard your thoughts, Chloe! Fill your head, force him out!"

'She clutched the sevenstar at her throat. "*The Lord is my shield, unb-breakable . . .*"

'Danton's riders swept before him, now only a dozen yards off our backs. Farmers and masons, a few militia members among them – once men with lives and wives and dreams, now naught but slaves to his will. I held my pipe between gritted fangs as I fumbled for a phial of sanctus. I'd no time to measure, tipping the whole lot into the bowl and spilling most, tamping it down with my thumb. I tried a half-dozen times to light my flintbox, finally dragging down a ragged, burned lungful, feeling that potency unfurl, the beast in me awaken. And reaching into my belt, I drew my wheellock, twisted in my saddle.

'Danton actually laughed to see the pistol in my hand. Against the skin of an ancien Voss, the shot would be less than worthless. And so I took aim, struck the trigger, black ignis flaring as the muzzle flashed and the shot cracked,

'"Sorry, boy . . ."

'. . . right between my target's big brown eyes.

'The lead horse dropped like a rock, brains smashed to pulp. As it collapsed, the horse behind it screamed and collided with its fellow, and I saw Danton's eyes grow wide, his smile fail as the horses collapsed in a tangle of snapping harness and bone. The lead spar crashed into the earth, the crack of splitting timbers rang out in the night, and Danton's carriage flipped end over end, that dark-haired lass with the pretty green eyes thrown like a ragdoll. I turned away before she struck the earth, closed my ears to the sound of her breaking, telling myself over and over that it's always better to be a bastard than a fool.

'*Her name . . .*

'"Better to be a bastard than a fool," I hissed.

'*Her name was Nahia . . .*

'Several riders stopped to help their fallen lord, but the rest rode on, crossbow bolts hissing through the air. Rafa cried out as one struck his shoulderblade, and Saoirse cursed as their horse almost spilled. Bellamy twisted in his saddle, unleashed his own crossbow into the closest thrall. The man bucked, coughed blood, but stayed upright. A dagger flashed through the night, struck the fellow in his throat and sent him tumbling, another already in Saoirse's hand.

'"How far to the river?" Chloe gasped.

'"That's Haemun's Hill ahead!"

'Reaching to my bandolier, I snapped the seal on a glass phial and hurled it. The silverbomb exploded, blasting thralls from their saddles in a blinding flash. But the others came on. And in the distance, among the riders who'd stopped to help him . . .

'"Fuck," I hissed.

'"Gaaaaaabe!"

'"I see him, Chloe!"

'"No, Gabe, ahead, *ahead*!"

'We'd rounded the bend at Haemun's Hill, horses frothing, hearts pounding, and ahead I saw a sheer, dark bank dropping ten feet into the black rush of the Dílaenn River. The mooring stones were intact, crusted with blooms of maryswort. But beyond . . .

'"Mothermoons, the bridge is down!" Saoirse roared.

'"Keep riding!" I bellowed.

'"But Gabriel—"

'"I'll hold them, Chloe! KEEP RIDING!"

'I pulled up on Jezebel's reins, slowing the dray and drawing my sword. Ashdrinker gleamed in my lanternlight, a silver smile on her hilt and a silver whisper in my mind. She seemed more certain tonight, her voice steadier, closer to what she'd once been.

'*No mercy begged, Gabriel. And none bestowed.*

'The first thrall reached me – a militiaman with a long ashwood spear and suit of stout chain. I split the man's spear in half, sent his guts spilling into the dark. I heard Bellamy whooping, Chloe yelling, "Hold tight, Dior!" the boy screaming as their horses plunged into the rapids below. Three riders barrelled past me, and I took one off his horse, another's arm off his shoulder as they flashed by. I grunted as a sword pierced my ribs, cutting leather and meat and bone, *twisting* as it came.

'*Much faster ye were in thy youth, Gabriel.*

'I lashed out at the man who'd stuck me, blood spilling warm and wet down my side. "Nobody asked your f-fucking opinion, Ash!"

'*Ye mayst use me as a walking stick if ye hast need?*

'The thrall gurgled as I drove Ashdrinker through his throat, twin arcs of blood fountaining into the sky as the blade scraped his spine.

'*Ah, much better, much b-better indeed. The snik and the snak and the red red red.*

'The swordsman clutched his split neck and collapsed into the road. But looking farther down it, I saw him coming again now, a black shadow, no smile on his face any more – the beast he'd been named for surfacing as he bared his fangs and roared.

'"De León!"

'"Gabriel!" Chloe wailed.

'"*Face* me, you callow wretch!"

'*The first of seven, Gabriel. First of s-seven. As Fabién took from ye, take like from him.*

'One scream in front of me. Another behind. The vengeance that had dragged me northwards into this lonely winter, or the promise of perhaps finishing it once and for all.

'One foe in sight. One friend in need.

'No choice at all.

'*This t-time, I swear I—*

'Ashdrinker fell silent as I sheathed her at my waist, slapping Jezebel's rump. The dray kicked up and bolted, her breath like a blast furnace. I thought she might have baulked at the edge – that I'd have to force her into the plunge or simply leap from her back to the water below. But she charged towards that broken bridge as fearless as any horse I'd ever known. And as Jezebel leapt out into the breach, dauntless, plunging towards those dark rapids after Chloe and the others, I held tight to her mane and whispered, "I need to give you a better name, love . . ."

'We plunged into dark water, all the world muted. The river was *freezing*, and I almost inhaled a lungful as the shock reached my spine. I crashed to the surface, slinging a whip of waterlogged hair from my eyes and dragging a shaking breath into bleeding lungs. I saw Jezebel beside me, reached towards her, trying to float with the flow when—

'A thrall crashed atop me, his sword plunging into my shoulder, scraping my ribs. I roared in pain and clutched his throat, dragging us both below. He slipped his blade free, stabbing again, into my belly this time. But my thumbs had found his eyes by then, and they sank in, knuckle deep, muted scream and a bird-brittle crunch rising over the rapids' roar. He stabbed me again before it failed him – that strength which he'd been gifted but to which I'd been fucking born. And then he went limp, the water warm around my hands. Kicking free of his arms, I lunged back up to the air.

'"Gabriel!"

'Chloe's scream, ragged with terror. I searched the dark, spied her a little ways downriver, clinging desperately to her panicking horse lest her chainmail and sword drag her to her death. But her eyes were filled with purest horror.

'"Dior can't *swim*!"

'"Oh, blessed face*fuckery* . . ."

'I looked about, kicking upwards for desperate vantage. I saw spitting spray and grinning rocks and tumbling black. But of the boy, there was no sign.

'"Gabe, you have to—"

'The rest of Chloe's words were lost as I plunged below the foam. The bloodhymn kept the agony of my wounds at bay, and I swam through sunken boughs and a cold as deep as tombs. For the longest time, I saw nothing save the dark, and the folly of all I'd done. But ahead, cresting the jagged edge of a long-sunk stone, I caught it – a flash of pale. Fangs bared, I lunged, kicking with boots full of water and pockets full of hope, and finally, *finally* seizing hold of a fine frockcoat, midnight-blue with silver curlicue.

'I surged to the surface with a ragged gasp. The rapids roared in my ears, the sword wounds in my belly and shoulder bled red into the rushing black, and my heart sang in my chest as I saw Dior gasp for breath. And then the boy realized where he was, water all around, water *beneath*, and I saw panic clench his jaw and he grabbed hold of my throat and dragged me right the fuck back under.

'He thrashed and bore us down, boots kicking my bleeding belly. We crashed into a sunken stone, something inside me ripping. I roared and tried to hold him, but his panic had him by the short and curly ends. His thumb found my eye and his heel crashed into my bollocks and I felt him slip from my arms. Half-blind, I seized a fistful of ashen hair, dragged us back up in an explosion of half-drowned breath.

'"You kicked my balls, you fuck-eyed little pigdick!"

'"I c-can't—" he gulped and gurgled as he sank again.

'"Stop arsing about and hold onto me!"

'He tore at me a moment more, two fingers hooked in my mouth and his other arm wrapped over my eyes. But I was yet my father's son, a strength beyond strength in the curse he'd gifted me, and with the boy gasping on my back, I swam. The bank was too tall, the current too swift, and so we ran with it, along a rising shore, searching for the others.

'And then, like a hammer on my skull, I felt him.

'Lonely dark and nightmare deep. The weight of blood-soaked centuries on the backs of my eyes. I peered into the gloom above and I saw him, smelled him, *felt* him, stalking along the high-flung bank like the father of all wolves. Clad in a long frockcoat and silken frills, a blood-red hunter just a few feet and a thousand miles from his kill.

'Danton Voss.

'The rapids rushed swift, but he flitted tree to tree, licking dagger-bright teeth and watching with large, liquid eyes. Dior saw him too, and I heard the boy gasp as Danton's gaze fell on him. Hand outstretched.

'"*Come here, Dior,*" the vampire breathed.

'"Listen to nothing he says," I warned, paddling backwards from the bank.

'"*Come to me.*"

'"He's Voss, he'll get into your head," I hissed, kicking hard to keep us afloat. "Think of nonsense, think of nothing. Fill your mind with noise, loud as you can."

'The vampire held Dior in his black gaze, and I felt the boy tense like steel. But strangely, I saw Danton's eyes narrow, his fingers clench. Dior stared back, ashen white hair plastered across his eyes, but I could tell in a heartbeat that, somehow, *he* was the stronger. That for all the centuries in Danton's veins, the lad's mind was a locked room.

'"'Tis true, then." The vampire smiled, bewildered. "*All* true . . ."

'I kicked away into the rapids, ever closer to the northern shoreline. Danton followed on the babbling river's edge, dark eyes swallowing Dior whole.

"'I've no wish to hurt thee," the Beast vowed. "'Pon my royal blood, I swear it, boy. My dread father bids me spirit thee to his side. A black crown shall he place upon thy brow, and do thee homage, as a priest to Gods of old. Fear. Pain. Hatred. Dread sovereign of *all* this shalt thou be. The Forever King himself shall bow to thee, Dior."

'"*Dead tongues heeded are Dead tongues tasted*," I spat.

"'Worthless *wretch*," the vampire snarled. "I speak not to thee." One hand, pale as marble, still extended. "Come to me, Dior. And I will show thee a life undreamed of."

'I felt the boy tense on my shoulders. And for one terrible moment, I thought he might let go. But instead, half-drowned, wheezing, he pulled himself up and spat like poison.

"'F-fuck *you*."

'The Beast of Vellene's lips twisted in a dark smile.

"'You must say please, love."

'Danton lowered his hand. His eyes fell on mine, and I could taste it between us – all that blood unspilled. What we each had stolen, and then had stolen from us in kind. The vampire pressed tongue to teeth and spoke into the black rainbows between us.

"'Thou shouldst have stayed buried, de León . . ."

'We reached the northern bank, low enough to the waterline that we could stagger onto it. I helped Dior, dragging the boy through the shallows by his collar before dumping him on the shore. When I turned to face Danton again, he was gone. But his shadow remained, heavy and cold as the water and blood pouring off me in floods. The Beast had forever, but he wouldn't keep me waiting that long. Still, he'd given me one more kernel. One more sign of how desperately important Dior seemed to be to these bastards.

'*They want him alive* . . .

'I glanced to the shivering rat at my feet. "You aright, boy?"

"'I'm all r-right," he wheezed.

"'Because you look like shit twice stepped in."

'Dior squinted up at me and coughed. "We look n-nothing alike, hero."

'I almost laughed, shaking my head in wonder at his front. "Most folk would spare a merci for the man who just saved their lives, Lachance."

'He dragged his sopping locks from his eyes, lips pressed thin. But he said nothing.

'"That fucking coat nearly drowned you. Why didn't you rip the damned thing off?"

'"Told you." Dior coughed hard, spat. "It's m-magik."

'I scoffed, looked up and down the river's edge. The night was black, the rapids' roar throwing chill mist into the air. But I saw distant movement, sighed with relief as I spied Jezebel wandering the bank. Her flanks were steaming, mane and tail soaking, but she seemed unhurt, tossing her head and nickering as she spied me in the shallows.

'"Lucky bitch . . ."

'"Gabe?" came a distant cry. "*Gabriel!*"

'"Chloe! Down here!"

'I grabbed Lachance's magik collar, hauled the boy upright with one hand. We'd cut it close to the bone, but Danton couldn't pursue us 'til he found another place to cross the river. My greatcoat was rent from those sword blows, blood dribbling over my leathers, but the wounds were slowly stitching closed. My pipe was safe at least, nestled snug against the curve of my . . .

'"Oh, shit . . ." I hissed.

'Dior blinked, his arms wrapped tight and shivering. "What?"

'I spun on the spot, heart sinking. "Oh, you saints-buggering, cack-gargling *TWATGOBLIN!*"

'"*What?*" Dior demanded.

'I knew not how it happened. Mayhaps it'd been cut away when that thrall stuck me with his pig-sticker. More likely, I lost it wrestling with this idiotic little turd as he tried to drown us both. But the *hows* of it made no difference at all.

'I'd lost my bandolier. And with it had gone my black ignis, my spare silvershot, my few remaining silverbombs, and worst, worst, *worst* of all . . .

'"God spunks in my spuds once again."

'I clawed the waterlogged locks from my face and sighed.

'"My sanctus is gone."'

✦ XII ✦

OLD MONARCHS, NEW
SOVEREIGNS

"'WE'VE LOST MOST of our weapons. All our food. And every horse we had, save Jezebel."

'Chloe sighed, head in hands. "You should really think of a better name for her, Gabe."

'We were gathered in the shallow belly of a sandstone cave, somewhere in the hills north of the Dílaenn. Dawn had broken like a bridal chalice at a wedding feast, bringing all the same ill fortune. The weather was running straight to hell, and our only meal was the mushrooms Saoirse had scrounged. Phoebe had managed to find us at least, the big cat purring like an earthquake as her mistress scratched her behind the ears. We'd got a fire going to dry out our freezing clothes, but that was the extent of our good news. And the bad news was piling up like bodies to the sky.

"'I lost my sevenstar," Chloe whispered, hands to her throat. "Of all things . . ."

"'My sanctus too," I spat. "My flail. Silverbombs. Shot. Everything."

'Bellamy looked about the cave with a hopeful smile. "I saved my lute, at least?"

"'So fucking help me, Bouchette . . ."

'Rafa was stripped down to his sackcloth leggings, shivering with cold. "There is nothing for it now. We *must* go to San Guillaume."

'Chloe dragged another damp log onto the flames, trembling in a thin, dark shift. "Trekking to San Guillaume adds weeks to our journey, Rafa. If we head for the Mère—"

"'We can't travel all the way to the Nordlund on foot, Sister." Bellamy stood at the mouth of the cave, wringing the worst from his doublet. "And

San Guillaume *is* a distillery. I know not about the rest of you, but I for one could use a good stiff drink."

"'We can follow the river northwest," the old priest said. "The monastery rests atop a cliff where the Dílaenn meets the Volta. We'll be protected by the water, at least."

"'That path will take us through Fa'daena," Saoirse warned. "The Forest of Sorrows."

'The slayer had stripped down to her saintsday clothes, utterly unashamed of her nakedness. There were fae spirals carved into her skin, stained with red pigment – one twisting all the way up her swordarm and encircling her right breast, the other down her left hip and leg, all the way to her ankle. She was sharp muscles and scarred bare skin, and I could feel a smile tugging at the corner of my mouth as Rafa furiously looked anywhere but at the naked girl while still trying to address her politely.

"'What about the forest concerns you, Mlle Saoirse?"

'The girl looked about the company, face underscored by flames. "My clan hear grim tales of the southern weald. A dark rises in the once-green places o' the world. Dreaming nights past, but nae longer. We take our lives in our hands entering Fa'daena."

"'We give up our lives completely staying here," I said. "Danton will return."

"'He knows our destination." Chloe shuddered, wrapping arms about herself. "He . . . took it. From i-inside my head. Blessed Mothermaid, I can still feel him . . ."

"'Spare your back the lash, Chlo," I said, patting her shoulder. "A vampire that old is a power almost beyond measure. It'd take real training and pale-blood in your veins to keep him out. But at least we now know the Beast wants the boy alive. And if he believes we're headed north, San Guillaume may be a wiser road. He's a fierce tracker, true. But the river and weald may throw Danton off our trail."

'Chloe shook her head, quietly furious. "The knowledge we need to end daysdeath is in *San Michon*, Gabe."

"'And we will get there, Sister," Rafa cooed. "But San Guillaume is holy ground. We can regroup there, strike out from a place of strength. We must tread cautiously now, with this evil at our back. Upon our shoulders rests the fate of all the world of men."

"'What about the world o' women?"

'Rafa glanced to Saoirse, then quickly away. "It's the same world, my child."

'"Really." The slayer scoffed. "I'll just go take a piss standing up, shall I?"

'"I . . . suppose anything is possible?"

'Saoirse stood, glanced about the fire. "There's another path we can walk. Another destination we might seek. Solid as mountains and safe as the Mother's arms."

'"What do you mean, Saoirse?" Bellamy asked.

'"We could shelter in the Highlands," the slayer replied. "Among *my* kin. We've the knowings of magiks that were old before yer God was born."

'"God was not born, my child," Rafa said. "He has *always* been."

'"My folk tell it different. My folk tell it—"

'"Enough!" Chloe snapped. "We are *not* going to San Guillaume, and we are *certainly* not trekking to the bloody Highlands. We avoid the forest, head northeast until we reach the Mére. San Michon is our road. One capitaine. One course."

'The sister glowered across the fire, a curtain of sodden curls about her eyes. I wondered at the bloody single-mindedness that seemed to drive her. Even blind her. She'd devoted the best years of her life to this, true. But she wasn't seeing reason.

'"Mayhaps we should let the boy decide?" I said.

'Chloe glowered at me, but all other eyes turned to Dior. The lad crouched beside the flames, skin prickled with cold. Soaked as he was, he'd refused to take off his shirt and britches, shivering like a lamb as he huddled close to the flames.

'He looked at me, eyes trailing the silver ink on my skin. The lion at my chest and the angels on my arms, the Mothermaid, the saintsrose and doves. But he made no reply.

'"He *is* the Grail," Rafa said. "If God should take the steerage of our path . . ."

'"What say you, boy?" I demanded.

'Dior swallowed hard, looked towards Chloe. He felt he owed the sister a debt; he didn't want to gainsay her, that much was plain. He was enamoured of Saoirse too, I could see that, sure and true. But beneath it all, there was that street-smartness to him. A gutter edge. He could see the wisdom in old Rafa's words. We needed food. Horses. Sanctuary. And when he spoke, his voice didn't shake. I had to spare the little bastard a grudging nod. Whatever else he was – liar, thief, ungrateful little shit – Dior Lachance was still no coward.

'"We head to San Guillaume," he said.

'Chloe pursed her lips and shook her head. But finally, she sighed. "As you like it."

'We rested 'til noon, then pressed into the worsening snows. I wanted distance from Danton before night fell, but I'd another reason to get us off the shoreline – one I was fretting on more each moment. For whatever reason, Dior seemed to draw the Dead like a corpse draws crows. And the sooner we got moving, the sooner we'd run into wretched.

'Twelve hours since my last smoke. I'd one more phial – a holdout of fledgling's blood in my boot. But once that was gone, I'd be hellbound. And while it was only a faint itch now, I knew the itching would soon become scratching, then clawing, and Redeemer help me if it got beyond that . . .

'Chloe and Rafa rode on Jez, clinging to each other for warmth, while Dior led the horse into the deepening wood, chattering to Bellamy all the while. Saoirse and I walked on the flanks, Phoebe ever scouting, and though I still found the slayer a surly cuss, I had to thank all Seven Martyrs for that she-lion of hers. The beast was often gone for hours at a stretch, but ever she'd return, sometimes with a scrawny rabbit in her jaws, other times with news, which Saoirse always knew the telling of. I wondered if it were instinct or something deeper between them – some bond scribed in Old World witchery, like the spirals on Saoirse's skin.

'Three days later, we crossed a crooked stream, Saoirse whispered a prayer to the Mothermoons, and we entered Fa'daena.

'At first, the Forest of Sorrows seemed no different from the other woods of the world – which is to say, a stretch of old trees, being slowly choked by a pale unwelcome lover. In the years following daysdeath, most of the green places of the empire had withered, starved of the sun that had once gifted them life. But that wasn't to say nothing grew in Elidaen any more. There's no end of successors waiting for old monarchs to fall, and in the breach left by those towering giants in their robes of whispering green, a new king had risen.

'Fungus.

'Luminous flowers of maryswort. Long, strangling tendrils of asphixia. Bloated pustules of beggarbelly and jagged, crawling runs of shadespine. These were the new sovereigns of the forest, the grand lords of decay, building castles on the rotting tombs of the kings who'd come before. Mushroom and toadstool, mouldweave and whitespore, running thick across the ground or flowering on the still-standing corpses, so thick you could barely see the shape of the tree beneath.

'"*Ishaedh*," Saoirse spat, stalking the thin and muddy road.

'"Eh?"

'The slayer glanced my way, shook her head. "'Tis what we name it,

Silversaint. *Ishaedh*. The *Blight*. Twisting and ruining all that was once green and good."

'I glanced around, shrugged. "They're just mushrooms, girl."

'The slayer scowled. "Keep calling me *girl* and you're going to wake one morn with yer lollies in yer mouth, de León, I swear it."

'"Every contortionist's dream," Bellamy smiled, stomping along in the chill.

'"Ye've no ken what ye speak of," the slayer said. "And still ye speak."

'"That's one of my most endearing qualit—"

'My throat seized tight as bright red pain lanced through my belly. I staggered to a halt, hissing as it spread through my veins like fire.

'"Gabe?" Chloe asked. "Are you aright?"

'Fumbling in my greatcoat pocket, I took a long pull of my last bottle of vodka, finishing off the lot. Tossing the empty, I drew a deep breath and nodded. "Never better."

'It was a lie, of course. It'd been almost two days since I'd smoked, and the holdout phial in my boot was a quarter empty now. My skin crawled with invisible lice, and I was sweating in the brittle chill. But I couldn't risk another smoke yet – I'd no idea how long we'd be marching through this accursed wood, nor when I might find more leech blood.

'Vampires had been a blight on my existence as long as I could remember. But now that I needed one, we hadn't seen a single wretched since that attack at Winfael.

'It was almost like someone up there hated me.

'"Great fucking Redeemer . . ."

'Chloe pursed her lips. "Blasphemy, Dior."

'"No," the boy whispered. "*Look*."

'Ahead of us, I saw a pale shape moving across the path. At first, I thought I might be dreaming awake – that the thirst was throwing phantoms on my eyes. But no, there it was, moving through growths of 'stools and whitespore, proud as a lord.

'A stag.

'The weather was still warm enough down in Sūdhaem for medium-size game, and beasts like rabbits and foxes lingered in the north. But I'd not seen an animal this magnificent in *years*. He stood as tall as I, sharp muscles and tan hide, a grand crown of antlers on his brow. Bellamy immediately had his crossbow out, the rest of us falling still as stones. Thirsty as I was, the thought of cooked venison almost banished my agony entirely.

'The soothsinger took careful aim. I held my breath. His crossbow sang, and the quarrel flew true, striking the beast right in his throat.

'"Ha!" Bellamy cried. "Did you see *that*?"

'"The soothsinger fell silent as the stag swayed on its feet, turning to look at us. And at the sight of it, he almost dropped his bow. "Great *fucking* Redeemer."

'"Blasphemy, Bellamy . . ." Chloe whispered.

'The left side of the beast's body was covered in pale growths, pustules linked by a lattice of cobwebs. Its left eye bulged from its socket, bloated with what might have been blood. The stag shivered, gore spilling from the quarrel in its neck. Rearing up on its hind legs, it threw back its head and screamed. But as its mouth opened wider, *wider*, it split apart entirely, chin and jaw and Holy God, even its throat unfurling like the petals of some awful flower to form a horrid, tooth-filled maw. And its scream . . .

'Its scream was a little girl's. A *human* girl's.

'I drew Ashdrinker, bellowing over that godless howl. "*Shoot it again!*"

'The soothsinger fired – a crack shot, the arrow *thunking* into that bloated eye and bursting it like a blister. But the beast only lowered its head and charged, crown of antlers scything towards us. Saoirse lifted Kindness and Jezebel reared up in horror and Rafa and Chloe both tumbled from her saddle. I roared warning as the beast came on, that awful screaming filling my ears. I'd faced the horrors of the dark before, but nothing of this thing's ilk, and in truth, I'd no idea how to kill it. But in a blood-red flash, a blur of fang and claw flew out of the rotten scrub like a spear, up onto the charging stag's back.

'Phoebe's weight made the beast stumble, the stag screaming louder as the she-lion's fangs sank into the base of its skull. The beast veered sideways, crashing into a twisted oak, that little girl's scream rising in pitch as Phoebe bit harder, shaking, *shaking*, as she bore down her prey, and with a final twist of her head, snapped the stag's neck clean. The thing thrashed a moment more, legs kicking feebly as it gargled its end.

'And then, it lay still.

'Phoebe shook her head, the she-lion coughing and trying to spit, as if the beast's very blood tasted foul. Chloe picked herself up, shaken, eyes on the fallen horror.

'"Great *fucking* Redeemer."

'"Blasphemy," we all chorused.

'We stood around the fallen stag, silent and horrified. Up close, I saw the growths covered much of its body – its sable hide was actually more like moss. Those pustules spread across its skin, and it smelled like mouldering leaves, threaded with a deeper stink, not unlike the wretched. A perfume of death and rot.

"'*Ishaedh*," Saoirse murmured. "The Blight."

"'You've seen this before?" I asked, holding my cramping gut.

'In my dreams," the slayer replied, glancing about. "Nae so bad down here. But up in the northern weald, near the Highlands and in the old forests o' the world, the Blight holds grim sway. Fiáin and fae, bough and branch, all corrupted. And e'er it grows."

"'And this Blight . . . it started with daysdeath?"

'She looked at me sidelong. "Why d'ye care, Silversaint?"

"'Why do you?"

"'Because I'm bound to. By blood and breath, Mothers and Moons."

'I nodded, understanding at last why this heathen slayer was dragging her arse about with a bunch of One Faithers and a supposed descendant of the Redeemer himself.

"'A *geas*."

"'Aye." Saoirse traced the tattoos on her face. "My oath is sworn to end the Blight, by the spirit of the Rígan-Mor and the All Mothers, carved in my own moonsblood upon my sacred skin. And until my vow is fulfilled, nae man can kill me. And nae devil shall dare try."

'I glanced to Dior, the boy patting and cooing to Jez to calm her.

"'And I take it little Lord Stickuphisarse is the secret to ending this Blight?"

'Saoirse dragged a braid from her eyes, still scowling.

> "'*Dead shall rise, an' stars shall fall;*
> "'*Weald shall rot to ruin ae all.*
> "'*Lions roar an' angels weep;*
> "'*Sinners hands our secrets keep.*
> "'*'Til Godling's heart brights hea'en's eye,*
> "'*From reddest blood comes bluest sky.*"

'I shook my head and sighed. "Always a fucking poem, isn't there?"

'Rafa had picked himself up off the ground, brushing the snow from his furs. He was a holy man, a believer who held no truck with ungodliness. Still, he was a scholar too, with all a scholar's wisdom burning in those dark eyes.

"'You see, Silversaint? Even those who worship false faiths believe we can end this darkness. These prophecies are scribed in the bones of this world. Words of power. Words of truth. When the sun shines bright in the sky once more, all this suffering shall end."

'"And Dior is the key," Chloe said, squeezing the boy's hand.

'I looked down to the infected stag at our feet. The dream of roast venison was long abandoned, and only faint horror remained, keeping company with the thirst in my veins. Perhaps this Blight was the reason no wretched entered these woods. Maybe because people didn't come here any more, there was no prey for coldbloods to hunt. Whatever the reason, the ache in me was spreading like burning poison. When I looked to Chloe, my eyes couldn't help but drift to the arteries pulsing swift below the line of her jaw. When Bellamy stepped up behind me, I couldn't help but hear the song of his heart, *lub-dubbing* under his rasping breath.

'My teeth were sharp against my tongue. My throat, ashen.

'"Let's get the fuck out of this forest."

'We trekked onwards, not daring to forage any more. We lit a fire, beacon be damned, and slept only a few hours a night, all of us unnerved. The dark was full of whispers, the sound of soft feet. Phoebe never roamed far, and I hadn't the heart to tell the others about the silhouettes I saw creeping around the edges of our firelight. But though they followed, watched, nothing actually moved on us. We were interlopers here, unwelcome, but the Forest of Sorrows seemed content to let us leave. I rationed my sanctus, keeping myself just above the precipice, my mood souring more each day.

'"Those spiders have human hands."

'"Shut the fuck up, Bouchette."

'"That tree . . . its face looks like . . . my mother's."

'"Shut. The. Fuck. Up. Bouchette."

'"Is it me, or are the feathers on that bird . . . tiny tongues?"

'"SHUT THE FUCK UP, BOUCHETTE!"

'Atop Jezebel, bowed against the cold, Père Rafa sighed. "The Book of Vows speaks that we are not made more by the God above us, but by the friends beside us. Yet in this case, Bellamy, I must concur with our good chevalier. *Please*, for the love of God, shut up."

'The forest about us deepened, the strangeness with it, and after a fortnight our tempers were frayed to single threads. We were almost out of food, and I was down to my last peck of sanctus – just a few blood-dark flecks in the bottom of my phial. But at long last, we emerged from the weald onto a snow-capped tundra, a long plane of undulating grey before us.

Phoebe bounded through the snow like an overjoyed puppy. Rafa clutched his wheel and turned his eyes skywards. Dior only sighed.

"'If I never see another tree in my fucking life, I'll die happy."

'To the south, the Dílaenn River could be dimly seen – a thin strip of silver in the noontime grey. And in the distance ahead, we saw a sight that birthed a collective sigh of relief. A series of hills – once barley fields, now thick with potato scrub. A long road wound up to a tall peak, and atop it, like the Laerd Lady of all the surrounds, stood our goal.

'It was tall walls and good stone. It was stout gates and civilization. It was food. It was fire. It was liquor. It was sanctuary.

"'At last."

'Rafa smiled and made the sign of the wheel.

"'San Guillaume.'"

✦ XIII ✦

SORROW AND SOLACE

'SAN GUILLAUME WAS a monastery, but it would still pass for a fortress in a pinch.

'The structure crowned a steep rise, unassailable save by the thin road winding up to its walls. On either side, the ground dropped away in sheer cliffs, the Dílaenn River branching away from the Volta at the fork and flowing towards the sea. The walls were pale limestone, battlements crusted with grey snow. Murder holes looked out like dark eyes on the ascent beneath. Around the walls stood a sea of shanties and tents – commonfolk seeking shelter in the monastery's shadow, by the look. San Guillaume stood, silent and imperial, a monolith to God's majesty in this wilderness.

'But I knew, as soon as I caught the scent on the wind . . .

'"Something is wrong," Rafa murmured.

'We quickened our pace, the ache in my belly and in back of my eyes worsening as the smell of stale blood thickened. Drawing nearer, I saw that those tents and shanties were all empty, and dark shapes hung on the walls – wagon wheels lashed to the battlements with iron chain. Upon them, nailed upside down so that their souls would be steered towards hell, hung the bodies of a dozen men in the same pale robes as old Rafa wore.

'The songs of fat, sable crows hung on the wind with the stench of death. The priest breathed deep, eyes welling with tears. "What devilry is this?"

'"Gabe . . ." Chloe whispered, drawing her silversteel.

'I hauled Ashdrinker from her sheath, my grip tight.

'*There are seven quarts of b-blood in a full-grown man, did ye know that?*

'"That I did," I murmured.

'*Although, it depends on whether one uses the Elidaeni or N-n-nordlund quart, I suppose. The commonly accept—*

'"Ash," I growled. "Eyes open, eh?"

'. . . *I have no eyes*, she whispered.

'I glanced to Saoirse as she slung Kindness off her back. Phoebe was a bloody shadow at her side, the lioness's hackles rippling as we drew up to the gates. They were broad, iron-clad, carved with the circle of the wheel. But they creaked open at my touch, and the slayer and I exchanged a grim glance.

'"Rafa, Chloe," I said. "Stay here with Dior."

'Phoebe loped inside, silence itself, and Saoirse and I followed with Bellamy behind. Stepping into a broad bailey that was quiet as graves, I could taste soot, rot, strong spirits. Buildings rose either side of us; the arched vaults of a library to the west, dormitories and distillery to the east. Ahead, the bailey opened into a broad, round garden – now snow-clad and silent. The great circle of a cathedral stood at the heart of it, all limestone and thin stained-glass windows. Beautiful mosaics depicting the lives of the Martyrs were set in the stone at our feet. But they were stained now – old blood soaked into the tiles.

'*A monastery*, Ashdrinker asked, *or a mausoleum?*

'More bodies. Dozens and dozens, most dressed in monk's robes. They'd been dead a week or so by the look, left to rot where they fell. The floor was thick with rats, black-eyed and plump. Crows sat upon the bodies, pecking at treasures in half-frozen troves. More men were strung up on the walls in here, inverted like those poor bastards on the battlements.

'"Bladework," Bellamy reported, kneeling by one of the bodies.

'"The men on the walls look flayed to the bone." I spat the taste of death off my tongue, my belly aching. "Tortured and left to bleed out."

'"What in God's name happened here, Gabriel?"

'"A massacre . . ."

'"Silversaint."

'I looked to Saoirse, standing on the battlements above the gates. The slayer was pointing to the bodies and bloodstains on the bailey floor. It wasn't until I climbed the stairs beside the gatehouse that I understood what she saw. From the ground, it appeared a simple carnage, but from on high, there was a method to this madness. Stomach turning, I realized the corpses were arranged in a pattern – a grim signature in dead meat.

'*Flower and flail, flail and f-f-flower.*

'I nodded. "Naél, Angel of Bliss."

'"This is the work of the Holy Inquisition," Bellamy whispered.

'"Oh, dearest *God* . . ."

'I glanced downwards at the moan, saw old Rafa in the gateway, dark skin blanched with grief. He stumbled into the bailey, holding the wheel at his throat so tight I thought the silver might bend. "Oh Heavenly Father, what hell is this?"

'He ran to the closest corpse, the rats scattering. Falling to his knees, he turned it gently, a long, shuddering moan slipping over his lips. "Ohhhhhhhh, no. Alfonse . . .?" He turned to another body, just a boy by the look, and Rafa's face crumpled like old vellum in a tightening fist. "Jamal? *Jamal!*"

'He seized hold of the body, rotting and lolling in his arms.

'"What is this? WHAT MADNESS IS *THIS?*"

'"Rafa!" Chloe ran to the old man's side, horrified. The priest clutched her, spittle on his lips as he began to come apart at his seams. "Oh, Rafa, Rafa . . ."

'"Ch-chloe, th-this is Jamal. He . . . writes poetry. H-he . . . Oh, God . . . oh *God* . . ."

'Dior stood at the gates, sleeve pressed to his lips. A bitter wind blew in from the valley below, the boy's magik frockcoat billowing about him as he met my eyes. And he knew it as sure as I did. As sure as the dark sun sinking towards the horizon must set. Every single person in this monastery had been slaughtered. And somehow, some way . . .

'"This is because of me," he whispered.

'The slayer took the boy's scarred hand. "Don't say that, flower." And as Dior met Saoirse's eyes, I saw tears welling in his lashes with the truth none could deny.

'"Saoirse," I murmured. "Stay here and watch the others. I'll look for survivors."

'Rafa began howling, gut-deep, animal sobs. I shared a glance with Chloe as she pressed the old man to her breast, hushing and rocking him like a mother might. The atrocity of it all was etched in her eyes, bloodshot and brimming, and my jaw was clenched as I lifted Ashdrinker and strode into the library.

'The door was burned to char, old smoke in the air. Ashes danced about my boots, windows blacked with soot. My heart sank, some part of me aching worse than I had at the sight of those slaughtered men. The sword in my hand whispered, silver and full of sorrow.

'*Blasphemy . . .*

'Books. *Thousands* of books. Brass-trimmed codices and woodblock cuts. Vellum scrolls and parchment tomes, each illuminated by loving hands. And they'd been hurled like dross to the library floor, and there, set ablaze. Every one of them. Burned to fucking ashes.

'I knelt by the charred pile, flipping through ruined pages. The knowledge of geniuses, holy men and heathens, thousands of truths and thousands of lies, each of them a story worth the telling. And now, they were nothing but soot in my mouth as I whispered.

'"A life without books is a life not lived."

'Searching the other buildings, I found only bodies and the leavings of lives undone. Plates with half-finished meals. A partly woven wreath in a monk's cell, never to be completed. I trudged out of the empty cathedral, my thirst stabbing at the relentless scent of old, wasted blood. Fountains carved in the likeness of angels spilled brackish water into long ponds. Beyond the cathedral, a tall wall ran along the lips of the cliffs. Beyond it, a drop waited, perhaps a hundred and fifty feet, down to the frothing rivers below.

'Rafa stood atop it, looking down into those grey, freezing waters.

'As I walked to the battlements beside him, the old priest met my eyes. He clutched the wheel strung about his neck, rubbing the silver between his fingers. His face was harrowed, cheeks wet with tears. I said not a word. I'd none in me for horror like this.

'And then . . . music.

'It began soft at first. A few notes echoing on bloodstained stone. But the chords slipped together into a bar, and the bar wove itself into a tune, and soon, I stood silent and amazed as that smattering of notes reached into the awful stillness and filled it.

'Young Bellamy was sitting up on the wall, playing his lute.

'But not just a song. A *spell*. Begun in the string-struck spiral of a melancholy refrain but ending, shivering upon my skin and loosing the anchors on the whole of my heart. It was a song I'd never heard like of, a song that might make stones weep and the wind cease its sighing for fear of missing one gentle, soul-sick moment. It was ache and longing, fulsome and wanting, each swell and shift sweeping you higher as it spoke – through no tongue of man or way as weak as words – a truth beyond telling. A sorrow-sweet circle, like the pearl-white crescent of angel wings, curving upwards towards crescendo and then down, soft and softest, back to those same few ember-warm notes that began it all. It whispered at the edge of hearing, and it pressed lips smooth as silk to your aching brow and told you that though all things must have their ending, so too must then end darkness, and here, now, in this bright and blessed moment, *you* were alive and breathing.

'Bellamy struck one final chord, like the warmth of a kiss lingering after the lips have left your own. And he hung his head and was still. Chloe sat with face upturned, weeping. Rafa and I had followed the song back to the bailey, entranced, Dior mopping his lashes on his sleeve. Even Saoirse was pawing at her eyes. And reaching up to my cheeks, I was astounded to find them wet. But somehow, no sadness in my heart.

'"Seven Martyrs . . ." I breathed.

'"That was . . . *beautiful*, Bellamy," Chloe whispered.

'"Merci, Sœur Sauvage."

'"Does it have a name?"

'Bellamy's fingers trailed along his silver necklet, lingering on the sixth of the musical notes strung upon it. "A soothsinger must pen seven songs to be considered a master by his peers in the Opus Grande. Seven songs through which they might speak the truth of the world. That was my sixth. *Sorrow and Solace*."

'I shook my head, looking Bellamy over with new eyes. "And your seventh?"

'The young man smiled, gently putting his lute away. "I've not found it yet, Silversaint. That is why I left my Augustin, and my empress divine. To sing the truth of the world, I must see it first. And when I find that song, to her arms I shall return."

'A strange silence fell then. Windswept, yet somehow warm. And into it, Dior spoke the question burning in everyone's mind.

'"What are we going to do now?"

'Chloe and Bellamy looked to me. Rafa stared yet at the carnage around us.

'"There are no horses in the stables," I sighed. "But there's some food yet unspoiled in the refectory. Vodka in the distillery. Things will look less dark with something hot in our bellies." I glanced to Chloe. "Mayhaps you and Dior could help Rafa cook a meal, Sister?"

'Chloe met my eyes and nodded. "Busy hands, busy minds."

'She walked across the carnage to Rafa, standing still and silent. Taking the old priest's arm, she murmured, and he blinked as if remembering where he was, allowing himself to be led away, beyond the arched oaken doors and out of sight. Bellamy came down from the walls. Saoirse joined me as Phoebe drifted out of the gates like smoke.

'I laced my collar up about my face, looked from soothsinger to slayer.

'"Let's get burning."'

✦ XIV ✦

LIATHE

'THE STINK OF charred meat was thick on my tongue. We'd set the bodies burning a few hundred yards down the hill, smoke drifting skywards into thickening snows. I was throwing the last of them on the pyre – a boy, maybe twelve years old – when Phoebe came bounding back up the road.

'The sun hadn't yet fallen; the lioness moved in a soft blur through the long shadows, all golden eyes and rust-red fur. Saoirse knelt in the frost as the beast loped up to her and circled once, growling, tail lashing side to side.

'The slayer's eyes narrowed, and she looked at once to me. "Strife comin'."

'"Danton?"

'She shook her head, slung her axe off her back. "The other one."

'I looked down the hill, jaw tightening as I saw a faint spot of blood-red stalking towards us through the falling grey.

'"The monastery is holy ground. Both of you, get back inside. Now." I glanced to Saoirse, flashed her a small smile. "Pretty please with sugar on top."

'The slayer scoffed, and we retreated back through the gates. Bellamy stood on the battlements with a tallow-soaked quarrel loaded in his crossbow and a burning barrel beside him. I waited with Saoirse just inside the open gates, armed and ready.

'The bodies were gone, but the scent lingered, the knuckle-deep clawing of old blood on the back of my throat. The thirst was a constant pain now, my fangs grown long in my gums. But I pushed thoughts of blood aside as best I could, watching that figure come on like wolf to wounded deer, until she stopped but a few dozen yards from the walls.

'The highblood stood in the dying light, locks of dull midnight-blue parted about her face, running thick to her waist. She wore her long red frockcoat and tight black leathers, silken shirt parted from her pale chest. Her face was obscured by that porcelain mask, black lips and dark, kohled lashes. She was slender, tall – just a maid when she was murdered. But her eyes were bleached with time – a dead thing's eyes, drained of all light and life. Looking to Bellamy on the wall above, Saoirse and me waiting just beyond the threshold, she flipped her frockcoat hem back and gave a formal, strangely masculine bow, like gentry at court. Her voice was soft as shadows, marred by that slight, slurring lisp.

'"Good evening, Monsssieur, Mademoissselle, Chevalier."

'I glanced to the sun on the still-warm horizon. "Not yet it's not."

'The vampire looked past me to the buildings behind. "Where isss the child?"

'"You've got balls, bitch. Coming to holy ground with the sun yet up."

'"The one who comesss behind us will not be so polite as to asssk at all. But we will repeat ourselvesss once." Those pale eyes fixed on mine. "Where isss the child?"

'Phoebe bared her teeth in a soft snarl as Saoirse rested Kindness on her shoulder. "I dare ye step across that threshold to look for him, leech."

'The vampire didn't blink. But my eyes were now fixed on the sword in her hand. The weapon was gently curved, long, graceful as its mistress. When I'd seen it in the dark by that watchtower near the Ümdir, I'd thought the blade had simply been soaked red with the blood of the wretched she'd killed. But now, with bones burning and tongue parched, I realized the sword wasn't just drenched in blood. It was *made* of blood.

'*Her* blood.

'"Who are you?" I demanded.

'The vampire bowed again, deeper this time. "You may call usss Liathe."'

High in the reaches of a lonely tower, a swiftly scratching pen fell suddenly still. The Last Silversaint drained his glass to the dregs as the historian of Margot Chastain, First and Last of Her Name, Undying Empress of Wolves and Men, blinked once. Jean-François's voice was still sweet as smoke, but a fury boiled beneath his honey-smooth tones.

'Liathe.'

Gabriel leaned forward to refill his glass. 'Oui.'

'I knew you were a fool, de León. Yet the mind still boggles to know you name me leech whilst having kept company with the queen of them. To think of—'

'Careful, coldblood. You want the truth of this tale, best let me have the telling of it. What you know and what you *think* you know are two different beasts entire.'

The vampire scowled. 'As you like it.'

Gabriel raised his goblet. 'Awfully generous of you.

'"You may call usss Liathe," the vampire said, bowing. "Though we suspect you care lessss for Who and more for What, and we have no time even for ssso small a thing as Why. Danton Vosss is scant hours behind us. He has been tracking you since the Dílaenn, and every maggot-ridden foulblood for miles has been gathered to hisss pale banner. And when he arrives, at the edge of night, the Beassst will murder you all and take the cup in his father's name. The child hasss but one chance to survive."

'Liathe combed a long, black lock from colourless eyes.

'"Usss."

'Saoirse scoffed. "So concerned with Dior's well-being, are ye?"

'"We have guarded your steps for weeksss now. An inquisitor's cohort out of Sul Ilham laid low by our hand. Another from León. The bloody band who committed the carnage upon which you stand has eluded usss, but since word of the ruckuss you caused in Lashaame reached the Tower of Tearsss, the entire Inquisition has been brought to bear against your little company." She tilted her head, eyes narrow behind her mask. "Why do you suppose you have ssseen neither hide nor hair of them?"

'I sniffed hard, spat thick. "I can smell your bullshit from here, leech."

'"We have eternity." The coldblood sighed, tossing her silk scarf over her shoulder. "And yet, not a moment more to waste on nonsense such as thisss."

'"Well, I'd invite you in. But holy ground and all . . ."

'"Law the Fifth?" she slurred.

'I nodded, fangs glinting. "*Even the Dead have laws.*"

'Bloody sword in hand, blood-red frockcoat flowing about her, the vampire slowly walked up to San Guillaume's gates. And despite the knowledge that this bitch couldn't enter, I still drew Ashdrinker from her scabbard with a crisp ring of razor-sharp metal. The monster's eyes flickered to the dark starsteel, the jagged edge where the blade's tip had snapped free.

'*Never trust a woman who hides her f-face, Gabriel.*

'"Never mistake a monster for a woman, Ash."

'*Aye. B-beware this one.*

'I needed no warning, sure and true. I could feel the power in this thing, that bloody blade and the darkling magik that had made it. Questions to which I had no answers were whispering in the back of my mind. But no

matter the age, no matter the potency, no coldblood could set foot on sanctified ground. Such was the law of Almighty God Himself.

'Liathe brought the toes of her knee-high boots to the monastery's
threshold. She looked about her, eyes running the length and breadth of the
gates. Chill wind blew a strand of midnight-blue across her mask, and she
brushed it behind her ear.

'And then she stepped right across the threshold.

'"What the *fuck*," I breathed.

'*Witchery* . . . Ashdrinker whispered.

'I looked to the blade in the monster's hand. Those unanswered questions
ringing louder in my head. And I gave one voice, eyes on the vampire as I
whispered.

'". . . Sanguimancy?"

'"So out of hisss depth." Liathe looked at me with something close to
pity. "'Tis a wonder you can ssstill breathe at all, Gabriel . . ."

'Saoirse raised her beautiful axe, and Bellamy lit the arrow loaded in his
crossbow, Phoebe growling as she circled the vampire's flank. Liathe seemed
completely undaunted by any of us, looking instead to the refectory doors
Dior was hidden behind.

'"You play a game you cannot win," Liathe told us, soft and poisonous.
"Bring usss the child now, and we will allow the res—"

'The vampire stepped back as Saoirse swung her axe, the blade skimming
barely a whisker from her chin. Silent, swift, Liathe sidestepped Phoebe, the
lioness's claws catching that blood-red coat and shredding it like paper. I
shouted warning as the vampire struck back, her bloody blade scything
towards Saoirse's throat. The girl raised her axe to block, but the vampire's
blade simply flowed *around* the girl's guard like liquid and re-formed on the
other side, leaving a splash of red on the haft as it kept cutting right for
Saoirse's neck.

'The girl's eyes widened, she bent backwards, that bloody blade slicing
two of her braids neat as a razor. Overextended, Saoirse squealed as the
vampire's boot crashed like thunder, right between her legs, sending her
tumbling across the bloodstained tiles.

'Bellamy fired, but Liathe sliced the burning arrow from the air. Ashdrinker
hissed and the vampire swayed, Phoebe leaping at her legs again. The monster
moved, sinuous and swift, rolling aside and back up to her feet as that
crimson sword flashed towards my chest. But I raised Ashdrinker, blood and
blade ringing like steel as I blocked her strike.

'*Well, well*, Ash whispered.

'I caught a glint of surprise in the coldblood's eyes. Her blade had flowed around Saoirse's axe like water, but Ashdrinker had stopped it dead. And the smug bitch staggered as my riposte caught her right across the cheek of that painted mask.

'Porcelain shattered, the coldblood flashing backwards, coat flowing about her slender body like smoke. Her mask had broken away, only her eyes still covered, and I looked in horror at the thing beneath.

'The skin on the lower half of her face was gone. She had no bottom lip; sharp teeth sitting in blue-grey gums, mangled flesh clinging to pale bone. Under her silk scarf, I could see the muscles of her neck exposed. It was as if someone had grasped a fistful of her throat and torn the flesh away in one long strip, up and over her chin. I saw fury break through the ice of her eyes as she looked to the broken mask on the stone at her feet.

'"You *dare . . .*" she snarled.

'Bellamy fired another burning arrow, and again the vampire moved like water around a river-smooth stone. Liathe brought her wrist up to her mouth, fangs piercing her marble skin. Blood welled from the wound, bright and beautiful as the vampire flicked her wrist and spoke a word, inverted, thrumming with power. And before my wondering eyes, that sluice of ruby red formed itself into a long flail, as solid as the bloody blade she still carried. The scent of it gripped my aching belly; my hunger surged as Liathe spoke.

'"You should have stuck to chasing bu—"

'Phoebe roared and pounced at the highblood's chest, but Liathe was the swifter, twirling beneath yet another burning shot from Bellamy and lashing out at me. I fended off a half-dozen sword blows – groin, chest, throat – but that crimson flail caught me about my forearm and I felt myself swept off my feet, flung across the courtyard and smashing a fountain to dust. Still wrapped up, I roared as she slung me again, down into the floor, teeth rattling in my skull as I shattered the mosaic beneath me.

'"Fucksakes *shoot her*, Bouchette!"

'The soothsinger fired again, striking close enough this time that the flaming shot sheared through a long lock of midnight hair. "God *damn* it, she's too fast!"

'*Cut thyself free, ye b-bloody fool!*

'I lashed out with Ashdrinker, severing the bloody flail in a spray of ashes. The highblood sent me sailing backwards, black stars bursting as I struck the wall and crashed to the floor. Liathe ducked another flaming shot, that skinless face snarling as Phoebe finally sank her claws in. The lioness tore long slashes through the coldblood's leathers, the pale flesh beneath, and

Liathe struck back with her fist, pounding Phoebe's head into the stone. The big cat buckled, groaning, the vampire raised her bloodblade, Saoirse's mouth opened in a scream, "PHOEBE, MOVE!" as the blade flashed down like the bloody hand of—

'"*G-g-godddd*," Liathe gasped, staggering backwards.

'The vampire stared bewildered at the four and a half feet of starmetal protruding from her chest. Ashdrinker quivered, shaking from the force I'd put behind the throw – enough to shatter the monster's ribs and burst out through her back. Liathe's flesh sizzled like sausage on a skillet and she staggered, her own bloody blade slipping from her fingers and splashing in a long crimson puddle on the floor.

'She looked up at me, wobbling now to my feet. "Y-you . . ."

'Liathe groaned, hands smoking as she closed them about Ashdrinker's hilt and dragged the sword from her blackened chest. She let my blade fall to the stone with a bright *clang*, fingers burned to charcoal twigs, dead eyes boiling as she spat ashes.

'"We sh-should *kill* you f-for that, you ungratef—"

'"*Know my name, ye sinners, and tremble!*" came a fierce cry. "*For I am come among thee as a lion among lambs!*"

'A silver-bright light sheared into the courtyard, and Liathe flinched like she'd been slapped in her mutilated face, charred hands held up to her eyes. Turning, I saw Chloe and Rafa both stalking across the stone, the sister brandishing her silversteel sword, the priest holding his wheel, burning with a light that was almost blinding.

'"Leave this holy place!" Chloe shouted, raising her blade in both fists.

'Liathe spat through bared fangs. "Wretched *foolsss*, you kn—"

'"In the name of God and the blessed Mothermaid," Rafa roared, "I say *begone!*"

'The vampire hissed at the priest's command, backing away from that searing light. Her chest was split wide, mask shattered, ribs and hands still smouldering from Ashdrinker's kiss. Rafa cried again, "I said BEGONE, devil!" wielding his wheel like a sword. And just as when we'd fought at the watchtower, Liathe's body seemed to tremble, exploding into a thousand blood-red moths, now whirring and spinning up into the pale snows.

'I bent double, spitting blood. And as I watched, that storm of tiny wings rose up through the feeble sunlight and scattered into the gloom.

'Phoebe stood on unsteady legs, the lioness shaking herself head to tail and snorting blood. Dior came barrelling across the bailey, skidding to a halt at Saoirse's side.

'"Saoirse?" the boy demanded, grabbing her hand. "Are you aright?"

'"B-bitch . . . kicked me . . . i-in the c-cunny . . ." she hissed.

'"Who the hell *is* that devil?" Dior demanded.

'"And how in God's name did she enter holy ground?" Rafa asked.

'"She was a blood witch." Chloe looked at me, green eyes wide. "Gabe, could she . . ."

'But the good sister's voice failed as I shook my head. I'd thought the same myself at first – some foul arte dark enough to break even God's law. But looking at the bloody stone at my feet, the stink of burning bodies still hanging in the wind, I'd realized the simple truth.

'"There's no magik at work here. Just murder."

'Bellamy stood above, crossbow in shaking hands. "What do you mean?"

'I looked around the bloodstained belly of San Guillaume and sighed. "I mean how can this ground still be sanctified, when it's been soaked with the blood of God's faithful? How could it remain hallowed, when defiled in the name of that very same God?"

'"The Inquisition . . ." Rafa whispered.

'"In murdering the monastery's brethren, flaying and burning and torturing them, those fools profaned this place. Soaked it in the blood of innocents and holy men." I shook my head, retrieving Ashdrinker from the stone. "San Guillaume is sacred ground no longer."

'*And d-doom rides t'wards it, on black black wings.*

'Saoirse dragged herself to her feet, wincing. "That bitch said the Beast of Vellene will be at our throats by nightfall. If she spoke truth . . ."

'Chloe looked to me, paling under her freckles. "How can we hope to stand against Danton without God beneath our feet?"

'"We could put those feet to use?" Bellamy suggested. "We could run?"

'"Cowards never triumph, Bellamy," the slayer growled.

'"They don't die very often either, Saoirse," Chloe noted.

'I scowled back down the hill. "The one path we have to flee by will lead us straight into Danton's arms. That bastard could track a piece of hay through a stackful of needles. And if he catches us in the open at night-time, he'll carve us up like springtime lambs. We've no choice but to make a stand here."

'"But that blood witch said Danton has gathered every wretched for miles," Bellamy protested. "We barely held back a few dozen at Winfael, and that was without a highblood leading them. We've trapped ourselves like bloody rats!"

'I looked around the group, saw Bellamy's fear seeping into them like poison. Dior's jaw was clenched, all colour gone from his face – it was his decision that had brought us to these walls, after all. Chloe was pacing, dragging one hand back through her curls as she looked to the walls behind us, the sheer cliffs, the hopeless drop into the river a hundred and fifty feet below. Bellamy spoke again, voice trembling with fear.

"'We should never have come here, mes amis."

"'Hold your nerve, Bouchette," I growled.

"'My *nerve*?" the lad scoffed, almost laughing. "Did you *see* that monster? She carried a blade made of *blood*! She turned into a storm of fucking *moths*! Perhaps such horrors are commonplace for a silversaint, but I'm only a soothsinger! I'm not even a soldier!"

"'Soldier?" I sighed. "Let me tell you about the soldiers I've fought with, Bellamy. All those great battles you sing about? The heroes who fought at Tuuve and Báih Sìde, Triúrbaile and Coste? They were *boys,* for the most part. Teenage boys, just like you. Stonemasons and carpenters. Farmers and fishermen. They fought because they didn't have rich fathers. They fought because they didn't have a piece of parchment with the Emperor's seal to save them. They fought because they *had* to. And they'd nothing to look forward to afterwards, most of them. All they'd be at the end of it was alive. But before every battle I ever fought, I'd look at the faces of those boys, and in their loyalty to each other, in their courage at the sight of those horrors, I tell you sure and true, I used to see the face of God."

'I walked to the monastery wall and thumped my fist against it.

"'We have strong stone around us, Bouchette. Liquor in the cellars and water to be blessed. Holy wheels and silversteel." I looked around the group, fire in my eyes. "We don't need soldiers to win through this. We need only stand together."

"'Véris, Silversaint." Père Rafa smiled, clutching his wheel tight. "Véris."

'Dior squared his shoulders and nodded. Chloe put her arm around the boy and squeezed tight. Even Saoirse stood a little taller.

"'Bouchette, I want you fetching as much water as you can. Rafa, get to blessing it. Saoirse, start hauling liquor from the distillery. There's barrels of it, pure and strong as sin. Chloe, Dior, I want you looking for tallow, wood, bedding – *anything* that will burn. We don't have long 'til sunset, and I want to be ready when His Majesty arrives."

'I looked at the soothsinger in the lingering still.

"'You've still got your seventh song to write, Bellamy. You're not dying tonight."

'The company set about it, Dior headed to the kitchens, Saoirse to the cellar, Bellamy following Rafa, still looking shaky. Only Chloe remained. She stood a foot and a half shorter than I, clad in chainmail and silversteel, hands on hips as she smiled.

'"You always did give a rousing speech, mon ami. You haven't lost your touch since the Battle of the Twins."

'I shrugged, turning away so I didn't have to watch that vein, pulsing just below the line of her jaw. "When you're playing your last song, always pick a crowd-pleaser."

'". . . Last song?"

'Still refusing to look at her, I murmured so none might overhear. "When Danton arrives, keep Dior close. I'll cut you a way out if I can."

'"What happened to standing together?"

'"Fucksakes, open your eyes, Chloe," I snarled.

'"I don't—"

'"We're pinned down. Cliffs at our backs and God knows what coming at our front. Most of the folk in this company can't fight worth a damn, and the ones who can won't be halfway enough. I've had nothing to smoke for days. And Danton won't strike until it's night. All his power, *all* his strength brought to bear. Odds are about perfect we're all going to die."

'She licked at dry lips, glancing down the hill. "Do you truly think we've no hope?"

'"Keep Dior close," I repeated. "You see a break, fucking *run*."

'Chloe chewed her lip, fear finally breaking through that rime of eternal optimism. She'd always been a believer. Always felt we were meant for greater things. And swallowing hard, she nodded to herself, slipped her gauntlet off her hand and offered me her wrist.

'". . . Here, then."

'My jaw clenched. Pupils dilating. "What the *hell* are you doing?"

'"I know it's a sin," she breathed, trembling. "But I've given seventeen years of my life to this, and the whole empire hangs in the balance of it. So Gabe, if you need the strength . . ."

'My fangs were bright and sharp against my lips. My heart suddenly dashing itself against my ribs so hard it made me gasp. My veins were fire, that thirst rising on crimson wings – to have it offered freely when it was all I could do to stop myself just *taking* it . . .

'"Chloe . . . get away from me . . ."

'"Gabriel, I—"

'"GET THE *FUCK* AWAY FROM ME!"

'She stumbled back as I roared, her mouth open in shock. I knew what

I must look like – eyes flooded red, canines flashing, the thing in me so close to breaking loose, I could feel it clawing through my skin. But not here. Not like this. I'd promised.

'Chloe stood aghast as I backed away. She seemed smaller then, closer to the girl I'd once known. There was still fire in her eyes. Faith. Fury. But there was fear now too – the fear that comes with knowing the world is much bigger than you could ever be, and that there are simply some truths you'll never understand.

'"I'm sorry, Gabe," she whispered. "I'm sorry I dragged you into this. I'm sorry I took you from Astrid and Patience. I should never have done that." Hanging her head, she slipped her leather gauntlet back on. "There are a lot of things I shouldn't have done, I suppose. But I did them all for the best. Because I believed. In Dior. In you. And I still do. There is nothing, *nothing* I will not do to see this done."

'Staring towards the falling sun, she sighed.

'"But I'm sorry."

'I closed my eyes, saying nothing as she walked away. The beast in me crashed against its bars, howling for me to follow, to take, to swallow, just one mouthful, just one *fucking drop*. And the awful thing of it was, I knew deep down Chloe wasn't a fool to offer what she had – that I was weak and starving, and I'd need all my strength if ever I hoped to make it through this night alive, let alone best a Prince of Forever. But I'd made a vow. A promise whispered in the dark, cold as tombs and black as hell. Never again.

'*Never. Again.*'

Jean-François ceased his writing, dipped his quill into the ink at his side.

'A promise to whom, Silversaint?'

But Gabriel only shook his head.

'Patience, coldblood.'

✦ XV ✦

A PRINCE OF FOREVER

'WE PREPARED AS best we could in the time we had. Which is to say, terribly.

'I'd fought a half-dozen sieges before, but never with so little. We had holy water in abundance, and that was welcome news. An elaborate pump ran down the cliff to the depths of the Volta, used by the monks for their daily needs. Bellamy turned the crank as fast as he was able, while Rafa called down blessings on the water, and the courtyard fountains besides. I'd found a little chymist's workshop in the distillery, scattered phials of salpêtre and sulphur – enough to mix up a few handfuls of black ignis, at least.

'Saoirse hauled barrels and bottles up from the distillery below. It smote my black and shrivelled heart to waste liquor as sharp as this, even if it *was* fucking vodka. But still, we soaked the battlements and forecourt around the gates, sluicing the stone with the stink of high-grade spirits, adding a sprinkle of sawdust from the monastery's coopery for punch. We used all they had, emptying every drop. And yet, I saved myself a single bottle, downing it all to dull the pain of my ever-growing thirst.

'The dark sun was setting now, only a few minutes of feeble light left before night fell like a headsman's blade. I glanced around the company, broken glass in my belly. Saoirse and Rafa looked steady, Bellamy and Chloe a little shaky. Dior was stone.

'"Right," I said. "If that Liathe bitch spat any kind of truth, Danton has gathered every wretched for miles to his side. They'll go where their blood-lord wills them, which means they won't come mindlessly this time. Saoirse, you and I keep them off the walls as long as we're able. But when they break through, and they *will*, Bellamy lights the spirits with his bow, and we fall back to the cathedral. It's not holy ground, but most of the windows are too narrow to crawl through, and there's only two passages in and out."

'Dior chewed a ragged fingernail, then spat. "Maggot trap."

"'You what?" I asked.

"'It's a grift I thought up with my friends back in Lashaame," the boy mumbled. "You get a pretty girl, have her flash around a heavy purse in a seedy taverne, leave after one drink. Some prick's bound to follow with intent of relieving her of her coin, probably more besides. But the girl leads the fellow down a blind alley, where you and your crew are waiting. And you roll him hard and take everything he's got, then go to sleep content you stomped a bastard who deserved it." Dior shrugged. "I called it a maggot trap."

"'And you did this for recreation?" Rafa asked.

"'We did it to eat. But there's nothing wrong with enjoying your job."

"'In military terms, it's called a bottleneck," I said.

'The boy sniffed. "My name's better."

"'As you like it." I sighed, waved to the circular building behind us. "Now, bad news is, after dousing the battlements, there was only enough vodka left to soak one passage into the cathedral. The *westward* one. Good news is, in a nice enclosed space like that and with time to evaporate, spirits that strong will burn like a trencherman's fart in a candleshop. So when you fall back, fall back through the *westward* doors. The wretched will follow. And Dior will be waiting with the spark."

"'And after that?" Chloe asked.

"'With fortune, we thin their number enough for me to get my hands on Dant—"

'I gasped, bending double as a spasm of pain ripped through my belly. I could feel my nails stirring at the tips of my fingers, my fangs in my gums. The thirst was all I knew for a moment – the warmth, the scent of the company around me, the thudding pulse of that luscious, hot crimson beating just below their skin . . .

"'Gabe?" Chloe asked. "Are you aright?"

"'I'm f-fucking w-wonderful . . ."

"'Ye look like puddled shite, Silversaint." Saoirse lifted Kindness, her face grim. "Leave the bonny Prince of Forever to me. It's not my fate to die today. Nor tomorrow, neither."

'Bellamy nodded, grim. "I will not go to my grave with my song still inside me."

"'Blessings to you all," Chloe said, watching me with wide, worried eyes.

"May God and Mothermaid and all the Martyrs bring us victory over this evil."

'I looked to Dior, my stomach still burning. "You be ready for my signal, boy."

"'I'll be ready, hero."

'I looked to Rafa. "Do me a favour, Father?"

"'Ask it, Silversaint."

"'If you should happen to meet our Maker tonight, kick him in the cock for me."

'Saoirse, Bellamy and I took to the walls, wreathed in the stink of evaporating vodka. Rafa and Chloe stood in the bailey's guttering torchlight, Dior hidden in the cathedral. The cliffs at our flanks meant there was only one path by which Danton could approach, but as darkness deepened, thick and frozen, I'd no clue if we had strength enough to stop him.

'And the thirst . . . Great Redeemer. I was so *fucking* thirsty . . .

"'Remember," I hissed. "Retreat through the *westward* passage into the cathedral. The doors for the dead."

"'Poetic," Bellamy muttered. "If we live through this, there's a *hell* of a ballad in it."

'Saoirse's jaw clenched, her grip tightening on Kindness's haft. "They come."

'I looked into the dark, saw a multitude swarming up the hill. Fangs bared, I drew my sword from her sheath, that silvered dame on the hilt ever smiling at me.

"'Good fortune, Ash . . ."

'*Die not on me n-now, Gabriel. We've bastards seven to slay, to s-slay.*

'They charged towards San Guillaume, dark figures rushing through the falling night. I counted a hundred or more wretched, but against our little company, they may as well have been an army of thousands. And somewhere in the dark, their grim general awaited. I couldn't see him yet, but I could feel him, like a shadow at my back. I'd fought things like him most of my life, and still, a part of me found the thought of Danton Voss utterly horrifying. Not frightening, mind you. Just . . . horrifying.'

'Why?' Jean-François asked.

Gabriel shook his head. 'I used to wonder what it was that drove people like him to become the monsters they became. If it was a consequence of all that *time*, maybe – the need to indulge ever-darker desires, just to stave off the crushing boredom of forever. But you live long enough, you look into the mundane murk of people's souls often enough, you see Danton didn't really *become* anything. He'd just had the shackles of consequence removed. Give someone the power to do anything they want, and they'll do exactly that. *That's* the horrifying part – the only thing holding some folk back from the worst atrocities they can imagine is the fear they might not get away with it.

'His wretched came on, half rotten and all silent. I watched them, tipping my last few flakes of sanctus into my pipe. Inhaling red smoke, I closed my eyes, listening to the feet coming through the snows, feeling tiny snowflakes melting cold upon my skin, the faint notes of death and blood in the air, Saoirse's leathers, Bellamy's fear—

'"Gabriel . . ."

'—the song of the wind above and the waters below, the weight of the sword o—

'"*De León!*"

'I opened my eyes, found Bellamy staring at me incredulous as the enemy came on, ever closer, dead eyes and rotting tongues and—

'"Should you not be silverclad? If never before, we need the aegis now! At the siege at Tuuve, your faith burned so bright, the Dead were struck blind. At the Battle of Báih Sì—"

'"Have ye not figured it out yet, Bel?" Saoirse asked.

'"Figured what out?"

'The slayer glanced to me and sighed. "What worth all that pretty ink? What use a conduit for faith? If a man has no' a drop of faith left inside him to give?"

'And then the Dead were on us, and there was no more time to talk. Some crashed into the gates and began battering, others flowed up the stonework like water. I lit an ignis bomb and tossed it over the wall, the powder igniting, nails and scrap metal ripping through the coldbloods. Saoirse and Bellamy rose up, letting fly with holy water and burning crossbow shots, and wretched began to fall. But others yet were climbing, dead eyes and hungry mouths, and soon enough, they began spilling over the walls.

'It was bladework then, and miles of it, running back and forth across the highwalk in a desperate attempt to stem the tide. Bellamy backed off along the eastern walk, no longer shooting flame for fear of igniting the liquor beneath us, Saoirse and I cutting into the Dead. A wizened old man, a skinny lad, a rotten mother with a belly still swollen from the babe she'd been carrying when she was murdered – all fell under Ashdrinker's edge. But an ill feeling was growing in the back of my mind, darkening with every moment.

'*Where the hell was Danton?*

'Bellamy gasped, hand to brow. "I . . . I can f-feel him . . . i-in my head . . ."

"'Force him out, Bel!" Saoirse cried.

"'I-I can't . . ."

"'Mothermoons, where *is* he?"

"'GABRIEL!"

'I turned at Chloe's scream, heart sinking. And there I saw him, like a shadow, perched behind us atop the western battlements. A host of wretched were scrambling up the stones around him, dozens of them. And with sinking heart, I realized the Dead had used their unholy strength to simply crawl around the cliffs on our flank, completely avoiding the firetraps we'd laid.

"'Clever bastard . . ." I whispered.

"'Back!" Rafa raised his wheel, burning silver in the dark. "Back now!"

'The foulbloods began spilling down into the bailey, but Chloe and Rafa stood tall, the sister brandishing her silversteel, the wheel in the priest's hands burning like flame. Phoebe pounced upon the first wretched to touch the courtyard stone, tearing it apart as Chloe sliced another off at the knees. I cut down a foulblood on the wall, roared to Saoirse, "We're outflanked, fall back!"

'Bellamy lit his crossbow shot, raising his bow. "He was in my head, he—"

"'LIGHT IT, BOUCHETTE!"

'Saoirse leapt off the battlements to the stone below. The gates began to buckle, more wretched spilling up over the walls as Bellamy fired at the highwalk under my feet. The liquor and sawdust burst into flames, bright and seething. Wretched fell, flesh catching like tinder, a few hissing in agony as they crashed among their fellows below and set more ablaze. But yet more came on, a relentless, starving flood. And so I turned away, eyes upon their general. Fire rising at my back, I charged along the western highwalk, set to slay this dark shepherd and watch his sheep scatter.

"'DANTON!"

'He turned to face me as his flock spilled into the courtyard below. Clad all in black, frockcoat and ruffled sleeves, cravat stained with the blood of the last poor wretch he'd killed. The strength of murders centuries deep unfurled in his veins and coiled behind his eyes.

'*Lay b-but one hand upon him, Gabriel . . .*

'He raised his sabre, met Ashdrinker on his blade and turned her aside. I was dimly aware of Bellamy on the eastern walk, firing flaming shots into

the courtyard below now. Silver light burned in Rafa's hands as Chloe and Saoirse fought side by side. But I had eyes only for my enemy. Our blades sang as we crashed across the highwalk, fury twisting my lips into a snarl. Danton's blade sliced my arm, and I felt not a thing. Another blow carved my cheek to the bone, and I didn't even blink.

"'Ye look thirsty, halfbreed," he hissed.

"'You look frightened, leech," I spat.

"'I like thy new nun. A little shorter than the last one. How does she taste?"

'His strike sent me skidding back across the boards, fangs bared.

"'No, tell me not," he smiled. "I shall learn for myself soon enough."

'I heard Chloe scream, Bellamy cry out. More wretched had flanked us, cresting the eastern walk now. The soothsinger was struck from behind, dropping his bow. The Dead came at him from both sides, and in desperation, he slung his lute off his back, dipped that beautiful bloodwood into the burning barrel beside him, and started swinging it like a club.

"'Back, you bastards! BACK!"

'They were overrunning us now, too many, too clever with this leech lord pulling their strings. Desperate, I threw myself at him, Danton's sword piercing my belly and bursting out my back as at last, at *last*, my hand closed about his throat.

'*Yessss . . .*

'Danton seized my wrist, my fingers brushing his skin. I lunged, snarling, but bloated with the kill, lips red, eyes flooded, the bastard was just stronger than I. And as I felt my bones grinding beneath his grip, I realized how terrible my folly was.

'I was starving. Weak. And he, the son of a Forever King. Shoulders crowned with all night's mantle, all his strength, all his power at his command.

"'Not tonight," he smiled.

'My wrist snapped like a twig. The blade inside me *twisted*. I heard Rafa roaring Bellamy's name, "Run! RUN!" the soothsinger crying out as his burning lute broke across one corpse's shoulder, and a multitude of Dead bore him down. The necklet he wore snapped, musical notes spinning into the night as they sank their teeth into his skin.

"'*BELLAMY!*' Chloe cried.

'I gasped in agony as Danton flexed, lifting me off the ground, his sabre hilt pressed against my belly, his blade buried in my bowels.

"'Blood is owed thee, de León. And blood shall be rep—"

'An axe crashed into the side of the vampire's neck, landing with the song of splintering stone. Danton snarled, and turning on the spot, he slung me with all his strength. I heard Chloe scream as I slid off his blade and flew across the courtyard, weightless, tumbling, crashing into the mosaic floor and smashing it like glass. I felt ribs break. Tasted blood. Black stars in my eyes.

'Saoirse faced Danton on the battlements, the slayer tearing Kindness from the vampire's skin. Her blow would have lopped an ordinary head from its shoulders, split a tree to its roots. But the Beast of Vellene was an ancien Ironheart, his flesh like stone. Still, his throat was shattered, cracks spreading across his skin like veins through pale marble. And fury lit his eyes as Saoirse slammed her shield into his face and her axe into his belly.

'The highblood staggered as the slayer came on, furious, fearless. They crashed atop the highwalk as Chloe reached my side, bloody silversteel in hand, crying, "*Gabriel, get up!*" She dragged me to my feet, my left arm broken, Ashdrinker barely clutched in my other hand. Above us, Rafa had gone to save Bellamy, wheel held out, the wretched hissing and scattering as the priest reached the soothsinger's bloodied body. My ribs were grinding under my skin, blood in my mouth. But I watched Saoirse twirl, strawberry-blonde braids spinning in the air about her as she swung Kindness at Danton once more.

'"Nae man can kill me, vampire!" The slayer grinned, feral, face spattered with his blood as she buried her axe into his shoulder. "And nae devil would dare try!"

'Danton's hand closed around Saoirse's like a vice, her fingers pinned tight on the haft of her axe. "No man nor devil, I," the vampire said.

'He battered her shield aside, drew back his other hand.

'"I am a Prince of Forever."

'And lashing out with clawed fingertips, he tore out Saoirse's throat.

'Blood sprayed, crimson, brilliant. Phoebe looked up from a wretched's torn body, the lioness roaring as her mistress staggered. Chloe reached out across the gulf towards Saoirse, screaming, Rafa watching in horror as Danton threw back his head, laughing as twin fountains of the slayer's blood gushed across his skin.

'Saoirse stumbled to her knees, leathers drenched red. Her hands were pressed to her sundered throat, her eyes wide with disbelief. Phoebe roared in impossible fury, bounding up the highwalk stairs towards her mistress. Rafa had his wheel raised, screaming as he retreated towards the cathedral.

'"Chloe! Back! Get *back*!"

'Turning, I saw that the gates had crumbled, wretched charging on through. Yet more dropped off the eastwalk atop me, claws and fangs tearing my skin. As I fought, desperate, punching and stabbing, I heard a scream of animal terror, and something heavy flew past me, smashing the oncoming wretched aside – Jezebel, whipped into a panic by the Dead and the flames. The dray had kicked free from the stables, charging like a spear now, through the wretched and out the broken gates. I couldn't fault her for fleeing, thinking at least one of us might make it through the night alive. But she'd bought me precious moments at least, enough to climb to my feet and stagger back towards the cathedral.

'"Good luck, girl. Should've g-given you a better name . . ."

'Chloe hauled me backwards, hacking with her silversteel. I followed, gasping, swinging Ashdrinker and taking a wretched's head off its shoulders, slicing another's hands free of its arms, and with a twist, splitting its torso from its hips.

'I stumbled, pushing Chloe away from me. "Get to the cathedral!"

'I hurled my last ignis bomb at the gates, rewarded with a deep roar as the spirit-soaked stones caught fire. Chloe joined Rafa in dragging a bleeding, blood-soaked Bellamy towards the doors for the dead. The young soothsinger was holding his torn throat, whispering, "I . . . I will not . . . will n-not go to my . . ."

'"Phoebe!" I roared. "Get BACK!"

'But the lioness paid me no heed, moving in a blood-red blur along the westwalk. Danton lifted his head from Saoirse's ruins, drenched in the slayer's blood. Reaching up, he tore Kindness from his shattered shoulder, the axe wicked-sharp and beautiful in his hand. And as Phoebe leapt at him, bloody claws and fangs bared, the Beast of Vellene hurled that axe with all his unholy strength.

'The blade sheared through the air, *whooshing* as it came, everknots gleaming upon the bloodstained steel as it tumbled over and over and slammed into Phoebe's chest. The she-lion roared and spun midair, crashing to the boards, a long trail of gleaming gore in her wake as she skidded along the highwalk.

'"Oh, shit . . ." I whispered.

'The lioness came to rest at Danton's feet, her mistress's axe buried in her ribs. She tried to rise, claws scrabbling at the polished tip of Danton's boot. The Beast of Vellene seized the lioness by her throat, hauled her up to dangle, limp and twitching before him. And with casual brutality, he wrenched Kindness free in a gout of blood and flung the fated blade off the cliff at his back. And raising Phoebe high into the air, he hurled the lioness into the courtyard below, her body shattering on the stone.

'I could barely walk, arm and ribs broken, guts hanging from the slice in my belly. Rafa and Chloe dragged Bellamy through the doors for the dead, me behind, all Danton's wretched on our tails just as we planned. I could smell sharp vapour, praying Dior was ready for our little maggot trap. Staggering against the cathedral doors, I turned to watch as Danton leapt down from the walls, soaked in Saoirse's and Phoebe's endings.

'He smiled at me, black eyes in a mask of crimson.

'"Fool ye must think me, de León, to fall for so simple a ploy."

'He lifted a hand, like a conductor before some unholy orchestra. And at his unspoken command, the wretched veered away from our pursuit. Instead of following us mindless through the western entrance, they surged eastwards, towards the dawndoors. Smashing against them now, timbers splintering as they spilled inside; a starving, clawing, flood of dead meat rushing into the tight corridor beyond.

'And Dior Lachance stood at the end of it, a lit cigarelle in hand.

'"Bonsoir, maggots," he whispered.

'The boy flicked the smoke into the liquor-soaked still and slammed the door behind him. Vapour exploded, white-hot and roaring through the corridor. The cathedral doors were blown inwards, Dior thrown to the stone as a long gout of flame scorched the air over his head, burning corpses flailing, falling. Incinerating Danton's wretched in an instant.'

Gabriel leaned back and cracked his knuckles.

'Just as I planned.'

Jean-François ceased his writing, raised one eyebrow.

'You said the *western* corridor was the one set to burn.'

'That's what I told the others.' Gabriel shrugged. 'You don't live for centuries by charging in blind. I knew Danton would get inside one of their heads before he struck us. But the ability to read minds isn't so useful when those minds have been filled with lies. So, save for Dior, I told my comrades what I wanted my enemy to think.'

The historian tapped his lip, gave a grudging nod. 'Rather clever, de León.'

'Danton didn't think so. The Beast of Vellene roared in rage, fangs bared as he stalked across the courtyard. His forces were in charred tatters, but the prince himself was barely scathed. And though Ashdrinker hung bloodied in my hand, I'd nothing left inside.

'*Back, Gabriel. B-back now back back back now.*

'And so I turned, and staggered into the cathedral's belly.

'It was circular, surrounded by pews, a stone altar at its heart. Stained-glass windows ringed the space, only a few inches wide, save one – a lifesize portrait of San Guillaume in the northern wall, tome in one hand, burning torch in the other. Rafa, Chloe, and Dior were knelt around Bellamy, the boy's hands soaked with blood. The soothsinger's throat and wrists and thighs were all torn, Dior pressing red hands to the wounds.

'"Bel?" he pleaded. "*BELLAMY!*"

'The soothsinger's eyes were open, staring at the ceiling. And though the Redeemer's blood had saved him once before – might bring a soul back from the very edge of death, in fact – that same blood seemed of little use once the soul had flown. And looking into Bellamy's empty eyes, I knew.

'"No," Chloe whispered. "*No* . . ."

'"Rafa," I gasped, staggering into the room.

'"Oh, God," he breathed, looking over my shoulder.

'Danton stood behind me, swathed in shadow. The priest rose to his feet, face grim and spattered with blood. And though he stood years past sixty, his back bent and skin wrinkled, Rafa seemed a fucking giant then. Beyond the faith in him, I saw fury, burning like heaven's fire as he raised the wheel in his hand. Light flared, silver-bright, and I staggered past the priest, falling to my knees in a puddle of Bellamy's blood. The thirst roared within me, and for a moment, just for a *second,* it was all I could do not to press my face to the stone and lap it up, like a beggar to breadcrumbs.

'Dior rose up from Bellamy's corpse, spitting at Danton. "You fucking *bastard!*"

'The boy took a step forward, held in check by a desperate Chloe. "Dior, *no!*"

'The Beast of Vellene loomed before us, backlit by the glow of burning corpses. Old Rafa stood tall, dauntless, bathed in the power of his god. They watched each other, priest and vampire, light and dark, flame and shadow, each the other's match.

'"Impasse," Danton breathed.

'"To a fool's eyes," Rafa replied. "And you certainly have those."

'The vampire smiled, red and sensuous. All I could see of him was his face, vulpine, that black widow's peak swept back from his brow, and his hands, ghost-pale and bloodstained as he reached up and straightened the cravat at his throat.

'"I see them in thy mind, priest. With these fool's eyes."

'Rafa refused to answer, standing with his wheel burning before him. But

Danton drifted around the edge of the glow, like a hungry wolf circling ancient firelight.

'"All those dead brothers," he whispered. "Alfonse and Jean-Paul. Old Tariq and little Jamal. Flayed and left for the crows. If thou hadst not set out in search of the Grail, if thou hadst but stayed here among thy little books, thy tiny words, the Inquisition would never have been unleashed upon thy brethren."

'The vampire sighed sadly.

'"They are dead because of *thee*."

'But the old man shook his head, defiant. "Speak not their names. Speak not a word to me. I am deaf to all but the voice of the Lord our God. I am his hand upon this earth, and my faith in his love shall waver not an inch at the deceits of a wretched *worm* like you."

'The priest stepped forward, and I watched in wonder as Danton wavered.

'"Go *back*," Rafa spat, his voice rich with righteous fury. "Go back to the abyss that suckled you, to the loveless father that birthed you, and tell him he may send a hundred sons to test me and I shall best them all. The Lord is my shield unbreakable. He is the air in my lungs and the blood in my veins. And you have *no* power over me."

'The Beast of Vellene narrowed his eyes, slicked back his hair with one bloody hand.

'"Thou hast nothing to fear from me, priest?"

'"Nothing at all, vampire."

'Danton smiled then, dark and poisonous. "Then cast thy wheel aside."

'Rafa blinked. His gaze shifting from the monster before him to the holy circle burning in his hand. I looked between them, bleeding, broken, dread uncoiling in my belly.

'"Rafa . . ." I whispered.

'"The Lord is thy shield unbreakable?" Danton hissed. "Surely then, he will not allow a wretched worm to touch thee? So throw it aside, priest. Face me upon even ground. Show me *true* power. Show me a god who will not let his beloved servant die."

'"Oh, Mothermaid . . ." Chloe breathed.

'Rafa glanced back to the sister, eyes meeting hers. And then and there, the old priest made his mistake. If he had done it – if he'd cast that wheel away and stood undaunted, unafraid, I've no doubt in my mind Danton would have broken like glass. The wheel was just a *thing*. It was Rafa's faith that mattered.

'But the priest hesitated. He doubted. He *feared*.

'And the glow in the wheel began to die.

'Just a flicker at first, like a shadow across the black sun. But the priest's eyes grew wide. A tremor passed through his hand. And he looked up to the vampire and saw him, not cowering now, but standing tall, a hungry smile on ruby lips.

'"Stay back!" Rafa cried. "In the name of God, I command you!"

'And hollow, drenched in blood, Danton threw back his head and laughed. The vampire took one step forward, and Rafa one step back, and with each step, the light in that wheel dimmed further and further still. Chloe moaned in terror, Dior cursing softly as that pale light died. And my heart sank as I saw the last of our hope die with it.

'The Beast of Vellene reached out and closed long, clawed fingers around the wheel in Rafa's hand. Pale flesh sizzling on silver, Danton closed his fist, and the metal crumpled. Rafa opened his mouth, perhaps to pray, perhaps to curse, but the Beast's other hand snaked out, seizing the priest's shoulder, and as Rafa cried, "Save me, God!" the vampire opened his maw and sank his fangs deep into the holy man's throat.

'"Rafa!" Chloe screamed, and "NO!" Dior roared, and mouth filled with blood, teeth gritted, I dragged myself to my feet. Our last bastion had fallen, the priest groaning as the kiss took hold, lifting his arms and throwing them, like a drowning man to driftwood, about the shoulders of the thing that was murdering him. Chloe raised her silversteel, screaming in rage, but I grabbed her, stopped her from throwing herself onto that same pyre.

'"Chloe, he'll kill you!"

'I looked about us, to San Guillaume's window in the wall behind us, and with the arm that still worked, I hurled Ashdrinker, shattering the glass to splinters.

'"Go!"'

'Dior grabbed Chloe, dragging the sister away, me limping behind. The boy scrambled through the window, pulling Chloe through, and I left a trail of blood as I hauled myself after them, shredding my skin. Chloe was gasping for breath, eyes wide with terror and madness as I picked up Ashdrinker . . .

'*FLY, GABRIEL!*

'. . . and slipped the blade back into her scabbard. We had nowhere to run, yet I grabbed Chloe's hand and run we did, dragging Dior away from the broken window where Danton now stood, drenched in Saoirse's and Phoebe's and Rafa's blood.

'"I told thee I could follow forever, de León!"

'We backed up the stairs to the monastery walls, the highwalk running the edge of the cliffs. The drop loomed behind us, jagged rocks like teeth, a hundred and fifty feet down into lightless black. Danton was on the stairs now, smiling, a single breath away.

"'W-we have to," Chloe whispered.

"'It's too high," the boy breathed. "The rocks . . . I can't swim!"

'I gritted my teeth. "Take my hand, boy."

'And gripping tight, wincing in agony as Chloe seized my broken wrist, I dragged them both up onto the battlements. The dark opened its arms below us, Dior's eyes wide with terror, Danton coming at us like a black wind. Kicking off the railing, I jumped far as I could, Chloe holding one hand, Dior the other. Out into the windswept night, weightlessness and vertigo, the scream rising in Chloe's throat suddenly cut short as a pale hand reached into the brink and seized the collar of Dior's fine magik frockcoat.

'The boy wailed as Danton's fist closed tight, jerking us to a halt. I roared in agony, wounds tearing, broken bones grinding. Chloe shrieked, both our hands slicked with blood. My muscles screamed as we hung, suspended in a chain, Chloe holding onto me, me onto Dior, and Danton onto us all. My hands were full – there was naught I could do as, with a triumphant smile and the strength of bloody centuries, the Beast hauled us back up.

'In a second, he'd have us.

'In a second, it'd be over, everything for nothing.

'And in that second, Chloe looked up into my eyes. Burning with familiar fire.

"'Dior is all that matters, Gabe."

'And letting go of my hand, she plunged down into the dark.

"'*CHLOE!*" Dior roared.

'No time to think. No time to mourn. Time only to reach up, broken hand and bloody fangs, taking hold of that ridiculous coat and the waistcoat and shirt underneath and seizing a fistful, agony flaring down my shattered arm as I ripped seam and thread, silvered buttons spinning into the night as, magik or no, the coat slipped away from his arms, my weight dragged him down, Danton spitting a black curse as he staggered back, left only with a torn coat of midnight-blue and silver curlicue in hand.

'Rushing wind in my ears.

'A screaming boy in my arms.

'And down, down into the dark, we fell.'

✦ XVI ✦

THE ONE THING

'WHEN I WAS a lad, I used to play a game with my sisters, Amélie and Celene. It was named Elements. You close your hand, count one, two, *three*, then form your hand into a shape. Fist for wood. Fingers upturned for fire. Flat palm for water. Water beat fire. Fire beat wood. Wood beat water. Having fallen a hundred and fifty feet into it, it's now my official position that water beats just about anything.

'It felt like stone as we hit it. I've been punched by ancien of the Blood Dyvok, taken silverbomb explosions to the chest, been inside a chymical still as the mad bastard who ran it blew it sky high, and I tell you now, I've never felt anything like it. If I were an ordinary man, I'd have been dead. Story finished. Song sung. But broken and bleeding as I was, I was still paleblood, and like old Master Greyhand used to assure me as he cut me to ribbons every night at spar, palebloods don't die easy. The impact was deafening, rocking my brain inside my skull, turning black to blinding white. I lost consciousness, I'm sure of it. But only for a second. The cold snapped me back into my body like a bowstring.

'All was freezing black, above and below. But as I opened my eyes, tumbling in the water, I saw him. Ashen hair adrift around his face, hanging limp as a boned fish. And hurting as I was, still I lunged, slipping my good arm around his waist and kicking desperately, piercing the surface with a ragged, bruised-bone gasp.

'"Lachance?" I roared. "Lachance!"

'He made no reply, eyes closed, head lolling on his neck. But miraculously, somehow, he was breathing. I looked around, desperate, bellowing over the river's rush.

'"*CHLOE!*"

'No sound. No sign. Nothing. If I dived below to look for her, the boy in my arms would drown. And if we stayed in this water, he'd freeze along with it. And so, roaring her name one last time, eyes burning, I held Dior tight and swam north across the Volta, broken arm trailing at my side. Away from those cliffs above, the slaughterhouse of San Guillaume, the poor wretches Danton had butchered. I'd warned them all, Chloe too, but still, I had to push it from my mind. The sight of Saoirse being ripped ear to ear. Bellamy's eyes wide open, blinded forever. And Rafa. That poor bastard. Dying with Danton's mouth on his throat and the name of the God that had failed him on his lips.

'I swam, bloody water behind me, every muscle screaming. My only solace was a familiar weight on my hip; Ashdrinker, slapping my leg as I kicked towards the shoreline. I'd lost them all, but I'd kept my sword at least. And as a sodden cough wracked his frame and a feeble groan spilled over purpling lips, I knew I still had . . .

'"Lachance."

'He groaned again, near senseless.

'"Hold onto me, boy."

'His eyelids were heavy, and he clung weakly to the arm I'd wrapped around his chest. But though I could tell he was terrified of the water about him, though he knew if I were to let him go, he'd sink like a stone, even with the cold, he didn't tremble.

'Whatever else, Dior Lachance was never a coward.

'We reached the shallows, and I found my footing, slinging the lad over my shoulder. He was still senseless from the fall, ash-white hair hanging lank over his face. I'd ripped every scrap of clothing off him from the waist up to free him from Danton's clutches, and I knew the little bastard would freeze soon enough. So staggering up the wooded bank, I thumped him against an old rotted tree, and wincing at my still-shattered wrist, I shrugged my greatcoat off my shoulders.

'And then, I saw it.

'The one thing that would change *everything*.

'Dior was coatless and shirtless. But not entirely naked. Chloe's bandage was still around his throat, but another bandage was wrapped about his chest, many times over. At first, I thought the boy might have been wounded; the bandage some holdover from an older battle. But then, beneath the wrappings, I saw it. Saw *them*. Bound uncomfortably tight, but unmistakable.'

Jean-François blinked, glancing up from his tome and snapping his fingers.

'Breasts.'

'Oui,' Gabriel nodded.

Jean-François smiled all the way to his dark eyes, and clapped as if delighted. 'Dior is a girl's name as well as a boy's, Silversaint.'

'Do tell, vampire.'

The historian laughed uproariously, slapping his knee and stomping his feet. 'You never suspected? But your dear Chloe *told you* that falling star had marked the Grail's birth! *That's* why he wouldn't take off his shirt to dry it. *That's* why Saoirse referred to him by a feminine endearment like 'flower'. *He* wasn't a fourteen-year-old boy, *she* was a sixteen-year-old girl! Oh, de León, you are priceless. How much the *fool* did you feel?'

The silversaint reached for the wine, muttering. 'No need to rub it in, prick.'

Jean-François chuckled, and returned to his tome.

'I stumbled back, greatcoat in hand, rocked onto my heels. I looked Dior over, eyes roaming the shoulders, the waist, the jaw. I'd thought her just a lad, androgyne perhaps, pretty, oui, but the way she spat, swore, smoked, swaggered . . . Great Redeemer, the little bitch had me fooled. And then those blue eyes fluttered open, widening as Dior realized that fancy coat and silken shirt were gone. Pale hands flashed up to cover her chest – some feeble attempt at modesty we both knew was doomed to fail.

'The girl looked up into my eyes, horror, indignity, fear.

'"Fuck," she said.

'"My," I replied.

'"Face," we chorused.'

✦ XVII ✦

REMEMBRANCE

JEAN-FRANÇOIS WAS STILL chuckling, the vampire shaking his head as he wrote in his accursed book. The cell about them was chill, silent, save for the gentle scratching upon the page. Dipping his quill again, the historian frowned, realizing his ink bottle was almost empty.

'Meline?' he called. 'My dove?'

The door opened immediately. The thrall with her long chains of auburn hair stood at the threshold; a puppet summoned by invisible strings. She was a beautiful woman, Gabriel realized, wrapped in black corsetry and lace. The blood she'd suckled from Jean-François's thumb had healed her entirely now; only the faintest scar marked the place where he'd bitten her wrist. But still, Gabriel could smell it – faint traces of rust and autumn's fading. He pictured the woman on her knees before him, kohl-rimmed eyes gazing up at him as she brushed those auburn locks back from the pale promise of her neck. His blood thrummed southwards at the thought, leaving him hard and aching in his leathers.

'Master?' she asked.

'More ink, my dove,' Jean-François said. 'And something to drink for our guest?'

Gabriel emptied his glass and nodded. 'Another bottle.'

'Wine?' Dark eyes drifted to the bulge below the silversaint's belt. 'Or something stronger?'

Gabriel's eyes flashed. 'Another bottle.'

Jean-François glanced to the thrall, and Meline dropped into a smooth curtsey, feet whispering as she retreated down the stairs. Gabriel counted the number of steps again, listening to the faint song in the château below – laughter, still echoes, faint screaming. The night was past its deeping now, and he could feel the distant promise of dawn on the horizon. He wondered if they'd let him sleep.

He wondered if he'd dream.

'The hope of the empire entire,' Jean-François mused. 'The last scion of the line of Esan. The cup that held the blood of the Redeemer himself. A sixteen-year-old girl.'

Gabriel poured the last few drops of Monét into his glass. 'Plot twist.'

'And Danton had no hint of this revelation either, I take it? I imagine his pursuit would have been rather more single-minded had he known the truth of things. Despite his age, the Beast of Vellene ever favoured the pretty demoiselles.'

'Chloe knew.' Gabriel shrugged. 'Saoirse, too. But Sœur Sauvage kept the girl's secret buried deep enough that Danton didn't pluck it from her thoughts the night he chose to visit them. He never bothered to rummage around in Saoirse's head. And Dior's mind was always a closed room to the Dead.'

'And so, Danton toyed with *you* instead.' Jean-François tutted. 'Allowing your little famille vendetta to distract him from simply plucking his prize, and instead watching it slip, literally and metaphorically, through his bloody fingers.'

'I wouldn't describe the vendetta between me and the Voss as *little,* Chastain. The bloodfeud between me and Fabién's brood had been brewing half my life.'

'And so.' Jean-François steepled slender fingers at ruby lips, watching the man opposite with hunter's eyes. 'We return. Back to the beginning. And San Michon.'

Gabriel sighed, looking at the empty glass in his hand. Wondering if he were numb enough. Cold enough. He could feel them both; the endings to the tales he'd begun, like old scars on tattooed skin. He wondered which would tear wider, bleed harder, and for a brief, moonstouched moment, he considered the glass in his hand, the blade he might fashion of it; not enough for a vampire's skin, surely, but enough for his own.

Not across the stream, but up the river. The shard digging deep, letting that accursed blood flow. But such thoughts were folly, and he knew it – knew it from bitter experience and long, lonely nights, watching the wounds close over before his tear-stung eyes, the curse in his veins not allowing him to die. To sleep.

To sleep and never dream.

Meline returned, footsteps soft on the stairs. She stepped through the door she'd left unlocked, golden tray poised on one manicured hand. The damask of her skirts rustled like falling leaves as she swept into the room, and Gabriel could feel the warmth of her body, hear the music of her pulse as she placed a fresh bottle of Monét upon the table between him and the historian. She sank to her knees then, head bowed, hands upturned like a priestess before the marbled statue of a god of old. And Jean-François plucked the fresh bottle of ink from her open palms.

'Merci, my dove.'

'Do you desire anything else, Master?'

The vampire reached out, running one long, sharp fingernail ever so gently down the woman's cheek. Her breath caught in her breast as he hooked his claw beneath her chin, lifting her face so she could meet his eyes.

'Oh, my darling,' he whispered. 'Always.'

Her lips parted, a trembling sigh slipped from her mouth. But the vampire withdrew his hand the way God withdraws a blessing. 'Leave us now.'

'I am your servant, Master.'

The thrall rose on shaking legs, curtseyed, and retreated from the room. The pair were left alone again, killer and monster, an ocean unsaid between them. The vampire watched Gabriel refill his glass, the wine dark as blood yet holding none of its promise, brought brimming to the edge. Leathered wings cut through the night skies beyond the window. The twin moons hung in the heavens, dipped crimson.

'We must return there eventually, de León,' Jean-François said. 'Back to the seven pillars and the Scarlet Foundry and the walls of the Gauntlet. To wise Master Greyhand and cruel Seraph Talon, to treacherous young Aaron de Coste and your final Hunt together. You had been sent out onto the frozen roads of the Nordlund, Silversaint. A Voss of ancient blood had been behind the malady in Skyefall. An Ironheart of immeasurable power was already east of the Godsend Mountains, when the Forever King himself was still massing his Endless Legion in Talhost. There is a secret buried within your vaults here, de León. A secret soaked in darkest blood and whispered with holy tongues. And I would like to unearth it before you are too befuddled with wine to remember.'

'But that's the problem, vampire. Hard as I try. Much as I wish.'

Gabriel looked to the bleak night outside. Hands curling to fists, ears ringing with the song of silver trumpets, tongue tingling with the taste of fruit forbidden.

'I remember *everything*.'

Book Five

THE ROAD TO HELL

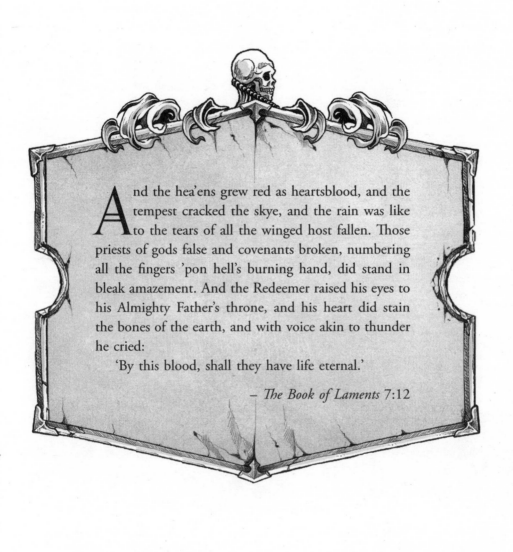

And the hea'ens grew red as heartsblood, and the tempest cracked the skye, and the rain was like to the tears of all the winged host fallen. Those priests of gods false and covenants broken, numbering all the fingers 'pon hell's burning hand, did stand in bleak amazement. And the Redeemer raised his eyes to his Almighty Father's throne, and his heart did stain the bones of the earth, and with voice akin to thunder he cried:

'By this blood, shall they have life eternal.'

– The Book of Laments 7:12

✦ I ✦

TRUTH BEYOND TRUTH

"'YOUR SISTER'S NAME is . . . Celene. But that is not what you call her."

'Seraph Talon sat across the fire from me, dark eyes on mine. The cave about us was small, warm, the blaze reflected in Master Greyhand's stare as he looked on. My brow was knitted as I met Talon's gaze, my head filled with as much noise as I could conjure.

"'Black hair," the thin man declared, stroking his moustache. "Black eyes. A troublemaker. An instigator. Hence, you call her . . . Hellion."

"'Shit," I whispered.

'I broke our staring contest, sighing as I massaged my temples. My head was aching, my heart low. Despite my best efforts, the seraph had once again plucked the images and truths out of my head after only a minute or so.

"'You're improving, my spud-witted little shit-bucket," Talon declared. "But not enough. If I can still pierce your defences, an elder Voss will shatter them in a bloody blinking. Work at it."

"'I *have* been working at it, Seraph. Every day since we left San Michon."

"'Day *and* night, then," Greyhand growled. "When we find our prey, you must be ready."

'I kept my face stone, but inside, I scoffed. *When we found our prey?*

'Great Redeemer, we'd been on this Hunt for months.

'Seraph Talon, Aaron, Greyhand, and me. A stranger company I'd never known. After setting out from San Michon, we'd headed northwest to the Godsend Mountains, following a month-old trail through a vista of chill black peaks and dying trees. Winter hadn't truly bitten when we set out, but now, the snows fell heavy, the roads, lonely and bleak.

'As we travelled, Frère Greyhand had used gifts of the Blood Chastain to track our quarry, murmuring to wise old owls and conferring with sly foxes as we bedded down. Many of the beasts had no clue about our prey; others whispered of different monsters, dark shapes rising in the southern weald and faekin stalking the moors with knives of gleaming bone. Still, a precious few had spoken of a woman – darkthing, deadthing – riding lonely roads in the company of other shadows. Heading north. Always north.

'And like good hounds, we'd followed.

'We'd visited the bustling town of Almwud and found a tale akin to Skyefall – the daughter of the alderman murdered, a bevy of highborn gentry fallen to a wasting sickness. The nest we'd burned out was small – a single fledgling who knew nothing of what it was. In the crossroad hamlet of Benhomme and the silver mining town of Tolbrook, we heard similar tales. And slowly, we'd begun to paint a portrait of the thing we stalked. This pale huntress who filled children's graves wherever she walked.

'This Marianne Luncóit.

'*Raven Child.*

'She was beautiful – all mentioned that, and ever first. A grace so perilous that men and women alike couldn't help but adore her. She hunted among high society, all flattery and silken finery, striking like a spider at their sons and daughters as she departed.

'A half-dozen kept her company. The first, another coldblood who masqueraded as her son – a dark-haired, gilded youth named Adrien. Five other men attended the pair as servants. In Tolbrook, Luncóit had informed the alderman she was surveying a claim in the hills above the town, just as she'd done in Skyefall. In the high-walled keep of Ciirfort, the charming madame and her handsome son had been treated to a tour of the garrison by an enraptured capitaine, whose daughter was later found murdered in her bed. We had no real certainty as to why this vampire was stalking towns along the Godsend, but she was doing so with intent. And we were always a few steps behind.

'The rivers were crusted with ice now, wintersdeep approaching on cold feet. We were camped beneath a snow-capped peak named for Eloise, the Angel of Retribution. A little farther north loomed the mountain named for Raphael, Angel of Wisdom. And in the valley between lay the next stop in our months-long search – the richest silver mining town in the province, and as fate would have it, high seat of Aaron's stepfather.

'The Barony of Coste.

'We were on bitter terms, Aaron and me. I was still sure the bastard had tried to have me killed back in San Michon, and got poor Sister Aoife murdered in the process. I was ill at ease with the idea that we were journeying to his former home, that I'd be laying my head down among his people. For his part, Aaron treated me as shitty as he always had. Watching me across the fire at night with silent menace. But as we'd travelled closer to his birthplace, I'd expected our lordling's mood to brighten at least a little. He'd always spoken of his mother fondly, and I thought he'd be joyous at the thought of reunion.

'And yet, the nearer we drew to Coste, the darker his mood became.

'That night before we arrived, we were camped in a cave on Raphael's eastern flank. Our sosyas were clustered at the entrance, snow clinging to their shaggy coats. Talon had been schooling Aaron and me in matters of mental defence along the road, and while I didn't like the seraph in my head, I knew vampires of the Blood Voss could read the thoughts of lesser men. Better Talon in my mind strengthening it than one of *them* pillaging it.

'Our lesson done for the night, the seraph held his hands to our fire. "Great Redeemer, it grows cold enough to freeze the blood in a man's veins."

'I rubbed my aching brow, glanced northwards. "And the rivers in their beds."

'Aaron met my eyes, nodding also. We may have been at odds like fire and ice, but in one dread, we were of accord. "The Forever King will march from Talhost soon."

'"Probably," Greyhand grunted. "Yet not a certainty. Patience is a quality that ancient vampires have in abundance. Fabién Voss will march when he is ready."

'"We should be doing more," Aaron scowled. "Not just chasing ghosts and shadows."

'"An elder Voss is not east of the Godsend at trivial purpose, de Coste," Talon growled. "In thwarting Luncóit, we thwart whatever part she plays in Fabién's design."

'We settled into silence, staring at the flames. I understood we needed to be as patient as our quarry, but like de Coste, I felt we'd been stalking Marianne Luncóit forever. The threat of the Forever King's legion hung over the Nordlund like a headsman's axe now. The Emperor's armies were split between the cityforts of Avinbourg in the north and Charinfel in the south, and we still didn't know where the blow would fall.

'"Blessed Mothermaid," I growled. "It's cold as a bog hag's tit in here."

'Seraph Talon's eyes glittered under the black arcs of his brows. Smoothing his long moustache, the little man rummaged in his saddlebag, produced a silver flask. Taking a deep swig, he offered it to me. I could smell the vodka from where I sat.

"'Merci, no, Seraph.'"

"'Come now, frailblood.'" The little man waved the flask in my face. "*Kindness spurned is ire earned*, so sayeth the Lord. And the Testaments name drink no sin.'"

"'It's not the sin of it, Seraph. I've just no wish to follow in my stepfather's footsteps. He was a devil on the drink.'"

"'Hmmf.'" Aaron reached for the flask in Talon's hand. "Mine also.'"

'I blinked at that, studying de Coste across the flames as he took a long, slow pull. Our lordling had only ever spoken of his mother, never the fellow who raised him.

"'My stepfather was a soldier,'" Greyhand declared. "Loved a drink. I remember he got right slovenly one eve, lost his key. So when he finally dribbled home, he dragged himself through the window, crawled into bed with what he thought was my mama. It turned out to be the magistrate's house, and the dame in question, his wife.'"

'Chuckles rolled around our fire. Even Greyhand managed a whisper of a smile.

"'The magistrate was not pleased.'"

"'Ah, but what about his wife, Master?'" I asked.

'Greyhand fixed me across the fire, deadpan. "You'd have to ask her, cub.'"

'I laughed again, spitting onto my whetstone as I sharpened Lionclaw. "When I was little, Mama got so fed up with my stepfather's drinking, she hid his clothes so he couldn't hit the taverne. He put on her church dress and went anyway. Just marched down the street in her prièdi best, proud as a lord. I remember it was white. Had blue flowers on it.'"

"'Sounds fetching,'" Greyhand nodded.

"'He *did* have fine ankles,'" I admitted grudgingly.

'Seraph Talon took another long swig, then handed his flask back to Aaron. "Do you remember that Hunt down in Beaufort, Greyhand?'"

"'With old Yannick? How could I forget?'"

'My ears perked up at that. I'd known Frère Yannick only as a broken man, put out of his misery in the Red Rite that first night I'd arrived in San Michon. But I always loved hearing the stories of old silversaints. Tales of horror and glory and blood.

"'You two hunted together?'" I asked, looking between the men.

"'I was not always a Seraph of the Order, shitblood,'" Talon growled. "I earned my aegis when you were still a tadpole paddling about in your godless father's janglesack."

"'It was many years ago, Little Lion," Greyhand said. "I was only newly sworn. A duskdancer had been stalking the Beaufort docks for months. Old Abbot Dulean sent the three of us down there to put a righteous end to it."

'Talon nodded. "The more a duskdancer takes the shape of his beast, the more the beast leaves its mark on him. This bastard was an old one. Wolfborn and hideous. Even when he wore the skin of a man, he had a wolf's eyes. Wolf's tail. Wolf's feet. So he'd developed a taste for streetwalkers, luring them into the shadows with the promise of coin and then gutting them like lambs. We decided to use bait to lure him out. So we drew straws, and old Yannick found himself in a wig and backless dress, smothered in whore's perfume and parading up and down the fucking jetty like ha-royale strumpet."

'Greyhand shook his head. "Finest legs I've ever seen on a man."

"'They worked too. Not even that bastard duskdancer could resist. Mark me now, frailblood. A good hunter uses the appetites of his prey against them. Want is a weakness."

'Greyhand sighed as he stared into the fire. "I miss that mouthy old dog. It was Yannick who named me Greyhand."

"'He was a good hunter," Talon nodded. "And a good friend."

"'Oui." My master shook his head, and I saw sorrow in his pale green eyes. "But Yannick made the right choice. I pray Almighty God and all Seven Martyrs grant me the same courage when the thirst calls and my time comes."

'I could still remember the horror I'd felt at old Yannick's ending; ritually murdered by the abbot and thrown to the waters of the Mère before the sangirè – the *red thirst* – could consume him. It was a silversaint's death. A man's death. But looking at the sevenstar in my palm, I found myself pondering that same paleblood curse in my veins. No matter how much sanctus we smoked to stave it off, I knew the sangirè would eventually drive all of us to madness. And before that, each of us would have to make Yannick's choice.

"'Better to die a man than live a monster," I murmured.

'Talon nodded, grim. "Véris."

"'Véris," Greyhand said, stirring the fire.

'*Truth beyond truth.*

'We sat with the sound of crackling logs, Greyhand and Talon now staring wordless into the flames. The silence stretched on, Aaron drinking deep from the flask, mute and sullen. I finally spoke again to break the uncomfortable quiet.

"'Why did old Yannick name you Greyhand, Master?"

"'Mmm. A tale not worth the telling, Little Lion.'"

"'You know, the stonemasons in San Michon have a wager. Whoever learns your real name wins a whole week's coin without labour.'"

"'Gambling is ungodly. And last I heard it was only three days' worth.'"

"'It seems your legend grows in the telling,' I smiled.

"'Legends always do, Little Lion. And ever in the wrong direction. But a man who sings his own song is deaf to the music of heaven. How shall I hear the word of God, if I am in love with the sound of my own voice?'

'I could feel Greyhand's quiet confidence. His unshakeable faith. He'd no need for mortal accolade or to strum his own lute – his service to the Almighty was enough, and sweet fucking Redeemer, I envied him that humility. But Talon spoke, eyes on our master.

"'I'll tell the story, then. Yannick shared it with me one eve over a cup of wine.'

"'Ah, such impeccable sources,' Greyhand scoffed. "Drunken gossip around the tankards of San Michon.'

'But Talon spoke regardless, his voice dropping as he leaned into the tale. "This was back when Greyhand was still an apprentice, see. Tale has it, he and his master were attacked by five coldbloods, deep in an old ruin near Loch Sídhe. His master Michel was slain in the ambush, and Greyhand retreated. But at dawn, he returned alone, nothing but his sword and faith to guard him. And when he emerged from that pit, the ashes of those five leeches were caked so thick on his fists, you couldn't see his skin. So." Talon nodded to our master. "Greyhand.'

"'Mmf,' he scowled.

"'I note a marked lack of denials, Master,' I said.

"'What point denial? When the gossips have already made up their minds? When next you tell the tale, Seraph, have me slay a dozen. Makes the number rounder.'

"''Tis a heavy burden, Master,' I smiled. "To be a hero.'

"'Hero,' he scoffed. "Mark my words, youngblood. You don't want to be a hero. Heroes die unpleasant deaths, far from home and hearth.'

'I looked into the flames. Thinking about what I was. The fate that had befallen old Yannick, and the madness that awaited us all. Greyhand spat into the fire, flames hissing.

"'Enough idle chatter. We reach Coste amorrow. What should your fellows know of the town that birthed you, Initiate?'

'All eyes turned to Aaron as he took another sip, grimacing as he swallowed. Again, the notion that I was stepping into this bastard's birthden felt like a stone in my belly.

'"Coste is the richest town in the province," Aaron said. "Its fortune made in silver and iron. The Baron is favoured at court, friend to Emperor Alexandre. My brother Jean-Luc is capitaine in the Golden Host at Avinbourg. My mother, His Imperial Majesty's second cousin. And then, there's me."

'"We've gained ground on our quarry this last month," Greyhand said. "It may be our Raven Child awaits us within the walls of Coste. And the Feast of San Maximille falls in two days. No doubt the town will be indulging?"

'Aaron sneered. "The Baron de Coste is never one to miss a chance to feast."

'"Be of good cheer, then. Our quarry is a bon vivant, lured towards the finer things like a bowerbird to shine. If she lurks in Coste's shadows, she should have occasion to be drawn into the light. So sleep now. Fear no darkness." Greyhand threw a warning glance to me. "And dream not of heroism, but of faithful service to the Lord your God."

'We settled abed. I listened to the crackling fire and tried not to think about the cold, the serpent sleeping across the flames from me. I knew not what awaited us in Coste, nor whether Aaron would try to finish what he'd started in San Michon, but I could sense our prey was near. I'd let impatience get the best of me during our hunt in Skyefall, and I was determined not to fail again. But despite Greyhand's warning, still I dreamed of glory.

'Glory, and a smile framed by a beauty spot, and locks of raven black hair.'

✦ II ✦

UNWELCOME GUESTS

'WE ARRIVED IN Coste the next day, just as the sun was sinking to sleep. The city was a grander affair even than Skyefall; a beautiful sprawl of dark stone and pale roofs carved at the banks of a magnificent waterfall. Winter hadn't yet turned the falls to ice, but they were almost there – huge sculptures of frozen water hanging over the drop, glittering like diamond. The great city was split in two, three bridges crossing the freezing river. A princely keep sat on a ridge above it all, flying flags of a quartered green field graced with two crossed warhammers – the crest of the famille de Coste. As we rode through the mighty gates, the whole city was ringing with song despite the chill.'

Jean-François wordlessly tapped his quill, raising one brow.

Gabriel sighed. 'The Feast of Maximille the Martyr is the grandest piss-up in the Elidaeni calendar. Less solemn than Firstmas or Wheelsday – the feasts of the Redeemer's birth and death – it's one of the most important festivals of the year. Maximille de Augustin was a warlord who, depending on who you believe, either received his commands direct from the mouth of Almighty God, or was just goat-fuckingly insane. Either way, he raised an army and seized control of Elidaen, Nordlund, and Ossway in the name of the One Faith.

'He was killed in battle by an arrow to the eye, which you'd think would be the sort of thing Almighty God would warn his Chosen One about. But his sons went on to conquer the Sūdhaem and Talhost, finally uniting the warring kingdoms into a single empire under the banner of the Wheel. They forged the Fivefold Throne, carved out the Augustin dynasty, and named dear old Papa the seventh martyr. Folk have been getting bowel-bustingly shitfaced on the anniversary of his death ever since.

'Aaron pulled his tricorn low as we rode beyond the walls, collar laced high so none could see his face. Some folk were suspicious at the sight of us, making the sign of the wheel as we passed. Others stared with want in their eyes, sensing the beast beneath our skins. But most were into their cups, and paid little mind. Coste was the biggest city I'd seen in my life. Thirty thousand people called it home, and most were in the streets that night. If a vampire hid among this multitude, it'd take the finest hounds to sniff her out.

'But I fancied us that and more.

'Riding through those gates, I was struck by how strange a turn my life had taken. Nine months back, I'd been sleepwalking; a blacksmith's boy with no clue of the future rushing at him headlong. And now, here it was, swathed in black and etched in silver. I confess I'd never felt so alive. A young lion at hunt, nose to the wind. And though I caught no hint of our quarry yet, if nothing else, I was awake.

'We took the winding roads up the hill, past overfull tavernes and rollicking bawdy houses. Aaron nodded to the keep above. "My stepfather throws a feast for his lords every year on this eve. Those halls shall be crowded with Coste's finest tonight."

'"So you're planning to wait outside, then?" I growled.

'"Stay up all night writing that one, did you, Peasant?"

'I flipped him the Fathers, and de Coste slapped his neck as if swatting a bug. I was fully aware it was foolish to be spitting at each other at a time like this. But I also knew I might find myself alone with Aaron watching my back tonight, and after the attack he'd orchestrated on me in the stables, I'd no trust he wouldn't put a knife in it.

'"Stop your squabbling," Greyhand growled. "We are at Hunt tonight."

'I waved at my greatcoat and sword. "If intent is to lie in wait among the sheep until the wolf shows teeth, it seems unwise to dress as shepherds?"

'Talon nodded. "We *do* stick out like four leather-clad thumbs."

'"I'm certain suitable attire can be acquired from the master of the house." Aaron rubbed his jaw and sighed. "So I suppose we'd best go speak to him."

'Our horses' shoes rang on the cobbles as we climbed the road upwards, and the light had well failed before we reached the keep. The portcullis was raised in welcome, the drawbridge lowered. Torches burned on the walls, lighting chill mists in the bailey. I could see men-at-arms, well-arrayed in steel finery and tabards of the house. The flag of the famille de Coste flew proud on the walls, spit and shine on every surface.

'An officer of the gens d'armes came out to greet us, clad in heavy mail. Before de Coste had even pulled down his collar, I saw recognition in the man's eyes. "Master Aaron . . ."

'"Well met, Capitaine Daniau. How is your son?"

'"Passing fair, my lord, merci." The man looked among us, and I could tell from his mix of fear and soft loathing that he knew *exactly* what we were. "What brings you home after so many months, Master Aaron? And in . . . such company?"

'"I have need to speak to my mother."

'"She is preparing for the feast, my lord, I fear she cannot—"

'"I fear manners have slipped in my absence, Capitaine." The blonde lordling sat taller, that familiar mix of arrogance and confidence oozing from his pores. "Unless it has become habit in Château de Coste for the manor-born to be questioned by the help?"

'"Forgive me, my lord. But your father left word if ever you were to . . ."

'The man's voice failed as Aaron leaned closer, a predator's gleam in his eyes. "*Send word to my mother I wish to see her, Capitaine.*"

'The man's face slackened, his eyes dulled. "At once, my lord."

'"See our horses stabled. If you've men sitting idle, set them to the watch. Mortal peril comes to your master's house this night, Daniau. And it wears no silver on its breast."

'I watched Aaron slipping into the role of the nobleson as easy as putting on an old coat, reminded of all the things I disliked about him. He spat orders to those men like he was their better, and I'd no doubt he believed it – of them *and* me. This prick was a snake. No matter if we were on the Hunt – I was damned if I'd give him chance to bite me again.

'Ten minutes later, we stood in the grand entrance hall of Coste keep, surrounded by fine tapestries and marble statues. A broad staircase led upwards, and to our left, I could see a beautiful ballroom, bedecked in finery and buzzing with servants. Long tables were being laid with pale linen, and beyond, a quartet of soothsingers practised above a dancefloor inlaid with bloodwood and gleaming mother-of-pearl.

'If the wealth of Skyefall had left me queasy, the opulence here was sickening. I couldn't imagine what it must've been to grow up in a place like this – no wonder de Coste acted as if the Mothermaid sucked his cock dry before mornmeal every day.

'"My son?"

'Aaron looked up, and I saw all tension melt from his frame. A stately woman stood on the landing, clad in a beautiful emerald gown, a spectacular powdered wig propped atop her head. She was perhaps forty, powdered pale, her eyes the same bright blue as Aaron's.

'"Mama," he whispered.

'"Aaron!" she cried, sweeping down and into his arms. Tears shone in her lashes as she held him tight, twirling him on the spot as if they danced. "When did you arrive?"

'"Just now. You remember Master Greyhand? These are my comrades, Mama. Seraph Talon de Montfort and Gabriel de León."

'The Baronne graced us all with a perfect curtsey. "Any comrades of my dearest are welcome within these halls. But praise San Maximille and the Mothermaid, I thought not to see you again so soon, my son. What have I done to deserve such a blessing?"

'"What indeed?" came a low, rasping voice.

'I turned to the stairwell above, and saw a man watching the reunion with narrowed eyes. The Baron de Coste was arrayed in a green frockcoat of finest cut, silken hose and shirt. He radiated cold authority, and dripped wealth from every gold-trimmed finger. But no amount of leaden paint could mask the burst capillaries scrawled on his cheeks or the strawberry plumpness of his nose.

'Growing up around a drunkard makes a lad an expert at spotting others, and I marked the Baron for a lush as soon as I laid eyes on him. He wasn't the kind who'd grown bloated with it; rolling to his cups like a whale through the surf. No, Aaron's stepfather was the breed whose disease eats him from the inside out. The Baron de Coste was a well-dressed skeleton, glowering at Aaron with undisguised contempt.

'"How comes it you visit on this of all nights, bastard?" He looked over our number with a soft sneer. "And what in the name of Almighty God possessed you to bring a bevy of halfbreed swine to my door?"

'"Baron de Coste." Greyhand bowed. "Well met again, seigneur. I apologize for—"

'"I have as little use for your apology as I have for your company, halfbreed," the Baron said. "You were welcome in my halls when last you visited only because you took this mongrel off my hands. Am I to understand you are returning him?"

'"We are here at our abbot's behest, Baron." Talon bowed. "We have reason to believe you may have an unwelcome guest at your feast this evening."

'"Several, it seems."

'"A vampire," Aaron said. "One we've stalked for months now."

'I saw de Coste's mother tense at that. But the Baron himself seemed unimpressed. "Well, it cannot be the one that despoiled your mama, bastard. Your rapist father was sent to his well-deserved hell years ago. The same that awaits you, I expect."

"'A woman," Aaron replied, undaunted. "An ancien steeped in murder, who has stalked the edge of the Godsend for moons now. Your guests may be in danger." He looked to his mama. "*You* may be in danger."

'De Coste turned his eyes back to the Baron. His jaw was clenched in defiance, and he stood taller, striking the pose of the proud young lord. But though I was again reminded of all the things I hated about him, I could see the little shit's pose for what it was now. A façade to hide the fear within. A fear I could sense in him, sure as breathing. Despite all he was, Aaron de Coste was afraid of his stepfather. Afraid, and utterly hateful.

'The Baron looked us over with papercut eyes. His lip curled.

"'Well, then. I suppose you'd best come in.'"

✦ III ✦

TROUBLE OF A DIFFERENT FLAVOUR

'THE GREAT KEEP of the Baron de Coste was filled to the brim, his peacocks and hens all on parade. Knights in green tabards and lordly finery, feathered caps and velvet crushed. Dames and demoiselles with lead-pale faces and cheeks rouged with blood, swathed in yards of old damask and chiffon and crêpe. And then, there was us.

'The Baron had graciously loaned a change of wardrobe, but he'd outfitted Greyhand, Talon, and me as servants rather than guests. I wore a simple black doublet and tight, pale hose, my hair tied in a long plait. The only weapons I could conceal beneath were my silversteel dagger and two silverbombs.

'Greyhand was posing as a footman, watching guests as they arrived at the Baron's door, and Archer soared the skies above, the falcon ever assisting his master. Seraph Talon was dressed as one of the house gens d'armes, patrolling within the keep should Luncóit seek entrance in secret. Aaron was attired as gentry, of course, arm in arm with his mother. And I was right there in the ballroom with him, serving fucking drinks.

'I watched the pair as they swept around the room, my eyes lingering on the Baronne de Coste. She clearly doted on her son, despite Aaron's being the offspring of her violation. Watching her, I thought of my own mama. And of my father.

'Who was she to him? Lover or victim?

'And in the end, what did that make me?

'The smoke of rêvre and whitepoppy hung in the air, entwined with the perfume of gilded ladies. Minstrel song mingled with the tune of gold-dipped fingers on crystal, of cruel laughter and cutting jabs. Wine was as rare as spun gold so long after daysdeath, and yet it flowed like water. I felt I swam in a bloody river, surrounded by hungry reptiles.

'But of Marianne Luncóit, there was no sign.

'"Terribly tedious, don't you think?"

'I blinked at the smoky voice, turned to find a pretty demoiselle regarding me with bored expression. She wore green silk, her corset pulling her curves into a perfect hourglass. Her long hair was the gold of autumn leaves, her eyes blue as old skies.

'"What's tedious, mademoiselle?"

'"All this." The girl waved about us. "The same old people having the same old conversations. It's just the same as it was last year. And the year before." She watched me through long dark lashes. "Except for you, of course."

'I proffered my tray. "May I offer you a drink, mademoiselle?"

'The girl took a glass, but raised one brow. "Come now. You're no more a servant than I. You arrived with Aaron and those others earlier today. The sour-faced man, and the thin one with the oily moustache. Who are you?"

'I was wondering the same of her, but turned my eyes to the floorboards as a good servant might. "Nobody of consequence, mademoiselle."

'"Hmm." She sniffed. "*I'll* be the judge of that."

'With one more glance for me, the young lady turned on polished heels and drifted into the throng. I shook my head, eyes returning to the crowd. Baron de Coste's ballroom was full of folk like that, all of the cut and colour I'd expected – the blushing ingénue, the handsome rake. The drunken lord and the smiling snake. My hand drifted to an inner pocket of my doublet, right over my heart, to the saintsday gift folded there. The portrait Astrid had drawn me. I was surrounded by beauties in old velvet and satin, corsets of whalebone and necklets of gold. And the only girl I found myself thinking of wore simple novice white.

'I missed her.

'The feast was done, the revels begun, couples sweeping about the dance-floor to beautiful song. The Baron de Coste sat among his lords, barks of laughter cutting the air like rusty knives. Hours had passed and still, not a hint of our quarry. But now, looking across the room, I realized I might have trouble of a different flavour.

'The Baronne de Coste stood among a bouquet of highborn dames holding court. Aaron had found his way free of his mother's side, and was now sitting at a round table, surrounded by beautiful young women. They flocked to him, silken and smiling, spellbound by the return of the handsome golden-haired lordling. But looking at the flush in his cheeks as he downed another goblet, there was no doubt about it.

'De Coste was getting shitfaced.

'I couldn't fucking believe it. Here and now? Spitting a soft curse, I walked across the dancefloor to hover beside his table, silent and glowering.

'"Ah, splendid." One of the demoiselles raided my tray, taking all the remaining drinks and nodding towards the kitchens. "Fetch more, garçon. And be swift about it."

'De Coste looked up at me and smiled. "You heard Mlle Monique, Peasant."

'I'd half a mind to drag the spoiled shit someplace private and kick some sense into him. But for all the apparent futility of it, we were still at Hunt. And so, instead of making a scene, I gave the silken gathering my best courtly bow – which isn't all that courtly, mind – and my best crooked smile, which I'm assured is crooked as an Ossian tax collector.

'"Pardon, mesdemoiselles. But I have a message for Lord de Coste from the Baron."

'The ladies looked to Aaron in question, and after a dramatic roll of his baby blues, the lordling begged leave and sent them away. I waited 'til the flock was out of earshot, then sat beside him, a polite smile painted on my face as I spat like I'd a mouthful of piss.

'"Have you taken leave of your fucking senses?"

'Aaron gulped another mouthful. "What troubles, frailblood?"

'"We're at Hunt, and you're so sodden you can barely stand!"

'"The hour grows late, and still no sign of Luncóit. Methinks the viper smelled the hounds on her tail. So, oui, I'm having a fucking drink." Aaron's eyes roamed the revellers about us, then sidelong to me. "You look ridiculous in those stockings, by the way."

'"Sweet of you to notice, shitheel."

'His sneer widened. "If it's of comfort, my cousin noticed too."

'I followed Aaron's eyeline, noting a clutch of pretty young femmes watching me over their fluttering fans. Among them, I saw that autumn-haired girl again, gazing at me with careful blue eyes. Looking about the room, I saw others staring at us too – the predator in our blood ever drawing attentions towards us. These folk knew not what we were, but *something* in their hearts told us we were not their kind.

'"Véronique has been gawping at your shapely calves all evening." Aaron raised his goblet, and the autumn-haired girl raised hers in kind, smiling sweet. "Expect a proposition when her father gets too drunk to notice. I adore the little bitch. Famille is famille. But her sort do *so* enjoy tumbling with the help."

"'Her sort?'"

"'Poor little rich girl." Aaron sighed and glanced about. "All of them. Such clichés."

'I gritted my teeth as de Coste finished his wine, eyes on his stepfather. The Baron de Coste was regaling his lords with a bawdy tale, and the noblemen roared with laughter on cue, like trained pups. Aaron shook his head in disgust.

"'*Especially* him."

"'I've no wish to cause alarm." I nodded to de Coste's empty goblet. "But from my vantage, you and your stepfather strike an awfully similar pose."

"'Careful, frailblood." Aaron glanced at me, his voice dark with malice. "You've no idea what it was to grow up under that bastard's roof."

"'Silk sheets. Servants hand and foot. I'm sure it was pure torture."

"'Know me so well, do you?"

"'I know you *exact*, de Coste. You spit at these folk behind their backs, and yet you're worst of the lot. The nobleborn bratling, above everyone and everything. The only folk you treat worse than the ones around you are the ones beneath you."

"'Would it shock you to learn, then, that my first love was a commoner like you?"

"'Talk about fucking clichés," I scoffed. "Just because you decided to slum it wi—"

"'Watch your mouth," Aaron slurred, slamming his fist down.

'A few of the gentry turned to stare as the glassware on the table jumped. Aaron gave them a princely smile and raised his glass until they turned back to their own business.

"'I *loved* Sacha," he hissed. "As the ocean loves the sky." His gaze returned to the Baron, glittering with rage. "And one night my noble stepfather caught us together when he was in his cups. And in his rage at finding me trysting with some *lowborn trollop,* he took up his tankard and beat me almost to death. But there was no *almost* for Sacha."

'I looked to the Baron, aghast. ". . . He killed her?"

"'I might've died too, if not for the blood in my veins. That was the night Mama told me what I was. So don't you *dare* compare me to that bastard, de León. *Ever.*"

'I stared at Aaron; this jealous highborn prick I so despised. I thought we'd nothing in common save the paleblood curse. And yet it seemed, in one more way, that Aaron and I were of accord: we both hated the men who'd raised us.

'Still, I could find little compassion for him. This prick had got Sister Aoife murdered for his jealousies. Instead of sympathy, I felt only fury at his hypocrisy.

'"Be that as it may, de Coste, if Greyhand comes in here and sees you getting ratarsed, he'll knock you out of your fucking shoes."

'"So concerned for my well-being?" Aaron reached for another goblet. "I'm touched."

'I snatched the wine away. "I give no fucks for your well-being, you stuck-up prick. But we're at Hunt here. Your clumsiness could spell the death of me."

'"Oh no. Wouldn't that be just *terrible*."

'"You'd like that, eh? If our prey saved you the trouble? I know your mind, bastard."

'Aaron rolled his eyes. "God, what are you bleating about now?"

'I hissed, the accusation slipping loose before I could stop it. "I *saw* you."

'"Saw me what?"

'Again, I knew it was foolish to unearth this trouble now. But I was furious. And if this cur had it in for me, I wanted to know it for certain. For him to *know* I knew.

'"The night I was attacked in the stables by La Cour and those wretched," I spat. "The night Aoife was *murdered*. I saw you sneaking out of the Armoury like a fucking thief. The same Armoury that La Cour escaped from moments later. Coincidence?"

'I saw my words strike home, a sliver of perfect rage piercing Aaron's eyes. For a moment, I honestly thought he might reach for the silversteel knife in his doublet. I could see it on his face then, sure as God was my witness.

'This bastard wanted to *murder* me.

'But then . . .

'Then . . .

'We felt *her*.'

✦ IV ✦

RAVEN CHILD

'IT CREPT ON me like sleep at the end of a quiet day. A chill prickling the back of my neck. Aaron felt it too, looking towards that passel of demoiselles. And among them, a figure stood now where none had before, as if conjured from the shadows themselves.

'She was silence. She was dead leaves fallen. She was a blood-red stain, spilling slow across the dancefloor and making my heart fall still. The drip of hot wax upon your naked skin. The first flicker of a lover's tongue into your open, wanting mouth.

'She wore crimson. A long and sweeping gown of lace and corsetry, like a bride all dipped in blood. Her skin wasn't just painted pale like the women about her, but white and smooth as finest alabaster. Her hair was the red of burning flame, flowing over her bare shoulders and past her slender waist. And she looked about the dancers on the edge of the ballroom's flickering light, and her eyes were black as the pits of hell.

'"Almighty God . . ." I breathed.

'I'd seen highbloods before, oui. But *never* the like of her. She drifted among the revellers, bewitching those she turned her attentions upon, passing through others like smoke. Nobody had announced her arrival, and I was struck with the notion that perhaps she'd *always* been there, waiting, watching. It was impossible to look away from her, but dread filled my belly even as I stared. This thing looked at the folk about her with the dispassion and cruelty that only the understanding of "forever" can bring.

'When she saw us, she didn't see people. She saw *food.*

'"*And I beheld a pale maiden,*" came a murmur behind us. "*Her eyes were black as midnight and her skin as cold as winter, and in her arms, she bore the nightmares of every sleeping babe, every shivering child, come ripe and fulsome unto the waking world.*"

'"*And her name was Death,*" Aaron whispered.

'I glanced to Greyhand in the shadows behind us. His pale green eyes were fixed on the newcomer, flooded red by the pipe of sanctus he'd apparently already smoked. "The Book of Laments hardly does her justice, does it?"

'"Nor the tales we'd heard on the road." I glanced back to the vampire, my mouth dry as ash. "Great Redeemer, I've never seen the like."

'"Ancien." Greyhand nodded. "No quarry under heaven more dangerous."

'Silently, we watched the monster seeping through the crowd, and all the world about her seemed colourless. A pretty fop dropped into a bow before her; a fly inviting a spider to dance. The vampire laughed, allowed the gent to sweep her out onto the floor, utterly oblivious to the peril he was in. Not just his flesh, but his very soul.

'Aaron and I rose to our feet as Talon joined us. The seraph's cheeks were flushed as he watched the vampire dance, his eyes also blood-red. "Almighty God, what a monster."

'"Forcing confrontation here . . ." Aaron gazed around the ballroom, looking first to his pretty cousin, then to his fair mama. "We put every person in this room in danger."

'"They are already *in* danger," I replied, eyes still on our quarry.

'"De Coste is right," Talon said, breathing quick. "Now I lay eyes upon her . . . we can provoke no fray here. To dance with such a devil in a crowded hall invites massacre."

'"What plan then, Seraph?" Greyhand asked.

'"Our Marianne is here to hunt," Talon replied, blood-red eyes still on the vampire. "We wait. We watch. And when the spider chooses her victim, we follow her back to wherever she spins her web and fall like hammers of God when the sun rises."

'I frowned at that. "We just let her . . . take one of the guests? Is that not a sin?"

'Greyhand glanced around us, uneasy. "De León raises a point, Seraph."

'"A good hunter uses the appetites of his prey against them. Want is a weakness. Look at her, Greyhand. This monster is too dangerous to confront in the dark."

'"She'll be less dangerous if we drive her to bed hungry, surely?" I asked.

'"Showing our hand here puts *everyone* at risk, shitblood," Talon spat. "We must not miss when we strike this blow. Losing one sheep tonight will spare the lives of thousands later. Almighty God will forgive us our trespass."

'I glanced to Greyhand and saw the notion sat just as ill with my master as it did with me. But Talon was a Seraph in the Ordo's hierarchy, and Greyhand only a Frère.

"'Master . . .'

"'The seraph has spoken. You will do as commanded, Initiate.'

'I could taste iron in my mouth. Cold dread pooling in my belly. But I'd disobeyed Greyhand on the Hunt once already, in Skyefall. I *dared* not do it again. "Oui, Master."

"'Do you think she's marked us?" Aaron asked.

"'Not yet," Greyhand murmured. "But standing here like flies around a corpse only invites it. De Coste, head outside where the footmen gather. The coldblood arrived in a hand carriage hauled by one of her thralls – an Ossian fellow with a dark beard. Turn on those Ilon charms of yours and see if you can glean the location of their abode. Press soft. If they know we've sniffed them out, they'll not return home."

'Aaron nodded, his tongue still slightly slurred. "Gentle as lambs, Master."

"'De León, watch near the entrance. The seraph and I shall mark the flanks."

'Talon grabbed my arm as I moved away. "Remember, mongrel, this thing is an elder Ironheart. If she even *looks* your way, mind the lessons I taught you. Think of toil, of tired feet and a domestic's drudgery. Build a wall of it and hide your secrets within."

"'By the Blood, Seraph."

'I slipped off through the crowd, carrying my empty tray. In truth, I felt sick to my heart. I knew this creature was deadlier than any foe I'd faced; that if we struck at night when she was strongest, she could butcher us all. But the idea that we were baiting our snare with one of these poor painted fools was a stone in my belly.

'I watched the coldblood circle the room, enchanting all about her. These folk had no knowing of the evil among them, instead, drawn towards it like moths to flame. But standing watch by the entrance, I noted another, surveying the ballroom just as I did. A dark-haired youth, a few years younger than I in appearance, clad in black velvet and pearl thread. The one who posed as Marianne's son, I realized.

'*Adrien.*

'He was beautiful. Timeless. And as our eyes met, I felt the press of his mind into mine, gentle as a first kiss. It was the strangest sensation – as if cold fingertips brushed my scalp, pushing through the jelly-soft dome of my skull. I crowded my thoughts as Talon had taught me, throwing up complaints about sore feet and the boorish manners of the nobleborn. But the thing's eyes flickered to my doublet, the weapons beneath. It could tell something was amiss – perhaps not what I was, but certainly that I was no mere sheep.

'He looked to the dancefloor, dark eyes fixed on the one who'd made him. And though Marianne Luncóit's demeanour changed not at all, I saw her exchange a swift glance with her spawn. Something passed between them, and her black eyes fell on me, and I felt her *see* me, as if I were stripped naked and bare before God Himself.

'Without a word, Adrien was gone, slipping off through the crowd like a knife. I looked to Greyhand, to Seraph Talon, not knowing whether to pursue or stand my ground. Marianne was moving now, a young girl spellbound on her arm, sweeping towards the doors as the guests parted before her like water.

'My master had told me to do nothing but watch. Talon had given express order to follow our quarry to ground. I wanted to prove myself worthy. I wanted to be a brother of the Silver Order, and I knew after my disobedience in Skyefall, the revelation of my strange bloodgifts, I was already dancing on a precipice. But I watched this monster approach, and I saw the lass in her embrace had hair the gold of autumn leaves.

'Aaron's cousin. *Véronique.*

'I thought of my sister Amélie then. Of my vow to Astrid that if I could spare one more mother the pain of what mine had suffered, I'd do it gladly. I didn't want to be a hero. Nor a fool. But neither did I want to become as monstrous as these things we hunted.

'Véronique was barely fifteen. Amélie would have been that age now. Perhaps I could've turned away, done what I was fucking told just *once* if I didn't know her damned name. But this girl's whole life lay ahead of her. Or no life at all.

'"Help me, God," I whispered. "Help me, please."

'I felt a heat then, burning and silvered in my hand and upon my chest. And looking down at my palm, I saw my sevenstar had begun to glow. I clung to that spreading warmth, filling my head with prayers to the Almighty. The leech drew closer, and I knew if I stood in her way, she'd shatter me like ice. But I could feel the breath of God upon my neck, silver burning in my skin. Reaching into my doublet, I drew my silversteel dagger, loosed my collar. And I stepped into the vampire's path, palm out, burning with cold, blue-white light.

'"Stop. In the Almighty's name."

'"De León!" Talon roared. "*Damn* you, boy!"

'The vampire narrowed her eyes. The music failed, folk about me gasping.

In the pale light blazing from my hand, at my throat, Luncóit somehow seemed not so beautiful any more. The monster spoke, and I was unsure if her voice rang only in my mind.

'"*No power hath thy Almighty over me, child.*"

'Where before I'd felt the soft press of the boything in my mind, now I felt a hammerblow, rummaging in my thoughts. I pushed back, trying to force her out as Greyhand and Talon came on through the crowd. The vampire took one step towards me, and the light in my palm flared so bright it made her flinch. Véronique blinked hard, the spell over her eyes burned away as she shrank in the monster's iron grip.

'"Release her," I spat. "By the Blood of the Redeemer, I command it."

'I could see the dark fury in Luncóit deepening as she took another step towards me. This was a creature old as centuries. I was an insect beside her. And yet, with God beside *me,* I stood a thousand feet tall. Light blazing before her, Talon and Greyhand rushing at her back, the vampire flung Véronique at the wall like a ragdoll. I cried out, diving and snatching the lass from the air as the force slammed us both backwards into the stone. The vampire moved in a blur, smashing onlookers aside and crashing through the ballroom windows. Shattered glass rained to the floor as Greyhand and Talon flew after her into the night.

'"Murder!" came a cry. "Murder, by God!"

'I shook my head to clear it, blinking about me. I saw one of the house gens d'armes staggering into the hall, the body of a serving lass in his arms. The girl was dead, drained pale as ash, twin punctures at her throat. The crowd about me gasped in horror.

'"N-nobody of consequence, eh?" Véronique moaned in my arms.

'With a moment to check on the bewildered lass, I pursued my master and Talon, flying through the broken window. I could see Aaron by the carriages, struggling with a tall, bearded man. Greyhand charged through the bailey past bewildered soldiers, Talon behind, both swift as hawks with the sacrament they'd smoked. Running to Aaron's side, I slammed my dagger's pommel into the thrall's head, allowing the lordling to lock up the man's arm and hurl him into the ground. I saw Aaron's doublet was soaked with blood – clumsy with drink, the lordling had earned himself a stabbing. But he seemed more furious than pained.

'"Damned *bastard,*" he spat, putting his boot to the thrall's head.

'"Are you well?" I gasped, looking at his bloodied clothes.

'"Unknot your gizzards, you quivering peon." He winced, pressing his chest with one bloody hand. "What in God's name happened in there?"

'"Luncóit spotted me . . . That is to say, I . . ."

'De Coste met my eyes. "Oh, Mothermaid, de León, you fucking *didn't* . . ."

'My stomach sank. I'd no regrets, but I knew my disobedience had landed me hip-deep in shite again. I heard a rush of footsteps, felt someone seize my throat. I was slammed back into the carriage, black stars bursting in my eyes. A fist struck my stomach, another blow cracked the side of my head so hard it almost popped my jaw loose. Blood in my mouth, I collapsed to the cobbles, crying out as a boot collided with my ribs.

'"You shitblooded little arsegrubber!" Talon spat. "I should've dragged you to Heaven's Bridge when I had the chance! You just cost us our fucking quarry!"

'I pulled myself up to my elbows, spitting blood. "I just s-saved a girl's l-life!"

'"And ended untold others!" Master Greyhand's stoic mask was abandoned, his fangs grown long as he loomed above me, drawing his silversteel sword. "What did I *tell* you, boy? What did I *say* would happen if ever you disobeyed me again?"

'Feastgoers had gathered out front of the manor house. Aaron looked to the steps, saw his cousin among the throng, her silken dress torn, her autumn hair in disarray. The Baron and Baronne themselves looked on as Greyhand raised his blade. But God had stood with me as I stared down that monster. He'd *willed* me to save that girl's life.

'Surely he'd not abandon me now?

'Dull moonslight glinted on silversteel, all my life flashing before my eyes. And as the sword began to fall, Aaron stepped into Greyhand's path.

'"Master, stop!"

'Greyhand held still, glowering as de Coste pointed to the unconscious thrall.

'"This bastard spilled where they nest! An estate near Falls Bridge, on the Silver Lane. If we move with haste, we can burn them out before they escape."

'"Presuming they return there, having now been discovered," Talon spat. "And presuming Luncóit does not tear us to pieces before e'er the sun rises."

'"All the more reason to spare this idiot." Aaron glanced to his cousin, back down to me. "At least for now. We'll need every blade we can muster to best this foe."

'Greyhand and Talon exchanged blood-red glances. I saw my master's grip on his sword tighten. He was so close to letting that blow fall, I could taste it. But in the end, he glanced to the gentry and soldiers about us, then to Aaron, standing now his way.

'"You'd best pray God that Initiate de Coste is right, de León," Greyhand growled. "Because if this monster and her brood elude us, every murder they commit thereafter is a stain upon *your* soul. And whatever happens tonight, when we return to San Michon, there will be a reckoning. Mark my words, boy. You will *never* Hunt as my apprentice again."

'I hung my head, nodded slow. "Oui, Master."

'Greyhand sheathed his sword. Talon turned back to the keep, eyes red as blood.

'"Gather your gear, brothers. We have a leech to kill."'

✦ V ✦

THE AGE OF THE FALL

'I LAY ON a rooftop in the Silver Lane with Aaron, both of us peering over the roof's ridge. The cobbles below were packed with feastgoers, their music and laughter muted by the rush of the nearby waterfall. But the estate across the way was pitch dark. All too silent. Archer sat on an iron weathervane nearby, watching me like a hawk.'

Jean-François quirked his lip. 'A falcon watching you like a hawk? Truly, de León, your wordsmithery is a marvel to behold.'

'My story, coldblood. I'll tell it how I like.' Gabriel finished off his wine and wiped his lips. 'And for your information "wordsmithery" isn't a real word.'

'Nor is "fuckarsery", but you hear no complaints from me.'

'Strange, I swear that's *exactly* what I just heard. Now, can I tell my tale or no?'

Jean-François sighed. 'As you like it, Silversaint.'

Gabriel topped up his glass, tapping his chin.

'So. We'd no knowing if Luncóit or her brood had returned here after the keep. But we had no other trail to follow. Aaron kept his eyes on the estate, stuffing his pipe with the sanctus entrusted to him by Greyhand. Guilt was gnawing at me as he lit his flintbox, dragged a deep draught into his lungs. I wondered again if our master was right – if my disobedience had saved one life only to cost hundreds more.

'But moreover, I was harbouring another guilt besides. I knew it made no sense for de Coste to have stepped up to my defence if he were behind the attack in the San Michon stables. If Aaron truly wanted me dead, he could've just shut his mouth and let Greyhand's sword fall. Despite how bad I wanted it to be true . . .

'Maybe I'd been wrong about him.

'Perhaps someone else had set La Cour free.

'Or perhaps she'd just broken free herself, as Talon always claimed.

'*So why the fuck had Aaron been sneaking around the Armoury that night?*

'When the lordling opened his eyes, I saw them washed red, irises almost swallowed by his pupils. I nodded as he handed me the pipe. "Merci."

'"You're welcome, Peasant."

'"No . . . I mean . . . for standing up to Greyhand on my behalf. Merci, de Coste."

'Aaron's eyes were back on the house, his breath coming like a racehorse's. But the sanctus seemed to have sobered him up at least. "You're an idiot, de León. A stubborn ass who thinks he knows better than men who've hunted these monsters for years. And that vanity is going to get you killed." He glanced my way briefly. "But you saved my cousin's life. Famille is famille. Now hurry up. They're already moving."

'Aaron spoke truth; I could see the dark silhouettes of Greyhand and Talon converging on the wrought iron fence surrounding the estate. And so, I drew a boiling red dose into my lungs, momentarily overcome with the rush of it, the thrum of it, uncoiling along my edges and filling every inch of me. And then we were moving, past the astonished merrymakers, burning torches and silversteel in hand as we reached the estate doors and blew them in like storm winds.

'Bloodstains on the carpet. Spatters on the wall. A dead servant lay on a chaise longue, our torchlight glittering on crystal chandeliers as we swept through the house. Greyhand and Talon were silverclad, tunics and greatcoats stripped off, but I could see no light in their inkwork, nor feel any heat in my own aegis. Greyhand descended into the cellar while Talon combed the lower level. Side by side, Aaron and I climbed the grand staircase.

'We split up, fanning out across the landing. I burst into what looked like the master boudoir, saw an elderly woman in the bed, red spatters on silk sheets. I knew she'd been slain earlier – that there was nothing I could've done to prevent this carnage. But the monsters who'd murdered these people were still at large. With every passing moment, the certainty that they'd eluded us was growing, and guilt over the ones they'd kill tomorrow night, the nights after, weighed heavier on me with every step.

'I heard a cry from Aaron, a thumping crash. I spun on my heel, dashing down the hall and bursting into a luxurious study. De Coste was on the floor, wrestling with a broad Sūdhaemi man. The fellow was twice Aaron's weight, and obviously a thrall – even with a dose of sanctus in him, de Coste was struggling. I put a kick into the big man's head, locked up one of his arms as Aaron seized his throat. And looking into the fellow's eyes, de Coste hissed.

'"*Be still now*."

'The thrall groaned, trying to throw off the compulsion, but by then, Greyhand and Talon had arrived. The man was brought to heel, Talon and I leaning on his arms as Greyhand sat atop his chest, a silver dagger to his throat.

'"Get off me, godpig!" the man roared.

'"Where is your mistress?" Greyhand growled, pressing with his dagger. "*Speak!*"

'The man hawked a mouthful of spit into Greyhand's face. Our master broke his nose with his dagger's pommel, glanced to de Coste. "Find her."

'Aaron nodded, kneeling beside the thrall's head. The man tried to close his eyes and turn away, but Aaron held him still. "*Tell us where your mistress is*."

'At the same time, Talon put his hand across the man's brow, eyes narrowed as he forced his way into the fellow's thoughts. I felt that familiar jealousy – seeing bloodgifts at work while I stood there, useless as balls on a priest.

'The thrall bucked and hissed, the blood from his broken nose lighting up the thirst inside me. He tried his best to resist – if Aaron and Talon were mere inquisitors with something as mundane as a rack or wheel, I'm certain the thrall would never have broken. But in the end, the Blood won through.

'"The bridge," Talon said, looking up. "They're at the Falls Bridge."

'"Why?" Greyhand demanded. "Why not simply flee?"

'"Because you're too late!" the thrall roared. "All that needs be known is known! The Master comes, you fucking godpigs! And blood and fire shall mark his passing!"

'Greyhand's fist crashed into the thrall's jaw, leaving him slack and sense-less.

'"This riddle makes no sense . . ."

'"We'll learn the truth of it," Talon spat, "when we bring this unholy beast to ground."

'The four of us flew into the streets, barrelling down packed thoroughfares. Aaron led us like an arrow, past dancing revellers and wandering lovers, towards the river cutting the city in two. Grey snow tumbled from the skies, Archer cut the dark with a piercing cry.

'Aaron slipped his coat from his shoulders, tearing off his tunic and leaving his tattoos bare. I stuffed Astrid's portrait into my britches and followed suit. All four of us were silverclad now, but the sanctus kept the chill away, the thought of what was to come rushing like fire through my veins. As we reached the Falls Bridge, I glanced at Greyhand and saw that glow in the silver on his skin; the telltale sign that evil was near and God rode with us.

'The waterfall was a rushing roar now, but above it, I heard laughter in the crowd ahead. My heart was pounding a hammersong as we pushed through the mob and finally, miraculously, saw our prey before us. The vampire we'd stalked since Skyefall.

'Marianne Luncóit.

'The Falls Bridge was dark stone, the railings lined with brass statues of saints and angels. She stood among them, all in red, her child Adrien at her side. A mob of drink-sodden feastgoers were gathered about her, cheering as she opened her hand like some corner magician and released a white raven into the air. The bird was beautiful, cutting down into the freezing spray and back up into the night. Three cages were lined up along the rail, two already empty. Squinting into the sky, I saw more birds winging westwards over Raphael's peak. And my heart sank in my chest as I realized what they were.

'"Messengers . . ." I breathed.

'A sharp cry split the air, and a thrall with a battleaxe came at me through the crowd. I met the blow with Lionclaw, the mob about me screaming. Blood sprayed as I struck back, kicking the fellow in the chest and tumbling him across the cobbles. A swarthy lad with lank hair was hewing at Talon with a broadsword, Aaron whipping out his wheellock and unloading into the face of a Sūdhaemi man charging him with punching daggers. The crowd roared again as the shot rang out, Greyhand bellowing over the panic.

'"Fly! For the love of God and the sake of your souls! *Fly!*"

'The crowd scattered as I plunged my sword into the big thrall's belly. All the world was moving as if in a dream, the sanctus rushing in my veins. The thrall's axe cracked the cobbles as I stepped aside, his jaw broke loose as I buried my pommel into his face. As the blood and teeth flew, I wondered if this man even understood what he was doing. If the poison he'd swallowed from his dark mistress's wrist allowed him the luxury of fear or regret, or simply made him a slave to her ancient will. Dying for the only God that mattered.

'But die he did, gasping his last at the end of my sword as the Maximille's Day revellers fled screaming, leaving only us and two monsters in the middle of the Falls Bridge. Grey snow swirled about us in freezing eddies, grey water rushed below us, over that frozen edge. Marianne Luncóit opened her hands again, releasing yet another white raven into the night, and I saw a small scroll of parchment tied to its leg with a bow of black ribbon.

'Her cages were empty now. Her stare too, as she turned to us, perilous and beautiful. Long flaming hair framed her face, somehow untouched by the howling wind. Her skin was white and hard as marble. And perhaps it was a trick of the light, but looking to the cobbles beneath her, it seemed she cast no shadow at all.

'"Too late art thou, oh children," she said. "All that needs be known is known. And now *he* shall know it too."

'"Rejoice." The child gifted me a dark smile. "The age of the fall has begun."

'I glanced to the white ravens soaring westwards, and I knew with awful certainty where they were headed. Who *he* was. The lion on my chest and the sevenstar in my palm burned with divine heat, warming my blood. And frightening and otherworldly as these two were, I could see the way their eyes narrowed as we closed about them. The way the boy's lip curled as a soft hiss slipped between his fangs.

'"Long nights hast thou harried my steps," the woman whispered to Greyhand. "Felt thee, like lips gentle on back of my shivering neck. And here thou art, my beautiful hunter."

'She held out her arms.

'"Kiss me."

'"The Lord is my shield, unbreakable," Greyhand spat. "He is the fire that burns away all darkness. He is the tempest rising that shall lift me unto paradise."

'The frère stepped forward, and the vampire edged back. Her chin was lowered, lashes fluttering as if somehow delighted by the pain that holy light caused her. Her ruby lips curled in a smile that was almost . . . affectionate.

'"I know thee, Silversaints. Talon de Montfort. Aaron de Coste. Gabriel de León."

'"Listen to nothing she says," Talon warned.

'"If the keeping of thy names have I, wouldst thou not know mine?" She ran her hands over the pale swell of her breasts, down to her hips as she smiled at Greyhand. "What name shalt thou whisper otherwise, Aramis Charpentier, when I love thee?"

'"We *know* your name. Luncóit? Raven Child? Hardly the deepest of riddles, Voss."

'The monster smiled, sly and wicked as she spoke the creed of her line.

'"All Shall Kneel, good Frère."

'She moved then, murder-quick, into Greyhand's light. Though the glow narrowed her eyes, curled her lip, still she struck, swift as a thunderclap. Greyhand gasped, bending backwards as diamond-hard fingernails whistled past his throat. Her other hand struck him in his chest, her flesh sizzling, sending him sailing back across the bridge as if he were made of feathers. I cried out as my master struck the railing, smashing the stone to dust and collapsing to his knees.

'Greyhand was back on his feet in a blinking, charging towards Luncóit. But the boy was moving too now, fast as a serpent's tongue. He drew a wicked dagger from his doublet in one hand, a wheellock pistol in the other. I cried out as he struck the trigger, Aaron whipped sideways as the shot hit him in the chest. And then the boy was flying at me. He slipped beneath the silverbomb I hurled, silhouetted in the explosion behind him. I danced backwards, keeping him at bay with Lionclaw as Seraph Talon charged Luncóit's back.

'Muscle memory kicked in; the countless hours of sparring entwined with the bloodhymn in my veins. But I fought highbloods now – the foes I'd heard so much of but had never truly faced. They moved hurricane-swift, and even though the light from our ink made that beautiful deadboy grimace in pain, still he came on. I hurled another silverbomb, swung my blade. I put all I had behind the blow, but though Lionclaw found Adrien's neck, his flesh was stone and his knife quicksilver as he struck back, too fast to follow.

'I staggered, hitting the flagstones, blood in my mouth. Adrien's shadow fell over me, and I saw death reach out its hand. But the flesh at his wrist cracked like glass as Aaron's blade crashed atop it, and Adrien hissed, slipping aside from the burning brand de Coste thrust towards his chest. Aaron struck again, silversteel sliding along the boy's cheek, trimming his dark locks. The vampire flashed backwards, one hand to his bloody face, the other still holding his bloody knife. De Coste stood guard over me, eyes lit by his burning torch. A bleeding hole was torn in his chest, angels of the host burning silver on his arms.

'"Are you well?" he hissed, eyes still on the glowering boy.

'I looked down at my belly, realized Adrien had stabbed me a dozen times.

'"Not r-really."

'"Take your time, Peasant," de Coste smirked, spitting blood. "I'll have this dance."

'Aaron charged the vampire, the pair moving like water and pale shadow in the silver light. Looking behind us, I saw Greyhand and Talon still entwined with the ancien, just a blur. The stink of ignis and silver caustic hung in the air, silverbombs roaring, flails and blades gleaming. The woman moved between them like a bloody knife, the red of her dress and hair and lips the only colour in the silvered glow.

'"Back!" Greyhand roared, cutting the air.

'"Say please," she smiled, cutting his arm with those wicked claws.

'"We are the light in the night!" Talon cried, lashing out with his flail. "We are the fire that rages between this and all world's ending!"

'"Kiss me then, hunter. And see who of us burns."

'Luncóit tore one of the brass statues loose from the railing, brandished it like a club. Greyhand was knocked aside, senseless and bleeding. Bringing back her arm, Luncóit hurled the statue like a spear. Talon cried out as the angel struck him, crushing him against the railing with enough force to kill any mortal man.

'I dragged myself upright, blood filling my boots, Lionclaw slack in my hand. Talon was on his knees, but Greyhand was back in the fray, coming at Luncóit like a thunderbolt. And so, I staggered back to help Aaron. For all his bravado, he was outmatched against that darkling boy, and wounded as I was, another sword might tip the scale.

'De Coste thrust his blade into the vampire's side, and I heard a sound more like cracking stone than splitting flesh. Jarred from his grip, Aaron's silversteel fell to the cobbles. Adrien's riposte ripped a red gash up the boy's ribs, through the weave of roses on his chest. Clutching the awful wound, Aaron stumbled to his knees.

'"*Close your eyes,*" he whispered, and the deadboy only laughed. Adrien lunged at de Coste, that dagger speeding towards Aaron's heart, and then I was on him, crashing into the vampire's chest and sending the both of us tumbling across the bridge. We hit the cobbles hard, a gong ringing in my ears as my head cracked the stone.

'"Insect," Adrien spat, turning on me. "*Cattle.*"

'I gasped as gore-slick hands closed about my throat, Adrien's flesh sizzling on the silver as he smashed my head back against the stone. I thrust my left hand into his face, rewarded with a wail of pain as light flared, as the warmth of God flowed up my arm and into my heart. The thing flinched backwards, hissing, and in a desperate stab, I lunged upwards and kicked him away, into the shattered railing.

'The boy flailed, arms pinwheeling as he tried to find his balance. Bleeding, his ribs torn to the bone, Aaron snatched up his fallen sword. The lordling hissed in his rage, fangs bared, and with one final blow to Adrien's chest, de Coste sent the monster backwards over the rail and into the freezing river below.

'I knew vampires couldn't cross running water. But I'd no idea what happened if they were submerged in it. Adrien began screaming, thrashing, as if he'd been tossed into a river of burning lye. The current swept the monster towards the falls, alabaster flesh running to soup and washing off his bones as he was hurled over that frozen brink.

'"*Adrien!*" came a scream. "*NO!*"

'I turned towards Luncóit, saw her eyes filled with fury. Greyhand took advantage, calling out to heaven as he brought his blade in a whistling arc across her throat. It was a blow that would have split an anvil in two, and the vampire's flesh shattered like ice. But she was an Ironheart. Ancien of the Blood Voss. And I saw now the terrible peril Greyhand was in: by risking his deathblow, our master had left himself off-balance. Bone-white fingers closed about his throat, sizzling on the silver. Her claws tore into the side of his head, ripped his ear clean off his skull, broke his jaw, pulped his right eye like a rotten egg.

'"Master!" I shouted, running forward.

'The vampire seized Greyhand's wrist, flinging him down onto the stone so hard the flagstones shattered. Greyhand cried out, blood on his lips. Luncóit slung him like a bag of rocks – once, twice, *twisting* as she did so. I heard bone breaking, saw Greyhand's red eyes wide with agony. And then he roared, head thrown back as the vampire thrust her heel against his chest and leaned away, tearing his swordarm out at the root.

'"Holy God . . ." I breathed, skidding to a halt.

'Talon staggered upright, bleeding from the eyes and ears. His shoulder was broken, chest staved in, left arm bloody at his side. De Coste and I joined him, gasping for breath. Aaron's skin was pocked with a half-dozen wounds, blonde hair plastered to bloodied cheeks. Greyhand lay broken on the cobbles as the vampire turned to us, tossing my master's severed arm over the railing and into the river below.

'"What do we do, Seraph?" Aaron wheezed.

'Talon shook his head, teeth red with blood. "I . . . I don't . . ."

'"We can't abandon Greyhand," I whispered. "The three of us can take her."

'The vampire laughed then. Her skin was spattered crimson, eyes searching mine as she raised her hand and licked the blood from her blackened fingers.

'"Take me?"

'The snow landed on her skin as if she were a statue. Her dress flowed about her like red smoke. She came to a halt at the edge of our light, beautiful and terrible, and she spoke with a voice that quickened my blood.

'"I am never taken. I only *take*. Such is the province of a Prince of Forever."

'My heart dropped in my chest as realization sank home.

'"Luncóit," I whispered. "Raven Child."

'"*His* child," Talon breathed.

'I saw the seraph's face growing paler, Aaron's bloodied sword tremble in his hand. We'd known the monster we hunted was powerful. But we'd never imagined . . .

'This thing had been old when the empire was young. The red sovereign of *centuries* of slaughter. And I whispered then, my voice quaking. The name of this beast we'd hunted since Skyefall. This vampire who now hunted us.

'"Laure Voss . . ."'

Laure Voss opened her arms. She slipped aside Talon's flail, moved swifter than a hummingfly past Aaron's sword. Her right hand tore through the seraph's guard, twisting his good arm so brutally the bone burst through his skin. Her other hand collided with his belly, claws tearing deep. She threw Talon backwards, loops of entrails spilling from the gaping wound. Aaron lunged with a bellow to the Almighty, aiming at the wound Greyhand had already begun. And at last, at *last*, the blade broke through, sundering that marble finish and opening Laure's neck wide.

'But the Prince of Forever struck back, and I cried out as those diamond-hard nails tore through Aaron's face, opening the lordling's cheek to the bone. I heard de Coste's ribs shatter as a blow struck his chest, sending him sailing back across the bridge.

'"De Coste!"

'"*Gabriel.*"

'I turned towards the vampire, once more circling the outskirts of my light. I was alone now, in an ocean of darkness. I remembered Skyefall, the blood of little Claude de Blanchet boiling under my hand. But if that gift was still mine, I'd no clue how to conjure it. Laure's eyes were fixed on me, framed by flame-red hair, lips parted ever so slight. She ran her tongue along her teeth, bloody fingertips across the gaping wound at her throat, roaming down the hourglass of her body and pressing hard between her legs.

'"I feel the want in thee, frailblood. I feel the fear. I know what thou didst to thy poor Ilsa. Thy terror, that ye might do the same to thy dear Astrid. But no weak and feeble flesh have I, to break upon thy stone. Thou canst *hurt* me, Gabriel. As *much* as ye want."

'She was hideous. She was evil incarnate. But God help me, she was beautiful and dark as the end of all days. I swallowed hard. Thinking of Ilsa's blood pulsing into my mouth. The perfume of Astrid's blood in the air. Laure prowled back and forth before me, but I swear I could feel her behind me, hands running down my bare chest, my belly, lower and lower still. She looked at the pocket where Astrid's portrait was folded. Biting her lip and shivering as her teeth cut deep, blood on her mouth.

'"Let me kiss thee, Gabriel. Let me kiss thee in places mortal girls fear to tread."

'I looked to my comrades, the fallen swords and broken bones. I could've run. Turned my back and fled to the cathedral, even now tolling the turn to San Maximille's Day. But to retreat was to leave my brothers to their deaths.

'"It shall be bliss," Laure promised. "I shall be the goddess ye die for."

'And looking at those bright red lips, those slender hands and bloody curves, I wondered again what it might be like, to die in pleasure instead of pain. How it might actually *feel* to have those teeth slip into my skin. Taken instead of taking.

'"Kiss me. Just once, Gabriel. *Kiss* me."

'I felt my hand falling to my side. The light about me fading, only the lion on my chest burning now, dim and water-thin. The vampire's smile widened, and she stepped closer. Her throat was shattered where Aaron and Greyhand had driven their blades into her flesh, and I could feel the chill off her skin, smell the blood and death and dirt as she enfolded me in her arms. Her lips drifted close and closer to mine. My whole body thrilled at her touch. And mouthing a prayer to the Almighty, I struck the fuse on my final silverbomb, and pushed it through the wound in her neck.

'The explosion tore through her body, blasting me backwards. Silver fire scorched Laure's flesh, turning marble to ebony. Her shoulder and throat split apart, a blow no ordinary coldblood could have withstood. But though she staggered, *still* that unholy bitch didn't fall, face twisted with pain and fear as her beautiful silken dress caught fire.

'I dragged myself upwards as the flames took hold, and Laure began to scream as I skidded to my knees at Greyhand's side. My master was unconscious, but still he breathed, and I slung him over my back as Laure whirled and shrieked, tearing at her dress before she became a pillar of flame. Next, I ran to Talon, the seraph gasping with agony as I hauled him up, "COME ON!" And last, I reached de Coste, his face ripped bloody, his chest shredded. Lifting him under one arm, Talon beside me and Greyhand over my shoulder, we ran. Down cobbled streets, past terrified townsfolk, and finally, out into the grand square. And there it stood, midnight tolling in the belfry: a circle of marble and gothic spires, reaching up to the heaven that had perhaps not yet abandoned us.

'Coste Cathedral.

'I kicked open the doors, staggered onto holy ground. Talon slumped across the threshold, his stomach a torn and bleeding mess. I lowered Greyhand to the floor, propping Aaron against the wall and pressing my hand to his bloody brow.

'"De Coste?" I whispered. "Do you hear me?"

'"*I* hear thee."

'My belly filled with ice as I turned to the square outside. And there she stood, naked and blackened. The once-flawless alabaster of her skin was a ruin, bone gleaming beneath the shattered façade. Her flame-red hair was ashes.

'But still, *still* Laure lived.

'"There is no God that shall save thee from me," she vowed. "I am a Prince of Forever, and forever shall I hunt thee. All thou hast, shall I take. All thou art, shall I unmake. And in the end, I shall have thee on thy knees, frailblood. I shall taste thee unto dying."

'Laure glanced down the street towards the sound of ringing horns, ironshod boots on snow-clad stone. Baron de Coste had at last mustered his men; soldiers with burning pitch and blazing torches. Wounded as she was, the vampire could still have sown ruin among them like a farmer in the fields. But in truth, she had no need to fight. She'd already done what she came to Coste to do. And after all, she could wait forever.

'"All Shall Kneel."

'She was gone. A blink, and she no longer stood there, leaving the square abandoned. My mouth was dust. Hands shaking. But against impossible odds, we lived.

'"F-foolish . . . l-little bastard."

'I looked to Greyhand. The wreckage of his face. The slowly bleeding gouge where his swordarm used to be. I searched about us, tearing a tapestry from the cathedral wall to wrap around his shoulders. He was paleblood, and the bleeding wouldn't kill him. But the fact that he was conscious at all proved how deep the silver ran in his bones.

'"I told you t-to run," he whispered. "Disobedience will be the d-death of you, boy."

'I looked to Aaron. To Talon. To my master. All of us such strange bedfellows, with little in common save the sin of our birth. But still. But still . . .

'"Perhaps so, Master. But my brothers are the hill I die on."

'Aaron managed a sneer. His wounds cut down over his brow and through his cheek, ripped by Laure's talons. I knew he'd carry that scar the rest of his life.

'"Fine s-sentiment. But I can't help n-noticing you're n-not dead, de León."

'"There's always tomorrow." My eyes returned to the place Laure Voss had stood. Her promise still hanging in the air. "This Hunt isn't over."

'"But so far, all for n-naught. We've still no idea why sh-she was here."

'A shrill cry split the night. I looked to the cathedral square, saw the first of the Baron's men moving in, swords and burning torches in hand. But above their heads, a grey falcon swooped out of the dark. Archer wheeled once, then flew in through the cathedral doors, wings whipping the blood-soaked hair about my face. Wounded as he was, Greyhand managed a smile, and I sighed in wonder when I saw what Archer carried in his talons.

'A dead white raven.

'"Clever boy," Greyhand nodded. "My clever, *clever* boy."

'The falcon rasped as I crawled over to his prize. I unpicked the black bow, unfurled the strip of parchment bound to the dead raven's leg. Looking over the message, I saw it was a tiny map of the Godsend Mountains, painted in an exquisite hand. Fine, flowing script detailed the towns that dotted the range – population, assets, garrisons of men. Black arrows swept down from the north, pointing towards Coste, Tolbrook, Skyefall, and then out into the Nordlund itself. And despite my wounds, I came to my feet, blood running cold as I realized what I held in my shaking hands.

'"De León?" Talon whispered. "What is it?"

'I looked to my fellows, uncertain whether to be overjoyed or horrified.

'"An invasion plan."'

✦ VII ✦

THE FAITHLESS

'WE'D RIDDEN HARD back to San Michon, Archer flying ahead bearing word of our discovery. And though our wounds closed along the road, the price of our almost-victory would be scribed on our skin always. My chest and arm were scored from the claws of Laure Voss's slain son. Talon's belly would bear the Wraith's touch the rest of his days, and Aaron's face was forever marred – a long, hook-shaped scar cutting through brow and cheek.

'But Greyhand had it worst of all.

'His swordarm was gone, his right eye and ear also, ripped free by the claws of the Dead. Our first night back in the monastery, Greyhand knelt in the front row at mass as if nothing were amiss. But he'd never be the hunter he once was. And all of us knew it.

'When the parting hymns were sung, Abbot Khalid and Seraph Talon bid Aaron and me remain. I tried to catch Greyhand's eye as he left, but he ignored me as he had on the road back home. I knew there were words unspoken between us – though we'd uncovered the Forever King's stratagem, the way things had played out in Coste was *my* fault. My master had vowed I'd never hunt as his apprentice again, and I feared I might be expelled from the Order for my disobedience. Strange as it was, hard as my struggles had been, San Michon was my home now. And I was in dread that I might be forced to leave it all behind.

'Khalid stood at the altar, Talon beside him. As ever, the Abbot of San Michon cut an imposing sight, dark skin glinting with the silver of his aegis. His green, kohl-rimmed eyes were lit with chymical light from the globes above, and the Cathedral was deathly hushed.

'"Seraph Talon has told me of all that transpired in Coste," he said. "To

stand against a daughter of the Forever King and live is no small feat. You
are clearly favoured of the Almighty, Initiates."

'My belly knotted itself tighter as Khalid's gaze fell on me.

'"That, or the devil loves his own."

'I swallowed hard as the abbot turned to Aaron.

'"Initiate de Coste, Greyhand has informed me you acquitted yourself
admirably these last months. You showed patience, valour, and discipline,
and dealt the deathblow to a grandson of the Forever King himself. He feels
you are ready to be sainted to the Order."

'De Coste glanced at me, clearly torn. "Abbot . . . it was Gabriel who
created opportunity for me to deal the deathblow to Laure's son. Gabriel
who staggered Laure herself long enough for us to seek holy ground. Without
him, we'd *all* be dead."

'"Greyhand has informed me of Initiate de León's conduct in Coste,"
Khalid replied.

'I lowered my eyes, stomach twisting again. Of course Greyhand had
told Khalid of my defiance. My rashness had cost my master his swordarm
and almost cost us our prey. Greyhand had stood up for me back when
Talon suggested I be taken to Heaven's Bridge, and in earning his ire, I knew
I might have lost my only benefactor. But still . . .

'"What will become of Master Greyhand, Abbot?" I asked softly.

'"I'd have thought you more concerned about your own fate, Little Lion."

'"I did what I thought was just," I murmured, gaze downturned. "God's
truth, I'd do it again. But . . . I know what happened to Greyhand was my
fault."

'"Greyhand has yet to decide his path," Khalid sighed. "He is strong as
silversteel. But it will take time to recover from what the Wraith in Red did
to him. In body *and* mind."

'"Godless leech," Aaron whispered.

'"We owe her a reckoning," I spat. "We should track her down and—"

'"You will do nothing of the sort, you gutterborn spunk-rag," Talon
snapped. "Count your blessings we do not flay the ink off your skin and
throw you from these halls."

'I blinked at that. "You mean . . . I'm not to be cast out of the Order?"

'"No," Khalid replied, sending my heart singing. "Your disobedience
warrants censure. But it cannot be denied you saved the lives of your fellows,
Little Lion, nor that your courage has given us a heaven-sent advantage
against the Forever King. But now is no time for vendetta against Laure
Voss. All our strength must be bent towards stopping her father. And thanks

to your efforts, we now know for certain where he and his Endless Legion will strike.'

'Elation filled me at the thought of my reprieve, that I might yet stand with my brothers in the battle to come.

'"Avinbourg," I whispered.

'Khalid nodded. "From the plan you uncovered, we know Voss intends to take the cityfort, then sweep south along the Godsend and seize Coste, Tolbrook, and Skyefall, cutting off silver supplies for the *entire* empire. And even with knowledge of his stratagem, we have precious little time to stop it. Wintersdeep is upon us. The Cherchant River is near frozen already. Emperor Alexandre has emptied all garrisons along the Godsend to reinforce Avinbourg, and a mighty host is being gathered from Dún Fas, Dún Cuinn, Redwatch, and Beaufort. They are to be led by the Empress herself."

'Aaron blinked at that. "Isabella is coming to San Michon?"

'Khalid nodded. "She and her forces will muster here in a week's time. So I trust your Hunt has not wearied you overmuch, Initiates. You will soon be called upon again to defend God's Holy Church."

'Both fear and exhilaration bubbled inside me at that thought. The idea of fighting a siege against thousands of Dead for the fate of the Nordlund was near overwhelming. But this was all I'd worked for. And we'd seen firsthand now, the depth of the evil we faced.

'"Initiate de Coste, you will be sainted into the Order next prièdi," Talon said. "If you have time now, I shall take you through your vows. And our expectations."

'Khalid turned to me. I knew in my thumping heart how close I'd come to the edge here, and I could see in his eyes that it was the abbot's word that had spared me the fall.

'"Get your sleep tonight, Little Lion. You'll have need of it."

'I bowed, numb with gratitude. "By the Blood, Abbot."

'I turned to depart, but then offered my hand to de Coste. After a heartbeat's hesitation, he shook it. Despite our differences, I knew Aaron had earned his induction. And since saving each other's skins in Coste, I was beginning to feel a faint kinship with him. We weren't friends. But there's a strange and fierce love forged in the fires of combat. A brotherhood written only in blood. Even among men who'd normally loathe each other.

'I left the Cathedral, into the freezing night. I could hear good cheer in the refectory, Smith Baptiste's laughter, Frère Alonso's pipes, but my mind was still unsettled. Travelling back from Coste, I'd been chewing on it incessantly. I *knew* I could believe nothing Laure Voss had told us. But the way

Talon had raged when Voss mentioned Sister Aoife . . . Despite my reprieve, there was still a mystery here. One I couldn't see the bottom of.

'Yet I knew someone who might . . .

'The wait was torture. Aaron and I bedded down in Barracks that night, and our fellow initiates all demanded a telling of the tale of the battle with the Forever King's daughter. It was hours before the bastards drifted off to sleep. But at last, I slipped from the Barracks, across the monastery, and into the Great Library's dark.

'All was silence as I stole among the shelves. That great map of the empire was etched on the floorboards, and my eyes drifted to the Godsend range, the name of a different angel scribed on every peak. I pictured the legion of the Forever King, marching even now towards Avinbourg, belly thrilling at the thought of the battle to come.

'But more, at the thought of *her*.

'It'd been months since I'd seen her, and those last few minutes as I stole into the forbidden section were by far the longest. What if she weren't here? What if she'd found a way out of this cage, just as she'd vowed? What if . . .

'But I rounded the shelves, and there she was. Seated at the great oaken table, surrounded by books. Her hair had been set free from her coif, long, ink-black locks framing pale cheeks. One hand traced the text she read, the other clutched a red-stained kerchief to her nose. Sisternovice Chloe sat beside her, poring over a dusty tome. The scent of blood and dreamweed hung in the air. And strangely, I saw a wheellock rifle near Chloe's hand.

'"Fairdawning, mesdemoiselles."

'Chloe startled at my whisper. Astrid looked up from her book, dark eyes meeting mine. She smiled at me then. And God, the way she did so . . .'

Gabriel leaned back in his chair, looking at the ceiling of his cell with shining eyes.

'That girl had a *thousand* smiles,' he sighed. 'A smile cruel as winter wind, that cut you down to shivering bone. A smile light as dove's down, just the softest hint of it across her cheek to let you know she was listening as you spoke. A smile that could make you fear, and a smile that could make you cry, and a smile that made you feel like you were the only man alive. And the smile she gave me that night was the first time she'd ever done so, and I've not forgotten it, not through all the blood and fire, not through all the nights from that one to this. A smile that whispered, and made me smile in kind.'

'What did it whisper?' Jean-François asked.

'That she was happy. And the sight of *me* had made her so.

"'Godmorrow, Gabriel,' she said.

"'It's good to see you both, Sisternovices. I pray God I find you well?'

"'Well enough.' Astrid swabbed at her nose. 'Minor blood loss aside.'

'Chloe smiled, her green eyes shining. 'I'm glad to see you returned safe, Initiate.'

"'Safer than some, at least. What's the rifle for?'

"'Oh.' Astrid grimaced. 'Don't mind that, it's Chloe's.'

"'. . . You stole a wheellock from the Armoury? Godsakes, why?'

"'I didn't *steal* it,' Chloe said, making the sign of the wheel. 'Theft is a sin, Gabriel.'

"'Abbot Khalid has been teaching us,' Astrid huffed. 'The sisterhood have lessons every findi since Aoife was killed by that highblood. It's fucking ghastly.'

'Chloe stared at the girl beside her. 'It was *your* idea, Azzie.'

"'I merely suggested within the abbot's earshot some of the girls might sleep easier if they knew how to defend themselves. I didn't think they'd make it fucking mandatory.'

'Chloe rolled her eyes at me. 'She's prevaricating now, bless her. She's actually a splendid shot. But heaven forbid she appear to be enjoying herself.'

"'You treacherous swamp donkey, how *dare* you? I'll be miserable all I like. *You're* the one who's enjoying herself. And rather too much, some might say. You're supposed to be betrothed to the Almighty, but you carry that thing about like you were bedding it.'

"'Oh, *stop*.' Chloe blushed furiously and repeated the wheel. 'I don't like such talk.'

'Stifling a smirk, Astrid threw me a sly glance. Taking Chloe's hand, she kissed it, pressed it to her cheek. 'I'm sorry, ma chérie. I'm only teasing.'

"'Well, I think training is a grand idea,' I said, nodding to the rifle. 'Aoife's death aside, the night grows dark outside these walls. And nights ahead bode darker still.'

'Chloe brushed a tight curl from her cheek, her voice growing hush. 'We heard tales of your Hunt in Coste. It sounded a frightful affair.'

"'I'll not dream sweetly of it, sure and true.'

'Astrid looked me over, head tilted. 'Are you . . . well?'

'I looked about our little sanctuary, then back to her eyes. 'Better now.'

'She smiled again, and I pulled up a chair. The metallic scent of Astrid's blood was knife-bright in the air, goosebumps prickling my skin. I could feel the thirst, like a slow-spreading crack through the ice beneath my feet. Even with all the sanctus I'd smoked on the road, those cracks seemed to be growing deeper, as if feeding it each night were helping awaken it. And though it stood in check, prowling behind the bars rather than throwing itself against them, the reminder of that beast in my blood made me ill at ease.

'Never once had I met him, but still, I was ever my father's son . . .

'"Well," Astrid declared. "Chloe and I have news that may cheer you further still. Two pieces, actually. I'll start with what I hope is the less dramatic one."

'She handed me a sheaf of parchment sealed with candle wax. As soon as I saw the handwriting, I knew who'd sent it. "Mama . . ."

'"She wrote back almost immediately," Astrid smiled. "I told you she'd miss you."

'The girls watched with curious eyes as I tore the letter and read, swift as I could.

'My dearest son,

'Your letter filled my soul with joy. The nature of our parting has been a stone about my neck, and I miss you as flowers miss the sun. Celene also misses you terribly, and assures you that she is misbehaving admirably to fill the hole of your absence. She also informs me you are deeply in arrears in regards to the letters she's sent you.

'I am glad you have found a home, my love. I am so grieved I did not tell you of your heritage. At first, I prayed God that your father did not pass his curse onto you. And when I could see you were destined to carry the weight of my sin, I was afeared of what you might think of me. I should have prepared you. I can only beg now you forgive me.

'I was little more than a girl when I knew your father, Gabriel. And love will convince a girl almost any lie is truth. But know I *did* love him, and in his way, perhaps he loved me too. I will tell you more, but God forgive me, I cannot do so without looking you in the eye.

'I pray you, seek leave from the abbot to come home for Firstmas. I will tell you all you wish to know. And then, I will beg you embrace me, and forgive me, and know I am your mother and love you more dear than you can imagine.

'The blood of lions flows in you, my son. I ask you to be brave a month or two longer. Then you will know all you need to, and more.

'With all my love

'Mama

'I finished reading with a dark scowl on my brow, my fangs stirring in my gums as the anger swelled. I could understand a letter was no place for so heavy a truth. But still, being left without answers was a bitter draught, and the sting of wanting something I couldn't have was becoming all too familiar.

'"Not the news you were hoping for?" Astrid murmured.

'I breathed deep to calm myself. "Just more questions," I sighed.

'"Well, then. We have one answer, at least." Chloe stood and fished about the dusty shelves. "Though we've had little fortune searching for daysdeath lore, Azzie and I *have* met some success on your task."

'I looked up, belly thrilling. "You found word of the fifth line? Why didn't you say so?"

'"She just did, Gabriel," Astrid said, her voice muffled by her kerchief. "All this blood is rather fortuitous, actually."

'"See here." From among the stacks, Chloe produced an ancient book, edged in tarnished brass and bound in pale, cracked leather. The title was embossed upon the spine in golden writing, almost completely faded with age.

'"I can't read it," I confessed.

'"There aren't many who can. It's a dialect of Old Talhostic, predating the Wars of the Faith. It took me days to translate a few fragments. But this book is a bestiary. Written by a vampire scholar named Lûzil. Or Lûsille. We're not sure which."

'Chloe opened the pages almost reverently. They were yellowed with age, creaking as she turned them. I saw anatomical illustrations of horrifying beasts, some entirely fictional, others variants of the faekin and duskdancers and fallen I knew full well to be real. The book seemed half folklore, half fact, all madness.

'"Strange vellum," I remarked, touching the page.

'"We think it's human skin," Astrid murmured.

'"Sweet Mothermaid . . ."

'"Here. Here it is." Chloe turned the book towards me. I saw heraldic crests in an archaic style, representing the four vampire bloodlines: the golden-crowned white raven of Blood Voss, the roses and serpents of the Ilon, the twin wolves and moons of Chastain, the bear and broken shield of the Dyvok. But the language was unreadable.

'"What does all this say? Does it mention the fifth line?"

'Astrid turned to the final page, blank and parched with age. "It appears not."

'I gritted my teeth, frustration rising. "Then why are you showing me this, Astrid?"

"*Because,* Gabriel, appearances can be deceiving." She took her kerchief away, and leaning over the book, snorted hard. Blood began to *drip, drip, drip* onto the blank page.

"'What are y—"

'Chloe held up her hand, eyes shining with excitement. "Just watch."

'I sat mute, trying to ignore the perfume of Astrid's blood, trying not to imagine how it might taste, silken and sticky-smooth upon my tongue. It gleamed like dark rubies across that dusty page, sweet as poison. And then my belly did a slow roll, my eyes widening.

'The blood was *moving.*

'Slow at first. Trembling. But oui, as if by some dark chymistrie, the blood took on a will of its own, sinking into the vellum as if it were a sponge. The stain spread, forming into unreadable words surrounding a sigil, much like the heraldry of the other bloodlines.

'Two skulls, facing each other upon an ornate shield.

"'Great Redeemer," I whispered. "What does it say?"

"'*Last, and verily, most contemptible of all Courts of the Blood,*" Chloe read. "*A broken line of sorcerers and cannibals, damned even among the damned. Spit their name from thy tongue as thou wouldst the blood of pigs, and guard thine own blood lest they wrest it from thy veins.*"

'Astrid pointed to a name scribed beneath the skulls.

"'*Esani,*" she said. "*The Faithless.*"

"'Esani . . ." I whispered.

'Astrid nodded at the page. "Courtesans pass messages like this. They use lemon juice or milk, painted onto parchment. The writing is invisible, but when held to flame, the juice chars and the letters become legible. We called it 'fire writing' in the Golden Halls."

"'I'd no idea ancient kith communicated this way."

"'I don't think anyone did. I was flipping through the pages when my nose started gushing. I saw the writing while I was trying to clean up the fucking mess. And within the hour, it had faded again."

"'Angel Fortuna smiles upon us . . ."

"'No, *not* the Angel of Fortune," Chloe said, her eyes shining. "Don't you see? It's just as I said the night that star fell from heaven! All this was ordained. *This* is the answer." She stabbed at the fading writing with her finger. "Somewhere in this Library, somewhere among these books, is the solution to daysdeath!"

'Astrid shrugged. "If it's hidden suchlike, it'd explain why nobody's found it yet."

"'But how will *you* find it? You can't bleed on every book."

"'I'm not certain." Astrid sucked her lip. "But perhaps Chloe's right . . ."

"'I *am* right," Chloe insisted. "You were meant to set us to this task, Gabriel. Astrid was meant to find this bloodscript, and through it, the way to bring back the sun. I *know* it."

'The fervour in Chloe's eyes was contagious. I swear I could sense the presence of God in that room with us, and looking at the bloody writing fading from that page, I found it easy to believe all this *was* ordained.

"'We should speak to the abbot about this," I ventured.

"'Are you *completely* mad?" Astrid waved about us. "Forbidden section, remember?"

"'There's too many books in here for you to test alone. If there *is* an answer to daysdeath hidden in these pages, you're going to need help finding it."

"'We're going to need help putting the flesh back on our bones if the prioress learns we've been sneaking out of an eve. Some of us don't heal quick as others, Gabe."

"'I'll tell Khalid, then. I needn't mention you two at all."

"'Oh, really?" Chloe asked. "You can read Old Talhostic, can you?"

'I looked at the fading writing on the page, lips pursed.

"'Archivist Adamo would never allow either of us back into the Library if he knew we'd been reading these books without permission," Astrid said. "If we'd something definitive to show, silver might outweigh blood. But I've no intention of having the skin flayed off my back just yet, merci."

"'And Abbot Khalid's mind is set on the defence of Avinbourg, anyway," Chloe said.

'I nodded reluctantly. They were right, of course – the whole monastery was bent on stopping the Forever King. "The Empress herself is en route to San Michon."

"'We heard," Astrid muttered. "Charlotte had every novice in the Priory polish every piece of silver in the refectory, in case that dragoncunt deigns to dine with us."

"'Blasphemy, Astrid," Chloe chided. "The Empress is chosen by divine right."

"'The Empress is chosen by the Emperor's idiot *cock*. And I pray God both she and it get chewed up and shat out by rabid dogs." Astrid glanced at me. "You might want to shave before she arrives, by the way. That *thing* on your lip does you no favours."

"'It's a moustache," I said, rubbing at my straggly whiskers.

"'It's a heresy."

'I met Astrid's eyes, offered a sympathetic smile despite the bitchliness. I suspected she'd be feeling bitter, knowing the woman who'd exiled her to this prison was now paying it a visit at the head of an imperial army. A change of subject seemed wise, and I had one more question before we got to work anyway.

"'Tell me . . . how well did you both know Sister Aoife?"

'Chloe bowed her head, again made the sign of the wheel. "She was very kind to me when I first joined the Priory. A goodly woman, God rest her."

"'The night I was attacked in the stable . . . perhaps an hour before she died, I saw Aoife weeping in the Cathedral. Asking the Mothermaid if she'd been given a blessing or a curse. And a few days before that, I saw her down in the stables talking to young Kaveh. He at least seemed nervous that I'd discovered them together. Do you know what any of this might have meant, Sisternovice?"

"'I've no idea," Chloe replied.

"'Well, Kaveh supplies me my dreamweed." Astrid frowned at me. "Perhaps Aoife had some bad habits also. But why are you asking about her now?"

'I chewed my lip, eyes narrowed. "The vampire we faced in Coste. She mentioned Aoife, and it drove Seraph Talon into a rage. I'm wondering if—"

"'Unless I'm mistaken, the Order has a law about listening to what vampires tell you," Astrid scowled. "Perhaps you should be focused on the impending battle against a bloodthirsty corpse army instead?"

"'Too many mysteries here by half . . .'"

'But I knew Astrid was right. If the battles I'd fought in Skyefall and Coste had taught me anything, it was that I needed to be patient. Stop. Fucking *think*. Charging in face-first was a good way to put the people around me and myself in danger.

'*The dead can't kill the Dead.*

"'All right, I've waited this long. Avinbourg first.'"

✦ VIII ✦

LIONHEART

'I WAS STILL uneasy as I stole out from the Library and back towards Barracks. My thoughts were filled with that image etched in blood – two skulls facing each other. A name echoing in my head, like a song I somehow already knew the words to.

'*Esani.*

'*The Faithless.*

'Looking skywards, I stared into the dark, to the heaven that must surely lay beyond it. Again, I wondered if all this had been ordained, just as Chloe said. If the key to ending daysdeath *did* lie in those dusty tomes – a secret only blood might tell. But all thoughts of bloodlines and divine plans and hidden truths were abandoned as I spied a familiar figure, moving like a thief through the dark. I recognized him by his silhouette alone now; after all, I'd hunted with him in the shadows for months.

'Aaron de Coste.

'I crouched in the dark of the Cathedral cloister, the angels in the fountain watching me with sightless eyes. De Coste glanced about, then slipped inside the Armoury's doors.

'I could've let it alone. He was still a pompous cock, but Aaron had bled for me in Coste. He'd stopped Greyhand from murdering me, and he'd defended me again earlier tonight in front of Khalid. I was certain he hadn't been behind the attack in the stable now. Nor Aoife's death.

'But I still remembered the rage in his eyes when I told him I'd seen him sneaking out of the Armoury. And as I'd once told Astrid, other people's business was ever my favourite kind. Curiosity had killed countless cats, I knew. But cats had nine lives, and lions too.

'Checking the Armoury door, I found it locked. But undaunted, I scaled to the roof. Just like the Barracks, the tiles were old, easy enough to shift. I made my way along the upper floor and down the spiral stair to the entry hall, bathed in gloom. Looking to the Scarlet Foundry's doors, I wondered how many vampires lay within there now, chained to that damnable machine to fuel our sacrament. But then, in the forge behind me, I heard a *thump,* followed by a pained cry.

'Wondering if devilry was afoot, I took a silversteel blade from the wall and crept across the foyer. Oaken shelves were lined with tools, stacked with barrels of black ignis. The forge beyond was kept warm by the embers, the smell of coal and sweat reminding me of my stepfather's house in Lorson. Four great furnaces burned within, still aglow from the day's works. I heard another gasp, a crash, a strangled hiss – what sounded like men fighting. And stealing towards the noise, I finally found Aaron and Baptiste Sa-Ismael, the handsome young smithy of San Michon, moving together in the glow of dying flames.

'But they weren't fighting, I realized.

'They were kissing.

'I could scarce believe what I was seeing. Aaron's hands were in Baptiste's britches, kneading and stroking, the smith groaning all the way from his heart. They moaned into each other's mouths, hungry as starving wolves. As I watched, Aaron shoved Baptiste backwards, the pair colliding with the stone wall. They were heedless of all but each other, lost in passion, too much body and not enough hands. I'd never imagined a scene like this, part of me appalled, part of me fascinated, watching them sway in the forge's light.

'Baptiste grabbed a fistful of Aaron's long blonde hair and slammed him backwards against a stack of crates. Aaron's breath came ragged as Baptiste turned him about, fumbled with his belt. De Coste's hands joined Baptiste's, tearing at his britches, dragging them down. Baptiste hauled off his own tunic, dark skin gleaming in the ruddy light as he spat into his palm. Aaron lowered his head, dripping with sweat, spitting into his own hand. I knew what was coming then. And I decided I'd no right to see more of it.

'I backed away, silversteel in my now-sweating palm. But fool that I was, and not watching where I was going, I stumbled on a bucket of scrap iron. Grabbing it to stop the clamour, I cursed under my breath. And then I heard footsteps, rushing breath, and I was slammed backwards into the wall so hard I saw fucking stars.

'"Treacherous *bastard,*" Aaron hissed, pressing his forearm to my throat.

'"G-get the fuck off me."

'"What did you see, de León?" he demanded, pressing harder. "*What did you see?*"

'"N-nothing," I gasped.

'It was foolishness and lies, and we both knew it. De Coste's britches were still loosed, his lips bruised red from Baptiste's mouth. My brother initiate was furious, just as he'd been in his stepfather's hall. Afraid his whole world was unravelling before his eyes.

'I know what that feels like now. I can't fault him for hurting me. But back then, I was enraged. And more, frightened. I was as big as de Coste now, maybe even stronger, but with Baptiste beside him, they were two to my one. I could see murder in Aaron's stare as he crushed his forearm to my throat, looking about to the hammers and anvils and any number of means by which a nosy lad could be ended quick and neat. Finally, his gaze settled on the silversteel I'd dropped as he'd struck me, gleaming in the forge light. He met my stare. His own sharpened by a predator's gleam.

'"*Close your eyes.*"

'But a soft voice spoke then. "Aaron. Let him go."

'"But he knows," de Coste spat, turning to Baptiste. "He fucking *saw*."

'Running a hand over the tightly knotted braids on his scalp, the young blackthumb heaved a sigh. He looked at the Armoury around him, back to the boy pinning me against the wall. "We both knew this couldn't last forever."

'"We can fix this, we can—"

'"Silence him? Is that what you're thinking? Buy our safety with sin?"

'"It's no sin," Aaron spat, his face twisted. "You and I are no fucking *sin*."

'"But what you're thinking is. Let him go, love." Baptiste shook his head. "Let him go."

'De Coste turned back to me, fury in his eyes. But I could also see the beginnings of tears. For a moment, he held on, squeezing tighter. But at last, he stepped back. Gasping, I slithered down the wall. Afraid. Horrified. Angry. These two were sworn members of a holy order of God. And they . . .

'"I locked the door," de Coste whispered. "I *locked* it."

'Baptiste stepped up behind Aaron, pressed his lips to the boy's bare shoulder. De Coste closed his eyes, cursed softly. And then Baptiste reached down to me.

'"Are you well, Little Lion?"

'I stared up at the smithy, at the small burn scars etched on his mahogany skin. There was no rage in his eyes. Sadness, maybe. Fear. I looked at the hand he offered. Broad and callused like the man who'd called himself my papa. A blacksmith's hand. A genius's hand. A hand that had forged the blade that saved my life in Coste.

'I took it.

'We stood in uncomfortable silence, and I pawed at my bruised throat. Aaron looked chagrinned, furious, but more than all, afraid. Baptiste met my eyes. "It would be . . . unpleasant," he said, "if Abbot Khalid or Forgemaster Argyle were to learn of this."

'I met the older lad's gaze. *Unpleasant?* We both knew that was a whisper telling tale of a hurricane. The One Faith was no jest to the men within these walls. The scriptures were clear, the word of God Himself; that God we'd all devoted our lives to.

'"The Testaments name it a sin," I said softly.

'"The Testaments also say it is God's place to judge. Not man's."

'"You're a brother of the Silver Order, Baptiste," I said, indignity rising. "You swore the Oath of San Michon. Obedience. Fidelity. Chastity."

'"I swore to love no woman save the Mother and Maid. And to that I hold." Baptiste took Aaron's hand and squeezed it, defiant. "'Tis no woman I love."

'"Nor I," de Coste replied softly.

'I looked into Aaron's eyes. This slick highborn bastard who'd spat at me every chance he got. This brother I'd fought and bled beside. "Then why stay here?"

'Baptiste frowned. "As you say, we are sworn to the Silver Order."

'"But why risk it? Why remain in a place where discovery might cost your lives?"

'Baptiste folded his arms and glowered. "Because we are *sworn* to the Silver Order. The dark is rising. A dark that threatens all men. And we *are* men, Gabriel de León. So, we choose to stand against it."

'Aaron squeezed Baptiste's hand. "Together."

'I remembered the tale Aaron had told me in his stepfather's hall. The lover that the Baron de Coste had beaten to death. And I realized that "Sacha" was a boy's name as well as a girl's.

'I understood now why Aaron stayed here despite his claims that all this would come to nothing. I understood now why he worked so hard to earn a place he seemed to have no real wanting of. And I understood in some small way the bravery it must have taken to remain within these walls. God only knows what Khalid and the others would do if they learned the truth. The vows of chastity that silversaints swore were to ensure we created no more paleblood abominations like ourselves. But still, the Testaments were clear.

'Aaron and Baptiste could have fled. Gone to live in Asheve or Augustin, where such a life would <u>not be so scowled</u> upon. But they chose to stand at the coal face and risk the flame. Because, despite it all, they believed that the dark must be fought.

'All my life, I'd been raised to see the word of God as law. But I was a sinner myself, wasn't I? I'd broken the rules of San Michon this very night. Astrid had broken the same in helping me, but through it, we'd found a way towards the truth of what I was. A meeting that, if Chloe were to be believed, was ordained by the Almighty Himself.

'And I wondered then: Could goodness come of sin?

'And if so, how could it be sin at all?

'What care I, the life these two lived? The Dead cared not for who we loved, nor creed nor kin nor any other measure. And if I were to risk all against them, I'd want the brothers beside me to be those who'd risk no less. Aaron de Coste and I weren't friends. At that moment, I still doubted we ever would be. But we *were* brothers. And as the old truth goes, you can choose your friends, but never your famille.

'"I'll not tell the abbot," I declared. "Nor Forgemaster Argyle, nor Master Greyhand either. I'll not breathe a word."

'Aaron and Baptiste looked at each other. Astonished. Uncertain.

'"Do you vow it?" the smithy asked.

'"I vow it, brother," I said, offering my hand. "On my fucking life."

'Baptiste waited a heartbeat longer, then took my hand and pulled me into a fierce embrace. There were tears in the young smith's eyes, and even though he smiled, Aaron's eyes were also shining. He slapped my back, sighed as if exhaling the weight of the world.

'"Merci," de Coste nodded. "Merci, Little Lion."

'I nodded to him, matching his smile. As I said, I didn't know if he and I could ever be friends. But perhaps now we might be something more than two boys who spat and sniped at each other while the shadow around them grew ever deeper.

'"You've a good heart, Gabriel de León," Baptiste told me. "A *lion's* heart."

'I only shrugged. "My brothers are the hill I die on."

'I took my leave, left the pair standing there etched in the light of the forges. And swift as I could, I stole back to Barracks under cover of darkness. My mind was awash with all I'd done and seen that night. But one thought called louder than the others – more than the mystery of my heritage, of shifting friendships and new allies, a question burning brighter than that star, falling from the black embrace of heaven.

'What is sin at all?'

✦ IX ✦

DRESSED FOR WAR

'SAN MICHON WAS busier than I'd ever seen.

'Silversaints were being recalled from all over the realm for the defence of Avinbourg, and there were over a dozen initiates bedding down in Barracks now. Big Theo Petit with his sandy hair and shoulders like an ox. Fincher with his mismatched eyes and carving fork under his pillow. Aaron's cronies: de Séverin, Big, Mid, and Lil Philippe – all those highborn lads who'd made my life a misery the last fucking year.

'Most didn't know what to make of me now. I was still a frailblood – the lowest of the low in a roomful of Dyvok, Ilon, Chastain, Voss. But they'd all heard of our battle with the Wraith in Red. And the first time de Séverin called me "Peasant", Aaron lifted his head from the Book of Vows he was studying, his voice velvet soft.

'"Leave him be, Sév."

'"What?" the big lad scoffed. "This lowborn boylover? He's lucky I—"

'"Sév." Aaron locked eyes with his fellow nobleson. "Leave him be."

'Three days later, it was famdi, the day before prièdi, and as the bells rang out the dawn, I found myself already awake. Tomorrow would be a landmark day – Empress Isabella was due to arrive at the head of her husband's army, and Aaron was to be inducted as a full-fledged silversaint. But today was special for me. I'd survived my first Hunt, and at last, was to be gifted the next piece of my aegis under the needles of the Silver Sorority.

'As I entered the Cathedral with de Coste beside me, I saw a familiar figure among the sisters at the altar. Looking through her lace veil, I saw a beauty spot beside quirked lips, and pride in dark, shining eyes.

'I didn't even glance at Astrid as they bound me down, dared not give away a breath of the secrets we shared. But still, I could feel her beside me, smell the rosewater and silverbell in her hair. After twelve hours under her needles, wrapped in incense and choir's hymn, I was near delirious with pain. But I couldn't complain. Aaron was having his entire back inked before the taking of his vows. He'd already suffered three days under Prioress Charlotte's needles, but now the piece was almost complete – a beautiful portrait of the Redeemer, surrounded by angels of the host.

'I watched Prioress Charlotte work, thinking on what Astrid had said about the role women played in San Michon. How little power they actually wielded. There were a dozen sisters about us, singing exultations or wiping off blood or mixing silver and ink.

'Who sang exultations for them?'

'What design did you choose, de León?' Jean-François asked.

Gabriel pulled up the sleeve on his left arm. Atop his hand was a wreath of roses. 'For the perfume of her hair,' he explained. His forearm was marred by scar tissue, rends and tears etched in his skin. But under the scars on his inside forearm, armour-clad, beautiful and bright, her wings outspread like burning silver ribbons . . .

'Eirene,' the historian nodded. 'Angel of Hope.'

'Such was the gift Astrid Rennier had given me. And when the deed was done, staring at that silver poetry she'd written on my flesh, I couldn't help but voice the thought. "You do beautiful work, Sisternovice."

'"The work we do is Almighty God's, Initiate," Prioress Charlotte replied, still bent over Aaron's bleeding back. "You, I, all of us are merely his instruments upon this earth."

'"Véris, Prioress. But the Order could not serve without the sisterhood. Without the silver in our skin, we'd be prey for the dark. So I for one am grateful, for all you do." I looked around the gathering, bowed low. "Merci, Sisters. To you all. We are nothing without you."

'Astrid smiled at me then, swift and secret. The look old Charlotte gave me made me wonder if any silversaint had ever actually said that to her before. The scars on her face twisted in an almost-smile, but clearing her throat, she returned to her work. "You are welcome, Initiate de León."

'I stayed with Aaron while Charlotte put on the finishing touches. The poor bastard looked like he was hanging on by the skin of his teeth. But finally, the Prioress leaned back, looking over the tattoo with a critical eye. It was a stunning piece; the Redeemer's stare seeming to burn upon Aaron's skin, candlelight setting the silver aglow.

'"Véris," she murmured.

'"Véris," came the reply from the sisters around us.

'I helped Aaron to his feet as he blinked like a newborn. "Aright, brother?"

'"I need a drink," he declared with shaking voice. "A very large, very strong drink."

'I laughed, easing my tunic over my own wounded skin. And with a bow to the sisters, a glance to Astrid, we left the Cathedral. It was snowing outside, and after the burning pain of the needle, the chill seemed a Godly blessing. As we walked towards the refectory, my eyes drifted northwards. I admit I was jealous that Aaron was to swear his vows amorrow; that he'd fight at Avinbourg as a full-fledged silversaint. But I also knew he'd earned it.

'"I'm happy for you, de Coste. Truly."

'He looked at me sidelong, words clearly fighting behind his teeth.

'"I owe you a debt, de León. And an apology."

'I shook my head. "You saved my skin in Coste just as I saved yours. There's no—"

'"I'm not talking about Coste," he said, lowering his voice. "I'm talking about Baptiste and me. I misjudged you. And I mistreated you. Frailblood or no, peasantborn or no. You are my brother, de León. And I ask your forgiveness."

'He offered his hand, and I grasped it tight. "Given. Gladly."

'Aaron nodded, jaw clenched. I knew three days under the needle had him feeling raw. Your walls are thin after an ordeal like that, and the person you are beneath can easily leak through. But I was still surprised to see tears in his eyes.

'"What Laure said to us on the bridge . . . about Sacha . . ."

'"It doesn't matter, Aaron. Whatever you did as a boy, you're him no longer. Your past is stone, but your future is clay. And you decide the shape of the life you'll make."

'He nodded, pawed his eyes. "I never thought I'd hear myself say it. But I'll be glad to have you beside me at Avinbourg, de León."

'"Beside you?" I scoffed, patting the sword at my belt. "Brother, I'm going to be in *front* of you. I've got more ink to earn. And Lionclaw is thirsty."

'"You're still an idiot, de León. And it's going to get you killed." Aaron shook his head and smiled. "But when you die, you'll die righteous."

'"But not tonight," I grinned. "Come. Let's get you that drink."

'I slapped him on the back without thinking, and he cried out in agony. I gasped apology, but not quick enough, and de Coste punched me in my left arm, sending a wave of flame up my shoulder. We fell to wrestling for a moment, exchanging friendly blows before falling off laughing. And side by side, we walked into the refectory.

'A rousing cheer greeted us as we entered, the assembled silversaints and initiates clunking tankards on tabletops. It wasn't often a new member was set to be sworn into the Order, nor so many of us assembled in San Michon at one time. Older 'saints offered Aaron congratulations; younger bucks gathered to get a glimpse of his new ink. Frère Alonso was playing a merry tune on a set of pipes. Abbot Khalid accompanied him on a beautiful blood-wood lute, with Forgemaster Argyle leading the song in his rich baritone. And though Greyhand was conspicuously absent, Seraph Talon was thumping the table with his ashwood switch, keeping time. He even smiled at us as we entered.

'Baptiste had saved us seats at table, beckoning us over. As we sat, the young smithy pushed a cup of vodka my way. But as ever, I demurred. "Not for me, Brother. Merci."

'"Oh, come now!" the blackthumb insisted. "Puts hairs on your chest! And it's not every day we see a new member of the Order ascend! One drink won't kill you?"

'"He has his reasons." De Coste spoke soft, taking the cup away. "Leave it, eh?"

'I looked between Aaron and Baptiste, the Brothers around me. The fires were warm and the smiles wide, and I knew a night like this came not often to walls like these. I'd grown up the son of a drunkard. But in truth, I wasn't even Raphael Castia's son. And the curse my true father had given me wouldn't be ignited by a mouthful of spirits.

'"One drink," I declared, reaching for the cup Baptiste had poured. "Won't kill me."

'Baptiste cheered, and I raised the cup to Aaron. But before I could offer toast, there came a loud thumping from the head table. Frère Alonso stilled his music, all eyes turning towards Abbot Khalid. The big Sūdhaemi was on his feet, smiling.

'"Tomorrow, we welcome a full-fledged Brother to the Ordo Argent!"

'Roars rang around the room as Khalid continued.

'"Then, we march to Avinbourg among the Emperor's armies, there to lay the Forever King to rest. I know each of you shall acquit yourselves with strength undying and faith unquenchable, and prove San Michon worthy of our Empress's patronage. But for now, let us toast our new brother, and know glory in the light of the Almighty's love."

'Khalid raised his cup to Aaron.

'"Santé, Aaron de Coste. May the dark know your name and despair!"

'"*Santé!*" came the roar, Aaron grinning like a child at Firstmas.

'We feasted into the night, and when Baptiste poured me another cup, I didn't turn it away. The drink was fine and the company grand, and I floated around, listening to the older 'saints tell stories of dark and blood and silver. I felt the love of God among that fellowship. I felt, for perhaps the first time in my life, I was finally where I belonged.

'It was then we heard horns in the Mère Valley, bringing stillness to the hall. A few moments later, the Cathedral bells sang out in answer, echoing across the monastery.

'"She's early," Baptiste murmured.

'"Empress Isabella," I realized.

'The brothers and initiates rose as one, bustling out of the refectory. The honour that the Empress did us was lost on nobody, and all wanted to bear witness to her arrival, see the army she'd brought to San Michon. Gathering on the Cathedral walkway, we heard them in the dark – tromping feet and steel on steel, a great multitude in the night-black valley below. We could see thousands of torches, illuminating thousands of yellow tabards bearing the unicorn of Alexandre III. A host the likes of which I'd never seen.

'"Now there's a fucken' sight," Fincher sighed.

'De Séverin nodded. "On golden banners, salvation comes."

'"Brothers!" Khalid called. "Prepare yourselves for Her Majesty's arrival, then assemble in the Great Library! Seraph Talon, Prioress Charlotte, with me."

'With some a little worse for drink, the brethren obeyed, the feast abandoned. Within the half hour, we were mustered in the Library, lined up with boots polished and silversteel gleaming. The Sorority was assembled also, sisters in their blacks, novices in white. I saw Astrid among them, lips pinched tight. Chloe stood beside her, nodding once to me. But looking about, I still saw no sign of Master Greyhand anywhere.

'The books stretched high above us, the great map of the realm at our feet. Archivist Adamo had arrayed wooden figures across the floor, representing the armies of the Forever King, the defenders of Avinbourg, and the great host mustering below.

'The impending battle was now on everyone's mind, and talk of it rippled among the gathering. But we fell silent as Abbot Khalid entered, marching swift to the front of the Library, Talon and Charlotte beside him. A brisk young man in courtly yellow satin entered, and beat a poleaxe upon the boards three times.

'"Her Imperial Majesty, Isabella, First of Her Name, beloved bride of Alexandre III, Protector of God's Holy Church, Sword of the Faith and Emperor of all Elidaen!"'

Gabriel shook his head.

'I'd never seen royalty. The way Astrid told it, Alexandre's court was a cesspit, filled with debauchery and corruption. I'd not have been surprised if the Empress was a serpent in a dress of human skin. But the woman who swept into the Library was nothing close.

'First, I was astonished at how *young* she was. Emperor Alexandre was in his middle-forties, but his bride must have been twenty years younger; only a few years older than Astrid, really. She was beautiful to be sure: long-limbed and graceful, with auburn hair styled atop her head in the seeming of a crown. But beauty was to be expected in an empress. What I didn't count on was her manner of dress. For though she wore a gown of royal yellow, crushed velvet rippling to the ground in waves, she was also clad in a breastplate of polished silver, and she wore a sword at her side. The weapon was more decorative than deadly, but her message was plain.

'Our Empress had come to San Michon dressed for war.

'She was surrounded by men and maids-at-arms, clad in the sunflower yellow tabards of the Emperor. On Isabella's brow sat a circlet of diamonds, and as she took her place at the front of the room, she looked over us with regal pride.

'"Our road has been long," she said, her voice low and sweet. "But our heart could not be filled with more joy to find so fine a company at the end of it. Deep is the faith we have bestowed upon your abbot, and we see it has not been misplaced. For in each of you, we see a hope that shines with the light of all God's grace, and through you, shall this land be redeemed from encroaching night. You have our thanks. And more, you have our love."

'Isabella gazed about the room, and you could have heard tears falling from an angel's eyes in that stillness.

'"We salute you, Silversaints. May God bless you and keep you safe from all harm."

'"Three cheers for Her Imperial Majesty!" Seraph Talon cried.

'A roar echoed in the Library, louder than I'd ever heard. Isabella had spoken for all of a minute, and I swear God half the men in that hall were in love with her. If she had bid us fly to Vellene and throw ourselves at the Forever King with naught but empty fists, we'd have leapt from the walls with smiles on our faces.

'"Attend now, Brothers," Khalid said, his voice like iron.

'Silence fell then. The assembled 'saints and initiates, the Silver Sisters who lurked like shadows – all watched as the abbot walked along the peaks of the Godsend Mountains. Raissa, Angel of Justice, and Raphael, Angel of Wisdom. Sarai, Angel of Plagues, and Sanael, Angel of Blood. All fell beneath his silver heels as he walked the length of the realm, arriving finally at Avinbourg. The cityfort sat at the northern end of the spine, barring the way into Nordlund, surrounded by wooden soldiers.

'"All royal garrisons along the Godsend are now emptied and marching north to reinforce Avinbourg. A snowstorm has fallen across Talhost, too bleak and dark to see through, even with the eyes we command. Some dark witchery is at work, obscuring Voss's host. Still, we have no doubt the Endless Legion is on the move."

'"How many do they number, Abbot?" Frère Alonso asked.

'"Ten thousand at least."

'Alonso squared his shoulders. He was a mighty man, Nordlund bred, with a great black beard and mane of long hair. "Forgive me, Abbot. My Empress. But we are hunters, not soldiers. What good will our number be against so vast a host?"

'"None whatsoever, good Frère," Isabella replied. "Those brave soldiers below and already manning the walls at Avinbourg will bear the brunt of the Legion's hunger."

'"We are a knife, Brothers," Khalid said. "Not a sledgehammer. But a creature so ancient as Fabién Voss does not risk himself in the vanguard. Not with ten thousand corpses to throw first. Like all those who fear death, the Forever King leads from the rear."

'The Empress nodded. "And while Voss hurls his host at the city's defences, this silvered company will sail around the mouth of the Cherchant, hit from behind Voss's lines in the light of the dawn, and with all God's grace, strike the hollow crown from his head."

'"An ambush," Alonso nodded.

'"An execution," Khalid said. "One upon which the Almighty Himself shall smile."

'The abbot's words filled my belly with butterflies. I could see wisdom in the plan; a way our small brotherhood could still deal a deadly blow. The Forever King was oldest of his line, controlling his brood like a spider in the centre of a grand and rotten web. With his death, his legion would be thrown into disarray, at least temporarily – easy pickings for the Golden Host. Slaying an ancien would be no small feat, but if we managed it, we could end the invasion at Avinbourg's walls.

'I spoke up, unable to contain myself. "When do we march, Abbot?"

'Khalid's eyes met mine. "You do not, Initiate."

'My belly dropped. For an awful moment, I feared my conduct on the Hunt had cost me my place among the chosen. But the abbot's gaze swept the initiates, each in turn. "None of you do. All initiates will remain in San Michon. Laure Voss is still loose in the Nordlund, and she *will* seek vengeance. It is unwise to leave this monastery unguarded."

'A murmur rippled among the initiates. This was the greatest battle of our age, and we were being left behind? Any sensible lad would've kept his fucking mouth shut then, but with a few vodkas in me, I was feeling less than sensible.

'"Abbot, I mean no disrespect. But just a few nights ago, you assured me we'd soon be called upon to defend God's Church?"

'Talon thwacked his switch on the floor. "De León, shut your damned m—"

'"Stay your anger, Seraph." Isabella regarded me, gaze roaming boots to brow. "*De León*. You were part of that brave company which uncovered the Forever King's plan."

'"One of four, Majesty." I bowed. "But I did my part."

'"A lion indeed. We understand your disappointment in remaining behind while others ride forth to fight. But there is no shame in tending home and hearth."

'"No glory either, Majesty."

'"We do not fight for glory, Initiate," Khalid growled. "We fight for God. We fight to redeem ourselves from the sin of our birth. Mortal accolade is meaningless. When you stand before your Maker, *he* shall know the role you played in the Forever King's defeat."

'"Presuming we defeat him."

'All eyes turned to the back of the hall. There, outlined against the night sky, stood Frère Greyhand. His jaw was unshaven, hair dishevelled. But fire burned in his remaining eye. The great doors swung shut behind him as he strode out onto the map of the realm.

'"Presuming the Forever King lets us," he said.

'"He will have little choice, Brother," Khalid replied. "We fight with God on our side."

'"You're assuming we get to fight at all, Abbot. We have no eyes to see through this accursed storm. No word from our allies upon the winds." Greyhand reached into his coat with his one good hand, fetching a familiar piece of parchment. "All we have to assure us Voss intends to crush Avinbourg is a single scribble."

'"Forgive us, Frère." Isabella eyed the invasion map Greyhand held. "But is that not a scribble you yourself stole? After a battle that almost killed you and your apprentices?"

'"Your pardon, Majesty, but that's what's been vexing me. The *almost*." Greyhand closed his fingers about the map, tossed the crumpled scrap of parchment to the floor. "The Wraith in Red is a Prince of Forever. If she was scouting towns along the Godsend to prepare for her father's invasion, why leave a trail so easy for us to follow?"

'"She needs to feed, Brother," Khalid said. "And vampires are creatures of habit, you know this. Perhaps she did not realize we'd track her so swift?"

'"Perhaps," Greyhand nodded. "But how is it two silversaints and two initiates faced one of the most powerful vampires alive, and all lived to tell about it?"

'I exchanged a glance with Aaron at that. Truth told, somewhere beneath the rush of our supposed victory, I'd wondered the same thing.

'"You think she used us, Master?" de Coste asked.

'"I think it's no wonder she took us for fools," Greyhand said, his one good eye fixed on mine. "Given the way some of us acted that night."

'I lowered my gaze, cheeks burning.

'Empress Isabella spoke into the silence.

'"You believe we are being misdirected, good Frère?"

'"I am certain of nothing, Majesty. Save the love of Almighty God. But these creatures know their prey. And I fear we guard our throat, yet leave our belly exposed."

'Greyhand walked to the Godsend's southern edge. And there, he stamped his heel on the cityfort that guarded the other passage to the Nordlund.

'"Charinfel," Khalid murmured.

'"Perhaps Voss *meant* for us to intercept that message," Greyhand said. "With this accursed storm, we've no way to be sure. But throwing all we have to defend Avinbourg sits ill with me, Khalid. Something about this smells foul."

'"What then do you suggest?"

'"Guard both passes."

'"We cannot strike Fabién Voss with less than full strength," Talon said. "Every silversaint here may still not be enough to end him. And if our battle goes ill, Avinbourg will need every soldier in the valley below to fend off the Endless Legion."

'"Then let *us* go, Abbot."

'All in the Library turned to me as I stepped forward. The boy I'd been might have quailed with those eyes upon me – generals and holy brothers and empresses. But after the things I'd seen, the blood I'd spilled, I was that boy no longer.

"'We initiates, I mean. If this is a ploy from Voss, *we* can defend Charinfel! Greyhand can lead us! We're doing nobody any good stuck here in San Michon!"

'Murmurs of agreement rolled among the initiates until Talon sliced the air and bellowed for silence. But Greyhand met Khalid's eyes.

"'If my fears prove true, they'll be more use on the line than behind it."

"'If your fears prove true, you and two dozen initiates will not *hold* that line."

'Greyhand rubbed his chin, looked to our Empress. Isabella stood among her advisers, eyes flickering between Greyhand and the abbot. A crag-faced general whispered in her ear, and she listened intently, studying the map. I could feel the tension in the lads around me – the idea we might be able to play a role after all filling us with fire.

"'General Nassar advises we can spare one thousand men," the Empress finally declared. "We are loath to reduce our numbers further. The last scout report we received told us the Endless Legion *was* moving northeast from Vellene. Despite your fears, all signs point to the Forever King striking Avinbourg, Frère, not Charinfel."

"'If this is true, I will consider myself gladly chastened, Majesty," Greyhand replied. "But in battle, the wise man prays to God, yet still raises his sword."

'My belly surged as Isabella inclined her head. "So be it."

'A small cheer went up among the initiates, and Talon again roared for silence. Our voices died, but our smiles remained, and several of the lads slapped my back in gratitude before returning to order. The counsel session rolled on, but in truth, none of us was listening. Where a moment ago we were set to be chained to the hearth like untrained puppies, now we were to be unleashed as a pack of wolves. And even if no evil ended up coming to Charinfel, at least we'd not be sitting like mushrooms in the dark.'

Gabriel dragged his hair back, tipped the last of his wine down his throat.

'It wasn't until the next morn I learned that's *exactly* what I'd be doing.'

✦ X ✦

THE SIN SHARED

'THE BARRACKS WERE abuzz that night, and I was treated to a dozen more slaps to my back as we bedded down. We all knew we'd be setting out with the dawn, but still, Theo and Lil Phil had smuggled some vodka from the refectory, and we shared a few more mouthfuls around our cots. Finch raised a bottle in my direction, and even de Séverin managed a smile.

'"Quick thinking and quicker talking, de León." The nobleson nodded. "Santé."

'"D'ye see Talon's face?" Fincher chuckled. "I thought he was about to shite blood."

'Petit grinned. "I fancy the Empress liked the cut of our kitten's coat, though."

'Aaron lifted the vodka in toast, the scar on his face twisting as he gifted me a rare smile. "To the brave, the bounty."

'I smiled in return. "One day as a lion is worth ten thousand as a lamb."

'We settled abed after a few more sips, and the liquor helped my brothers to their dreams. We were to march on the morrow, and I knew I should be about my sleep too. But there was one more visit I needed to pay before night took me. One more word that needed speaking. If all Greyhand feared was true, this journey could be my last.

'The Library was quiet as I stole inside, wooden troops still arrayed on the great map. My belly fluttered as I saw the parchment Greyhand had left crumpled on the floor.

'I picked it up, smoothed the map out, thinking of the price we'd paid for it. I turned my eyes to the empire beneath my feet; to Avinbourg, to Charinfel, wondering which the Forever King would actually strike. Greyhand might have been right. Laure Voss was ancien, and it *did* feel that perhaps she'd toyed with us in Coste. But still . . . something about all of this struck an ill note. Something I couldn't yet ken.

'I smelled rosewater and rêvre as I stole through the forbidden section, a small smile on my lips. And rounding the shelves, there I found her; sitting with chin in palms, long black hair tumbling about her face. The books before her were unread, the scent of dreamweed heavy in the air. Looking at her eyes, I could see she'd smoked more than usual.

"'Bonsoir, Majesty," I bowed.

'Astrid glanced to me, back to the candleflame. "What's so fucking good about it?"

'I held up the remnants of Theo's vodka. "I come bearing gifts?"

'Astrid looked to me again, lip quirking. "You may be seated."

'The drink from the feast was still quick in my blood, the pain of my new tattoo a faint throb beneath it. I handed Astrid the bottle, watching the candlelight playing upon her throat as she took a long, slow pull. Her eyes were heavy lidded, bloodshot, and she finished half of what was left before passing the bottle back to me.

"'I suppose you think you're terribly clever."

"'What exactly is terrible about being clever?" I asked, taking a mouthful.

"' *Tsk*. Boys." She took the bottle back, shaking her head. "Getting Isabella's attention like that is unwise."

"'I didn't realize I'd *got* her attention."

"'She knew your *name*. But have a care, Gabriel de León. Our Empress breaks the toys she plays with." Astrid drank deep, wincing. "I mean, honestly, did you see that sword she was wearing? She'd be lucky to find the pointy end. Showy cunt."

"'I didn't notice. My eyes were elsewhere."

'She scoffed. "Indeed."

"'I mean it. I've no use for pretty dresses and painted lips. Give me silver and blood. Give me a mind quick as the turning of the sky and sharp as the blade at my side."

"'Well, fancy that. A few sips of homebrew piss, and he turns into a poet."

"'I don't think any of that rhymed."

"'A terrible poet, then." Her smile failed, and she took another mouthful. "Apologies. I'm being a bitch again. Although Mama did tell me: In life, always do what you love."

"'You're no bitch, Astrid Rennier."

"'All right, *now* I'm insulted."

'"You strike the pose well enough. But if you're so bitchly, why are you in here every night, looking for the salvation of the empire that abandoned you?"

'"There's little else to do in this hole. Save torturing myself with fancies of escaping it."

'"You don't fool me, any more. A blackheart doesn't make people saintsday gifts, nor arrange swordplay lessons for their friends, nor spend time convincing the abbot to let your sisters learn to protect themselves. There's pure gold beating beneath your breast."

'"Oh Mothermaid, you *are* enchanted, aren't you?"

'She met my gaze, and I didn't look away. I could sense a precipice, and though I knew we both enjoyed this game, I was wary of the edge. I should be abed. I'd need my strength for the ride ahead, perhaps the battle at the end of it. But the liquor was warm in her cheeks, and the thought of leaving her again so soon was a stone in my chest.

'Astrid offered the bottle. "Another? Or is the rest for your queen?"

'I shrugged. "One more won't kill me."

'"Famous last words, Little Lion."

'"I don't plan on dying tonight, Majesty."

'"And what about tomorrow?"

'I looked at her then. Into the haze of those long, shady eyes. She was upset, that much was plain. But I thought she'd smoked herself numb because of Isabella – the sight of the Empress who'd exiled her to this prison, the thought of what might've been. Astrid Rennier was a royal bastard who but for a quirk of fate, might well have been a princess.

'But looking at her now, I saw no self-pity. That wasn't Astrid's way. Instead, gazing into the bloodshot dark of her eyes, I saw fear. Not for her. But for me.

'"I've been thinking," she declared.

'"I wondered what that grinding noise was."

'She scoffed. "Prick."

'"Bastard."

'"Touché. But I like it better when you call me Majesty."

'I leaned back, laughing. "What have you been thinking?"

'Her tone turned serious, the small smile dying at her lips. "About your tale of what you did to that fledgling. And what Chloe and I found in that book."

'My smile died also. Thoughts returning to Skyefall, and the blood of that deadboy boiling at my touch. With the Forever King rushing at us headlong, all the noise and bustle of the last week, it was hard to find time to fret on it. But aside from that strange name – *Esani* – I still had no true idea what I was. Nor what I could do.

'"I was thinking," Astrid continued. "If it's a bloodgift, then you must train it like any other. And I know you've got no one here who can teach you, nor any real idea how to conjure it. But if you wish help to master it . . . I'll offer."

'"You mean . . . try to use it on you?"

'"You need practice if you've intent to wield it with any skill."

'"I don't want to hurt you, Astrid."

'Dark eyes glittered as they met mine. "A little pain never hurt anyone."

'Despite myself, my belly thrilled a touch at those words. I matched her stare, and I could see it, sure as I could see my own reflection in the dark of her pupils.

'*Want.*

'This was dangerous now. I knew all too well the peril that came when such talk was mixed with smoke and drink. This girl was promised to God, and I was soon to be sworn as his soldier. For all the thrill of our little flirtations, there was no future in this. Nothing to be gained, and everything, *everything* to be lost.

'But Great Redeemer, she was beautiful. Smoky lashes, framing pools of midnight black. My gaze traced her cheek, down the line of her neck to the secrets beyond.

'I should have told her no.

'She should never have offered in the first place.

'But in truth, that was the allure of it all.

'"All right, then," I said.

'She pushed the bottle and books aside, climbed up onto the table in front of me. I could smell vodka on her lips and dreamweed in the air as she offered her hand. I felt a frisson through her fingertips as we touched. I thought of Skyefall, of the surge of heat running up my arm as I boiled that fledgling's blood.

'But sitting this close, all thought of bloodgifts and practice melted away. As I've said, not even God Himself can come between a girl and a boy truly in want of each other. And looking into Astrid's eyes, I knew what she wanted. And God help me, I wanted it too.

'"This is foolish," I whispered.

'She wove her fingers through mine, thumb brushing feather light along my skin.

'"Let's call it reckless."

'I don't know who moved first. I don't know who followed. I know only our first kiss was more a collision, a meeting of powder and flame. She sank down into my lap and crushed her mouth to mine, dragging her fingers through my hair. I pulled her closer, hard as I dared, the strength of the dark blood in my veins singing. And the taste of her, the smell of her, the feel of her, alive and warm and wanting in my arms awoke it inside me – that same hunger I'd known in Ilsa's bed. I felt that thirst rise like a flame, roaring through me, fangs stirring in my gums, heat in my veins. Wishing became wanting, and wanting became needing, and all of it, *all* of it was need of her.

'But this was madness. This was *wrong*. This was against the rule of the monastery and the commands of our betters and even the will of heaven itself.

'"Astrid," I whispered. "We cannot do this."

'"I know," she breathed, kissing me again.

'She reached down between us, and I gasped as I felt her fingertips running up and down me through my leathers. Her kiss deepened, desire bleeding into me, and though we knew this was a sin, somehow that only made us burn the brighter with it. Her mouth was open, her kisses hungry, and I heard her hiss as my fangs scratched her lip and a stab of impossibly bright and burning blood splashed upon my tongue.

'I gasped and tried to pull away, terrified of hurting her. But her hand slipped inside my britches and closed around me, holding me still. She could have steered me with the lightest touch then. She could have killed me with a whisper. She looked me in the eyes and I could see the truth of it, curled at the edge of her bloody smile.

'There's no sin so dangerous as the sin that is chosen.

'No sin so glorious as the sin that is shared.

'"How does a man pray, Gabriel?"

'I was breathless, speechless, licking her blood from my lips and shaking my head.

'Astrid took my hands, pressed them to her body. Guiding my touch over the swell of her breasts, down her ribs to the maddening curves of her hips. She licked her bleeding lip, eyes fluttering closed, hips rolling as she swayed against me. Leaning close, she pressed her bleeding mouth to mine, the taste of her almost driving me mad.

'"How does a man pray?"

'"I don't know. I don—"

'"He prays on his knees, Gabriel."

'And then she pushed herself back up onto the table, slid her hands over my shoulders, pulling me closer, down. The taste of her blood crashed and burned upon my tongue, and her eyes looked deep into mine as she whispered the words that made me completely and finally fall.

'"Pray to me."

'And a part of me was just a sixteen-year-old boy then. Begging only to serve and wanting only to please. But the rest of me, the most of me, was filled with a hunger darker than any I'd ever known. I ran my hands up over her legs, slowly rucking her robes up around her hips, her breath coming quicker as I slipped to my knees. The scent of her crashed upon me, the need of her filled me utterly. And she shivered as she felt the first feather-soft touch of my tongue, her pulse thundering beneath her skin, fingers slipping into my hair as she dragged me in tighter. "Please," she sighed. "*Please.*"

'I kissed her, adored her – soft, languid, her every sigh and moan an invitation to coax yet another from those lips, louder and longer. She was mine then, not God's, wholly and solely mine. Honeyed petals beneath my tongue, nothing and no one between us. Looking down into my eyes and shivering harder between every breath, her hips swaying, toes curling as she parted her legs wider, one hand in my hair, the other now finding her breast, stroking and plucking through her holy vestments. I was lost in the taste of her, the thrill of it all, so silken smooth and velvet soft I could barely breathe. I'd never known any sin so sweet as this. Never wanted anything in my life as much as I wanted her.

'"Touch me," she begged, and I obeyed.

'"Inside me," she pleaded, and I almost lost my mind.

'She mewled my name, head thrown back, shaking so hard I could barely hold on. Drowning, begging, God, she was so warm there. Her every soft secret at my fingertips, moaning in time with every burning kiss. She sank back onto the table, books scattering, spine arching as she began to shake, legs rising skywards, eyes rolling back in her head, lips parted as she called my name again, so long and loud I knew for certain we'd be undone . . .

'And then the bells began ringing.

'Our eyes met over the plane of her heaving belly. Confusion breaking through the swell of hunger, the rush of need. My pulse was hammering, my lips and chin drenched, sweet nectar and hot blood and salty sweat as the tolling rang out over the monastery, echoed through the empty Library.

'"What's that?" she whispered.

'The hour was late, but dawn was nowhere close; this was no mass being called. And helping Astrid up from where she lay, ignoring the thirst that surged ever brighter as I looked to her still-bleeding mouth, I spoke with creeping dread.

'"Something's wrong . . ."'

✦ XI ✦

WHICH YOU WILL BE

"'OATHBREAKERS! FUCKING BLASPHEMERS!'"

"'Shut your mouth!'"

"'Bastard, bog-grubbing sinners!' 'Ware ye! 'Ware now, Brothers!'"

'Those were the cries that greeted Astrid and me as we stumbled from the Library and into the night. The air was freezing after the fire of her lips, and I could still feel her body pressed against me, taste the sin of her in my mouth as we spied a mob of silversaints and initiates in the snow outside the Armoury.

"'Best get back to the Priory, Majesty," I told her.

'She nodded, squeezing my hand. "Be careful, Gabe."

'I circled about the monastery bridges, approached as if from the Barracks. Nearing the Armoury, I saw Seraph Talon on the steps, fury in his eyes. And beside him . . .

"'Oh, no . . ." I whispered.

"'Ware!" Talon roared. 'Ware now! Foul sin and oaths broken, by God!"

'Aaron and Baptiste stood together, clothes dishevelled, Aaron's lips red and raw. I joined the back of the crowd, more 'saints and initiates now spilling from the Barracks. Talon was shouting pure venom, spittle on his moustache. Baptiste looked distraught, Aaron furious as Abbot Khalid and Forgemaster Argyle finally forced their way through the throng.

"'Seraph, what be the meaning o' this?" Argyle demanded.

'Talon pointed his switch at Aaron and Baptiste. "Bastard boylovers, I saw them!"

"'Saw what?" Khalid spat. "Speak plainly, man!"

"'I had work in the Foundry! A batch of sanctus to accompany Greyhand to Charinfel. But I heard tumult in the forge and sought the source. And there I saw them, bare in each other's arms." The seraph stabbed one callused finger as my heart sank. "De Coste and Sa-Ismael! Rutting like mongrels in heat!"

'A dark mutter rumbled among the assembly. Argyle blinked in astonishment, rubbing his chin with his iron hand. "What madness is this?"

"'No madness." Talon spat on the stone. "Transgression and treachery, that's fucking what! Hellbound bastards, the pair of them!"

"'Baptiste?" Khalid asked. "Aaron? Of what does Seraph Talon speak?"

'My belly was curling into a small cold knot as I saw the lovers exchange a desperate glance. Aaron was afeared, heartsick, watching all he'd trained for going up in smoke. Baptiste's jaw was clenched, flame-scarred hands balled in fists. Frère Alonso demanded explanation. I heard Big Phil spit on the ground. De Séverin and Aaron's other cronies whispering "Oathbreakers" and "Boylovers" and "Fucking dandies".

'And though I knew it foolish, still I couldn't remain mute. Aaron was my brother. Baptiste my friend. I knew not what I'd say, yet still, I pushed through the throng. But the young smithy caught my eye, and the look on his face begged me to be still.

"'This was my doing!" he declared.

'Baptiste stood taller, met the Forgemaster's eyes.

"'Aaron was in his cups after the feast, Master. I took advantage, I admit it."

'Argyle's lip quivered with rage. "You broke your holy oath to San Mich—"

"'I broke no oath. I swore to love no woman, and to that I hold."

"'To lay in sin out of wedlock is sin enough! But to lay with another man is a sin doubled!" Talon shouted. "And on holy fucking ground? With the Empress abed in the valley below, no less? You shame us all, you cock-gobbling little whoreson!"

'The mob growled in agreement, the tide around us turning dark.

"'This is mortal sin, Baptiste," Khalid growled. "You damn your soul with it."

"'I know the Testaments name it so, Abbot. But God shall decide my fate upon my day of judging, no other." The young smithy glanced to his lover, and my heart ached at the pain in his eyes. "But Aaron is blameless. He was soaked with drink. Befuddled with the pain of his ink. He knew not what he did. I beg you spare him for it."

'I looked to Aaron. The lordling's eyes downturned to the snow at his feet. All he'd worked for hung in the balance. His very life might be at risk here. And I knew he stood back on that bridge in Coste then. Laure Voss smiling as she circled the edge of our light.

'*It's not my fault, Papa. I didn't want it. Sacha made me, Papa. Sacha* forced *me.*

'Aaron shook his head. Bracing himself as if to throw a punch.

'"No," he whispered.

'"Aaron . . ." Baptiste pleaded.

'"No," he said again, firmer, looking Khalid and Argyle in the eye. "Baptiste speaks lies to spare me punishment. But only because he loves me. As I love him." His voice rose over the growing clamour. "And that is no fucking *sin!*"

'"Whoresons!" cried Frère Charles, and "Take them to the Bridge!" roared Frère Alonso, and the mob surged forward. I fought against them, crying out as rough hands seized Baptiste and Aaron, blows falling like rain as Khalid bellowed for order. I punched and flailed, all descending into chaos when a pistol shot rang out over the tumult.

'*BOOM.*

'Stillness fell. Turning, I saw Greyhand, his smoking wheellock raised in the air. His good eye was bloodshot and pouched in shadow. But his hand was steady.

'"Still yourselves, Brothers."

'"But they're sinners, Frère!" Lil Phil spat. "Bastard *oathbreakers!*"

'"They've admitted guilt, Brother," Frère Alonso said. "This sin is theirs to own!"

'"It is," Greyhand nodded. "But Aaron de Coste is still my apprentice 'til he swears the silver rite before God and San Michon. I'll not see him judged by the madness of the mob."

'"Greyhand speaks truth, Brothers!" Khalid bellowed. "That this sin warrants sanction is not in doubt! But no measure shall be meted without prayer and contemplation! Lock them both beneath the Cathedral!" The abbot gazed around the throng, eyes flashing. "We march *tomorrow!* Look to your own reflections, and your own souls! For soon *all* of us may stand bare and bloodied before God's judgement!"

'Rough hands dragged Aaron and Baptiste to the Cathedral, led by Seraph Talon. The rest of the mob lingered like carrion eaters above a battlefield, unsatisfied, but unwilling to break faith with Khalid. And with muttered curses, they began drifting back to Barracks.

'I remained there in the chill. The memory of Astrid's lips lingering with the blood on my tongue. But Greyhand lingered also, Archer perched upon his good shoulder. The falcon peered at me with golden eyes, gave a rasping screech. I looked at the place my master's swordarm had been. The gulf between us. The words unspoken.

'"Master . . ."

'"Did you know?" he asked, his voice like old boots on gravel.

'I wanted to tell him the truth. I wanted to trust him as once I had. He'd been a cruel bastard with me, no doubt. But unlike my stepfather, Greyhand's cruelty served a purpose. There's a difference between being ground underheel and ground on a whetstone. I was harder and better than I'd ever been because of him, and I wanted to beg forgiveness for my diso- bedience in Coste. Despite saving that girl's life, I wanted to tell him I wished I could have taken it all back. To ask if he blamed me as I blamed myself.

'"What will become of them?" I asked instead.

'Greyhand narrowed his good eye, empty sleeve whipping in the wind.

'"I will plead for clemency. But the Order's rules are clear. They will suffer the fate of all oathbreakers upon Khalid's return. Aaron will be taken to the Bridge, bound to the wheel, and flayed with silvered thorns until nothing remains of the aegis that marked him as part of this Brotherhood. And then, they will both be cast out of San Michon."

'"But that's madness! Baptiste is the finest smith in the monastery! And Aaron was set to be inducted among the brethren on the morrow!"

'"Baptiste broke his vows," Greyhand spat. "And speak not with a weasel's tongue about man and woman, he knew full well it was wrong. And Aaron knew also. It's a fool who plays at the precipice. But only the prince of fools blames another when he falls."

'The wind sang a heartbroken hymn. A part of me couldn't believe Aaron and Baptiste had been reckless enough to meet again so soon after I'd discov- ered them. But I'd risked the same myself with Astrid tonight, thinking I might be going to my death tomorrow. I couldn't fault my brother for doing the same. My chest ached at all of this. But I tried to take solace in the Faith, as I'd always done. Whatever became of Aaron and Baptiste, that was the Almighty's will, was it not? They'd broken the law of God, hadn't they?

'I thought of Astrid again, the taste of our collision lingering on my lips. I felt like I'd had cold water dashed over my head, the want I'd been drenched with now sobered by the certainty of how foolish it had been. How selfish. How dangerous.

'Chloe, the falling star, the bloodscript – all of it told me we had a greater role to play in this. Was it right to risk all that? Wasn't it the darkest kind of wicked?

'No sin so dangerous as the sin that is chosen.

'No sin so glorious as the sin that is shared.

'But still . . .

'"Master . . . I don't know if I can ride to Charinfel and leave Aaron behind to rot in a cell."

'"Good," he growled. "Because you're not riding anywhere, de León."

'I blinked, meeting Greyhand's cold stare. "Master, I don—"

'"You don't get to call me Master, boy. Not any more. I told you in Coste that you'd never Hunt as my apprentice again." He walked closer to me, a strip of dark leather about the place where his eye should have been. "You thought I'd forgotten? That perhaps the Wraith in Red had knocked the thought loose from my skull while she ripped my arm off and tore the eye out of my head?"

'"I saved your life."

'"And cost me these," he said, waving to eye and arm.

'"Master, I'm sorry f—"

'Greyhand's fist collided with my stomach like a battering ram to a city's gate. Hitting my knees, I gasped as he smashed a backhand across my face, sending me sprawling in the snow. I tried to scramble to my feet, but his boot collided with my ribs, left me curled on the freezing stone in agony.

'"*Damn* your apology, boy," he hissed, slapping the hollow socket at his shoulder. "This is the Almighty's will, and I accept it as a faithful servant should! What I will *not* accept is an apprentice who seeks his own glory when he should seek God's!"

'"I d-don't—"

'"Of course you do! You spoke so tonight before the Empress herself! Even now, even here, your first concern isn't for your Brothers who march towards war and death without you, but that you'll be left behind! You have no patience, de León! No discipline! You do not *think*, save to think that you know best! Well, you will *learn* to think, boy! And I will ensure you have all the time in the world to do so!"

'The frère eased back, taking a grip on his growing rage.

'"*Better to die a man than live a monster*, we say. But there are many kinds of monsters in this world, boy. A man does what he must. A monster does what he wills. A man serves his God. A monster serves only himself. And I do not ride with monsters."

'I spat blood off my tongue, fangs bared in my rage. But Greyhand only scowled.

'"While your Brothers are gone, choose which you will be."

'And with that, he turned his back, and left me bleeding in the snow.'

✦ XII ✦

NOW DANCE WITH ME

'SAN MICHON WAS empty as my sister's grave, my heart, heavy as the stone that marked it.

'Khalid, Talon, and the other silversaints had set off at dawn, marching northwest to the song of silver horns. Golden banners billowed in the twice-biting winds, men and wagons and horses charging to Avinbourg's defence and the murder of the Forever King. Greyhand and my fellow initiates had set out soon after, a thousand soldiers behind, heading towards the gambit at Charinfel. I'd watched it all from Heaven's Bridge, columns of men streaming like ants across the chill grey snow. And when they were out of sight, I'd spat over the drop into the waiting Mère, cursing beneath my breath.

'Four days, I skulked about the monastery like a ghost. Aflame with the injustice. Aaron and Baptiste were locked beneath the Cathedral until Khalid returned, and I tried to visit. But Keeper Logan barred the way, informing me that Seraph Talon had forbidden anyone should see "them bastard boylovers". Prioress Charlotte held the key to their silver-shod cells, and she visited only to feed them, and give Aaron his nightly sacrament.

'I attended mass every eve in an almost-empty Cathedral, avoiding Astrid's eyes. I wasn't ashamed of what we'd done. I dreamed of it nightly. But I *was* ashamed at the punishment I'd been meted, and boychild that I was, I feared I'd be the lesser in her eyes – to have been left behind while my Brothers fought to decide the fate of the empire.

'I tried filling daylight hours in the Library, but the map upon the floor was a constant reminder of the battle to come, and besides, Archivist Adamo was a horrid bastard to be around. He was the kind of librarian who believed the best libraries were ones bereft of people. The sight of orderly shelves was a joy to him. Someone dog-earing a page was a fucking nightmare. It's a strange truth, but some folk enjoy the notion of *owning* books more than reading them, and I soon tired of him glowering at my back.

'So in the end, I spent most days praying in the Cathedral, asking God and Mothermaid to grant me humility. Patience. Serenity. I found none of it, no matter how hard I begged. I filled the rest of my time in Barracks, staring at that scrap of parchment we'd stolen in Coste. Looking at the map of the Forever King's invasion, I could feel wheels spinning, the machinations of minds centuries deep behind them.

'Had Laure Voss meant for us to find this map?

'Had we been hunting her, or had she been baiting us?

All Shall Kneel.

'Despite my prayers, I burned with fury at it all. And finally, I hurled the parchment to the floor, spitting every curse I could conjure. I felt like stabbing someone so something else could bleed. After all my trials, I'd been left in the rear like a disobedient child, and a part of me supposed that's exactly what I'd been. But I'd not disobeyed my master purely out of pride. I'd saved Véronique de Coste's life. I'd saved *his* life for godsake, Aaron and Talon besides.

'But where had it got me? Despite all Greyhand had warned me about, I *did* want to prove myself. I *did* want glory. And to be denied it because I'd refused to consign an innocent girl to her coffin filled me with rage. In the end, it got the better of me. And with nothing else to loose it upon, I loosed it on the things about me.

'Like a fucking child.

'I smashed my cot to splinters. Hurled my war chest like an unwanted toy. And finally, I turned to the wall and punched it. Again. Again. Feeling my knuckles rip and skin pulp, the pain of my bones grinding on stone overwhelming the hurt of the notion that perhaps this *was* my fault. I was born of sin, after all. And I'd indulged more than my fair share, God knew. Perhaps he was punishing me at last.

'I fell to my knees, gasping and spent. The wall was dented and cracked, my knuckles shredded. I held up my hands, watching blood running red and thick down my fingers, spattering on the floor, on that cursed scrap of crumpled parchment that had cost me so much. And squinting through my shameful tears, at last, I saw it.'

'. . . The blood,' Jean-François realized.

Gabriel nodded. 'Oui.'

'. . . It was moving.'

'Of course it was,' Gabriel sighed. 'By some dark chymistrie, my blood took on a will of its own, sinking into the parchment and exposing the message hidden upon it.'

'The sin of pride, de León.' The historian smiled. 'Ever it served you well.'

'Or the devil loves his own, vampire.' Gabriel shrugged. 'Either way, I picked up the parchment with shaking hands. And on the flip side of Voss's map, just as I'd seen in the Library's forbidden section with Astrid and Chloe, the blood formed itself into words.

'In justice and hope, no hope there be,
'In mercy and bliss, no bliss for thee,
'In death and truth, no truth I see,
'Through blood and fire, now dance with me.

'I stared down at those words as if to burn a hole in them, my mind all atumble. This was a secret message from Laure Voss, meant for the eyes of the Forever King himself.

'*But what did it mean?*

'I was already waiting in the Great Library that night as Astrid and Chloe stole inside, careful as cats. I stepped from the shadows before the door was even closed behind them, that scrap of parchment in hand, the writing now faded to naught.

'"This is it," I said.

'The pair both startled as I spoke, Chloe fumbling with her wheellock, Astrid's hand pressed to her breast. "Oh, you cunting *bastard*, Gabriel . . ."

'"This is the answer. Look." The girls watched, wincing as I sank my teeth into my thumb hard enough to break the skin. And dropping the blood onto the parchment, I held it up in the dim light so the sisternovices might see that riddle take shape once more.

'"A hidden message for the Forever King from his daughter," I said.

'"Great Redeemer . . ." Chloe whispered.

'Astrid took the parchment from my hand, eyebrow rising higher. "Not much of a poet, is she? A few centuries to practise, you think the bitch wou—"

'"Azzie . . ." Chloe sighed.

'"Apologies. I need a smoke."

'"What does it mean?" Chloe asked.

'"That's the problem, Sisternovice," I said. "I've no idea."

'I paced into the Library, Chloe trailing behind, Astrid standing in a puddle of dimmest moonslight and squinting at the writing. "I've been pondering it all day," I said. "And I think Greyhand was right. These bastards know their prey. They're playing us for fools."

"'So it was all a ploy?" Chloe asked. "Laure Voss left a trail along the Godsend wide enough to follow, just in the hopes you'd catch her?"

"'These creatures have been hidden in the shadows for centuries. So I think Laure *was* trekking the Godsend at purpose. Scouting garrisons, taking the measure of the forces the Emperor could muster. The fact Fabién Voss set his beloved daughter to the task shows how important it was to him. Laure was her father's eyes in the Nordlund."

"'But this riddle speaks of something deeper than the plan you found," Chloe said.

"'I *know*. Else why hide it? But Laure said she *knew* we were stalking her. And she sent a dozen ravens to her father, presumably carrying a dozen copies of this message. I think she was anticipating we'd intercept at least one of them. I think she left the map for us to find, and hid the true message for her father in the blood."

"'Avinbourg is a ploy," Astrid said. "Isabella's army *is* marching to the wrong place."

"'Oui."

"'Charinfel, then?"

'I walked out onto the great map, along the Godsend, until my silver heels were at rest atop the southern cityfort. I could picture Greyhand and my fellows marching to the garrison's aid. If Voss attacked Charinfel, he might well take it with only a thousand extra men and a handful of initiates to bolster it. But I was still uneasy.

"'I fear it's not that simple. It's lies within lies with these leeches."

"'*In death and truth, no truth I see, through blood and fire, now dance with me.*" Astrid scowled. "This reads like child's prose. I mean, honestly . . ."

"'Mediocre poetry aside, the answer clearly lies within this riddle," Chloe said.

"'And I've not the eyes to see it," I spat.

"'Well, we must *find* the eyes. Perhaps this is why God brought us together."

"'Sisternovice, you're not telling me anything I don't already know."

"'Well, *think*!" Chloe cried. "Did Laure say anything that might prove a clue? Because while we stand here, the imperial army charges towards a battle that will never come, and if the Forever King makes it around the Godsend, all the empire is set to fall before his accursed host!"

'Astrid and I looked to each other. And I saw the thought form in her eyes just as it spilled from my lips. "Host . . ."

"'Chloe," Astrid declared. "You're a genius, ma chérie."

"'. . . I beg your pardon?"

"'The angels of the host," I whispered. And looking to the sisternovice, I began walking the length of the Godsend, stamping my heel upon each peak as I passed. "Each mountain is named for one! Sarai, Angel of Plagues. Evangeline, Angel of Temperance. And look here! Justice and Hope. Mercy and Bliss. Death and Truth. They're pairs! Mountain passes!" I knelt by Mont Sanael and Mont Gabriel, the Angels of Blood and Fire. "Laure wasn't just scouting our forces, she was looking for the best path to cross the mountains! One of Voss's thralls said it in Coste. *The Master comes. And blood and fire shall mark his passing!*"

"'The Forever King doesn't intend to go around the Godsend," Astrid breathed.

"'The bastard's going *over* it." I stabbed the map with my finger. "Here, at the Twins."

'Chloe frowned. "But it's the dead of winter. The wind atop the Godsend would freeze your blood to ice, and the snows lay a hundred feet thick. No army could cross it."

"'No living army. But our enemies are the Dead."

'Chloe stared at the map, her voice a whisper. "Almighty God . . ."

"'We must send word to Isabella," Astrid said.

"'We must," I nodded. "But Voss would've got his daughter's message weeks ago. The Endless Legion is already on the move. Even if we send a rider now and the Golden Host comes about, they may not reach the Twins in time."

"'What do you propose?" Chloe asked.

"'To stop them, of course."

"'*Alone?*"

"'The Brothers of the Hearth are still here. Argyle, Keeper Logan and others."

"'Nightswatchmen and blacksmiths?" Astrid demanded. "Against ten thousand wretched and Mothermaid only knows how many highbloods?"

'I turned my eyes to the window, to the Cathedral beyond and the cells beneath. "There's at least two other brothers in San Michon who can yet help me."

"'This is madness. This is absolute bloody *foolishness!*"

"'Let's just call it reckless."

"'Oh, pack that schoolboy smile a lunch, Gabriel de León!"

"'If you've a better notion, I'm all ears, Majesty. We'll send a rider to the Empress, to be sure. Another to Greyhand. But until word reaches them, the only people standing between Fabién Voss and the Nordlund are the three of us in this room."

'I stood and dusted off my hands.

"'So if you'll excuse me, mesdemoiselles, I have a prioress to wake.'"

✦ XIII ✦

BLOOD AND FIRE

'TWO HOURS LATER, we stood in the snow outside San Michon's stables, our breath winter white in the night air. I looked among our company, saw the weight of the world on every shoulder. Keeper Logan and Keeper Micah. A dozen blackthumbs from the Armoury. Archivist Adamo's assistant, Nasir, a few kitchenhands, the two grooms, Kaspar and Kaveh. And of course, Baptiste and Aaron, newly freed from beneath the Cathedral.

'Old Charlotte hadn't taken kindly to having her vigil interrupted by my banging on the Priory door. But once Astrid and Chloe were back in their bedchambers, that's exactly what I'd done. Charlotte had listened intently, her scarred expression darkening as I explained my fears, Voss's strategy, the desperate counter I'd hatched, and my declaration that I'd need every man I could get. The likelihood of my plan proving anything but suicidal was almost none. But to her credit, the prioress had handed over the keys to Aaron and Baptiste's cells with little resistance. And along with it, she gifted me a dozen phials of sanctus, dark as chocolat, sweet as honey.

'"May Almighty God protect you, Initiate."

'"May he protect us all, Prioress."

'I stood beside young Kaveh now, pushing Laure's crumpled map into his hand. His brother Kaspar was already ahorse. "Ride hard, Brothers. Kaspar, seek the Golden Host. Kaveh, you chase south after Greyhand. Swift as the wind."

'"Almighty God be with you, Little Lion." Kaspar looked to his brother. "And us all."

'I squeezed Kaveh's hand, spoke soft. 'When you return, Brother, I'd have a quiet word. About you and Sister Aoife. On the odd chance I'm still alive, of course."

'The boy looked at me, his expression dark. But he nodded, just once.

"'Go. Ride!"

'I slapped the horses, whispered a prayer as the lads galloped into the night. Baptiste's brother blackthumbs had loaded up our wagons, and I was checking the barrels within when the rumbling of iron chains caught my ear. Looking upwards, I saw the sky platform once more descending from the Cathedral.

'I looked to Logan in question. "Keeper?"

"'Nae ken, laddie," the thin man growled.

'The platform *thumped* to rest on the snow. Two dozen sisters from the Silver Sorority stood upon it, clad in winter greatcoats and silver-heeled boots – raided from the Armoury, no doubt. They carried wheellock rifles, horns of black ignis, pouches of silvershot. Charlotte, Sister Esmeé, Chloe Sauvage among them. And strangest of all, Astrid.

"'Prioress? What is this?"

"'Exactly what it appears, Initiate."

'A murmur rippled among the men as I met Charlotte's eyes. "Prioress, I—"

"'I am not here for debate, Initiate de León. In the absence of Abbot Khalid and Seraph Talon, *I* am senior luminary of this monastery. You once told me silversaints could not serve their purpose without the sisterhood. I wholeheartedly concur. And if your fears prove true, by the blessed Mothermaid, you shall need all the help you can find."

"'No disrespect, Prioress," Aaron said softly. "But what help can you be?"

'Charlotte threw him a disapproving glance, hefted her wheellock. "Abbot Khalid has spent a great deal of time teaching us to defend ourselves with these abominable things. But I rather think God intended we defend this empire instead. And with the Almighty's grace, and the blessings of the Martyrs, that is precisely what we shall do."

'I looked among the sisters and novices, there in the falling snow. I saw fear, of course. Shaking knees and wide eyes and pinched lips. But I also saw set jaws and clenched fists and faith that the Lord God would see them through. I saw *belief*.

"'We'd be blessed to count you among our company, Sisters," I said.

'Charlotte turned to her charges. "Those of you who can ride, fetch a saddle. The rest of you, pick a wagon. Quickly, now."

'The sisters and novices did as commanded, most climbing into the wagons with our stores. But a few saddled up sosyas, assisted dutifully by the brethren. I sidled up to Astrid, helping her to saddle a brave mare named River. I was aware of the folk gathered about us, keeping my voice a whisper and speaking most with my eyes.

'"What in the Almighty's name are you doing?"

'"Lovely weather for a ride in the country."

'"This is no jest. Wasn't it you who told me war should be left to the warriors?"

'Astrid looked to the women about her, the boys; this pitiful band riding towards the open jaws of hell. "That's difficult to do when the war is at your doorstep."

'"What happened to the blackhearted bitch who wanted only to escape these walls?"

'"Oh, Gabe." She smiled sadly. "If this ends the way it's likely to, I *will* have."

'My heart was sick with fear for her. She met my stare, and I could see the memory of our night in the Library on her face, a sliver of want in her eyes that made my blood sing. But with Charlotte watching, sisters and brothers around us, I dared not give away anything of what we shared. And God knew we'd no time to argue.

'With a sigh, I resigned myself to this desperate throw of the dice. I finished with Astrid's saddle, climbed onto Justice's back. Baptiste caught my eye, lacing his collar about his lips. "I pray all Seven Martyrs you're wrong about this, Little Lion."

'"None pray harder than I," I replied, pulling on my gloves. "But it's as Greyhand said, Brother. In battle, the wise man prays to God. Yet he still raises his sword."

'"Greyhand also had words on the topic of heroes, if I recall," Aaron growled.

'I looked around our band; one tiny sliver of flame in a sea of darkness. The fear of it all was like ice in my insides. I knew we were almost certainly riding to our doom. But I also knew that if we let our fear rule us, we'd never ride at all. *Someone* needed to speak. And so, I gripped Justice's reins hard to stop my hands from shaking, and standing in my stirrups, I raised my voice.

'"I know not what awaits us at the end of this road. We will look upon the face of horror, that much is sure. But courage is the will to do what others will not. And in the arms of heaven's host, we are invincible. I have looked into the eyes of the Dead and not flinched. I have faced down a Prince of Forever and lived. And I tell you now and true, I have never known such pride, as to ride with a company such as you."

"'Véris, Little Lion," Baptiste smiled. "Véris."

"'Aye, fine speech." Logan scratched his whiskers and tipped me a wink. "For a Nordish-born prettyboy sheep-fucker, like."

"'. . . Merci, good Keeper."

'And with that, we were away.

'A host of barely fifty, facing an army of ten thousand. And still we rode as if towards heaven's arms. Prioress Charlotte led the sisters in hymns as we stabbed westwards, the road bitter cold, the snows falling thick. We rode with barely enough pause for food and sleep, so cold by the time we stopped for the night that some could barely move. Tenting by the roadside, the grim shadow of the Godsend rising before us, I found myself picturing the hungry horrors amassing beyond it. Knowing every minute we rested was a minute wasted.

'Days and days on end.

'The Twins rose up before us as we rode into broken foothills, and I prayed the angels Sanael and Gabriel would watch over us as we slept. The wind was a blade, the air so thin it hurt to breathe. Our lead wagon broke its axle, and we forged on with only one. Two sosyas froze to death in the night, and four sisters and a brother blackthumb had to turn back, too frostbitten to ride on. I thought for certain Astrid must break, pleading silently every time I caught her eye. But she remained hunched in her saddle, shivering, hard as steel. And still we climbed, up into the pass between Blood and Fire. Higher. Colder. Bleaker.

'A storm hit on the twelfth day, and if the sun rose, we could barely tell. The cold was so fierce that another half-dozen of our company couldn't get ahorse, little Chloe among them. It was decided they should remain behind to direct the Golden Host if they arrived, while the rest of us pressed to the passage on foot. The way was too perilous for the wagon, and my brothers and I had to drag the barrels we'd brought with us through the grey drifts. For once in my life, I was grateful for the dark strength my father had blessed me with.

'Night fell, and there were no hymns around the fire that eve. The thought of what might be coming over those mountains was pressing on us all now, and the snow above was so thick that none dared make a sound. My stepfather had taught me ice. He'd taught me snow. How it falls. How it kills. I knew the notion that loud noises could cause avalanches was a fiction, but who knew what was listening, out there in the dark. And so, silence.

'We struggled on the next day, only two dozen in our company now, fighting against the frost and screaming wind. Even at noon, we were only able to see by the pale glow of our lanterns and the brief flashes of lightning immolating the peaks. But at last, towards sunset, the wind slackened, and we finally reached the pass between Fire and Blood.

'Twin watchtowers stood tall against the storm, thrust up from the mountainside like black fingers raised to heaven. They were wrought during the Wars of the Faith, fashioned in the appearance of the angels these peaks were named for. The storm blew southerly, and the tower of Gabriel was almost entirely buried, only one dark hand outstretched from the snow piled about it. The snowpack rose up in a sheer cliff, a hundred feet deep, untold tons. So we sheltered in the lee of Sanael's looming wings.

'Aaron huddled beside me, collar laced high against the gale, leaning on his barrel to catch his breath. Baptiste crouched in his frozen furs, peering down into the vast valley on the other side of the pass. Prioress Charlotte stood hunched against the screaming wind with her holy sisters, Astrid among them. That she'd made it so far spoke of a strength in Sisternovice Rennier I'd never dreamed of.

'At first, we saw nothing. Even as the lightning crashed, illuminating the expanses of grey snow on the Talhost side of the peak, there was no movement. The slope below was a vast plane of frost and swallowed trees, packed hard by the wind and piled impossibly deep, impossibly heavy – no army of men could cross a divide that treacherous without freezing to death or setting off an avalanche.

'My teeth were chattering so badly I could barely speak. "Anyone g-got a drink?"

'"N-n-not any m-m-more," Logan hissed.

'"I see nothing," de Coste said, his breath steaming. "And w-we c-cannot tarry l-long. This chill will b-be the d-death of us, Gabriel."

'"What n-news, Brothers?" the prioress called.

'Baptiste drew out a silver-trimmed spyglass. I fetched my own and crouched beside him, peered into the valley below. For long minutes, I saw no sign, no peril across that frozen expanse. The thought occurred that the Endless Legion had already passed over, but that was foolishness; we'd have run across them on the way. A vain hope occurred to me then – that perhaps I'd been wrong, and even now, the Forever King's forces were crashing like waves against Avinbourg's walls. And then lightning struck, and as the swirling grey lit up before us, one brief heartbeat, bright as the long-lost day, my breath caught in my lungs as I saw what was coming up the mountains towards us.'

'And that was?' Jean-François asked.

'Vampires.'

Gabriel swallowed.

'Thousands upon thousands of vampires.'

✦ XIV ✦

THIS MOMENT

'"SWEET REDEEMER," I whispered.

'"What did you s-see?" Charlotte demanded.

'Baptiste lowered his glass and spoke soft. "They are c-coming."

'"How many?" Astrid asked.

'I swallowed hard, meeting her eyes. "*Many.*"

'"And we are two dozen." Baptiste turned to Aaron. "Two dozen against thousands."

'I looked among our company. They were afeared, all of them. And I realized they were looking to me, who'd brought them here. All knew how thin the ice we stood upon was. How like it was we were facing our deaths. I learned a lesson there on that frozen slope, sheltered beneath an angel's wings. About leading men. About leading anyone.'

'And that was?' Jean-François asked.

'When your whole world is going to hell, all you need is someone who sounds like he knows the way.

'"In the Trial of the Blood," I called, "Seraph Talon told me that the greatest horrors forge the greatest heroes. But Frère Greyhand always said it's foolish to be a hero. That they die unpleasant deaths, far from home and hearth." I raised my voice above the winds, trying to light a fire that might burn away this chill. "I think the truth lies in between. One or two moments of heroism – that's what the wise seek. One or two heartbeats that last a lifetime. And *this* is one. A moment to bring a smile to your face on your deathbed. A moment that others will rue they were not here to share. A moment of which you will say, many years and miles from here, that *then*, if never again, I stood among heroes. And I was one."

'I looked among them, fangs bared in a fierce smile.

"'This moment."

'Aaron nodded. "This moment."

"'Prioress Charlotte," I called. "Form your 'lock line along this ridge, from tower to bluff. Half firing, the other half reloading. Keep them off me best you can."

"'What do you intend to do?" Charlotte asked.

"'Hold them off long enough for our brother blackthumbs to save our backsides." I turned to Baptiste and his fellow smiths, thumping a fist upon the barrels of black ignis we'd dragged from San Michon. "The snowpack is heaviest along the north ridge. Up there, beneath Gabriel's tower. A few barrels should bring the whole damned lot of it down on these bastards. Hundreds of thousands of tons. Just make sure you run your matchlines long enough to be clear when it all comes down." I swallowed hard. "And try to give me warning before you blow it. It's going to be bloody down there."

"'There are thousands of them," Charlotte frowned. "It's going to be *slaughter*."

"'Maybe." I nodded, looking about the group. "But my friends are the hill I die on."

'Aaron checked the silverbombs in his bandolier. "I'm coming with you."

"'And I." Baptiste hefted a mighty silversteel warhammer. "Sunlight here is thirsty. Brother Noam and Brother Clement can handle the setting of the charges."

'Aaron frowned. "Baptiste, you're a blacksmith, not a—"

'The big lad pressed his lips to Aaron's. "Shut up, love."

'I reached into my greatcoat, produced a silver pipe. Aaron's breath quickened as I packed it with the sanctus Charlotte had given me – a deeper dose than either of us had dared before. Astrid watched as I struck my flintbox, breathing down, her dark eyes on mine as it crashed into my lungs and out through my veins; that monstrous perfume, that divine madness, lifting me up into the frozen heavens.

'I packed another dose for Aaron, looking on as he drew down the entire bowl in one draught. De Coste's whole body tensed, canines growing long and sharp. He breathed a plume of scarlet smoke into the freezing air, tendons in his throat stretched taut. And when he opened his eyes, I saw them washed scarlet, pupils so dilated his irises were almost gone.

"'Oh, God," he breathed, red as blood. "Oh, *God*."

'Aaron stabbed his silversteel blade into the snow, unbuckled his greatcoat and sloughed his tunic off his shoulders. I did the same, both of us silverclad amid the grey. The smiths hefted the ignis barrels and charged up towards the snowpack under Gabriel's tower. Charlotte, Astrid, and the other sisters formed their line along the ridge, Keeper Logan and Micah set to defend them. As I met Astrid's gaze, all the words I wished I could say were held behind my sharpening teeth. The memory of her lips burning brighter than the sacrament in my veins. And she smiled at me then. One of her thousand smiles – a smile that caught me up and held me tight, banishing anything remaining of the fear inside me.

'"*This* moment, Gabriel de León."

'The whole world was trembling as Aaron, Baptiste, and I ran down the slope towards the Dead. I didn't remember drawing it, but Lionclaw was in my hand, a burning brand in the other. There was no terror in me then. No memory of friend or famille or even Astrid's smile. There was only the bloodhymn. Pounding so fierce I found myself laughing – actually fucking *laughing* as we charged together to our deaths.

'I saw shapes in the darkness, heard running feet in grey snow. The Dead had seen our light, and they were coming, oh *God*, they were coming, and my fingers were wrapped about Lionclaw's hilt and my heart crashing against my ribs as I looked to my fellows and saw their shining eyes on mine.

'"Now," Baptiste hissed. "*Now* you can slay me something monstrous."

'The air was freezing, but we felt no cold, goosebumps rising instead at the sight of the designs upon our skins: roses and serpents, the Redeemer on his wheel, angels singing and lions roaring, throat to wrist to waist in silver ink.

'And they were glowing.

'Mild at first. But as the footsteps rushed closer, our light grew stronger, a circle of illumination twenty, thirty, forty feet about us. I felt my left hand growing hot, and I saw the sevenstar on my palm and the silver angel up my arm, the lion on my chest – all burning with that same fierce and terrible light.

'"God stands with us, brothers," Baptiste breathed. "We cannot fall."

'"No fear," I whispered.

'Aaron nodded. "Only fury."

'And then, they hit us.

'Out of the dark, hissing and clawing. A swarm, dead eyes full of hunger, fangs glinting as lightning split the sky. The wretched of Talhost wore the clothes they were murdered in – courtly dresses or peasant rags, frockcoats or threadbare tunics, acres of pale and bloodless skin. There was no form to their ranks, just numbers and teeth and sheer, unholy strength, set to drain all the world to dust and bones.

'But mighty fucking Redeemer, we were *untouchable*. That rotted host came on like a flood, and as they reached our light, they broke like water on stone. Our inkwork blinded them, our silversteel cut them like scythe to wheat. The air was ashes and blood as we fought, snows drenched red. Looking to the northern ridge as lightning cracked the sky, I spied the tiny figures of Brother Noam and the other blackthumbs burying their barrels of black ignis at the snowpack's base. Silvershot whizzed past our heads from the sisters above, and at the edge of our light, I saw wretched fall, skulls shattered, bones splintering.

'Everyone knows war is hell, coldblood. But there's a heaven in it too. A savage joy in standing on the ground where your enemy wants you to fall. I couldn't feel my body. I might have known the scrape of a claw or the brief twinge of a cracking bone. But pain? Pain was for the enemy. Pain and silver.

'And then, I felt him.

'The kiss of serpent's fangs to my skin. The bleak infinity of countless years, the dust on the tombs of forgotten kings. The weight of a presence impossible, a mind unknowable, pressing in on mine out of the long and lonely black.

'The mind of a Forever King.

'I saw him, as if he stood before me. His skin, hair, eyes – all bleached snow-pale by years beyond counting and sins past reckoning. A youth, fey and eternal, beautiful and terrible, wreathed in an unlight so cold and bitter-bleak my heart felt frozen in my chest. And I heard him speak in my head then, across the blood-drenched snow between us, and his words were the song that would unmake the world.

'"*I see thee.*"

'"Great Redeemer . . ." I whispered.

'"I feel him too," Aaron gasped.

'The wretched came on, and our silversteel gleamed, blood-red and holy-bright. But they were nothing, I realized, *nothing* compared to what walked behind them with steady tread, implacable, inescapable, no impulse so base as haste to ruin the portrait as he strode towards us, surrounded by his children, his grandchildren, his brood entire – a dread court of the Blood, with all the time in creation upon their side.

'And then I heard screams. Behind.

'"Gabriel!"

'*Astrid . . .*

'"GABRIEL!"

'Heart dropping into my belly, I looked back up the slope, saw torches burning against pale grey – Brother Noam and the other smiths dancing in the dark. And by their light, I saw a figure, familiar, weaving among them like a shadow and cutting them down into the snow.

'A shadow wrapped in red.

'"Laure . . ."'

✦ XV ✦

IN RED

'I CURSED MYSELF. Of course that unholy bitch would be here to meet her father as he crossed the Godsend. Laure Voss had come upon us from behind like a thief, and I'd left our backs exposed like a fool. From the look, Noam and the others had set the ignis charges, but now Laure was tearing them to pieces, and with none to light the fuse . . .

"'Can you hold them?" I roared to Aaron, cutting down another wretched.

"'Or die trying!"

"'When I give the signal, you run back up this slope!"

"'Go, Little Lion!" Baptiste bellowed. "Almighty go with you!"

'Turning from my brothers, I dashed back up the ridge. I saw the bright blooms of silverbombs, sluices of blood. The blackthumbs fought bravely, but they were Brothers of the Hearth, not Hunt, and they stood now against a daughter of the Forever King.

'Their torches sputtered and failed, plunging the ridge back into darkness. Lightning split the sky, a brilliant arc, and I saw a blood-red shadow flickering across the snow towards the tower of Sanael, and the sisters firing from its shelter.

"'Charlotte, get back! Astrid, *RUN!*"

'I heard a scream in the black, heart twisting in my chest, but then I was among them, sword high, scything towards that figure bathed in my aegis's light. Laure was drenched to the armpits in gore, chin and throat painted scarlet, all semblance of the beauty I'd seen in Coste cast aside. A monster now, bleak and true.

'Slipping aside from my blow and flashing back to the fringe of my light, the Forever Prince drew herself up to her full height. Her scarlet gown flowed about her like mist in the freezing winds, long red hair plastered to the blood soaking her skin.

'"Get back!" I spat. "In the name of God and Redeemer!"

'"I told thee once, boy. No power hast thy God over me."

'The sisters gathered behind me in the shelter of my light. I could feel Astrid there, and I breathed a prayer of thanks. But the bodies of other sisters were split and bleeding in the snow, Keeper Logan and Keeper Micah beside them. Glancing down the slope, I could see Aaron and Baptiste had lost their ground, falling back now before that relentless tide. We had only moments before the legion swept up the pass and overran us all.

'Laure smiled, and I felt the venom of her, seeping into my mind.

'"I shall have thee on thy knees, frailblood. I shall taste thee unto dying."

'A grey crust of ashes and blood was on my skin, and my aegis burned with holy fire. Laure's eyes narrowed against it as I hurled my last silverbomb, feeling the heat on my skin as I swung my blade. I threw all I had behind that blow, and it landed true. But her flesh was ever stone as I struck her, and her fist was a battering ram as she hit me back.

'The breath left my lungs. I felt something tear. And then I was flying, hitting hard. Black stars bloomed as Laure leaned over me, arms open to break me.

'Tiny thunder blasts rang out across the ridge, a half-dozen shots of pure and blessed silver crashing into Laure's face, chest, throat. She reeled backwards, a cobweb of cracks across her skin. I blinked the blood from my eyes, Prioress Charlotte roaring, "Reload!"

'All heaven held its breath. All time stood still. I rose up out of the snow, Lionclaw in my fist, and with all my strength and the name of God upon my lips, I drew back my blade and plunged it into Laure's chest.

'Again, she struck me, claws tearing my skin and sending me flying back into the tower. The masonry smashed to dust as I hit, blood in my mouth, ribs shattering. The ancien staggered as she clutched Lionclaw, now buried to the hilt in her chest. But still, this Ironheart bitch wouldn't fucking *fall*. Her face twisted, and my heart sank as she took hold of the blade with smoking hands and dragged it from her shattered breast.

'"I am a Prince of Forever. Think ye a sliver such as this can end *me*?"

'Prioress Charlotte stepped forward, the wheel about her neck like silver fire, the clawmarks across her face twisting as she bellowed, "In the Mothermaid's name, I say back!"

'The vampire hissed, one hand up against the light. And with the other, she lifted the blade she'd just pulled from her chest and hurled it. I heard Astrid cry out as the sword ploughed into Charlotte's skull, splitting it in half and sending the prioress's body sailing back like a ragdoll. And as those bottomless eyes fell on Astrid, I dragged myself to my feet.

'My silverbombs and holy water were spent; I'd nothing left to throw. And so I threw myself, crashing into Laure and bringing us both down into the snow.

'Her fist collided with my skull, and she climbed astride me, black eyes narrowed against my aegis, gore-slick hands sizzling as they closed about my throat. Her breast was shattered where my sword had struck, but still she lived, her strength the sum of ten thousand stolen lives. I could feel the chill off her skin. See death in her eyes.

'"Is this the best of thee? So feeble, thy final gasp? E'en the babes of thy beloved Lorson fought fiercer than this afore I bathed in them."

'My heart froze in my chest. ". . . What?"

'Her lips curled, all the horror of hell in her eyes. "Vowed did I, that all thou hast I wouldst take, Gabriel de León. Thy home. Thy mother. Thy little Celene . . ."

'"You *lie*!"

'Laughter rang across the frozen peaks, black and bleak. "A palace shall I build of thy suffering, frailblood. Upon a throne of thy misery shall I reign. All sh—"

'Lionclaw crashed across the back of Laure's head, bone splitting, blood splashing. The vampire reeled, hissing, fangs bared.

'"The only queen on this mountain is *me*," Astrid spat.

'Standing above us, she drew back my bloody blade for another strike.

'"And he's no frailblood, you unholy *cunt*."

'There's a liberation in death. When you *know* you're going to die, the fear of it departs. All that remains is the rage. And as I seized hold of Laure's throat, that was all I felt. *Rage*. I pictured my mama, braiding my hair on my saintsdays, teaching me to wear my name like a crown. I saw my baby sister, my little hellion, my Celene, laughing as I told her some bawdy tale, hearing her voice in the letters I'd never answered. And last, I thought of my other sister. My sweet Amélie. The girl who told us stories of an eve, who danced as if to music only she could hear. Ma famille. My heart. And this leech had ripped all of it away. I was back in the mud of Lorson then. The day what was left of Amélie came home. And I felt it, ringing in my head like a song to which I already knew the words. A promise. A name.

'*Esani*.

'My hand tightened about her throat and I felt it; all my hate and all my fury seething under my skin. Laure's eyes grew wide and her mouth opened as her throat began to blacken under my touch. She seized my hand, but still I squeezed, steam rising from the cracks as her blood began boiling beneath her skin.

'"*Release me!*"

'She screamed, immortal flesh burning in my grip, that porcelain charring to the bone. Boiling blood spilled down my arm, scalding, steaming, but still I held on, pushing her off me now and down into the snow, her flesh crumbling in my hand. Those ageless eyes melted and ran down her cheeks like candle wax as she cried out again.

'"*FATHER!*"

'And across the black between us, I heard a roar of purest rage ring out in reply. I could hear the anguish in it. The hatred, an eternity wide. But with one final scream, the Wraith in Red's spine arched, and her boiling tongue lolled between her fangs, and with all the fury of centuries denied, Laure Voss burst into ashes in my grip, leaving little but a smoking wound in the snow and the remnants of a tattered gown, red as blood.

'I staggered to my feet, and Astrid met my eyes. "Gabe . . ."

'"Take shelter in the tower," I gasped. "Go!"

'Breathless, bleeding, I ran across crimson snow towards the ignis barrels. Aaron and Baptiste had abandoned the fight below, the Endless Legion howling behind them. I roared "RUN FASTER!" as I reached the snowpack, searching the powder for the matchline cords. Fumbling for my flintbox, I pressed flame to fuse. The line spat sparks, fire hissing down its length towards those buried barrels and the doom inside.

'"De Coste! Baptiste!" I roared. "*RUN!*" And then I was sprinting up the slope, snow crunching beneath my boots, towards the only salvation I could see. The ignis detonated behind me, muffled by storm and snow. But beneath, I heard a fearsome sound, like the tread of mighty boots. A great cracking, as the fresh powder from that raging storm fractured, a split cascading across Gabriel's peak and loosing the weaker snows beneath.

'I felt the ground giving way, trying desperately to keep my footing. But the whole pack crumbled, and I flung myself across the brink towards my only hope – the outstretched hand of that towering angel, still buried beneath the snow. It was the bloodhymn that saved me, I think. That, and perhaps the hand of God. And I crashed against Gabriel's open palm, digging my fingers into the tower's stone as all the world came apart.

'The whole Godsend rang with the thunder of it. God only knows how much snow was loosed. A tidal wave of grey, a calamity crashing down the mountain's face, ever picking up more weight and speed. And as the Endless

Legion was swept back down the mountain, I felt him, like clawed and frozen fingers digging into my skull.

'The vow of a father eternal, to the one who'd murdered his daughter beloved.

'"*I have forever, boy.*"

'"*I* am *forever.*"'

✦ XVI ✦

LAST SON

'I CURSED MYSELF a fool the entire ride. All seventeen days of it. Aaron one side of me, Baptiste the other. And like a shadow at our back, unexpected, perhaps unwanted, came Greyhand, followed by a cohort of Her Majesty's soldiers in sunflower-yellow tabards.

'They'd found us only a few hours after the battle, bloodied upon the eastern slopes with Chloe and other sisters who'd not made the ascent. Greyhand and our brother initiates arrived first, a breathless Kaveh leading them. Outriders of the Golden Host galloped out of the dawn soon afterwards, Khalid and the other silversaints at their head. And they'd stood amazed as Astrid told them the tale – a tale of two dozen against ten thousand, sweeping the Endless Legion back down into Talhost beneath hundreds of thousands of tons of snow.

'The abbot and brother silversaints remained behind with the Golden Host to guard the crossing. The Endless Legion was not defeated, and all knew those corpses would dig themselves free of the frozen tomb we'd built. But as history tells, Fabién Voss didn't press into Nordlund that year, instead, retreating back into Talhost to bide his time.

'He had forever, after all.

'But our victory was no comfort. And though I knew the Dead were foxes and serpents all, I had to ride back to Lorson to see. We stopped to rest only enough to spare the horses. I barely slept or ate, sick with the thought of what we might find, of ma famille, my home, and darkest among them, the thought that this was my fault. Laure had snatched the image of my village from my own head in Coste. I had *led* her there.'

Gabriel looked down at his open hands. And he sighed from the bottom of his soul.

'The ruins had stopped smouldering by the time we arrived. The scent rising on the horizon, and my sobs already trying to claw loose from my throat. I leapt into the fresh-fallen snow and tasted air like ashes, choking me as I roared into the emptiness.

'"Mama? *Celene!*"

'Only fat crows answered, staring at me with black and hungry eyes. The corpses lay where Laure had left them; a great multitude in the town square, thrown atop one another like broken dolls. I saw familiar faces among them, horror freezing my heart. Luc and Massey, my childhood friends. My sweet Ilsa, crumpled as if she were made of sticks and rags. The bodies of dead babies scattered like rose petals across the snow.

'"Almighty God," Aaron breathed, making the sign of the wheel.

'Baptiste's eyes were full of sorrow. Behind him, I saw the chapel's walls were intact, stone blacked by flame. Looking up through my tears, I saw the roof was gone and realized at once what had happened – the godly folk of Lorson had fled to sanctified ground or barricaded themselves inside their homes, where an uninvited coldblood could not enter. And the Wraith in Red had set fire to their roofs, leaving them a simple choice: flee the inferno and into her waiting arms, or stay within and burn.

'I walked among the charred pews of God's own house, searching the dead. My mind shied away from the horror that must have been their final moments. I recognized very few, their bodies ashen. But in the church's heart, I saw a figure crouched before the altar's wreckage. Burned almost beyond recognition. A priest.'

'Good Father Louis,' Jean-François murmured.

'Oui.'

'You prayed he'd die screaming, Chevalier.'

Gabriel glanced up, eyes grey as steel. 'Oui.'

'And your famille?'

Gabriel exhaled, holding his breath with no air in his lungs. He seemed a smaller man, then, broad shoulders hunched under the weight of years and loss.

'I looked at Father Louis's remains, there on the hallowed ground that hadn't saved him. And my heart sank as I saw another figure, cradled in his arms as if to shield it from the flames. It was charred like firewood, charcoal skin stretched over kindling bones. But I could tell it had been a girl. A candlemaid.

'"No," I whispered. "No, *no* . . ."

'My baby sister. My little hellion. My Celene. Her hair was black straw and dust, and her fingers burned to sticks. And I sank to my knees in her ashes and screamed so hard I felt my voice crack, reaching out to touch her cheek and watch the skin flake away in the cold winter wind. I'd never taken the time to answer her letters, I realized.

'And now I never would.

'I walked like a man to the gallows. I was aware of the men who'd come with me only as ghosts. I remember someone trying to bar my way, shoving them aside and spitting fury. And I stumbled through the ashes and snow until I found it. My stepfather's house.

'They were in the yard. Of course they were. Once they saw the church burning with my sister inside, they'd never have remained locked behind closed doors. My stepfather lay with his old warsword a few inches from his hand. He'd seemed so huge to me when I was a boy. A giant, ever casting his shadow upon me. He'd never been the finest man, nor the finest father, and yet he'd stood as mine for his part. And the sight of him lying broken and bloodless just a few feet from the forge he'd given his life to . . .

'But it was nothing. Nothing compared to what came next. If the sight of my sister's body had gutted me, the sight of my mama shattered me like glass. Her hand was outstretched towards the chapel. Her eyes frozen in her skull. And the look on her face was not one of fear or pain or anguish. It was *rage*. The rage of the lioness she'd been, trying to get back to her burning cub.

'I'd known fury the day Amélie came home, coldblood. I'd known hatred. But now I felt it wash over and through me like holy water. Like the fires of heaven sent. And I tell you now and tell you true, the boy I'd been *died* that day. Died as if he'd burned in that church with his sister. I was dismantled. I was unmade.

'The last son of Lorson.

'Greyhand sat with me as soldiers piled the bodies and put them to the torch. I watched the flames consume my mama's dark curls, my stepfather's hands, the smoke and sparks rising up into the daysdeath sky as Greyhand patted my shoulder, awkward, like a father who'd never had any desire to be one.

'His face was streaked with ashes, ravaged with scars, a strip of leather covering the hollow of his stolen eye. I stared up into the dark, the smoke of those pyres, wondering if this was all some nightmare from which I'd wake if only I prayed hard enough.

'"I'm sorry, Greyhand," I said. "I'm sorry for what I let her take from you."

'"It is God's will, de León. Who are we to know the mind of the Almighty?"

'I hung my head. "This is his will then? My baby sister burned like tinder? My mama butchered like cattle? How can it be so? How can he want this?"

'"My mama died when I was a boy," he told me softly. "She was all the stars in my sky. I remember wondering, if I loved her more than life itself, how could I go on living with her gone? But that is what we do, Little Lion. We carry the greatest burdens not on our shoulders, but in our hearts. But those taken from us never truly die. They await us in the light of God's love."

'He leaned close and sought my eye.

'"That is *true* immortality. Not the dark counterfeit to which our enemy lays claim. Eternity lies in the hearts of those who cherish us. Love them, Gabriel. And know they await your arrival at the throne of the Almighty. But not yet." He shook his head. "*Not* yet."

'I looked at my old master, and through my tears, I saw the truth of his words. There is a time for grief, and a time for songs, and a time to recall with fondness all that has been and gone. But there is a time for killing too. There is a time for blood, and a time for rage, and a time to close your eyes and become the thing heaven wants you to be.

'"I will love them." I licked the ashes on my lips. "And I will avenge them."

'I heard silver-heeled boots scuffing snow and char. Looking up to find Aaron and Baptiste, side by side. Their faces were drawn with grief and horror, but they stood tall, together. Brothers I'd risked my life besides. Brothers I loved.

'"Will you return with us to San Michon?" I asked.

'Baptiste looked to Greyhand. "Would we be welcome?"

'Our old master sighed. "The Testaments are clear, Sa-Ismael. The word of God is law. The sin is yours to own."

'"I felt him on that mountainside, Greyhand," Aaron said. "Bathed in his holy light. God stood with us, Baptiste and me, as we faced down a dark that seeks to consume all men. *All* men. And if your God would name my love a sin, then he's no God I know."

'"Where will you go?" I asked.

'"South perhaps?" Baptiste shrugged. "You could come with us, Little Lion."

'"No." I smiled, though my chest was aching. "I have monstrous things to slay."

'"You have a lion's heart, mon ami." The big lad took my hand, pulled me into a fierce, tear-stained hug. "See to it those monstrous things do not take it from you."

'"Hearts only bruise. They never break."

'I patted Baptiste on the back, released my hold. And then I turned to Aaron. This stuck-up lordling prick I'd so despised, who I'd fought and bled with, who I'd once never dreamed of thinking of as a friend, let alone famille.

'"Adieu, brother."

'Aaron took my arm and led me away, and though Greyhand watched sidelong, he didn't follow. When we were out of earshot by the horses, Aaron released his grip, meeting my eyes. "I pray God and Mothermaid watch over you, de León. But more, I pray you watch over yourself. And above all, watch Seraph Talon."

'". . . Talon? Why?"

'"The night the Empress arrived at San Michon. The night he . . . caught Baptiste and me. At the feast, I *swear* I felt someone in my head. A touch light as feathers, but still . . . I fear Talon didn't discover us by accident as he said. I fear he wanted rid of me."

'"To what end?"

'"I know not. But he is not to be trusted, Gabriel. Watch your back."

'I swallowed thick. Nodded once.

'Aaron embraced me, and I hugged him back, gutted at the thought of one more loss. "I say you then farewell, brother," he told me. "But not goodbye. We *will* meet again."

'I watched Aaron and Baptiste ride together, off into the dark and the cold, side by side. And I wondered if it was true, that our paths would cross once more. I asked myself if goodness could come of sin, and if so, what sin was at all. I asked myself if God loved us, how it was he could hate that we found love ourselves. How he could allow such suffering to go unanswered. How he could have deemed it wise to create a world that cradled horrors such as these.

'I asked myself, but I heard no answers.

'I wasn't ready to listen yet.'

✦ XVII ✦
SWORD OF THE REALM

'ABBOT KHALID STOOD before the convocation, the Redeemer's statue above, the faux Grail behind. All eyes were downturned as he spoke the gospel in his booming voice, but still, I found my gaze drifting from the altar to our honoured guests. None could blame me, of course. San Michon Cathedral had never played host to such an entourage.

'Empress Isabella, First of Her Name, beloved bride of Alexandre III, Protector of God's Holy Church, Sword of the Faith and Emperor of all Elidaen sat in the first row, a host of a hundred soldiers and maids-at-arms about her. Isabella was resplendent in royal yellow, her brow graced with diamonds, eyes glittering like sapphires as she watched the mass. The honour being done to me by her presence was lost on no one.

'My heart was thudding in my chest, palms damp with sweat. And at gospel's end, when the notes of the choir had dimmed like sunset light, the abbot turned his eyes to the gables high above, the heaven beyond.

'"Almighty Father, Mothermaid and Martyrs, hear my prayer. Through trials of Blood and Hunt and Blade, there stands one faithful servant among us deemed worthy to be sainted silver. Hear him now and judge him true in this, his pledge."

'I felt all in the Cathedral watching as I stood. But I stole a glance at the choir loft and saw the only one who mattered. The distance between us seemed impassable. But still, I could feel Astrid beside me as I walked to the altar. My mouth dry. My belly, butterflies.

'"Kneel, Initiate de León," Khalid commanded. "And speak your holy oath."

'I'd worked myself bloody to carve my place here. I'd almost broken upon this wheel. The loss of ma famille and friends, the trials I'd faced

– all had burned away anything of the boy I'd been. The sin of my birth, the knowledge that God would punish me for it, the dark truth of what I was – I accepted all as a price to be paid to protect the things I loved. And though I hadn't realized it at the time, I knew every fall I'd taken and mistake I'd made along the way had led me here, to this moment. I'd looked into the eyes of forever and seen the depths of the evil we faced. I knew the dedication it would take to send it back to hell. And so, as the choir raised their voices in song, I made the sign of the wheel before the Redeemer who'd died for my salvation. And I sank to my knees.

'"*In the sight of God Almighty, creator of heaven and earth, of all that was and will ever be, I pledge my life to the Order of San Michon.*

'"*I am the light in the night. I am hope for the hopeless. I am the fire that rages between this and all world's ending. I shall know no famille, save these my brothers. I shall love no woman, save our Mother and Maid. I shall seek no respite, save in paradise at the right hand of my Heavenly Father.*

'"*And in sight of God and his Seven Martyrs, I do here vow: let the dark know my name and despair. So long as it burns, I am the flame. So long as it bleeds, I am the blade. So long as it sins, I am the saint.*

'"*And I am silver.*"

'"Before Almighty God, the Mothermaid, the Seven Martyrs and all the angels of the heavenly host, I name you Brother of the Hunt. You knelt as but an Initiate of the Faith." Khalid stepped back, cheeks twisted in his scarred smile. "Arise now—"

'"Hold."

'Stillness fell across the Cathedral, all eyes turning to Isabella. The Empress rose, and making the sign of the wheel, stepped to the altar before me.

'"Blood spilled is blood owed," she said. "Valour proven must be valour repaid. There is no doubt in our eyes that the hand of heaven is upon you, Gabriel de León. All our empire stands in your debt. So our empire gives what reward it can."

'Isabella drew her sword with a flourish.

'"In sight of God and Mothermaid and Martyrs, we name you defender of our empire and keeper of our holy faith. We bid you be just to our subjects, and merciless to our enemies, and true in all measures under heaven. You are our sword. Our shield. Our hope. Arise, Gabriel de León, Silversaint of San Michon, and Chevalier of Elidaen."

'A great roar went up among the congregation, and I felt my heart soar in my chest. Looking about, I saw their faces as they came to their feet: Theo and Fincher, de Séverin and the Philippes. Khalid's smile. Talon's grudging nod. Even Frère Greyhand's thin, cruel lips seemed to be suffering a slight curvature, though I was certain he'd put it down to a trick of the light. The Empress stood, beaming like the long-lost sun, all her host applauding. And I stole another look up into the choir then, past Chloe Sauvage and Sister Esmeé, at last finding the one who mattered most. The only one who mattered at all.

'Astrid Rennier. Smiling at me.

'Though I could say nothing with all eyes upon me, I hoped she knew. And glancing to the Empress, I vowed I'd repay that girl for all she'd done.

'No matter what it cost me.

'We feasted in the refectory, a spread fit for royalty, though Isabella herself didn't attend. The initiates who'd called me frailblood, who'd pissed in my boots and shit in my bed, all raised their tankards, and I put my grudges behind me, knowing these lads were better my brothers than my enemies. I was a sixteen-year-old boy. A hero. A sword of the fucking realm. There's no glory so sweet as glory earned. And yet there was a weight on me that needed lifting. Words that needed speaking, yet unspoken.

'I stood slow, and a hush fell on that hall.

'"To Prioress Charlotte," I said. "To Keeper Logan. To Michelle and Micah and Tally, to Robert and Demi and Nicolette and all those who marched there, but did not march back again. To Aaron de Coste and Baptiste Sa-Ismael." I raised my goblet and looked among the gathering. "To the courageous dead. And to brothers lost."

'A shadow fell over the hall then. But Greyhand stood and called "Santé!", and soon all took up the shout. And we drank then, because we were alive and we were breathing, and even in darkest nights, that can be cause enough for triumph. The fare was fine, and the smiles were broad, and the peace I knew was complete. But after an hour or so, a hush fell over our number, and I turned to find four men in the Emperor's livery behind me, a stout Sūdhaemi man with a craggy, battle-scarred face at the fore.

'"Her Imperial Majesty demands your presence, Chevalier."

'To hear that title truly brought it home to me – what I was now and what I'd done. We marched to the Great Library, and I saw maids-at-arms on the door. Walking inside, I found the entire hall lined with soldiers, wooden figures scattered on the great map at their feet. Abbot Khalid and Seraph Talon were already waiting, Forgemaster Argyle and my old master Greyhand too. But my attention was drawn to the woman at the end of the room.

'"Well met, Chevalier," Empress Isabella smiled. "Our congratulations upon your ascension. We and our realm entire owe you a debt."

'I dropped to my knee, bowed my head to stop it spinning. I wondered what my mama and Celene might have thought of me then, to see me knighted before the Empress. My chest ached at their loss. But I knew they'd be smiling upon me from heaven's shore, Amélie beside them. That they'd have been proud of me.

'"You honour me, Majesty."

'"We do. But it is honour earned." Isabella toyed with a silver ring on her finger. "De León. *Lion* in old Nordish. The goodly abbot informs us it was your mother's name?"

'I looked down to the signet ring my mama had given me – those lions flanking those crossed blades. "If it please Your Majesty, I did not know the monster who was my father. And my mother . . ." I sighed. "She never had the chance to tell me of him. But she told me the blood of lions flowed in my veins. To never forget it, no matter what else might come."

'"She sounds quite a woman."

'". . . She was, Majesty."

'"You have our sympathies, Chevalier. But rise now, we pray you. We would hear of the Battle of the Twins from your own lips. How is it you unearthed the Forever King's plan when all other eyes were blind to it?"

'I looked to Khalid, uncertain, but he only nodded. And so, I spoke of all that had happened from the moment I discovered Laure's hidden message. I left out Chloe and Astrid, of course, but told all else – the blood missive, our desperate ride from San Michon, the Wraith in Red, and the vow of the Forever King, ringing in my skull like funeral bells.

'The Empress stood mute the entire time, and again, I was struck by how young she was. Isabella was a woman but in her mid-twenties, and yet she sat upon the throne of an empire. Her capitaines and aides-de-camp watched me like hawks, and I was conscious of the weight in the air, the scrutiny upon my every word. I felt a small fish then, in a great dark water. And in the end, Isabella turned to the Sūdhaemi man beside her.

'"How is it de Fronsac did not know of this gambit, Nassar? What does our general in Avinbourg do all day, we wonder? How is it Capitaine Belmont and his scouts could not tell us the direction an army of *ten thousand* corpses marched until it was too late?"

'"I fear I do not know, Majesty," the man confessed.

'"No? It seems there is much our commanders do not know, despite its being their business to do so. And were it not for the insight of a *sixteen-*

year-old boy, Nordlund would already be overrun. How much of our empire is already thralled to these monsters? How much of our army? How many in our court?"

'I glanced to Abbot Khalid, but his eyes told me to hold my tongue. I began to get an inkling of what was happening here. Looking more carefully at the figures on the map at our feet, I saw wooden wolves on the coast of Sūdhaem, wooden bears in the Ossway. A scattering of wooden roses inland. And my stomach sank as I realized what I was seeing.

'"The other bloodlines have begun to strike."

'"De León, you will speak when spoken to!" Talon snapped.

'"All is well, good Seraph," the Empress said. "Were it not for the quick thinking of our young paleblood here, Fabién Voss would be marching on our capital." She inclined her head to me. "It is true, Chevalier. Dyvok, Ilon, Chastain – all are on the move. The bloodlords of those dread lines fear being left behind if Fabién Voss stakes too deep a claim. So now, our enemies come at us not on one front, but four. And we know not whom we can trust." Her eyes fixed me to the floor. "But it is not for naught we have named you our sword, Gabriel de León. And we shall call upon you soon to stand in defence of our empire."

'I kept silent then. I'd no inkling of the factions at court, the politics in play. I looked to the Empress, and beyond the beautiful dress and painted lips, I saw an iron fist in a silken glove. Astrid and her mother had been swept aside like deadwood in this woman's path, and a part of me hated her for that. But it was not Alexandre III, Emperor of Elidaen and Protector of God's Holy Church who'd ridden to Avinbourg's defence.

'"Merci for your testimony, Little Lion," Khalid said. "Leave us now."

'"Little Lion?" Isabella asked, one eyebrow rising.

'"So we call him, Majesty," Talon replied. "A nickname, from when he arrived."

'Isabella looked me up and down, lips curling in a careful smile. "Not so little any more, we think." She nodded to the seraph, then back to me. "We are pleased. You may go, and with our heartfelt thanks, Chevalier. May the Almighty bless and keep you."

'"Majesty, if it please . . . might I beg a favour?"

'"Impertinent wretch!" Talon blustered. "Silence your tongue, de León, before—"

'The seraph's tirade was halted as Isabella raised a gentle hand. Instead of being offended, she actually seemed . . . entertained. "Little Lion indeed. Yet most would hold we have shown you favour enough?"

"'I beg it not for me, Majesty."

"'Ah. Charity. A respectable trait for a true knight of our empire. Speak, then, Chevalier. Let us see your selflessness rewarded."

'I opened my mouth, but looking to Khalid, to Talon and Greyhand, I found no words would come. To beg this favour put me in peril, but I feared for others besides myself. Empress Isabella watched me carefully, eyes like knives.

"'Leave us," she commanded, glancing around the room.

'I saw the Brothers look to each other, uncertain. And yet they obeyed, silversaints and soldiers, courtiers and handmaids marching out into the brittle night air. But as they left, I felt a touch upon my mind. So cotton-soft as to be almost unnoticeable. So silver-swift as to be almost imperceptible.

'But still. I felt it.

"'You seem an uncommon man, Gabriel de León," Isabella told me. "Would that some of our loving husband's generals were so bold."

"'A friend of mine told me recklessness is a more admirable quality than foolishness, Majesty," I said, eyes downturned. "Though I often fail to see the difference."

"'Your friend sounds a wise one."

"'It is for her I'd beg favour, Majesty."

"'Ah. A *her*. Now you are descending into cliché, Chevalier. Who is this maid for whom you beg? No wife you can claim now your vows are sworn, that much is sure."

"'. . . Astrid Rennier."

'Isabella's smile wavered. Only for a second, but yet, I saw it. And more, a hint of something darker behind those beautiful blue eyes.

'Displeasure.

"'Astrid has yet to make vow to the Silver Sorority. I'd beg Your Majesty for mercy and an end to her exile. She fought bravely at the Twins, standing where almost no one else dared. And Astrid's peerage is not her fault. She does not belong here."

'The Empress regarded me carefully.

"'I should have known. Such was her mother's nature also. The serpent sinks her fangs wherever she lays her head. Even, apparently, in a house of God." Isabella studied her fingernails, lips pursed. "In love with her, are you? Know that you are not the first fly to fall into that pot of honey, Little Lion. She had many favourites at court, your dear Astrid. And she played them all like fiddles. As she now plays you."

"'I most humbly beg your pardon, Majesty," I said, swallowing hard. "But the sisternovice had no knowing I'd speak on her behalf."

'I was terrified to talk so, but it wasn't fear of an empress's wrath. If my wish were granted, I'd never lay eyes on Astrid again. I thought about our meetings in this very library, wondering how empty this place might feel without her in it. And yet, I couldn't forget the debt I owed her, nor how miserable she was, looking at the walls that had become her prison. I'd miss her like a part of me had been cut away. But hearts only bruise, she'd told me. And if she were happy, that was a price I'd gladly pay.

'*Sweet Redeemer, I do love her . . .*

'"What will you give us, Chevalier, should we grant you this boon?"

'"Loyalty. Loyalty unto death."

'"We are your Empress, Gabriel de León. You owe us *that* already." Isabella paused, looking down at those wooden wolves and bears and roses scattered across the realm at her feet, the ravens lurking yet west of the Godsend. "And yet, we cannot deny that God Himself seems to have set you apart. It was not by chance alone that you discovered the Forever King's ploy, nor that you survived the storm where so many others fell." Her eyes met mine, glittering like the jewels on her brow. "We think perhaps the Almighty has a plan for you."

'I thought of little Chloe then. Her words that night the star fell from heaven.

'Isabella inclined her head. "So be it."

'My heart rushed so hard at those words that it ached, and I wondered if it would have hurt less if Isabella had denied me. I bowed low, hair sweeping to the floor.

'"I am in your debt, Majesty. Your mercy knows no bounds."

'"Oh, be sure and certain it does, Chevalier." The Empress gazed out upon the map of the empire, her voice hard as iron. "Our mercy is quite at its limits. So grow not too comfortable here in San Michon. We shall call upon you, Gabriel de León. And soon."

'Isabella offered her hand, fingers dipped in jewels and silver. I couldn't help but think of the first night I'd spoken to Astrid then, here beneath this very roof. The hand she'd offered and I'd then kissed, and that I was now letting go of forever.

'I pressed my lips to Isabella's knuckles. "Empress."

'"Leave us now," she commanded.

'And like a good little soldier, I obeyed.'

✦ XVIII ✦
A STORY YOU CAN LIVE

'I RETURNED TO the Library later that night, at the hour we usually met.

'I wasn't certain I was doing the right thing. My belly was a cold fist, my heart punching on in my chest. This last year, I'd made more than my fair share of mistakes, reckless gambits, blind assumptions, thinking in my vanity that I knew better. And though I was now a knight of the empire, a sworn silversaint, though I'd seen through the machinations of a Forever King, I still waited there in the shadows of the forbidden section, staring into the light of our single candle, wondering if I was a fool.

'But I wasn't left to wonder long.

'My pulse ran quicker as I heard careful footsteps. Quiet and quick. A now-familiar tread, working its way through the warren of shelves and curiosities and dusty books, into our little sanctuary from the world. I wondered if she'd be angry with me. Wondered what she'd say. Wondered if this was going to end the way I thought it might. And as the footsteps reached the end of the warren, he stepped out into the light, faux outrage already on his face, accusation already spilling from his lips.

'"What *devilry* is this?"

'I eased my boots off the table. "Bonsoir, Seraph."

'Talon looked about the room, moustache quivering as he realized I was alone.

'"Expecting someone else?"

'"This section of the Library is forbidden, de León."

'"I'm not an initiate any more, Seraph. I go where I please."

'"And what are you doing in here in the middle of the night?"

'"Waiting for you."

"'Me?'"

"'I felt you in my head earlier.'"

'The thin man looked me up and down, spat through sharpening teeth. "How dare you accuse me of such? Brother 'saints do not use their gifts upon each other in San Michon without consent, you frailblooded little arselicker."

"'I know that's why you're here, Talon. Hoping to catch me and Astrid like you caught Aaron and Baptiste. A good hunter uses the appetites of their prey against them. Want is a weakness, isn't it? How better to be rid of me with hands white as angels' wings?'"

"'So you admit it. You *have* been meeting a sisternovice in here."

"'But how could you have known that? Unless you've been in my head?'"

"'I have eyes, de León. I see the way she looks at you."

"'Oh, oui. I've no doubt you've been watching *all* the sisternovices. Deciding which to take for your new aide? It's been months since Sister Aoife died. That girl you murdered in Coste probably didn't do much to scratch the itch.'"

'Talon's eyes narrowed to slits in his skull. "What did you just say?"

"'The serving girl in Coste keep. You framed it well enough with vampires on the loose in the château. But you were on the loose too, Talon. Alone. And when you showed up in the ballroom after Laure arrived, your eyes were red as blood.'"

"'So were Greyhand's. I'd just smoked a pipe of sanctus, you filthy bog-skank.'"

"'Except you didn't smell of it like Greyhand did. Your eyes weren't flooded because of the pipe. They were flooded because you'd just *fed*. Like you fed on Aoife the night she died." I rose from my chair, stalking towards him. "I wondered when Aaron warned me that you'd slipped into his head. I wondered why you'd want rid of him, and me. And then I remembered. Greyhand was out cold, but Aaron and I both heard what Laure said to you on that bridge: *I would promise you pleasures no chaste and holy brother could dream of. But you're already ours, paleblood.* And when she mentioned Aoife's name, you charged at her headlong like an idiot. Not because you were angry. Because you wanted to stop her from saying more in front of Aaron and me.'"

"'You little bastard . . .'" Talon hissed.

"'How long?'" I demanded. "How long were you feeding on Aoife? How long were you *sleeping* with her?'"

'Talon's eyes grew wide with rage. "How dare y—"

"'I saw her in the Cathedral the night she died! On her knees before the Mothermaid, arms around her belly. *Is this a curse or a blessing you've gifted me?* she asked. But it wasn't until I talked to Kaveh that I learned the truth. Dreamweed isn't the only herb he can wrangle on his supply runs to Beaufort. Sister Aoife asked him to get her honeywell. Rowanwhite and rainberry. You're a master of chymistrie, Talon, so tell me! Why would a young woman want herbs of that ilk?"

'Talon met my eyes, his own welling with furious tears.

"'You've no idea what it's like, boy," he hissed, hands in fists. "You are *young*. The sacrament still sates you. You do not know what it is to lie awake and feel the sangirè inside you, spreading like flame. But you *will*. Already you hear that whisper, gentle as spring rains, but oh, it *grows*, boy. It grows with every sunset until its scream is all you can hear."

"'She was pregnant, you bastard!"

'Talon dragged his fingernails across his stubbled scalp, a snarl at his lips. He took a step towards me, and every inch of me bristled with threat. The beast I was prowled back and forth behind the cage of my ribs, my teeth now sharp as razors.

"'You killed her," I spat. "And the child you put inside her."

"'It was not a child, it was an *abomination*! Its ending was mercy!"

"'And the maid you killed in Coste? What mercy did you give her? You murdered two innocent girls, and all because you didn't have the stomach to face the Red Rite as Yannick did! You shame that sevenstar and all who wear it, you fucking coward!"

'Talon snarled and lunged at me, and we collided in a hateful embrace. The seraph was older, stronger, but my old friend rage was at my back, willing me on. We crashed against the shelves, timbers splintering, parchment flying as his hands closed around my throat. I pummelled him with my fists as his fingers crushed my larynx. My knuckles crashed against his jaw as he buried his knee in my crotch. As I squealed and doubled over, his knee smashed my nose to sauce, and I found myself flying, crashing through another shelf and sending the ancient tomes tumbling.

"'I told you, boy," he spat, sitting astride my chest. "I earned my aegis when you were still a dribble in your unholy father's cock."

'I clawed his eyes, and he grabbed my wrist. I screamed as his fangs sank into my flesh. Blood sprayed as I tore my hand loose, but as that red touched his tongue, I saw the monster surface in Talon's depths – that hunger to which he'd found himself a slave. His face twisted, his strength terrifying, a bloodshot scrawl spreading across the whites of his eyes as he seized my neck. I roared as his fangs sank into my throat, punching and bucking even as the kiss took me: that bliss, that horror, that awful, bloody *wanting* bid me be still, *be still,* to close my eyes and hold my breath and pray it didn't end too soon.

'A kick crashed into Talon's ribs, so hard I heard bone splinter. With a bloodied cry, the seraph rolled free, tumbling across the scattered pages. I gasped for breath, pressed a hand to the ragged gouges he'd ripped in my throat. Looking upwards, I saw silver-heeled boots, an empty sleeve in a leather greatcoat, a pale green stare.

'"I didn't believe it when the boy told me," Greyhand growled. "Not Talon, I thought. He'd have the courage to do what was right when his time came."

'"Greyhand . . ." The seraph smiled and tried to rise. "Let me explain, old frien—"

'Talon gasped as Greyhand's sword sank hilt-deep into his chest, out through his back, red and bright. The seraph's bloodshot eyes grew wide as Greyhand *twisted* the silversteel blade up through his ribs, cleaving his treacherous heart.

'"Better to die a man than live a monster." Greyhand wrenched his sword free and sighed. "I'm sorry I couldn't spare you that, old friend."

'Talon collapsed on the floorboards in a widening pool of blood. His chest was split by silversteel, heart sundered. Bloody fangs bared, his eyes fell on me.

'"You w-will understand one day, b-boy." His chest rattled with one final gasp, sticky and red. "I-I will await you in h-hell . . ."

'I lay on my back in a slick of dark red, hand pressed to my savaged throat. My nose was smashed across my cheeks, legs shaking, blood thick on my fingers. Looking at that bastard's body, I could feel nothing close to pity after what he'd done. But I *did* feel a cold horror at the thought that a silversaint so high had fallen so very far. If a brother so dedicated could succumb to the madness of the thirst, anyone could.

'*Anyone.*

'"Can you walk?"

'I looked up into Greyhand's eye, his face as ever stone. "I th-think so."

'The silversaint offered his good hand. "Let's get you to the Infirmary, Little Lion."

'I met his hand with mine, my other still staunching the blood. "Merci, Master."

'"I'm not your master any more, Chevalier." He slung my arm around his shoulder, thin lips twisting. "In fact, technically, you probably outrank me now."

'I nodded to the corpse behind us. "He might have killed me if you hadn't been there to stop him. It seems you've still a few lessons to teach."

'"Know no shame, Little Lion." Greyhand shook his head, the ghost of a smile at his lips. "Old age and treachery can always overcome youth and skill."

'"I'll remember that."

'"I'm sure you will."

'We shuffled from the Library towards the Infirmary, blood running down my throat and chest, red footprints behind us as Greyhand sighed. "I've known him since I was your age. I'd not have believed it unless I heard it from his own lips. Not Talon."

'I shook my head, sticky hand pressed to my bleeding neck. "If we spend all our lives in darkness, is it any wonder when darkness starts to live in us?"

'"Mmm." Greyhand looked to the heavens above. To the one watching over us. "Nothing is certain in this, save the love of God. Life is not a story you can tell, de León. It's only a story you can live. The bright news is, you get to choose what kind yours will be. A story of horror, or a story of courage. A story of indulgence, or a story of duty. The story of a monster. Or the story of a man."

'The doors to the Priory opened before us, and I saw light and warmth inside.

'"What will your story be?"'

✦ XIX ✦

ON THIS FIRE

'I OPENED MY eyes, floating in the dark between dreaming and waking.

'I sensed her before I saw her – the scent of her hair and the faintest notes of blood, entwined with the gentle perfume of dried herbs from the Infirmary outside. Turning my head, I found her beside my cot, quiet and still in the dark. For the thousandth time, I wondered what this place would be when she left it and me behind.

'"Astrid," I whispered.

'She simply stared, her expression inscrutable; that mask she'd learned to wear as a mistress's daughter in the Golden Halls. But her eyes were shining, deep and dark as the night above. And I wondered at the mystery of it all – that I'd come to these walls so far from home to meet a girl such as this. A girl I must now say goodbye to.

'"I should dump that pisspot on your head," she said.

'". . . What?"

'"Of all the shit-brained, dropped-as-a-babe, pig-skulled, *fucking* . . ."

'She stood swiftly, biting her lip to halt her tirade. The Infirmary was quiet as tombs, and raised voices would surely bring curious cats. But I could see fury in Astrid's eyes as she glowered down at me, knuckles white at her sides.

'"They told me what you did. What you said to that hell-bitch Isabella."

'". . . I thought you'd be pleased. I've ended your exile."

'"Nobody asked you to do that, Gabriel!"

'"Nor should you need to? I know how you feel about San Michon, Astrid. No hell so cruel as powerlessness, remember? You said you'd tear the wings off an angel to fly this cage. Well, now you can leave whenever you want."

'Her lips pressed thin, eyes glittering with anger. "Suppose I don't want to leave?"

'"But you *hate* this place."

'"And if hate had the steerage of my course, I'd already be gone. But it doesn't!"

'"What are you talking about?"

'She met my eyes and sighed. "Do you truly not know?"

'I saw the plea in her gaze, and my stomach was lit by the wings of a hundred burning butterflies. I knew what she spoke of. Of *course,* I did. If I tried, I could still remember the bliss of her mouth on mine, the lonely, empty ache of wanting something I could never have. But I *couldn't* have her. Because this was wrong.

'All of this, *wrong*.

'"Astrid . . . there's no future for you here. There's no future in . . . this."

'"You mean *us*."

'"I mean I swore an oath before the Mothermaid and Martyrs and God Himself to love no woman. And if you stayed here, you'd soon be wed to him besides."

'"You *do* love me, then . . ."

'I turned away lest she see the answer in my eyes. But she sat on the bed beside me, pressed her hand to my cheek and forced me to look at her. To *see* her. She was the shadow on my thoughts when I tried to sleep. The fire in my dreams that bid me never wake.

'"Tell me you do not want me," she whispered.

'"Astrid . . ."

'"Tell me, and I will leave this place and never think of you again." A tear spilled down her cheek, caught trembling at the bow of her lips. "But if you do want me, Gabriel de León, then *say it*. Because only a coward would cherish the wanting of a thing and yet send it away. And I will not give my heart to a coward. I will give it to a *lion*."

'God and Martyrs, she was beautiful. That face shaped like heartbreak, like a secret unshared. Her eyes were darker than all the roads I'd walked and all the monstrous things I'd seen, and in them I knew I'd find a heaven if only I were willing to risk a hell.

'"Tell me you do not want me."

'"I can't," I whispered. "God help me, I can't."

'"Then *take* me, Gabriel." She lifted her chin, fierce and furious. "Take me, and God and Mothermaid and Martyrs be damned with us both."

'And there was nothing left then: no restraint, no law, no vow that could have held me anchored through her storm. I kissed her, hungry and hard, and in that kiss, I knew salvation and damnation. A vow I could truly keep.

'On this fire, I would burn.

'And there in the dark of that cell, we stripped each other bare, skin to skin. Her teeth nipped at my lip and her fingers wove through my hair, and she sat astride me and kissed away my every thought and fear. All hope abandoned to the flames between us. My fingertips traced her body, curve and valley, down to the shadow between her legs, the softness that had haunted my dreams. We were silent, the two of us, speaking only with eyes and hands and desperate, whispered breath, the fear of discovery thrilling us both, the glorious, wanton guilt of it somehow making all of it the sweeter.

'Her lips were flame and frost upon my skin, kissing me in all the places mortal girls feared to tread. I kissed her just the same, sinking between her thighs as she plunged me into her mouth, and the taste of her near drove me mad. We moved slow in the dark, smothering our sighs in each other's secrets until there was nothing but the inevitable, nothing but the fire awaiting us both. She clawed and she pleaded "Fuck me, *fuck* me' and as I slipped into her, slow and deep and hard, there was nothing else in all the world that mattered. No divinity but the want in her eyes. No eternity in hell I wouldn't have gladly suffered if I could have lived just one more moment of the heaven inside her.

'We swayed together, her atop me now, the razors of my teeth brushing the satin of her skin, feeling her shiver as she whispered my name. And as the rush took hold, as I felt it singing inside me, she pressed her hands to my cheeks so she might meet my eyes. Desperate. Needing. Lips bruised like cherries.

'"Bite me," she breathed.

'". . . What?"

'"Bite me, Gabriel."

'My teeth were sharp against my tongue, and I could see the pulse thudding down the milk-white silk of her throat. I wanted it, God help me, I *wanted* it so badly it was all I could see, all I could taste. But there was still enough of me left to push it back, away, my breath ragged in my lungs as she swayed atop me, deeper, faster, warm and so impossibly smooth, dancing me ever closer to my brink.

'"They'll see," I whispered. "The mark . . ."

'"Here," she begged, running one hand over her breast. "*Please.*"

'There's no need deeper than to be desired. There's no sweeter word under heaven than *please*. And I gave myself over to it utterly. Feeling her shiver as a dark growl rose up in my throat and the hunger took me whole. I seized a fistful of her hair, smiling as I dragged her in. A need on the edge of madness. A want on the edge of violence. And she groaned and pushed herself down onto me, deeper, harder, and my tongue slipped over her pebble-hard nipple and her nails clawed my back as the monster I was sank its fangs into her breast, piercing the white and birthing the red.

'She crushed us together, back arching, mouth open in a silent scream as the Kiss took hold. Her whole body began shaking, her legs wrapped tighter around me as she lost herself in the fire of it all and her blood – God, that impossible burning *life* – crashed across my tongue and into the very heart of me.

'And I knew the colour of bliss then. And its colour was red.

'I drank her, as a river drinks the rain. Drawn up into the crimson light of a sun long faded, so lost that I was only dimly aware of her slipping me free, finishing me with her hand, the death of me spurting across her skin as I swallowed just one more mouthful, just one more drop. Gasping, she tore herself loose from my mouth, and wounded, wanting, she crushed her lips to mine, iron and rust and salt between us. We sank into the ruin we'd made of my bed, our bodies slick, her cheek against my chest, and all of her wrapped in my arms.

'We lay there for an age in silence. In truth, I'd no knowing what to say. This was the road to hell, I knew. And both of us now walked it.

'"This is sin," I told her. "They will punish us for it. And God beside them."

'Astrid lifted her head, met my eyes.

'"But I don't care," I breathed.

'Her fingertips brushed my face, making me shiver. "We could leave?"

'I shook my head, giving the answer she already had the keeping of. "You said you'd not give your heart to a coward. We couldn't leave even if we wished it. And I don't think either of us truly does."

'"This will be our lot, then? Loving in the dark? Like liars?"

'I kissed her brow, eyes closed tight. "Until the war is won. Until the song is sung."

'"And then?"

'"Then us. Forever."

'She kissed me again, melting in my arms. A kiss of flames and tears, of sweetest sin, a kiss to which all others would be compared and found wanting. And if this was wrong, I decided, then let it be the wrong I'd die for. There, with that girl in my arms, I swore to God I would give all else – my blood, my life, my everything – if only he would let me have her.

'Just. Her.'

BROKEN GLASS

GABRIEL FELL SILENT, staring at the silver she'd scribed on his skin. He heard the cry of a lovelorn wolf; a solitary howl out in that long and lonely dark.

He held his empty wineglass in numb fingers, feeling the liquor rushing bloodwarm in his veins. If he tried hard enough, he could reach out and touch her now. He had but to open the window to his mind's eye and find her there, waiting, smiling, untouched by the teeth of time. Long black hair and deep black eyes and a shadow that weighed a ton.

'You served San Michon five more years,' Jean-François said, drawing long, smooth lines in his accursed book. 'Five years in which your name became legend. You led the attack on Báih Sìde and liberated the Dyvok slaughterfarms at Triúrbaile when you were only nineteen. You freed Qadir and broke the siege at Tuuve at twenty. You slew elders of the Dyvok in Ossway, Chastain in the Sūdhaem, burned out a nest of ancien Ilon that threatened the Crown itself. *The Black Lion*, they called you. Your name was a clarion call. A hymn in the houses of the holy, and a curse in the Courts of the Blood.'

The vampire stopped drawing long enough to meet Gabriel's eyes.

'How did it all come undone?'

'Patience, coldblood,' Gabriel replied.

Anger flashed in the vampire's gaze, swift and black. 'No, Silversaint. I have shown the patience of angels eternal. You will finish this chapter *now*. How did it end?'

Gabriel met the monster's eyes, lifted his tattooed hands into the light. '*Patience.*'

Jean-François blinked at the name across the silversaint's fingers.

'Your daughter.'

Gabriel reached to the bottle, spilling the wine into his goblet, deep and red. He pressed the glass to his lips and drank deep. The wolf sang again out in the dark, alone and heartsick. It was an age before the silversaint conjured voice enough to speak.

'We didn't plan it. Astrid and I. We never imagined it. She swore to the Silver Sorority, became Mistress of the Aegis in San Michon. I, the young paragon of the Ordo Argent. We lived as she prophesied, stealing our moments in the dark when duty allowed. Fucking like thieves. But it was enough. *She* was enough.

'We were careful. So careful that when she told me, hand to belly, I wondered if it was a sign from God. For one foolish moment, I thought it might not matter. My accolades were too many to count by then. Someone told me there were more babes named Gabriel that last year I served in San Michon than were gifted the name of the Emperor himself.'

The Last Silversaint shook his head.

'But of course, it changed *everything*. I had enemies aplenty by then. Outside San Michon, and within. The vanity Greyhand had warned me about was ever my weakness. I wasn't a lamb, I was a fucking lion, and I walked the earth like one. But the light that burns twice as bright burns half as long. And the poppy that grows too tall gets cut down to size. *Oathbreaker*, they called me. *Blasphemer*. There's a great deal you can get away with if your name grows large enough, coldblood. But this wasn't some pretty painted courtesan who'd welcomed me into her bed. This was a sister of the Silver Sorority. And no matter how many hymns they sing for you, no matter how many babes are named for you, it's a forgiving priest indeed who pardons the man who makes a cuckold of God.

'The brethren demanded I set Astrid aside. Even Greyhand. And I told them where they could shove their fucking demands. So, she and I were excommunicated. They let me keep my aegis at least – probably for fear of losing their hands. But all those years of service, all those lives I'd saved, and no one in San Michon was even allowed to come wish us farewell. Finch, Theo, the Phils, Sév, Chloe – *nobody*. We climbed onto Justice, Astrid's arms about my waist, and alone, friendless, we rode into the dark.'

Gabriel's smile was like the sun rising.

'But we weren't alone for long. And never again. God still gave us one more blessing. A tiny, beautiful blessing, with her mama's smile and her papa's eyes, and no hint of the curse that flowed in his paleblood veins.'

Gabriel shook his head, voice soft with wonder.

'The first time I held her in my arms, I cried more than she did. I used to watch her while she slept as a babe. Just stand above her crib for hours and wonder how the hell someone like me had made something so beautiful. And as she grew, I realized *she* was the reason I'd been put on this earth. Not to lead armies or defend cities or save an empire. Looking into her eyes, I knew it, like I knew the taste of my wife's lips or the song of the blood. Goodness *could* come of sin, and she was proof. She was perfect. Great Redeemer, she was *everything*. Our Patience.'

Gabriel stretched out his legs before him, ankles crossed, leathers whispering. Tipping his head back, he finished off his wine, a droplet running down his chin. Reaching for the Monét, he found it empty, cursing under his breath.

'Hearts only bruise,' the vampire murmured. 'They never break.'

Gabriel nodded. 'So Astrid would often tell me.'

'A pretty sentiment.'

'A fucking lie.'

'Where did the three of you go?'

Gabriel's eyes were fixed on the goblet in his hand. The reflections of the lantern's flame playing like fireflies on the blood-dark drop in the bottom. Thumb tracing the arc of the teardrop scars down his cheek, he looked to that pale moth still beating its wings in vain upon the lantern's chimney, heedless and hopeless.

'De León?'

'Your voice will never feel so tiny as when you're screaming at God,' he whispered.

'. . . What?'

Gabriel blinked, his eyes coming into focus. He looked up at the historian and slowly shook his head. 'I don't want to talk about them any more.'

'Must we do this again? My Empress demands her tale.'

'And she'll have it.' Gabriel's grip tightened on his empty glass, knuckles white. 'But I don't feel like talking about ma famille right now.'

'You are a prisoner here. Completely within our power. For all intents and purposes, Chevalier, you are my slave. So apologies,' the vampire said, leaning forward, 'but has it somehow been conveyed to you that it makes any difference at all how you *feel*?'

The wineglass shattered in Gabriel's hand. A hundred glittering shards splintering in his fist and falling to the stone. The silversaint winced and opened his fingers, looking at the blood dripping, dark and sweet and thick.

Jean-François was suddenly standing. Though he barely seemed to move at all, the historian was across the other side of the room, bristling with threat. A black hunger filled his eyes as he watched the red *drip, drip, drip*.

'Are you *insane*?'

Gabriel smiled, held out his wounded hand. 'Frightened of a little blood, vampire?'

Jean-François hissed, pearl-white fangs bared, 'If I fear anything, de León, it is what I would do to you if I let my hunger have its head.'

'And what do you think you'd do to me, coldblood?' Gabriel's eyes narrowed. 'Before your Empress has the whole of her tale?'

The Last Silversaint rose from his chair and stepped forward, bleeding hand outstretched. Jean-François took another step back.

'Seems we're all *someone's* slave.'

'Meline!' Jean-François bellowed.

The door flew open in a heartbeat, the thrall woman on the threshold in her long, black gown. Her eyes were wide. One hand beneath her bodice. 'Master?'

The vampire blinked, the dark shadow that had filled his eyes dimming. He smoothed down his frockcoat and plucked at the ruffled hems of his sleeves.

'Our guest has cut himself.'

The woman released the weapon she had hidden in her bodice. A dagger, mostlike, though it was difficult for Gabriel to tell. She dropped into a curtsey, made her way to the silversaint's side, taking his hand. Gentle as she was, Gabriel could still feel the terrible strength in her grip; the power gifted from nightly sups at her master's wrist. The silversaint's eyes were still fixed on the vampire's, his lips curling into a grim smile as he saw that, despite regaining his composure, the creature still refused to move closer.

'It is deep, Master,' Meline reported. 'It will heal in time, but it's best I—'

'Swiftly, then.'

The thrall curtseyed once more, rushing from the room.

'And bring another fucking bottle!' Gabriel shouted.

The woman fled down the stairs in a flurry of black damask. Again, she left the door unlocked behind. Gabriel listened to her descend, forty stairs, seventy, his senses still sharp as razors. He heard iron keys. A heavy lock. Door slamming.

He turned pale grey eyes back to the historian. Jean-François still lurked on the other side of the prison cell. The historie had fallen on the floor, open to a sketch of Dior back in the Perfect Husband, wrapped in her ridiculous frockcoat. The silversaint picked it up, marvelling once again at the vampire's artistry.

'It's a fine likeness.' He smiled, heart aching. 'The little bitch would be flattered.'

'Put that down. You'll get blood on it.'

Gabriel dropped the book onto the vampire's chair. 'Heaven forbid.'

The historian dragged a long golden curl from his eyes and whispered, soft with menace. 'I shall see you punished for this, de León. I shall have you on your knees.'

'I'm sure you can taste me already. But you know this is all a waste of time, don't you?'

'Time is something my Empress has in abundance.'

Gabriel shook his head, smearing crimson across his chin as he stroked his stubble. 'If that were so, I'd already be dead, vampire. Your Empress needs the secret of the Grail. But you said it yourself. The cup was broken. The Grail is *gone*. This is your world, leech. Your here and your now and your forever. And when the monsters you've birthed drain every last drop from it, you'll have none but yourselves to blame.'

Gabriel glanced over his shoulder.

'That was quick.'

The thrall woman stood on the threshold again. 'Master?'

Gabriel met Jean-François's eyes again. 'I don't want to speak of ma famille any more, vampire. So, you can sit and watch me get quietly shitfaced, or I can stop wasting our time and return to the story I'm actually here to tell.'

A moment passed, long and silent, before the vampire spoke again.

'. . . As you like it, Chevalier.'

The silversaint returned to his chair, dripping blood. As he sat with a wince, the thrall knelt beside him. He saw a bowl of steaming water, bandages, smelled the antiseptic perfume of witchhazel and fools' honey. And beside the bowl . . .

'Merci, Mlle Meline,' he said, reaching for the new bottle of Monét. 'When they usher me into hell, I'll be sure to put in a good word for you.'

Jean-François returned slowly to his seat, eyes on the silversaint's bleeding hand as he picked up his historie. The vampire straightened his beautiful coat, took the span of three breaths to regain his composure, then spoke.

'So. Your gambit at San Guillaume had turned into a massacre, Silversaint. Sister Chloe, Père Rafa, Saoirse, Bellamy, Phoebe – the entire Company of the Grail. All butchered by the Beast of Vellene. The only ones to survive Danton's wrath were you and Dior.'

Jean-François's lips twisted into the faintest of smiles.

'And *he* had turned out to be a *she*.'

Gabriel winced as Meline fished a long splinter of glass from his palm. He stared at the sevenstar etched there, silver ink glinting in the lantern's golden light.

'I don't suppose I could have another smoke?'

The historian lifted his quill and simply glowered.

Gabriel shrugged. 'Can't blame a man for trying.'

He lifted the Monét to his lips and took a long, slow swallow right from the neck.

'So. The end. The beginning. The Grail.'

Book Six

AS DEVILS CAN FLY

From holy cup comes holy light;
The faithful hand sets world aright.
And in the Seven Martyrs' sight,
Mere man shall end this endless night.

– AUTHOR UNKNOWN

FEAR NO DARKNESS

"'YOU'RE A GIRL."

"'I noticed."

"'Fuck."

'I skimmed my good hand through my sodden hair, my breath hanging pale and heavy between us. Dior looked up at me, drenched bone deep, her lips purpling from the chill. We were crouched on the banks of the River Volta, shoreline crusted with ice like a frosthunter's beard, a deadwood rising beyond. The night was black as sin, black as the river behind us, black as the heart of the thing that had torn our little company to ribbons.

"'*Fuck*."

"'You s-said that already. What happened to Saoirse?"

"'She's dead," I sighed.

'Dior's eyes widened. "Are you s-sure?"

"'Danton tore her and Phoebe apart right in front of me. So oui, fairly fucking sure."

'The girl swallowed hard, jaw clenched. "Sister Chloe?"

'I stared out to the dark waters that had claimed my old friend, rushing past us, silent and hungry. And eyes burning, I shook my head.

"'*Fuck*," Dior hissed.

"'That's what I said."

'The girl hung her head, arms wrapped around herself, shivering. For a moment, I thought she might begin to weep. To break. None on earth could've faulted her for it. She looked very small then, and very alone. But instead, she dragged herself to her feet, and shaking, half-staggering, waded out into the shallows, blue eyes fixed on San Guillaume's silhouette on the cliffs across the river. She raised one finger to the monastery, screaming at the top of her lungs. "I'm going to *kill you*! You hear me, bastard? I'm going to rip out your fucking heart and feed it to you, you sonofabitch, you *whoreson*, you—"

"'Enough,'" I said, putting a hand on her shoulder.

"'Get your fucking hands off me!' she flailed.

"'She was my friend too!' I roared. "I knew her since before you were *born*! But you're shouting at the wind, and every minute we waste is another Danton will use to cross this river and be at our throats again! We need to move!"

"'Who the fuck is *we*?' The girl stomped up and down, knee-high in freezing water. "This is the Volta! This is as far as you go, remember?"

"'. . . You think I'd leave you here? How rotten a weed do you take me for?'"

"'Well, why would you stay? You don't give a damn about me! You kept your word to Chloe. Back to your wife and famille, no? Pack your shit, hero!'"

'I looked at this girl: half-naked, frozen to the bone, furious. And I could see myself in the mirror of her eyes. I couldn't fault her for thinking I'd abandon her, for believing I was that kind of monster. Broken. Selfish. Faithless. Cruel.

'She'd known me barely a month, and already better than most.

"'Here,'" I held out my greatcoat. "You'll catch your death."

"'I don't want your pity. And I don't need your help.'"

"'Pride never filled an empty belly, nor kept a man from freezing to death. Girls neither, I'll wager." I held the coat out again. "Don't be a fool.'"

'She glowered a moment longer, then snatched the coat from my hand.

"'Most folk would spare a merci for the man who just saved their lives, Lachance.'"

'Her scowl softened a touch, but still, she gave no thanks. Instead, she slung my coat around her shivering shoulders. Too big by half, hanging on her narrow frame, snow-pale hair dripping in pale blue eyes. She was making a good show of it, and I knew better than most how rage can warm your body for a while. But if we didn't find shelter and get a fire going, this girl was set to freeze to death. And I'd follow soon after.

"'Come on,'" I nodded. "There's cliffs up this way. If we're lucky, we'll find a cave."

"'And if we're not lucky?' she asked, teeth already starting to chatter.

"'Then we can thank God for his consistency.'"

'We trudged up the frozen banks, leaving the shadow of San Guillaume behind us. Great Redeemer, it was freezing. My tunic and leathers were sodden, blood trickling from my punctured belly, every breath a great cloud of frost from my lips. That final, tiny speck of sanctus I'd smoked on the monastery walls was all that kept me going, but Dior was shivering so badly she was soon stumbling. Within a mile, she had her first fall, face-first over a tree root into the snow and dirt. She pushed my hand away when I offered it, snarling and rising to her feet. But a few hundred yards later, she fell again. And again.

'Her lips were blue now. Trembling so hard she could barely breathe, let alone walk. My wrist was still broken from Danton's thrashing, and so, I knelt beside her, lifting her onto my shoulder with my one good arm as she snarled protest.

'"G-get off m-me."

'"Technically, *you're* on *me*."

'"Y-y-you w-w-w-wish, you f-f—"

'"Shut the fuck up, Lachance."

'The snow came thicker, chill creeping into my bruised bones. My feet were numb, my troth ring like ice on my aching finger. But finally, blessedly, we reached the cliffs above the river, and stumbling, shaking, I found a thin crack in the red sandstone, widening into a crevasse beyond. It was almost black within, but I spied bones on the floor, smelled old spoor and faint animal musk – a wolf den, long abandoned.

'I placed Dior on the ground, brushed the frost-rimed hair from her face.

'"Lachance? You hear me?"

'She moaned in reply, eyes hollowed, lips purple.

'"I've got to find something to burn. Stay awake, you hear?"

'Again, the girl only murmured, her eyelids bruised deep blue. I knew if she lost consciousness there, she might never find it again. So, with a curse, I drew Ashdrinker from her sheath. Placing the blade in Dior's lap, I squeezed the hilt, knuckles white.

'"Keep her awake, Ash."

'*Fingers not for the pinching, nor hands f-for the slapping. Blade for the cleaving and edge for the cutting and song for the d-dancing and the red, red—*

'"Just . . . tell her a fucking story, aright? Don't let her sleep."

'*Tales for the t-t-telling? These have I, abundant.*

'I wrapped Dior's hand around the broken sword's haft. The girl's eyes fluttered open as her fingertips touched worn leather, breath rushing as she whispered. "Oh . . . oh . . . *God*."

'"Nothing too dark, Ash," I warned. "Happy endings only, understood?"

'*No such thing, such thing, Gabriel.*

'"I mean it."

'*As do I, my friend. And I am sorry f-for it.*

'I let go of the hilt and ran. Out into the dark, looking for anything dry enough to burn before the last hint of sanctus wore off. Stomping through the woods, snapping branches, I tried not to picture Chloe letting go of my hand and plummeting into the dark waters below. Her final words echoing now in my aching head: *Dior is all that matters, Gabe.*

'She'd believed, Chloe Sauvage. Believed in that girl deep enough to die for her.

'*What the hell was I going to do now?*

'When I'd gathered a bulging armload, I hobbled back to the cave, fast as my numb feet would take me. Dior was huddled inside, shaking head to toe. But she was still awake, her hands on Ashdrinker's hilt, wide eyes fixed on me as I set the fire. I'd managed to keep that old capitaine's flintbox, striking it now on the kindling I'd gathered. For a moment, I was put in mind of my stepfather, his lessons out in the Nordlund wilds when I was a little boy.

'Lorson. Mama. Amélie. Celene.

'Lifetimes ago now.

'"She's singing to m-me," Dior whispered, soft with wonder. "Ashdrinker."

'I glanced at the sword in the girl's shaking hands. The silvered dame on the crossguard. Beautiful. Infuriating. Utterly mad. "And what's she singing to you about?"

'"The b-b-battle at the Twins."

'I scoffed. "Believe not a word, then. Ash wasn't even there for that one."

'"You k-killed her. Danton's s-s-sister."

'I blew gently on the flames, my broken arm throbbing, hands numb.

'"You saw him," Dior insisted. "The Forever K-k-king."

'I pictured him then. Much as it pained me. That perpetual youth, beautiful and terrible, wreathed in an unlight so bitter-bleak it froze your heart. And I heard it again; the vow of a father eternal, to the one who'd murdered his daughter beloved.

'*I have forever, boy.*

'I took the sword from Dior's shaking hands. "I told you no unhappy endings, Ash."

'*I am sorry, Gabriel, but she must learn the t-truth of it sooner or lat—*

'I sheathed the blade, placing her at rest against the wall. Turning back to the flames, I stoked them higher, sensation creeping into my fingers, throbbing in my broken arm. The smoke drifted through the cracks above, heat bleeding into our little refuge. I dragged my sopping tunic off, prodding the slowly closing wound in my aching belly. Danton had stuck me good, the bastard. But not fucking good enough, and I vowed he'd regret it. The whole time, Dior watched, silent, shaking a little less in the budding warmth.

'"Ten thousand," she finally said. "You beat an army of ten *thousand* vampires."

'"Not alone. Not just me."

'"The Forever King would've taken Nordlund if n-not for you."

'"He *did* take the Nordlund, girl. Three winters later the Bay of Tears froze solid, and he swept across the north like a dose of the salts. All I did was make him wait."

'"You were sixteen."

'"So?"

'"So *I'm* sixteen, and the most impressive thing I've ever beaten is my . . ." The girl looked down at herself, sighing. ". . . Actually, I s'pose penis jokes are a little redundant now, aren't they?"

'"Boys tend to make them a lot." I shrugged. "Good way to pretend to be one."

'"I noticed."

'"But why would you?"

'"Notice?"

'"Pretend to be one."

'Dior looked at the ink on my fingers. "How old's your daughter, hero?"

'I stared at this strange girl across the flames. Pretence abandoned, there was still that edge to her, street-hard and gutter-sharp. A fearlessness. A swagger. "Why?"

'"Younger than me?"

'I nodded slow. "She's almost twelve."

'"She'll be noticing by now, then. You probably won't for a while longer. Most fathers would rather tear the sky down than see their daughters grow up. But her mama has marked it, I'll wager. She knows what a world like this does to young girls."

'"There's *no one* who loses more sleep over that than a father, girl. Believe me."

'"If that were true, you'd never ask why I pretended to be a boy."

'Dior plucked at the beaten leather around her shoulders, sighing.

'"You ruined my magik coat, hero."

'"That coat almost got you killed. Again. And it was as magik as a pig's arsehole."

'"You're wrong." She stared across the flames, shaking her head. "Oh, it wouldn't stop an enchanted blade or let me walk across worlds or anything impressive enough for poor Bel to write a song about." She hung her head then, scratching at well-chewed fingernails. "You want to know what that coat did?"

'"I suppose you'll tell me, regardless."

'"It let me walk a dark street without having to watch over my shoulder. It let me step into a room and not feel eyes crawling every inch of my skin. It let me raise my voice without being laughed at, let me threaten to kill you if you didn't get your filthy fucking hands off me. It let me do all the things your daughter is starting to figure out she *can't*, because your daughter is starting to figure out what a world like this does to young girls."

'Dior sighed, scraping ash-white hair over her face.

'"I *loved* that coat."

'". . . Someone put their hands on you?" I asked softly.

'Her eyes were hard as diamond. "My mama had excellent taste in terrible men."

'I smiled sadly at that. "Mine too."

'Dior softened, her ice melting a little. "Far as I know, mine never brought any vampires home. So, I suppose yours has mine bested."

'"Was she like you?"

'"I'm *nothing* like her," Dior glowered.

'"I mean . . . Esan. The line of the Grail. Did her blood—"

'"Heal people?" Dior spat into the flames, vicious. "If it did, she didn't know it. Else she'd have bottled and sold it like she did every other part of herself."

'". . . She was a courtesan?"

'"She was a poppyfiend. And a drunk. And if you want to call a mother who sells her body to feed her habit while letting her daughter starve a *courtesan*, then as you like it. But I've a simpler word for it."

'". . . Your papa?"

'The girl just shrugged, and flipped me the Fathers.

'She'd no knowing who he was, then. One more thing we had in common.

'"What happened to your mama?"

'"What happens to *all* addicts, hero."

'"Bad?"

'". . . Worse."

'Dior looked into the fire, flames crackling as her voice grew hushed.

'"She was like a ghost near the end. Grey skin. No teeth. Dead without dying. But she stayed a slave through it all. To that god she prayed to. That devil she blamed. Too stupid to know they were one and the same.

'"I'd been away for days. I'd took to looking after myself by then. Found my own friends. But I'd come back to check up on her. I found her on the ground beside her bed. Eyes rolled back in her skull. I thought the worst, soon as I saw her – I knew it'd kill her in the end. But I could still see her lips moving. I thought maybe she was dreaming. So I shook her to wake her, and her mouth opened and a rat crawled up out of it."

'My stomach turned a slow, awful roll. "Sweet Mothermaid . . ."

'Dior shook her head, breathed deep. "I dream that shit almost every night."

'"How old were you?"

'"Eleven, maybe. It was the streets of Lashaame after that." She flipped her fringe from her eyes, swagger returning. "A stolen coat. Haircut with a rusty knife. Simpler that way. Not easy. But easi*er*. The gutter doesn't fuck boys the same way it fucks girls."

'". . . I'm sorry."

'"Are you really?"

'"Of course I am," I growled. "I'm a bastard, not a monster."

'Dior reached into the greatcoat I'd loaned her and pulled out my silver pipe. "Then you should throw this thing in the river, hero. Go back home and kiss your wife and hug your daughter and tell them you're never going to leave them again."

'"And abandon you?"

'"Everyone else does."

'There was no self-pity in those words. Fury, maybe. But wallowing in sorrow didn't seem to be this girl's way. A quiet came over her. Soft as shadow. I tried to remember what I'd been like at sixteen, and I could see she was older than I'd ever been at her age.

'"You know, when Sister Chloe and Père Rafa found me, I was looking for their angle right away. I ran with a pack after my mama died. Gutter rats and pickpockets. We used to play a game at nights to keep the hunger away. Talk about what we were going to do when we got older. Meet a handsome prince and marry him. Become a famous pirate, sail the Eversea, that kind of bollocks. But no matter how grand those dreams got, not a one of us imagined we'd be the saviour of the damned world when we grew up."

"'What *did* you want to be when you grew up?"

'Dior shrugged, looked me in the eye.

"'Dangerous."

'She turned her gaze back to the flames.

"'After Sister Chloe and Rafa told me about the prophecy, for a minute I genuinely thought it was going to be aright. So *stupid* of me. Everybody leaves. Mama. Saoirse. Chloe. Toff." She gritted her teeth, furious. "Everybody."

"'Who's Toff?"

'But Dior was lost, staring into the flames.

"'So *fucking* stupid . . ."

'I sighed. Tired. Bloodied. Brimming with anger and sore with sorrow. Chloe was dead. Rafa, too. This wasn't why I'd come north – getting dragged into ancient conspiracies and babysitting the descendant of the Redeemer himself? I never wanted *any* of this. The Volta was as far as I'd agreed to go. I should just cut my losses right now.

'*Always better to be a bastard than a fool.*

'But this girl had nothing left. For all her front, she was hanging by a thread. And strange as it seemed, unearned as it was, that thread was me.

"'You should sleep," I sighed. "Things will look brighter come the dawn. And we want to be moving during the day."

'Dior's voice was dull as old iron. "We."

"'There's a cityfort northwest of here. Redwatch. Was a rough place a decade back, and I can't imagine it's got softer. But we get there, we work out what comes next."

"'I told you, hero," she warned. "Go back to your wife and daughter."

"'And I told *you*, girl," I growled. "I'm a bastard, not a monster."

'Dior clenched her teeth, jaw squared. I could see the wheels inside her head spinning. But more, I could see sadness. Fear. All the weight of this rotten world on those scrawny shoulders. And finally, she pulled my greatcoat tight around her and met my eyes.

"'I'm too cold to sleep."

"'Well, tough shit. Because you need to."

'Dior gazed at me across the fire. "You could warm me up?"

"'. . . What?"

'My belly took a sickening lurch as she traced one hand slowly down her neck. Fingertips drifting along her collarbone. Her lips parted, now. Her voice a purr.

'"Tall. Dark. Damaged. You're just my kind of poison."

'Her fingers reached the bandages about her chest, then rose up, one by one. And with a sigh of relief, I realized she was flipping me the Fathers again.

'". . . Had you worried there, didn't I?"

'A bubble of nervous laughter burst on my lips. Hanging my head, I chuckled as the girl wiggled her fingers. "You little bitch."

'"Oui, *I'm* the bitch," she scoffed. "Shave off ten years and that disaster-piece of a beard, and you still wouldn't have a prayer in hell, hero."

'I scowled, scratching my stubble. "I lost my razor."

'The mischievous smile on her lips dimmed. "Jesting aside, now. I'm fucking freezing. And your virtue's safe with me. You're married, for starters. And you've too many cocks."

'"Last I checked, I'd only the one."

'"As I say. Too many."

'Her eyes narrowed just a sliver, watching me in the flickering firelight. I recalled seeing her and Saoirse then. Lost in each other's arms.

'"Ah."

'"Ahhh," she echoed.

'This was a testing, I knew. Most folk didn't hold truck with such a life, especially not the devout. But it hadn't bothered me when I was a believer. Sure as hell didn't bother me now. Of all people, who was I to judge someone for who they tumbled?

'"Get comfortable, then," I said.

'Dior stared a moment longer, then pulled herself off the cave wall. Skinning off her sopping boots and britches, she shuffled closer to the fire. I kept my eyes averted, looking to the dark outside. When she was settled, I fetched Ashdrinker and lay down facing away from Dior, spreading my greatcoat over both of us. We weren't much to each other in all that cold and dark and empty. But better than nothing.

'We lay in silence for a time, back to back, crackling flames the only sound.

'"I'm sorry," I said eventually. "About Saoirse."

'Dior sighed. "I'm sorry about all of them."

'". . . Oui."

'More silence. But Dior spoke again, her voice small.

'"Hero?"

'"What?"

'"What if Danton comes?"

"'He won't. Not yet. The river."

"'But if he does?"

"'I'll keep watch. Sleep now, girl. Fear no darkness."

'More quiet. Lifetimes long.

"'Hero?"

"'What?"

"'. . . Merci.'"

✦ II ✦

A ONCE-GREEN KINGDOM

'"*GABRIEL.*"

'The whisper woke me from bleak dreams, stained with blood's perfume. The dark was waiting when I opened my eyes, my body stiff and aching with cold. There was warmth at my back, and I heard her murmur as I shifted, and for a second, I fancied myself back home in the bed we'd made and the life we'd built, the song of the sea in my ears. But the voice came again, not behind, but out in the night beyond the cave.

'"*Gabriel.*"

'I eased my greatcoat off us, tucking it around Dior's back. Again, the girl stirred, frowning, eyes flickering beneath her closed lids. Dreaming of rats and mothers' mouths, I supposed. I dragged the last log into the embers to warm her, dragged myself to my feet. And quiet as cats, I slipped into the dark outside.

'The world was still and frozen, dark as dreaming. I saw the silver ribbon of the Volta below, a thin clifftop leading to a lonely drop. And she called again, whisper soft.

'"*Gabriel.*"

'I followed her voice, along the freezing stone and up to the very edge of that precipice. And on the other side of the river, back across the freezing Volta, I saw her on the shoreline. Just a pale shadow in the frail dawning, face framed by long locks of midnight. A beauty spot beside dark lips, one eyebrow arched as always. She stood among the snow-clad boughs and the ruins of a once-green kingdom, watching me. And she spoke then, lips moving, her voice a warm whisper in my mind.

'"*My lion.*"

'"My life," I sighed. "How did you—"

'"*Always, Gabriel. I will always find you.*"

'She looked at me across that dark and frozen gulf. My boots edged closer to the fall. The sun was struggling to raise its head over the worldsend, through the daysdeath shroud. All the horizon was the colour of blood, as if the whole world were drowning in it. Beautiful. Horrifying. And I realized I couldn't remember what real dawn looked like any more.

'"*Tell me you love me.*"

'"I *adore* you."

'"*Promise you will never leave me.*"

'"Never," I breathed. "Never!"

'Her hand drifted up to her face, one long fingernail tracing the arc of her lip. I realized she was weeping, tears of blood streaming down her face.

'"*I miss you so much . . .*"

'"Hero?"

'I turned at the call, Dior's voice echoing within the cave behind. I looked back to Astrid, standing on that bleak shore, the wind blowing long locks around her pale curves. For a second, it was all I could do to not fling myself off that edge, swimming back across that black expanse and throwing myself into her arms.

'"*If I can find you,*" she warned, "*Danton can too.*"

'"Next time, I'll be ready."

'"Hero?"

'I could hear the slight tremor in Dior's voice now. Glancing to the cave.

'"I have to get back," I whispered. "She sounds frightened."

'"*She's not your concern, love. Remember why you left us.*"

'"Astrid, I . . ."

'My voice failed as she turned, slipping away like a ghost, bare and pale between the trees. Nothing but an empty shoreline and the drop into the Volta below. Hands shaking, I wiped the tears from my face, dragged my hair back, squeezing through the crack and into the warmth of the cave beyond. Dior was by the flames, huddled inside my greatcoat.

'"There you are," she said.

'"Here I am. You aright?"

'She shrugged, like she was donning a suit of armour. "I thought maybe you'd . . ." Dior frowned, noting my bloodshot eyes. My haggard face. "Are *you* aright?"

'"No. I'm thirsty."

'The girl looked at me, suspicious. "You know . . . you talk in your sleep."

'"And you snore. But you don't hear me complaining." I glanced to the breaking dawn outside while Dior made small noises of outrage. "If you're awake, we should get moving. It's a long walk to Redwatch. And I need to find something to smoke."

'Her face soured at that, all concern vanishing. "Have to feed the need, eh?"

"'It's not like that," I growled. "I'm not your mama. I'm a paleblood, girl."

"'Maybe. But I can still see a shadow on you."

"'This thing is in my veins. It makes me what I am. I don't do it for fun. I do it because I *have* to. You give the beast his due, or he takes his due from you."

"'But . . . your foundry, your chymicals, they were in your saddlebags."

'I sighed, throwing a mournful glance back across the river. "Oui."

"'We could go back to San Guillaume? Jezebel is still in the stables. We cou—"

"'No," I said flatly. "Too dangerous. Jezebel broke loose during the battle anyway. She's fucking miles away by now. I visited Redwatch years back, and there's folk there who truck in dark places. We get to the Night Market, I'll find what I need."

"'What happens if you don't?"

'I swallowed hard. The burn was already beneath my skin, soon to spread out through my spine, all the way to my fingertips. I glanced to Dior's lips, the pointed chin beneath, that thin, throbbing vein just below her jaw.

'I snatched Ashdrinker from the wall.

"'Let's get moving.'"

✦ III ✦

BLAME THE BLACKSMITH

'THREE DAYS LATER, we were barely moving at all.

'Freezing. Stumbling. Nothing to eat but a few frozen mushrooms. Nothing to smoke at all. As ill fortune would have it, we'd been hit by wretched on the second day – a pair of them coming at us through the dead trees. Farmer folk – mother and son by the look, seen off by me and Ashdrinker without too much drama. But with nothing to collect their blood in, no way to cook it, I had to waste it in the snow.

'My wounds had healed, but the thirst sat in my belly like a knot of flame now, roiling ever wider. We followed frozen banks, me staggering in front, Dior stumbling behind. The deadwood was silent, the river sluggish; a grey dress hemmed with frost. Wintersdeep was biting at our heels now, and even a river mighty as the Volta would soon freeze solid.

'If we didn't reach Redwatch, we'd be frozen long before.

'Dior was huddled in my greatcoat, shivering and miserable. She didn't complain, which was a mark in her favour, but she seemed possessed of an irrepressible need to chatter. To *question*. About the Silver Order. About San Michon. About vampires, the capital, anything that entered her damned head. I don't know whether she did it to keep her mind off the cold or my mind off my thirst, or simply to torture me. But you remember what I said about the problem with most men being they never shut the fuck up?'

Jean-François nodded. 'Oui.'

'Turns out that's also true for teenage girls.

'"How can she do what she does?" she asked on the third day.

'"Eh?" I growled, stumbling along the riverbank.

'Dior's eyes were fixed on the sword at my waist. "Ashdrinker. How can she hurt the Dead so easily? When you fought that masked vampire in San Guillaume, those wretched in Winfael, it looked like her blade *burned* them. I thought only silver did that."

"'She's magik," I growled, breathing a cloud of frost. "And I'm talking true magik, now. Forged from the heart of a fallen star, long before the empire was born."

"'She's . . . impressive to watch."

"'You should've seen her when I was younger. She could cut the night in two." I sighed, my gaze roaming the silvered dame on the hilt. "She never used to stutter, you know. But she's not what she used to be since she broke. She gets confused sometimes now. About where we are. Or when. Truth told . . . I think she's gone a little bit mad."

"'How'd she break?"

"'I pushed her down the stairs after she asked too many questions."

"'Is it true what Bellamy said?"

'I sighed. "Probably not."

"'About you finding her in the grave of a dead barrowking?"

"'Barrowking graves are called barrows. Hence the name. And no. Utter bullshit."

"'You won her in a riddle contest in the Everdark, then?"

"'Never been to the Everdark. I'm not that suicidal."

"'So . . . you sexed some deadly faequeen so expertly that she passed out and—"

"'Fucksakes, grow up, will you?"

"'Well, what about her knowing how everyone will die?"

'I sighed again, glancing down to Ashdrinker. "That much is true."

"'. . . Really?"

'I peered over my shoulder. "Want to know?"

"'How I die?" Dior swallowed thickly, teeth chattering. "I . . . suppose s-so?"

'I stopped and stared. "You certain? It's not a truth you can unlearn, girl."

'She looked me in the eye. Squared her shoulders and nodded.

"'Give me your hand, then," I said.

'Dior complied, her fingers trembling. I took hold, wrapped my other fist around Ashdrinker's hilt. Snow fell gently about us, melting on our skin as I scowled, murmuring under my breath. Then I opened my eyes, and foretold Dior's death.

"'You keep asking me bullshit questions, and I drown you in this fucking river."

'"*God*, you're a prick," she spat, snatching her hand away.

'"Serves you right."

'"For what?"

'"Tall, dark and damaged?"

'She scoffed. "Truth is the sharpest knife."

'I raised a warning finger. "I'll have you know I'm—"

'I gasped, doubling over in agony as a wave of flame swept up my spine. Holding my belly, eyes squeezed shut, just struggling to stay upright. I felt Dior's hand on my shoulder as all the world around me buckled and swayed.

'"Getting worse?"

'"It only ever gets worse, girl."

'". . . Is there something I can do?"

'I inhaled through gritted teeth so I wouldn't have to smell her. "Short of conjuring a nice, fat wretched and something to cook with, m-maybe shut up a while."

'She chewed her lip. "I can do that."

'"I've a g-gold royale says you don't last an hour."

'We staggered on, freezing and aching, the thirst clawing the insides of my skin. I'd never gone more than seven nights without sating it, but I knew what would happen when I broke. And the pure, black dread of that thought had me tied tighter than a hangman's noose, every step, every minute, harder and harder to breathe.

'"Hero . . ." Dior said.

'"Forty-seven minutes, girl," I growled. "You owe me a g-gold royale."

'"No, *look*!"

'I pawed the frost from my lashes, glanced to where she was pointing. And out in the middle of the freezing Volta, maybe half a mile downriver, I saw a sight that almost made me believe the Almighty's favourite pastime wasn't spitting in my spuds.

'"A barge," Dior breathed.

'She was right. A flat-bottomed boat was ploughing its way upriver, manned by a dozen crew with long-poled oars. The bargemen sang as they worked, and I could hear them now if I tried, over the rushing pulse in my ears.

'"There was a fine maid from Dún Fas,

'"Who had a remarkable ass;

'"Not rounded and pink,

'"As well you might think—"

'It was grey, had four legs, and ate grass?' Jean-François interrupted.

Gabriel smiled, gulped his wine. 'Heard that one before, have you?'

'It's older than I.' The vampire tutted. 'River folk.'

'They don't change much,' the silversaint chuckled. 'The Volta is the grandest river in Ossway, and folk have been plying boats along it for centuries. It was a harder way to make a living than it'd once been, but river trade had become the lifeblood of the empire since the wars grew thick. Coldbloods couldn't fuck with it. Until wintersdeep arrives and the waters freeze solid, of course. Then the revels begin.

'"Oi!" Dior shouted. "Over here!"

'I joined her shouting as best I could, my belly still burning. But I sighed with relief as one of the polecats pointed at us. The bargemen set to it, punting closer while Dior jumped and waved. The vessel was good oak, maybe seventy feet, her prow sweeping up out of the water in the likeness of a beautiful swan. Trade goods crowded her decks, but she carried passengers also; two score or more. As the barge drew closer, I saw they were refugees, no doubt fleeing the bloodlords of the Dyvok and their war for the Ossway.

'The barge slowed perhaps thirty feet off the shoreline, the polecats watching us with suspicious eyes. An Ossian fellow with a grizzled, bearded face stepped forward, hands on hips. He had flaming red hair and was dressed as a navyman, replete with a tricorn hat and heavy duster, sea green with brass buttons and trim.

'"*Nice* coat," Dior murmured.

'"Fairdawn, travellers," the man called in a thick western brogue.

'"Godmorrow, Capitaine," I nodded.

'"Where d'ye head?"

'"Redwatch. But anywhere other th-than here sounds lovely right now."

'"Angel Fortuna smiles on ye, then. Other than here's our destination. Ye've coin?"

'I patted the purse hanging on my swordbelt beside Ashdrinker. The man's gaze lingered on the blade, drifting now to Dior. I studied the passengers behind – grubby men and women, thin children, all watching with something between hostility and curiosity.

'"Well, swim oot with yer purse and ye're welcome aboard," the capitaine declared.

'"Swim?" Dior scoffed. "That water's fucking freezing."

'"It's also fuckin' *running*, bairn. And ye must think me seven shades o' shitewit to pick up two strangers pale as ye in days dark as these without a testin'."

'My fingers were trembling too badly to manage it, so I pulled off my glove with my teeth. The capitaine's eyes widened at the sight of my seven-star.

'"You're safe enough with m-me aboard, Capitaine."

'"*Silversaint . . .*" came the whisper among the refugees.

'The capitaine scratched his thick ginger beard, then turned to the polecat beside him, ordering him to fetch their skiff. Dior watched the dark waters beneath us with nervous eyes as we were punted out to the barge, but soon enough, we were aboard, my shaking hand thumping into the skipper's. "Merci, mon ami. We're in your debt."

'"Nae debt, Silversaint," the man bowed. "'Tis my honour to grant ye passage. Name's Carlisle á Cuinn. My brother fought with two of yer lot at the siege of—"

'I grabbed my stomach, staggering as another wave of pain swept through me. Dior caught my arm, Carlisle my other. ". . . Ye aright, Frère?"

'I gritted my sharpening teeth, vision flooding red. "How far to Redwatch, Capitaine?"

'"Two days," the big fellow replied. "If we move wi' haste."

'Dior looked Carlisle in his eyes. "Might I humbly request you do so, monsieur?"

'The capitaine threw a worried glance in my direction, but he was soon barking orders. Dior and I got the hell out of the way, threading among the tight-packed cargo and refugees. They were a motley lot, empty eyes and dirty hands. They watched with curiosity, suspicion, awe, as Dior and I made our way to the bow and slumped down near the figurehead.

'"You look like shit," she whispered.

'"We look n-nothing alike," I managed.

'Her smile was water-thin. "Can you last two more days?"

'I curled over into a ball, arms around my belly. "Want a bet?"

'The girl looked at her hand, running a thumb down her forearm. I could see the vein beneath her skin, light blue, pulsing with that maddening, beautiful life. "Maybe you c—"

'"*Don't,*" I snarled, my fingers snapping around her wrist.

'"You're hurting me," she whispered.

'I released my grip, ashamed and sickening. "I'm sorry, just . . . don't ever offer me that again, aright? Don't even *think* it."

'"Why? If it's the choice between that and starv—"

'"Because I'm not a *fucking animal*. So just promise me."

'She looked me over, her lips thin. "I promise."

'And so, it began. Two days of hell as we punted up the Volta at what seemed a snail's pace. Carlisle came by to check on me after an hour or so, but I gave monosyllabic answers until he got the message and let me be. I was probably the first member of the Ordo Argent these folk had ever seen in the flesh, and I'm sure the good capitaine and crew were disappointed in the show I was putting on. But I was just struggling to hold myself together. I kept my head down, conscious of Dior sitting vigil beside me. The girl didn't move an inch until the bell rang for dinner, and then she was gone only a moment.

'"There's a man dying back there."

'I blinked through the haze, looking up as she handed me a wooden bowl of – you fucking guessed it – potato stew. "What?"

'"Back there." She nodded. "At the arse of the boat."

'I lifted the bowl and forced a mouthful down. "A boat's arse is called a s-stern."

'"He's with his famille. Refugees from Dún Cuinn. All these people." Dior brushed her hair down over her face. "The man got his leg broken on the journey. It's turning black."

'I glanced down to the stern, saw the famille Dior was talking about among the mob. A snaggle-faced fellow with a slender wife, two young lasses with eyes of old sky blue. The poor bastard was laid out in his love's lap, sheened with sweat despite winter's chill.

'"I can smell him from here," I nodded. "Leg's gone septic. He's a d-dead man."

'"His name is Boyd. His wife is Brenna. Their eldest is—"

'"You're not contemplating what I think you're contemplating . . ."

'Dior looked down at those scars on her palm. Up into my eyes. "And what's that?"

'"Something that'll get you *killed*," I growled, low and deadly. "Look around. These are peasantfolk, girl. They don't hold truck with magik, and they don't believe in miracles. What they believe in is devilry, and dark sorcerie. You start opening veins and laying on bloody hands to heal folk their ills, they'll burn you for a fucking witch."

'"I don't need lectures from you, hero."

'"Then pull your head out your arse," I hissed.

'"Right, I know you're in a state? But I'm going to need you to march *all* the way off my tits here."

'I glanced down at her thin chest. "You've *got* no tits."

'Dior gasped, gobsmacked with outrage. "You fucking—"

"'Listen, you get to San Michon, you do whatever bullshit they need you to. 'Til then, keep your head all the way down. Because I'm not sure if you've noticed, but if we hit trouble, I'm going to be as useful as a taddysack on a priest."

'Dior scowled and started scoffing her dinner. Pouting. Sullen. She was a piece of work, this girl. A thin streak of seagull shite with scabs on her knuckles. Always ready for a scrap, to answer back, to spit. But, turns out there was a good soul under all that front. Eyes that saw the hurts of the world, and a heart that wanted to fix them. For a moment, she reminded me so much of my own Patience I had to catch my breath.

"'Look." I gritted my teeth. "Apologies. I'm shabby company when I'm thirsting."

"'I've news for you. You're not a bucket of chuckles when you're *not* thirsting either." She glowered. "I've tits that'd make angels cheer, you grumpy shit."

"'I'll take your word for it. But I'm not riding your scrawny arse for the fun of it. We're in a world of enemies here, girl. Danton aside, there's that masked bloodmage chasing you, and as far as we know, the Inquisition are still hounding your trail." I scowled, gulping down a scalding mouthful. "Fucking Rafa. Why he and his brethren sent word to the Pontifex about you is beyond me. Augustin is a nest of vipers. Always has been."

"'Welllll." Dior gave a sad sigh, chewing her lip. "The Inquisition isn't really Rafa's fault. Those two bitches who chased us out of Dhahaeth . . ."

"'The ones I shot? You knew them?"

'She looked at her wrist. That thin scrawl of blue, like cracks in pale marble. "Let's just say I don't need a lecture on what folk do to witches these nights."

"'All the more reason to keep your gift on the quiet."

"'. . . Maybe."

"'You can't save the world one inch at a time, girl. Believe me, I've tr—"

'The thirst surged again, blood-red and stabbing. I clenched my teeth, felt them growing long in my gums, doubling over so my hair might hide my twisting face.

"'Maybe you should sleep?" Dior murmured.

"'Maybe you could b-beat me unconscious?"

"'God, *gladly*."

"'Just not the f-face, aright?"

'She sighed. "Will this do?"

'I glanced up, saw a beaten tin flask in her hand. "Is that . . . ?"

'"It smells like dog shit soaked in flaming hair, but I'm fairly sure it's liquor."

'I unscrewed the lid, my nose burning at the scent. "Where'd you get it?"

'"Six years on the streets of Lashaame, remember?" She shrugged thin shoulders. "Picked it from the capitaine's pocket. So maybe you'd best down it quickly and . . ."

'Her voice faded as I tipped back my head, guzzled the entire flask. The liquor burned like fire, but still, it helped douse the flame in my belly a little. I lay down and curled into a ball, aching and miserable, wanting only to be numb.

'Dior sighed. "You're a bloody mess, hero."

'"Don't blame the blade. Blame the b-blacksmith."

'She sighed, drummed her fingers on her knees.

'"I'll keep watch. Sleep now."

'I closed my eyes, sinking into the black behind them. Searching for quiet. The Almighty hadn't been doing me many favours lately. And as I'd told Rafa, it was only a self-entitled fool who fancied the bastard would listen.

'Still, I almost prayed anyway.'

✦ IV ✦

THE PRICE

'THEY CALLED IT Martyr's Cradle. They called it the City of Scarlet, Saintsholme, the Isle of Seven Sins. But mostly, they just called it Redwatch.

'It had started like most river cities do – as a fishing town. But it rose to fame as the birthplace of the fourth martyr, old San Cleyland himself. He was a brick shithouse of a man by all accounts, a few drunkards short of a bar fight, but he had a remarkable talent for slaughter. Visited by the Mothermaid in a dream, Cleyland raised an army of faithful lunatics and marched into Ossway, intent on bringing the One Faith to the pagans of the west.

'He died, of course. Being a martyr and all. Perished in valiant battle against a coalition of Ossian clans, or choked to death on a chicken bone during a victory piss-up, depending what you read. But not before he'd converted half the country at swordpoint, and built a series of priories to the Mothermaid that stand to this day. In return for his faithful butchery, the Almighty gave Cleyland the key to hell, and the big man stands guard over its grim gates to this day. And if you think designating the safekeeping of the abyss to a pin-headed twatgoblin who doesn't know which part of the chicken is safe to eat sounds a terrible idea, you and I are in total agreement.

'We reached his birthplace near the end of the second night, punting into a crowded dockside sprawl. Redwatch might've started as a village, but now it was a cityfort, and one of the empire's finest. Built on a broad island in the middle of the Volta, its walls and towers were made from red river clay, hence one of its many names: the City of Scarlet. Its buildings were tight-packed and towering, citizens living atop one another like rats in a bloody maze. On its eastside, a foreboding keep punched holes in the sky, and northwards, the Priory of San Cleyland kept a mother's watch over the city of his birth.

'I was in some of the worst shape of my life. The thirst had me so tight by then, all the world was washed scarlet. Dior gave thanks to Capitaine Carlisle in my stead, and the man looked me over with something between pity and fear as I shuffled past, hair tumbled about my face. All around me, I could smell it, feel it, taste it. Blood.

'*Blood.*

'Still, there was enough of me left to notice Dior share a small nod with a grubby fellow passenger as we shuffled onto the jetty. Last I'd seen him, the man had been laid out in his bride's lap, dying of infection. One look at him told me his once-broken leg was now straight as a spear, and I could smell no sepsis in his veins. He bowed, hand to heart, as we stumbled past. His wife had tears on her cheeks; his daughters made the sign of the wheel, watching Dior with awestruck eyes of old sky blue.

'I glanced down at Dior's hand, saw a fresh strip of bloody cloth about her palm.

'"You didn't . . ."

'"Tits," she said, motioning to her chest. "*Right* off them."

'"You fucking *idiot.*"

'"I was careful," she hissed. "I spoke to them at night. Nobody else saw."

'I shook my head. "I'm going to tell you something now, girl. And you mark these words, because they're ones to live by: it's *always* better to be a bastard than a fool."

'"You're not my fucking papa, aright? I don't need words to live by from you. Now, tell me where this damn Night Market is so we can get you what you need. Because if you fall over here, I'm leaving your surly arse for the bloody rats."

'"There," I managed. "Up that alley."

'It'd been over a decade since I'd visited Redwatch, and like everywhere in the empire, all was worse than when I'd left it. It was far more crowded, for starters, streets jammed to bursting even after dark. Beggars with open sores and refugees with stricken, battlesick faces, street preachers and honey-girls, fisherprinces and riverthugs, and everywhere you looked, burly bastards in the sunflower yellow of the Emperor's troops. We pushed through the crush, and all about me I could smell it, thrumming in every vein, rushing beneath every suit of skin.

'*God help me . . .*

'"Which way?" Dior asked.

'"The squeezeway," I winced. "P-past the hucksters."

'We passed a bevy of thieves selling charms against the Dead – pendants of churlsilver, braids of virgins' hair, necklets of "duskdancer teeth" plucked from the heads of dead dogs. Nonsense all, sold by crooked bastards and bought by desperate fools. But beyond the grifters and frauds, in the damp shadows off the Redwatch drag, a fellow with eyes could find it. A tiny puddle of dim but true magik, hidden in the dark.

'The Night Market.

'A single street. A few faceless shops. Women with needle eyes and ill-favoured men with tattooed faces, snatches of spells carved into swarthy skin with ink-stained knives. Iron in the air. Ash and the dreams of pale gods, dead long before we discovered there was only One. My every bone was aching, eyes red as river clay as we staggered up to a thin black door and I hammered six times. The sign above the threshold simply read THE PRICE.

'"Souris!"

'"This place makes my skin crawl," Dior whispered.

'"*Souris!*"

'". . . His name is Mouse?"

'"*Her* name. Just keep your eyes on the w-well side of down and your mouth on the right side of shut. This is d-deep water." I pounded again. "Sour—"

'The black curtain in the window beside the door was pulled aside, and I saw a pair of eyes, utterly white and apparently blind, peering through the grubby glass. I pressed my sevenstar to the window, leaving sweat misted on the pane. Even my *gums* were aching.

'The curtain closed. A moment as long as my life passed before I heard six locks and six chains being loosed. With a slow creak, the door opened, revealing a woman, ancient and wrinkled, bent back draped with a smoke-grey shawl laced with charms of silver. But though her pupils were white with age, still she narrowed her eyes at the sight of me.

'"Lion Noir," she purred, smiling with empty gums.

'"M-madame," I winced. "I've a will to b-buy, if it please you."

'Those blindworm eyes turned to Dior, roaming head to toe. And finally, Madame Souris shuffled aside. "Enter freely and of your own will."

'We stepped within, Dior whispering a soft curse. The scene was chaos; like a junk store had a drunken hate fuck with a lunatic asylum. Every square foot was packed with shelves, and every square inch of those shelves was filled – books and bottles, herbs and scales, tiny pickled things in cloudy jars, hourglasses in skeletal hands. The store was lit by a hundred softly burning chymical globes, and stank of cat piss and insanity.

'"We heard you were dead, Lion," Souris called, shuffling ahead.

'"They t-tried."

'She smiled over her shoulder. "Well. God loves one of those, doesn't he?"

'We followed the old woman through the mess, Dior close on my heels and studying every nook and corner, until Souris propped herself at a long counter. Among the twisted curios and dusty jars and books of skin, sat a rocking chair. Seated in it, wearing a pretty dress of timeworn silk and a powdered wig, was a human skeleton.

'"Look who it is, Minou," Souris cooed. "Our Black Lion, back from the dead."

'I bowed at the bones. "Good seeing you again, madame. You haven't aged a night."

'"Whereas you," Souris tutted, "have seen far better days."

'"I'm hoping you can r-remedy that."

'"Hoping not praying?"

'"Not my business any more."

'"So we hear." Blind eyes flickered to Dior. "What *is* your business these days?"

'"All due respect, madame. But none of yours."

'"Fair play." Lighting a bone pipe, she breathed a plume of thin yellow smoke into my eyes. "Your desire? We're fresh out of pretty nuns with bad taste in men, I'm afraid."

'I spoke the word as if it were chocolat melting on my tongue. "Blood."

'"Plenty of that for free right outside. Presuming you're willing to dodge the soldiery and risk a tickling from the Inquisition."

'Dior tore her eyes from the curios about us. "There's Inquisition in this city?"

'"Arrived six nights back." The old woman tilted her head. "That troubles you, girl?"

'"I'm not a girl."

'Souris chuckled at the skeleton. "You hear that, Minou? She's not a girl."

'"Our *concern*," I hissed, "is commerce. And the blood I need is of a darker sort."

'"Mmm." Madame Souris rose and wandered along her shelves. Taking down a timeworn, dust-covered book entitled *A Complete and Unabridged Historie of Elidaeni Floristry*, she opened it to reveal a dozen phials of desiccated blood inside a carven hollow.

"'All from foulbloods, I'm afraid,'" Souris declared. "Slow trade these nights. The Dyvok have made a sow's ear out west, and the Voss a terrible ruckus eastways."

"'They'll serve,'" I whispered, wiping the sweat from my cheeks. "I'll need a chymist's foundry, too. Mortar and pestle. Hollyroot. Some redsalts and—"

'The old woman raised her hand and nodded. "Blood for blood?"

"'Blood for blood,'" I replied, dragging up my sleeve.

'Souris fished about beneath the countertop, produced phials and a glass tube tipped with a silvered blade. Then she turned to Dior, staring with blind eyes.

"'One should do it, ma chérie.'"

'Dior frowned at that. ". . . What?"

"'That's the question isn't it, Mlle Notagirl. *What.*" The old woman leaned closer, smoke drifting from wrinkled lips. "I've walked the halls of the king in yellow. Tasted delights in the arms of bleakborn princes and danced naked 'neath black stars with brides of the Neverafter. And not *once* in all my years have I smelled the like of you. So what *are* you?"

"'Not for t-trade is what she is,'" I growled.

'Souris tilted her head, watching the empty air just above my left shoulder. "That's the price, Lion Noir. I've no need of what's in you. I've plenty of paleblood a'ready."

'I clenched my teeth. "That's the only blood on offer, madame."

'Souris sniffed, packed the foundry and phials and herbs below the counter. "Pity."

"'Hold now.'" Dior glanced at me, back at Souris. "He needs those."

'The old woman held up a needle-tipped phial between ink-stained fingers. "Everyone needs something, Mlle Notagirl. And every need comes with a price."

'Dior rolled up her leather sleeve. "Then I'll—"

"'No,'" I growled. "Not like this. N-not for me."

"'As you like it.'" Souris smiled like the cat who stole the cream, sold the cow, and fucked the maid. "They'll be waiting here when you change your mind. I'll even wrap them up for you, Chevalier."

'Dior had sense enough not to dance a fuss before the old woman, and after a small bow, we were limping out of the Price. But as soon as we were back in the dingy streets, the girl clutched my wrist and hissed, "Are you *mad*? You need that blood!"

"'N-not that badly.'"

"'You can barely stand! How bad does it need to get?'"

'"Listen to me, girl." I grabbed her arm, fury in my eyes. "I know Souris well enough to buy from her, but that doesn't mean I trust her. Forget gibbets and pyres, forget peasant superstition. There's a whole *world* beneath the one most folk see around them, and there's *true* witchery in it. Coldbloods aren't the fucking half of it. Duskdancers. Faekin. Fallen. Leave aside the Forever King, Chloe's prophecy, all the rest. What do you think would happen if that world knew what you could do?" I shook my head, wincing. "The cure to any ill, any wound, just the stroke of a knife away? God, the things they'd do to own you . . ."

'"But you *need* it!"

'I gritted my teeth, coughing. "I'll figure s-something out."

'The hour was late, and the ache in me was blinding as we trudged back out into the crush of the Redwatch streets. We found a dockside dosshouse – a nowhere fancy affair called Mandy's Kiss, its walls crusted with dead hollanfel vines and runs of shadespine. I paid the publican twice the owing, told him we weren't to be disturbed, and with a knowing glance to the "boy" at my side, he winked as we trudged upstairs. Locking the door behind us, I fell on the bed, curling into a very small, very miserable ball.

'Dior plucked the curtains, muttering. "This place smells like someone died in it."

'"Someone probably d-did."

'"What are you going to do now?"

'"Repeat p-performance?"

'"Fucksakes, hero, you're—"

'"I'm thinking!" I snarled.

'"Well, think quicker! Because you've the look a man half dead and all dying!"

'I growled between clenched fangs, threw her my purse. "If you've a need to make yourself useful, go find me something to drink instead of pissing in my fucking ear."

'"How about I piss in a cup and save you the coin, you surly prick?"

'"Great Redeemer, girl—"

'My half-hearted moan was silenced as the door slammed. Thirsting, miserable, I curled up tighter and tried to think past the crushing pain in my skull, the cold lice in my skin. I was in no shape to threaten violence, and Souris wasn't a dame to be gently fucked anyway – a man who brought quarrel to her door had better be carrying more than a broken sword. I could offer a greater sum, but the old bitch had those blind eyes fixed on Dior now. A tie of service might suffice, but I'd no wish to bind myself to the likes of her, and besides, I'd business to the east. Business bleak and all kinds of bloody. Business that had dragged me far from home and hearth already, and still, not even begun . . .

'As if to remind me, I heard scratching at the window. Sharp fingernails drifting across cold glass. My stomach did a burning roll, and lifting my head, I expected to find dark eyes staring back at me, reminding me of that debt due. But there was only the wind, blowing a dry hollanfel vine across the pane.

'I closed my eyes. Cursed it all. This beast I was and must soon become. The door opened, and something cool and heavy cracked me across the cheek. Gasping, I squinted at what had hit me, saw a bottle of paint-thinner that might've passed for vodka. Dior stood on the threshold, glowering.

'"Anything else, Majesty? No? Good."

'She made to close the door again as I croaked, "Where you going?"

'"It stinks in here," she spat. "And there's a pretty maid downstairs with a pouch of cigarelles who seems a damn sight more pleasant company than you. So when you've done your thinking and pulled a civil tongue into your head, come find me. 'Til then?"

'She slammed the door harder, making me wince. And like a beggar, like a dog, I cracked the wax on that bottle and downed the lot of it without pause. It was nothing close to what I needed, nowhere near the thing I craved. But it served enough to drown me, push me down into soft black arms, where the pain might not find me. The fear in me was rising, one thought beyond all others – the thought of what I'd do when I broke. Dark rising around me, cold stone, wet and sticky, the colour of my lady's lips the last time I kissed her.

'And though there was naught but dark outside the window, still I heard her voice, echoing in the black behind my eyes.

'"Remember why you left us."

'*Remember why you left us.*'

+ V +

CLEVER AS CATS

'"HERO."

'The voice broke through the sweats, the brittle rime of sleep.

'"*Hero!*"

'I opened my eyes, gasping, sitting up in bed and regretting it dearly. Blinking, bleary-eyed, I dragged the hair from my fevered brow and stared. Dior stood at the foot of my bed, ashen locks tossed back from twinkling eyes. She dumped an armful on the mattress at my feet; a packet wrapped in dull burlap tied with string. And I stared in gobsmacked bewilderment as she stripped the bow and showed me what lay within.

'Mortar. Pestle. Foundry. Hollyroot. Redsalts. A dozen more herbs and chymicals. And at the last, like a cluster of jewels in a stolen crown, a dozen phials of dark, dried blood.

'"The old lady wrapped it," Dior smiled. "Just like she said."

'"Tell me you did *not* give those dusty bitches your blood."

'Dior planted her boot on the bed, fished inside, and twirled a thin leather wallet between her fingers. I recalled us sniping at each other outside that pub in Winfael.

'*You've got a key, smartarse?*

'*To every lock in the empire, dumbarse.*

'"You *stole* these?" I hissed.

'Dior grinned, proud as a lord and twice as crooked.

'"Did they fucking see you?"

'She shook her head. "Clever as three cats, me."

'"Cheeky *bitch* . . ."

'"Flatterer."

'It was a fool who filched from the likes of Souris and the Night Market, but God's truth, I could worry about the spill later. Instead, I lurched from the bed like the Redeemer risen, snatched up the mortar and pestle, and set to work.

'Breaking the wax seal on the first phial, my hands were shaking so hard I almost spilled my prize. The blood looked to be the poorest kind, but the scent still flooded my tongue. I mixed the hollyroot, redsalt, queensong, the recipe as familiar as my own name, almost disbelieving that after days of thirst, sweet relief would soon be mine. Spreading the thick red paste onto the foundry's heating plate, I set it by the hearth and started pacing.

'Ten minutes.

'Ten minutes and I'd be *home*.

'Dior had flopped down on the mattress, spread-eagled, eyes closed. I looked at her sidelong, shaking my head in disbelief. "I don't even want to ask how you did it," I sighed. "It'd take a wagonload of foxes with diplomas in cunning from Augustin University to get inside the Night Market without invitation."

'Dior murmured, eyes still closed. "Careful, hero. That sounded a little like praise."

'"It was."

'She opened her eyes at last, levered herself up onto one elbow. "Sweet Mothermaid. You really *are* sick, aren't you?"

'It was shameful how good I felt. How just the *promise* of a fix had me light as clouds. I stalked back and forth before the hearth, toying with the flintbox in my britches, watching the flames, the foundry, the sanctus desiccating within.

'But still, there was a doubt looming now, just beyond the window. I looked towards the empty glass, still half-expecting to see her there. The shadow that had followed me all the way from Sūdhaem, drawing closer and closer with every step.

'*Remember why you left us.*

'"I've been thinking . . ."

'"Me too," Dior murmured.

'I crouched against the wall, arms wrapped tight around my stomach as a new wave of flaming agony swept through me.

'*Just a few minutes more . . .*

'"Mesdames b-before messieurs."

'"As you like it." Dior sat up in the bed, chewing on a broken nail. "Now . . . please bear in mind, you're still the surliest prick I ever met. You're a drunk. And an addict. You act a fucking bastard, and yet you somehow seem proud of it. By my reckoning, the people who hate other people usually just hate themselves. But still . . . you stood by me when you'd no reason to. After what happened at San Guillaume, you could have left me behind, but you kept your word to Sister Chloe. Went beyond it, even. I'd be dead if not for you."

'I held up one shaking hand. "You don't have t—"

"'No, no, let me finish. You might act a fucking bastard, but I've been a bitch to you too. I didn't treat you fair. Growing up the way I did . . . Let's just say the men Mama brought home didn't leave me with the finest opinion of them. But you're an honourable one. Every bit the hero people say. So," she breathed as if exhaling poison, "I'm sorry."

"'It's aright, girl."

"'You know, I have a name. And you never use it. Nor I yours, for that matter."

'She clomped across the room in her beggar's boots, extended her hand.

"'Apologies, Gabriel de León."

"'Accepted, Dior Lachance. And returned."

'She smiled, crooked and pretty. Turning on her heel, Dior walked to the window as if a weight had been lifted off her shoulders. She looked to the dim dawn outside, down at the beaten leather she was draped in. "You know, this coat of yours *is* possessed of a certain air of dangerousness and all, but I should get my own before we set out. The whole tall, dark, and tattooed look works well for you, but you must be freezing your bollocks off in just that tunic. And it's bound to be cold as a snowman's jollies up north."

"'Dior . . ."

"'Apologies." She smiled, tucking her hair behind her ear. "I know I talk a lot sometimes. You said you've been thinking too?"

'I chewed my lip, fangs brushing thirsty skin. "After we rest up, w-we should head to the keep. Talk to the capitaine."

"'About the road to San Michon?"

"'About finding some soldiers to escort you there."

"'. . . You mean to come with us?"

"'I mean there's bound to be a few of the officers I served with in the Ossway campaigns still hanging around in a fort this big. I can put in a good word. Get you some well-hard bastards to watch your back. A solid horse, some—"

"'Wait . . ." She stared hard, all her world falling still. "You're leaving me?"

"'Not alone," I insisted. "These are good men. Veterans. They'll see you through t—"

'"You're *leaving* me."

'I clenched my teeth, hung my head. This wasn't why I came here. Babysitting this girl wasn't why I'd left home. I had a famille. A *debt*, dark as night and red as murder. No matter the blood in Dior's veins, this task wasn't mine. I was no believer. No zealot. Prophecies were for fools and fanatics, and after all God had done to me, I was the last bastard alive he'd be choosing to safeguard his own flesh and blood.

'I had a daughter of my own to think about.

'But still, the look in Dior's eyes struck me to the heart. So wounded that I had to turn away. A tear spilled down her cheek – the first I'd ever seen her cry, even with all the blood and pain we'd lived through. And her lip curled, and she looked down to those knife scars carved across her palms, and she sighed.

'"I fucking *knew it*—"

'The door smashed off its hinges, crashing along the floor. I rose to my feet as a dozen soldiers burst into the room, dressed in scarlet, cudgels in hand. Ashdrinker was leaning against the wall, and I lunged for her, desperate. But the thirst was still red and raw within me, my muscles weak as four of the bastards crashed atop me.

'"Get off me!" Dior screamed. "Let *go!*"

'I heard a crunch, a deep-throated squeal that told me someone's crotch had met Dior's boot. I thrashed, feeling a jaw pop as my elbow crashed into it. But the cudgels fell like rain, and above the sound of my pulping flesh, I heard slow footsteps coming along the boards towards me. They stopped just before my face, and I squinted through the bloody haze: tall-heeled, knee-high, wrapped in strips of spiked hide. My eyes roamed the leather-clad legs beyond, up to their owners.

'Their hair was black, cut in pointed fringes, eyes hidden by tricorns with short, triangular veils. Ornate black gauntlets covered their right hands, fingertips sharp like claws. And my belly ran cold as I saw that their blood-red tabards were marked with the flower and flail of Naél, the Angel of Bliss.

'The first inquisitor stalked into the room, lifted Ashdrinker from the floorboards where she'd fallen. "You've done the Almighty's work this day," the woman declared.

'"Merci, godly daughters," said the second, glancing over her shoulder.

'I heard Dior curse as I saw two refugee lasses in the doorway, staring with eyes of old sky blue. The eldest nodded, made the sign of the wheel. "Véris, Sisters."

'"You treacherous fucking sows!" Dior roared. "I saved your papa's *life!*"

'The first inquisitor slapped Dior. The girl's head whipsawed on her shoulders, blood spattering. "Silence, witch. You've led us a merry dance. But now the song is done."

'I sighed, looking up at the other. She was staring at me, finger toying with the ragged boulette hole in her tabard. "Had a f-feeling I'd see you bitches again."

'"Bitches?"

'The woman smiled, lifting her foot.

'"Oh, the hymns we shall sing, heretic."

'And her boot came down like thunder.'

✦ VI ✦

CHURCH BUSINESS

'ICE-COLD WATER CRASHED into my face, and black flared into burning white.

'Sputtering, spitting, I tossed sodden hair from my eyes. I was in a dark room, freezing – underground, from the sound. Iron hooks were fixed in the rafters. The walls were red stone, and through the heavy door, I could hear women singing hymns above.

'This was no prison cell, I realized. I was beneath the San Cleyland Priory mostlike, in what looked to be their old meat cellar.

'And *I* was the meat.

'I'd been stripped naked, wrists manacled, dangling from one of those iron hooks so only the tips of my toes touched the flagstones. My head was throbbing, my thirst a living, breathing thing. The inquisitor who'd danced on my skull stood before me, clad in black leathers and her blood-red tabard. She still wore her tricorn, features mostly hidden by her veil, but I could see red lips, curled and cruel.

'Her sister was nowhere to be seen, but a brick mansion of a man stood at a butcher's bench along the wall. Beside a bundle wrapped in burlap, I saw an impressive collection of real and makeshift torture implements. A ten-tail whip, a bonesaw, a hammer, thumb screws. A poker was thrust into a brazier of burning coals, the iron red-hot.

'"All the makings of a jolly weeksend," I hissed.

'The inquisitor tilted her head. "You can last longer than that, surely."

'"My wife b-been telling stories about me again?"

'"Your whore, you mean?"

'My face darkened at that, my soft smile vanishing.

'"Oh, oui," she said. "We know who you are. *What* you are."

"'If that were true, you'd be speaking more polite about my wife."

"'I am Sœur Talya d'Naél." She raised her right hand, scraping one iron claw along my whiskers. "It will be a pleasure to make your acquaintance."

"'Where's D-dior?"

'The inquisitor ignored my question, eyes shining behind her veil. "You . . . *shot* me."

"'Not well enough, apparently."

"'It hurt. A very great deal." She dug the claw in, lifting my chin and staring into my eyes. "*Merci*, Monsieur de León."

"'That's *Chevalier* de León to you. I s-suppose that's why you've got me stashed under a nunnery, instead of taking m-me up to the keep? The local capitaine might not appreciate you baby-killing bitches torturing a Sword of the Realm."

"'You are no Sword," Talya scoffed. "You are an apostate. Disgraced and excommunicated. This is *Church* business. To be conducted upon *Church* grounds."

"'Like the business you conducted in San Guillaume?"

'Talya smiled, dark and bleak. "We supposed your priest might seek succour there. A drowning man will clutch even at straws. But straw burns, halfbreed. Just like heretics."

'I swallowed hard, my stomach full of broken glass. This close, I could see the vein thumping along Talya's neck, smell her blood under her perfume of leather and misery. Her razored claw drifted down my collarbone, tracing the lines of the lion inked on my chest.

"'Beautiful," she breathed.

'And with a small smile, she pushed one sharp claw right through my nipple.

'I gasped in pain, bucking against my manacles. The inquisitor's claw dug through muscle, scraping bone, blood spilling down my belly. She leaned in close, whispering in my ear. "I owe you *pain*, heretic. I owe you bli—"

'She gasped as I smashed my brow into her nose. I felt a satisfying crunch, heard a gargling squeal as my headbutt sent her stumbling backwards. Her thug stepped forward, ready to dismantle me, but Talya held up her hand to stave him off. She pressed her palm to the blood gushing over her lips, face twisted in fury.

"'You . . . b-broke my *nose* . . ."

"'Come closer, bitch. I'll kiss it better."

"'Faithless *bastard*."

'I thrashed, wild at the scent of her blood. It filled the cell, my lungs, my head, fangs gleaming as I bucked against my restraints. "*Where's Dior?*"

'Talya's lips twisted in a bleeding smile. "My sister Valya is taking her confession."

'"You're torturing her? She's an innocent *child!*"

'"Innocent?" Talya spat blood, the scent near driving me mad. "Dior Lachance is a heretic. She is a witch. And she is a murderer."

'"The *fuck* are you babbling about? She didn't kill anyone."

'The inquisitor sneered. "Dior Lachance murdered a *priest,* halfbreed. A bishop who ran an orphanage, no less. Ritually slaughtered him, mutilated the corpse, and painted the walls of his home with his blood. And were it not for the confession of her conspirators, she may still be conducting her deviant rites on the streets of Lashaame to this very day."

'"Bull*shit.*"

'The inquisitor produced a sheaf of parchment, covered in black script.

'"You will name Lachance a witch," Talya said. "A practitioner of profane blood rites, sent to sow discord among the Almighty's faithful. You will name the ones who assisted her in escaping justice in Lashaame – namely, Sœur Chloe Sauvage of the Order of San Michon and Père Rafa Sa-Araki of the Order of San Guillaume – as slaves to Lachance's dark will. You will confess your involvement in the girl's coven, and beg God's absolution for your heresy."

'My eyes narrowed, fangs bared. "The fuck I will."

'"How I *prayed* you would say that."

'Talya smiled, nodded to the thug by the torture implements.

'"Philippe?"

'The thug dragged the burlap aside, and my stomach churned as I recognized everything Dior had stolen from Madame Souris. Beside my foundry, my ingredients, I saw glass phials brimming with chocolat-red powder. The thug lifted one between forefinger and thumb, smiling as he loosed the stopper.

'"We took the liberty of bottling it for you," Talya purred.

'The man waved the open phial in front of me, and the scent of the sanctus within – God, it struck me like a spear to the chest. I actually moaned, gasping as the thirst roared through me, fangs long and pointed, heart hammering, so close, so *close.*

'Talya picked up the ten-tail whip, and my jaw clenched as I saw that the thongs were spurred with metal. The leather creaked as she coiled it in her fist, walking slowly behind me, heels clicking stone. My skin prickled as I felt that clawed gauntlet on my skin again, tracing the inkwork on my naked back. Angel's wings across my shoulders, the Mothermaid and infant Redeemer below, carved a lifetime ago by hands that loved me.

'*Crack!*

'I gasped as iron and leather bit into my skin.

'"Do you confess?"

'"Could you aim a little higher, S-sister?"

'*Crack!*

'"Nono . . . a t-touch to the left."

'*Crack!*

'". . . th-that's it."

'*CRACK!*

'*CRACK!*

'*CRACK!*

'Iron doesn't hurt palebloods the way silver will, but by that stage, I was starving, weak, ready to break. Instead of stitching closed, my wounds bled like a butchered hog's. I thrashed at my chains until my flesh tore, blood spilling down my arms, the back of my legs, pooling on the stone beneath me. And always, the scent of that sanctus filled my lungs.

'I'd felt hunger like this only once before in my whole life. No mere human can imagine the agony. No smokefiend or bottlebride or poppyhound can even *begin* to understand.'

Jean-François pursed his lips, spoke soft. '*I* understand.'

'I knew this was bullshit. I knew Dior well enough to know she was no cold-blooded killer. If someone had handed her to the Inquisition, it was a betrayal, not a confession. And I remembered her words in the cave, then. What she'd said about everybody leaving her.

'I'd done the same, I realized. Too wrapped up in my own dark. I'd been ready to turn my back on that girl, like everyone else had. And I realized I'd forgotten the most important lesson. A lesson learned through trials of ice and fire. A lesson that should've been carved into my bones with blood and silver.'

'What lesson?' Jean-François asked.

The Last Silversaint took a swallow from his bottle. It was a long while before he spoke again.

'I found myself in darkness. Drenched in bloodscent. I felt my daughter's hand in mine. Her fingers, soft against my calluses, the echoes of her laughter ringing in my head. I saw Astrid's face floating in the black before me. Lashes fluttering upon her cheeks as if she were waking from a dream. Red lips. Two little words.

'*Do it.*

'*I can't.*

'*You must.*

'*Come in.*

'*COME IN.*

'"Who's there?"

'I blinked hard, drenched in blood and the perfume of want. The pain had stopped, the rhythmic crack of the lash across the tattered meat of my back had stilled. I looked up through curtains of sweat-drenched hair, saw the thug before me, scowling. I could feel Talya behind me, and I swear under the stink of gore and leather and sweat, I could smell desire; the sadistic bitch was wet as spring rain.

'But she'd stopped now. Her voice soft.

'"Who's there?" she asked again.

'A reply came from beyond the door, and I realized someone was knocking. The voice was muffled, shy – a young sister from the priory, I guessed.

'"Pardon, Inquisitor. But your holy sister sends urgent word."

'The pair looked at each other, Philippe stalking to the meat cellar door as Talya twisted the ten-tail in her hand, wringing a thick soup of blood from the leather onto the stone at her feet. The thug opened the door, scowling. "This had best be im—"

'The fellow gasped as four and a half feet of jagged metal was jammed into his belly. The strike was nothing poetic, but the sword still cleaved his mail like a razor through silk. He clutched his gut, the blade slipping free as he fell backwards, blood and bowel spilling from the rend. And through my starving haze, my heart surged as a figure came through the door, bright blue eyes wild with rage.

'Dior lifted Ashdrinker in her hands, pointed the blade at the inquisitor.

'"Your sister said to tell you the witch is loose."'

✦ VII ✦

BLEEDING BUT UNBROKEN

'HERE'S A TRUTH about sword fighting, coldblood: even if you're bad at it, when the person you're fighting doesn't have one? You're still going to be pretty good.

'One glance at her form told me Dior Lachance had never swung a longblade before in her life. Her grip was for shit. Her stance was woeful. And as I've said, it's only in storybooks some little bastard picks up a sword and wields it like he was born to it. Still, that blade was forged in an age long past by the hands of legends, and broken though she was, Ash remembered something of what she'd been. I could tell by the way she glanced at her, Dior was listening to Ashdrinker in her head. Stepping forward with blade raised.

'Talya shouted a prayer to Naél, lashed out with her whip. Dior flinched as the thongs snapped the air, inches from her throat. I cried warning as the girl struck, almost collecting me on the backswing. But undaunted, Dior stepped up, carving the air with broad blows, and Talya's whip was sent spinning from her grip. The inquisitor backed away, snatching up a hammer from the bench and roaring to her brethren for help.

'Dior brought Ash down in a clumsy overhand swing, and the inquisitor darted aside, slammed the hammer into the side of the girl's skull. Dior staggered, gasping, swinging Ashdrinker in a backhand arc that forced Talya away. To her credit, the inquisitor was no slouch, and alone, even armed only with a hammer, she might've proved Dior's match. But in dodging Dior's strike, she'd brought herself close to me.

'I dragged myself up on my chains, bleeding, gasping, scissoring my legs around the woman's throat. She roared again for her men, slamming her hammer into my leg, my belly, struggling to break free. And Dior took her chance, lunging with Ash and spitting Talya like a Firstmas hog. The blade sheared through that blood-red tabard and into the blood-red meat beyond. The woman wobbled, slipped from between my legs and down to the floor in a puddle of blood – hers and mine.

'The scent of the murder, the sheer, maddening flood of it overcame me. I gritted my teeth, vision flooded, fangs aching in my gums. Dior looked about, snatched up my pipe from the table. No care taken for measure, she upended a sanctus phial over the bowl, and I whimpered at the sight of the powder spilling on the floor. She stuffed the pipe into my mouth, striking my flintbox.

'"Quick. Breathe."

'I needed no urging, almost weeping as that smoke hit my lungs. My eyes rolled back in my head as it crashed into me and over me, deep as the darkest river, falling upwards into a burning sky. I cursed it even as I loved it, days of agony vanishing in a heartbeat as I dragged down another lungful.

'I heard Dior twisting Talya's key, felt my restraints come free at last, slithering to my knees in a pool of red. Head bowed. Just trying to breathe.

'"M-merci, mademois—"

'I flinched as my britches crashed into my head, my boots skittering along the stone.

'"Get dressed," Dior spat. "Can't have lil' Gabriel flapping about while we're running for our lives through a nunnery."

'". . . lil' Gabriel?"

'"Fucksakes, just get dressed!"

'I hauled on my britches, my boots. Wincing as I pulled my tunic over my bloodied back, I watched Dior from the corner of my eye. She was gathering up the foundry, the sanctus phials, tying off the burlap with shaking hands. She'd stolen some nun's nightshirt from the look, but it was soaked with her blood, and I could see her eyes were bright with pain – our captors had been no kinder to her than me.

'"How'd you get loose?" I murmured.

'"Good thing about shoes as shitty as these." She patted her beggar's boots and the slim leather wallet stashed within. "Most folk don't want to go poking around inside them."

'"Clever bitch," I whispered.

'The priory bells started ringing. Not the tolling for mass or the song of the dawn, but an alarm, frantic, echoing in the cellar around us. Dior looked up, cursing.

'"They know I'm loose."

'"Those bells will have the whole city garrison down on us."

'Dior tossed me Ashdrinker, snatched up the burlap bundle, and we ran from the cell, red footprints behind us. Bolting down the corridor, we passed another member of the Inquisitor cohort, dead from a single swordblow to his back. I glanced at Dior, but she avoided my gaze. Pounding up a stairwell with Ashdrinker in my hand.

'*Judge her not, Gabriel. The girl d-did what needed to be done, be done.*

'"I know."

'*She has fire, this one. Fury. She r-reminds me of thee in younger days.*

'". . . I know."

'Cresting the stairs, we found ourselves on the priory's ground floor. I could see flickering torchlight ahead; the inquisitorial troops already searching the courtyard. And the bells were bringing more soldiers as I feared – already I could hear them distant, heavy boots tromping up through the streets of Redwatch below.

'"Not the grandest idea to try fighting our way out of this," I murmured.

'Dior nodded to the shadows. "This way."

'I limped up another stairwell behind her, my minced back still raw and bleeding. Cresting the first-floor balcony, we ducked low and ran along it, avoiding the crowded courtyard below. At the end of the landing, Dior led me through a small doorway and back down a thin flight of stairs, and we found ourselves in the priory kitchens. Someone was still ringing those bastard bells, and I knew we didn't have much time before we were overrun.

'Dior snatched up a burlap sack by the door, stuffed with spudloaves and dried goods. I realized she'd been here already, raiding the stores. Wounded, bloodied, beaten as she was, she'd still had her wits about her. But I also realized she must have been fixing to leave me behind – that she'd got almost as far as the gates before coming back for me.

'God's truth, I wondered why she'd done it.

'Somewhere distant, I heard a scream echoing in the dark. Boiling with rage. "Methinks Inquisitor Valya just discovered her sister," I murmured.

'"Sick bitches," Dior spat. "Wish I'd got them both . . ."

'We slipped out the kitchen's rear, along the priory's walls. I saw torchlight on stone, heard an inquisitor screaming that we must be found, *found!* The first wave of soldiers was arriving – young scraps all, sunflower-yellow tabards, brand-new swords. If they cornered us after we'd murdered inquisitorial troops, they'd be in no mood for talk.

'We passed a laden clothesline, and running to the fluttering cloth, Dior tossed a bundle at my head. Rough homespun and lace. Black and white.

Though the habit was a squeeze, the veil covered my scruffy beard at least. And clad as sisters of the San Cleyland Sorority, we crept along the walls to a stairwell, then up to the battlements above.

'Peering over the edge, I saw a forty-foot drop to the cobbles below. Handing Ashdrinker and our bags to Dior, I patted my minced shoulders.

'"Climb aboard."

'The girl met my eyes, wondering a handful of heartbeats before finally clambering onto my back. With her arms around my neck and the sacrament in my veins, I wormed my fingers into the brickwork and scaled downwards. I could feel Dior's heartbeat hammering against my back. Smell our blood, red and fresh in the air.

'"I'm sorry," I murmured. "That they hurt you."

'She made no reply, simply holding tight until we reached the ground.

'Snow began falling as we stole through the Redwatch streets, quiet and quick. The cityfort about us was waking, those damn bells echoing down thoroughfares and off red-brick walls. More troopers charged past, up towards the priory, but swathed head to foot in our stolen vestments, we were paid little heed. Making our way through the wending dark, we'd soon reached the grubby sprawl of the Redwatch docks.

'"We can steal a boat," Dior whispered. "Make for the north shore."

'"Wait," I told her, looking at the stores about us. "Hold here a moment."

'I left her in the dark, slipping up to a fancy shopfront and twisting the door handle until I felt the lock pop clean. Inside, I grabbed a swift armload: furs, cloaks, blankets, bundling them under my arm and tossing a handful of royales onto the countertop as I left.

'Stepping back outside, I saw Dior had already boarded a small rowboat, pushing herself out into the Volta. I caught a few strange looks as I bolted down the pier after the girl, nun's habit streaming behind me as I took the leap and landed in the boat with a *thump*.

'I watched the City of Scarlet fade into the snow and mist behind us. The priory bells were still ringing, the perfume of blood hanging in the air. But it seemed we'd avoided pursuit. I took over the oars, watching Dior as I rowed towards the northern banks. The girl sat hunched in her vestments, dragging off her veil and casting it into the river.

'Ice crunched on our hull as we neared the shallows, our prow breaking through the thick rime of dirty frost. I climbed into freezing water, dragging our little dingy up onto the bank. But Dior just sat in the boat, watching the snow falling all around us.

'"Dior? You aright?"

'She looked at me, mute and unblinking. Her lip was split and swollen. Her eyes bruised black. Her face pale and spattered with red. I knew not what those inquisitors had done to her, but I'd had a taste myself. For a moment, I wondered if they'd broken something inside her, the wound only felt in the aftermath.

'"Come on." I held out my hand. "I've got you."

'But she pursed her split lips. Rubbed her bruised eyes. Gutter-hard and street-sharp, and I saw the truth. Though she'd no clue how to swing a sword, still she'd picked one up to defend me. Though she'd no reason to come back for me, still she'd returned. And though they'd beaten on her hard as they dared, still, she wasn't broken.

'"*I've* got me," she said.

'And standing, she leapt onto the frozen shore.'

✦ VIII ✦

MAGIK

'IT TURNS OUT nuns' habits burn quite well.

'Dior sat and watched while I got a fire going, ably assisted by the vestments I'd worn in our escape. It had been deadwood and drudgery for miles after fleeing Redwatch, freezing cold, and the pair of us had been too tired and beaten to talk much. The woods about us were long decayed, frozen, but as the sun's light began failing, we found a place to stop – an ancient oak with a great hollow in its belly. Two branches rose from its flanks, and it reminded me of a penitent man; arms outstretched, head thrown back to heaven.

'I foraged in the gloom for a while before I found what I was looking for – tiny brown caps sprouting in the trunk of a fallen pine. Grinding them into a paste, I boiled the leavings in my foundry, then handed the steaming brew to Dior.

'"What's this?" she asked.

'"Idleshade." I motioned to the awful bruises on her face. "It might befuddle your wits a little, but it'll help with the pain."

'I broke out a couple of spudloaves, and we ate in silence for a time. The night was bitter cold, snowflakes hissing as the sparks rose skywards, pale moths dancing around the flames. There was something peaceful about it all, but I knew this serenity would be fleeting. Inquisition aside, Danton was still on our trail, and even now, he'd be hunting for a way across the Volta. It might take time. Hell, it might take 'til the river froze over. But wintersdeep was breathing bitter cold upon our heels now, and sooner, not later, the Beast of Vellene would be at our throats again.

'"You came back for me."

'Dior glanced up as I spoke. She'd been nursing her tea, eyes on the laughing flames. Her face and lips were black and blue, dried blood under her broken fingernails.

'"In the priory," I murmured. "You came back for me."

'"Of course I did."

'"I thought I told you it's better to be a bastard than a fool."

'"And I thought I told you, you're not my papa. Don't tell me what to do, old man."

'I chuckled at that. She smiled weakly in return, but it soon curdled to a sneer.

'"I decided I owed it to you," she said. "It was my stupidity that landed us in that shite to begin with. You warned me too. About trusting those ungrateful fuckers on that barge. You told me to keep my head down, and I didn't listen. I don't know why I do that. Don't know why I haven't learned my lesson yet. Everybody betrays. Everybody leaves."

'"Not everybody. Not always."

'"*You* were going to."

'I breathed deep, nodding. "And I'm sorry for it, Dior. Truly."

'"You needn't be sorry." She shrugged. "*I'm* the fool who keeps making the same mistakes and expecting something different to happen."

'I studied her then, across the crackling firelight. The clenched fists. The tiny sparks of rage in her eyes. And I realized she wasn't even talking about me any more.

'"You're talking about Lashaame."

'She met my stare. "They told you, eh? Those inquisitor bitches told you what I did?"

'"A version of it." I shrugged. "One I didn't put stock in."

'"They tell you I killed someone?"

'"A bishop."

'"He wasn't a bishop, he was a *bastard*. A fucking . . ."

'Her voice failed, and she clenched her jaw, turned back to the fire. She looked tired and beaten then, all the weight of the world on her shoulders. I could see a scab here, one she wanted to pick at. But I'd no ken how much it might bleed if she tore it loose.

'"You don't have to tell me, Dior. I'll not judge you ill."

'She sighed, pawing her hair down over her eyes. I'd noticed she did that when she wanted to stop people from seeing her. A shield, ash-white, hiding her from the world, like that damned magik coat. "You remember you asked what I wanted to be when I grew up?"

'"Dangerous," I nodded. "And you proved yourself that today, sure and true."

"'It was a lie, though. I never really cared about being dangerous. I just didn't want to be alone. That's how my mama went out, you know. Even *I* abandoned her in the end." She laced bloodstained fingers together, voice soft. "Everybody leaves. Even me."

'Dior spat into the fire. I stayed soft and still, just listening.

"'After Mama died, I fell in with those gutter runners I told you about. Ten of us, living in a warehouse in the Lashaame docks. The place was run by an old locktalker. Called himself the Narrowman. He was a grumpy bastard like you, but God . . . I *loved* it there. He gave us jobs, took a cut, kept us off our backs and knees. Even taught us how to read with an old copy of the Testaments. It almost felt like we were famille for a few years."

"'Sounds . . . an interesting place."

"'It was educational," she smirked. "I learned the game there. Shadow-work and rip-runs. Maggot traps and honeypots." She chewed a fingernail for a moment, her voice dropping a little. "There was a pickpocket in Narrowman's mob. Smart. Silver-quick with a knife. She used to dress as a boy too, but I spotted her right away. She wore an old top hat and halfcoat, like gentry." Dior smiled faintly. "Called herself Toff.

"'I didn't know girls could love girls. I just knew I loved being with her. And one night, she and I were sitting on the warehouse roof talking and laughing, and she touched my cheek and told me I was beautiful. And then she kissed me."

'Dior shook her head, trailing fingertips along her lips.

"'Nobody ever kissed me like that before. I didn't know you *could* get kissed like that. It was like . . . like my whole body was powder and she was flame. One of those kisses you're going to compare to every kiss that comes afterwards, you know?"

'I smiled softly. "Oui."

"'But I could see a shadow on her." Dior glanced at me. "Same as I see on you. Toff used to have nightmares. And sometimes she'd wake up crying. I wanted to help, to make it better. I'd always ask her what was wrong, but it took almost a year before she told me. About a man. A *priest*. Named Merciér." Dior spat the name like poison. "Toast of the city, he was. Guardian of the poor. Bishop of Lashaame. He made his bones running the city orphanage. Toff used to stay there, before she shacked in with the Narrowman."

'Dior snarled a little, running her thumb over the scars across her palms.

"'Turned out the toast of the city liked little girls. And when Toff was younger, he . . ."

'I shook my head and snarled. "Fucking bastard."

'"I was *so* furious for her. I said we should stomp the prick. Just . . . snuff him out like a fucking candle. But even after everything that happened to her, Toff still believed. In God. In the Testaments the Narrowman used to read us. She used to drag me to mass every prièdi. Killing a priest was a sin, she said. It was God's place to judge him. Not ours.

'"But I convinced her we could roll Merciér, at least. Man of the cloth. Fat cat. Toff deserved some payback after what that fucker did. So we broke into his estate one night while he was at a private service. We were halfway through cleaning the place out when the bastard came home. Forgot his spectacles, the stupid pig. We could've run. Made it out clean. But when Toff laid eyes on him . . . she just . . . snapped.

'"Like I said, she was silver-quick with that knife of hers. And she drew it and just *went* at him. Screaming. Stabbing. She stuck him a dozen times before he fell. When she was done, she left the knife buried to the handle in his privates."

'Dior's voice was a whisper now, edged with tears.

'"I was *so* scared. All my front, all my talk of being dangerous . . . fuck . . ." She stared down at those stained hands again. "You know how much blood there is inside a person?"

'I nodded, my voice soft. "I've a notion."

'"I tried to drag her away. Get the hell out of there. But Toff was staring at the blood on her hands. And while she stood there shaking and crying, Merciér dragged himself to his feet and put that shiv right in her chest. Once. Twice. I tried to take the knife away, and he cut my hands up pretty bad before the blood loss got him. But when he fell, he stayed down, and I grabbed Toff and ran, dragging her back to the Narrowman's. And I put her on the floor and our friends all came out, and Toff . . . she was just lying there trying to breathe and there was so much *fucking blood* and I just wanted to stop it. So I pressed my hands over the holes, screaming for someone, anyone, to help me."

'"Your palms were cut up," I murmured, looking to her scars. "Your blood . . ."

'Dior nodded. "That's when I learned what I could do. There in a place I called home, surrounded by people I thought of as famille, saving the life of the girl I thought I loved. And they all stared, pale as ghosts, as Toff's wounds closed over and she sat up and blinked at me with those eyes I used to drown inside."

'Dior shook her head, tears spilling down her cheeks.

'"And they called me a w-witch. All of them. Even . . . even *her*. Toff looked at me like I was the one who'd hurt her, not saved her. I tried to take her hand, tell her I loved her, and she flinched away like I burned her. Like she was . . . scared of me."

'I nodded, remembering the terror in Ilsa's eyes that night I learned what I was.

'"I know what that feels like."

'Dior wiped the tears from her cheeks. "They handed me over to the magistrate. I got blamed for Merciér's murder. All Lashaame was baying for my blood. They hung me in one of those fucking gibbets for people to spit on, throw shit at. The church sent word to the Inquisition, and those twin bitches arrived to burn the Bishop Killer. The heretic. The witch."

'She shrugged, chewing a ragged nail.

'"Then Sister Chloe and the others showed up. Busted me out of my cage in the dead of night and we hightailed it, hard and fast as we could. All the shite I'd been through, and I still let myself think it might be aright with them. Sister Chloe saved my life. Bel was sweet as honey. And Saoirse, she . . ." Dior shook her head. "But the same thing happens. Again and again. All the people I care about leave, or they get taken away. And like an idiot, I keep doing the same thing over and over and expecting it to be different. I don't know why I do that. I don't know why I don't just learn my lesson."

'"You've a good heart, girl. That's why."

'"For all the good it does me. I've dragged my arse halfway across the empire over this prophecy shite, and for what? People who'd lock me in a gibbet or burn me at the stake? I should just be like you. Do what you need. Take what you want. Fuck the rest."

'"You don't want to be like me, Dior."

'"Why not? You're doing aright. You've a wife. A daughter. A few people who love you. But the rest of the world? Just . . . fuck it *all*."

'I hung my head then. Seeing what she saw in me.

'"My wife used to tell me hearts only bruise. They never break. I don't know if I believe that any more. I know this world is cruel. That saints and sinners suffer one and the same. I know every time you give a piece of yourself to someone, you risk them breaking it. I know there are some wounds that never truly heal, and sometimes all that's left of people are their scars. I know time eats us all alive."

'Dior watched me rub the ink across my knuckles, toy with my troth ring.

'"I've seen the worst this world can conjure, girl. I've seen people kept in cages and farmed like cattle to slake the thirsts of monsters spat straight from hell's belly. I've seen armies of faithful men slaughtered like hogs while God stood by and did *nothing*. I've seen parents eat their children. And I can't say it gets better. I can't tell you I believe like Chloe did – that you're going to be the one to fix all this. I won't lie to you like that."

'I tore my gaze from the flames, looked the girl in the eye.

'"What I *can* tell you, is that the only heaven I've found in all this hell was in the people I loved. Friends. Famille. So, you need to keep on thinking the best of folk, despite seeing the worst of us. Hold onto that fire inside you, girl. Because it makes you shine. And once it goes out, it goes out forever. Know you'll make mistakes. Understand that it will bruise – hell, it might even break. But don't lock it up inside your chest."

'I reached across and squeezed her hand.

'"Aim your heart at the fucking world."

'Dior pawed at her eyes, and I saw that fire still burning in them. She was bloodied, oui. Battered. But yet unbroken. She looked down at my fingers wrapped around hers, eyes shining with unspent tears as she read the name etched across them.

'"That's your daughter? Patience?"

'I nodded. "Astrid inked it after Patience was born. All the rest of this . . ." I pulled up my sleeves to show the edges of my aegis. ". . . angels and Mothermaids and Martyrs, none of it mattered in the end. I wanted something that did."

'Dior chewed her lip, pensive.

'"You know . . . Ashdrinker told me." She glanced to the blade at my side. "About what the Silver Order did to you and your wife. I understand why you wouldn't want to go back to San Michon after that. I don't blame you for wanting to get back to your famille, Gabriel. You didn't ask for any of this. And it isn't your fight."

'"If what Chloe said is to be believed, you're *everyone's* fight."

'"But you *don't* believe."

'I looked into the fire, sighed from somewhere old inside. "I can't believe in a God that loves us. Not after all I've seen. But I believe this: my friends are the hill I die on. I forgot that lesson for a while. But I vow it now, *never* again. So if your path is San Michon, I'll walk it with you." I squeezed her hand again, hard as I dared. "I won't leave you."

'She smiled. "We're friends, then?"

'"The strangest sort. But oui. Friends."

'She brushed the hair from her eyes, lips pursed in thought. "You know . . . you treat me different now you know I'm not a boy."

'"No. I treat you different now I know you're not a cunt."

'She laughed, and it made me laugh in turn to see. I could tell she was letting go of something heavy inside with that laughter. Something she'd carried a while.

'"Here." I smiled. "I got you something."

'I turned to the bundle I'd nabbed from that dockside storefront in Redwatch. It was wrapped inside the folds of a heavy foxfur coat I'd taken for myself. But I threw the rest at Dior, one by one across the flames.

'"New britches," she breathed. "And boots!"

'"Can't have you running around the provinces dressed as a nun. I've a bad enough reputation for that kind of nonsense as it is. I got you a shirt too. And this."

'Her eyes lit up as I proffered a fine-cut gentleman's frockcoat. It was snow grey, knee-length, embroidered with beautiful golden curlicues. The buttons were embossed with designs of tiny roses, a neckpin of the same motif for the cravat. The fabric was stout but soft, the inners lined with fur, warm and fine. It was a coat fit for a lord.

'"It was the fanciest they had," I said. "Wasn't sure about the colour."

'"No . . ." She looked up at me with shining eyes. "No, it's *perfect*."

'"Try it on, then."

'With a grin wide as the sky, Dior hauled off her priory vestments. I winced to see the wounds and bruises beneath, but the girl still moved like she was dancing, slipping the shirt and coat onto her shoulders and bracing up the buttons. She stretched out her arms, adjusted the line and twirled on the spot, whooping with delight.

'"You'll have the whole forest down on us," I growled. "Calm your tits."

'"I've *got* no tits, remember?" She kicked a toeful of snow at me, did another graceful pirouette. "Well? How's it look?"

'I simply smiled.

'"Magik."'

✦ IX ✦
A SHADOW MOVING SLOW

'A CRACKLE SOUNDED in the deadwood behind us, and Dior fell still, her eyes growing wide. I was on my feet in a second, all joy from our tiny festivities forgotten, drawing Ashdrinker from her sheath and cursing myself a fool, an idiot, a—

'*There was a fine maid from Dún Fas, who had a r-remarkable ass; not rounded—*

'"Shut up, Ash!"

'I narrowed my eyes, peering out beyond the circle of our fire. The forest was black, chill, frozen to its bones, and again I heard it; something heavy, snorting and trudging through the dead scrub towards us. Dior snatched up a burning log from the fire.

'"A coldblood?"

'"No," I whispered. "I can hear it breathing."

'*Not the Beast of Vellene, at least, at least . . .*

'"A beast of some sort, though. That's the sound of four feet, not two."

'"Another one of those deer?" Dior hissed.

'I remembered that rotten stag we'd faced in the Forest of Sorrows, its head peeling apart as it screamed with a little girl's voice. Saoirse had warned us that the Blight up here was far worse than in the south. And though we weren't yet in the northern weald, still I wondered if this was some new horror stalking us in the dark, Blight-riddled and twisted.

'I saw it coming now; a shadow moving slow towards us. My grip tightened on Ashdrinker, and as Dior hissed warning, I stepped out to meet it, teeth growing long in my mouth as I raised my blade . . . only to lower it again just as swiftly.

'"Sweet Mothermaid," I whispered.

'"What is it?" Dior hissed.

'"*Jezebel . . . ?*"

'The mare nickered as I spoke her name, tossing her head and stomping one hoof. She stood there in the falling snow, a grey shadow against the deeper dark. Her legs were bramble-scratched, her mane tangled, her hide filthy. But still, I couldn't believe my eyes, laughing as I stumbled through the frost to her side. Dior shouted in amazement once she recognized the dray, running into the dark and throwing her arms around Jez's neck. The mare nickered again, apparently just as happy to see Dior as Dior was to see her.

'"Seven Martyrs, how did she *get* here?"

'I shook my head, just as baffled as the girl. "Last I saw this dame, she was charging out the gates of San Guillaume like her tail was afire. She must have been so frightened by the Dead that she swam across the Volta to escape them. Poor wretch."

'"She's not a wretch, wash your mouth out!" Dior scowled. "Come on, love, come over by the fire. Let's get you warmed up, eh?"

'We led the mare back to the light, and I watched Dior fret and fuss, combing out the tangles from Jez's mane, feeding her a handful of dried mushrooms from our supplies. Again, I shook my head in wonder. The mare had always shown the grit of ten stallions, but her survival, letting alone finding us here . . . well, it was nothing short of a miracle. And though I wasn't one to put stock in miracles, still, I cast one wary eye towards the heavens, wondering if our luck had finally changed.'

Gabriel sighed, gazing into the lantern's flame.

'I should've fucking known better.'

✦ X ✦
DIM AND DIMMER STILL

'"VALIANT?" DIOR OFFERED.

'"No," I replied.

'"Aright, what about . . . Courage?"

'"That means the same thing as Valiant."

'"Chivalry, then?"

'"It's the worst kind of tosser who names his horse Chivalry, Dior."

'The girl rolled her eyes. "This from the man who named his sword Lionclaw."

'"I was fifteen, what the fuck do you want from me?" I growled. "And I told you, stop talking to Ashdrinker about my childhood. She wasn't even *there* for most of it."

'"If you want Ash to stop telling me about you, you should stop loaning her to me."

'"Well, someone's got to stop you from falling asleep on watch."

'"That's happened *once* in two weeks. Climb off my tits about it, merci."

'We'd abandoned the frozen edge of the Volta, turned north onto a long, lonely road. A fortnight trekking through northern Ossway, and we'd seen few signs of life. All was silence, save the songs of starving crows, and all was stillness, save the eddies of falling snow. We passed bone-filled gibbets. Ghost villages, abandoned by all but corpse-fat rats. The hollowed wrecks of once-mighty castles. Old farmers' fields that had become mass graves, the bodies frozen where they fell. Even the Dead had abandoned this place – just a few stray wretched to harry our steps, the best of which now resided in small glass phials inside my saddlebags. God was nowhere to be seen.

'This was the empire I'd fought so hard to save – an ever-growing sea of ice and darkness, in which humanity's light grew dim and dimmer still. But the Nordlund was looming ahead of us, and I knew that in that shadowed sea, a few tiny flames lingered.

'I'd taken to loaning Ashdrinker to Dior when the girl stood watch at night. I knew she'd no real idea how to swing a sword, but the blade would speak to her in the small hours, keeping her alert while I stole some sleep. I snatched only a handful every night, but thank fuck for the little I *did* get. Because God's truth, Dior was close enough to sending me mad without adding sleep deprivation to the mix.

'"What about Gallantry?" she asked.

'"No," I replied.

'"Greatheart?"

'"*Terrible.*"

'"Well, if you don't like my suggestions, make your own," the girl snarled. "We can't keep calling her Jezebel."

'"Lower your voice, for fucksakes."

'Dior spoke again, two octaves lower, "What, like this?"

'"She's a horse. She doesn't give a shit what we call her."

'"She's brave. She's strong. She's loyal." Dior gave the mare a fond scratch behind the ears. "She deserves a name that says something about who she really is."

'"If that's the way names work, why isn't yours Annoying-the-Fuck-Out-of-Gabriel?"

'Dior rolled her eyes. "You're *such* an arsehole."

'"See, that'd work too."

'My lips twisted in a secret smile, and we set back to it. But trudging onwards, I soon found that smile fading. The dead trees were slowly thinning, and through the swirling snowfall, I could see what lay ahead. It was inevitable, of course – I'd been chewing on what to do about it for days. But I'd hoped we'd get farther before this particular bucket of cocks hit us full in the face.

'"Shit," I breathed. "The Ròdaerr."

'In front of us, the road dropped away to a steep bank and a broad river. The bridge had been torn down, twin mooring stones thrust up from the shoreline, one smeared with a bloody handprint. The Ròdaerr was only eighty yards wide. But it was trouble nonetheless.

'"Should be easy enough to cross," Dior said. "It's frozen solid."

'"Not solid," I replied. "And that's one problem."

'"We've more than one?"

'I looked to the falling snows, shivering in the bone-cracking cold.

"Wintersdeep has finally caught us. Every river north of the Ūmdir is in the process of freezing." I met the girl's eyes, shook my head. "We can't reach San Michon like this, Dior."

"'But if the rivers are frozen . . . that'll make it *easier* for us to travel, not harder."

"'Easier for us,' I nodded. "*And* the things chasing us. The coldest nights of the year are about to fall. The Beast of Vellene will be over the Volta and right up our arses with whatever strength he can muster along the way. Danton moves faster than we do. He *knows* where we're headed. We won't reach San Michon before he runs us down."

"'Is there someplace we can shelter?"

'I sighed, taking my old map from my britches. It was beaten, water-stained, crumpled, but the lines of the empire were still visible on the parchment. I tapped a small black star on the banks of the Mère.

"'Château Aveléne,' Dior murmured. "What's there?"

"'Maybe, just maybe, a fire bright enough to burn Danton to ashes."

"'That path leads through the northern weald. Saoirse warned us not to go there. She said the Blight was far worse, that the—"

"'We're beggars, Dior, we don't get to choose. But after the beating he gave us at San Guillaume, the Beast will think we're shattered. Fleeing for our lives. And in truth, that's all we've been doing. I came north to kill this bastard and his whole accursed famille, and I'm sick of running. Do you trust me?"

'The girl met my eyes and nodded. "I trust you, mon ami."

'I looked to the stretch of grey ice before us. "Aright, then. *This* is our road."

"'One that's liable to crack right under our feet."

"'Right you are. So I'll go first."

'Dior raised an eyebrow, looking from me to the frozen river, then back again. "Don't be daft, Gabriel."

"'I can find a safe path. I grew up in the Nordlund. I know ice."

"'*I'll* go first. I'm faster. And smarter, just quietly. Hence not wanting to be stuck on this bank holding the horse while you bugger off alone."

"'You ever done this before?"

'She shrugged. "The Lashaame River freezes in winter. They held a fair on it once."

"'Soft city girls," I tutted.

'She scoffed, brushing snow off her frockcoat. "Tell me what to do then, bumpkin."

"'Walk slow," I smiled. "Legs wide. If the ice cracks and you hit the water, the cold will knock the breath right out of your lungs. If that happens, keep your head. Kick upwards. Turn around, and go out same way you went in. Still got that pig-sticker of yours?"

'Dior shook her head. "Those bitches took it in Redwatch."

"'Here." I unbuckled my dagger and sheath from my swordbelt. "If you hit water, stab it into the ice, pull yourself out. Just be mindful of the current."

'She hefted the blade, looking at the sevenstar embossed on the pommel, the Angel Eloise with wings spread across the hilt. "It's beautiful," she murmured.

'I nodded. "Forged by the finest smith San Michon ever knew. I've owned that blade seventeen years. Wore it through the Battle of the Twins. Báih Sìde. Triúrbaile. Tuuve. Not many folks in the empire deemed worthy to carry silversteel."

"'I'll give it back on the other side, I promise."

"'Keep it. It's yours."

'Dior gazed at the dagger in her hand, fingertips running over the coat I'd given her. She brushed her hair down over her face, pressed her lips thin.

"'You're not going soft on me, are you, Lachance?"

'She scoffed, dragging her armour back on. "Hard as fucking stone, me."

"'Just don't sink like one. I don't fancy diving in after you."

'And she smiled then. Because she knew I would.

'Dior slipped down the frozen bank and took her first steps out onto the Ròdaerr. She moved in a crouch, lithe, fearless, sweeping the snow off the frozen surface with her palms as she went. The ice was pale grey, darkening as it grew thinner, and I imagined the river's current, still rushing deadly and swift below that frozen crust.

'Her path across the ice was wandering, zigzag, and my heart was climbing up into my throat watching. But finally, she reached the opposite bank, waved to me in triumph.

"'Come on, old man!"

"'I'm thirty-fucking-two!"

'She snapped a branch off a nearby tree, held it aloft. "Walking stick for you!"

"'Little bitch." I scratched Jezebel's chin. "Aright, girl. Sunset waits for no saint."

'Taking the horse's reins, I led her carefully down to the icy shore. The mare knew not what to make of the frozen water at first, but she followed faithfully as I shuffled slowly out onto the glass-smooth grey. It was easy going to begin with, the river frozen solid close to shore. But as we walked farther out, the crust grew thinner, shifting from snow grey to a deeper iron. The ice groaned a little under us now, bright ticking sounds ringing in my ears as tiny fractures began appearing under our feet. But Dior was no fool, and the path she'd chosen was true. If it hadn't been for God's insistence on shoving his prick into my earhole at every opportunity, we'd have been gold as a sailor's best teeth.

'Jezebel sensed them first, ears pricking back, snorting. I caught something on the wind, tilting my head to listen. And I heard it then, soft as a feather and quick as a knife in the dark. Footsteps. Behind.

'"*Gabriel!*" Dior shouted.

'I turned, eyes narrowed as I spotted them: a ragged boy, an old man, a woman, young and broad. Three wretched were stumbling down the frozen banks behind me, hands and mouths black with dirt and old blood.

'Now, normally this wouldn't have meant more than a daily session of sword practice. Like I say, we'd stumbled across a few rotten coldbloods on our road. But *none* of those bastards had appeared while we were halfway across a frozen fucking river.

'I drew Ashdrinker, the sword glinting in my hand as the rotten little boy took his first step out onto the ice.

'*R-r-run, Gabriel.*

'"They're only three," I growled. "Why the hell should I run?"

'*Because* she *w-will.*

'I realized it too late. I was too used to riding with Justice, see. But Jezebel was no bold sosya, raised in the belly of San Michon to be fearless of the Dead. And after the massacre at San Guillaume, she seemed to hate and fear them more than most beasts. So when she caught a good whiff of those wretched on the wind, she huffed and reared up, and Dior's path be damned, Jezebel thundered right the hell across the ice.

'The ticking sounds turned to snapping, and the snapping to splintering. Deep, white cracks spread out like spiderwebs as a thousand pounds of terrified mare galloped across the river glass. The wretched were sprinting towards me, the old bastard slipping and scrabbling, the boy loping on all fours like a wolf, clawed fingers digging into the frozen surface. I felt the ice shift, pitching underneath me like the deck of a storm-tossed ship as Dior roared warning, as Ashdrinker's voice rang inside my head.

'*Run, ye blasted fool!*

'I turned and bolted, skipping across the shattering surface. The ice was breaking apart ahead of me; I saw it give way under Jezebel's hindquarters, the mare screaming as she plunged through. A chunk of ice splintered under my silver heels and I stumbled, leaping onto a buckling shelf. And then, the entire world gave way under my feet.

'I made a jump for it, sailing through the air as the shelf collapsed. But not quite far enough. The surface flipped and shattered as I struck it, splintering in maddened spiral patterns as my boots smashed through, the rest of me following, Ashdrinker roaring in my head as she slipped from my fingers and went skittering across the ice. And with a short, pitch-black curse, I plunged into the frozen Ròdaerr.

'The shock punched me hard in the chest, and just as I promised Dior, all the breath fled my lungs. I'd cracked my skull on the shelf as I went under, tasting blood in my mouth as the cold stabbed my bones. It was a few heartbeats before I pulled myself together, shook off the shock, looking about the gloom and kicking upwards towards the light. But I cursed as I cracked my skull again on the ice overhead. With sinking belly, I realized the current had me, dragging me downriver away from the hole I'd plunged into.

'I kicked hard, punching with all my strength, ice splintering under my fists. But I had no air in my lungs, black spots bursting in my vision as I punched the surface again.

'*Thump*.

'*Crunch*.

'Nothing.

'I was being dragged, fighting the current now, pressed against the ice above. The surface was smooth as glass under my gloves, nothing to cling to, and I cursed as I reached for my dagger, remembering I'd given it to Dior. I could see a dark shape through the crust above me now – a dim shadow and dimmer voice, barely heard above the fearful tempo of my pulse. Of all the places I'd been, the horrors I'd faced, it seemed idiotic that this was the way I might end; suffocating under a mere foot of frozen water. I cursed myself a fool for not having taken the sacrament – if I were fresh sated, I could have punched my way out. But as it was, even paleblood fists weren't strong enough to tear free of this tomb.

'I slammed my fist into the ice again, again, hearing cracks reverberate along the frozen grey. Black flowers were blooming in my eyes now, beautiful, paralysing, the pressure in my chest, the need to *breathe* burning like flame.

'I was slipping along in the current's loving arms, the light growing dim. All fire was fading. All hope was lost. Hell beckoned, forever arms open wide, but I supposed it might at least be warm there. And then came a crashing sound, and through the black veil over my eyes, I saw the ice above me split, shattering like a comet had crashed upon its face. And though I'd no breath in me to scream, still I tried as four and a half feet of razored starmetal came plunging through the ice and speared me right through my gut.

'I was jerked to a sudden halt, pinioned on the steel, mouth open in agony. I heard Ashdrinker's voice ringing in my head then, silver bright in the crushing black.

'*FIGHT!*

'I squinted in the dark, saw that the blade had created a webwork of cracks in the grey above. And I thought of Astrid. Of Patience. Furious and snarling, shredding my gloves and ripping my knuckles bloody as I smashed my fist upwards again, again, again.

'*I refuse to die here,* I told myself.

'I.

'*Thump.*

'Refuse.

'*Crunch.*

'To die here.

'My fist broke through the cracks, stripped back to the bone, and I felt someone grab hold. Agony flared as the blade was dragged free of my gut. I tore at the frozen lid of my coffin, lungs burning as the pieces came apart, as dim light broke through, as at last, kicking and dragged from above, I pushed my head up into the blessed air.

'"*Gabriel!*" Dior roared. "*Hold onto me!*"

'I could do nothing but gag, stabbed and bleeding as the girl dug her fingers into my forearm and hauled me back. Dior was on her belly, Ashdrinker thrust into the ice like a piton, and finally she hauled me free, out of that frozen black and onto the blinding surface.

'"Hold on!" Dior pleaded. "Hold on, Gabe!"

'Clutching my split belly, I left a long trail of crimson on the grey as she dragged me towards the shoreline. And at last we came to rest, just a few feet from the frozen banks. I curled into a ball, holding my stomach, freezing cold, skull ringing, drooling blood.

'"Can you hear me?" Dior squeezed my hand, her eyes wild. "*Gabriel?*"

'"Fuck . . . m-my . . . f-f . . ."

'I felt hands fumbling with my coat pockets, blinking up at the daysdeath light. I could taste my own blood, feel broken glass in my belly, heart thrashing on my ribs.

'"Here. Here, breathe . . ."

'She pressed my pipe to my lips and the taste of sanctus washed over me, sweet and merciful red. I coughed, blood spattering on the frost, taking the pipe from Dior's shaking hand and inhaling another lungful. I felt that accursed strength, the agony in my belly fading, able to breathe easier. I pressed my hand to my sundered gut, blood dribbling through my fingertips.

'"You . . ." I squinted at Dior, my teeth sticky. "Y-you . . ."

'"It's aright," she said. "I got you, Gabe. You're safe."

'"You . . . f-fucking . . . stabbed me."

'"Wait . . . you're getting *tetchy* with me now?"

'"Tetchy?" I coughed, spitting red. "You *stabbed* me!"

'"It wasn't my fault!"

'"You stabbed me *accidently*?"

'"No." She scowled, shrugging. "It was Ashdrinker's idea."

'I glowered at the blade, now thrust into the snow at the girl's side. "*Was* it now . . ."

'"I just grabbed her to break the ice," Dior said. "But the current had you. We needed to hold you still so you could punch free. So, she told me to . . . you know . . ."

'The girl made a circle of her left forefinger and thumb. Poked her right index finger through it repeatedly. The silvered dame on the sword's hilt smiled at me as always.

'"Bitch," I hissed.

'Dior gave a sympathetic wince. "Does it hurt?"

'"You STABBED me!"

'"Fucksakes, don't be such a baby! There won't even be a mark by the morrow. You know, most folk would spare a merci for the girl who just saved their lives, de León."

'The shock was fading now, the fear of almost drowning paling to a dull ebb. Surly prick that I was, I was still realizing this girl had indeed just saved my sorry arse, and the least I could do was refrain from acting a complete bell-end about it.

'"Merci," I scowled.

'She pursed her lips, climbed to her feet and offered her hand. "Get up, old man."

'Dior hauled me upright as I gasped in agony. One hand to my bleeding gut, I blinked about in the dim light. "What happened to the wretched?"

'The girl nodded to the shattered ice. "Went under. All three. Didn't make a sound." She shook her head, horrified. "But it was like they just . . . melted."

'"And what about—"

'I heard heavy hooves, crunching in crisp snow. Dragging the hair from my eyes with a bloody hand, I saw Jezebel plodding up the frozen bank towards us, a little waterlogged, a little shaken, but apparently none the worse for wear.

'"God's truth," I sighed. "You are the luckiest bitch I ever met."

'Dior met my eyes, the thought occurring to her just as it did to me.

'"That's *it*!" she cried.

'"*That's* it . . ." I nodded.

'I limped to the mare's side, scruffing her ear with one bloody hand as Dior threw her arms around her neck.

'"Fortuna."'

✦ XI ✦

NIGHT AND KNIVES

'ONE DEGREE IS the difference between fluid and solid. The divergence between water and ice. But those who've grown up in the coldest places will know the shift that comes with wintersdeep, and the way we who live through it, shift with it. Dim days grow dimmer still, bleak nights bring bleaker thoughts. And as the landscape about you changes, so does the limit of your spirit. The dark weighs heavier when your cloak is soaked with melted snow. Laughter is best avoided when your beard is so caked with frost that it hurts to smile. Spring blooms, and autumn rusts. But winter?

'Winter *bites*.

'We'd entered the northern weald ten days past, and all was night and knives. Growths of maryswort lit the dark with ghostly blue luminance. Beggarbelly pustules and jagged runs of shadespine covered every surface. I was a knot of nerves, all of me on edge as I led Dior and Fortuna through the twisted wood.

'The deeper we trekked, the harder this twist of fate struck me – that I of all people would end up guiding this girl to safety, and that the salvation of the empire had somehow fallen into my hands, so many years after that empire turned its back on me. I didn't know the truth of Dior's blood, how it might bring all this to an end. I knew only that I wanted to keep her safe. And so, I barely slept, sitting with Ashdrinker in hand at nights, keeping vigil over Dior as she dreamed. Every snapping twig quickened my pulse. Eyes flickered like candles in the gloom, winking out as I looked at them. Footprints would be etched in the snow around our fire when we rose in the morn – wolves, maybe, save the tracks had too many toes and smelled of rot and sulfur.

'On the eleventh day, we found a clearing, an ancient tree in its heart.

Its limbs were hung with sculptures made of twigs . . . and with dead bodies, some almost fresh. The other trees were bent towards it, branches pressed together like penitent hands, asphyxia growths hanging like curtains of hair about bowed heads. Voices pleaded at the edge of hearing. I *swear* that tree whispered to me as we passed. Saoirse had warned that the Blight in the north was far worse than the south. But in truth, she'd not told the half of it.

'Dior looked about and shivered. "And you wonder why I never left the city."

'"No," I replied. "No, I really don't."

'"I don't think we should've come this way."

'"Well, don't blame me," I hissed.

'"And why not?"

'"Because . . . I'd rather you didn't?"

'*A stunning riposte.*

'I glowered at the sword in my hand. "Bitch, you stabbed me. I'd be laying off the lip for a few more days if I were you."

'*Apology I gave ye. What m-m-more wouldst thou ask?*

'"How about never fucking do that again?"

'*This . . . I c-c-cannot vow.*

'"Can you smell that?" Dior asked.

'I lifted my nose to the wind, nodded once.

'"Death."

'We stopped for the night, tied Fortuna to a tree that looked like a weeping woman, arms up over her face. The sky was black as sin, the snow coming down relentless, wind howling all about us through the twisted boughs, the creaking branches, the tombs of kings that had once ruled this place when all was green and good.

'After a cheerless meal, I smoked a red pipe while we sat and shivered. All the night was alive, all my senses ablaze. I caught notes of decay entwined with a dozen breeds of fungus, thin embers of strange animal life, Dior's blood. But beneath, faint as whispers . . .

'"You should get some rest," I said. "I'll wake you when it's time for your watch."

'"You promise?" she scowled. "Because you didn't last night."

'"You needed the sleep. Being the saviour of the empire is hard work."

'Dior scoffed. "Saviour . . ."

'The girl sucked her lip, blue eyes glazed as she watched the crackling flames.

'"You really think it's going to be like Chloe said? Just show up at San Michon, mumble some phrase from some dusty book, and huzzah, au revoir daysdeath?"

'"I've no idea," I sighed. "But someone less cynical than me would point out you must be *some* kind of threat, else the Forever King wouldn't have his son chasing you."

'"Nor that bitch with the mask you fought at San Guillaume." Dior chewed a ragged nail, spat it into the fire. "She seemed to know something."

'I nodded, remembering Liathe and her bloodblade, that pale mask and the paler eyes beyond. Sanguimancers. Vampires of ancien blood. Mysteries within mysteries, as ever. I looked down at the sevenstar on my palm, the veins beneath my skin.

'"It could all be lies. Maybe everyone playing this game is a fool. We'll learn the truth when we get to San Michon, I suppose. There's deceit and madness aplenty in that library. But there *are* truths too. Astrid and I found a few. When we were young."

'"*Esani*," Dior murmured.

'I glowered at the sword on the frost beside me. "You talk too much, Ash."

'"I think she gets lonely," Dior smiled. "Stuck in that scabbard all day."

'"My heart bleeds." I flicked snow at the silvered dame. "Along with my *stomach*."

'"It can't be coincidence, though, can it? A fifth bloodline, with almost the exact same name as Michon's daughter? Esan. *Faith*. Esani. Faith*less*."

'"I don't know, Dior. We looked for years in that library, Astrid and Chloe and me. We found mostly nonsense. There's power in my blood, and I've learned a trick or two. If I ever get my hands on Danton's throat while I'm at my best, he's in for a reckoning. But truth is, my bloodline never made much difference to the way I lived my life. Astrid used to tell me that was what made her proudest. Raised among those Dyvoks and Chastains and Ilons, and I stood tallest of all." I tapped the veins at my wrist. "Not because of this."

'I thumped a fist over my chest.

'"Because of *this*."

'"Aim your heart at the world," she smiled.

'I nodded. "One day as a lion is worth ten thousand as a lamb."

'Dior lay down by the fireside, cloak beneath, fine coat draped over her. A mop of ashen white covering eyes that were the blue of long-lost skies. Scrawny shoulders and clever hands and the blood of a dead fucking godling in her veins.

'"Tell me about your daughter," she murmured.

'"Go to sleep, Lachance."

'"I *will*." She smiled, eyes closed. "But I like your voice. It's smoky. Relaxing."

'I looked at the name tattooed across my fingers. Drawing down another draught and exhaling a plume of scarlet. "What do you want to know?"

'"Anything. What's her favourite colour?"

'"Blue. The water around our house was almost blue some days."

'"You live on a river?"

'I shook my head. "Lighthouse. Just off the southern coast. Tide came in with the moons, covered the bridge to land. So nothing could cross over at night."

'"Clever."

'"I have my moments."

'"Does she like it there?"

'"I hope so. It's south. Down past Alethe. Sometimes we got flowers in spring."

'"I've never seen a flower," Dior sighed. "What's her favourite?"

'I could smell it stronger now – that scent Dior had caught on the wind. Truth told, it had been following us all day. Like a shadow. Like a ghost. I looked to the dark beyond the firelight and saw it – a shape I knew as well as my own name, silhouetted against the corpses of fallen trees, dead emperors mouldering in frozen tombs.

'"Gabe?" Dior asked.

'"What?"

'"What's Patience's favourite flower?"

'"Silverbell. Like her mother."

'"You must miss them."

'I shook my head. "I'll be back with them soon."

'"I'm sorry," she sighed. "That I took you away from them."

'"No more questions, girl. Go to sleep."

'Dior curled up in her coat, face towards the flames. And I sat there in the cold, watching the eyes that were watching me. I could see her more clearly now; no longer a dark shadow, but a pale one, porcelain skin draped with bolts of black hair, soft as silk and thick as smoke. She said nothing, just waiting until the breath of the girl beside me slowed and smoothed, breast rising and falling in the peaceful cadence of sleep.

'The shape drifted back, deeper into the shadow.

'And I stood, following into the dark.'

✦ XII ✦
EVERYTHING FALLING APART

'SHE STRUCK ME from behind, slammed me into the skin of a crumbling oak, perhaps fifty yards from the fire. The light was still bright enough to catch in the black flint of her eyes, her strength as bleak as the storm above. And she crushed her lips to mine, and I could feel the razors in her mouth as she snarled like a wolf and pressed herself naked against me.

'"My lion," she whispered.

'She bit my lip, cold hands at the buttons of my greatcoat, at my tunic now, slipping up inside and running her fingers over the muscle and ink beneath. She hissed softly, cold hands burning on silver ink, fingernails digging into my skin.

'"You'll hurt yourself," I whispered.

'"A little pain never hurt anyone," she breathed.

'My hair tumbled about her cheeks as she kissed me again, like the sun once kissed the silverbell that grew around our home. She brushed burning lips across the ink at my throat, my chest, fingernails drifting to my belt and dragging the buckle free as she sank slow, ever so slow to her knees.

'"Stop," I begged. "Please."

'She looked up, pupils so wide with hunger her eyes were black. "I've missed you."

'"And I you," I whispered, heart breaking. "More than anything."

'She kissed me through my leathers, root to aching crown, and as she pulled my britches lower, the want in me was so real I felt my knees buckle.

'"Just a little," she pleaded.

'"I can't."

'"Just a mouthful, love."

'"I *can't*."

'She hissed, dark and shivering, rearing back like a serpent. I had to close my eyes against the sight of her anger, the break too close to the surface.

'I never wanted any of this.

'When I opened my eyes, she was standing off in the dark, slender arms folded, the storm wind blowing long locks around her. God in heaven, she was beautiful. It was all I could do to stop myself from sinking to my knees, to plead, to pray. Everything fading. Everything falling apart.

'"I love you," I told her.

'"If that were true, you wouldn't tell me no."

'"Astrid . . . please . . . I need my strength."

'Black eyes flickered to the distant fire. "For her."

'"She has no one else."

'"She's not your daughter. She's not your famille."

'"I *know* that!"

'"*Do* you?" She glanced to me, a strand of long black hair caught at the edge of her lips. "You're coming apart, love. You've given too much of yourself to this already, and you're still nowhere close. You're forgetting why you left us, Gabriel."

'"No," I replied, voice like iron. "I remember."

'She turned to face me, and I could see bloody tears in her lashes. "You're headed to a place I can't follow. I don't want you to go."

'"Dior will be safe in San Michon. And next time Danton comes, I'll be ready, I'll—"

'"That girl isn't why you came here. Why you left Patience. Why you left me."

'My hands curled into fists. "I *know* why I came here. I don't need you to remind me. I see it every time I close my fucking eyes!"

'"Please don't be angry," she whispered.

'I hung my head, shutting my eyes against the burning tears, her whisper the only sound in the dark. "Tell me you love me."

'"Of course I do."

'"Promise you'll never leave me."

'"How could I?" I sank to my haunches, head in my hands. "You're all I ever wanted. The two of you . . . you were the pieces I never knew were missing. You—"

'"Gabe?"

'I opened my eyes, saw Dior standing in the dark, staring at me. She looked frightened, cold, that fine frockcoat dusted with snow. Ashdrinker was unsheathed in her hands, dark starsteel gleaming in the light of the distant flames.

'"I heard you shouting. Were you talking to someone?"

'A glance told me Astrid was gone; a wraith vanished into the gloom.

'"Myself," I replied, rising to my feet and buckling my belt. "Just myself."

'"You're bleeding," she said, pointing to her lip.

'I licked at the scratch, the blood, my fangs still long and sharp in my gums. "It's nothing. You shouldn't be away from the fire. It's freezing out here."

'I grabbed her hand, dragging her along beside me.

'"Are you aright?" she asked.

'"I'm fine. Just . . . don't leave the light again. It's dangerous."

'"Gabriel, I'm worried about you."

'"Stop fretting on me, girl." I snatched Ashdrinker from her hand with a snarl. "And give me that bloody sword. You've no ken how to fucking use it, anyway."

'*What is thy game, Gabriel?*

'"Shut up, Ash."

'*Thy threads unravelling. Thy knots undone. Long years did we face the d-dark together, and I tell thee true, tell thee true, I am sorry for my part in it. But at the end of this road lies madn—*"

'I sheathed the blade, silencing her voice. Dior stared at me as we made it back to the circle of the flames. I crouched close to the crackling heat, shivering, licking at the bite on my lip. The girl stood opposite, hands folded inside her fine-cut sleeves.

'"You know . . . you could teach me," she murmured. "If you were so worried."

'I glanced up, meeting bright blue eyes. "Teach you what?"

'She waved at Ashdrinker, risking a small smile. "How to use a sword?"

'"I don't think so."

'Her smile dimmed. "Why not? I can handle a knife."

'"Because a blade and half a clue are more dangerous than no blade or clue at all."

'"Gabriel, listen to me—"

'"No. It only encourages you."

'"Enough people have already died on my account," she snapped. "I don't want other people fighting my battles for me."

'"And yet, here I am."

'Her jaw dropped a little at that, swiftly clenched. "You know, I survived for years without a soul to help me. I was raised in *shit*, and I clawed my way out myself. I've saved your arse three times now by my counting, and you still give me no credit. You *do* treat me different now you know I'm a girl. You're not my papa. I'm not your daughter."

'"Damn right you're not. She'd make ten of you."

'She took a step back then. Like I'd struck her. "Goddamn, you're a sonofa*bitch*. I'm trying to be nice. I tell you I'm worried, and you just spit in my face like a fucking—"

'"Shut up."

'"You don't tell me to shut up! Who the hell do you th—"

'"No, shut up!" I hissed, raising one hand. "*Listen!*"

'Jaw clenched, scowling in fury, still, she took it in check. Tilting her head, Dior strained to hear. The storm was blustering above, whipping through the trees, but there, above the clamour, it came again, dim, off to the west.

'She met my eyes, breathing a little quicker. ". . . Thunder?"

'"Those are footsteps."

'Dior frowned. "*Big* ones."

'I lit the wick of the hunter's lantern at my belt. Snatching up a burning brand from the fire. Dior remained by the blaze, eyes narrowed as she strained to hear.

'"I think . . ." She shook her head. "I think they're coming closer."

'"They are." I slung a blanket onto Fortuna's back, patted it. "We need to go."

'Our quarrel forgotten, Dior grabbed another burning branch from the blaze, skipping up onto Fortuna. The mare stomped, ears pricked back as I took her reins, leading her on foot through the scrub and snarl. The wind was screaming, the snow drifting through the tangles above as we moved, me guiding us through the dark with wide paleblood eyes.

'"Where are we going?" Dior asked.

'I pointed west, to whatever was thudding towards us. "Away from that."

'The footsteps were drawing closer, distinct now under the raging storm. I could hear whispering through dead trees, a chill rising in my belly. Risking a glance over my shoulder, I saw shapes; a multitude, distant through the snarl. At first, I feared the Dead – some legion raised by Danton to run us to ground, come upon us in the deep of night. I wasn't certain whether to be relieved or afraid as I saw that the things behind us were nothing near human. Shadows within shadows, the whispering growing louder. Eyes like storm lanterns in the dark, mighty shapes moving through tangled boughs, skin run through with pustules, too many legs, too many mouths. Close and closer.

"'Hold on!"

'We ran now, Fortuna's eyes grown wide, the mare straining against the reins in my hand. She wanted to gallop, fear stealing her reason, but charging blind through these woods by torchlight was insanity. Still, those shapes, those *things*, spider-limbed and owl-eyed, they came on in a flood, sliver claws and dagger teeth too many for counting, and though I'd no ken from what horrors they'd been born, I knew they were hungry.

"'Gabriel!" Dior roared.

"'*Fuck* my . . . Move!"

'Dior shuffled forward as I scrambled up onto the mare behind her, slinging my arms about her waist as Fortuna broke into a gallop. Branches whipped and clutched, my face torn and bloodied, Dior's head bowed as she bent double and rode like all hell came after us. She risked a glance behind, eyes wide with fear.

"'What the *fuck* is that?"

"'Don't look!"

"'God, Gabriel, they—"

"'DON'T LOOK!"

'Animal shapes, twisted beyond all measure of light or reason. The dreams of screaming trees, raised in the mouldering grave of a cradle once green. Mushroom skin and toadstool eyes, faces inside open mouths, slack with spore and madness. I'd trodden the darkest paths of this world. I'd looked into the eyes of hell and seen it looking back. And great fucking Redeemer, I swear I'd never seen the likes of them.

'If not for Fortuna, they'd have taken us. But the mare ran hard as always, weaving among the rotten hulks, the boughs like grasping hands. And though the dray was never the fastest horse I'd ridden, she was ever one of the steadiest. Her flanks were soon damp with sweat, chest heaving like a bellows, but though we could see only a dozen feet ahead in the strobing light of my lantern, she didn't stumble. Instead, we wove like a needle through a loom, twists and gullies, leaping over tumbled trees while the snow fell thick about us and Dior and I held on for dear life. I could hear the girl praying, and I found her hand, squeezed it tight as she squeezed back.

"'No fear," I bid her. "I've got you."

'Blinding snow. Thundering hooves. Twisting shapes at our back. We couldn't see a thing, and still we rode, tears frozen on our cheeks. I heard a shift in the wind, no longer hissing through the wood but howling instead. The trees about us thinned, and for a second, I thought we'd made it clear, only to feel my heart sink as I realized why. Fortuna charged on, true to her name, true to the last, true to the moment her luck finally failed her.

'I roared, grabbing at the horse's reins . . . but too late, *too late*, as the cliff's edge loomed before us. And with a terrified bellow, the panicked mare galloped out into the breach and flung us all over the edge, into the black gulf beyond.

'Dior screamed and I roared "HOLD ON!" and we were falling, out into the snow-strewn dark. I clutched the girl's waist, twisted us as we came free from the mare's back, as poor Fortuna screamed again. Curling over Dior, clutching her tight, I gasped as I felt us strike a surface, jagged, brittle, snapping loose and spinning us about. Something crashed against my skull, splintering, and I realized we'd struck the boughs of some naked pine, hurling down, branch by snapping branch. It spun us, pierced and tore me, and still I held on, refusing to let Dior slip from my arms. I heard her gasp, felt us twist, my leg caught between grasping limbs and *snapped* clean in two, and I roared in red agony as all the world spun blinding, and at last, we crashed into a thick drift of new-fallen snow.

'All was fire. The pain every colour under heaven. I could see bone thrust up through my torn thigh, out through my leathers – a jagged shank of femur, glistening red. Blood in my eyes and my mouth. Cold and dark all around us. Fear stabbed my heart as I squeezed the girl in my arms, called her name, desperate.

'"Dior? *Dior!*"

'She lay still, hair strewn across her face, not white now but red. Her brow was cut, but still, still she breathed. I closed my eyes, held her tight, shaking with relief. The snow was piled high around us, the wind a funeral dirge. I looked about, my nose alight with the scent of death. And I saw her, twenty yards away – our poor Fortuna, crumpled in a drift of snow.

'I couldn't see the ridge above. I'd no idea how far we'd fallen, nor if we'd been pursued. There was only thin scrub and dead pines about us, no blighted wood nor glowing eyes, and I realized at last we'd reached the edge of the weald. But even if the horrors chasing us hadn't followed us down here, death still loomed a few heartbeats away.

'My leg was broken, bone sheared up through bleeding meat. I could straighten it, but it would take time to heal – time we didn't have. The night was black, my blood freezing on the snow about us, and there was naught to feed a fire with, nor shelter to seek.

'I fumbled for my pipe, thoughts racing as I inhaled a bloody lungful. And dragging off my gloves, I clenched my teeth, gasping as I reset the bone in my torn thigh. The pain was blinding, my bloody hands shaking as I pushed my shattered femur back inside my torn muscle. I could hear a sound under the wind, ragged and guttural, and I realized at last it was me; screaming as I felt bone meet broken bone.

'The bleed was sluggish now, bright red. I ripped off my belt, pressed Ashdrinker in her scabbard against my leg and bound her to my thigh, cinching tight as I could. With shaking scarlet hands, I took another hit, feeling the pain ebb like blood in warm water. Still listening for pursuit, knowing full well if those things followed us, we'd be torn to pieces.

'*No time to fret*, I told myself. *No time to fear.*

'*When there's little you can do, do what little you can.*

'Face twisted, I took hold of Dior's coat, dragged us closer to Fortuna's corpse. I checked the girl over, looking for broken bones, bleeds, but my body had spared her the worst of it. And so, taking the dagger I'd given her, I turned to the fallen mare. She'd carried us longer than we could've hoped. She'd been a friend in dark places, and I hated to ask her for more. But there was yet one thing she could do for us.

'"I'm sorry, girl," I whispered. "I wish your luck could've held longer."

'I plunged the knife into her belly, met with a greasy rush of blood and shit. I tore the blade up to her ribs, sawing through bone. Steam rose from the wound as I thrust my hands into that awful warmth. Swallowing my bile, I took hold and heaved – long coils of gleaming intestine, then up, up into her chest, the great swollen bags of her lungs, her dauntless heart, until the snow was piled with a great heap of steaming viscera.

'Dior's lips were blue as I dragged her out of her furs and coat, boots and britches. I cracked Fortuna's ribs wide, holding them apart with shoulder and elbow, my broken leg screaming as I dragged Dior out of the cold that would kill her and into the only shelter we had. Drenched and gasping, at last I lay back against poor Fortuna's flank, dragging her guts atop me for the warmth. Stroking her cheek. Murmuring above the howling wind.

'"Merci, girl."

'*Better to be a bastard than a fool.*

'I lay there in the slowly cooling gore. Nothing to do but wait and heal and hope.

'Hope, but never pray.

'I reached inside Fortuna's ruin and found Dior's hand, squeezing tight.

'And together, we waited for the dawn.'

+ XIII +
FORWARD NOT BACKWARDS

'NO DARKNESS FOUND us before daylight did.

'I'd kept a weary vigil, my leg slowly mending, the cold and fatigue still threatening to drag me down into a sleep from which I might not wake. The storm rolled on unabated, but now that the black sun had raised its head, I could see a little better at least. In the distance, a broad, dark strip of frozen river snaked through the scattered pines and stubborn tundra scrub. And as I gazed upon that icy shore, I realized at last where we were.

'"The Mère . . ." I breathed.

'My thigh still ached, but the sanctus had healed the broken bone well enough. And so, staggering to my feet, I looked around us. It had been ten years since I left this place behind me: the majestic frozen flows, the snow-clad expanse, the shadow of peaks looming far to the freezing north. The land that had borne me, lit a fire inside my chest, and in the end, cast me out like a beggar into the cold.

'"Nordlund," I sighed.

'At last, I'd come home.

'A muffled shout came from the corpse behind me, followed by a horrified wail, and turning, I saw blood-streaked hands clawing their way from Fortuna's gut.

'"Hold on!" I called, prising the ribs and frozen flesh apart, and frost crackling, bones snapping, Dior dragged herself free of the wreckage. She was gasping, drenched in slime and blood, one side of her face swollen black and blue. As I hauled her to her feet, she looked at herself, horrified, scarred hands held out before her. It seemed she might retch.

'"Sweet f-f-fucking M-mothermaid . . ."

'"All's well, girl. Breathe easy now."

'She looked to the cliffs above, the broken pine we'd smashed through, and at last, to Fortuna's ruins. I saw her eyes close, her cheeks balloon. She fell to her knees in pink snow, bending double. But still, she clenched her teeth, finding someplace iron deep inside and swallowing hard. I tore off Fortuna's blanket, wiped the worst of the gore off her skin as she heaved and swallowed again.

'"Can you walk?"

'"W-where?" she whispered.

'"That's the Mère River. We're close to Aveléne. I can carry you if you've a need."

'"And who's going to c-carry you?"

'I waved vaguely. "A technicality, Mlle Lachance."

'Dior managed a smile at that. And I watched, marvelling as she dragged gore-streaked hair from swollen eyes and stood on shaking legs.

'"We've come this f-far. Forward, not backwards."

'She scrubbed her skin and hair in the snow as best she could, and I handed over her boots and clothes. Dior kissed her fingertips, kneeling to press them to Fortuna's cheek, and I could see tears in her eyes as she murmured thanks. It might've seemed a foolish thing to some – for this girl to cry over a horse she barely knew when she'd lost so much already. But in truth, we weep not for those departed, but for we who remain. And it's ever best to take the time to say goodbye. All too often, fate robs us of the chance.

'We kept to the banks, Dior and I limping side by side. This part of the river was once rushing rapids, frozen now into a still life, in stasis, like the things yet hunting us. I looked to the ridge above, the frost behind, knowing he was still back there. I could feel him now, drawing close, cold and relentless as the snows. The storm rolled on, chilling us to the bone. A snow hawk circled overhead, almost lost against the grey skies.

'Four days we walked those banks, and by the end, we were both fit to fall. But finally, cresting a snaking bend, I took Dior's hand and pointed. "Look!"

'A jagged mont rose up from the Mère's shoreline like a tower to heaven. Good, thick walls encircled the base, and on the road spiralling up its slopes, little houses stood; solid Nordlund stone with black tiled roofs. Atop the chill rock loomed a castle carved of the same dark basalt it stood upon.

'"Château Aveléne," I breathed.

'It had seen better days, to be sure – no enchanted castle from a faerie story, nor a place a king would gladly hang his crown. Aveléne was a grim, foreboding place, keeping stoic watch over the frozen river snaking from the

north. But any light was welcome in a sea of darkness, and even from the valley below, we could see tiny flames upon the walls that told us here, despite all odds, humanity endured.

'"Who built this place?" Dior whispered.

'"An old Nordling king," I told her. "Centuries past. Lorenzo the Fair, his name. He intended this castle as a gift for his bride on the arrival of their first child. But Lorenzo's queen and the babe both died in the birth. She lies buried within, along with the child she bore. The castle still bears her name to this day. Aveléne."

'"You've been here before?"

'"Years back," I nodded. "Astrid and I stopped here, after we left San Michon. She was heavy with Patience by then, and there were few places in the empire that would've welcomed us in our disgrace. But within these walls, we found sanctuary. Peace. It may not look much, but the two happiest days of my life, I had right here."

'Dior met my eyes. "You mean . . ."

'I nodded and swallowed hard, trying to dislodge the lump in my throat. Thumb running across the tattoos on my fingers as the echoes of laughter rang in my head.

'"This is where Astrid and I were wed. And where Patience was born."

'We trudged up from the frozen bank, past a long wooden pier, now mired in the ice. Barges were dragged up onto the shoreline, and heavy sleds were now lashed to the jetty instead of boats. The snow sat two feet deep, and the going was slow, but at last we hitched up outside the trench and walls encircling the mont. Braziers burned along the battlements, cross-bowmen with quarrels dipped in pitch stood the watch. My heart lifted to see it – not a muddy village with a palisade of twigs, nor a gutted monastery with corpses on the walls. But the first true sanctuary we'd found since we left Sūdhaem.

'"Hold!" cried a voice from above the gates. "Who goes?"

'She was a stout Nordish lass, dark of hair and pale of skin. She watched as I pulled the glove off my left hand with my teeth, held my palm up in the freezing air.

'"A friend," I called.

'The lass looked me over, scowling. "If you knew our capitaine, Frère, you'd know how little weight that star holds beyond these walls. No friend of Aveléne bears it."

'"I know your capitaine, mademoiselle," I replied. "Better than most. I pray you run now, and bring news that Gabriel de León is come to see him."

'"The Black Lion . . ." someone whispered.

'The watchlass looked me over, growled to the boy beside her. "Run, Victor."

'We stood in the freezing cold below the walls, Dior shivering on my shoulder, my breath frozen at my lips. I was relieved beyond measure to be here, but as I looked at the youngsters along the battlements, my guilt gnawed me to see it – this tiny spark of light to which we'd brought such danger. I could only hope my friends would understand the peril we faced, and why I'd dragged it to their door.

'Truthfully, we had nowhere else to go.

'After an age, I heard metal on metal, a dim cry. And with the splintering of ice upon frozen hinges, the drawbridge lowered. I saw a figure, broad-shouldered, dark-skinned, squeezing through the gates before they were barely open, and in a rush, he was running at me, his smile so bright it almost made me cry. He was older now, as we all were, flecks of grey at his temples, a few wrinkles in mahogany skin. But damned if he wasn't still as handsome as he'd been the day I walked into his armoury all those years ago.

'"*LITTLE LION!*" Baptiste roared.

'He crashed into me, knocking the breath from my lungs as he roared. And I laughed as he lifted me off the ground, howling, and Great Redeemer, the joy in his eyes was enough to break my heart. I simply held on, tight as I dared, his baritone deep in my chest as he bellowed my name, and God, try though I did, I couldn't hold back my tears.

'Baptiste let me down after an age, and he kissed me on both cheeks, bewildered. "Good God Almighty," he breathed. "I never thought to see you again, brother."

'"Nor I you," I grinned. "But never in my life have I been happier to be wrong."

'"Admitting you were mistaken?" came a voice. "Well, that's a first, sure and true."

'I looked beyond Baptiste's shoulder, and saw him striding across the drawbridge towards me. As princely as he'd ever been: long golden hair swept back from his scarred brow and cheek, his jaw set, his features proud. But his eyes were tempered with wisdom now, shining with tears as he opened his arms.

'"Fairdawning, Peasant," Aaron grinned.

'"Godmorrow, Lordling," I laughed.

'And he threw his arms around my shoulders and dragged me into an embrace, and all the years between us were nothing then. We were but boys again, paleblood born, brothers-in-arms, who'd stood side by side and stared into the face of hell together. Hard as iron. Strong as silversteel. Still unconquered.

'"It's so fucking good to see you, brother," I whispered.

'"And you, brother," Aaron breathed, his voice breaking.

'I grabbed his cheeks, pressed our foreheads together. And at last, reluctantly, he broke from my embrace. "Last we heard, you were down in Sūdhaem with your wife and girl. What in God's name brings you back here, Gabe?"

'"We need your help, brother." I looked to Dior behind me, huddled against the chill in her lordling's coat. "She needs your help."

'Baptiste raised one heavy brow. "She?"

'Dior gave a graceful curtsey, like a lady in the Emperor's court.

'"Best fetch a few bottles," I told them. "We've much to talk about."'

✦ XIV ✦
CHÂTEAU AVELÉNE

'"I SWEAR BY the Almighty, Mothermaid, and all Seven Martyrs," Aaron sighed, "I've never heard a tale half so strange as this."

'"The Holy Grail of San Michon," Baptiste breathed, making the sign of the wheel.

'Aaron stood beside a roaring hearth, staring at Dior with curious eyes. Baptiste was likewise studying the girl, firelight gleaming on dark skin. The pair had brought us through the gates without question, ushering us up the mont to their crumbling keep, and we were now seated in a great stone hall. Threadbare tapestries hung on the walls beside a grand map of the empire. Regions fallen to the coldbloods were marked – by Aaron's hand, no doubt – bears to the west, snakes and wolves to the south, and to the north and east, the white ravens of the Blood Voss, sweeping ever closer to the capital, Augustin.

'Château Aveléne was old, her stone cracked and her halls draughty, but good God, it was a welcome change from the weald. We'd been brought drink, fresh food – real, actual *meat,* no less – and Aaron and Baptiste had listened intently as I told our tale.

'They looked well, my old brothers. Aveléne had been near a ruin when they settled here years ago, but they'd reclaimed it from the hands of time, and now it stood like a lighthouse in an ocean of darkness. The bailey had been full of folk as we'd been ushered inside, not just soldiers, but women and children – familles, carving out a little life beside this burning hearth. In truth, it was a marvel to see.

'Baptiste was still hard as nails – he'd obviously kept up his smithing in the years we'd been apart. He'd cropped off his hair, stubble across his scalp now, salt and pepper at his temples. He wore old dark leathers trimmed with pale fur, hands still broad and callused from his hammer.

'Aaron's hair was longer, and he'd grown a short beard, trimmed razor sharp. He still wore lordling's attire: a fine frockcoat in the emerald green of his famille and a cloak of grey fox. If the cloth was old, a few buttons missing, he still cut the noblest sort of pose. And though his face was still scarred from the Wraith in Red's claws, though this castle was not so fine as the ancestral keep at Coste, my brother still stood proud as ever he'd been.

'"The tale strikes me just as strange as you," I told them, swallowing another mouthful of vodka. "And I'm living it. But on my life, on my *name*, I've seen it with my own eyes. Dior's blood turning vampires to pillars of flame. Bringing back men from the verge of death. And the Forever King believes it too. Hard enough to set his son on our tail."

'"The Beast of Vellene," Aaron murmured. "Laure's baby brother."

'"He must be across the Volta by now." I nodded to the map upon the wall. "I know not if he'll find us here, but he's been at us like a damned hound up to this point."

'"There's something in my blood," Dior said quietly. "It draws them, like beggars to silver. It happened near Lashaame and Dhahaeth. Again at Winfael, and all the way through Ossway. Wherever we are, coldbloods seem to find us."

'Aaron stared at the map with one brow raised, sipping from his iron goblet. Baptiste sighed heavy, gentle eyes on Dior. "What does the Beast want with you, mademoiselle? Why does Fabién Voss care for you at all?"

'"I don't know." She swallowed, looking at her scarred hands. "Danton said something about a black crown. That even the Forever King would do homage before me."

'"Lies drip from the tongues of the Dead like honey. We can put stock in nothing he's told you." Aaron met my eyes, firelight reflected in his own. "What of this masked one who hunts you? Liathe, you said? I've not heard the name before."

'"Nor I. But she's powerful, and has gifts of the blood I've never seen." I shook my head. "I don't know her game. But she and Danton seem at odds. Both want Dior alive, and *neither* can be trusted. We need to lure the Beast in, put him in his grave, then get Dior to San Michon before more enemies descend."

'"I'm surprised you put any trust in the Ordo Argent, brother," Aaron said, watching me carefully. "After all they did to you and Astrid."

'"How is your lioness, brother?" Baptiste asked, sparing me a smile. "And your cub? She must be a proper little dame by now."

"'Almost.' I smiled, water-thin. "She's eleven."

"'Give her a kiss from Uncle Baptiste when you see her, eh?'"

"'I know the Order didn't treat Gabriel fair," Dior interrupted. "But Sister Chloe believed the answer to daysdeath was inside those walls. She *died* for that belief, and not alone. Rafa, Bellamy, Saoirse, Phoebe – I owe it to all of them to see this through."

"'Poor Sister Chloe," Baptiste murmured, looking into his glass.

'Aaron nodded, making the sign of the wheel. "I was ever fond of her."

'Dior chewed her lip, looking to my old friends. "Listen, I'd no idea Gabriel was going to bring me to a place like this. We had nowhere else to go. But still, you've every apology I can muster for putting all this on your shoulders. I'm sorry for—"

"'No apologies, Mlle Lachance," Aaron replied. "I trust Gabriel de León with my life. If he vows you're a cause worth fighting for, then fight we shall, and with all heaven's grace."

"'I don't want anyone else dying for me . . .'"

"'A good thing we've no plans to." The Lord of Aveléne drew up his sleeves, and I saw the silver tattooed there, the story of his youth and faith and fire still etched upon his skin. "I know it doesn't look much, but if the Beast of Vellene thinks he'll storm this castle with a few rotten mongrels, he's in for a reckoning, sure and true."

"'God is on our side, mademoiselle." Baptiste smiled, squeezing Dior's hand. "And a few of my own innovations besides. I'll show you before mass, if you like?"

"'Mass?' I frowned, pouring another cup.

"'It's prièdi, brother." Aaron scratched his neat beard, thoughtful, looking to Baptiste. "And after that, a feast, I think. What say you, love?"

'Baptiste slammed a fist on the table, making the goblets jump. "A grand idea!"

'Dior frowned. "I don't want to put you to any trouble . . .'"

'Nonsense!" the blackthumb bellowed. "Too long has it been since we had an excuse for song and laughter. And in nights dark as these, who knows when we'll have occasion again? A feast, Mlle Lachance! We insist! To embrace old friends, and welcome new."

"'We may not have an emperor's larder." Aaron smiled to me. "But I'll wager our fare is a damn sight better than this bastard's cookery."

"'Here now,' I growled. "I'm not that bad."

"'He *does* try," Dior sighed. "But his mushroom ragout . . . isn't the best."

"'If you think that's bad, you should try his trailbread," Aaron laughed. "Old Master Greyhand almost wrote to the Pontifex to have it declared a crime against God."

"'Fuck yourselves," I chuckled. "All of you. Treacherous dogs."

'Baptiste grinned and slapped my back, and I couldn't help but stand and embrace him once more. I'd no ken just how much I'd missed these men, this brotherhood, and the thought that they'd put all they had on the line simply because I asked them . . . God help me if I almost didn't weep again, then and there.

'Baptiste led us on a tour of the château as promised, and I could see he and Aaron hadn't been idle. Aveléne had been impressive when Astrid and I first visited, but in the decade past, Aaron and Baptiste had turned the old ruin into a fortress. Beyond the walls around the mont's base, only a single winding road led to the castle gates. If pressed, the folk from the town below could fall back inside the keep, and Baptiste's grand design.

"'Engineering works all along the battlements," he said proudly, striding the walls with one hand entwined with Aaron's. "Fire throwers and ballista, barrels full of coal. We've a chymical still where the old stables used to be, churning out wood alcohol pure enough to burn like tinder." He glanced to me. "I *don't* recommend you drink it, mon ami."

'I winced, sipping from my new flask. "Couldn't be worse than this vodka."

"'It'll send you blind, Gabe. And mad."

"'As I say . . ."

"'We've a hundred brave warriors," Aaron continued, leading us through the crowded bailey, the song of soldier and steel. "Well trained, well armed. We have scouts afield, so we'll spot any army long before they arrive. Eyes to see and fangs to bite."

"'I could use a few phials, if you've spare," I said softly.

"'No fear. We've a goodly stash." Aaron nodded, patting my arm. "Not the finest quality, but wretched often wander this way, and I still enjoy the H—"

"'Oh, Mothermaid, they're *beautiful!*"

'Dior ran across the bailey to a broad covered pen. Inside were more than two dozen dogs – stout and hardy Nordlund hounds with thick fur, grey and mottled, and bright blue eyes. Dior knelt beside their pen, and the big dogs sniffed her hands, licked her face as she grinned in delight. "I've never seen so many, so big!"

"'We've been breeding them a while now," Baptiste smiled. "We use them for sledding on the river when it freezes over. Trade runs down to Beaufort, so we're not cut off come the winter snows."

'"Could you use them to get to San Michon?" the girl asked.

'Aaron and Baptiste exchanged a glance, and the blackthumb rubbed his chin. "We've not much occasion to visit there, chérie. The monastery still stands – the Forever King took one look at it and decided it wasn't worth besieging. Fabién's eye has ever been on the east, and Augustin. The silver-saints guard our north flank, and for that we give thanks. But Aaron and I have no desire to eat at a table where we're unwelcome."

'I shook my head, still angry for them after all these years. Aaron was one of the finest initiates that Order ever saw. Baptiste their greatest smith. I looked at what these two had built here, at the dark closing in all around us, and I marvelled San Michon had ever turned their backs on these men. And of all things, over love.

'We meandered on, Aaron's arm around Baptiste's waist as the blackthumb proudly showed me his forge and a small glassworks beside it. We arrived at a long storehouse laden with supplies: dried foodstocks, large barrels of vodka and wood alcohol from their distillery, smaller barrels marked with black crosses. Dior finally finished fussing with the dogs, returned to my side. Looking about the storehouse, she wrinkled her nose.

'". . . What's that smell?"

'"Yellowwater and nightsoil." Aaron pointed to a wooden shed across from the dog pens. "We farm that too."

'The girl looked at Aaron as if he were moonstouched. "You're farming piss and shit."

'"For the salpêtre," I realized.

'Aaron nodded, drumming his fingers on the stack of smaller barrels. "Old Seraph Talon's chymistrie lessons weren't wasted on me, brother. We've sulphur from the mines near Beaufort. And charcoal aplenty."

'Dior simply looked baffled, but I found myself grinning. Looking closer at the smaller barrels, I realized they weren't marked with crosses, but with the twin scythes of Mahné, the Angel of Death. "You cheeky bastards are making your own black ignis."

'"For years now." Aaron took in the château with a sweep of his hand: the armed soldiers, the engineering works, the baying dogs, the good, thick stone. "As I say, woe betide our Prince of Forever if he seeks to ruck up these skirts."

'I looked about the town, breathing the smoke, listening to the laughter and bustle, the hymn of metal on metal, and I allowed myself a small smile.

It'd been a bloody journey to Aveléne, sure and true. And it was still a good trek up the Mère to San Michon. But it seemed we'd found a kind of sanctuary. Here at last, we might finally be safe.'

The Last Silversaint leaned back and took a long pull from his bottle of wine.

The historian continued writing in his book.

'You should have fucking known better?' Jean-François murmured.

Gabriel sighed. 'I should've fucking known better.'

✦ XV ✦

SUNSHINE AND POURING RAIN

'EVERY WOBBLY CHAIR and crooked table in the mont had been dragged into the hall for the feast. Piecemeal utensils laid on patchwork tablecloths. Cracked crockery and mismatched tankards. Save the sorry guards upon the walls, most of Aveléne turned out that night.

'I could see familles in the hall, little children, even a few newborn babes, and again, I was stricken with the thought that I'd brought evil to this door. But once the meal began, I forgot the taste of guilt a moment and simply let myself breathe. As Baptiste had said, there was little cause for celebration those nights, and though folk had no clue as to why, still they came, feasting on rabbit stew, mountains of button mushrooms, and hot potato bread. I knew not the secret, but whoever worked the keep's kitchens was a sorcerer – I even went back for a second helping of spuds.

'A trio of minstrels began belting out merry tunes, and the floor was cleared for dancing. Dior sat at my right side, her plate empty, her belly full. Some poor sod was busy trying to clean the bloodstains out of the clothes I'd bought her, and Dior had been offered a dress to wear. But instead, she'd borrowed an old frockcoat from Aaron. That alone told me that for all the warmth and merriment, she was still ill at ease. Dior wore that coat like armour, hair dragged down over her face. She was also well into her third glass of Baptiste's homebrew vodka.

'"Go easy on that stuff," I warned. "It's got a kick like a lovesick mule."

'"I like mules," the girl smirked.

'"Fine, don't blame me if your head's splitting come the dawn."

'"Ariiiiiight, old man," she sang, flipping me the Fathers.

'"I keep telling you, I'm only thirty-two."

"'Could've fooled me with that beard, Grandpapa."

'I scowled, scruffing at my road whiskers. "I told you, I lost my razor."

"'Well, find another, you look like a robber's dog." She raised her cup and grinned. "Would your wife let you get away with a monstrosity like that?"

"'No, Astrid hated it," I smiled. "She used to call my moustache a heresy."

'Dior screwed up her nose. "You had a moustache?"

"'Not after she called it *that*."

'Dior laughed as I poured myself another glass.

"'That was one of my wife's many talents, see. She always knew just the right thing to say to get her way. That woman had me wrapped around her little finger, and it only got worse when Patience learned how to do it, too. She took after her mother, that one, sure and true. One look into those eyes, and I'd melt like springtime snow."

'I laughed to myself, shaking my head. But as I knocked back another cup, I saw Dior was sucking her lip, looking at me twice-strangely.

"'. . . What?"

"'Might I beg this dance, mademoiselle?"

'The pair of us broke our staring contest as Baptiste swept into a low bow before us. Dior blinked at the smithy, rubbing at the bruises on her face. ". . . Me?"

"'If it does not offend?" The smith gifted the girl a smile that would've melted the Mère. "My heart belongs to another, Mlle Lachance. But he's not the jealous sort. And no flower so divine should be left to wilt in the corner."

'Baptiste's dark eyes sparkled with gleeful mischief as he proffered his hand. The crowd cheered as the music about us shifted pitch, the minstrels quickened their pace. But Dior glanced to me and shook her head. "Perhaps later."

"'You're certain?" the big man asked, astounded his smile had failed.

"'Oui," she nodded. "Merci, Baptiste. Later, I promise."

"'As you like it, mademoiselle. But I shall hold you to that vow." The blackthumb swept into another bow and retired. I saw him grab another lass's hand, waving to Aaron as he swept her out onto the floor. The dancers swayed and seethed across the boards, all the room clapping in time.

"'You don't like to dance?" I asked Dior.

"'I don't know how," she admitted. "Not many galas in the gutters of Lashaame."

"'I'll teach you, then," I declared, holding out my hand. "It'll be good practice."

'"Practice for what?"

'"At root, dancing and swordplay are one and the same."

'Dior blinked as slow realization dawned. She glanced down to Ashdrinker on my hip, and she whooped, planting a swift kiss on my cheek.

'"You're a good man, Gabriel de León."

'"I'm a bastard is what I am. I'm just your kind of bastard."

'We stepped out onto the floor together, fumbling through our first steps, the room about us awhirl. And though she was three cups in, still Dior followed with an innate rhythm that told me she might one day be a fine sort of blade. She trod on my feet a few times, of course, but her laughter was brighter than the music around us, and to see her happy made me happy in turn. I couldn't remember the last time I'd laughed as hard as I did that night, and for a while, it was enough. But the whole time, it was growing in me – a shadowed melancholy that deepened with every cup I snatched from a passing tray, every burning mouthful I swallowed in my quest to drown it.

'And so it was, when Baptiste returned and asked Dior to dance again, I gratefully made my escape. I'd had too much by then, and I knew with a few more, I'd be stumbling. The smiling faces about me seemed like death masques now, the music a dirge, and as the minstrels broke into a merry jig and all the crowd began stamping in time, I realized there was nowhere on earth I wanted less to be. Dior howled as she twirled arm in arm with Baptiste, spinning and stumbling through the throng, and I snatched a bottle from a table and pushed through the great wooden doors, out into the lonely chill.

'The wind made my eyes water as I trudged the cobbled path, shoulders hunched for warmth. I knew where I was headed, walking without thought, tugging another swallow from the bottle as it rose up before me like a lodestone. I could see candlelight through stained glass, smell the votive incense, hear echoes of the mass long sung.

'The Chapel of Aveléne.

'It was a tiny affair, nothing so grand as the Cathedral of San Michon. Still, it had seemed a palace not so long ago. And as I stepped inside that wintersdeep night, I saw myself as I'd been all those years past. Walking on colt's legs through the dawndoors, Aaron at my side, down to the altar and the angel waiting there. She'd stood in a beam of dimmest daylight, hands over her belly, and I know it sounds clichéd, but she'd been *aglow* with it. The Order had cast us out like bones and chaff, and I should've been ashamed. But walking to Astrid's side that day, promising to be with her forever, I knew only love. Purest love.

'I stood now in that empty church more than a decade later, and all was cold and silent. A wheel of rowan wood still hung above the altar, a carving of the Redeemer lashed upon it, spinning gently in the wind as the doors creaked open behind me. I took another pull from the bottle, swaying on my feet. I knew I'd be a sorry bastard come the morrow.

'"Fairdawning, Aaron," I called.

'"Godmorrow, brother," he replied.

'I could feel him standing beside me now, as he'd done on that happiest of days, carrying the troth rings Baptiste had forged with his own hands. I offered Aaron the bottle, and he took it, drinking from the neck. We stood side by side, and I stared up at the wheel spinning over our heads, slowly shaking mine.

'"Did that ever strike you as odd?"

'"I'm not sure what you mean."

'"The wheel." I nodded to it. "Why they chose *that* as the symbol for the One Faith."

'"It's a symbol of the Redeemer's sacrifice. The offering that laid the foundation for His Church on this earth, and our salvation. *By this blood, shall they have life eternal.*"

'"But doesn't it strike you as a little morbid? Seems to me maybe they should've found something that celebrated the days he *lived*. The words he *said*. Instead, the symbol of his Church is the thing that killed him." I shook my head. "Always struck me as strange."

'Aaron handed me back the bottle. "Are you aright, Gabe?"

'I looked at him then. My friend. My brother. I'd never visited the ruins of Coste, but I'd heard the tales of what Voss had done to the city after he crossed the Bay of Tears. I'd always wondered if Aaron wished he'd been there. Falling into ruin along with his famille before the advance of the Forever King. And I sighed, staring up at the Redeemer again.

'"How can you still pray to this bastard, Aaron?"

'"He is my God. All I have, I owe to him."

'"All you have?" I scoffed. "They took *everything* from you. They cast you out of the Order you'd devoted your life to. You stood in defence of this empire and his Church, and the men of both were set to flay the skin off your back for who you loved. Because of a few words in some dusty fucking book. All you are is what God made you to be, and yet they turned on you for it. How can you pray to him after that?"

'"It's as you said, brother. It was *men* who did that to Baptiste and me. Not God."

"'But he allowed it to happen. *All on earth below and hea'en above is the work of my hand. And all the work of my hand is in accord with my plan.*"

'Aaron gazed at the Redeemer above us, shaking his head.

"'You're looking at it wrong, Gabe," he sighed. "God may have sent the storm, but he gave me arms to swim for shore. He might bring the winter snows, but he gave us hands to light the flame. You see the suffering all around you but not the joy right beside you, and you curse him for the worst but don't thank him for the best. What the hell do you want from him?" Aaron looked to me, searching my eyes. "If Baptiste and I had never been cast out of the Order, we'd not have been here all those years ago when you and Astrid came pounding on our gate. And I'd not have been standing here beside you when you swore your love for that woman, nor had the chance to see you weep as you held that baby girl in your arms. If we'd stayed in San Michon, we'd not have been here to answer when you and Dior came stumbling in out of the snow today. And if that girl is the answer to ending all this suffering, isn't *my* suffering worth that?"

"'You're telling me there was no other way to get Dior where she needed to be?"

"'I'm telling you I've made my peace with him. You only appreciate the sunshine after you've stood in the pouring rain. Everything happens for a reason, Gabe."

"'Bullshit!" I spat, rage rising. "This isn't about reason, it's about *retribution*, Aaron! He sets you up to fail, and when you break his damned rules, he punishes you for it. He makes you want, and when you take, he takes it all away. What kind of sick fuck does that?"

"'Such is the price of sin, Gabe."

"'If it's sin, how can goodness come of it? And who'd let that goodness flower a moment only to tear it out of the earth? A sadist! A blacksmith who blames his own blade! What kind of bastard punishes the people you love in order to punish you?"

'I flung the bottle, the glass shattering on the Redeemer's wheel. One of the stays came loose, and the wheel dropped, twisting lopsided as I spat in fury.

"'No fucking brother of mine!"

'Aaron looked at me carefully, a scowl on that handsome brow. "Are we talking about me and Baptiste now? Or are we talking about *you*?"

'I made no reply, staring at that holy fool spinning above us.

"'. . . Where are Astrid and Patience, Gabriel?"

"'Waiting for me.'"

"'At home?'"

"'Where else would they be?'"

"'If they're at home, why are you here?'"

"'I know a king who needs killing.'"

"'. . . Voss?'"

"'Voss,' I hissed, the name like poison on my tongue. "Once Dior is in San Michon, I head east to take that whoreson's head. To end this once and for all."

'Aaron stepped between me and the wheel so that I'd be forced to meet his eyes. "Gabe, Fabién Voss sits at the heart of a legion ten thousand strong. The greatest armies and generals in the empire have fallen back or simply fallen before him. No man of woman born can slay the Forever King. You know this. It's madness. It's *suicide* even to try."

"'And yet, here I am.'"

"'. . . Is that what you want? To die? What about your famille?'" He reached for my arm, seizing tight. "Gabriel, look at me. Where are they? Why did you leave them?"

"'Let it alone, brother,'" I growled.

"'Gabe—'"

"'*Let it alone!*'" I bellowed, slapping his hand away. Grabbing his coat, I slammed him against the altar, my face inches from his. "You want to huddle here in your crumbling halls until the end comes, so be it! You want to waste your life praying to a God who doesn't care, as you like it! But I'll not hide in the dark for fear of sleep, nor sing the praise of a bastard who'd call himself Lord of an earth such as this! By my hand, Fabién Voss will *die*! By my blood, by my soul – *not* by your fucking God – I vow it!"

"'I love you, Gabriel,'" Aaron said low, deadly. "But *take your hands off me.*"

'That predator's gleam, that old gift of the Ilon stirring in his veins. Paleblood, through and through. And I let him go, ashamed at myself, at all I was and had become. I couldn't bear to look at him, staring at my hands instead as I whispered.

"'Forgive me.'"

"'Brother, there is nothing to forgive,'" he said, putting his hand on my shoulder. "I know you speak from hurt, and though I fear the cause, I'll not add to it by asking for its name. I'll not tell you what to believe, either. Each man's heart is his own, and in the end, only he has the filling of it. But I tell you this, and if never you have listened to me before, by all the love you bear for me, I beg you listen now. Because I see a shadow on you, brother. And I am *afraid*."

'He took my hand, squeezing tight as he searched my eyes.

'"It matters not what you hold faith in. But you must hold faith in *something*."

'I met his gaze, the truth fighting behind my teeth.

'To speak it would make it real.

'To speak it would be to live it again.

'"The Worst Day," I whispered.

'A chill clanging split the air, brittle and sharp, metal on metal. The spell between us broke, Aaron's pupils dilating as the song grew more fevered. And through the rushing in my ears, the echo of my brother's words, I realized at last what I was hearing.

'Aaron looked to me, jaw clenched. "Alarm bells."

'I glanced to the Redeemer hanging on his lopsided wheel, and then to the night awaiting us outside. Hissing through sharpening teeth.

'"Danton."'

LORD OF CARRION

'THE GREAT HALL was emptying as Aaron and I rushed from the chapel. The merrymakers, the minstrels, young and old – all were making their way through the torchlit dark to the château gates. I saw Baptiste among the throng, and Aaron and I pushed our way to his side. Men and women were gathering arms, the bells still ringing on the outer walls, a great multitude now trekking down the winding road to the mont's base. I looked for Dior among them, even calling her name, but I couldn't see her anywhere.

'We reached the outer walls of Aveléne, and I followed Aaron up onto the battlements. The bells ceased their ringing as he and Baptiste arrived. Watchmen saluted the pair briskly, nodding, "Capitaine." I could see their loyalty to Aaron was fierce and true, that they loved him to a man, no matter who he loved in his turn. But I could also feel a sliver of fear among them. And squinting through the bitter-bleak snows to the edge of the torchlight off Aveléne's walls, I could find no way to fault them.

'The Beast of Vellene stood in the road. He was clothed all in black, his duellist's cloak whipping about him in a wind that seemed to moan all the louder as it touched him. His eyes were darker than the night above, his skin so pale it gleamed like pearl. Any who looked on him, prince or pauper or poet, would know him for what he was: a lord of carrion, heavy with centuries, crowned with menace and malice. And the sight of him cleaved all but the boldest heart with despair.

'Danton stepped forward, his flint-black gaze roaming the walls. Men quailed as he looked upon them, women trembled, the chill of him like a knife in their minds. His eyes fell on me, and a smile, cold and pale and sharp, curled his ruby lips.

'"Where be the lord of this . . . hovel?" he asked. "I would treat with him."

'Aaron stepped forward, golden hair blowing in the wind. "I am he."

'Danton's gaze fell on my friend, and I saw Aaron grit his teeth, fangs bared. I felt the air crackling between them; a battle of wills, ancien versus paleblood born. And at the last, I saw Danton's smile grow sour.

'"Who art thou, mortal?"

'Aaron took off his glove, held up the sevenstar on his palm, now burning with a pale and fierce light. "A mortal, oui," he answered. "But no mortal's son. My name is Aaron de Coste, son of House Coste and the Blood Ilon, and my mind is not yours for the plundering. I have been slaying your kind since I was but a boy, and I am a boy no longer. Now speak your piece and be done, vampire. My dinner is getting cold."

'"De Coste?" Danton gave a small bow. "Well met, monsieur. 'Tis rare to find folk of breeding so far west these nights. Please accept my condolences upon the fall of thy home, thy famille, thy legacy entire."

'"*This* is my famille," Aaron said, waving to folk on the walls. "And my home. You come to its gate with empty hands and liar's tongue. What do you want, Voss?"

'"Dior Lachance."

'"Then I fear you've come a long way for a longer wait." Aaron placed one hand on the hilt of his sword. "Like all within these walls, the girl is under my protection."

'"Girl?" Realization dawned, and a flicker of dark delight glittered in Danton's eyes as he glanced at me. "Oh, de León, thou art not destined to lose an—"

'"Speak not to him," Aaron spat. "You treat with me. If you call this display of beggary *treating*, that is."

'"Beggar thou wouldst name me?"

'"Beggar?" Aaron shook his head. "No. *Louse*, I name you. *Worm. Leech.* A parasite, grown fat and foolish enough to stand alone before my walls and beg anything of me. I was there at the Twins the day your sister died, Voss. I heard the music of her screams. And I've a will now, to see if I can make you sing as sweet."

'Aaron drew his sword – that same beautiful silversteel blade he'd carried through his apprenticeship in San Michon, the Angel Mahné on the hilt, blessed scripture down the blade. Beside him, Baptiste hefted his silversteel warhammer, and all around him, the men and women of Aveléne drew steel, set arrow to torch, raised wheellock guns.

'"Be off, maggot," Aaron growled. "Afore I set my dogs on you."

'Danton smiled, bleak and empty.

'"Call thy dogs," he said. "They can feast upon thy corpses."

'The dark behind Danton moved, and I felt my belly turn. I saw them coalescing from the snows behind the Beast, like darker shadows in his wake. Cold skin and colder hearts. Faces white as bone and beautiful as a dreamless sleep, clothed in all night's raiment. Their eyes were keen and merciless, and they wore fear like cloaks, the terror of them washing over the walls in a fog. A tall, dead-eyed brute. A slender woman with wheat-gold hair and blood-red eyes. A boy, not more than ten when he died. Near a dozen in total, called by the Beast from across the Nordlund no doubt – children, grandchildren, cousins. Ironhearts, all.

'"Highbloods," Baptiste breathed.

'Behind them came a rabble. Rotten and hollow-eyed. A multitude of wretched, slaved to the highbloods' will. More than I'd seen since my days of silver. There were soldiers among them, clad in the Emperor's colours – the remnants of cadres and cohorts slain in the wars. But there were plain folk too, men and women, children and elders, all dragged away from the bright shores of heaven and back to this hell on earth.

'Hundreds upon hundreds of them.

'"Such a force . . ." someone whispered.

'Danton stood now in the falling snows, his dark majesty unveiled. He seemed to swell in stature; once a single shadow at the edge of the torchlight, now the vanguard of a darkness set to swallow that light whole. His gaze roamed the walls, slow, piercing, those men and women who had but a moment ago stood fierce and tall as their capitaine roared like a lion. But now, as those eyes fell upon them, as the dark mind behind them pierced their own, every one quavered at the horror of him.

'"I see thee all. I know thy hearts. I know thy sins." Danton's eyes drifted back to Aaron, glittering and hard. "But more, I know thy strength. There is no preparation beyond those walls now hidden from me. If thou wouldst stand against me, Aaron de Coste, thou shalt fall. As the city of thy forebears did. As thy once-noble line did. And for the vengeance of my sister beloved, I shall mete like suffering from thee. I shall slay thy flock, one and all. I shall make their children watch as I feed them to the teeth behind me. I shall make castrati of their sons, I shall gut their parents like hogs, I shall build mountains of their babies' bones. But their daughters . . ."

'He looked to the wall once more, to the folk who stood shivering in his chill.

'"Them, I shall loose into the snow and the dark. One by one. And when I find them, each agony they endure shall upon thy heads be. I shall make thy daughters *bleed*, Avelène. I shall gift them a suffering from which God and angels shall avert their gaze. Or . . ."'

'The shadow around Danton diminished, his smile returned, sly and red.

'"Or, thou canst give me what I seek. One little girl seems not so small a price? One tiny life, for the life of every man, woman, and child beyond those walls? For in the end, what is Dior Lachance to thee, Avelène? Save a noose about thy neck, tightening?"'

'I heard a commotion, a murmuring along the battlements. And looking behind us, down to the cobbles below, I saw Dior now standing in the street. The stares of the city's folk were fixed upon her, pale and slender, all alone among them. But she stood with eyes on the gates, listening to the voice beyond.

'"I feel thee!" Danton roared out in the dark. "I feel thee in their minds, girl! Shall their lives pay the forfeit of thy courage? Shall their blood stain thy hands like thy Saoirse? Thy Bellamy? Thy Rafa? I shall take thee anyway, girl! I am a Prince of Forever, and forever shall I hunt thee! Ask thy dear Gabriel what in the end that means!"'

'I drew Ashdrinker from her sheath, roaring into the wind.

'"You don't get to bleat about courage and threaten children in the same breath, *coward*! And you set one foot inside this city, I'll teach you how short forever can be!"'

'Danton looked along the walls, shaking his head sadly.

'"Oh, de León. I will not need to set foot in there at all."'

'He raised his voice, calling over the clawing wind.

'"One night I gift thee, Avelène! Let it not be said Danton Voss is without mercy. Amorrow shall I return with all hell's fury in my wake! If thou wouldst still deny me my prize, I shall make red slaughter of thee all! And those who rise thereafter? Dogs shalt thou be! Fed only the dregs of carcasses long rotten, lower than worms, for all eternity!"'

'He looked to me, black eyes like yawning pits in his skull.

'"For now, behold what becomes of those who defy me."'

'One of the highbloods came forth – the tall Nordlund brute with thick dark hair, carrying a figure over his shoulder. It was wrapped in homespun cloth, bound in chains, bloodstained and filthy. I knew who it was before the sackcloth was torn from his face, before his body was thrown into the snow, still wrapped in irons, tongue blackened and long fangs glinting as he opened his rotten mouth and moaned.

'"Rafa . . ." I whispered.

'The old priest lay in the grey, gabbling nonsense as Danton pressed his boot to the back of his head and forced it down into the snow. "In one night shall I return, Aveléne. Consider carefully, if thou wouldst live to see nights thereafter."

'He stepped back, back into the shadows at the torchlight's shivering edge. The dark seemed to swell, reaching out and swallowing him whole. The highbloods slunk back after him, hungry eyes fixed upon the walls. I heard the multitude of wretched retreating with their masters, leaving only one behind, wrapped in chains, staring up with soulless eyes at the folk on the walls and screaming in mindless hunger.

'"Oh, God . . ."

'I turned and saw Dior behind me, looking with horror at the fallen priest.

'"Oh, Rafa . . ."

'The old man howled, thrashing against the chains they'd wrapped him in. It had been a day or two before he Became, by the look of him – the intellect, the wit, the will, gone the way of all flesh. Only the hunger remained now. The hunger and the hate, shining in his gaze as it roamed the walls, falling at last on Dior and me. He roared again, too weak and starving to break his bonds. But I knew, and she knew it, too – if there were no chains or steel or walls between us, he'd drink us both to dying.

'"We can't leave him like that," Dior whispered.

'She looked down to the old man, twisting and howling in the snow. Tears shone on her cheeks as she turned to me, a silent plea in her eyes. And unable to stand it any longer, I snatched a bow from the watchman beside me, lit one of his tallow arrows in the brazier, drew the string back to my lips. Poor Rafa looked to me, and beyond the madness and murder in his eyes, I like to think that whatever was left of him inside might have nodded, might have begged me, do it, *do it*.

'"Better to be a bastard than a fool," I whispered.

'The arrow flew true. The flames spread on those bloodstained robes, the undying flesh beyond. I gave the bow back to its owner, took Dior's hand to draw her away from the sight. But she forced herself to stay, to watch, to breathe the smoke and bear witness to Rafa's end. And when it was over, when naught but ashes remained, she looked to the folk around her. Every man and woman on those walls, gazing now to her, weighing her in their minds. They knew nothing of what she was, what she *could* be, only that she and I had brought this peril to their door.

'Aaron caught my eye, glanced back up the hill.

'"Perhaps you two had best await us in the keep, brother."

'I nodded. "Come along, Dior."

'She looked at me as I squeezed her hand, tears for poor Rafa shining in her eyes. And together, we walked through the murmuring crowd, back up to that old château and whatever safety now lay within. Behind us, the priest's remains smouldered in the snow, the smoke rising slow towards the sky. But, as always, heaven was silent.

'And beyond the scent of char and ashes, I caught it then.

'Just a whisper on the wind that set my heart racing.

'The scent of death.

'Death and silverbell.'

✦ XVII ✦
A SHOULDER TO CRY ON

"'YOUR HEAD IS so far up your arse, that lump in your throat must be your fucking nose.'

"'You can't leave, Dior.'

"'Well, I sure as hell can't stay, Gabriel!'

'We were stood in my bedchamber, glowering at each other. A fire was blazing in the hearth, the curtains open to the night outside. Through the window, I could see the chapel in the courtyard where I'd been wed, and beyond, braziers burning on the walls of Aveléne, illuminating the brave souls standing watch. But every now and then, one would cast their gaze up towards the keep, scowling black or muttering to a comrade. I knew the words they spoke. The fear they fought. But I didn't care.

"'You leave the shelter of these walls, you're giving that sonofabitch exactly what he wants. You might as well tie a bow around your throat and deliver yourself to the Forever King!'

"'I can't ask these people to die for me, Gabe!'

"'You're not asking! Aaron's commanding! They're soldiers, that's what they do!'

"'They're not soldiers!' she shouted. 'They're fathers and mothers! Sons and daughters! You heard what Danton will do to them if they stand against him!'

"'He's saying that to get inside their heads. The Beast won't fight a battle when he can have you handed over without him risking his skin! I've been killing vampires half my life, and I tell you now, there is *no one* more afraid of dying than things who live forever!'

"'Tell that to the people who are going to die on those walls.'

"'Mighty fucking Redeemer, will you listen to me? You've seen the defences

Aaron and Baptiste have built. Every single one of those deathless bastards is shitting blood at the thought of hitting these walls. Danton wants you to blink! He wants someone to break!"

"'And who says someone won't? You think I matter more to those people than their own *children*? Who says they're not gearing up right now to give me over?"

"'Let them try,' I growled, hand on Ashdrinker's hilt. "Let them fucking *try*."

"'I am not going to hide up here like a rabbit while strangers risk their lives for me!"

"'So where will you go, then?' I demanded. "Out into the snow on foot? San Michon is two hundred miles up the Mère, and they'd run you down before you got twenty!"

"'I don't know, I didn't kill these things for a living!"

"'That's right, *I* did! And I say the safest place for you is *exactly* where you are!"

"'I won't have it! Enough blood has been spilled on my account! Saoirse, Chloe, Bel, Rafa." Her voice broke then, and Dior turned away from me, eyes on the flames. "Sweet Mothermaid . . . didn't you see what they d-did to him?"

'My voice fell, my temper with it. ". . . Of course I did."

'I looked out beyond the window, and saw a pale shadow moving in the dark. The scent of rosewater and silverbell hung in the air with my whisper.

"'It's what they do, Dior. They hurt you through the people you care about."

'I saw her outside now, waiting for me. Floating, as if submerged beneath black water, arms open wide as she trailed her fingernails across the glass. Pale as moonlight. Cold as death. No breath on the window as she drifted closer.

"'*My lion*."

'I turned my back, looking instead to the girl by the fire. "I can't have more blood on my hands, Gabriel," she declared. "I can't ask these people to die for me. I won't."

"'This is war, Dior. Peasants starve so soldiers can eat. Soldiers bleed so generals can win. Generals fall so emperors can keep their thrones. It's the way it's always been."

"'I'm not a soldier, or a general, or an emperor."

"'You're the Holy Grail of San Michon."

"'You don't even believe that! That's not what this is about, Gabe, and you know it!"

"'I know you need to grow the fuck up!" I roared. "Because if you are what Chloe believed, this is only the start of it! And it may not be just, it may not be right, but some pieces on the board just count for more than others! It's no matter how many pawns were lost when the game is done! All that matters is who fucking *won*!"

'Dior looked at me hard, firelight gleaming in her eyes.

"'I'm sure that's poor solace for the pawn's wife. Or husband."

'She glanced down at the ink on my hands, swallowing hard.

"'. . . Or father."

'I scowled at that. "What are you—"

"'I heard you and Aaron talking in the chapel." She'd stopped her pacing now, standing etched against the dancing firelight. "And I know what Danton was trying to say to you when he found out I was a girl . . ." She shook her head, tears shining in her eyes. "*Oh, Gabriel, you're not destined to lose another?*"

"'*Dead tongues heeded are Dead tongues tasted,*" I growled.

"'You told Aaron they were at home. Astrid and Patience."

"'They are."

"'Then why would you leave them?"

"'If you were eavesdropping, you already know."

"'You're going to kill the Forever King."

"'That's right."

"'But why? You left this war behind half a lifetime ago." She clenched her teeth, lips trembling. "I'm sorry, Gabriel. I truly am. But what you're doing isn't fair."

"'Fair, what's not f—"

"'I know why you want to protect me now, when you never gave a damn about me before. I know why you treat me different now you know I'm a girl." The tears were falling now, streaming down her face as she glanced to the ink below my knuckles. "And I'm sorry, but you can't ask me to do this. I'm not her. I'm not *them*. I can't fill that hole. I never will."

'My hands were fists at my sides. Her pale shadow pressed against the glass behind me. Her soft whisper inside my head.

"'*Don't listen, love . . .*"

"'I don't—"

"'You lied to Aaron," Dior said, her voice breaking. "I know what happened to them."

"'*Don't go someplace I can't follow . . .*"

'I turned back to the window, the shadow floating in the night beyond. Her skin was pale as the stars in a yesterday sky, her beauty of edgeless winters and lightless dawns, and my heart hurt to see her – that fearful kind of hurt you couldn't hope to bear, save for the emptiness it would leave if you put it behind you.

'"*Tell me you love me*," she begged.

'I turned to look at the girl, jaw clenched. "You stop this now."

'"The Worst Day," she insisted. "The day *he* found you. That's why you left home, why you've come all this way. Why you drink. Why you don't believe any more. All of it. This isn't about me, none of it is. It's about *them*, Gabe. Astrid and Patience."

'"*Promise you'll never leave me*."

'"Astrid and Patience are at home, Dior."

'"I know. I *know* they are."

'She breathed deep, tears spilling down her cheeks. Eyes that saw the hurts of the world, and a heart that wanted to fix them. But she couldn't fix this. No one could.

'"That's where you buried them, Gabriel."

'The words were a knife to my chest. I felt my teeth clench so hard I feared they'd crack. A war drum beat in my temples, heart rushing as I turned to that shadow watching me from beyond the glass. She looked at me with pleading eyes, long hair floating about her like ribbons of silk, tearing now between my fingertips.

'"*Don't*," she begged me. "*Don't let me go, love* . . ."

'The taste of betrayal was venom in my mouth, my fury white hot in my chest. I looked down to the blade at my waist, that silver dame on the crossguard. And I tore Ashdrinker from her sheath, starsteel glittering in the firelight.

'"You *told* her?"

'*Gabriel, n-never.*

'"You talk about them in the past tense, Gabe," Dior whispered. "You talk in your sleep. All the time. About that day. The Worst Day."

'"Shut up," I whispered.

'*Gabriel, p-put me down. Ye are upset, upset.*

'"Gabe, I'm sorry. I didn't mean to hurt you . . ."

'"*My lion . . . please . . .*"

'"*Shut* up."

'*Think now, what ye do. Think of what she—*

'"I hear you talking to her sometimes. I know it hel—"

'"*You promised you'd never leave me. You—*"

'"SHUT UP!"

'I roared at the top of my lungs, turning and hurling the blade through the window. The glass blew outwards, a million glittering pieces falling like snow as the sword sailed through the empty black outside. The wind blew through the shattered panes, and I slipped to my knees. Looking into the dark where she'd never been.

'Because she was at home.

'*Where else would she be?*

'I felt it rising inside me, pressing the walls of the dam I'd built. The denial, the drink, the smoke – all of it, anything to keep it at bay. But still, I stared out that broken window, that hole they'd left behind. I felt Dior kneel beside me, heedless of the broken glass as her fingers slipped into mine. My fangs had torn my lips, blood in my mouth, hair about my face as I bent double and tried to hold it inside.

'"I don't want to hurt you, Gabriel," Dior whispered. "I know what they meant to you. I can't let other people die for me because you're afraid to lose someone else you care about. I can't be what you want me to be. But I *am* your friend. And I *can* be more than just a hill to die on."

'"What else is there?" I whispered.

'"A shoulder to cry on."

'She shrugged as if it were the simplest thing in the world.

'"If you want. I'll not judge you ill for it."

'I felt the words behind my teeth. Trying in vain to swallow them.

'To speak it would make it real.

'To speak it would be to live it again.

'But still . . .

'But still.

'I spoke.'

✦ XVIII ✦
THE WORST DAY

'IT WAS AN ordinary day. I'd spent it working in the loft of the lighthouse. The brick was warm under my bare feet. The sweat cool on my skin. I could see our house below, the spire of stone it was built upon, falling down into the ocean. Patience and Astrid were feeding the chickens together. The water was almost blue. That's the awful part about it: the worst days of your life start out just like any other.

'It'd been fifteen years since the Battle of the Twins. My service in San Michon felt a lifetime ago. The war was creeping closer, year by year, but we'd gone as far south as we could. I hadn't smoked the sacrament in ten years. Despite all they'd warned me of – the thirst within, my father's curse – all of it was held in check by the bliss Astrid nightly gifted me from her veins, and in the simple joy of her arms. The Forever King's war, the things I'd been and done – it was almost far enough away to forget, and in truth, I was happy to let myself. And that's the thing that wakes me up at night, see. I should've known there'd come a reckoning.

'He told me he had forever, after all.

'I don't know how he found us. Nor how long ago he'd learned where we hid. Maybe he'd always known – allowing me a few years to taste happy, to delude myself into thinking he might forget. I know only that it was springtime when he came. The breeze off the ocean was soft and cool. The silverbell trying to bloom among the stones.

'We had a rule to always be inside by dark. *Always*. But Patience loved the scent; Astrid, too. And while my wife finished in the kitchen and I set the table for supper, Patience had gone outside to gather flowers for the centrepiece. Just for a minute. That's all it takes for your world to turn upside down, you know. A second's distraction. A single moment that haunts you every moment for the rest of your life.

'The waves were crashing on the rocks, but there were no gulls singing in the air. That was what crept on me first; a small silence, a tiny note of wrongness that planted a sliver of ice in my gut. Astrid was singing in the kitchen, and what was left of the sun was pressing dark red lips to the horizon, and I fell slowly still, listening. And that splinter of ice became a stone, sitting cold in the pit of my belly as Astrid called over the song of the sea.

'"Patience, dinner!"

'Not a sound, save shushing waves and whispering wind and the silence where the gull song should've been. And I felt it then; the dread I should've cherished all those waking years. The tiny part of me that had known, that had *always* known, bid me walk to the fireplace, to reach to the dark wooden plaque above it, to the blade I'd hung there so many years before with a prayer I'd never need draw her again.

'But as my hand closed on Ashdrinker's hilt, I heard it, quiet on the breeze. A voice soft as silverbell blooms, laced with a brittle note of fear. "Mama?"

'Astrid turned to the door. "Patience?"

'"Mama?"

'And there came a knocking, gentle as feathers upon the door. Three raps on the wood – I remember that clear as daylight: *One. Two. Three.* And I felt a heat then, like I'd not felt in years; a fire long dormant now flaring like a phoenix in the ashes of what I'd been. I looked to the ink on my hands, and the icy stone in my belly became a knife as my aegis began to glow. And our eyes met, my love's and mine, across the flagstones of the home we'd built, and in that moment, I think a part of us both knew.

'Astrid flew to the door, and I roared at her to stop, knowing in my heart she never would. And as she flung it wide to the night fallen outside, I felt him, like snow upon my skin, I saw him, like every nightmare waking, I knew him, like I knew the teeth of time and the taste of blood and the warmth of hell awaiting. Standing upon the threshold of the little home we loved, the little life we'd built: a debt long since due. A fond smile was on his lips, and his eyes were heavy-lidden coals, sharp as the sword sheathed in my hand.

'"Papa?" Patience whispered.

'"Oh, God," Astrid breathed. "No . . ."

'He stood on the cusp of night, arm about my daughter's shoulder. He held the flowers she'd picked in one pale hand, like a courter come calling. Clad in long, white, satin brocade, unblinking, unmoving, unchanged from that moment I'd first laid eyes on him so many years before. As if all the moments and miles between then and now were but a dream from which I'd finally woken.

'"*May I come in, Gabriel?*"

'"Oh no, NO!" Astrid screamed, and I lunged, stopping her from flinging herself against his stone. And I held her tight as she thrashed and roared, and the thing outside our door drew Patience closer and ran one bone-white claw down the curve of her cheek.

'"Oh, God . . ." I breathed.

'Fabién Voss looked skywards, searching all the gables of heaven. And his gaze returned to mine, and he whispered the question I've been asking ever since.

'"*Where?*"

'"Please," I begged. "Don't hurt her."

'"*Let me in,*" the vampire promised, "*and I vow I shall release her.*"

'The greatest lies are the ones we tell ourselves. The deadliest poison the one we swallow willingly. And yet sometimes we clutch at those deceits like a drowning man at straws, because the alternative is simply too awful to fathom. We believe in life after death, because oblivion is too dark an abyss to stare into. We tell ourselves our creator cares, because the thought of a maker who doesn't is too terrifying to consider. And standing there, with Astrid trembling in my arms, I convinced myself Fabién Voss spoke truth. That he was only here for me, that ma famille were blameless, that he would let them go. Because the alternative would've simply shattered me like glass to look at.

'Instead, I looked into my daughter's eyes, wide and frightened and fixed on me, her papa, her mountain, the man who would do anything, give *anything*, to keep her safe.

'"Papa?"

'"*Shhhh,*" the vampire cooed. "*Hush, child.*"

'"All will be well, love," Astrid told her. "Listen to me. All will b-be well."

'The vampire stared at me, the windows to his soul looking in on an empty room. The ink upon my skin burned with cold radiance, but his eyes were narrowed only slightly against it; the dark power within him stronger than mine. I glanced to Ashdrinker in my hand, desperate thoughts awhirl in my mind. But Voss only shifted his hand on Patience's shoulder, fingertips drifting slightly closer to her neck.

'"*May I come in, Gabriel?*"

'All that stood between us now were two words. So much power. So much peril. How many hearts have been made complete by words so small as "I do"? How many more have been shattered with a breath as tiny as "It's over"?

'Two little words.

'*You mustn't.*

'*No choice.*

'*My baby.*

'"Come in," I told him.

'He smiled. Beautiful. Terrible. And scuffing his boots politely upon the doormat Astrid had woven, the Forever King stepped across the threshold and into our home. I saw shapes behind him in the dark, other figures, half a dozen; Princes of Forever all, steeped in terror and blood. I knew their names: Alba, Alene, Kestrel, Morgane, Ettiene, Danton. But none made to step closer, hovering on the edge of night, bearing silent witness as their dread father walked slowly inside. I can't tell you what I felt to see it – that monster with my baby on its arm. So much terror and fury I could barely bring myself to speak.

'"Let her go."

'"*Soon,*" he replied.

'"If you hurt her . . ." Astrid hissed, teeth bared. "God help me . . ."

'The Forever King smiled then, waving to the dining table.

'"*I have interrupted thee at repast. Apologies, I beg. May I sit?*"

'I nodded, my hand still on Ashdrinker's hilt. Fabién moved, liquid, the preternatural grace of centuries at his call. There was nothing unconsidered about him; no wasted motion, no squandered breath. He moved like a statue come to life, every part of him bleached bone-white by the hands of time, save those eyes, black as the holes between the stars. One hand wrapped around my daughter's waist as he settled her upon his lap.

'"*Wouldst thou do me the honour of joining me, old friend?*"

'I sat opposite, tense as a bowstring. My eyes locked on his. Terror in me, then. Complete and total terror.

'Voss gazed about the room, at the roaring fire, the pots and pans, the hook where I hung my coat; these tiny fragments of our life, now so inconsequential. He took the silverbells Patience had gathered and slipped them into the vase.

'"*A bright little lair thou hast crafted thyself, I see. A pleasant clime to while away thine autumn, afore cruel winter comes.*" He glanced to Astrid, hovering beside me, anguish and horror in her eyes. "*We have travelled far to be here. My throat, I fear, is parched. Might I trouble thee, dearest madame, for a glass of wine?*"

'"We have none," Astrid replied.

'"*The Beaumont, my dearest. Hidden in the pantry?*"

'Astrid paled a little at that, and with a desperate glance into my eyes, she slipped towards the kitchen. Voss turned to me, a conspiratorial smile on bloodless lips.

'"*She intended it as surprise for thine anniversary. Touching, no?*"

'I knew he was in her mind then. I could feel him in mine also. Slipping like a thief through our secrets, our thoughts, nothing sacred, nothing hidden. The images of murder filling my head, the sword in my hand buried in his throat, the lunge for the burning logs in the fire, the desperate maths of how I might save them – my daughter, my love – all unveiled. Patience looked at me, and she whispered again, "Papa?" and a tear slipped down her cheek. Voss turned to her, his voice like black silk.

'"*Oh nono, hush now, little flower. It pains thy Uncle Fabién, to see thee cry. Tell me, my sweet, my love, my angel dear, how old art thou?*"

'She looked to me, and I nodded, bloody agony in my chest.

'"Eleven," she whispered.

'"*Oh, precious love. Oh, such an age! All childhood's brightness still cherried in thy cheek, all womanhood's promise budding 'pon thy horizon. Thy name is Patience, aye?*"

'"Oui . . ."

'He looked at her sadly, fingers brushing back her long black hair.

'"*I had a daughter once. Oh, aye, I had a daughter, just as beautiful as thee. And I loved her, Patience. I loved her just as dear as thy brave and noble father loves thee.*"

'Astrid placed the goblet of wine on the table, bright and red as blood. And Voss broke his stare with my daughter, looking instead to my love.

'"*Oh, not for me, dear madame.*" His grateful smile vanished, and for a moment, his face was a mask of pure malevolence as his gaze slipped to Astrid's throat. "*For thee.*"

'"Voss . . ."

'"*She is a beauty, Gabriel.*" He was smiling once more, placing a kiss so cold upon Patience's cheek that I saw her skin pale where his lips touched her. "*Both of them, radiant as the sun. Proud art thou? Of this lair, this life thou hast made?*"

'"I am."

"'*Love them, dost thou? As God loves his angels?*'

"'I do.'

"'*And what wouldst thou give to keep them safe, thy angels, thy loves?*'

"'Anything.'

"'*Thy life? Thy liberty?*'

"'Anything! Everything! *Please!*' I slammed Ashdrinker on the table. "*PLEASE!*'

"'*Four. Centuries.*'

'I blinked, my belly grown far beyond chill. ". . . What?"

"'*That is how long I knew my Laure. My* angel. *My* love. *My Wraith in Red. Four. Hundred. Years.*" He caressed Patience's cheek, whisper soft. "*Thou hast had the keeping of this flower for but eleven, and already thou wouldst give thy soul for her. Nothing from which thou wouldst shirk, Father, to save thy precious daughter's life. What then, think ye I would not do to avenge my daughter hers?*'

'That claw rested still upon her throat. And every desperate notion, every bleak fantasy I could conjure ended only in horror. I knew he wanted me to beg, but still, I did. Hoping for some reprieve, and praying, oh mighty fucking God, *praying* with every part of me, every mote of my wretched soul that he would spare them this.

'I would have given *anything* to spare them this.

"'Voss. Please . . . Your quarrel is with me."

"'*Quarrel?*" The vampire blinked. "*Like clerks over a bill? Nay. No thing so shallow as quarrel twixt thee and I. Call it what it is, Silversaint.* Vendetta."

'He turned black eyes to the glass of wine, then up to Astrid.

"'*Thou art not drinking, madame.*"

'His gaze drifted to the hand she held quivering behind her back.

"'*What is the knife for?*"

"'You," Astrid promised. "*You.*"

"'Voss," I whispered. "Listen to me. Damn it, *LOOK* AT ME—"

"'*Know thee the name of thy sin, Gabriel? Thy soul hath the stain of them all, but know thee thy greatest? Come now, and speak its name. If thou wouldst give thy life for theirs, first I shall take thy confession. I shall be thy priest, and thee, my son. Gabriel de León. The Black Lion. The Saviour of Nordlund. Liberator of Triúrbaile. Redeemer of Tuuve. Sword of the Realm. Silversaint. What sin, sweetest, is thine?*"

'I clenched my teeth, fangs grown long in my gums. Thinking upon my life, the answer that might buy me reprieve, the confession he sought of me. "Pride," I whispered.

'"*Once perhaps. But no more. Speak again, and true.*"

'I looked to Astrid, my breath trembling. The vows broken between us. I'd never think our love a sin, but still, I spoke, desperate now. "Lust, then . . ."

'"*Thy sin, verily. But not the worst. Thy God is listening, Gabriel. Thy trumpets sing. Shalt thou die with soul unshriven?*"

'My grip tightened on my blade as I hissed, the things I wanted to do to this bastard and all his wretched kind aflame in my head. "*Wrath.*"

'Voss shook his head, as if disappointed.

'"*Tis Sloth, Gabriel. That was thy sin in the end, and worst among them all. Not Pride. Nor Lust. Nor Wrath. Simple Sloth.*" He waved his hand about him, lip curled in disgust. "*To slink ye here, to this hovel at earth's end, like a mongrel to its flea-struck bed? To foil my design, to stand in my way – verily, to take my daughter's life – all these wrongs might I have forgiven had ye but stayed thy course. Long centuries have I sought an adversary worthy of my ire. And for one bleak and blessed moment, as I heard my daughter scream through the death ye gifted her, my hollow heart sang as it hath not for centuries at the thought . . . perhaps I had found him. That man who could give me but a second in which I might once more taste life through fear. I hoped. Verily, I prayed.*"

'He shook his head.

'"*And* this *is what becomes of thee? This pitiable, ordinary life? Nay. Nay, this, I cannot forgive, old friend. To turn thy back with deed undone? To step from stage with song unsung? Magnificent were ye, Gabriel. And now? Thou art a lion, playing at being a lamb. And that is why by God thou art abandoned, and why he hath unleashed me upon thee.*"

'"Voss, please . . ."

'"Please," Astrid whispered. "*Don't.*"

'"*So beautiful,*" he whispered, running a claw along Patience's neck. "*But already, ye fade, Patience. The sweetness of the fruit is but the prelude to decay. Dying hast thou been, since the day ye were first born.*"

'"Almighty fucking God, Voss, you said you'd let her *go!*"

'He looked at me. His eyes black glass, like mirrors in which I saw myself. Wretched. Begging. And he spoke then, the words that would unmake my world.

'"*And unlike thee, I keep my vows.*"

'His hand moved. Just a flicker. And he . . .'

Gabriel's voice faltered. Ashes on his tongue.

To speak it would make it real.

To speak it would be to live it again.

'He . . .'

Jean-François sat with one pale hand pressed to his chest, a sliver of pity in his soulless eyes. The cell they sat in was cold as tombs, the pale light of dawn not long from the horizon. But the dark in that stone room was deep as any the vampire had known, as long and empty and bleak as a lifetime unloved. And he stared at this man, this broken wretch, leaning forward in his chair and covering his face, shoulders shaking in silent sobs. And a single, bloody tear spilled from the vampire's eyes as he whispered.

'Almighty God . . .'

The Last Silversaint drew a shuddering breath.

Looked to the skies above.

'Where?'

+ XIX +

UNMADE

'THERE'S A HATE so pure it's blinding. There's a rage so complete it's all-consuming. It takes you, and it breaks you, and the thing you've been is forever destroyed. Burned to ashes and then reborn. And that was all I knew as I rose up and drew Ashdrinker from her sheath, the sword an extension of my arm, my arm an extension of my will, my will a summation of that hate, that rage, that desire to unmake. Not kill. Not destroy. To *annihilate*. Ashdrinker screamed with me as she sliced through the space between us, too red for me to look at. A blow that might've cut the earth in two. A strike so perfect it could have split the sky.

'The blade struck the Forever King across his throat. Starsteel, fallen from heavenly skies, pitted against immortal flesh, ancient when the empire was a madman's dream.

'I heard the sound of steel striking stone.

'The song of dreams undone.'

Gabriel looked at his hands.

'And Ashdrinker shattered.

'Astrid struck, screaming, the silver knife in her hand flashing. All hell's fury in her eyes. If she could have given her life to make him bleed a drop, she would have died ten thousand times. But for all her rage, my love was a child's fist upon a mountainside. And Voss's hand snaked out around my throat, cinching like an iron vice. I roared as he seized Astrid with his other hand, drawing her to his chest as he looked into my eyes and smiled like all light's dying.

'"*There he is*," he whispered. "*The lion awakened*."

'I snarled, blind fury, strangled rage. And with all the dark might of his ancient blood, Voss lifted me high and hurled me down, his strength so great I was sent crashing through the floor and into the cellar below. My skull smashed upon the stone, and I felt my bones shatter, my body break, my heart inside it. His voice drifted down through the dust, the blood, the hurt, a whisper in my rising dark, too soft for any but us two to hear.

'"*I shall await thee in the east, Lion.*"

'And though I would have given my last drop of blood, my very soul to fight it off, still I felt it take me. The awful arms of darkness, reaching up from that splintered stone and dragging me down into sleep unwanted. And the last sound I heard before it took me was not my broken, ragged breath, nor my love screaming my name, nor the sound of all we'd built, all we'd done, all we'd wished for, crashing down around my ears.

'It was laughter.

'Voss's laughter.

'And then, blackness fell.'

✦ XX ✦
A PROMISE IN THE DARK

'I WOKE IN darkness. Blood in my mouth. Blood in the air. And I wondered if this was hell. No flames, no fallen, no lake of brimstone. Just dark and silence unending. But then I moved, and pain lanced through me, broken bones and bleeding meat, and I realized life, cursed and hateful, still coursed through this wretched body.

'I felt a weight upon my chest. My fingers roaming old leather, cool metal, familiar. A razored edge, a jagged tip with six inches now missing – my sword, laid out upon my breast as for a king in a barrow of old. My eyes began to pick out details in the black. Shattered bottles and crumpled shelves. I was in our cellar, I realized – the ruins of it, anyway. Ceiling beams held an avalanche of broken stone but a few feet above my head. It looked as if the entire house had been brought down atop me, the lighthouse also – tons of fallen masonry held in check by only a few slivers of wood and the accursed hand of God.

'"God . . ."

'*Gabriel . . .*

'Ashdrinker whispered in my head, her voice now broken like she was.

'*Gabriel, I am s-s-so sorry I f-failed thee, failed thee.*

'And then I saw her. Lying on the stone beside me.

'My love. My life. My Astrid.

'My heart, splintering inside my chest.

'She looked more beautiful than she'd ever been. But it wasn't the beauty of a thousand smiles, nor of the mother of my child, nor of the light of my life. No. Hers was a dark beauty now. Those lips that had once breathed life into mine? Now red as murder. That face shaped like heartbreak? Not milk-white and soft, but marbled and hard. I saw no rise and fall of breath in her breast, no pulse at her throat, still marked by the press of his teeth and the leavings of his feast. And I reared back, almost breaking at the final, awful horror of it. Because she wasn't dead. She was Dead.

'And I knew the colour of desolation then. And its colour was red.

'I'll not give breath to the dark thoughts that entered my mind. Not even for your pale Empress, vampire. I'm sure you can imagine the desperate, vain hopes, the evil, selfish dreamings, as far from heaven as devils can fly. All smothered at last by simple despair.

'This was not her.

'This was not my Astrid.

'I pictured her as once she'd been. That first night we met in the Library of San Michon, that beauty, that smile, that girl who wielded books like blades.

'I kissed her lips, red as rubies, cold as midnight.

'I saw her lashes stirring on her cheeks.

'And I picked up my sword.

'Two little words.

'"Forgive me."

'*Do it.*

'"I can't."

'*You must.*

'"Oh, God."

'And I did.

'I looked to the heaven that hadn't answered when I begged. The God who'd let it come to this. I felt them rise up like poison inside me, shuddering sobs spilling through bloody teeth. I wept like a father untethered, like a son betrayed, like a husband widowed, until my throat closed over and my voice was broken and I longed for death.

'But through the roaring in my ears, I heard a voice inside my head, clinging to the words she now spoke. Words like *vengeance*. Words like *violence*. Words like *promise* and *purpose* where, otherwise, there was only madness. Not for me to lie quiet in my grave while the one who had buried them yet walked. Not for me to close my eyes and sleep, to consign myself to this tomb. Not until the song was sung.

'If he wanted a war, I would be it.

'If he wanted a fear, let it be me.

'One last gift my love gave to me. One last sacrament, taken with burning tears in my eyes, and revulsion for all I was boiling in my soul. I'd no other way out of that grave, no other path towards the vengeance of which she whispered. But if there was some tattered remnant left of my heart before then, it turned to ashes as her taste crashed upon my tongue one final time. I made a vow then and there, a promise to them both, my Astrid, my Patience, my angels. Whispered in the dark, cold as tombs and black as hell, that never again would the blood of another touch my lips. Never again would I feed this monster I was.

'*Never again*.

'And with the strength she'd given me, bloody tongue and trembling hands, I tore my way free of that grave he'd buried us in. And with the smoke of the fires I lit rising to the sky behind me, I dragged on the shape of what I'd been, and I remembered; there is a time for grief, and a time for songs, and a time to recall with fondness all that has been and gone.

'But there is a time for killing too.

'There is a time for blood.

'And a time for rage.

'And a time to close your eyes and become the thing hell wants you to be.

'And so. I did.'

✦ XXI ✦

ALL AND EVERYTHING

'I FELL SILENT, still staring out that empty window of Château Aveléne. The place she'd never been. The chapel where we'd been wed. Echoes of my happiest day. Dior still knelt on the floor beside me. Squeezing my hand so tight I thought she might break it. Weeping so hard I feared she might never stop.

'"I'm sorry, Gabe. God, I'm so sorry."

'"Now you see," I whispered. "Why I'll not give you over to him. Why I'll not lose one more drop to this. Why I must see this through to the end. Because I miss them, like a piece of me is missing. And I love them, like love is all I was. And there is nothing I'd not do, no depth to which I'd not sink, no price I wouldn't pay to have them back and here with me. Because they were my all and my everything.

'"But they're gone.

'"They're gone, and they're never coming back. And that bastard *took* them from me. And for that, he will die, Dior. He and every one of his cursed line will die."

'"God, Gabriel," she whispered. "Forgive me if I . . ."

'I shook my head. "So long as you understand. This is where you're safest, so this is where you stay. No matter the cost." I met her eyes, iron in my voice. "You hear me?"

'"Oui." She sniffed hard, pressed her head against my shoulder. "I do."

'I looked to the broken glass, the night outside. The scabs were torn away now, the sight of that empty window a hole in my chest. But the rage did a little to cauterize the bleed, and the thought of what was to come did the rest – enough for me to put aside the grief for one breath longer and do what must be done.

"'I have to go find Ash. Then talk to Aaron. I need you to go to your room and stay there. I'll have Baptiste send his best people to watch your door until I get back. Answer to no one 'til I return."

'She nodded, eyes downturned. "Oui."

"'Promise me."

"'I promise."

"'I *mean* it."

'She met my eyes, her own flashing. "I promise."

'I nodded once, swallowing the taste of salt and blood. Pushing aside sorrow and focusing on that fire within as I rose to my feet, drawing Dior up with me. "It's almost light. I know it's hard, but try to get some sleep. Tomorrow will be a long night. The longest of your life. But I intend you see the dawn."

'Silver heels crunched on broken glass as I made to leave.

"'Gabriel."

'I turned at her voice. And as I did, she threw her arms around me and pressed her cheek to my chest and squeezed for all she was worth. "You're a good man, Gabriel de León. Merci. For everything."

'I tensed at her embrace, then sank into it, blinking hard at the burn in my eyes. I'd wept oceans already. And tears were no more use here than prayers. Still . . .

"'I'll return soon," I vowed. "And I'll not leave your side afterwards 'til I've seen you safe inside the walls of San Michon. Sleep now, girl. Fear no darkness."

'I saw her to her room, closed the door tight, and casting a wary glance around the shadowed halls, I trudged out into the night. I could taste the fear in the air, hear the soft murmurs at my back as I walked through the falling snow. I found Ashdrinker in a drift beside the chapel, the silvered dame glittering in the muted moonlight. A few of Aaron's soldiers rushed past, looking at me strangely as I fished the sword from the snow, wiped the blade clean.

'*Is all well?*

"'Well as it ever is."

'*Ye t-told her, told her?*

"'Like you said, Ash. No such thing as a happy ending."

'*I am sorry, Gabriel. Always and ever. That d-day was my greatest failure.*

'I looked down into her face, her shattered blade, the words etched down her length that only she and I knew the telling of. We'd waded through rivers of blood together, she and I. We'd carved our names into the pages of history.

'"Never blame the blade. The failure was mine. But I've a will to set the ledger to rights amorrow night, if you've a will to help me. I've a need to slay something monstrous."

'*Always. Always.*

'I sheathed her at my side, her weight a comfort on my hip as I stalked back to the keep. I found Aaron and Baptiste and their sergeants-at-arms in the Great Hall, gathered around a map spread out on the feasting tables. I had a quiet word with Baptiste, and the blackthumb nodded once and immediately sent three heavy-set, hammer-fisted bladesmen to keep watch at Dior's door. And then we set about planning for the assault.

'There were voices raised and angry curses and dark glances thrown my way – I knew at least half these folk rued the day I'd ever set foot inside Aveléne. But still, they loved their capitaine fierce, and they hated coldbloods all, and between those two measures, Aaron held them steady. All knew the strength of the force set to crash against these walls amorrow night. All knew victory would be hard won if it were won at all. But Aaron and his men had been preparing their defences for years, and Baptiste was the genius he'd always been, and as the dawn's frail light pushed through the tall windows, I knew we had a fighting chance. But more, with a full dose of sanctus in me, with all my strength at my command, if I could have but one moment, one tiny window in which to get my hands around the Beast's neck, I'd be one step closer to the vengeance I came north to find – one step closer to the end of the Forever King's accursed line.

'We ate breakfast together, Aaron, Baptiste, and I. And though the memory still held pain, it reminded me of days in San Michon. There's a strange and fierce love forged in the fires of combat. A brotherhood written only in blood. And I didn't realize how much I'd missed it until that moment, nor how glad I'd be to have it back.

'"You have my thanks, brothers," I told them. "And all the love I have to give. You risk everything for me, and on thin promise at that."

'"And gladly," Aaron replied. "But not just for you, Gabe."

'He shook his head, staring at the sevenstar on his palm.

'"I know you have your doubts, but I feel the will of the Almighty in all this, brother. I feel the weight of providence, the hand of fate itself. I swear to the Mothermaid, I cannot explain it. But somehow I know that all this . . . every moment of our lives has been leading to this night." He met my eyes, fierce and proud. "And I am *ready*."

'"God stands with us, Gabe," Baptiste said, squeezing my hand. "As he did when we stood together at the Twins. Then as now, with him beside us, we cannot fall."

"'No fear,' I murmured.

"'Only fury,' Aaron nodded.

"'You should sleep, brother,' Baptiste murmured. "No offence, but you look like hell."

'We shared a weary chuckle, and I gave my thanks again. And embracing them both, sick with sorrow, I retired upstairs. I bathed properly for the first time in as long as I could remember, blood and grime so clouded the water I had to change the bucket three times. Dragging the tangles out of my hair. Shaving off my road whiskers with a razor Aaron loaned me. I looked at the man in the mirror and saw the scars within and without. I wondered if he would ever find peace. If he would ever forgive himself. If it would ever be over.

'And then I trudged to my bedchamber, wanting nothing more than a few blessed hours on clean sheets in a soft bed . . . God, the thought of it seemed like heaven. But I stopped off at Dior's room first, nodded to the bladesmen on duty outside her door. They looked at me with faces grim and eyes narrowed, resentful and sullen. But one of them finally spoke; a gruff Ossian fellow with a beard like a brace of badgers.

"'You'd nae remember,' he grunted. "But we fought alongside each other at Báih Sìde."

'I looked at him, bleary-eyed and exhausted.

"'Redling,' I finally said. "Redling á Sadhbh."

'He blinked in surprise. "That's right. How'd you—"

"'I remember,' I sighed. "I remember everything."

'The man looked me over, flint eyes and bristling beard. "I'll give ye nae thanks for bringing such evil to our door," he growled. "But if I must fall tonight, I'm proud to do it at the side of the Black Lion."

"'Oui,' said the second bladesman. "God bless, de León."

'I nodded thanks, shook their hands, told them to know no fear. And then I opened Dior's door a crack, peered into the dark of her bedchamber. She faced away from the door, bundled up under her blankets, soundless and still. I watched her a moment, reminded of the nights I'd stood at the door to Patience's room, just listening to her breathe and wondering how in the name of heaven I'd made something so perfect.

'Again, I felt my eyes burn.

'Again, I blinked away those useless tears.

'And then I realized that Dior wasn't breathing at all. That her coat wasn't hanging on the peg, nor her boots sitting at the foot of her bed. And my belly turned to ice and I stormed into the room, already knowing what I'd find as I ripped away the blankets.'

Jean-François dipped his quill into the ink and smiled faintly. 'Pillows.'

'Dior Lachance was no coward. But she sure as hell *was* a liar.'

Gabriel shook his head, taking a long gulp of wine.

'And the lying little bitch was gone.'

+ XXII +

THE LION RIDES

'MY FURY WAS terrible. Not for the bladesmen outside Dior's door who'd failed to hear her climbing from the window, nor for the kennelmaster who'd lain sleeping as she stole the dogs from their pen. Not for the watchmen who'd turned a blind eye as she led the hounds down the hill, nor for the soldier who'd helped her hook them up to the sled she'd loaded.

'No. My fury was for the fool who'd believed that girl would cower inside a castle while another drop of blood was spilled for her sake.

'We stood on Aveléne's highwalk now, peering out through the crenellations to the glittering Mère in the frozen valley below.

'"She rode out at dawn," Aaron reported. "Into the snow, headed northeast towards the Maidsroad. She can take that all the way to San Michon if—"

'"No," I scowled. "She's riding on the river."

'Baptiste shook his head. "Our scouts report she was trekking—"

'"She's switched back. The little bitch is clever as cats. And after getting an eyeful of that map in your hall, she knows the Mère will see her all the way to the monastery."

'"How do you know that, brother?"

'I breathed deep, sighed a cloud of rolling frost. "I offered her a phial of my blood, way back in Winfael. She refused it. So when I got her that new coat in Redwatch, I slipped the phial into the lining instead." Shaking my head, I remembered Master Greyhand's lessons. "Old age and treachery can always overcome youth and skill, Lachance."

'"Forgive me, Gabe," Baptiste said. "But what good is a phial of your blood?"

'"Because I can *feel* it."

Jean-François stopped writing, glanced up from his chronicle. 'Feel it, de León?'

Gabriel nodded. 'I'd never had a teacher. Never met anyone who could unlock the secrets of my bloodline. But still, I'd learned a few tiny invocations over the years; scraps and whispers, hidden in the pages of San Michon and unearthed by my love.'

'Sanguimancy,' the historian murmured.

'Oui. And atop the walls of Aveléne, I reached towards the horizon and felt it sure and true; a tiny piece of me inside a prison of glass, headed north along a road of grey ice.

'"She's on the river," I said. "And the Dead are following."

'"The watchmen said she'd loaded her sled with supplies," Baptiste murmured. "But even running heavy, the Dead won't move faster than a team of dogs on ice in daylight."

'"Day won't last forever," Aaron warned.

'"I have to reach her by nightfall," I said, marching down the stairs. "That's when they'll hit her. I need the rest of your dogs, Aaron. And a sled. Quick as you may."

'"I'll come with you," he declared, and again, I marvelled at the trust and love my brother bore for me. I smiled at him even as I shook my head.

'"She has a two-hour head start. I need to run light as I can."

'"Gabe, you can't take Danton and that army alone."

'I patted Ashdrinker's hilt. "I'm not alone."

'Baptiste shook his head. "Gabe—"

'"I'll not waste time arguing, brothers. Mothermaid knows what I did to deserve friends so true as you. But you've not dogs enough to follow me, nor horses that can run safe on a half-frozen river. And every minute we waste is another minute Danton draws closer to that girl's throat. So get me those dogs. *Please*."

'The kennelmaster worked swift, stripping a sled back to the bones so I might run lighter. I stood with my brothers on the frozen pier, the Mère stretching away into falling snows, the folk of Aveléne watching from atop their walls. They felt guilty no doubt; that they'd turned a blind eye and let Dior leave alone. But more, they were conscious that the girl had drawn the shadow away from their walls, that she'd thrown herself over the brink to spare them slaughter. And their voices were raised up now, a clamour along the ancient stone and ringing somewhere in the hollow of my chest.

'"Godspeed, de León!"

'"Mothermaid bless you!"

'"The Lion rides!"

'"THE BLACK LION RIDES!"

'Baptiste threw his arms around me, hugged me fierce. "Angel Fortuna ride with you, Little Lion. May God and all his heavenly host watch over you."

'"Merci, brother. Look after this prettyboy for me."

'But Aaron wouldn't share the smile I shot him. "This is foolishness, Gabriel."

'"Let's call it reckless. Such was ever my nature. Now tell me farewell, brother, and bid me Godspeed, and if you've a will to pray for her, I'll not curse you for it."

'"For her but not for you?"

'"He doesn't listen, Aaron." I smiled, sadly. "He never has."

'Aaron slipped a bandolier over my shoulder, loaded to bursting with silverbombs, holy water, sanctus phials. And then he dragged me into an embrace, squeezing tight.

'"Remember, Gabe," he whispered. "It matters not what you hold faith in. But you must hold faith in *something*." He kissed my brow, eyes shining. "Godspeed. Ride hard."

'The wind was at my back as I charged out, as if the storm itself spurred me on. The dogs were that dauntless Nordish stock known as lancers, and they ran swift, my sled blades hissing across the ice as we barrelled down the frozen curve of the Mère.

'The riverbanks were crags and cliffs at first – the good black basalt of my homeland's bones – and the fresh powder in front of us was unmarred by track or tread. But a few hours upriver, the cliffs gave way to lowlands and frozen deadwood, and I saw the twin arcs of sled blades and a multitude of dog tracks veer out from the banks onto the ice – Dior's trail, sure and true. She'd carried her sled over the rocks and onto the river, hoping to hide her passing. But I knew a bloodhound as skilled as Danton wouldn't be thrown off by so simple a ruse, and soon after, her tracks were lost in the tread of the things that followed her – a great host flooding out from the woods and pursuing her up the Mère. I pictured the highbloods and wretched Danton had brought with him, looked to the meagre supplies I carried, the broken blade at my waist. In truth, I didn't know if it would be enough. But when there's little you can do, do what little you can.

'A snow hawk cut through the skies above me, mottled white and iron grey, calling upon the frozen air. My lancers ran onward into the blinding snows. The wind had shifted now, a howling northerly cutting like a sword down the Mère's gut, the falling snow like razorblades. My collar was up about my face, my tricorn pulled low, but my eyes still burned, tears frozen on my cheeks, the chill making my knuckles ache.

'The blackened sun was slinking towards its bed now, a moonsless night waiting in the wings, and still, no sign of my quarry. But as the daystar dipped towards the horizon, long shadows blurring in the muted light, my heart surged as I saw it in the distance; the faint churn of powder thrown up by hundreds of feet. And I realized I'd caught them, caught them both: Danton's horde running hard on Dior's heels, the girl fleeing before them as if the devil himself came behind.

'She was bent over her sled, roaring for her dogs to "Run! RUN!" and spurred on by their fear of the Dead, the hounds barrelled down the ice like lightning. But as the sunlight failed, the Dead grew stronger, ran faster, drew closer, ever closer to their prize. The wretched ran first, like beasts before their masters' whips. The highbloods came next, those dread cousins and children Danton had mustered to his aid, Ironhearts all. And at the last came the Beast of Vellene. I could see him now if I squinted. Rage flaring at the memory of him standing outside my home the night his father knocked three times on my door, bearing silent witness to the atrocities within.

'I owed his famille blood. And tonight, *tonight,* I vowed, I'd begin to repay the sum.

'The pipe was full and at my lips, and I breathed the colour of murder into my lungs. All the night came alive, every sense aflame, the smell of dogs and fresh sweat, the sound of thundering footsteps and galloping pulse, the sight of the enemy before me and the blade I bore, now naked and gleaming in my hand. But with sinking heart, I saw the last breath of sunset flee the sky, and my mind rang with the echoes of my childhood in the halls of San Michon; one of the first lessons I ever learned, before my name became legend and my love burned like summer flame and my pride brought it all to an end.

'*The Dead run quick.*

'They were at Dior's heels now, claws outstretched. I saw they'd catch her long before I did, and in desperation, I roared her name. She looked back to me through the falling snow, and I thought perhaps I might see fear in her eyes at last. But instead, I saw a gleam, glass-sharp and gutterborn. Not the saviour of an empire nor the descendant of a God, but a street rat. A girl who'd grown up in dingy alleys and rotten hovels far from here, who'd survived by wits and guile, thief and trickster and incorrigible liar.

'The flintbox she'd stolen flared, and her fuses began to spark. The silver dagger I'd given her flashed, and her dog team was cut free from their moorings. The breath left her lungs as she leapt free, dragged by the hounds along the ice and away from her sled as it wobbled and flipped behind her, the barrels she'd loaded and lit now spilling across the ice, branded with tiny Xs – the twin scythes of Mahné, Angel of Death.

'"Black ignis," I breathed.

'"'Ware!" Danton roared. ""WARE!"

'The powder ignited, deafening blasts rippling across the valley and lighting the dark bright as the day. The closest wretched were engulfed or ripped to pieces by the explosion. But as the concussion struck the ice, reverberating hard enough that I felt it beneath me, at last I realized the genius of what Dior had done. The frozen surface of the Mère shattered in spectacular spirals, just as when Fortuna had bolted across the Ròdaerr. And just as I'd done that day, Danton's legion found themselves plunging below the surface and into the icy depths of the still-running river below.

'"Maggot trap," I smiled.

'A hundred at least, two of the highbloods among them, the entire shelf beneath them breaking apart. Only a few had mind enough to scream as the water washed the flesh off their bones and death, long-denied, wrapped them at last in loving arms.

'But others scattered, Danton among them, veering away from the gulf and skipping across the shattering surface. Like shadows, fleet and deadly, they danced along the cracking frost closer to the shore, where the river was frozen all the way to its beds, and there, they continued pursuit. Dior's gambit had carved a bleeding gouge through Danton's force, but dozens of the vampires still remained – most of the highbloods and the Beast himself among them – and now, Dior's folly was laid bare.

'She was dragged along the ice behind her dogs, desperately clinging to the severed harness. I bent double, roaring at my own lancers to run onwards, swerving around the gulf in the shattered river glass and riding on. But Danton was filled with fury now, he and his cohort drawing closer, ever closer.

'"I said I would hunt thee forever, girl!"

'"F-fuck you!" she sputtered, holding on for dear life.

'"You must say please, love!"

'"Danton!" I roared. "Face me, coward!"

'But the Beast ignored me, save to glance over his shoulder and gift me a murderous smile. I was still too far away to help her, barely keeping pace while the vampires gained with every step. If they caught her, those highbloods could keep me busy while the Beast made his escape with Dior, and all this, everything, would be for nothing. I heard that snow hawk calling again somewhere in the dark above, Ashdrinker's voice ringing in my mind over the clamour of my pulse.

'*Ride, Gabriel! We m-must save her! RIDE!*

'And then, the inevitable happened. Dior's dogs pounded onwards, terrified of the Dead, heedless of the girl they dragged behind. They dashed towards a drift of snow, a foot or two high across the ice, veering around it. But Dior shrieked as she swung wide on the harness, closing her eyes as she ploughed into the drift. Her grip failed, and with the sound of snapping whips, the harness broke free, sent her tumbling, sprawling, spilling through the snowbank and rolling to rest on the other side. She cracked her face on the ice, split her brow, blood on her hands and cheeks. I roared in horror as Danton howled in triumph, his highbloods swooping towards the fallen girl, his wretched scrambling, claws unfurled.

'One of the highbloods seized hold of her – an elderly fellow dressed like a country gent – lifting her up by the collar as if she weighed a feather. Dior cursed, scrabbling at his face, the vampire shrieking as her fingers painted crimson lines across his cheek. And where her blood kissed his flesh, fire bloomed, white-hot and blinding. He staggered back, howling, Ironheart flesh carved with great ashen rents by the merest touch of her blood.

'A silverbomb burst among the wretched, blasting a few to pieces. Another exploded, another, sailing from my hand and lighting up the night, silver caustic scalding Dead skin and eyes. Danton's flock scattered as I unleashed another volley, leaping from my sled and roaring, "DIOR!" And the girl cried, "GABRIEL!" and scrambled to her feet. A tall, dead-eyed brute made a grab for her as she dashed towards me through the silversmoke, her fine frockcoat shredding in his fist. A wretched leapt atop her, trying to bring her down. But again, she lashed out with those blood-slicked hands, and again, the vampire fell back, its flesh burned black where her blood had touched it.

'She made it to my side, crashing into my arms, face slicked red. Ashdrinker sang in the air, scything through the wretched at her back, leaving them in smoking pieces on the ice. I hurled my holy water, my silverbombs, cutting through the rabble that charged me headlong, soulless eyes and open mouths. Dior lashed out with her silversteel dagger as I cut more wretched down into the bloody snow, the pair of us standing back-to-back as the song of the blade rang in my head: steel as mother, steel as father, steel as friend. I'd been killing these bastards since I was sixteen years old, and near the first of them I'd ever slain was a Prince of Forever – there was no way under heaven I'd fall beneath the teeth of a few dozen mongrels with a full dose of sanctus in me, with my swordarm whole and the fury of a widower, of a father undone burning within. And though I made a red fucking slaughter of those dogs, still, I knew it was no kind of triumph. Danton and his highbloods hung back, watching as I spent the last of my arsenal, backing away onto the ice now with nothing left to throw, no more tricks up my sleeve.

'And still almost a dozen highbloods to kill.

'They fanned out about us as we backed away, slowly encircling. I knew a few by name, by bloody reputation. A dark-bearded brute named Maarten the Butcher, who wore mail and carried a great two-hander in hammer fists. Another warrior named Roisin the Red, swift and sharp, her body clad in fur-trimmed leathers and her hair in slayer's braids. A slender woman with wheat-gold hair and blood-red eyes called Liviana. A boy known only as Fetch, not more than ten when he died, dressed in pale finery spattered with blood.

'Ironhearts all, each the father or mother of decades of murder, each a nightmare to slay alone, let alone with ten siblings beside them. And at their head, a Prince of Forever, son of their dread liege himself. The butcher of a thousand maids, the bloodhound of the Forever King, the Beast of Vellene, now stalking towards me across the ice as his fellows slowly closed their circle around us.

'"I warned thee, Silversaint," he said. "Ye should have stayed buried."

'I clenched my fangs. "Papa should have killed me when he had the chance, bastard."

'"But he *did* kill thee, de León. Not the hero who songs were sung for, the chevalier who defeated undying armies, the man who became legend. Not even the boy who slew my sister dear do I see before me." Danton shook his head, their circle drawing tighter. "A shadow is all that remains of thee. A hollowed cur, a drunkard and a wretch, sodden with spirits and with spirit broken."

'Danton raised his blade, the sabre's edge gleaming.

'"But ye may still live to see the dawn, de León. Thou hast business with my dread father in the east, do ye not? Debts unpaid?" He circled around us now, behind the wall of his highbloods, his smile ruby red. "Thy Patience? Thy Astrid? Thou didst slumber in thy cellar as my father had his way with thy bride, but still, certain am I thou hast imagined the sweet sufferings he bestowed before planting her in the ground beside thee. And more certain am I, thou doth desire *nothing* so much as to see my king again."

'The leather on Ashdrinker's hilt creaked as I squeezed it tight.

"'A chance for vengeance I offer thee," Danton said. "Put up thy sword and step ye aside. Give the girl over to me, and ye may yet live to see thy vow fulfilled. Ye need not die for her, de León. For in the end, what is Dior Lachance to thee?"

'I glanced to the girl at my back, bloodied and shaking.

'Eyes wide and blue, rimmed with tears.

"'Gabe . . ." she whispered.

'And I saw the truth then. The truth of it all. No matter the vengeance I'd sworn, nor the life that had been stolen from me, nor the endless ache inside my chest. Because even in darkest hours, that ache let me know I was still alive. It was as my love had told me, as she'd *always* said. Hearts only bruise. They never break.

'And in the end, I knew I'd not take back a breath of it. Not the bliss I knew then, nor the pain I felt now. Not all the forsaken hours I'd spent without them, the ache of my lips without Astrid's kiss, the emptiness of my arms without Patience's embrace. In those few moments I had them, and if only then, I was immortal. Because they were immaculate. And they were mine.

'And no matter the God I'd turned my back on. No matter the father I cursed and the heaven I defied. Because in the end, it matters not what you hold faith in. So long as you hold faith in something.

'I tore off my glove with my teeth, wrapped my bare hand in Dior's.

"'I will *never* leave you," I vowed.

'It began as an ember, just a spark to tinder, finite and small. But like to the summer-bleached grasses of my youth, the spark began to smoulder, and that smoulder became flame, burning down my arm and into the palm of the hand that now held Dior's. I felt it like fire in the ink Astrid had scribed upon my skin. I felt it like her lips upon mine. And releasing my grip, looking to the sevenstar on my palm, I saw it burning with light – not cold and silver as in days of old, but hot and crimson. Tearing my coat away, the tunic beneath, I saw the lion on my chest ablaze with that same furious light, red as the heat of my stepfather's forge, as the blood I'd spilled and seen spilled in kind, as all the fires that surely burn in the hate-drenched heart of hell.

'I raised my hand, ablaze. And I saw them tremble.

"'Which of you unholy bastards wants to be the first to die?"

"'Kill him," Danton hissed. "Kill him and bring me the girl."

'The vampires wavered, crimson light reflected in narrowing eyes.

'"Obey me!" the Beast roared. "You are ten, he is one!"

'Dior raised her dagger. "You mean *two*, bastard."

'"Count again, girl."

'The whisper drifted across the ice. Danton turned, glowering as a now-familiar figure strode out from the tumbling snows. Locks of midnight-blue ran thick to her waist. Her long red frockcoat whipped about her in the howling wind, silken shirt parted from her pale chest. She'd fashioned herself a new mask; white porcelain with a bloody handprint over her mouth, red-rimmed lashes. And beyond, those pale eyes, drained of all light and life.

'Liathe still looked injured from our brawl in San Guillaume – her chest yet marred from Ashdrinker's kiss, her hands yet charred from the blade's touch. But she held her sword and flail nonetheless, both sculpted from her own blood, glistening red in my burning light.

'"Who art thou?" Danton snarled.

'"Call usss Liathe."

'The Beast of Vellene pressed his lips thin. He could sense the power in this one, wounded though she was. "Step aside then, Liathe. This prey belongs to the Blood Voss."

'"We will not," she replied. "The child comes with usss."

'"Us?" Danton spat. "Thou art but one, cousin. Know ye who I am? Know ye my dread king and father in whose affairs ye now meddle?"

'The vampire tilted her head, long black locks flowing in that howling wind. "We know Fabién. Knew him, long before he laid claim to his hollow crown. Long before *you* did, Danton." She stepped forward, raised her bloody blade. "Tonight we drink your heartsblood, little prince. Tonight your father grieves another child."

'Danton's face twisted – fury and perhaps the slightest trace of fear. But a prince of the Blood Voss wasn't about to be denied when so close to his prize, nor, I suspect, did he have any desire to explain to his father that the Grail had been plucked from his very fingertips by another leech. And so, he turned to his black circle and snarled with all the weight of the sovereign blood in his veins, "*Butcher her!* And *I* shall take the girl myself!"

'The highbloods obeyed, moving like a storm of crows, black and swift. I had time to see Liathe raise her bloody blade, sling back her bloody flail, and then Danton was upon us. I raised Ashdrinker to meet his charge, roared to Dior "Get behind me!" as the Beast came on. His sabre crashed upon my blade, sparks flying as the edges kissed. We stared at each other a moment over crossed steel, eyes burning with purest hatred.

'"Tonight you sleep in hell, de León," he hissed.

'"This *is* hell, Danton," I smiled. "And the devil loves his own."

'And then, it began in truth.

'When last we'd faced each other, I'd been starving, weak, and he'd spitted me like a pig. The time before, with the weakling sun in the sky, I'd taken his arm off at the elbow and torn the heart from his daughter's chest. But now there would be no excuses, no measure found wanting. The night was bitter cold and sin-black, the Beast's full power at his command. But I burned like a beacon, my aegis aglow, the bloodhymn ringing in my veins. No mercy asked, no quarter begged, the debt I owed hanging above us like a headsman's blade, and a pale shadow – a beauty of edgeless winters and lightless dawns – standing at my shoulder.

'"*My lion,*" she whispered.

'I could feel them, I swear it. My angels. Their love. Their warmth.

'And with that inside me, I was unbreakable.

'But alas, so was the skin of my foe. It'd been years since I faced an enemy like this; an ancien Ironheart, a prince of the Dead. His flesh was stone as I struck it, Ashdrinker almost jarred from my hand with every blow, and though deep cracks appeared in his marble skin after each strike landed, I felt like I was chipping away at a mountain. Danton's blade flashed quick as silver, reflecting the burning red light of my aegis, and though the glow kept his eyes part blinded, burned him as he drew close to strike, still he did, like thunder, like the monster he was – a bleak lord of carrion, too heavy with the weight of centuries to be bested by my faith alone.

'Ashdrinker caught him across the throat, a chunk taken from his pale skin. His riposte cut through my shoulder, blood sluicing across the snow and the burning lion on my chest. I reached towards him, desperate to get a grip and unleash my bloodgift. But the Beast of Vellene knew the fate that had befallen the Wraith in Red – knew that for me to get my hands on him might spell his end. And so, he kept his distance, circling like a snake and rearing back as I drew close, almost taking my hand off at the wrist as I reached towards him.

'He smiled, wagging a finger. "Learn a new trick, dog."

'"No dog, leech. The blood of lions flows in these veins."

'"Thou art weak, de León. So weak ye could not even defend that which ye loved most dear. And I shall make thee *watch* as I take another from thee."

'Behind me, Dior raised her silversteel. "I'll burn your heart out, bastard."

'The Beast laughed, and we clashed again, sparks and blood raining into the black. I could hear screams behind me, the sound of snarls and steel – I knew not how Liathe fared, but nor could I risk a glance to tell. Danton came on again, again, his sabre cutting a bone-deep gouge though my chest, another across my arm, and I felt the slack weight of muscles sliced loose from their anchors of bone, my left arm hanging heavy now, my speed failing. Ashdrinker's voice rang in my mind, spurring me on, silver-bright.

'*They knew us, Gabriel. The b-blade that cleft the dark in twain. The man the undying f-feared. They remembered us. E'en after all these years.*

'The silvered dame smiled in my mind.

'*And so do I.*

'We feinted, shifted, and finally lunged, everything we had behind that strike. Ashdrinker split the night in two as once she had, arcing between the falling snowflakes and towards the Beast's chest. With snarling, sinuous speed, Danton raised his blade, turned Ash aside, and instead of sundering his long-dead heart, the broken blade pierced his shoulder, driven in to the hilt. The Beast roared in agony, fangs bared bloody. But I saw my folly now – same as Saoirse on the walls of San Guillaume. My blade was stuck in the stone of his flesh, his hand locking about mine on the hilt. His claws whistled as they came, speeding towards my throat, Dior screaming my name as I tore myself loose, talons shearing across my chin as I tumbled backwards and landed with a crunch on the ice.

'The Beast towered above me now, gasping as he tore Ashdrinker free. His hands smouldered at her touch, and with a dark curse, he flung her away into the dark. And on he came, plunging his blade towards my heart. I rolled aside, kicked his knee with silver heels, rewarded with a crunch, a curse. But he swung again, again, blinded by my aegis, by his fury, at last striking true, his sword spearing my bicep and pinning my left arm to the ice. I roared in pain, thrusting my free hand towards his throat as he lunged atop me. We struggled, fangs bared, breath hissing through my teeth. All I needed was one moment, one *second* with my fingers around his neck.

'"I'll k-kill you, bastard," I spat.

'"Bastard?" He smiled ruby red as he leaned in harder. "Nay, halfbreed, no bastard, I. I am of the Blood Voss. The blood of *kings*. I am a Prince of F—"

'The vampire grunted as Ashdrinker plunged down through his back. His black eyes grew wide, and he stared stupidly at the blade of broken starsteel protruding from his chest, bewildered at how Ash had bested his flesh.

'But still, still, he was the son of Fabién Voss, ancien Ironheart, and the bastard didn't *die*. He snarled at the girl who'd stabbed him – Dior, standing behind him now like a thief come in the night. She was gasping, ragged, her hands slicked with blood as she tore the blade loose. The Beast reared up towards her, serpent-swift, furious.

'But he staggered as the wound in his chest began to smoulder, and I saw Ashdrinker's blade doing likesame; as if the gore upon it burned. And I realized at last that the blood on the blade wasn't his, it was hers – *it was hers*, her palms sliced open and the blood of the Redeemer Himself smeared upon Ashdrinker's broken edge.

'Danton clutched his chest as it burst into flame, and the scream that tore up out of his throat came straight from the bowels of hell. Dior swung again, no master with a sword but still, silver-quick. And Ashdrinker, forged in an age long past by the hands of legends and now blessed by the blood of the Grail herself, split his throat from ear to ear. The Beast staggered back, trying to scream, trying to curse, trying to beg through the ruins of his neck as those flames spread, as his flesh turned to ash, as he stumbled and fell onto the ice. His body convulsed as if the thing inside him – that dread animus that had propelled his corpse through countless years – refused to let go its broken shell. But the fire laid claim his skin. And dread time laid claim his flesh. And by the terror in his final, croaking wail, I like to believe the dread emperor of hell itself laid claim his wretched fucking soul.

'I dragged myself to my feet, trembling, staring at the bloody waif before me.

'"Great Redeemer," I whispered.

'"Flatterer," she gasped.

'The Beast of Vellene was dead.'

✦ XXIII ✦

RÉUNION DE FAMILLE

'A SCREAM TORE the night behind us, the sound of fat boiling in a fire. Dior tossed me Ashdrinker, the hilt still sticky with her blood, and we turned towards the ungodly wail, my eyes widening at the sight before us.

'"Fuck my face," I breathed.

'Liathe still brawled with the highbloods, ten against one. And though besting foes that many and powerful would take a miracle, it seemed to be raining miracles on the Mère that night. In fact, though her black hair was now soaked with blood, her red coat and pale flesh torn by dead claws, Liathe seemed almost to be . . . winning.

'Maarten the Butcher was now a smear of ashes inside a suit of smoking chainmail. Roisin the Red had lost an arm, using her other to hold in the contents of her sundered belly. Liviana lay curled in the snow, clutching the smoking ruins of her right hand. And I watched in fascination as Liathe hauled the boy Fetch off the ice, his pale finery now red with blood, squealing like a stuck piglet as her hand closed about his neck. I felt my belly surge as I heard a familiar sound, caught a familiar scent – that of boiling blood.

'"Sanguimancy," I whispered.

'The boy screamed again, little legs kicking, jaw distended in agony. And Ironheart though he was, I saw Liathe's fingers digging deeper into the blackening flesh of his throat, that marble turning to ashes, blood rising in gouts of red steam from his bleeding eyes.

'The elderly gent flashed out of the snow, snarling, and Liathe was forced to fling the boy away before she could finish him off. But he hit the ice, wailing and thrashing, red smoke wafting from his ruined throat.

'"My Prince . . ." Liviana whispered.

'The highbloods turned at her voice, looking at the ruins of the Beast at my back. I stalked towards them across the ice, Liathe backing away from the glow of my aegis, hissing in soft rage. The enemy of my enemy was just another enemy, and I'd never stand willingly beside a vampire in battle. But if this unholy bitch happened to kill a few of these leeches for me while I cut the rest to pieces, then as she fucking liked it.

'The Ironhearts quavered, staring in bleak amazement at the ruins of their lord. Pondering whether to fight on or simply flee into the dark.

'"The Lord is my shield, unbreakable!"

'The roar rang across the frozen Mère, a small flare lighting the distant dark. A glow I'd long ago forgotten brightened the night, silver-blue and charging towards us. Goosebumps prickled my skin – not at the freezing cold, but at sight of the Mothermaid and Redeemer, the angels of the host, bears and wolves and roses, throat to wrist to waist. That holy magik, wrought by the hands of Silver Sisters. The armour of the silversaint.

'Four figures ran down the ice out of the north, the holy light on their skin burning like ghostflame. They carried silversteel blades, and their eyes were fierce and wild.

'"I'll be damned . . ." I breathed.

'At the sight of the charging silversaints at their back, Liathe and I at their flanks, the Ironhearts took one last look at one another and made their choice. Their dread capitaine was slain. Their advantage lost. And you don't live forever by being a fool. Like shadows, they fled back into the deeper dark, content to live another night. And though I was loath to let them escape, I still felt some grim satisfaction at the thought of their bearing news to the Forever King – his prize lost, his ambition foiled, his youngest son slain. And I vowed under my breath, blood on my hands and the ashes of a Beast on my skin.

'"Only the beginning, Fabién . . ."

'"Come with usss, child."

'I turned, incredulous. Liathe stood in the snow, fingers outstretched, bloody handprint painted across her mouth. Dior exchanged a glance with me and raised her silversteel dagger. I almost laughed.

'"Surely you're jesting."

'That snow hawk cut through the skies above as the 'saints dashed towards us. Liathe fixed me with pale, lifeless eyes, narrowed against my light. "There is but one place in the entire empire this girl is sssafe, and it is *not* in the crumbling hallsss of your wretched Ord—"

'"Bitch," I sighed, "shut your *fucking* mouth."

'I raised Ashdrinker between us, her blade drenched blood-red.

'"If you think I've dragged my arse halfway across this empire, murdered priests and been tortured by inquisitors, fought off hordes of wretched and fled deepweald horrors, battled Princes of Forever and eaten my weight in fucking spudloaf just to hand this girl over to you now, you're madder than the sword in my hands, vampire."

'*The snik and the snak,* Ash whispered. *And the red, red, red.*

'"You have no clue as to what thisss girl mea—"

'"This girl has a name," Dior snapped. "And she's standing *right here.*"

'"Gabriel!" came a distant cry.

'"They have no comprehensssion of what you are," Liathe hissed, glancing at the oncoming silversaints. "Come with usss, child, I beg you." That pale hand reached through the falling snow. "*Come with usss or die.*"

'But Dior shook her head, lip curled. "You fuckers murdered Rafa. Saoirse. Bellamy. Sister Chloe. I may not know much about this silversaint game yet, but I learn quick, and I've learned this: *Dead tongues heeded are Dead tongues tasted.*"

'"Gabriel!" came that cry again. "*Dior!*"

'"Foolsss," Liathe hissed. "*Foolsss . . .*"

'The silver cadre reached us, bathed in divine light. Outnumbered, wounded, and nobody's fool, Liathe snarled behind her mask, swept her shredded coat about her, and blew apart into that storm of blood-red moths, winging upwards into the tumbling snows.

'"Sweet Mothermaid . . ." one of the 'saints whispered. "What was *that?*"

'I looked to the four of them, silverclad in the cold. One was a Sūdhaemi youngblood I'd no knowing of, dark of skin and black of eye. But the other three, I knew from days of glory. Big de Séverin, the bear of the Blood Dyvok ablaze on his chest, and his mug's face split in a stupid smile. Sly little Fincher, a gleam in his mismatched eyes as he lifted the silver carving fork his grandmama had gifted him, flashing me a rogue's grin as he twirled it between his fingers. And last, of course, the one I knew best of all.

'He was older now; ever skin and bone, hair that was once dirty straw now almost grey. But still, he'd charged with all the faith and fury of his youth, a silversteel longblade in his one good fist, and righteous fury burning in his one good eye.

'"Greyhand . . ." I whispered.

'"Gabriel de León," my old mentor breathed. "By the Mothermaid and all Seven Martyrs, I never thought to see you alive again . . ."

'"How in the name of God did you find us?"

'He lifted his good arm, and the snow hawk that had been circling above alighted on his wrist. "Old Archer passed a few years back. This is Winter. She's been following you since before you reached Aveléne."

"'But how did you know to even look for us?" the girl beside me asked.

'I nodded to her by way of introduction. "This is Dior Lachance. She—"

"'We know who she is," Greyhand said.

"'Gabe?" came a wild cry. "Dior?"

'My heart dropped and rolled in my chest, Dior's eyes lit up, and we both turned towards the shout. And stumbling down the frozen riverbank, among a cadre of Silver Sisters armed with wheellock rifles, I saw a face I never thought to see again.

"'Sister Chloe!" Dior cried.

'The girl broke into a limping run, and the little sister dashed across the ice, slipping in her haste. Dior slid as she tried to stop herself, tumbled into Chloe, and the pair fell again, laughing and weeping as Chloe whispered, "Merci, oh merci, Almighty God . . ."

"'A river runner brought the good sister to San Michon weeks back," Greyhand murmured. "He found her on the banks of the Volta, half drowned, mostly frozen. But he was a godly man, and he took it upon himself to carry her back to us. We thought she might not pull through, but her faith burns strong. And when she regained consciousness, Sœur Sauvage told us of your travels together, that you and the girl might yet live. And so, we sent our eyes to look for you, by all the roads you might travel."

'I smiled as I watched Dior and Chloe roll in the snow, my heart grown warm.

"'Is it true, Gabe?" Fincher looked to me. "What Sister Chloe told us about the girl?"

"'Is she truly the Grail of San Michon?" de Séverin asked.

'I looked to the ruins of Danton's corpse, shaking my head. "Her blood burned a Prince of Forever to ashes. Brought men back from the brink of death. If she's not what Chloe says, then I've no other explanation for what she does."

"'Redeemer be praised," Finch whispered, making the sign of the wheel.

"'The end to daysdeath," the youngblood breathed.

"'. . . Maybe," I sighed.

"'It's good to see you again."

'I looked towards Greyhand as he spoke, my jaw clenched. Reunited after all that time, I didn't know what to feel. He'd been my teacher, this man. He'd saved my life, and I'd saved his in kind. And though in truth, I'd surpassed him in my days of glory, a part of every son will feel ever trapped in his father's shadow. But there was still a gulf between us. Greyhand had been among those who ordered me to set Astrid aside, who'd passed judgement on me when I refused, who'd sent my love and me out into the cold and dark. And though I remembered Aaron's words, though I was more conscious than ever that every moment of my life seemed to have been leading to this, that all I'd suffered and all I'd lost might simply have been so I could be the one to deliver Dior to San Michon, still, still . . .

'"I wish I could say the same, Frère," I murmured.

'"Nae Frère," Fincher said. "Nae longer. Greyhand stands as abbot now, Gabe."

'I looked to my old master in question. "Khalid?"

'"His thirst grew too loud." Greyhand signed the wheel. "He took the Red Rite four years back. God granted him the strength for a silversaint's death."

'"Better to die a man than live a monster, eh?" I asked.

'"You *did* it!"

'I grunted as Chloe barrelled into me, throwing her arms around my neck in a fashion most unbecoming a sister of the Silver Sorority. But I caught her and laughed, the joy at seeing her alive overcoming the shadow on my heart at this strange reunion with the brotherhood who'd abandoned me. Chloe kissed my cheek, heedless of the blood and ashes, her eyes sparkling like cut crystal.

'"I *knew* it!" she shouted, laughing and crying. "Did I not tell you all those years ago? Did I not say it then as now? God intended *great* things for you, mon ami. And you have done a greater service to this empire than any holy brother, any chevalier, any hero or emperor in all the pages of history!" She kissed me again, squeezing tight. "You're a good man, Gabriel de León. The *best* of men."

'"He's a bastard is what he is," Dior grinned, limping towards us.

'"Watch your tongue girl," I growled, mock-serious. "I owe you a bollocking for breaking your promise to me. And you owe Aaron and Baptiste a sled and a team of dogs."

'Greyhand's jaw twitched as he glanced downriver. "San Michon will compensate the Lord of Aveléne for his losses. You may give him my word when you return to the château."

'I frowned. "I'm not going back to Aveléne."

'Chloe nodded, climbing down from my neck. "Gabriel has business in the eas—"

"'I'm not going east, either." I glanced between the pair, a slow frown creasing my brow. "I'm going to San Michon with Dior."

'Chloe smiled soft, shaking her head. "Gabe, she's safe with us now. You've done more than I could ever have asked, but there's no need to trouble yours—"

"'It's nothing close to trouble." I trudged across the ice to stand at Dior's side. The light in my aegis had faded now, and the cold was creeping in. But as she slipped her hand into mine, I could still feel fire in my chest. "I'm not leaving her."

"'All is well, Sister," Greyhand said. "Though we parted beneath a cloud, Gabriel served San Michon for long and storied years. 'Tis no sin to seat him at our table for a night. I've no doubt a few of our youngsters would like to meet the infamous Black Lion of Lorson."

'*Not famous,* I thought to myself. *Infamous.*

'Chloe pressed her lips thin, but nodded. "Véris, Abbot."

"'Let's be about it, then," Greyhand grunted. "Sunset waits for no saint."

'The Silver Sisters had brought a spare sosya, and as Chloe bandaged Dior's wounded hands, I wrapped myself in a blanket for the ride back north. Dior climbed aboard a stout grey fellow, and I caught her looking back across the Mère. The shattered ice and cold ashes, the remnants of immortal monsters, proven all too mortal by her hand. Her coat was dusted with snow and spattered with blood, and I had the almost irresistible urge to brush her hair the fuck out of her eyes.

'Instead, I proffered Danton's sabre and bowed like a gentle at court.

"'What's this for?" she asked.

"'To the victor the spoils. It's the finest sort of blade, good to practise with." I smiled, dried blood cracking on my cheeks. "We've lessons to begin, you and I."

'She grinned in return, took the sabre and looked it over. "It *is* pretty."

'I handed over the Beast's scabbard. "Just don't cut your fucking hands off."

'She chuckled and hung her head, ashen hair over her eyes.

"'I'm sorry, Gabe," she murmured. "I'm sorry I lied to you."

"'Apology accepted. So long as you don't do it again."

'She raised a bloody right hand. "I do solemnly swear: no more lying to Gabriel."

"'Good." I winced as I climbed up behind her. "Because dramatic chases with immortal hordes gets the blood pumping and all, but I'm not as young as I used to be."

'"Should I fetch your walking stick, old man?"

'"Cheeky bitch."

'"Coming after me was foolish, you know. You said it's always better to be a bastard."

'"Privileges of being a father. Don't do what I do, do what I say."

'She smiled faintly, blue eyes still on the bloody ice. "Merci. For following me."

'"I told you. My friends are the hill I die on."

'"We're still friends, then?"

'"The strangest sort. But oui." I breathed deep and sighed. "Still friends."

'She smiled wider, impish, and leaning up, she kissed my bloody cheek.

'"The fuck was that for?" I growled.

'"No reason," she lied.'

✦ XXIV ✦

THIS ENDLESS NIGHT

'IT ROSE UP before us like it had that findi seventeen years ago, wreathed in snow-grey fog. And though I'd seen it a thousand times, still, I knew what Dior felt as she looked to the bluffs above and breathed a frozen sigh.

'Simple, jaw-dropping awe.

'"Fuck *my* face," she whispered.

'Seven lichen-covered pillars towered above the frozen valley, crowned with the familiar haunts of my youth – the Gauntlet, the Armoury, the Cathedral. I remembered the years I'd spent here: quiet moments in the Library's dusty stacks, feasts of victory and hymns of praise and stolen moments of bliss in the arms of she who was my love.

'Before I'd lost it all.

'I felt a wave of nostalgia, that sweet poison seeping into my heart, that vain and selfish desire to dwell among glories of the past, when days were better and simpler, when all the world seemed bright, tinted rose-red in the halls of memory. But it's a fool who looks with more fondness to the days behind than the ones ahead. And it's a man drenched in defeat who sings that sad refrain; that things were better then.

'Fincher told me that Kaspar and Kaveh had both married, moved back home to Sūdhaem, and I didn't know the lads who came out from the stables to take our horses. I didn't know the gatekeep who winched us up on the sky platform, nor any of the Silver Sisters who stood with Chloe and watched me sidelong as we rose up from the valley floor. They knew *me* of course – the Lion the dark had feared, the boy Empress Isabella had knighted with her own blade, the fool who'd stolen a bride from God. And in returning to this place, I felt like a man who'd found an old coat he wore as a boy, slipping it onto his shoulders and discovering it no longer fits.

'Sad for youth lost.

'Proud that he has grown.

'But most of all, uncomfortable.

'"We must begin our preparations with Dior," Chloe said, her voice almost trembling with anticipation. "The Rite must be conducted at dawn, and there is much to make ready."

'"What is this Rite?" I asked. "Where does it come from?"

'"Unearthed in the depths of the Library's forbidden section. An ancient text written in bloodscript, penned by a Grail scholar before the rise of the empire, and translated with poor Rafa's help over many years." Chloe made the sign of the wheel, hung her head. "The book is very old. So fragile the pages might turn to dust if you touch them ungentle. Hence, I couldn't bring them with me in the search. But this is fitting anyway." She smiled at Dior like a mother twice proud, waved to the grand Cathedral as we rose into view of it. "It is here, in the church of the First Martyr, that San Michon's descendant shall put an end to the endless night."

'As ever, Chloe's fervour was contagious, and the 'saints and sisters around us murmured, staring at the girl beside me in soft awe. "Véris."

'Dior gazed at the Cathedral in wonder. With Isabella's patronage, it had been restored to its full glory, thrust skywards like a spear unto heaven, black stone and beautiful windows of glittering stained glass. "Do I . . . do I need to do anything?"

'"Perhaps a bath is in order?" Chloe chided. "But no, love. You need only be yourself. Almighty God, the Mothermaid, and Martyrs shall do the rest."

'Dior looked to me, and I nodded. "Go with Chloe. I'll not be far." And taking Dior's hand, the sisters led her across the rope spans towards the Priory. Greyhand murmured that he must prepare for duskmass, that we would talk anon. De Séverin slapped me on the back, and Fincher grinned. "What say we buy ye a drink meantime, Brother?"

'"Throw in a tunic and new greatcoat, and I'll get the first round," I smiled.

'The Brothers laughed and saw me to the Barracks to wash the blood and ashes from my skin, and from there, to the Armoury. Seraph Argyle was in the forge, among his blackthumbs as ever – an old man now, but still broad as barns and hard at work, his iron hand wrapped about the blade he was hammering. He nodded greeting, but seemed not overjoyed to see me, even after all those years; the stain of my sin didn't wash out that easily. But he didn't protest at least as I grabbed myself some fresh leathers.

'Looking about me, I saw again the mark of coin in the walls and the works – San Michon was a splendour once more. Yet I couldn't help but notice it seemed emptier somehow. Emptier even than in the days of my youth. Paleblood numbers had always been thin, but it seemed that here, like everywhere else in Elidaen, the war had carved its mark.

'The sun was sinking by the time I was done, and the bells were rung for duskmass. I knew I'd need to attend the Cathedral for the Rite at dawn, but I'd no stomach for prayer that night. And so, I fetched a bottle from the refectory beneath the stares of curious kitchenhands, and made my way to the Library. I wandered among the stacks for a time, drinking from the neck and thinking on all that had been. The great map of the empire was laid out at my feet, the wolves of Chastain and the bears of Dyvok and the ravens of Voss spread like a bloodstain across all the five countries of the realm.

'*What will this world be*, I wondered, *if the sun were truly restored on the morrow?*

'*What if it has all been worth it?*

'God Almighty, I couldn't even remember the colour the sky had been . . .

'I walked into the forbidden section, my old boots heavy on the creaking timbers. I navigated the dusty shelves, the books and scrolls and strange curios. I remembered the scent of blood hanging in the air the first night I came here, half-expecting to see my love as I rounded the corner to the room we'd first spoke, first kissed, first sinned. But it was empty, of course – empty save for the long table we'd once sat at years ago, looking into each other's eyes and welcoming the fall that awaited us both.

'I looked at the tome laid out on the table, thicker than my thigh, trimmed in tarnished brass. It was so old the leather had been bleached grey, the vellum turned brown with countless years. The book was near falling to pieces, but the lettering was still visible, faint and faded, oui, but still there. This, too, was a strange immortality, I realized. Poems, stories, ideas, frozen forever in time. The simple wonder of books.

'I ran my fingertip just above the page's surface, a breath shy of the spidery lettering. I could read not a word of it save one.

'*Aavsunc.*

'I remembered Rafa explaining the word's meaning to me in Winfael: Old Talhostic for *essence*. The essence caught by the First Martyr in her womb. The birthright Dior now carried in her veins. The blood of the Redeemer himself.

'From holy cup comes holy light;
'The faithful hand sets world aright.
'And in the Seven Martyrs' sight . . .

'"Mere man shall end this endless night," I murmured.

'The bells rang to end the duskmass, and I wondered about Dior. She'd eat in the refectory maybe, or perhaps the Priory. And though there was no safer place for her in all the empire than upon the holy ground of San Michon, though she'd proven more than capable of looking after herself, I was ill at ease at not having seen her for a time.

'I left the Library, intent on the Priory. But I found my feet dragging me towards that great spire of granite and stained glass in the monastery's heart. I walked past the fountain of angels – Chiara and Raphael, Sanael and my namesake, Gabriel – through the dawndoors, and into the belly of San Michon Cathedral. Trudging up the aisle, emptying the last of the vodka into my belly, I found myself before the altar. The place Astrid had scribed the aegis into my skin, where I'd sworn the vows we'd broken. I stared up at the Redeemer on his wheel, my fingertips drumming Ashdrinker's hilt. I let the bottle fall from my hand and roll along the stone at my feet.

'"Still no brother of mine, bastard," I said. "But I hope your blood rings true."

'"How is Astrid?"

'I turned at the voice, saw Greyhand climbing the spiral stairs from the sacristy beneath the altar. It was his duty as abbot to speak the mass, of course – he must have been down there changing out of his robes. He was back in silversaint garb now, his eye flooded red from the sacrament the brethren all took at services, the gouge Laure Voss had torn through his empty socket covered by a patch of black leather.

'"Sœur Sauvage told me you two had wed?"

'I looked at my old master, tongue thick in my mouth. "What of it?"

'"She said you had a daughter. Patience?" Greyhand shook his head, fixing me with his one good eye. "Thank God and Mothermaid for the small mercy she was not a son, I suppose. To bring another paleblood into this world—"

'"Spare me the sermon, Abbot. I'm not drunk enough for it."

'He sucked his teeth, nodded slow. "So how is she? Your beautiful wife?"

'"I didn't think you cared, old man."

'"Astrid Rennier was Mistress of the Aegis in San Michon for five years, Gabriel. I knew her well as any, and better than most. Of course I care."

'"Care so much you cast us out into the cold without a thought?"

"'I had *thoughts* aplenty," he said, eye flashing. "First among them being that you both knew what you did was wrong, and yet you did it anyway. Second, that you lied to me with every breath you could muster after the night you took her into your bed. And last, that I had been a fool to place the trust in you I did. I thought the years between then and now might have cooled your head on the matter. But I see that was vain fantasy." He looked me up and down, shook his head. "You are as you ever were."

"'What should I have done, then? Forgive? Forget? Fuck that. And fuck you. You turned your backs on us. After all we did."

"'I told you once and I'll tell you again," Greyhand said. 'It's a fool who plays at the precipice, but only the prince of fools blames another when he falls. You cost us dear when you walked out those doors, Gabriel. The war has been going ill ever since, and our numbers dwindle by the year. Theo Petit, Philippe Olen, Philippe Clément, Alonso de Madeisa, Fabro—"

"'There's a reason I didn't attend mass tonight. Don't preach at me. And don't you dare try to paint me with their blood. That's on *your* hands, not mine."

"'And when was the last time you *did* attend mass, Gabriel?"

'I blinked, frowning. "What year is this again?"

"'Tis true, then, what Chloe said. Faithless as the blood that flows in your veins." He glanced at the empty bottle at my feet. "You could've been the greatest of us . . ."

"'I *was* the greatest of you."

"'*Was*," he snapped, fire in his pale green eye. "And now? An oathbreaker. A drunkard. Ever you lacked the humility to think beyond your own desires. To put aside your pride and do what truly needed to be done. I once told you that you had the telling of your own story. That you could choose what kind it might be. And *this* was *your* choice." He shook his head again. "God, what a disappointment you are."

"'I gave my *life* for this empire!" I roared. "And I'm still giving it! I dragged that girl halfway across hell to these walls, and still you give me no credit!"

"'And yet still you seek it, as you always have!" We were nose to nose now, the bitterness of resentment that had festered over long years rushing forth, like poison from a wound. "Even now you dare to speak of sacrifice when that girl shall pay a thousand times the sum of your own on the morrow! *She* shall be the one to spill her blood in the name of this empire, not you!"

'The Cathedral rang with Greyhand's words, like the echo of a wheellock shot.

"'. . . What did you say?"

'Greyhand lowered his gaze, teeth bared.

"'What the fuck did you just say?" I demanded again.

"'Too much," the abbot growled, turning away. "I'll speak no more of it."

'I grabbed his arm, incredulous. "You're going to . . ."

'Greyhand snatched his arm free, a dangerous glint in his bloodshot eye. "Get your hands off me, Gabriel."

'My mind was racing now, and I thrice cursed myself a fool. I thought back upon that dusty tome in the Library, the word *Aavsunc* scribed on the faded pages. Again, I remembered Rafa explaining the word's meaning in Winfael, but this time, I remembered true. *Aavsunc* wasn't Old Talhostic for *Essence*. It was the word for *Lifeblood*. And *that* was what they intended to spill in this ritual come the dawn.

"'You're going to *kill* her," I hissed.

"'. . . Such is the price." He turned his head to avoid my gaze, his voice a wet-gravel snarl. "For the end of daysdeath. For the salvation of the empire."

"'Does Chloe know about this?" I demanded, incredulous.

"'T'was she who unearthed the ritual, Gabriel."

'My heart felt cleaved in two at that, my belly turning cold and hard. "And what about Dior? Does *she* know? Did you tell her?"

'Greyhand glowered, his silence speaking all.

"'Fuck me," I hissed. "Fuck *me*, you cannot do this. She's sixteen years old!"

"'*One* life," he spat. "One life for the sake of thousands . . . nay, *hundreds* of thousands! I have been sending men to their deaths for a decade. I am fighting a war against an enemy who does not die, who turns our own dead against us. Think of the suffering that could be averted! If the sun rises true on the morrow, the war is *over*, Gabriel! Every coldblood abroad in the land, wretched and highblood alike, will be burned to ashes with a single stroke of the blade!"

"'The blade! At the throat of an innocent child!"

'He raised his chin, defiant. "Almighty God will forgive us our trespass."

"'No, this is wrong. This is purest evil, Greyhand, and you know it! Better to die a man than live a monster, you taught me. Well this? This is fucking *monstrous*!"

"'I vowed to defend this empire, Gabriel. To be the fire between this and all world's ending." Greyhand scowled, dark as dusk. "And unlike you, I keep my vows."

'My fist crashed into his jaw, splitting his lip. Greyhand staggered, the sanctus in his veins keeping him on his feet. But my sword was drawn now, Ashdrinker gleaming in the light of the chymical globes, that silver dame seeming to glower at my old master.

'*Broken-black, twisted-true, rotten rotten rotten to the core.*

'"I won't let you do it," I growled. "There's no chance in hell I will let you do this."

'I backed away down the aisle, eyes locked with Greyhand. I'd not smoked since morning, and he'd a duskmass dose in him, but I had two hands, not one. And so, he simply followed, roaring, "Gabriel, don't be a fool!" as I turned and ran. I burst from the dawndoors as he dashed into the belfry tower. Bells began ringing; an alarm echoing across the monastery, entwined with the bitter, howling wind. I ran, ran from the Cathedral and across the rope span towards the Priory, shouting at the top of my lungs.

'"Dior! *Dior!*"

'I heard running feet, Greyhand bellowing, circling off to my right and moving sanctus-swift. The nightswatchman loomed out of the dark ahead, lantern high, sword in one hand as cries of "traitor!" and "treachery!" rang on the walls. I'd no wish to hurt him, swooping low and kicking his legs out from under him, breaking his nose with a punch that left him senseless on the bridge. But I could see silversaints now: Finch and de Séverin, that Sūdhaemi youngblood, all descending. I ran, but Winter swooped out of the dark, carving a furrow down my cheek with her talons. I gasped and lashed out, the snow hawk retreating quick as lies, and when I'd blinked the blood from my eyes, I saw that Finch stood before me, sword drawn and feet apart, his faeling eyes on Greyhand.

'"Abbot, what the hell—?"

'"Take him in hand!" Greyhand bellowed, running towards us.

'"Get out of my way, Finch . . ."

'"By the Blood, man, I said bring that oathbreaker *down!*"

'"They're going to kill that girl, Finch. Get *the fuck out of my way!*"

'We'd fought side by side, Fincher and I. He was at Triúrbaile with me when we liberated the Dyvok slaughterfarms. And like I said, there's a bond between men who've placed their lives in a brother's hands, and asked that brother to do the same. But there's fanaticism, too. There's faith unbridled and minds unquestioning; the soldier at the order of his commander, the faithful at the word of their priest. And after breaking my vows, my brother trusted me not so much as once he had.

'In truth, I couldn't fault him for it.

'Finch raised his sword, and though I was his better with a blade, he was dosed with the sacrament. We clashed, both bled, both cursing. I struck again, and he fended me off, roaring, "Have ye gone fuckin' mad?" as Winter struck again at my back. I lashed out again, furious, smashing Finch's blade from his hand and slicing his arm bone-deep. But by then, the youngblood had arrived, and Greyhand too, and the old bastard slung his flail and caught my sword hand at the wrist. I roared again, "*Dior!*" and flipped Ashdrinker to my left, spitting the youngblood as he came on headlong and leaving him in a bleeding puddle on the stone. I whirled on Greyhand, trying to wrest my hand free from his accursed flail, and finally, de Séverin arrived, striking with the strength of the Dyvok blood in his veins.

'"*DIOR, RU—*"

'De Séverin's blade plunged through my back, out through my belly, and I gasped, coughing blood. He hauled me up off the ground as I tried to gut him on the backswing, sliding down that great two-hander until my spine was arched upon the crossguard. I swung again, and de Séverin slung me into the wall with the strength of the Untamed, the brick smashed to powder where I struck it. And wild-eyed, furious, Finch loomed up over me, his silversteel raised in his bloody hand and his fangs bared and gleaming.

'"HOLD!" Greyhand bellowed.

'I tried to get to my feet, bleeding and spitted, but Greyhand's boot crashed into my jaw, sending me sprawling. Again, I tried to rise, and again he kicked me, splintering my ribs. I clawed snow and stone, tried to call for Dior, but I couldn't drag breath enough into my punctured lungs. And Greyhand kicked me again, again, again, so fucking hard I saw black stars, felt bone crack, tasted hot blood; his old boots dancing, and all the fury of a former master upon his most disappointing student ringing on my skull.

'They stood about me, gasping, bloodied. They could have killed me then and there. But for all his faults, all his flaws, old Greyhand was ever an adherent of San Michon's law.

'"This man bears the aegis," he growled. "We will not despoil this holy ground by murdering him like a dog in the street. Though he has fallen far from grace, Gabriel de León was once our brother. He will not die as a monster. He will die as a man."

'De Séverin hauled me to my feet, bloody drool at my chin.

'"That is the best I can offer you, Gabriel," the abbot said.

'They dragged me half-senseless, cracked skull still ringing with the dance of Greyhand's boots, long spools of blood swinging from my chin. I could say my mind was racing, desperately searching for some way out of this. I could say I roared again for Dior, my thoughts only for her. But that would be a lie. In truth, the old bastard had kicked the living shit out of me, and I could barely conjure my own name, let alone hers.

'By the time we stopped walking, some semblance of clear thought returned. I blinked hard, trying to understand why my hands wouldn't move.

'"We beg you bear witness, Almighty Father," I heard Greyhand say. "As your begotten son suffered for our sins, so too shall our brother suffer for his."

'"Véris," came the reply around me.

'And at last, I realized where they'd brought me.

'Heaven's Bridge.

'I'd been chained to the wheel, the wind moaning in the gulf behind me, that long drop down into the frozen Mère. I remembered my first night in this monastery, old Frère Yannick giving himself over to the Red Rite and the arms of God. But let's be clear now: this was no ceremony, no celebration, no blessed journey to meet my Maker. This was a murder, plain and simple. And my old friend rage rose up inside me, and I roared and bucked against the bonds that held me. Denying with every inch of me, every scrap of breath in my bleeding lungs, every drop of blood in my furied heart that it could end like this.

'*I refuse to die here,* I told myself.

'*I. Refuse. To die here.*

'Greyhand pressed his flail to my shoulders – seven ritual touches for the seven nights the Redeemer suffered. A flintbox was kissed to my skin, to mimic the flames that burned God's begotten son. And then, my old master raised his silvered sword.

'"From suffering comes salvation," he intoned. "In service to God, we find the path to his throne. In blood and silver this 'saint has lived, and so now dies."

'"Fuck you," I hissed. "*DIO—*"

'The blade flashed.

'Pain flared bright.

'My eyes closed.

'And my throat opened wide.'

✦ XXV ✦

GENTLE AS STARLIGHT

'A RUSH OF impossible warmth cascaded down my chest.

'I felt the bonds at my wrists loosened.

'I felt a hand upon my chest, like a father guiding his son to sleep.

'I felt myself falling.

'And as the wind filled my ears, as I began that long tumbling drop down into the mother's arms, as I closed my eyes and the tears came at the thought that finally, *finally*, I might see them again, I felt one final sensation.

'Gentle as starlight.

'Soft as first snows upon my cheek.

'Moth wings.'

✦ XXVI ✦

BROKEN VOWS

'MY TONGUE WAS burning as the dark receded. A fire, rushing down my gullet and flooding out through my veins. It was copper and rust, autumn burning red, a hymn both familiar and like nothing I'd known.

'Blood.

'*Blood.*

'My eyes flashed open, realization crashing down – that I wasn't dead, that this was no life hereafter, that I'd been denied my well-earned sleep and the warmth of ma famille's arms. But more, I realized that vow I'd breathed in the ruins of my home, that promise I'd whispered as my lady gave her last gift to me, had been broken. I'd sworn no drop of it would pass my lips again, and yet it had been *forced* upon me, flooding down my slit throat and dragging me back from the very edge of death.

'The blood of an ancien.

'She knelt above me with wrist pressed to my lips, that masked monster in a maid's body, bloody handprint across her mouth, pale, dead eyes fixed upon mine. I lunged upwards from the bloodstained snow, but she stepped away, long, dark whips of hair flowing about her like oil on water. That bloody sword now gleaming in her hand.

'"L-liathe," I gasped, my larynx tight and aching.

'She bowed like gentry, and again, the masculine gesture from a form so feminine struck me as odd. But such thoughts were whispers under the rush of my fury: that the vow I'd sworn to my bride had been broken for me by this deathless leech.

'"You dare," I growled, staggering towards her. "You f-fucking *dare* . . ."

'"Why the rage, Silverssssaint? We just saved your life."

'"It wasn't yours to save! Not like *that*!"

'I spat red onto the snow, the wondrous, awful fire of her still flooding my mouth, tingling at the tips of my fingers. Even though my throat had been sliced clean through by a silversteel blade, the wound had closed over; chilling testament to the power in this thing's dead heart. I'd tasted the blood of ancien before – smoked in a pipe, true, but still, the thrill and strength of blood thickened over centuries wasn't a stranger to me. But this was a potency I'd *never* felt before. I dragged my sleeve across my lips, sticky and red, spitting again as my voice shook with hatred.

'"You bitch," I snarled, hands curling into fists. "You leech, you *fucking*—"

'"Snatched from the fall by our thousand wingsss, dragged from death's door by our opened vein, and yet, you spit insult at usss, like a boychild denied sweets after sssupper." Liathe shook her head and tutted. "You were raised better than that."

'"You know *nothing* about me. Not the mother who raised me nor the home I grew up in. Not the blood in my veins nor the price that I've paid. So speak like you know me again, vampire, and I'll rip the lying tongue out of your dead fucking skull."

'"A part of us hatesss you enough to let you try." She shook her head, her voice almost sad. "But not tonight."

'"Hate me? You don't even *know* me."

'"Are we ssso different?" she asked. "Ssso changed you do not recognize usss?"

'The vampire reached up to that mask she wore, dragged it aside. Again, as at San Guillaume, my eyes went immediately to the lower half of her face, the awful wound there. Her bottom lip and the skin below it were simply gone. The edges of the wound were ragged, perpetually bruised, as if the flesh had been not cut away but *ripped*, like a troublesome glove. The teeth in her lower jaw were exposed, and I could see the cartilage and bone, the muscles of her throat flexing obscenely as she spoke again.

'"It was worssse once. So awful you surely wouldn't have known us. But we're closer to what we were now. Ssso look again, Gabriel. Look *again*."

'My eyes drifted up, locked on hers now, pale and bleached by death. But there was something in their shape, something . . . as she reached up with one slender hand and parted that long, dark hair from her face, something in the cut of her cheek or the arc of her brow that stirred it within me. A faint spark of recognition.

'"Do you truly not ssssee?"

'And it hit me then, like a hammer between my eyes. Memories of a childhood lost, of a home gutted by flame and a town in ashes. But I shook my head. *Impossible,* I thought, *impossible,* remembering the day I'd returned to Lorson and beheld the vengeance Laure Voss had meted for my sins. My mama dead in the snow, one hand outstretched towards the chapel. And within, cradled in old Père Louis's arms, another figure. Charcoal skin stretched over kindling bones. But I could still tell it had been a girl. A candlemaid.

'My baby sister.

'My little hellion.

'"Celene . . ." I whispered.

'My stomach turned as she tried to smile with but half a face.

'"Well met, brother."

'She'd been but a girl when I left for San Michon, and girls grow quick at that age. With half her face missing, her eyes bleached, I might have been forgiven for not recognizing her. Still, I could scarce believe what I was seeing. After all these years . . .

'"But . . . I saw your body, burned in the church!"

'"Not I," she said, shaking her head. "I was not in chapel that day. I wasss off tumbling with the mason's boy, Philippe. You remember him."

'Those pale eyes narrowed as if in remembered pain.

'"She found usss first. Before she struck the village. Laure was *delighted* when she discovered I was your sister, Gabriel. She made me watch while she made Philippe sssing. She made me cry. She made me beg. She made me think she might let me live. And then she told me why she'd come to Lorssson. What *you'd* done to earn her wrath. And she kissssed me, and she ripped my face off with her clawsss and drank me slow so I might feel it to the last. And then, she left me dead in the sssnow."

'"Celene," I whispered, utterly aghast. "Sister, I . . ."

'"But I didn't die, brother. I woke, but an hour or sso after the Wraith slaughtered me. Trapped in the body I died in. *Thisss,*" she hissed, waving to the ruins of her face, "body."

'"You said your name was Liathe."

'"My title. Not my name."

'"But your blood," I breathed, my tongue still aflame with it. "Even if you were the child of an ancien, you're still only a fledgling. And your gifts . . ." I looked to the blade in her hand. "Sanguimancy is province of the Blood Esani, not the Voss."

'"*Sso* much you do not know. An ocean beneath your feet you do not sssee. But while you hid in the shadowsss after your fall, brother, I *embraced* them."

'She lifted her hand, and that blade carved of her blood shivered and moved, snaking through the air like a living thing, circling her body in long, sluicing arcs before coalescing into the shape of a sword once more.

'"Unlike you, these last fifteen yearsss, I spent my time wisssely."

'My mind was awash, a thousand questions, an awful guilt. A joy to learn my baby sister wasn't dead, a horror to see she was Dead instead. And more, above all, that blood she'd given me, the strength of it, the fire, the fear and the hate of it – first, that my vow had been broken by her hand, but more, the knowledge that I was now *bound* to her, at least in part. And that with two more sups from her wrist, I'd be her slave.

'"Why did you not say anything when first we met?" I demanded. "When we fought at San Guillaume? We're blood, you and I. Why didn't you *tell* me, Celene?"

'"Because everything I have sssuffered, everything I am, is because of you."

'Again, she gifted me that hideous smile.

'"Because I *hate* you, brother."

'I dragged a hand across my bloody chin, spitting red again. "Then why save me?"

'She looked at me as if I were simple. "Because your former brethren have the Grail on holy ground, and I cannot go up there and take her myssself." Pale eyes roamed my body, the blood-spattered snow. "Why did they try to murder you?"

'"They intend to kill Dior at dawn. I tried to stop them."

'"*Kill* her?" Celene's eyes grew wide. "Why?"

'"A ritual. To end daysdeath."

'"Those fools," she breathed. "Those wretched *foolss* . . ."

'She fixed me with her dead gaze, death-bleached eyes imploring.

'"You must stop them. You *mussst*. They have no comprehension of what they do."

'"Celene, how do you—"

'"There is no time!" she snarled. "The sun rises! If that girl's blood is spilled on holy ground, then *all* will be undone! *All* of it!"

'I clenched my teeth, desperate for answers but knowing she spoke truth – at least in part. If I didn't stop them, Chloe and the others would murder Dior. No matter my sister's game, whatever role she imagined Dior might play in it, whatever scheme this *vampire* who'd been my blood was behind, I couldn't let Dior die.

'Simple as that.

'I looked to the monastery above, the pillars rising five hundred feet into the sky, the Cathedral crouched atop it like a black spider at the centre of a horrid web. There was no way to ascend on the sky platform undetected, and I'd need to come quick and quiet if I were to best a monastery full of my brethren. But still, the potency of the blood Celene had forced me to drink was rushing in my veins, filling me with a strength unrivalled. And I conjured another way I might ascend those heights and do what must be done.

'I looked to Celene, now fixing that mask back over the ruin of her face.

'"I'll return," I told her. "And then you and I will speak of the last fifteen years. Of those oceans unseen."

'The snow fell grey in the dark about us; the wind howled in the gulf between us.

'". . . It's good to see you again, Hellion. I'm sorry I never answered your letters."

'"Go, Gabriel."

'I walked to the base of the Armoury's pillar.

'I dug my fingers into the rock.

'And with the strength of stolen ages inside me, I climbed.'

✦ XXVII ✦
A FOND FAREWELL

'THE ASCENT WAS a blur, in truth. As I raced the dawn up that spire of black granite, dreading the moment I might feel bleak daylight break the eastern sky, I remember only cold; bitterest cold. My fingers grown numb, every breath making my teeth ache, my lungs burn, the vague thought that one slip might spell my doom flitting at the back of my mind like a troublesome firefly. But more, and most, my mind was filled with the thought of my brethren's betrayal: Greyhand's sword at my throat, Finch, de Séverin, and the others bringing me down like a dog, and the bitter knowledge that Chloe had known Dior's fate all along.

'*I'm not that little girl any more, Gabe. I know what I'm doing. And if I can't tell you all, then I beg you forgive me. But God above, truth told, it's best you don't know all.*

'Little Chloe Sauvage.

'A believer that one, through and through.

'I crested the pillar's cusp with the dark still at my back. The blood my sister had given me was the only way I could have made that climb. And taking a moment to gather myself in the Armoury's courtyard, I gazed about the ancient buildings of San Michon. The Great Library. The Priory. This place I'd once pledged my life to and was now set to undo. Even when they'd cast me aside, I'd never wanted the Order to actually fail. I'd still believed in what they did. But now, I was set to burn this place to the fucking ground.

'Dawn was a fearful promise at world's edge, and at any moment, those Cathedral bells might begin their dreadful song. But it's only a fool who walks towards a battle barehanded, and one hand holding a sword is worth ten thousand clasped in prayer.

'I climbed the Armoury walls as I'd done as a boy, and though the old tiles had been replaced, they still came away easy enough. I crept down into the forge, took a moment to warm my freezing hands by the fires, let the cold leach a little from my bones. And then, I stepped out into the main hall, those rows of beautiful swords forged by the hands of the saintsmiths, taking up a longblade in each hand. The first was a beauty, the Angel Gabriel at the crossguard, a well-worn verse from the Vow of San Michon upon the blade.

'*I am the fire that rages between this and all world's ending.*

'But the second blade was a wonder, the Angel Mahné upon the hilt, twin scythes bared, death's head grinning, a grim promise from Laments etched down its length.

'*I am the door all shall open. The promise none shall break.*

'I threw on a new tunic, greatcoat, bandolier, and silver-heeled boots. And like all hell's reckoning, I strode towards the Cathedral.

'It rose into dark skies, seeming to glower at my approach. The northern wind pressed me back, whipped my coat about me. The angels in the fountain stared in reproach as I ascended the stairs – not to the dawndoors in the east, but those for dusk in the west. The doors for the dead. Such they'd left me for twice, these brothers of mine. And now, I'd see that favour returned. Here, I'd lay this to rest.

'I could hear a voice within, raised up in prayer. A woman I'd taught the art of the blade, a woman I'd let myself believe in, a woman I'd called a friend.

'"*From holy cup comes holy light; the faithful hand sets world aright. And in the Seven Martyrs' sight, mere man shall end this—*"

'The doors boomed like thunder as I kicked them in, smashing against the walls as I stepped into the Cathedral. The bells began ringing as the choir fell silent, as the Brothers in the front row rose to their feet, eyes wide at the sight of me: Finch and de Séverin, the youngblood, Seraph Argyle and a passel of smithies and watchmen and Brothers of the Hearth, and last of all, Greyhand, his pale green eye wide with astonishment. Chloe stood at the Cathedral's heart, arms upheld towards the statue of the Redeemer, reading from the ancient tome on the podium beside her. Dior was laid out on the altar, strapped down like a young 'saint about to be gifted his aegis. She was dressed in white robes, ashen hair brushed back from bright blue eyes, looking up at Chloe with total trust. But she turned as I strode up the aisle, swords in hand.

'"Let her go!"

'"Gabriel," Chloe whispered.

'"Gabe?" Dior frowned. "What are—"

'"Dior, they mean to murder you!"

'"Almighty's name, bring him down!" Greyhand bellowed.

'Four 'saints charged me, and I silently thanked the Angel Fortuna that the rest of the monastery's complement must have been abroad at the Hunt – I'd no knowing if I could have taken more of them. But that ancien strength burned in my veins alongside my fury at these bastards – brothers I'd once fought and bled beside, who'd now tried to murder me. They came not one at a time like in the theatre plays, no, all together, tooth and nail, but the aisle wasn't wide enough for more than two at a stretch. The headstrong youngblood came first, de Séverin beside him, that Dyvok strength in his swordarm. But it wasn't just in taverne tales and soothsinger songs that I was named the greatest swordsman of the Ordo Argent – I'd earned that part of my legend, sure and true. And hungry and strong and swift as they were, I left both those silvered 'saints in puddles of their own blood and shite, sprayed across the Cathedral's blackstone floor. Finch came next – little Finch with his mismatched eyes locked on my own. The Voss blood in him had grown thick over the years, and I felt his mind pushing into mine, looking to see my strikes before I made them and counter with his own. But for all his faults and all his weaknesses, old Seraph Talon had trained me well. I called up a wall of noise inside my head, left a tiny crack for Finch to peer through – enough to see the feint I conjured to throw his way. But I feinted not at all, striking true instead, and the counter he'd readied was left unsaid as my swords plunged into his belly and chest.

'Finch snarled in desperation, spitting blood, drawing that damned silver carving fork from his coat and thrusting it at my throat. But I grabbed his wrist, hearing bone splinter, stabbing back. And with the fork buried to the hilt under his chin, I left him split and bleeding on the Cathedral tiles.

'A cry echoed on black granite – the screech of a snow hawk – and lines of fire were ripped down my scalp as Winter swooped from the gables. The silverbomb I lifted to hurl slipped from my fingers as a barrage of wheellock shots rang out from the choir loft; the assembled sisters unloading at my back with a dozen blasts of silver. My bomb exploded beside me, ripping my flesh and blinding me in a cloud of silver caustic, and through it charged my old master, his eye alight with fury, silversteel in his hand.

'He'd taught me from a cub, this man. Singing me the hymn of the blade in the Gauntlet, day after day, until my fingers bled and my lungs burned and my hands grew hard as iron. And we crashed against each other now, like waves on a storm-tossed sea. I recalled the kindness and the cruelty he'd shown me. That he'd been more a father to me than any man alive. And in truth, a part of me still loved him like one, despite it all.

'We danced back and forth among the pews, the stone ringing with the song of our swords. The sisters above risked a few shots, but most were afraid of hitting the abbot now. And though he was one-handed, I had a half a dozen silver slugs in my back, and the old bastard was proving my match. I risked a glance to Dior, saw that she was struggling with her bonds now. Chloe still stood with arms raised, still reading aloud in Old Talhostic from the tome, rushing through the final words of the Rite.

'"Chloe, don't you dare!"

'"Sister Chloe, let me go!" Dior shouted.

'"I'm sorry," Chloe whispered, drawing a gleaming silversteel knife from her habit. "But all this was ordained, Dior."

'"No, don't, let me *go*!"

'"It's for the good, love," she whispered. "It's God's will. All on earth below and heaven above is the work of his hand."

'"CHLOE!"

'Winter swept down from on high as I roared, slicing my brow open with her talons. Gasping, blood in my eyes, I felt another lucky shot from the loft strike me behind my knee. As I stumbled, Greyhand took his chance, spitting me in the chest and driving me back into one of the mighty stone pillars.

'"I warned you about being a hero, Gabriel," he growled, twisting the blade. "Heroes die unpleasant deaths, far from home and hearth."

'I grabbed his hand in one bloody fist, keeping it locked on the hilt. Drooling blood, I dragged myself forward on his sword until the crossguard was pressed against my belly, and with my other hand, I seized his throat.

'"Who the *fuck* told you I was a hero?"

'The old man's eye grew wide, his mouth opened in a scream as the flesh of his throat began to blacken. Frantic, he tried to get his hand free of my grip, but I held on, grim, hateful. He'd chosen to grant me a silversaint's death, this man, this mentor, this father mine; supposing that after all the blood and love between us, at least he owed me that.

'But I owed him no such thing. Not a man's death but a monster's; a monster who'd cut my throat and given me to the waters, a monster who'd stand watch while a bride of the Almighty butchered a sixteen-year-old girl in God's own house. And the blood boiled in his veins, and steam rose crimson and roiling from his eye, and the flesh of his throat turned to ashes in my fist. Ruined, smoking, he crumpled to the ground – the Abbot of the Ordo Argent, dead by my hand.

'"Au revoir, father," I whispered.

'I dragged his blade free from my belly as Winter swooped out of the rafters again, screeching in rage at the death of her master. A dull *thwack* rang out as I swung, limping forward now in a cloud of tumbling feathers. Shots rang out from the loft, and I hurled a handful of silverbombs, sisters scattering whole or in pieces among the blinding concussions. And still I stalked towards the altar, blood-red eyes locked on Chloe now, the sister standing above Dior with silversteel knife raised, as her voice faltered, as she stared at me with wide green eyes and spoke with bloodless lips.

'"Gabriel, all this was meant t – *hrrrrk*!"

'I drove the sword into her chest, pinning her to the podium and the tome laid upon it. Chloe grasped the blade, palms sliced bloody, a look of utter disbelief upon her face – as if even here, even now, she expected God to intervene.

'Always a believer was little Chloe Sauvage.

'"N-no . . ." she gasped. "All the w-work of his hand is in ac-ccord with his p-plan . . ."

'I leaned in close, whispered through bared fangs. "*Fuck* his plan."

'She tried to speak, a line of crimson spilling down her chin as she slumped back on the tome and sighed her last. Turning, I tore off the straps binding Dior to the altar, and she surged up into my arms. I held as tight as I dared, trembling, almost weeping with relief.

'"Are you aright?"

'"I'm aright," she breathed, looking in wide-eyed horror at Chloe's body. "She . . . was going to kill me. Why would she do that?" She shook her head, tears in her eyes. "*Why?*"

'"It's not your fault, love. The ritual demands the Grail's lifeblood to end daysdeath."

'I turned with a snarl, spitting through bloody teeth.

'"This fucking book . . ."

'I kicked the podium over, sent it crashing to the floor. Chloe's body tumbled, the ancient tome's spine cracked, splitting and splaying the old pages across the bloody stone. I snatched up a burning candle from the altar, set to drop it into the book's ruins.

'Dior grabbed my wrist, looking into my eyes.

'". . . Would it work?" she whispered.

'"I don't care," I replied.

'And I let the candle fall.

'The flames spread, the vellum burned, the ritual upon it turned to char and ashes. We stood side by side, Dior and I, watching the smoke rise into the stained-glass light. And I felt not one drop of regret. I'd find another way to end the endless night, to bring the Forever King to his knees. Or I'd fall trying. Because some prices are simply too steep to pay.

'I looked at this girl beside me. My hill to die on. My shoulder to cry on. I'd no clue what I believed, save only that I believed in her.

'"What do we do now?" Dior asked softly.

'I stared up at the Redeemer and sighed.

'"I suppose you should come meet my sister."'

✦ XXVIII ✦

TOMORROW AND TOMORROW

GABRIEL UPENDED THE empty bottle of Monét over his open mouth. The light of the weakling dawn was creeping through the window like a thief now, refracting in blood-red droplets, falling slow onto his tongue.

Drip.

Drip.

Drip.

That skull-pale moth was still flitting about the lantern's light, beating upon the glass. With a speed belied by the four bottles he'd downed, Gabriel snatched it from the air and squeezed. Opening his fist, he let the broken body fall to the stone, ruined wings dusting the sevenstar on his hand.

He felt as if he'd been in this room all his life.

The Marquis Jean-François of the Blood Chastain dipped his quill into his ink bottle, scribing the last few words the silversaint had spoken. The pages were filled with his story now, word by word, line by line. Gabriel thought it strange, and in truth, a kind of wonderful; that all he was and would ever be could be distilled into a few elegant lines on a page. The summation of his youth and his glory, his love and his loss, his life and his tears, captured like an errant moth and bound as if by magik into so small and plain a thing.

The simple wonder of books.

Jean-François finished his writing, scowled at the window, as if offended by the daystar's interruption. Blowing breathless breath upon the ink to dry it, the vampire placed the tome upon the table, steepled pale fingers at ruby lips, and smiled.

'A fine night's work, Silversaint. My pale Empress shall be well pleased.'

Gabriel dropped the empty bottle to the floor, wiped his lips on the back of his hand. 'You honestly can't imagine the relief I'll feel at meeting her approval, vampire.'

'There is still much ground to cover. Your truck with the Liathe and your ties to the Faithless. The battle of Augustin and the treachery in Charbourg. The death of the Forever King and the loss of the Grail. But . . .' Again, Jean-François cast hateful eyes to the dawn rising through the thin window. 'Time has caught us for now, I fear.'

'I told you, vampire.' Gabriel smiled, his tongue thick with wine. 'Everything ends.'

'For tonight, perhaps.' The historian nodded, smoothing the tall feathers at his collar. 'But we have tomorrow. And tomorrow. And tomorrow.'

Jean-François reached into his frockcoat, produced a wooden case carved with the Blood Chastain coat of arms. Twin wolves. Twin moons. With a monogrammed kerchief, he fastidiously cleaned the quill's golden nib, packed it away, and secreted the case within his coat once more. Reaching forth to gather up his tome, he rose to leave.

'Before you go . . .'

The vampire looked into the Last Silversaint's eyes. 'Oui, Chevalier?'

Gabriel breathed deep, shame burning his cheeks.

'. . . Could I have another smoke?'

The monster looked at the killer with narrowed eyes. So still, he seemed carved of marble. Gabriel clenched his wine-stained teeth, the want in his skin, the need on its way.

'Please,' he whispered.

Jean-François inclined his head. And though he never seemed to move at all, he now held one hand outstretched. And there, on the snow-white plane of his upturned palm, lay a glass phial of reddish-brown dust.

'You have earned it, I suppose.'

Gabriel nodded, wretched and thirsting. Reaching slow towards the phial. 'You know, you never answered my question, Chastain.'

'And what question was that, de León?'

'When your dark mother and pale mistress set you this task . . . did you think she was locking me in here with you, or you in here with me?'

Gabriel's fist closed about the vampire's wrist, silver-swift. And with a speed belied by the four bottles he'd downed, he seized hold of Jean-François's throat. The vampire's eyes widened, and he opened his lips to shout, but that shout became a scream as the marble of his flesh began to blacken, and the blood within his veins to boil.

Gabriel rammed the vampire back into the wall, the brick crushed to powder. The chronicler bucked, roaring and trying to break loose. The table had upturned, the historie spilled, the glass lantern crashing to the floor. Gabriel bared his fangs, teardrop scars twisting on his cheek, inhaling deeply of the red smoke rising from the vampire's skin.

'I told you I'd make you fucking scream, leech,' he spat.

A roar of fury rang out as the cell door was flung wide, and Meline flew into the room. She held a gleaming dagger in hand, eyes burning with the ardour of a mother for her child, a lover for her beloved, a thrall for her master, plunging her blade through Gabriel's greatcoat and into his back once, twice, three times. The silversaint turned and slapped the woman hard enough to send her sailing across the room, slamming Jean-François into the wall again. But as pain lanced through his chest, bubbling now into his mouth, salty red, he realized the blade she'd stabbed him with was no mere shank of pig iron.

'S-silversteel,' he gasped.

Jean-François burst apart in his hands, the vampire's body collapsing into a tumbling, jumbling mass. As Gabriel staggered backwards, pink froth at his lips, he realized he was holding only the vampire's feathered mantle and frockcoat; dark velvet embroidered with golden curlicues. A horde of rats was swarming about his feet now, spilling from the legs of the historian's britches, the sleeves of his fine coat, rushing in a flood from the cell. Meline had rolled to her feet, clutching the historie to her bosom as she dashed from the room and slammed the door, a few rats chittering and squealing as they squeezed below the jamb. And wheezing, drooling blood, Gabriel found himself alone in the cell once more.

The Last Silversaint limped to the fallen table, took up the bone pipe, the glittering sanctus phial. Loading the bowl with a healthy serving of the sacrament, Gabriel sat cross-legged among the upturned furniture and broken bottles, long hair draped about his face, leaning towards the puddle of burning lantern oil. His belly thrilled as it began: that sublime alchemy, that dark chymistrie, the powdered blood bubbling now, colour melting to scent, the aroma of hollyroot and copper filling the cell. And Gabriel pressed his lips to that pipe with more passion than he'd ever kissed a lover, and oh sweet God in heaven, breathed it down.

The hatch across the barred window in the door slammed aside. Glancing up, Gabriel saw a pair of chocolat brown eyes, bloodshot with pain and rage and stained by bloody tears.

He raised his pipe and gifted Jean-François a grim smile.
'Can't blame a man for trying.'
The historian narrowed his eyes and hissed.
Gabriel breathed a plume of bloody smoke into the air.
'Until tomorrow, vampire.'

DAWN

IT WAS THE twenty-seventh year of daysdeath in the realm of the Forever King, and his murderer was still waiting to die.

The killer stood watch at a thin window, hands stained with new blood and ashes pale as starlight. The floor was scattered with broken glass, splintered furniture, the stone under his feet marked by soot and spilled ink. The door was iron-clad, heavy, still locked like a secret. The killer watched the sun rise from its unearned rest, and pressing a thin bone pipe to his lips, he remembered how good hell tastes.

The château below him was sleeping now. Monsters slinking back to beds of cold earth and slipping off the façade that they were anything close to human. The air outside was pale with flurries of falling snow, with the chill of winter unending. Thrall soldiers clad in dark steel still patrolled the battlements below, and the killer's lip still curled as he watched them. But in truth, he knew who was truly the slave.

He looked down at his hands. Hands that had slain things monstrous. Hands that had saved an empire. Hands that had allowed the last hope for his species to slip and shatter like glass upon the stone.

The sky above was dark as sin.

The horizon, red as his lady's lips the last time he kissed her.

He ran one thumb across his fingers, the letters inked below his knuckles. 'Patience,' he whispered.

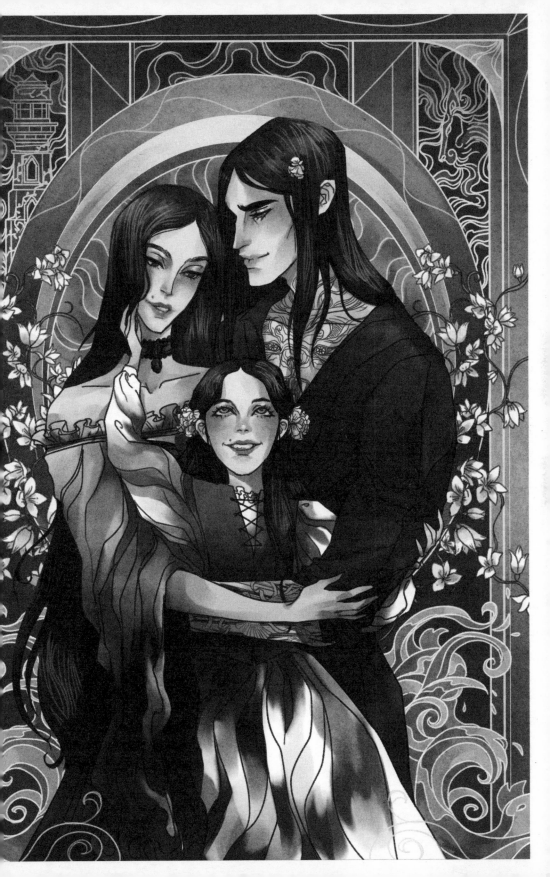

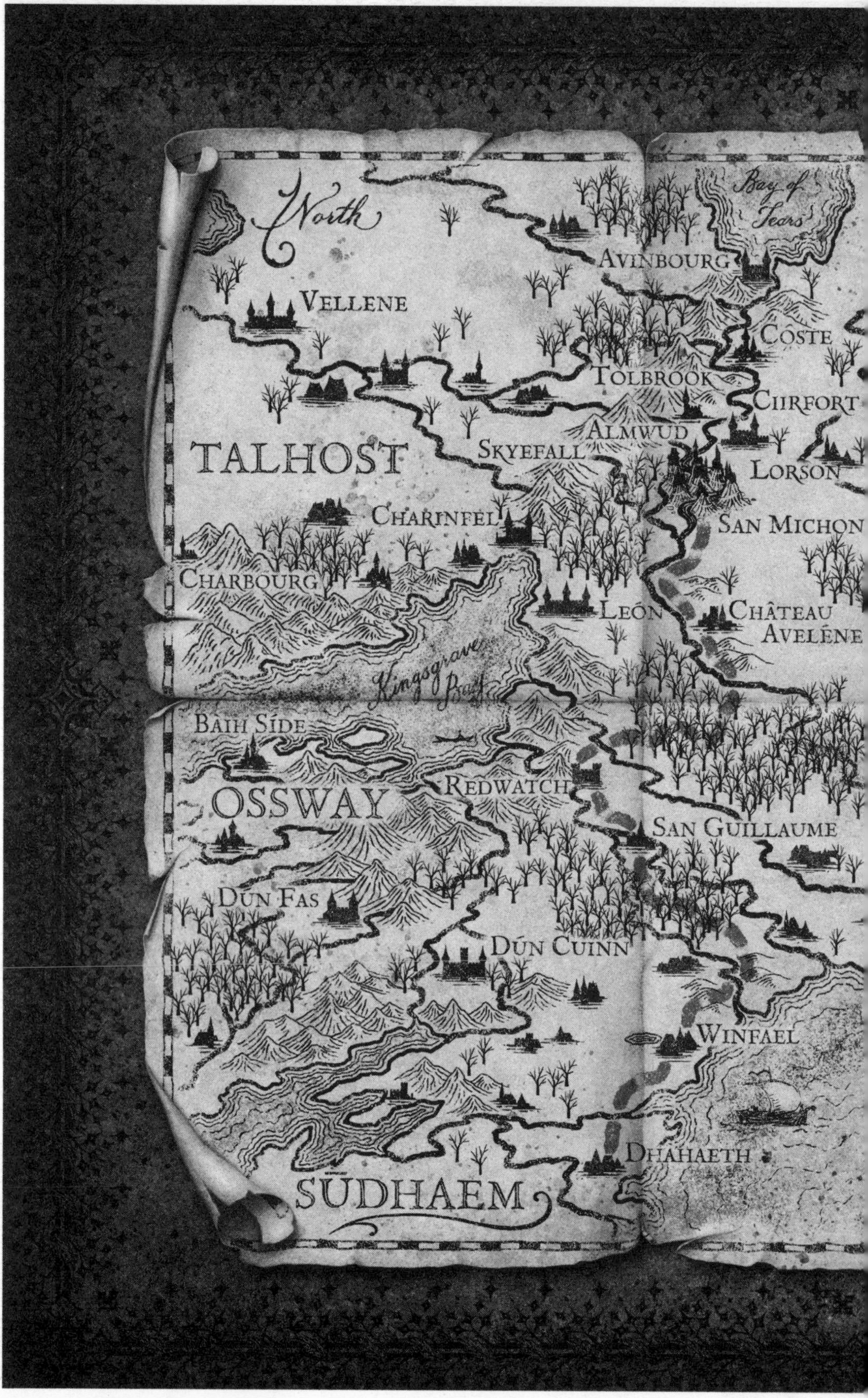
North
Bay of Tears
AVINBOURG
VELLENE
CÔSTE
TOLBROOK
CIIRFORT
ALMWUD
TALHOST
SKYEFALL
LORSON
CHARINFEL
SAN MICHON
CHARBOURG
LEÓN
CHÂTEAU AVELÈNE
Kingsgrave Bay
BAIH SÍDE
REDWATCH
OSSWAY
SAN GUILLAUME
DÚN FAS
DÚN CUINN
WINFAEL
DHAHAETH
SŪDHAEM

Mothersea
Bay of Tombs
NORDLUND
BEAUFORT
SAN MAXIMILLE
Bay of Antoine
MONTFORT
Gabriel's Journey

ACKNOWLEDGEMENTS

Thanks and bloody kisses to the following:

Peter, Lily, Joe, Sarah, Jeff, Paul, Tom, Young, Jennifer, Lisa, Andy, George, Tracey, Rafal, Lena and all at St. Martin's Press, Natasha, Vicky, Jack, Micaela, Claire, Sarah, Jaime, Fleur, Isabel, Alice, Fionnuala, Robyn, and all at HarperVoyager UK, Michael, Thomas, and all at HarperCollins Australia, the amazing Marco, Sam, and all my foreign publishers, Bonnieeee, Jason, Kerby, Virginia, Orrsome, Cat, Lindsay, Ursula, Piéra, Fiona, Laure, Josh, Tracey, Samantha, Steven, Toves, Catriona, Tiffany, Clarissa, Sara, Minh, Morgana, Ash, Bill, George, Anne, Stephen, Ray, Robin, China, William, George, Pat, Anne, Nic, Cary, Neil, Amie, Anthony, Joe, Laini, Mark, Steve, Stewart, Tim, Chris, Stefan, Chris, Brad, Marc, Beej, Rafe, Weez, Paris, Jim, Eli, Tom, Joel, Astrid, Ludovico, Mark, Randy, Elliot, CJ, Mitch, Pete (RIP), Tom (RIP), Dan, Sam, Marcus, Chris, Winston, Matt, Robb, Oli, Robert, Maynard, Ronnie, Corey, Chris (RIP), Anthony, Dez, Chino, Jonathan, Ian, Briton, Trent, Phil, Sam, Tony, Kath, Kylie, Nicole, Kurt, Ross, Jack, Max, Poppy, Leila and Indy, my readers for the love, my enemies for the fuel, the baristas of Melbourne, Sydney, Paris, Lyon, London, Birmingham, Manchester, Edinburgh, Glasgow, Roma, Milano, Venezia, and most importantly Praha.

Finally and especially, Amanda, my blood and fire.